CW01176841

Darkness Resides
Book Three of the Morhudrim Cycle
by A D Green
1st Edition – 1st November 2023
Release Version 1.0 1st November 2023
© Andrew Green (A D Green)
ISBN:9798868096242

All characters in this work are fictitious and any resemblance to any real persons, living or dead is purely coincidental.

All Right Reserved.
No part of this publication may be reproduced or transmitted in any form or by any means, without prior permission in writing of the Author.

Map artwork by A D Green

Edited by M.C. Green, BSc and Graduate Diploma in Arts (English)

Acknowledgements

Cover artwork by Midjourney

Vikncharlie for book cover design

My Beta readers Jordan Green, Ian Firth, Ian Hodgson and Martin Walls

"You can make anything by writing"

C.S. Lewis

Contents

Map of the Rivers	iii
Map of the Norderlands	v
Map of the Cumbrenan	vii
Prologue	1
Chapter 1: Brikka's Blood	10
Chapter 2: Awakened	20
Chapter 3: White Heron	29
Chapter 4: Bitter Parting	39
Chapter 5: Blood Has Been Spilt	49
Chapter 6: Death Road	59
Chapter 7: Leave The Dead Behind	70
Chapter 8: Hunters Hunt	79
Chapter 9: Fallen Cardinal, Fallen King	90
Chapter 10: The Abyss	99
Chapter 11: Connections	106
Chapter 12: Blood Money	118
Chapter 13: A View From A Hill	125
Chapter 14: The Conduit	132
Chapter 15: Eastern Promise	143
Chapter 16: A Small Matter Of The Succession	154
Chapter 17: The Prince and the Mouse	170
Chapter 18: We Are The Grim	183
Chapter 19: Death Comes In Darkness	193
Chapter 20: Hot Rocks and Ice	201
Chapter 21: The Road to Thorn Nook	212
Chapter 22: River City	221
Chapter 23: Lady White Crow	231
Chapter 24: The Morqhill Sallies	247
Chapter 25: Everything Is Soup	259
Chapter 26: Of Mouse and Murder	269
Chapter 27: Fire Flight	274
Chapter 28: The Wylders	286
Chapter 29: To Spar or Not To Spar	298
Chapter 30: Redwood Sunset	310
Chapter 31: The Rider	319
Chapter 32: A Thousand Barbed Thorns	328
Chapter 33: The Hungering	345

Chapter 34: Ruminations, Cogitations and Lies	349
Chapter 35: One Last Hunt	358
Chapter 36: A Road Hard Travelled	371
Chapter 37: Lost Innocence	386
Chapter 38: I Wish I Had Known Her Name	395
Chapter 39: Master of Birds	409
Chapter 40: Winter-Meet	422
Chapter 41: The Mouth Of The Viper	433
Chapter 42: An Endless Path	442
Chapter 43: The Sanctuary of Caves	454
Chapter 44: Fire and Ash	470
Chapter 45: Better Not Get Yourself Killed	486
Chapter 46: From Sea to Sky	498
Chapter 47: The Envoy Tree	505
Epilogue	518
Principal Characters	522
Ilf dictionary	530

Map of the Rivers

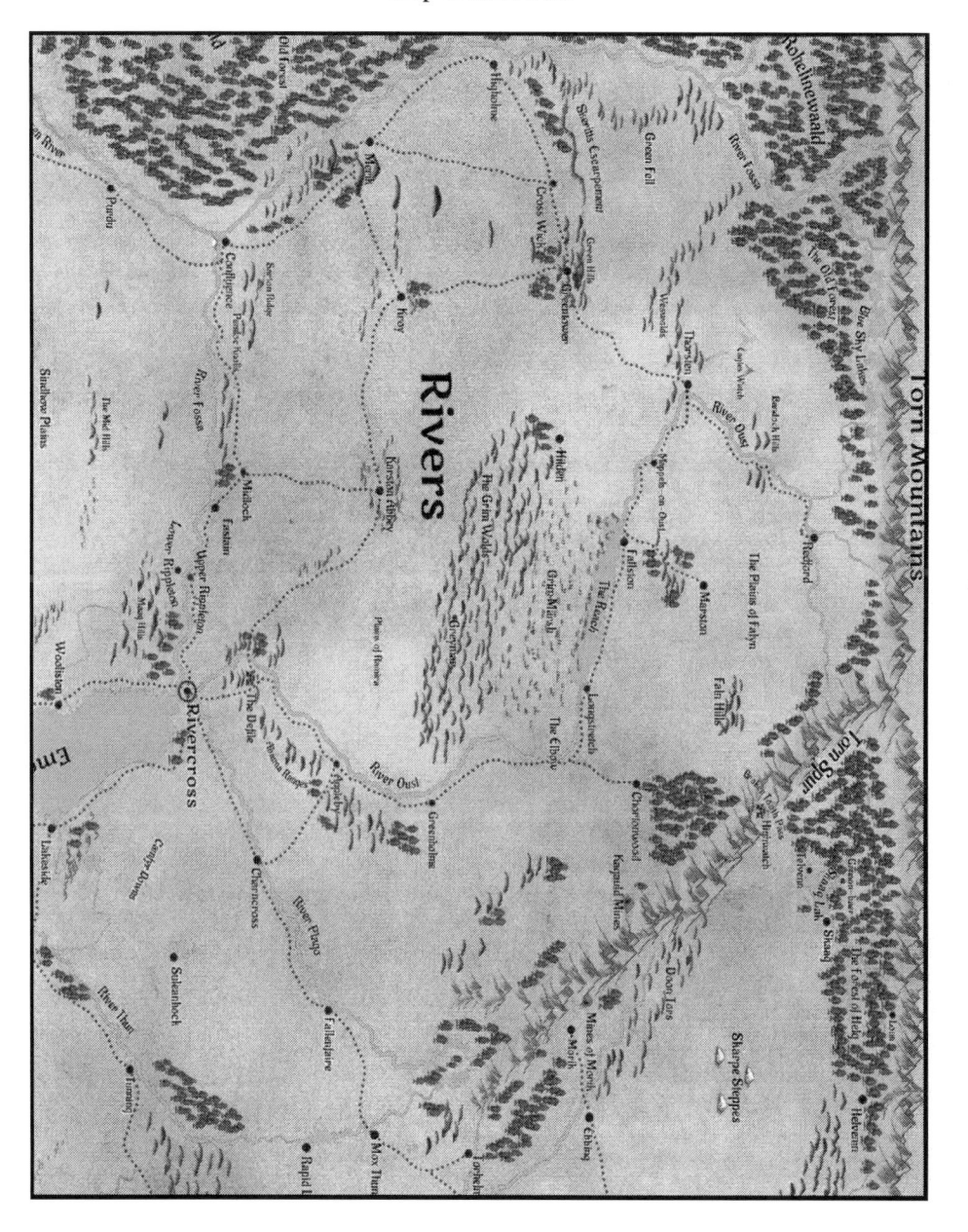

Map of the Norderlands

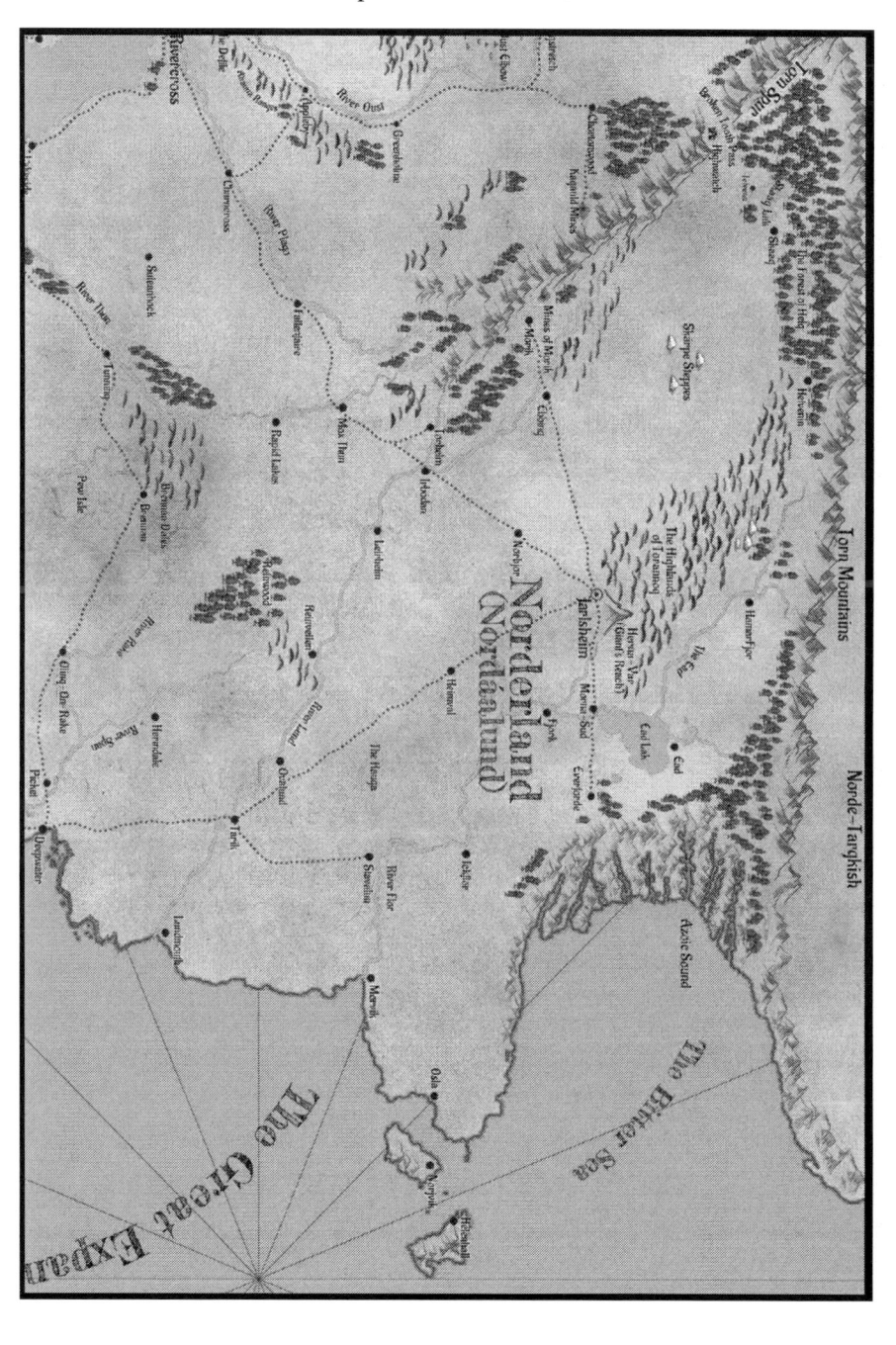

Map of the Cumbrenan

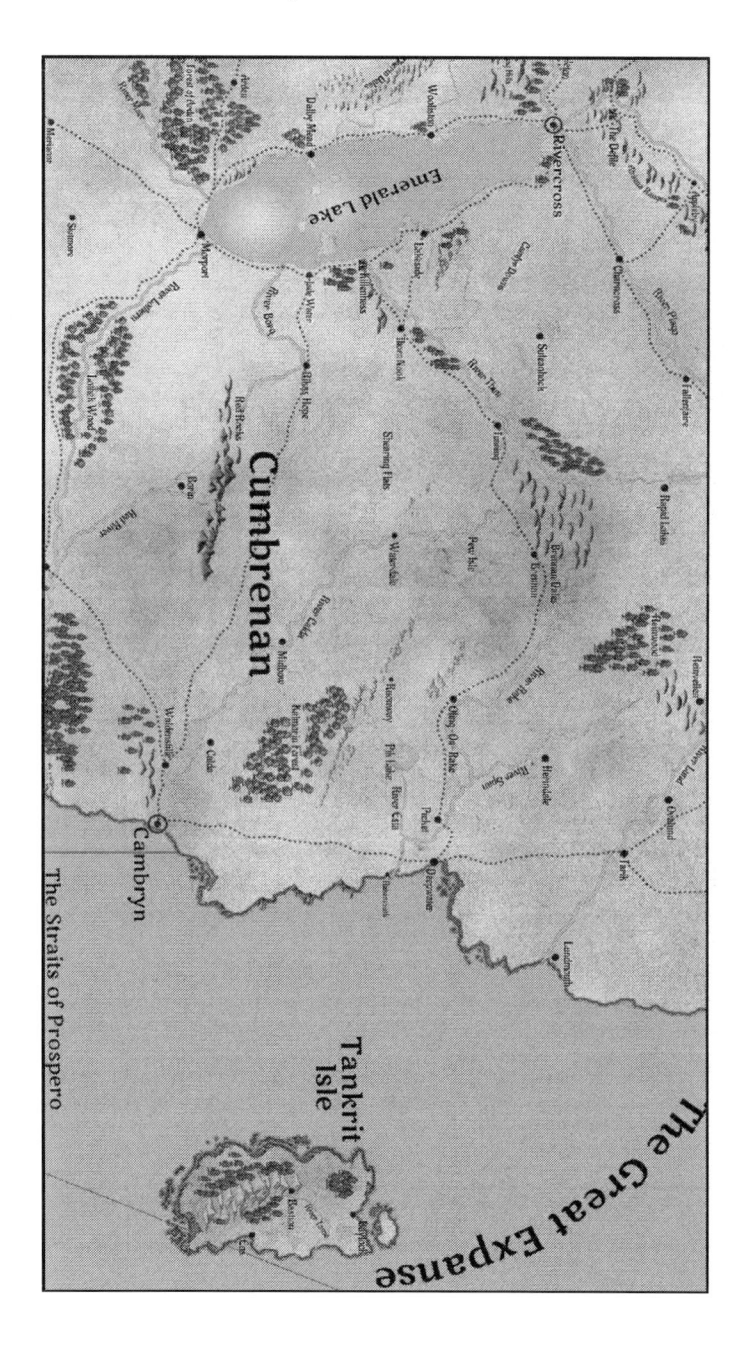

More maps can be found at http://adgreenauthor.com

When the Forgotten One returns, then shall the rivers run red and the shadows fall. And where the darkness resides there too shall chaos reign and all shall end, lest the light that was lost be found again.

Excerpt from the Gnarhlson Prophecies

x / Darkness Resides

Prologue

1007th Cycle of the 4th Age
1st Cycle of Ankor (Jud'pur'tak) (The Return - Spring)
Ick-Báal Mountains, Norde-Targkish

It was early in Jud'pur'tak's cycle and it signalled the new life of spring. The largest of the tri-moons loomed heavy in the sky, the silver disk a counterpoint to the burning glory of Marq'suk, the life-giver.

Torq observed the skies with interest. The shamans named the moons 'The three eyes'. Celestial bodies from which it was said the gods beheld all things. It gave Torq comfort knowing they watched over him and it hardened his resolve. He would not fail.

He pulled his cloak tight. The first day of the Return it might be, but the Bite was reluctant to relinquish its hold just yet. The air was bitter. The ground too was hard with snow, the shrubs and rocks coated in hoarfrost.

Hefting his pack, Torq trudged on. His bag was light, carrying only a tinder box, one day's rations, a waterskin, a rope, and a blanket made of longhair. The blanket was not for him. He carried a knife in his belt and a spear in his gloved hand, his weapon of choice to aid in his trial.

The dark blemish of a forest lay ahead, settling like a skirt around the Ick-Báal Mountains. It promised shelter but Torq knew the distant treeline was further away than it appeared; the vast plains and tundra of the Norde-Targkish were deceptive. Its gullies and dells lay hidden until you stood almost upon them.

This cycle, for the ritual of the passing, there had been thirty-two hands and three, participating in the trials. Not all would succeed but those that did would become named. Only the named could speak in council or receive a share from raids. Only the named could become warrior caste.

Not all would make it though. The Norde-Targkish was unforgiving and would claim its share in blood price. Those who survived but failed would be outcasts, no longer of the Sartantak. Forsaken, they would be without a tribe unless by chance another took them in, though never to be named, for the gods willed it so.

I will not suffer that fate, Torq resolved.

That night, he settled in the shelter of the woods, its tall trees untroubled by the snow. He lit a small fire to warm himself, his skin aching in its glow. Above, through the canopy, the red moon of Naris-Krol cast a baleful eye upon him and he felt humbled by it.

The shamans taught that, Marq'suk the life-giver, was all-powerful but that the sun had to replenish itself each day. In the beginning, it left the world in darkness before the gods created the three moons to traverse the void and shine light in the dark. Then, in time, as the worthy passed Nos'varqs Gate and entered the Hall of Varis'tuk beyond, each would place a light in the void. The shamans foretold that when enough had passed through there would be no more darkness. That until this time, wherever darkness resides, the gods would continue to watch over them.

The following morning Torq foraged, eating a frugal meal of blaa-den'wort, finding the hardy fungus at the base of a conifer. Setting out once again, he followed the border of the forest eastward, enjoying the weak warmth of the life-giver on his face.

Throughout the day, the forest edge turned slowly northward, following the Ick-Báals as the mountains retreated leaving a wide vale, Nordrum. Ancient and legendary, Nordrum was the site of a great battle, its soil reputedly soaked in the blood of the fallen. It was the first time Torq had been here and looking at it he was unimpressed. It seemed no different to his eyes. The land was as white and featureless as the rest.

The ragged outline of a ruin lay at the vale's northern apex. Tal'Draysil, the fabled lost city of the humans. Entry was forbidden, as ordained by the gods. Torq felt uneasy just looking at it. His gaze turned to the blunt capped mountain directly behind the ruin, Furous, and recalled the shamans' challenge.

'You must gather a fire-stone from Furous. Its crown was cloven by Varis-tuk and its heart ripped out. Climb the mount's fiery slope and at its centre you will find what you seek.' It sounded simple but he'd seen the uneasy exchange of looks between the elders and Kor-tunq, the tribal chieftain. Only the shamans seemed unperturbed.

'The gods have spoken,' Torq had replied in ritual acceptance.

Approaching Tal'Draysil, he saw the tall spire of a tower rising from its epicentre. In contrast to the rest of the ruins, it appeared untouched by the fury of nature. It added to his sense of foreboding and Torq found himself repeating those self-same words of ritual like a mantra, as if saying them aloud would ward off the hidden miasma that hovered over the ruin.

Skirting the broken stone of Tal'Draysil, Torq entered the trees that covered the slopes of Furous. He made camp in the lee of a large, frost-coated boulder that felt strange to the touch. Curious, Torq ran his hands over a small nub and was surprised when it broke loose. The freshly exposed rock was jet black and peering close, tiny holes permeated its surface. Torq hefted the nub; it felt light enough that it could float. He placed it in his pack, resolving to show it to Tar. His friend would be fascinated. Probably even trade a skin of garkís milk for it.

The thought turned his mind to food and grabbing his spear, Torq ambled back down the slope. He'd spied a rigut burrow near some hardy bracken bush. Settling above the hole with the wind strong in his face, Torq waited whilst Marq'suk painted long shadows on the ground and the light turned a sullen yellow.

As twilight faded to night the chill seeped up from the ground and into his bones. The wind numbed his face, and his arm ached from holding his spear poised. Finally, he was rewarded with a faint scrabble of noise. Moments later, a long-eared, white-furred head appeared at the entrance to the burrow. The whiskered head twitched before inching out further to sniff the air. A hop and the rigut was halfway out.

The spear jab was short and fast.

That night Torq ate well. He should have saved some of the meat but whilst the rigut had seemed a good size, it was scrawny from the Bite and, after skinning and gutting it was half what it was. Roasting the carcass over the campfire, his stomach throbbed. Hungry, smell taunting, Torq gave in and devoured it, bones and all. Afterwards, he dressed his campsite, lopping bracken bush off and placing it around its edge, before settling down for another freezing night.

He thought of his task. The feast of passing would be in seven turns and he must return before its start or he'd be cast out. The tribe was encamped two turns to the southwest leaving plenty of time to climb Furous, locate a firestone, and return. Stacking the fire with fallen branches that hissed and steamed, Torq huddled closer to the flames and closed his eyes.

The following day was overcast and the life-giver was a sullen orb hidden by cloud. Stacking wood by the strange boulder, ready for his return, Torq set off. He foraged leaves from an accacha bush and with a mouthful of water chewed it into a cud, admonishing himself for not saving some of the rigut.

As Torq ascended the slopes of Furous, the forest came to a sudden end, revealing a barren, rocky landscape that rose imposingly. Hard snow packed the ground between outcroppings of rock. Outside the cover of the trees, the wind gusted, swirling a fine brume of ice crystals into the air. Shielding his eyes, Torq looked upslope. A notch marred the lip of the mountain. A natural draw, it would be his path.

Leaning into the wind, Torq set off. The higher he climbed, the steeper the slope, until he was scrabbling using stony handholds to pull his large frame from rock to rock. A tiny nugget of fear lodged at the back of his head. If he were to fall it would mean the end. Even should he survive, he would likely break something. It would finish any hope of completing his trial and make him an outcast. Death was preferable.

Dismissing his fear, Torq climbed on. Worry would only hinder him. Besides, whilst he wasn't renowned for his climbing skill it was something all urak learned and he'd tackled far harder paths than the one Furous offered.

Reaching a wide ledge, Torq rested briefly, gathering his strength. Sipping on his waterskin, he looked downslope at the distant forest to judge how far he'd come. He stared. Something had moved down there; a shadow?

The life-giver broke through the cloud cover, casting a ribbon of light that fractured off the snowy mountainside. Rubbing a callused hand over bony eye ridges, Torq squinted. Perhaps it had been a trick of the light or a mist whipped up by the wind. Or maybe he'd just imagined it. Whatever it was, it was gone now, but it left him feeling unsettled. It was not unheard of for more than one to be given the same trial or for another tribe to offer a similar challenge to their own. If it was a rival, then vigilance would be needed.

The rest of the climb was arduous. The defile he moved up was plentiful with rock holds but many were treacherous and more than one boulder was sent tumbling after testing his weight upon it. Despite the cold, Torq felt sweat gather on his back and noticed that the icy wind did not trouble him in the draw of rock.

Reaching the cleft at the top of the mountain, Torq rested briefly, whilst considering his surroundings. Behind, stretched the Vale of Nordrum and Tal'Draysil, the light of the life-giver breaking through the overcloud to caress the plains with golden fingers. Ahead, the Ick-Báals rose, like guardians around its fallen sister. As for Furous itself, Varis'tuk had indeed gutted her. The crest he sat upon was a giant rim that circled the summit to its northern edge which was cracked and split.

The inside was carved hollow and sloped down several hundred paces before levelling out into a flat, concentric circle. Strangely, there was no snow covering the belly of the crater and at its middle was a lake, covered with mist. Torq felt his breath catch at the sight, moved by it. It was not quite what he expected. There was no liquid fire as the shamans had said, though several vents belched bilious smoke into the air. Maybe what was sought lay buried or hidden?

The day was late. The life-giver soon to fade and diminish. Torq needed to decide; climb down and camp in the centre, or stay where he was until Marq'suk renewed? A gusting blast of icy wind decided him and Torq set off.

The journey down proved more hazardous than the path up. The rocky sides were easy to navigate at first. But the rocks slowly grew smaller and more broken, eventually turning into a shale of stone and pebble. There were no handholds and each step crunched and slipped, scattering tiny avalanches of gravel. The cascade of stone slowly grew with each of Torq's steps, until he was slipping, borne down on a river of scree. The best he could manage was to slide; keeping his body flat, until the slope tapered off and he came to a bruised halt.

Picking himself up, Torq removed bits of stone from his harness and clothing whilst looking about. It seemed darker and smaller now he stood at the base. The sides appeared steeper and taller than they had from above.

The faint sulphurous smell, which tainted the air soon after starting his descent, was much stronger at the base of the crater. Torq moved to the steaming lake. Several pools were scattered around its edge and bending low over one, Torq trailed his fingers through it before snatching his hand back. The water was hot. He sniffed his fingers and touched a tongue to them. Bad, the water held some taint to it. He had drunk sparingly on the climb but nevertheless, Torq had little more than half a skin left. A turn at most before he must return to the forest. Six turns to complete his task, yet the next would decide it. He'd not have time to make a second trip.

The pungent smell and steam off the lake warmed the air and Torq found himself stripping out of his cloak, over vest, and two of his tunics, making a bed of them in a small hollow of rock. The air barely whispered and the light faded quickly, the heavens obscured in cloud.

Breaking his rations out, Torq ate half, relishing each morsel before washing it down with a sip of water that he held in his mouth as long as possible. He did not like this place.

The night was uncomfortable and Torq woke from a fitful sleep at first light, dry-eyed with a sore throat and nose that was crusty with blood. The foul smell had gone, though in truth he couldn't smell much of anything.

Head pounding, Torq started searching the crater for a fire-stone. They were sacred, used by the shamans in some manner unexplained but crucial to their art. What did one even look like?

"Ascend the mount's fiery slope and at its centre, you will find what you seek," Torq muttered irritably. Well, the slopes had not been fiery and he could not find what he sought. He searched around one of the gas vents, the thick smoke making his eyes sting as he drew near. There was no opening, no hidden way underground that he could see.

Walking a circuit of the lake, Torq searched its shoreline, but it was just stone and boulders and black scree, nothing more. He sat on a grey-coated rock to think.

Maybe he needed fire to find the stone. If the guts of Furous were fiery, as the shamans said, maybe the stone would reveal itself, but with no flame, it lay hidden. Fidgeting, he gave a dry cough and rubbed his face. His head ached and he didn't feel so good.

Glancing up at the rim of Furous, Torq wistfully followed it around till he found the cleft he'd entered from. For the first time, he wondered how to climb the gravel slope. The nugget of fear at the back of his mind twisted, turning to doubt when something drew his eye in the notch. Staring hard, Torq could see nothing, a gust of snow in the wind maybe?

Rising wearily, Torq resumed his search and shortly thereafter happened upon a rock that caught his attention. It was black and pitted, like the one he had camped beside in the forest and the piece he had broken off. Only this one was perfectly spherical and as big as his head. He hefted it easily. Like its tiny brother, the rock weighed little. He laid it next to his pack. He would not have room to carry both it and the firestone, if ever he found it, but it was interesting to look at and somehow the black rock called to him.

Torq lay down and closed his eyes, needing a moment to rest.

He awoke, eyes gritty and swollen, to find the light was fading. High above the rim of Furous, the red eye of the killing moon was a glare of reproach.

The gods watched.

Chastened, Torq rose and gathered himself. His whole body ached and the taste of iron was bitter in his mouth. This place was killing him. He had something to do but his mind was vague. What was it? He'd been looking for … something. Torq tripped, falling over a small boulder, sending it rolling across the gravel. It was jet black and unnaturally round. Reaching out, he laid a hand upon it and found it hard and solid, yet it weighed almost nothing. It seemed familiar. As he grasped it, so too did his mind. This must be what he sought.

Eager to be gone, Torq packed it in his bag. He gulped water from his skin to rinse the taste of blood away. Slinging his pack over his shoulders, Torq stumbled, before catching his balance. Why was he so hot?

Glancing about to get a bearing, Torq spied a notch atop the crater. Opposite the notch, the crater's rim was cracked and jumbled with fallen stone. For no good reason, other than a sense it was right, Torq took a step towards the cleft. His foot crunched, settling in the gravel. Now he was moving, Torq was eager to be gone and he staggered up the slope.

Soon enough purchase became difficult as the sides rose. Boots sinking into scree, Torq sent gravel cascading behind, each step slipping back a little so that soon, two steps were needed to make one. He paused, resting forward on his hands. His limbs ached and he coughed blood onto the ground. *That's not good*, Torq thought.

Looking up, the cleft seemed far away. A shadow filled the gap. It stood, unmoved by the wind; a dark, foreboding presence that did not belong. *It waits*, the errant thought broke through the fugue of his mind. Torq's foot slid, setting the shale tumbling, threatening to drag him down with it. He crouched low until the click and clatter of stone subsided.

Weary, his body cried for relief. His head felt too heavy to hold up and throbbed, each pulse sending stabbing pain through his eyes. Gritting his teeth, Torq took another step forward and felt the whole mountain shift. The scree hissed, laughing as it dragged him, tumbling, back into its maw.

* * *

Torq opened his eyes on a bed of stone. Breathing was difficult, his throat was swollen and dry. He lurched, rolling over onto his back. Lying still, he sucked in ragged breaths. Rock dust stung his eyes.

He must have been there a while, for Naris-Krol had moved to the western edge of the crater's rim. The killing moon leered disdainfully at him and Torq felt shamed by it. Why was he so weak? He could barely move. Voice hoarse, he cried out to Naris-Krol and whichever of the gods might be watching.

And they answered.

Darkness filled the moon, swirling like blood in water until just a crescent remained. A red smile. The gods laughed at his weakness, his failure. He was unworthy. He would hang no light in the heavens.

The roiling shadow loomed, filling his vision until he saw nothing but darkness. His face felt its caress as it kissed his skin, soothing his agony but not his disgrace. The smoke eddied, shrouding his eyes. It covered ears and nose and mouth. Torq reeled upright, eyes flaring, mouth bared. The scream, when it came, was primal and base. A howl of pure terror ripped from the soul. The last thing Torq remembered was Naris-Krol's smiling countenance.

* * *

It was the feast of passing and most of the watchers had left to join it. The last to return from their trial had arrived a turn past and none since. No more were expected.

Nuupik-tarn was one of the few that remained. Head Shaman of the Sartantak, he waited patiently. The stones never lied.

Nearby, a young urak sat and although he was still, Nuupik could sense his anxiety. Tar-Tukh he was named. No longer chala, the urak had chosen his path and should have been celebrating with the other new warriors.

Tukh was a popular name to take. A bird of prey that hunted the vast plains, it was a name of strength and power, though uninspired. That Tar-Tukh was here and not celebrating meant he waited for someone, that much was obvious and it pleased Nuupik. All too often his people gave in to their baser, more violent instincts. But this urak was loyal to a friend and loyalty was to be nurtured. It was a true sign of strength, not the bird flying alone in the sky hunting for itself.

He watched Marq'suk kiss the hills to the west. The golden sun was fading fast. Once it was gone the trial of passing would be over and the feast of passing officially begun. Then it would be too late. His eyes turned back to the north, where the stones foretold he would return. Nuupik prayed silently to Muruin, the god of fate, to make it so. For time was fading with the light.

The young warrior rose suddenly, tense and rigid. Head fixed and unmoving. Cursing his failing eyes, Nuupik gathered to his feet and peered myopically. He could see nothing.

Tar-Tukh took a step out.

"No." The word stopped the urak in his tracks. Nuupik glared at him until Tar-Tukh took a rueful step back.

"Forgive me, Revered. I was not thinking."

Nuupik grunted but said no more. Something moved out there, an indistinct blur. It would barely have registered if it had been still.

It grew steadily, slowly morphing into the shape of an urak. It seemed in no hurry, unconcerned with racing the setting sun and Nuupik felt anxious. The few remaining watchers were also on their feet and one had no fear expressing Nuupik's worry.

"Must be injured to be so slow? It'll be a close race with the life-giver."

A look from Nuupik was all it took to still the voice and together the watchers waited in silence.

It seemed an age, the sun seemed to slow in its descent as the figure walked ever closer. At several hundred paces it was clear to Nuupik the urak was Torq. He was larger than most and unmistakeable for it. Size mattered to the urakakule but did not always bear out. Nuupik knew the fight masters thought little of him, Torq being too slow to capitalise on his bulk. That he never made it past three rounds in the training circle meant they considered him ordinary at best. The stones said otherwise.

At Torq's approach, Nuupik's eyes widened. Half the layers of clothing that protected against the cold were gone. He wore no cloak, overcoat, or the larger, layered tunic all urak wore in winter. Just his harness, a few woollen layers, and his pack. He had no weapon except for the knife strapped to his harness.

If he was affected by the cold, Torq showed no sign. Trudging on, he came to a stop in front of the shaman just as the life-giver dipped its head from view.

None spoke. All were waiting to hear the shaman.

"If you possess a fire-stone you are in time," Nuupik declared, his voice gruff and challenging. Close up, he saw that Torq's eyes were red-rimmed, his face ashen and covered in dust. He made no answer and showed no sign of hearing his words.

The watchers shifted with several placing hands on their weapons. To ignore a shaman was intolerable.

"Show me," Nuupik commanded.

A silent moment passed and the air filled with agitated menace as the surrounding urak tensed. There were more of them than before, Nuupik saw, and realised many must have wandered out from the campfires at seeing the watchers rise. One was Kor-tunq, the chieftain. Past his prime, he would be challenged soon. A pity, thought Nuupik, he was wily and missed nothing. A good leader was difficult to replace. He returned his gaze to the front.

Dropping his shoulder, Torq slipped the pack from his back and let it settle at his feet. He bent, untied the flap, and dug around inside. Straightening, he held his hand out. In it, between thumb and finger, was a small black rock. He held it like a trophy to the gathered. An urak laughed then stilled. With a flick, Torq sent the stone spinning towards the shaman.

Nuupik heard the crowd gasp at the audacity, even as he snatched it from the air. He knew as soon as he caught the rock what it must be. He smiled. Opening his palm to confirm it, he saw the small lump of fire-stone. It was sacred. To be so negligently tossed like that. A pity too, for the stones, had hinted at more, this specimen was barely adequate.

The stones do not lie.

His eyes glanced at Torq, then slowly traversed down to his pack. It looked full.

"Show me," Nuupik commanded, a second time.

"Name me. Then I will gift you what is in my bag," Torq replied.

There was a rasp of drawn weapons at the insult and Nuupik raised his voice in anger.

"This is a matter for the gods, not the tribe. No blood will be shed this night and no blade will be drawn. When I turn, I will see that it is so, else there will be an accounting."

With exaggerated slowness, Nuupik turned. The crowd had grown immeasurably. No weapons were in view. His back ached abominably from his long vigil, but he dismissed the pain. Realising he prevaricated, Nuupik returned to Torq.

"Speak."

"I lay in the belly of Furous watching death approach. Naris-Krol bore witness above and smiled at me. A smile of untold death and killing. It told me 'Now is not your time'."

Nuupik's jaw was slack; the stones did not foretell this. "Only the shamans may speak with the gods."

"The gods speak to who they will." Torq bent, dipping once again into his pack. This time, he lifted out a bundle wrapped in a coarse-haired blanket. Uncovering it to reveal a black sphere of rock that was perfectly round.

"With this firestone, Nuupik-tarn, the Sartantak will become the mightiest of all tribes. We will usurp the Manawarih and lead the Red Skull. Forsake me and this firestone will be cursed and the Sartantak will fade into obscurity. Now name me."

A murmur rose, growing louder as urak spoke over urak. Nuupik heard none of it, his mind only for the firestone. It was completely spherical and larger than any he'd ever seen. Just for a moment, the eyes of Torq seemed to swirl black; a reflection, a shadow of the fire-stone? An omen, the gods had spoken what the stones had foretold.

"So be it. I name you Krol."

Chapter 1: Brikka's Blood

1017ᵗʰ Cycle of the 4th Age
4ᵗʰ Cycle of Ankor (The Bite - Winter)
Highwatch, Norderland

The jagged spine of the Torns stretched from the Endless Sea in the west to the Great Expanse in the east. Ancient guardians, the mountain range divided the hard lands of the Norde-Targkish from the Nine Kingdoms, presenting a snow-capped barrier that was difficult to breach in the heights of the summer months and was all but impregnable outside of them.

From its immensity, and like a tributary of a great river, thrust the Torn Spur Mountains. Stabbing like a blade into the kingdoms, they split the land, creating a natural border between the Rivers and the Norderlands. The only blemish in its serrated skyline was a notch, as if a tooth had been snapped from a gum. Here the mountains were narrow creating a high pass that granted a way through.

Johanus Ulrikson stood upon the enduring stone walls of Highwatch staring westward as if his eyes might pierce the veil covering the road and declining slope. Above him, should he look to his left, rose Eracus and to his right, more distant but no less towering, her sister Ocanik.

Ulrikson stamped his feet to chase the numbness from his toes, his breath billowing like the sea of fog he gazed upon.

"It was said by druids of old that we stand upon the head of Brikka. Do ya know this legend, Ser?" he asked the man who stood beside him.

Tannon Crick had heard it, many times. But sometimes a man needed to talk and Crick sensed this was one of those times. Ulrikson, Barle of Highwatch was a tall, lean man with wide shoulders. Like many of his brethren, he had dirt-blonde hair and blue eyes and his bush of a beard had been pulled tight, plaited, and knotted. At his silence, the Barle continued.

"Brikka was the smallest of all her sisters, but so too was she the fiercest. It was said if ya stood upon her, ya could feel her wrath shakin' yar insides and turning yar legs ta jelly. A man could'nae stand when her anger showed." As he spoke, Ulrikson raised his eyes to the mountains, his head nodding imperceptibly to the giant sentinels.

"Her sisters Eracus and Ocanik tried ta calm Brikka, fearing the gods she raged upon would lose patience with her. But Brikka wanted more and would'nae listen ta their wisdom. Why should I be so small when I have the biggest heart and the hottest fire? she'd challenge them, I can feel it burning inside me,

"One day, tired of Brikka's ceaseless demands ta be the greatest and tallest of all her sisters, the gods smote her down, drivin' her deep beneath the earth 'til only her head rested above. Now Brikka could'nae see past her sisters' skirts ta look out upon the world and her fire was trapped far below. A fitting punishment for her stubbornness, the gods declared."

Ulrikson turned and looked at Crick. "But the fire still burns in her. These walls we stand upon are made of Brikka's gneiss and granite and are older by far than ya can imagine. We were dust in't heavens when this rock was birthed and yet if'n I lay naked upon it, I can feel Brikka still, raging below. She will rise again one day. Until then my people will wait and watch. So it has ever been."

Tannon Crick scowled, "You suffer the same affliction as Brikka, Johanus. She did not listen to her sisters and suffered for it. If you do not heed me, your people will never see her rise again, for you will all perish here. I urge you, at least, send those who cannot fight away; the mothers and children, perhaps with a small guard. High Barle Janis has pledged to shelter them."

"All here will fight. None'll leave, Order man. We'll nae abandon Brikka, her sisters will aid us. If ya dinna have the stomach fer battle take yar men and leave."

Crick snorted, the words, though a challenge, had been said without malice. It was one of the things he admired most about Norders. Blunt and to the point, they often said what they thought without regard for the offence it might cause.

He gazed out over the walls. It was difficult to see where the snow-covered ground twisted into the pale mist. It gave the appearance that the fortification floated upon a soft white cloud. Falsely of course, for Crick knew the walls were built upon a bed of hard rock that extended a hundred yards, one end anchored to a rising cliff face and the other finishing at a yawning chasm of splintered rock. Should he turn and look behind, he would see the wall's twin, guarding the eastern approach.

Crick had been here many times in the past; the last was when Johanus Ulrikson was little more than a babe in swaddling clothes. Highwatch had not changed much in the interim.

Life here was hard, even by Norder standards. The air was thin, the ground gave no yield for crops and there was not much else to live on besides. Barely a hundred souls resided here, in solid stone huts with slate grey roofs, all built within the relative shelter of the walls of Highwatch.

Crick had arrived the day before and after a brusque greeting, Ulrikson had invited him to eat and rest in the old tradition. Over a flagon of mead and a salted stew of tubers and fox meat, the Barle of Highwatch told him they'd seen more Rivers folk in the past ten days than in the past ten years. Ordinarily, they saw few outsiders. The people of the Rivers had better, more established trade routes to the south. Use of the high pass at Broken Tooth tended, almost exclusively, to be Norders from the banks of Skaag Lak and the forests of Helg. All this, Crick already knew of course. The point of it though was Ulrikson had learned of the urak incursion from a bunch of outsiders, the messenger from Jarlsheim turning up a day later to corroborate their disjointed tales.

"I've only eighty of ma own ta hold the wall with spear and bow. I'll need more'n the two score ya've brought and the two hundred from Skaag and Helg," Ulrikson had raged. "Where is Janis and where are his warriors?"

Crick had thought his claim exaggerated at the time. He'd seen barely fifty people when he rode into Highwatch and half were mothers and children. As for the warriors from Skaag and Helg, they'd arrived shortly after him with an oath from their Barles promising more would be sent. But time was running out.

He grimaced thinking of the night before. He'd been forced to intervene when Marlik Riekason had taken offence at Ulrikson's tone toward his Barle. Ai, they were fierce folk.

The gusting wind brought Crick back to himself. He wiped the moisture from his eyes before it could freeze. It would snow again soon. He could smell it. Already tiny crystals formed in the air, scratching at his face as they were swept by.

He squinted into the sky. The high cloud was lowering, sinking down the sharp slopes of Eracus and Ocanik, their peaks already vanished.

Closing his eyes to focus his mind, Crick phased into ki'tae, his hidden sense. Colours blossomed in his mind, a swirling riot dominated by shades of golds and blues and azures. He extended out looking for any tell-tale but found none. He phased back, a momentary pain pulsing through his eyes and into his brain as he opened them.

Ulrikson had said the last people to climb the pass had come two days ago. It left Crick with a hollow feeling in his chest and his guts roiled like they hadn't for many a year. Old tells from battle. The urak would not be far away. He turned to Ulrikson.

"Think I'll stay. At least until the wall is breached."

Ulrikson grunted. "It's cold. Ma balls are tucked up tight and both are telling me it'll only get colder this day." He slapped Crick on the shoulder, cracking the frost forming on his thick cloak. "Come, Ser Tannon. If'n our blood is soon ta feed Brikka let us drink ta it while we can."

The two men walked the wall to the gatehouse, passing the sentries standing watch, Ulrikson acknowledged each by name. They descended stone steps gritted with crushed rock and dirt, walked past a war engine next to the smouldering coals of a fire, and covered the short distance to the roundhouse, which, like everything in Highwatch, was stone-built.

Warmth and noise hit them as soon as they entered; the one as comforting as the other. In the centre was an open-hearth fire, the smoke cleverly captured by a metal hood that funnelled it up and through the rafters above. Enough escaped its rim, however, to leave wood smoke flavouring the air, seeping into clothing and skin alike.

Six long tables, bracketed with benches, spread out from the hearth like spokes on a wheel, and not a seat was spare.

Crick spied the five knights that comprised his Hand sitting at one of the tables with Marus Banff, his steward, at the end. Dressed as they were, they stood out; grey dogs in a brown pack. The five were wearing dark clothing beneath tarnished grey armour and thick sable cloaks. Banff was dressed in a similar fashion but without any armour. As Crick approached with Ulrikson by his side, his steward rose, followed immediately by the five.

"Sir Tannon. Barle Ulrikson." Banff ducked his head. "Here take my seat."

Banff nudged an elbow into the grey knight at his side, Katal Zakpikt, whose brown eyes stared back. In the torchlight, his dark skin looked deeper than it was. He puffed his cheeks out. "And mine, it seems I'm no longer in need of it."

Crick grinned. "It seems not, Kat."

They sat and Ulrikson bellowed for mead and food, deafening the table. Before it had a chance to arrive, the door to the roundhouse groaned open and a man in brown furs entered, snow dusting his cloak and shoulders, eyes searching the room.

Ulrikson immediately got up.

"Helge is back. Something is coming."

* * *

The fog was thicker than before. Rising against the walls it ate the sky and Crick could only see ten paces to either side.

Marus Banff was behind, somewhere in Highwatch, but Crick knew he'd not stray far. His Hand stood on either side of him, Jon Hodden and Katal to his right with David Sanction, Karl Hubert, and Merin Somar to his left. They were all armoured. Tannon Crick in his gold, his men in grey. All wore brushed steel cuirasses with matching vambraces on their arms and greaves on their legs. Quilted gambesons, black and full-bodied, sat beneath, providing an extra layer of padding and protection and covering their upper legs.

"Can't see shit in this," Jon Hodden growled.

"Urak could be twenty paces away and we wouldn't see 'em," David Sanction agreed. "Probably smell 'em though."

"The wind is at our backs," Merin said pointedly. "Best you keep quiet and listen instead."

No one said anything for a time. The fog swirled, snow fell and the cold sucked at their bones. A howl rose, both muffled and echoing so it was unclear whether it came from in front or behind.

They waited. Five minutes turned to ten when a voice rang out by the gatehouse close to their right. "Two of the dogs are back."

Ulrikson had sent five out not thirty minutes ago. That only two returned boded ill. Crick focused, slipping into ki'tae and the world changed. Gliding through the colour blooms he extended his awareness outward and found that which he sought. One or two may have blended into the kaleidoscope of colours and been missed. Not so the hundreds. White blemishes, laced through with blood reds and deep purples, were everywhere and he sensed hundreds more behind.

Tannon Crick rubbed his eyes. Taking a long breath he called out, loud enough that Ulrikson would hear from his position over by the gatehouse.

"They're here. Two hundred paces."

"Ready the nags," Ulrikson cried.

Behind came a roar of flame as the fires were doused with oil and a dozen flares fractured the mist. This was followed almost immediately by the subtle, grind of cording as the arms on six mangonels were wound back, the ancient war machines groaning under the stress.

A loud crack sounded, like lightning splitting a tree, and piercing screams filled the air as one of the engines tore apart, collapsing in on itself.

Crick turned round, they all did, but there was nothing to be done. As if the screams were a signal, arrows suddenly clattered against the stonework. Jon Hodden was struck and flew backwards off the wall; the heavy crump of his armour as he hit the ground softened by the snow. Crick and the rest of the Hand ducked low, taking cover behind the battlement. Katal crawled to the far edge of the rampart and stared down.

Marus Banff was there, knelt beside the fallen grey knight. Somehow, he'd dragged Jon into the lee of the wall sheltering them from the still falling arrows.

There was a loud snap, whoosh, thud, all in a heartbeat as a mangonel released, causing Banff and Katal to flinch. The war machine propelled its load of fire stones, sending them arching high into the air where they were swallowed by the mist.

Glancing up, Banff gave a quick shake of his head to Katal, who could see for himself that his friend's wound was mortal. A thick-shafted arrow had struck just below the left eye. Jon Hodden was still alive, body twitching, rivulets of blood running down his face, teeth red. But his wide eyes were glazed and unfocused. Death approached. Katal watched Banff draw a thin knife from his boot. Without hesitation, he thrust it through the knight's eye. His body gave a final shudder and went limp.

The crank of the mangonel intruded and Katal shuffled back to the wall. Dave Sanction and Karl Hubert were returning fire, launching arrows blindly from behind the battlements. Crick stared at him.

"Jon?"

"Gone," Katal murmured.

They all heard. Crick said nothing.

"Mercy take him," Merin muttered.

"Fucking hellspawn," Karl snarled, launching an arrow.

Another snap, thud, as a war machine unloaded. The clack of arrows on stone petered out. A roar, deep and guttural came from the mist and Ulrikson was screaming. "Here they come."

The Norders all rose up, Crick and his four with them. Shields were held out and spears brandished. Between them archers notched and drew, launching arrows into the fog as the roar grew closer.

The mangonel behind fired another hail of burning stone into the heavens but gave an ominous whine, then snap, as cordage broke. Loud curses replaced the expected crank of the gearwheel.

Like a surging wave, urak appeared from the mist, battle cries rising. They appeared huge, bestial things, standing a head taller than most men and half again as heavy. Most wore fur and leather with bands of metal sown in places. Their large heads were bare and their faces red as if dipped in blood and left to run, dripping down their torsos. They carried round shields colourfully emblazoned and were heavily armed.

As the urak rushed forward, Crick could only see those to his immediate front, but from the sounds of it, they attacked the whole breadth of the wall. David Sanction moved past his shoulder and angled his bow down. Crick followed the arrow as he released it, watching as it buried into the chest of an urak. At the next crenel, Karl was notching and launching as fast as he could. From this range and with the urak so thick, he hardly had to aim.

Sanction staggered suddenly as an arrow glanced off his helm. Crick grabbed a fistful of his cloak to stop him from stumbling backwards off the wall.

Wincing, Sanction grunted in pain. He shrugged, shaking his head to clear it. "Son of a whore," he cursed. With a glance and nod to Crick, he returned to the fray, keeping tight this time to the merlon for cover.

A head appeared at the opening in front of Crick, and he thrust his sword, short and sharp, into its face. He felt the blade bite and watched the urak fall away. He spared a brief look to his right. Katal stood with sword and shield on his back, a pace back from the embrasure. In his hand he held a short-handled spear, covering both his and Hodden's post. Beyond Katal was Marlik Riekason, who led the two score bannermen that High Barle Janis had sent with him and next along, the murky outline of another warrior. The mist swallowed up everything further along the wall.

Difficult to fight a battle like this; impossible to command one when you can see nothing, he thought.

He stabbed again as another head appeared. The urak ducked to avoid it but Crick smoothly followed, slicing into its neck. It dropped away spraying blood.

A hail of arrows, thick-shafted and dark in the muted light, swept the wall. Sparks flew off the stonework. Crick took a blow on his shield.

Pained cries rang out along the ramparts. Some arrows had found marks and warriors fell. A mangonel released nearby and Crick watched its fiery cargo streak into the sky, tearing a hole in the fog before it was swallowed. Somewhere out there fire rocks would be falling to deadly effect.

For days now, Ulrikson had been slicking the walls down with water, which cooled and turned to ice. It made the facing stonework slippery and the footing below treacherous. It seemed, however, not to bother the urak, their hooting calls were loud as another wave tried to scale the walls.

The ring of steel on steel sounded and Crick was thrusting again as an urak appeared, managing to latch a meaty hand over the rim to lever herself up with surprising dexterity. His sword dipped beneath her blocking hand and opened up her throat. He slashed downwards, his blade edge slicing into fingers and she fell away.

The chill in his bones was gone, he felt sweat on his back and his brow. "Sanction, cover my wall."

David Sanction stabbed, his sword coming back bloody. He stood to the side using the stone for cover. Breathing heavily, he grunted in response.

Crick slipped past him, then Karl Hubert who gave him a grin and a nod as if he was enjoying himself. He'd discarded his bow for a shield and his favoured axe, not the best weapon for this type of fight but Karl would use nothing else.

Merin, when he passed him, was covering two crenels like Katal. Crick stepped over a man sprawled across the rampart with an arrow in his chest, dead eyes staring at nothing. The dead man's cloak and clothing were the thick, brown fur of Highwatch, but his armour was mismatched and ill-fitting. Unlike Marlik Riekason and his warriors who held the right, and who were well-trained, seasoned men, this poor bastard lying at his feet was clearly a holdsteader, more used to hunting and gathering than fighting.

Crick moved on, encouraging the defenders as he went, clashing and fighting, bolstering them as needed. He ducked behind a merlon as a shower of arrows peppered the wall in front. A woman glanced at him; a line of blood marred her cheek. She looked tired and drawn but her eyes were fierce. An arrow thunked, punching through her breastplate and pushing her, spinning, off the rampart to the ground below.

An urak appeared where the woman had been and Crick's sword bit, slicing into skull and ear. His blade was almost wrenched from his grasp as the urak toppled back.

He spared a glance below for the woman, an old habit and a dangerous one. Only his reflexes saved him as he spun around a spear thrust. He crashed his shield into the urak that had slipped in behind him and then opened its belly with his sword. The urak howled. Crick slammed his shoulder into his shield and, with the aid of the icy stonework, pushed the urak from the wall.

He'd not seen the woman when he'd looked before, his eyes spotting instead the broken frame of a war machine, with fires burning either side to heat its shot.

The wall shivered suddenly and the ground trembled, forcing Crick to a knee. As if the mountains rumbled their disapproval, a tremendous groan rolled out, low and deep. A moment of stillness hung in the air, a resounding boom of thunder split it, immediately followed by a roar and a crash.

The walls shook. Warriors were thrown to the ground as the noise extended. The mist came billowing over the ramparts in a sudden thick rush and on its tail rode a cloud of snow and rock dust.

Disbelieving, Crick staggered to his feet. His ears were ringing. The urak would be coming; he started screaming, urging warriors to their feet, rushing along the wall, pulling men and women upright. The ramparts ran abrupt and sudden into the cliff face, he'd reached the end.

A bellowing of war cries rang out and the urak renewed their assault. The defenders, bruised and shaken, met them with sword and spear. The fighting turned brutal and desperate as urak gained the ramparts. Oversized, eyes filled with bloodlust, they wreaked havoc. Arrows started flying from below as women and the older children took aim at them. It was enough, barely, to hold the balance as urak were struck and dispatched only to be replaced by more.

Up ahead of Crick, two more urak cleared the wall. One took a spear to its left shoulder. Enraged, it seized the spear with one hand and smashed the man holding it with the axe held in its other, cleaving him from shoulder to sternum. Another urak clambered over the ledge.

Crick phased. Time slowed as he strode into battle. His sword swung from reverse guard to high point forward, punched through leather and sinew, scraped bone, and pierced heart. Turning, his momentum dragged the blade free and into the face of the urak who had a leg hooked over the battlement.

The remaining urak slashed, its heavy blade cutting the air. Crick ducked low, bringing his shield up, angling it to deflect the blow wide and into the merlon. Turning, twisting, he slipped past the urak dragging his blade edge through the tendons behind its knee. The urak roared in pain and swung an elbow back. Crick slipped to the side, his blade licking out again and taking it under the armpit, the urak's own mass sinking the blade deep.

Crick emerged from the chaos bloody, with warriors staring at him all around.

"Fight or die!" He bellowed.

"Fight or die," a woman screamed, baring her teeth. She held a spear that was half again as tall as her and thrust it violently through the crenels at an urak.

The shout went up and rippled down the wall. Crick gave a grim smile, he'd meant it as a warning, but it made a good battle cry.

More black-shafted arrows swept the walls and warriors fell impaled, the woman with the spear taking one in the throat. It sent her teetering and gurgling backwards off the wall.

Too many, Crick said to himself. Too many fallen and too many urak. Already half a dozen had reached the top and more were joining them in a sudden surge. The wall had moments before it was lost.

Focusing his mind, Tannon opened himself to ki'tae, this time drawing on the tae'al from the fires below, fires that fed the war machine their ammunition. The flames guttered and a dozen glowing coals, shimmering with heat, rose into the air. With a thought, he sent them, searing retribution, one after the other into urak. The stones struck, burrowing through leather and melting into skin and flesh, with force enough to knock each urak from its feet.

A moment passed. The wall was clear. Warriors rushed to plug the gaps and Crick sucked in a breath. His mouth was dry and he felt a great weariness. He needed a drink.

His consciousness prickled and a shiver ran through his body. Something moved in the aether; something fast, something unnatural. Crick turned to the west and looked up into the leaden sky. He could see nothing through the cloud. He crouched, bringing his shield around and triggered sigils, black runes hidden in a black face, and felt them shimmer into life. A bubble of energy rippled into being around him just as a ball of hellfire struck from the heavens, so loud and so vicious, it sent a shockwave out that incinerated everything inside twenty paces and blasted everyone within fifty from their feet, urak and human alike.

Crick was spared the heat and the fire but was sent hurtling from the wall and through the air. He landed with a crushing impact against the wall of the roundhouse, breath exploding from his body.

He awoke momentarily from where he lay crumpled on the ground. His ears were ringing and he felt blood dribbling out of them. It streamed from his nose too. One of his legs was numb and twisted at a funny angle and acute pain throbbed in his shield arm. He tried to stand and a sheering ache split his skull. His eyes closed and consciousness left him.

* * *

Marus Banff found his Lord during a lull in the fighting, broken and looking all but dead. He snorted a plume of breath into the air. They should all be dead.

Marlik Riekason had reinforced the left side of the wall with twenty men near the end. Even so, defeat had seemed inevitable when the urak inexplicably pulled back. Of the three hundred and twenty defenders only a hundred and ninety-eight survived. Most of those carried wounds and fifty or more were serious.

It was only a matter of time.

Dave Sanction had met his end. A cleaver blow rang his helm before deflecting into his shoulder. Katal had taken his assailant, but Sanction had bled out and died on the wall as the battle raged.

Banff brought the wagon around and between Katal and Merin they half lifted, half dragged Tannon Crick onto its bed.

"Does he live?" Riekason asked, watching from the side of the roundhouse.

"For now," Banff replied.

"Yar leaving?"

Banff nodded his reply.

"I've ten wounded that canna fight. If I strap them to they'n horses they can accompany you. There are many more besides. I'll speak ta Ulrikson."

"I dinna have any horses," Ulrikson complained when asked.

"Let them walk if'n they can. Better still, they can take some of our horses. We'll nae need them," Riekason replied grimly.

"If they can walk they can fight," Ulrikson argued.

In the end, Marus Banff left with his Lord, Hubert, Somar, and Zakpikt, thirty wounded and ten of the younger children. As the gate at Highwatch boomed shut and they took the rocky road eastward, Banff was glad to see the back of it. Only death was left in that place.

Chapter 2: Awakened

The Grim Marsh, The Rivers

Tom Trickle lurched. He gagged, throat burning as he tried sucking in lungfuls of air. They came, but only in short sharp gasps; each barely enough to sustain him. And, whilst each ragged breath felt a miracle, the air inhaled tasted warm and sour in his mouth.

His eyes slid open. Above was a mottled stain of greys and browns that shimmered in and out of focus. Tom groaned, his back was stiff and his shoulder blades ached. Whatever he was laid upon was hard and unforgiving.

Which of the seven hells is this, he wondered?

"You're alive then?" The voice was like gravel and instantly known. Black Jack.

With the name, his memory came rushing back. He would have wept, only tears took energy he didn't have and showed weakness that needed to be hid. Tears led to death and he very much wanted to be alive.

I'm in the first hell, Tom thought.

"It was a close thing. A moment more an' you'd be lying there dead, nought but a lump of meat."

Tom felt the still air move. A shadow loomed and peered down at him. It was a handsome yet rugged face, but all Tom saw in it were cold, calculating eyes and hard edges. His father crouched, kneeling over him.

"You know what occupied me mind, watchin' you? Waitin' to see if you decided to live or die?" A glint of teeth, "I'm in an expansive mood, so I'll tell ya.

"The world thinks ya gone and wouldn't miss ya none for it. Better a dead lump a meat than a livin' one. I was thinkin' how simple it'd be ta end ya. Then, I says to meself, 'Jackson,' I says, 'the world has shit on you so fuck the world.'"

"So, much as I might want to slit your throat and watch ya drown in ya own blood, I'm given ya a last chance. Think a yaself reborn, Tom. All I ask is loyalty, eh." Black Jack leaned over and patted Tom on the cheek. "You hear me boy, don't you?"

Tom glared, unable to stop the hate from filling his eyes.

"That's the spirit. Now, stop arsing about my little redwing and get yaself gone, afore I change me mind."

Tom watched his father rise, eyes conveying the threat in his words, and knew he had to move. He grunted and strained but his limbs felt numb, detached as if they belonged to another.

In the end, it was Black Jack that saved him. The dead, predatory gaze was penetrating, evaporating his fear, for Tom suddenly felt none. In its place lay a calm certainty; he would move or he would die.

Tom was not ready for death.

He rolled his body, easing the pain in his back and shoulders, then levered himself onto his hands and knees. He rested briefly, then struggled to his feet. Staggering, legs struggling to bear his weight, Tom swayed for the door.

Tom couldn't remember how he got home. He held a vague recollection of dim corridors and stone steps, of the sun in his eyes and the wind on his skin and voices calling to him. It was a discordant montage that failed to penetrate the fog that clouded his mind.

* * *

Tom awoke from a deep sleep, his body reluctant to acknowledge the hands roughly shaking him. With a groan, he cracked his eyelids and was relieved when the pounding, grinding pain he expected did not materialise. It was a small mercy.

The concerned face peering down at him had been beautiful once. But a harsh life and too much knorcha weed had taken its toll, pulling the skin tight around the woman's mouth and eyes, leaving her face stretched in permanent severity. Her smile was thin-lipped and Tom could smell the smoke tang on her breath and see the rotted gums and stained teeth.

"Quit shaking me, Ma." His throat was raw, his voice a pained hiss.

"Well, why dint ya answer," her words whistled as she spoke. "Thought you was dead."

"I feel it. Now leave me be." Tom rolled over, making his back a wall between them. Annoyingly, she began shaking him again.

"Why you keep pissin' on Black Jack's wrong side I'll never know. There's summat wrong in your head, Tom. I've always knowed it and the gods can see I've raised ya best I could; kept a roof over us. Well, I can't have it no more. You're a man growed and trouble I don't need no more."

Tom shrugged her hand from his shoulder and closed his eyes. "I said leave me be, damn it."

"No." She might have stopped shaking him, but something in her tone caused Tom to twist and look at her. "Witch stopped by yesterday with a face like someone pissed in her vinegar. Took one look at ya 'en said to send ya when you woke. Now, there's talk of murder up at her place and your name mixed in it all. I don't know the how or why, but I want ya gone. I've packed ya things, take 'em with you when ya leave."

"Where am I meant to go?" Tom said, hating the whine in his voice. He searched her face. In the veiled light, his mother's brown eyes looked soft and sad, but her jaw was set firm and her mouth was pinched tight. She didn't answer.

Tom sat up and watched her retreat to the flap of sackcloth covering the entrance to his room. She wasn't much of anything. Most days he despised her. Weak, self-serving, she'd shown him no love and Tom felt none in return but still, she was his mother and this was the only home he'd known.

Stood like a gargoyle in the doorway she watched as he laced his boots, cinching them tight. Tom wondered as he did so when he'd taken them off? He couldn't recall but he still wore the rest of his clothes, even his brown cloak, and hood. A glance around his sparse room was all it took to show that what few possessions he had were gone.

As if reading his mind, she spoke. "You got nothin' worth stealin'. They're in a sack by the front door." Stepping through the curtain she stood back, holding it wide, and waited.

Tom's feet felt heavy and his blood coursed slow and reluctant through his body. He took a step forward and felt his resolve harden. Fuck her, he didn't need her anyway. His next step was firmer and with the next he was through the flap, brushing past his mother and into the musty interior of the main room.

Tom froze, his heart thumping loudly. Busk stood in the doorframe leading to his mother's room. He wore a torn undershirt that started life white but was now a stained yellow and tan. It was tucked roughly into a pair of brown britches that sat unbuttoned and loose on his hips. One of Black Jack's bruisers, Busk had a face that looked like it had met a tree at some point, giving him a squashed, grumpy look that was uglier for the sneer painted across it.

Spying the sack bag by the front door, Tom moved towards it, suddenly eager to be gone. Busk followed his movements, dark eyes glinting as they caught the paltry light from the fire. He stank of sweat and stale mash and other things Tom didn't want to think about.

"Don't come crawling back." Busk held his arm out. "Sayzan," he called.

Tom watched his mother slip to Busk's side and into the crook of his body.

What did he care? Snatching his bag up, Tom didn't bother to check its contents. Anything missing was a moot point. With Busk there, it would do no good to argue and he'd suffered enough beatings already. Sparing a final glance at his mother, Tom levered the door open and shuffled out feeling torn and alone. He blinked in the harsh light. It was hardly glaring; the sky was cloudy and sullen but it was bright after the inside. There was snow on the ground still, apart from the pathways where it had vanished into the mulch. Tom judged it to be early morning. He must have slept the day and night away, his mother had said as much.

"'Bout frigardy time. My ass is froze off," declared a voice.

Spinning around, Tom found Nadine Varla rising from a log beside the woodpile. She grinned, the faded red bandana she wore struggling to contain her mane of black hair.

Tom couldn't help but return the grin. As sorry as he felt right then, Varla was one of the few faces he was pleased to see. She was as wild as her hair and her smile was a balm, for it was meant.

"Hey, Var."

Her eyes creased. "'Hey, Var' he says, ya little shit. Thought you was dead this time."

Tom tried for flippant but annoyingly his voice caught, "Ai, me too." He felt his eyes water in the wind and wiped a sleeve across them. "Wonder why I fuckin' bother livin'."

Varla crossed the space between them and slapped him on the arm. It hurt.

"Life is one big turd. Still, I'm glad you did bother." Varla said. "Now, stand tall, dry ya eyes. Don't give no-one nothin'. Ya hear me, Tom?"

Tom rubbed a hand where she'd struck him, "Don't know about hearin' ya, but I certainly feel ya." He sniffed then gave a wry smile and changed the subject. "How's little Aousa?"

"Good. Helpin' with the Millers." She smirked, leading Tom away. "Now, come on, this ain't a social call. Hett wants ya…" Her head turned and her voice trailed off.

Tom twisted, looking back. Busk stood at the door to his mother's house, watching with a leering grin on his face.

"Come on," Varla repeated. "Busk is too dumb to be evil but I swear, every time that man tries ta smile some furry creature somewhere keels over dead."

She led them through the Grimhold, past the dilapidated walls surrounding the keep, through the village, and onto the path to Hettingly's cottage and apothecary. All the while, Tom felt eyes on him and heard the conversations stop as he passed by. He did his best to ignore it all. Everyone knew everyone in the Grimhold and he didn't want to acknowledge their stares. He'd only see the all too familiar scorn or pity in their eyes.

Trees and bushes rose, lining the path as they left the holdstead and its jumbled mess of wood and stone cottages behind. Tom was warm despite the cold breeze but then it was always warmer in the Grimhold than its surroundings. Snow rarely settled long and the waters never froze except in the coldest, darkest of winters. According to legend, the Grimhold was protected from the harshest of the elements by the magics that lay hidden and dormant beneath the mire. Something Tom was not entirely convinced about.

Passing a bend in the path, Hett's stone-built cottage came into view. A finger twist of smoke from the stack in its thatch was the only sign it was occupied. Next to it, lower and smaller, was another building of similar construction that, but for its size, was almost its twin. No smoke rose from this roof but it immediately drew the eye, for its solid, heavy wooden door was flanked by a man and woman. Both wore the studded leathers usually reserved for raiding and both were armed with swords, their small wooden shields slung across their backs.

Varla had been mostly silent on the walk here and Tom had been grateful for that, absorbed as he was in self-pity. Now though, her silence rang like a warning bell as he surveyed the apothecary. Why were guards here? His mother's words from earlier echoed in his mind 'talk of murder and your name is mixed in it all'. It wasn't Hett; his ma said she had come by to see him. Immediately his thoughts turned to Wraith. Was she okay? Who was murdered?

He glared at Varla, "What's happened?"

"Hett will explain. No point hearing it twice," Varla said. "Come on."

She slapped him on the back, urging him on towards the cottage and Tom followed, his mind darting over possibilities and growing more unsettled with each of them.

They passed the guards, Mattie Nieker and Rogar Sanning, Tom giving both a distracted nod.

"What mood the witch?" Varla called out.

"If'n I said sweeter than wormwood I'd be lying," Mattie replied.

"Best keep me head down and mouth shut then." Varla laughed, her eyes flicking to Tom.

Her words were meant for him, Tom knew, but he didn't care. All he could think about was Wraith. He longed to open the door to the apothecary. To check she was there still and alive, but he knew Nieker and Sanning would stop him. They were there to keep folk out as much as the occupants in. Knew as well that any answers he needed lay with Hett.

Tom trudged by, head low, and marched up to the cottage. Its shutters were closed blocking any view of what might lie within. He licked dry lips and wished he had something to drink. Stepping in front of the door, he lifted his hand to knock when it flew open and the beetle-browed face of Hett appeared. She stood aside and jerked her head at him to enter. Varla didn't follow.

It was the first time Tom had been inside Hett's cottage. A brightly burning oil lamp hung from a beam in the centre of the room with a round, solid wood table beneath it. On the far wall, a hearth fire hissed sending warmth out that tickled his face. Cupboards and a rack with an oddment of garments hanging from it occupied the left sidewall. Its opposite held an internal door and was framed each side with pictures. Above him, the central beam had all manner of objects pinned or hooked to it. The room smelled of wintersweet and honeysuckle which stood in a wooden vase near the window. It was… homely and so far removed from anything Tom had ever seen or envisioned that he stood like an idiot with his mouth ajar.

The door slammed, bringing Tom back to himself. One of the chairs by the fire was occupied he realised; he could see the head of the person rising above the backrest. It didn't so much as twitch at the loud noise and seemed shaded despite the light in the room.

Hett jostled him as she moved past, hooking a stool out from under the table with a foot.

"Sit."

Tom moved to obey.

"Hang your cloak up fool, did your mother never teach you no manners?"

The reference to his ma smarted but Tom found his mood lifting despite it. Hett's manner, brusque and familiar, was oddly grounding. His eyes tracked to the shadowed figure as he unfastened his cloak. He knew it was her, could feel it in his blood.

"Stop gawping boy," Hett confirmed, "Now sit. Let me look at you."

Tom promptly sat and Hett immediately latched a gnarled hand to his chin and yanked his head up and around. Standing uncomfortably close, breath snorting out her nose, she peered into his eyes. Tom squirmed but her grip was fierce. After a time she released her hold and stepped back. Closing her eyes she held her hands out and Tom instantly felt a shift, the hair on his head and arms tingling. It was gone in an instant and Hett's clear blue eyes snapped open.

"Thought you was dead." Hett scowled.

"You're not the only one. Yet here I am," Tom said. He flinched as Hett moved but it was only to take a step away.

"You've some bad bruising around your neck and some itch foot but otherwise you seem whole," Hett replied. "The first will heal of its own, the second I'll give you a powder to rub in your toes and sprinkle in your wraps."

Not knowing what to say, Tom said nothing at first. His eyes drifted to Wraith. "She's sitting up. When did she awaken?"

"Bout the time Jackson was choking the life out of you, I'd say." Hett moved across to Wraith as she spoke and sank into the blanket draped over the opposite chair. "Come, sit here. Feast your eyes, Tom."

Rising from the stool, Tom picked it up, walked around the table and settled it between the two chairs. Sitting on it was like getting into one of the hot pools beneath the keep; the heat of the fire radiated against his exposed skin, sinking through his flesh and into his bones. Ordinarily, he would have taken pleasure from it but his thoughts were only for Wraith.

"What's wrong with her? Why is she sat staring into the flame? Does she not hear or see me?" Tom asked.

She looked changed. The black tendrils marking her eyes and mouth seemed darker in the firelight, or else the flame-glow against her pale skin made it appear so. Reaching out, Tom touched a hand to her shoulder and felt a jolt through his fingertips.

Wraith's head turned slowly, as if moved by some ancient mechanism, then tilted until it aligned perfectly with his. Her eyes were all black and danced with reflected firelight. Unblinking, they held his own, piercing him, rendering him powerless to move. Her head canted a fraction to the side.

"Tom."

Her lips hardly moved and the sound was barely audible but he heard it.

"Hmmm, interesting," Hett muttered. Then, as if tired of waiting for Tom to ask, Hett spoke. "Wraith awakened yesterday morn and called out but has uttered nothing else since. Until now, that is."

Tom's eyes flickered to the side, but he held Wraith still in his periphery. "She spoke. And she can sit. Can she walk? What did she say?"

"Just your name. Until now I wasn't sure she was aware it belonged to you; whether it was said consciously or whether it were just an echo of summat she'd heard and repeated. But you've disproved that I think." Hett sighed, "As for the rest, she has tension in her body. I walked her here, but her movement was uncoordinated, like that of a newborn foal, and with no volition of her own. It was only at my prodding and prompting she's here at all."

Tom couldn't keep the excitement from his voice. "That's something right? I mean, she turned to look at me and that was on her own. She sees me, knows who I am. I feel it. Does she understand us do you think?"

"Steady, Tom. We know nothing and must assume nothing. In answer, I think not. Whatever Wraith is, my sense is she is newly awakened. I suspect she understands tone more than actual words, but I expect that will change. Already she knows your name." Hett rubbed a hand over the back of her neck. "There's more. And much that remains unanswered."

"What?" Tom asked, hearing the disquiet in Hett's voice.

"The child is dead. Murdered."

"Child? What child." But Tom knew and Hett remained silent.

"Millie? Millie was murdered? By who? Why?" Tom bowed his head, angry all of a sudden and confused. She was an innocent. Death was a constant in the Grim but despite the violence of their world, the murder of a child was almost unheard of; there was barely a two score of them as it was. The Grim took its own dues.

"Found her mutilated body atop Lord Sandford. Her neck was broke, snapped like a twig and him lying there, drenched in her blood."

Tom twisted away from Wraith, his face red with more than just the heat of the fire, but Hett was not done.

"Found Sofia huddled in the far corner shaking like a leaf in a gale. Don't know what she saw but it broke her mind an' she's not said a word since."

"Gods save us. What if he'd killed Wraith?" Tom said. He knew he'd erred when Hett's face wrinkled into a frown, "Or Sophia. Where is she now? Is she safe at least?" He deflected.

"She's safe. Maybe, if her mind mends, she can give us some answers, eh?"

"Answers? But we know. You said yourself Sandford was covered in blood. Black Jack will kill him for this. Stake him in the stench for the Sallies to take."

"Sandford is awake and talking. He tells a different tale to the one you assume," Hett said.

"Bastard'll say anything to save his skin. Who wouldn't?" Tom hissed. Hett was quick, but Tom sensed her movement and ducked enough that her blow missed the back of his head, clipping him instead just above his ear. "Ouch."

"Engage that head of yours, Tom. I know you feel invested in Wraith but don't let it cloud your judgement," Hett berated.

"I thought I was?" Tom griped, rubbing his scalp. "If not Sandford then who? You said yourself Wraith hasn't moved excepting by you."

Hett glared. "Sandford claims no memory of what happened, only that he dreamt of a shade filling the room. A malevolent entity, he called it. One he claims knowledge of."

Tom shook his head at that but knew better than to interrupt.

"I can see you thinking about it, Tom. It's writ on your face like charcoal on wood. Ya probably right. The shade he speaks of is his own black soul. Thing is, he don't deny it. Last night he insisted we kill him, 'before I kill anyone else' he said. Cried like a babe, if you can believe that," Hett said.

"So do it. He's right, slip a blade in his heart or put something in his water. Let's be done with him."

Hett shook her head, "Despite all his tears and pleading, Sandford doesn't know what he did or even what happened. There is darkness in him, something other which does not belong. Given what we've witnessed, something evil. It has the same taste and scent as the darkness in Wraith only Wraith's is unfettered. Would you have me slip a knife in her heart too?"

"What do you mean, unfettered? I don't think Wraith would do this, you're wrong. She's not evil."

Hett barked and Tom knew her well enough by now to know that she laughed. Then, the humour left and she glared.

"Do I need ta slap ya again? You know I hate to repeat myself," Hett said. Then, in a more conciliatory tone, she continued. "I mean, that Sandford's darkness blackens his soul, but he is alive, there is a man inside still. Wraith on the other hand has no soul to taint. There is no humanity residing in her. Now do you understand?"

Hett turned and stared at Wraith who had not moved. Her head was still locked on the boy.

"Something happened in that room we don't understand, Tom. All we know for sure is an innocent girl was butchered and that the demons inside Sandford and Wraith have both awakened. Do you remember our vow? Because I do and I will hold you to it, only now, if one dies, they both must."

Tom's heart twisted at her words. He'd sworn an oath and meant it at the time and a man's word was not lightly given or broken. Now though he wasn't so sure. Looking back at Wraith he stared into the oblivion of her eyes and wondered if he could see it through. Hett would, the witch could have ended her anytime and Sandford for that matter. He recalled that Sanning and Nieker stood guard at the apothecary and with sudden clarity knew they had been posted there by Black Jack. Wraith and Sandford were alive because his father wanted it so.

He glanced again at Hett, her bright eyes a contradiction to Wraith's dark ones. The look she returned was a knowing one and he felt his face flush. She gave a tiny nod, and a chill of premonition ran like water down Tom's spine.

Alive for now but Hett would bide her time. She wanted them dead and expected his help when called.

Chapter 3: White Heron

Kingsholme, The Holme

The banging was loud and made Tomas jump. He was in Renix's apartment reading one of the many volumes in the Order ambassador's study. Books were endlessly fascinating. This one 'The History of Royce, First High King' fired his boyish imagination. Royce was only a handful of years older than him when first he campaigned, waging heroic battle.

The banging sounded again. Urgent, insistent, Tomas reluctantly closed the book and placed it on the side table. Rising, he headed for the entrance hall and wondered who it might be. He'd not answer the door, that would be foolish and Tomas was nobody's fool. He was wanted, the price on his head staggering and he was only twelve. With the temerity of youth, it had impressed him greatly. That was until Sparrow. Sparrow changed everything.

Whenever he closed his eyes and thought of Sparrow, Tomas vividly recalled her limp body hanging in the bell tower, skin flayed, tortured, murdered; could still smell the sweet repugnance of her decay. It ruined his memory of her and Tomas was bitter about that. They were young street thieves with nothing and no one except each other. Their friendship was unspoken for 'what is unsaid cannot be broken,' but their bond was deep; forged by the daily struggle to survive in a world that cared not whether they lived or died. The strife they got into, the hunger they shared and the pain they endured, were all the easier because they had each other. But that was lost now, superseded by the violence of Sparrow's death. And it was all his fault.

The thumping came again, this time accompanied by a voice that was deep and familiar. "Tomas, it is Horyk, Horyk Andersun. Lord Renix sent me. Do not make me batter the door down. It's urgent."

Empty words, the door was strong, made of an unknown hardwood and infused with energy, or at least that was what O'si told him. It wasn't beyond the realms of possibility that the Sháadretarch lied but Tomas had convinced himself it was true and thinking the door magicked made him feel safer. Besides, he'd tried picking its lock once and failed miserably, so it must be spelled.

The air shimmered in front of Tomas and the tall, imposing figure of Horyk Andersun appeared.

"You ain't funny, O'si," Tomas hissed, unamused.

"I am a little," Horyk said in the voice of the sultry, dark-skinned princess the demon liked to taunt him with.

"I can hear you speaking; I know you're in there Tomas," came the real Horyk. "Come on lad, open up. Renix sent us. By the Andersun Hearthstone, I swear an oath on it. I mean no harm boy."

Tomas glared accusingly at O'si and groused. "Don't s'pose you can take a peek. See if he's alone."

Horyk shrugged his wide shoulders and the princess answered. "Told you already, the door is infused with energy, I cannot penetrate its weave without destroying it and that would kill whoever is on the other side. Worse, it would make a mess of the entrance hall, and Renix, now you have told on me, would not best be pleased."

There came another bang on the door, this one less forceful, and a new voice, louder brasher. One Tomas had no trouble recognising, even if it hadn't announced itself.

"Boy. It is I, Herald, Crown Prince, and your liege. I demand you open this door immediately or I will have you flayed to within an inch of your life."

There ensued a loud whispered discussion. "Please, my prince, lower your tone. We need to be as unobtrusive as possible," the Norderman warned.

"Don't, 'my prince' me, Horyk. How dare he disobey my direct order?" Herald demanded. "I'm left standing like a vagabond on a street corner. It's intolerable."

Glancing at O'si, Tomas whispered. "Well, that's the Prince alright, it's impossible to fake pompous prig that well. Be ready."

"For what exactly?" the demon asked.

Tomas walked the hallway to the door and placed his hand on the lock bar. He couldn't help himself. "Who is it? Who's there?" The muffled splutter of indignation on the other side of the hardwood was immensely satisfying.

"You know it is I, you little guttersnipe. Now open this door before…."

"Your highness, pray-tell is that you?" Tomas gushed, adding in a flash of inspiration, "My prince."

A scuffle sounded and some hissed invective. It was Horyk who answered him. "Enough games, Tomas. Let us in."

Something in the Norderman's tone warned Tomas not to push further and so he slid the lock bar back. Turning the handle, he pulled the door wide. The prince barrelled in elbowing his way past with a glare for good measure.

Horyk, with a glance back down the stairs, grunted before ambling leisurely through the doorway. He stopped beside Tomas. "A boy was speaking, who was it to?"

"Myself," Tomas muttered, then when the imposing bulk beside him didn't move, elaborated. "When I get nervous I talk, even if it's just to me."

Horyk listened to the sounds of the street ebbing up the stairwell. "I need a red cloth or blanket. Think you can find one?"

"Sure, I'll go look," Tomas said. Horyk stopped him with a callused hand to his shoulder.

"Good. The Crown Prince and I will wait in the study."

Tomas scowled. "The solar is better. The study is private and Lord Renix ain't here."

As if not hearing a word, Horyk sauntered past him into the study.

"Bloody pox on 'em," Tomas cursed, slamming the door shut and sliding the lock bar in place. He didn't need to look either, recalling a red-dyed cloth in the study, in one of the cupboards from when he'd first 'explored' the room.

After handing it over to the Norderman, Tomas watched as Horyk shook it out and hung it from the window. In his world, a coloured thread tied to a post or an old boot on a dry line and a hundred other tells, told those in the know, where was safe, where was not, who was selling, who was buying and what. To Tomas, the red cloth was too loud and obvious. May as well stand naked on the roof, wave your arse in the air and say, look here I am, Tomas thought. He switched his attention to Herald.

The prince was pacing and clearly agitated, Horyk too though he hid it well. 'Information is the richest currency' Benny Four Fingers told Tomas once, 'but picking it can be harder 'un-picking a lock. Too many questions are like to get ya killed, even more so if they be givin' answers. Boy's gotta listen with his eyes.'

Sitting, Tomas picked up 'The History of Royce, First High King', opened it randomly then started reading.

It incensed Herald. That the street rat sat calmly, pretending to read. Pretending to be what he wasn't. The tome in the boy's lap looked weighty and old, its vellum fragile.

"Hey, boy. Don't touch what's not yours. That book's worth more than your life."

'I live here, you bloated windbag and I'll touch what I like,' Tomas wanted to shout, only life had taught him that answering back to a 'big' got you beat real bad and, as much as the prince irritated him, it was hard to forget those early lessons. Closing the book instead, Tomas lifted it back onto the stand, crossed his hands, and waited. It seemed to rile the prince even more.

"Don't just sit there like an idiot. Go, fetch me some wine. Horyk, you want some?"

"No."

Herald glared at Tomas until the boy got up and disappeared through the door.

"Leave the lad alone, my prince, tis unseemly to pick on him and bad ká to insult a host," Horyk said.

"Bad ká?" Herald snorted, "Leave your superstitious nonsense in the north where it belongs. Coming here was a mistake. I don't know why I listen to you."

"Hear that?" Horyk replied. He was stood to the side of the window where he could watch the square below unobserved. Herald paced closer until his first sword guided him with a hand to the opposite side of the window. "Do not stand in front of an open window, my prince."

"You're being overly dramatic, Horyk. This is not like you." Even as he said it though, Herald picked out the distant clamour of bells. It was not the deep toll of the Trinity Bells which called the people to worship every ten-day and holy day. These were higher, faster knells.

"The signal bells from Anglemere," Horyk stated. "The castle calls the garrisons to arms. The gates will be sealed and the city locked down. It bodes ill. If, it is as Renix suspects, then very ill for you, my prince."

"Your wine," Tomas stood in the doorway with a goblet in one hand and a carafe in the other.

Herald startled at the sudden interruption. Horyk's words disturbed him and it was almost a relief to focus on the boy again. "How long have you been eavesdropping?"

The chunk of the lock bar sounded from the hallway, loud in the interlude. It was followed by the squeak of a hinge.

Horyk signed for Herald to be silent. Moving, he occupied the centre of the room. Facing the door, he pulled his sword slowly and quietly from its scabbard.

The hinge sounded again, a click as the door shut followed by the lock bar dropping back into place.

Herald's shoulders were tense and he found himself holding his breath. It was bloody Horyk, putting him on edge with that drawn sword. It was probably just Renix returning. He spared a glance at the boy. No wine in his hands now, replaced instead by a small sharp blade. Where had that come from and when did he draw it? The boy faced the study door and it belatedly occurred to Herald to draw his own knife.

"I mean you no harm," a voice called from just outside the study. It was a woman's voice, calm and reasonable. A figure filled the door frame.

She was ordinary. Her brown hair neatly plaited into a tail, her face plain but friendly, eyes warm. She wore grey leggings and a long smock cinched at the waist with a black belt that held several pouches. To Herald, the woman seemed unthreatening, looking like a merchant or stallholder or any of a dozen professions, but the boy did not put his knife away and Horyk did not return his sword.

"Who might you be?" Horyk asked.

The woman wet her lips as she considered the question. "The giving of names can be a dangerous thing. Or so a little mouse tells me?" Her eyes swivelled to Tomas.

"I know who you are. I've seen you before," Tomas threatened.

"It is often better to say less, not more, Tomas. You of all people should understand that," the woman replied. "Still, since I know who you all are, it seems only fair to share my name. But first, tell me why you are here, Highness?"

"Lord Renix bid me come. He…" Herald's voice trailed off as Horyk held his fingers up to still him.

The woman's eyes danced. "I knew but had to ask. There is a form to these things that must be observed. I suspect you know my name already but I will tell it freely. I am Tasso Marn and you, Prince Herald, are a hunted man. Now, tell me everything Renix said."

Herald recounted events with Horyk adding bits missed here and there. Afterwards, Marn sat in thoughtful contemplation for a moment before looking up at them all.

"We must move quickly. That the bells still toll bodes ill. The streets will be filling with the city watch and Kingsguard if they aren't already. The three of you will need to change into something less, conspicuous."

Herald shook his head. "Just two, the boy's not coming. Got a price on his head and we don't need the attention that will bring."

"He comes, no argument," Marn said.

"With him? Na," Tomas thrust his chin in the direction of the prince, "Think I'll take me chances on me own."

"What part of 'no argument' did you not understand?"

The woman's eyes lost their soft edge and Tomas knew to shut his mouth. An opportunity would present itself soon enough, he told himself. Hopefully.

"Good." Marn said at his silence, then to all of them. "I will return soon with something you can wear. Until then, do not leave this room."

Whilst Marn spoke, her eyes never wavered from Tomas' as if she could read his thoughts and his cheeks flushed.

* * *

"A wagon is outside ready to take you to a safe house. We need to move now, time is crucial," Tasso Marn stressed.

With a grimace, Herald picked at his clothing. Ill-fitting, the coarse cloth was rough against his skin. Thankfully the woman had allowed him to keep his undershirt else he was sure he would break out in a rash.

"Rald," Marn called. When Herald didn't answer she poked a hard finger in his chest and watched his face redden in anger. "Rald, is your name now, your only name. Pay attention."

"When you get to the wagon, lie flat in the back. Do not dawdle, do not look about, and under no circumstance must you talk or utter a single sound. I will cover you over. You will not be able to see. That is both for your safety and mine. The ride will be uncomfortable and feel longer than it is. Endure it in silence. If we are discovered because of your moaning, I will stick a knife in you myself. Understood?"

Herald's neck flushed. Tasso Marn addressed them all but her eyes held his. A trickle of fear had feathered its way into his bones however and it tempered his anger. How had things come to this?

"Tomas, you lead, Rald next. Wait inside the arch until I call you, then Horyk." With that Marn ushered them out. "Leave the pack," she ordered Tomas.

"No, if the pack stays so do I," Tomas declared, shifting it on to his shoulder, the reassuring weight of 'Sházáik Douné Táak' pulling at the straps.

With a flick of her head, Tomas surged through into the entrance hall before Marn could change her mind. He heard Herald shuffling behind. At the door, Tomas pressed his ear to the hardwood. Detecting nothing he slid the lock bar up, turned the handle, and pulled the door ajar.

The darkened maw of the stairwell yawned, still and empty. Moving quickly, Tomas descended the steps. At the bottom, he waited until he felt the prince at his back. He glanced past the archway.

A wagon, ladened with a dozen bales of cloth awaited a mere arm's length away, a horse fidgeting in its traps. A hunched figure sat on the riding board, dark-skinned, black-haired. A brown cloak settled across his shoulders and gathered on the seat around him. He was armed. His head was still but Tomas got the distinct impression the man knew he was there.

With a swish and brush of cloth, Marn passed him. She moved directly to the wagon's backboard and Tomas watched as she shifted the bales. Standing back, her head twisted a fraction giving a quick surveil of the plaza before giving a curt nod.

Unhurried, Tomas moved to Marn. Hopping onto the flatbed he slid through the gap in the bales. The wagon was half empty. A large tarp was laid out and Tomas knew to wriggle beneath it. Moments later, the boards shifted imperceptibly as a weight settled upon it, followed by a grunt of exertion and shuffling. Then, the florid face of Herald appeared under the covering. The prince's dark eyes slid off Tomas as he crawled to the opposite side, his distaste obvious. Horyk was last and despite his size moved easily, squeezing in between prince and thief. It was tight, his shoulders broad and it earned him a glare from both sides.

Jumping up on the wagon, Marn checked the covering and re-positioned the cloth bales. Satisfied, she jumped down and latched the backboard up. Moments later she was clambering up onto the bench seat.

"All set, my love?" The man's voice was sonorous.

"Ready, Chiguar."

"White Heron?" he asked.

"Yes," said Marn.

The man clicked his tongue and with a shake of the reins, the wagon rumbled down the street and out of the square.

***

Tomas wasn't sure what the White Heron might be. It sounded like an inn, which was a worry since most had some kind of tie with the Syndicate. With a bounty on his head, an inn would hardly be a safe house for him or the prince. Tomas knew most of the taverns, at least in the Old Town districts of Gloamingate and Highgate. The Morngate area he knew less well but in none could he recall a White Heron.

The wagon proved to be as uncomfortable as Marn promised. The air was close, stale with breath and sweat, and the boards grew harder with every bounce and jostle. The prince grumbled but was quiet enough that the grind of the wheels over the cobbles drowned it out.

A voice called out and the wagon drew to a sudden stop. Tomas listened in trepidation.

"Hoo, Sergeant. What's all this?" The wagoner called, his deep voice jocular and friendly.

"Trouble at the top is all I know. Can't say no more than that, Chiguar," the voice replied.

"Good to see you, Sergeant Adler," Marn said. "I hear tell there was trouble at the Red Conclave and some of the Cardinals murdered. That true?"

"Nice to see you too, Marn, still with this reprobate I see," Adler joked.

"Reprobate… I seem to recall it was me helping you back to barracks last time you got blind drunk and what thanks do I get for it?" Chiguar protested.

"You make my point for me, my friend. It was you pouring that evil stuff down my neck. It gave me a mouth like sawdust and a head thick as porridge the whole of my next shift."

"Well, we'll have to do it again, eh! Maybe this time you might even buy a few rounds."

"Cheeky sod," The sergeant swore. "But I'll take you up on that. Once all this business is finished with."

"So what's happening?" Chiguar asked.

"Well to answer Marn, summat's up with the red priests only they're keeping tight shut about it. But this is something else. Captain has gone for a briefing and says orders is coming down the line. We're to hold the gates till then. Sorry folks."

Tomas heard an audible gasp from Marn.

"Damn it, Adler, business is tight. I don't deliver this order, Marn could lose the shop," Chiguar said in sudden angst.

There was a pregnant pause from the sergeant. "Pardon my language Marn but shit and damn." Another delay, "Go on, hurry then, quick afore I change my mind. If the captain hears tell he'll have my nuts in a noose."

The wagon rumbled to life and as they rolled beneath the arch of the gate, Tomas heard the sergeant. "Not a word of this. Captain hears I'll have you all emptying latrines for a month."

"If the Cap'n hears, you'll be joining us." a woman replied.

"If'n that's so Sayers, you'll be waking up with no teeth." The threats continued but trailed off as the wagon rolled through.

The rest of their journey was slow but uneventful. For Tomas, who was used to sitting patiently for hours on end whilst casing a place, it was the longest two hours of his short life. A handful of times Horyk had to caution Herald, who fidgeted and moaned constantly. At least until a ripping, tearing sounded and the thin-tipped blade of a rapier appeared. It parted the tarp and slipped unerringly between Horyk and the prince, its point lodging in the wagon bed. After that it was ten whole minutes before the muttering started again, only this time more subdued.

* * *

The White Heron was neither white nor a tavern. It was a dilapidated room on the second floor of a wood and thatch tenement.

The smell was enough to tell Tomas they were somewhere in Old Town, and most likely Gloamingate. The cloying whiff of tanneries and abattoirs meant they must be near Blood Row. It coloured the air, an overlay to the stink of soiled waste and refuse, the former clogging the central gutter that ran down the middle of the lane and the latter heaped in piles against walls and bracketing an alleyway just ahead.

The lane and alley had been the only visual clue to exactify where he was but Tomas was given no time to orient himself before Marn ushered them through a rickety door that threatened to cut loose from its hinge. Then, up a flight of stairs that groaned under Horyk's weight, along a corridor, and through a scarred but solid oaken door.

"Trinity save me," Herald gasped, "You don't seriously expect me to stay in this squalor? There are rats in that corner - and the smell!"

"It's better than my old place," Tomas observed.

Chiguar entered the room with an armful of bedrolls. "Here, take one. You'll be here until morning at least. Light no lamps and make as little noise as possible." Close up, Chiguar was of average height but heavyset with broad shoulders and thick arms. His hands were rough and callused; a working man's hands.

Taking a bedroll, Tomas picked a corner near the shuttered window and laid it out before slinging his pack on top of it. His body was stiff and sore from the wagon ride and he didn't want to lie down just yet. Instead, he stood stretching his back out and casting a discrete eye over Marn and Chiguar. He'd seen Chiguar once before, leaving Marn's shop. He'd thought nothing of it at the time, just another customer and Marn just a shopholder. Clearly, they were more.

Everything had happened so fast once Horyk and Herald turned up and he'd gone along, meek as a mouse, no questions asked. After the initial rush of leaving and clearing the gatehouse into the Trades, their escape had been far from dramatic, or fast. It had left plenty of time to think and all of it was troubling.

Renix was in Anglemere castle unpicking some plot. The High King lay poisoned, possibly dead and the prince whisked away in secrecy. Even Blind Pete the Leper could see Herald was up to his neck in shit and here he was with him. If there was one thing the streets taught, it was not to stand next to the person holding the can. And what of Renix? Where was he? What if he didn't show? Where would that leave him? Tomas eyed the shuttered window. If needs be, he could be out and away if he timed things right. It would take nothing.

An unfamiliar pang settled over him at his thoughts and in sudden clarity, he realised it was guilt. He would have died the night he fell but Renix had saved him, placed him under his protection and treated him well. Better than well; he'd given him a place to live, clothes, and freedom. And he had taken Sparrow and given her a proper burial, not left her to burn on the pauper's pyre. Renix had even given him his token.

The guilt was that he thought only of himself and of escaping. It was unworthy. Renix deserved better from him and it gave him the strangest feeling. Since when had he ever felt worth?

Herald spoke then, eerily echoing his own questions. "What of Renix? How will he find us here, wherever the hells here is? What if… what if he doesn't come?"

Marn looked at the prince. Her eyes guarded but she understood his meaning. "We wait, Rald; Chiguar will go and find out what he can. Plans have already been made to leave the city if needs be. Please, do not concern yourself."

"Don't concern myself!" Herald spluttered. "My father…"

Chiguar took two steps and stood face to face with the prince. Horyk pulled Herald back placing a hand on his sword hilt.

Ignoring the Norderman, Chiguar placed a finger to his lips, his eyes never wavering from Herald.

"Don't shush me," Herald spat.

The skin around Chiguar's eyes tightened but it was Marn that spoke. "My husband is being overly polite, Rald. What he means to say is, you talk too much and too loudly. You are not in control here, we are. You do what we say when we say, or we will take Tomas and leave you to your fate. Is that understood? Please answer quietly."

Herald's jaw chewed, then, he responded in a more measured tone. "I will not leave the city. I should never have come. I need to see my father not hide in some decrepit, foul-smelling hole. I am guilty of nothing."

"If you wish to leave, Chiguar will take you to the All-Ways. The city watch was closing down the market stalls when we passed it and there was a contingent of Kingsguard as well. Decide, now."

"We will wait," Horyk said. Herald started to object but before he could open his mouth, Horyk turned on him. "I am your sword, oath sworn to protect you with my life. And I am telling you, we wait here till morning's light."

Feeling outnumbered, Herald sat despondently on his bedroll. He could feel everyone's eyes on him, judging him, thinking him a fool. He glanced at the boy over by the window.

"What are you staring at?" he hissed.

Tomas looked away.

Chiguar spoke. "I must move the wagon. I'll be back soon." He embraced Marn briefly and then he was gone, his steps softly receding on the floorboards outside.

Closing the door, Marn slipped a bar across it. Resting her head against the wood she whispered under her breath.

"Be safe."

Chapter 4: Bitter Parting

Lower Rippleton, The Rivers

"No, absolutely not," Darion growled.

Face reddening, Nihm snarled back. "It's not your decision to make. You've made choices for me all my life. Now I make them." Each word hammered her father like a body blow.

They had been arguing for a while, each as stubborn as the other but now her Da sat heavily, shoulders slumped. They were in the Jaded Fish tavern at Lower Rippleton, in the room Darion shared with the Black Crow Sergeant, Kronke and the White Priest, Father Melbroth. Nihm was thankful neither was present.

It was unfair on him, yet even as guilt washed through her, Nihm knew she would not be moved. The girl her Da had left behind at the homestead all those many weeks ago no longer existed. The naive simplicity and innocence of her life were gone. She was not who she once had been. She had changed. She had killed. The thought was sobering.

Still, Nihm couldn't help but try to soften the blow a little. The abject misery on her Da's face was like he'd just received a death sentence.

"I'm not saying I won't ever go to Tankrit, just not now. Hiro's right; if I go, the Order will make my choices for me. Direct me, teach me. Tell me who I am. Well they had their chance. Now, I decide. I choose."

Eyebrows knuckling, Darion shook his head. "Would it be so bad? The Order taught me and your Ma. They're a force for good in this world and can teach you so many things. Make you the best you can be."

Nihm grimaced. "You told me yourself, I was tested and didn't have the ability. The Order rejected me when I was six. Ma didn't want to, yet every year she asked Keeper again and each time he said no. I'm sorry Da but they've had ten years of chances. I'm too old for this academy and even if it suits the Order now, it doesn't suit me. If and when I come to Tankrit, it will be for you, to see you. Not Keeper and not the Order."

"If ya tryin' ta appease me you're doing a lousy job." Darion sniffed, wiping a hand under his nose. "Well, better tell Mercy at least. She's a right to know. Hiro too, though I'm not sure he'll take you on this fool errand of his."

Rising, Darion hugged his daughter tight. Held her for a time as if it was all he need do to keep her safe with him. Finally, he let go. Holding her at arm's length he gazed at Nihm with sad eyes as if to imprint her face in his memory. He kissed her forehead.

"Enough," he rumbled.

They walked downstairs and into the inn's common room. It was early morning and still dark outside with the remnants of last night's storm blowing through. The room smelled of wood smoke and straw and despite the early hour, it was busy. Darion took the only free table by the window. The reason for its vacancy was obvious as they sat, with a draft blowing through the window joints that chilled the skin.

Catching sight of Mercy, Darion signed for the mage to come over. Excusing herself from Father Melbroth, she walked across, looked between father and daughter, and sat.

"You both look as miserable as a red sinner. What is it?" Mercy raised a hand to the innkeeper and signalled for food; thought about it and held up three fingers. If there was one thing she knew, misery loved company, they may as well eat.

"Nihm will explain once Hiro joins us," Darion replied. R'ell and M'rika entered, still wearing their white priest garments. He watched as they surveyed the room, found a quiet corner, and moved towards it. This must all seem so strange to them, Darion thought.

The conversation was stilted, only Mercy tried to engage in small talk and after a time she stopped trying. She was comfortable with silence. The food arrived, oatmeal with goat's milk, almonds and honey to sweeten it. Mercy tucked in, observing as Nihm pushed her spoon around the bowl.

"Whatever it is, eat. It's cold out, you'll need the energy whether you feel like eating or not." Mercy spooned a mouthful to illustrate her point.

Hiro and Maohong appeared and needed no prompting to make their way over.

"We should talk," Hiro said to Darion, "in private. No offence, Mercy."

The mage shrugged her shoulders and took another mouthful of oatmeal.

Darion was more direct. "Sit both of you; Nihm has something to say that Mercy needs to hear. Whatever you have to say can wait till after."

Hiro pursed his lips, absorbing the sombre mood around the table. Brusquely, he sat, sliding along the hardwood plank that served as a bench seat to make room for Mao.

"Just tell it straight." Darion patted Nihm's arm and, without preamble and full of nervous energy, she did.

"Since Ma saved me I've been different. You know it, even though we don't speak of it, Master Hiro aside," Nihm started. "In Fallston, I made a connection with Renco. I don't know how, but ever since I've been dream walking. At least, that's what I call it. At first, it was just dreams, nightmares really and I thought them my own, only they weren't. Sometimes, when I dream walk, I see through his eyes. I know Renco lives and have a vague sense of where he is. What I see is real," Nihm asserted.

Mercy was no longer eating. Her spoon rested in the bowl, the scar lining her cheek and jaw, stationary. Whilst Hiro regarded her with furrowed brows, a sure indicator that questions would follow once she was done.

"Girl no eat?" Mao asked, pointing at Nihm's bowl.

It broke the intensity of the moment. With a wry grin, Nihm slid her bowl across and watched as Maohong tucked in with gusto before restarting her tale.

"Renco was taken by the Red Priest, Zoller. A woman was with him with golden hair and blue eyes. She is important to him, I think. About five days back, when I dream walked, he was with an army of Red Cloaks. They were travelling north."

"North?" Hiro's hand cupped his chin.

"Yes, at least the river was on his left and the sun setting. When he looked back, I saw a fortress atop a hill."

"The Defile, it must be," Hiro exclaimed.

Encouraged that Hiro did not dismiss her claim out of hand, Nihm continued. "My next dream walk was a day past. Renco was still with the Red Cloaks but this time heading south and in a snowstorm. The sense I got was that they were running from something.

"Then, this morning I dream walked again. Renco and the woman were no longer with the Red Cloaks and somehow on the opposite side of the river. They were not alone." Nihm looked across into Mercy's eyes. "Amos was with him, Jobe and Jerkze too, and others, a stout woman in a robe and two girls. One I know, a child I met in Thorsten."

"You're sure? My brother lives…" Mercy's voice trailed off. Hope burned in her chest that had not lived there since Fallston.

"There is more," Nihm murmured. "Jerkze was injured, an arrow strike. I don't know how badly but he still lived when I awoke."

Mercy sat deep in reflection and Nihm waited, giving her time. When the mage looked up again her eyes were bright, face stern. "Thank you. I have kept my oath and you are safely returned to your father. Now, I must look to my brother."

"I'm coming with you," Nihm blurted.

"No," Mercy shook her head. "No, you're not. We've just brought you to safety. I'll not take you into danger again."

Nihm shrugged, "It's vast out there, a lot of wilderness. You'll never find them. Even with me and my dream walking, the chances are slim. Still, that's better than none."

Mercy rubbed a hand across her face, fingers tracing the livid scar on her left cheek. Troubled, she regarded Darion.

"And you're okay with this? After losing Marron, you're just gonna let Nihm go?"

Darion's jaw clenched and his steel-grey eyes were like flint. *'No, I'm not. I hate it,'* he wanted to shout. *'I want her with me, safe on Tankrit where she has a chance of belonging to something, of living without fear. Free to learn and become who she should be. But she won't go and I'll not force her. She's a woman grown and, damn it, it's her decision, not mine or Keeper's or anyone's.'* He sighed expansively and leaning across, Nihm placed a hand over his and squeezed. Instead, he answered simply.

"Ai."

A look of exasperation crossed Mercy's face. "That's all you've got to say?"

Darion's eyes flickered to Nihm. "Mercy's right," he muttered, "it's cold out. Eat, you'll need it." He slid his bowl across.

"Saint's light preserve me," Mercy blasphemed, "Hiro; tell them, this is madness."

Darion slammed a hand on the table and the bowls and drinking mugs rattled and danced. The sudden noise drew many eyes in the room.

"It's Nihm's choice and was not easily made. Take her with you or do not but don't undermine her because you disagree or think it reckless. And if you decide not to take her, I'll stake my ilf bow, Nihm will find your brother before you do."

A stilted silence followed, broken by Mao's scraping of the bowl with his spoon. He smacked his lips then probed and prodded, working at a bit of almond stuck between his teeth.

Hiro looked about the table. "Well, if that's settled, I suggest like friend Mao here, we eat whilst we can. I'll see Lord Inigo about getting across the river and acquiring some horses. If my memory serves, there's a landing just east of the Ripples. From there the Defile is a day's hard ride due north. Darion, I would have that word if I may?"

Gaining his feet, Hiro led Darion outside. It was bitterly cold and the snow a foot deep. They followed a forged path to the stables and storage barn. Once Hiro was satisfied it was empty, he turned to Darion.

"You'll be leaving us here then?"

Darion nodded. "I'll go south to Wooliston and seek passage across the Emerald Lake. I'll not risk the ilf in Rivercross."

"That is wisest," Hiro said agreeably. "What you did back there was brave and, I imagine, unbelievably hard. But it was right."

"Master Attimus taught me once that brave and foolish are two sides of the same coin," Darion said.

"Did he indeed?" Hiro muttered.

"That right and wrong is a matter of perspective," Darion continued.

"That old fossil says a lot of things," Hiro complained, "But now is not a time for philosophy. Tell me, what of the priest?"

"Father Melbroth? Ironside says Keeper has agreed to see him. He's coming with me. Now, ya gonna get to the point, or are we going to dance around all morning?"

Hiro sighed. "I should have made more effort to see you and Marron over the years. Sometimes I turn around and it seems a whole decade has gone by."

"Anyway, my point, lad, is Ironside and Castigan. They were here quickly, neh? Keeper only knew of the ilfanum a week ago. That means they were sent for something else. I think that something else is Nihm, though they know it not, or at least, not yet."

Darion paced, chewing on Hiro's words. Why Nihm and why now? It was Marron. In saving their daughter, she had awoken something inside of Nihm. Her abilities and powers seemed so very like those of an Order Knight, yet he knew she was different again. Did Keeper? Facing his old mentor, Darion cocked an eyebrow in query.

"Keeper sensed a power in the north unlike any before," Hiro answered his unspoken question. "I was sent to investigate and found Nihm. Keeper does not know the power is hers. He may have felt her awakening in the aether, but he does not yet understand it. With our relationship being somewhat fractious at the moment, Ironside and Castigan were dispatched. Of the Order Knights, they must have been closest to have arrived so quickly, neh?"

"Why hide her? Surely Keeper will protect Nihm. Instead, she follows you into danger," Darion growled.

Hiro nodded sagely. "We are all pieces on a board to Keeper. The intent might be for the greater good but Nihm is young and growing still and Keeper would have her be what is needed rather than allow Nihm the freedom to become what she is meant to be."

"And what is that exactly?" Darion asked.

Hiro shrugged. "How should I know? But I've seen her aura. It is true and I believe it should be for her to decide."

"With you guiding her I suppose," Darion hissed, "Because your purpose is so much purer than Keeper's?"

"Keeper and I are ancient, Darion, witnesses to the history of this land. We have raised kings and toppled tyrants. Yet look where we stand. Is humanity any better for our interventions?" Hiro sat on a hay bale.

"The Kingdoms have stagnated for centuries and now it is assailed once again by an ancient foe. Things must… evolve. I have faith that Nihm will do what is right for her. And maybe, just maybe, that is good for us all and the natural order of things, neh?"

Darion resumed his pacing. How could Hiro show such blind faith in Nihm, yet he, himself, be beset by doubt and turmoil? The cold metal on his ring finger ached. A reminder of what he had already lost. He didn't wish to lose his daughter as well, yet knew he could not keep her. As painful as it might be, Hiro was right. If faith was all he had left, he too would place it in Nihm.

Hiro watched the dawning acceptance in Darion's eyes and was moved by it. Should he say more? Should he say that the ilfanum had not set foot on Tankrit Isle in over seven hundred years? That sending an envoy was hugely momentous. That if Ironside and Castigan did not escort the envoy, it meant Keeper placed more importance on finding 'Nihm' than in mending fractured relations with Da'Mari? Relations that were vital if they were to combat the Morhudrim.

Rising from his straw seat, Hiro approached Darion. "I will say my goodbyes now, my friend." They clasped arms, then roughly embraced, Darion's large frame engulfing Hiro's.

Afterwards, alone, Darion sat and thought about everything they had discussed. On reflection, his friend and former master had not told him everything. It was not his way. But Hiro had told him what was needed. It would have to do.

Resolved, he went in search of Kronke.

* * *

"Lord Inigo has offered us work and we've taken it until we know what's what," Kronke rumbled. "Smee, that mage of his, says Lord Bouchemeaux still holds the Black Keep and that it'll be spring before the High Lord can move against the urak. I guess then, we'll go too."

Darion had gotten to know the Black Crow sergeant pretty well; they'd been through much together. He saw the flicker of hope cross his face. Kronke's wife lived and worked in the Black Keep. If the Black Crow lived, maybe she did too.

The two men were stood in private discussion on Lower Rippleton's dockside, surrounded by throngs of people as they were organised and then boarded on the small flotilla of boats.

"What of the lad? I was thinking James could come with me. There's nothing left here for him," Darion offered.

"He's asked me to take him on. If I want to see Thorsten again, I'll need him and many more like him." Kronke shrugged, uncomfortable but committed. "I got my oath and he wants to kill urak. The poor fool thinks that blood will ease his suffering."

An uneasy silence fell but it was how it had to be, and Darion knew it. He held his arm out and Kronke clasped it.

"If we both live through this thing, we're getting seriously shit-faced drunk," Kronke promised solemnly.

"Ai," Darion said agreeably. He glanced at the depleted remains of the Black Crows, who stood unobtrusively to the side. A ragtag bunch of misfits in black, travel-stained tabards and light armour that had seen better days.

Jess Crawley, as handsome as her mouth was foul, if not for the glower she wore. Morpete, fresh-faced and innocent to look at but for his eyes, those had seen the horror of death up close and he was a boy no more. Pieterzon, Zon, Deadeye, weasel-faced and whip-thin. Darion was mildly surprised to see him; he'd half expected the sneak thief to have absconded in the night. And, finally, James Encoma, Kronke's newest recruit. He was as young as Morpete, only with more anger than innocence and was the only Black Crow not in colours. *If he receives training, he'll do alright*, Darion thought, *make a good soldier if he lives long enough.*

He had spoken to them in farewell already. Brief words but heartfelt. They had shared a journey. He lifted a hand and it warmed him when they returned it, even Pieterzon. Five Black Crows, a single hand. They were maybe all that was left, outside of the Black Keep.

Looking around, Darion spied his daughter aboard the *River Arrow*, standing at its prow. Nihm watched him back. They had said their goodbyes in private. Stoic, both strong, each for the other, no idle words wasted. Hiro and Mao stood next to her and it eased Darion's soul a slither knowing they were there. Mercy, with her men Lucson and Stama also stood nearby. At least Nihm was in good company.

Darion's eyes snapped amidships. Ironside, Knight of the Order strode purposefully towards Hiro. His frame hinted at trouble and Darion was instantly moving.

* * *

"That is not acceptable," The larger knight was saying. "Keeper has instructed me to escort you to Tankrit and that is where we're going," his face was calm, his voice reasoning.

"I'm not," Nihm said. "Thank Keeper for his kind offer, but I'm afraid my answer is no."

"You are young and foolish to spurn such a generous proposal. Your father goes to Tankrit, why would you not wish to go with him?" Ironside asked.

"What I wish is none of your concern or Keeper's. I've nothing more to say on it." Nihm saw his right eye give a single twitch, *a sign of annoyance?*

<A strong probability.> whispered her mind. Already Sai was reading the Order Knight, the inflexion of his tone, every twitch of his body, stance, and posture. <I assess a high chance of physical confrontation.>

Nihm expelled a warm stream of breath through her nose watching it billow in the frosty air. At least Sai had learned not to put percentage numbers to it, knowing how it annoyed her. It must be serious, the thought abstractly popping into her head.

There was a hint of teeth as Ironside smiled. "This is not about wants or desires. It is about what must be. So, don't make this any harder than it should."

Twisting, he turned and extended his arm, holding a hand out for her to take. "Come, I don't have time to mollycoddle a young, reckless girl."

Nihm was entirely aware of her surroundings. There was little room in the prow to manoeuvre. Sliding her right foot back, Nihm turned side on and leant away from his hand.

"You have called me foolish, reckless, and twice, young," Nihm said. "I'm all of those things but it is not for you to say. I don't know you and care not what you want or must do. Please leave."

Mercy stood quietly, watching. Staff in hand, her dark leather cuirass singed, the burn marks framing the sigils etched at its centre; scars from before Fallston. The mage's face was pinched but otherwise, she showed no sign of intervening.

<*She has sworn an oath to the Order. She is bound by it not to interfere,*> Sai observed.

<*Nice one.*> Nihm bemoaned. She spared a glance at Hiro, observing Mao just behind who was idly picking at a feather that had speared his cloak. As if sensing her angst, Hiro stepped forward until he stood beside Ironside.

"Where's Lyra?"

Ironside tilted his head but his eyes never left Nihm. "Gone to meet Rutigard and Ansel. She'll be back with the wagons and horses before the sun is halfway high."

"A pity, maybe she could talk some sense into you," Hiro exclaimed. It caused Ironside to break eye contact and regard him instead.

The knight's green eyes were hard. "You've taken yourself away from the Order, Hiro. I don't understand why Keeper tolerates it but I'll warn you once, for old time's sake. Don't get in my way."

"You forget yourself. Nihm is my student, not Keeper's. She stays with me," Hiro stated.

Ironside shook his head. "Keeper was less than pleased about that when we spoke. I said it was a ruse that the girl is your student and Keeper did not deny me. So, unless you are coming to Tankrit with us, step away."

"That is two warnings," Hiro replied. He didn't move.

Watching the byplay, Nihm felt the tension crackle in the air between them. She was not the only one. Mercy stepped back and the people closest to the prow edged away. Nihm spotted R'ell and M'rika in their priest robes, their dark eyes unknowable, and wondered where they had come from. Last she'd seen they were on the shore near her Da. Thinking of him, she glanced and found him elbowing and shoving his way up the gangplank. Her heart skipped; she was not alone at least.

Sensing the moment was escaping him, Ironside was the first to move. Inhumanly quick, his arm shot out.

As fast as she was now, Nihm was not fast enough. By the time she reacted and phased, Ironside had already seized her arm. It was lightly held though and his grip easily broken. In a swirl of motion, Nihm threw her free arm up over his and twisted her body.

In the same instant, Hiro stepped between them, his movement a fluid blur as he too phased. He thrust a blocking hand against the Knight's forearm.

Ironside was waiting. His lunge had been precise, premeditated, and loose. As Hiro struck, so did he. Relinquishing his hold sent Nihm's counter off balance. Ducking beneath her arm, the Order Knight slammed his free hand, palm out, into Hiro's ribs.

Hiro saw it too late to block, his focus intent on protecting Nihm. It was a basic error; one he would have berated and chastised Renco for. Managing to turn with the blow, Hiro deflected enough to avoid the full impact. A sharp pain exploded in his side, taking his breath away. It was all he could do to fall back and roll, avoiding by a hair, Ironsides follow up.

Nihm cried out as Hiro went down. It happened so quickly it seemed one motion, the old monk, thrown across the sandalwood decking into Mercy's legs, skittling the mage.

As she tumbled, Mao hopped forward. Mouth open, he thrust his arms out, hands splayed. Nihm wasn't quite sure what it was she saw. The air shimmered, translucent and shifting, into a form that was hard to define. The hairs on her arms stood on end as an ionised charge filled the air.

Ironside instantly sensed the raw power building behind and like a spring trap released, spun to face this new threat.

Mao screamed. High-pitched and undulating, a wave of energy pulsating from where the air obscured and shivered. The pulse struck Ironside flush, making the skin on his face ripple and compact. His nose crunched, exploding blood as he was lifted and propelled out and over the prow railing. Flopping like a rag doll, Ironside crashed into the water.

There were screams and shouting followed by confusion and a mad rush, as the people closest tried to get away whilst others further back strained to see the commotion.

Somehow, through it all, Darion barged his way through. Nihm was standing, flushed but otherwise okay. Mercy was picking herself up, Lucson hauling her upright, none too gently. Hiro was down clutching his side whilst Mao stood, silent and slack-faced.

"What in hells happened? Are you alright?" Darion asked. Then at Nihm's nod of assurance, "Where are Snow and Ash?"

"They're in the barn. Morten's with them. They don't like the boat so much," Nihm murmured.

"And Ironside?" Darion couldn't see him anywhere. When a dozen pairs of eyes swivelled to the prow rail, he rushed to the side.

Immediately, Darion pulled his boots off and unclasped his cloak. Ironside was laid face down, half-submerged. Blood plumed ominously, streaking the water as it was teased away by the current.

Clearing the railing, Darion jumped and plunged into the river. The intense cold hit in a biting rush. Fighting to the surface, he gasped, sucking air in before panting it out again.

He'd landed near the body. Reaching out, Darion grasped a handful of fabric and pulling Ironside close, turned him over. His face was a mess. Darion couldn't tell if he was breathing or not. Looping a hand around, he paddled for the side, remembering to turn his head away.

* * *

Whilst the confrontation had been short its aftermath proved to be far-reaching. Ironside lived but was unconscious, his breathing ragged as he was carried back inside the Jaded Fish where Father Melbroth attended him. Hiro too was injured with two cracked ribs that pained him with every drawn breath. Mercy sought to bind them with cloth strips but Hiro waved her away.

"Leave them be. They will heal in their own time whether they are bound or no." It had forced a change in Hiro's plans, and he was sour about it. The ribs would take time to heal, and the injury would impede him too much to allow him to go after Renco. Not through rough country, buried beneath a blanket of snow. He needed rest, which he wouldn't get, there was no time for it and the binding oath he'd sworn dragged at him, pulling and urging him south.

In the end, Hiro decided to await Castigan and travel with the Order Knights and Darion to Wooliston. There it was agreed, he would wait five days for Mercy and Nihm. It would make for an interesting journey with Ironside for company.

Darion had hoped, briefly, that Nihm might follow Hiro, but one look was enough to tell him otherwise. A brief hug was all he allowed himself and some final, parting advice.

"Remember, the hunter must always consider the hunted, what they are, what they have, what they could do, and prepare accordingly," Darion said, invoking a saying uttered many times in the past. He smiled ruefully, eyes creasing. It was not enough to hide his concern.

"I will," promised Nihm. "When I'm done, I'll come find you."

Now, Darion was stood alone, watching as the *River Arrow* grew ever smaller; it was strange, he thought. No one that had boarded the vessel in Confluence remained with her now. Lord Idris had already left with Kronke, westward, back to meet his people as they travelled the south bank of the Fossa. According to Kronke, Idris felt he'd abandoned them and it impressed Darion that the young Lord looked to them now.

He inhaled deeply, the air crisp in his lungs, clean with the smell of new snow. His heart panged for a final glimpse of Nihm but she was hidden from view, the boat too distant. Mercy is with her, he consoled himself. A Duncan. Darion prayed it would be enough.

Chapter 5: Blood Has Been Spilt

Northwest of the Defile, The Rivers

Renco was surprised and more than a little chastened to discover his rescuers included a frumpy young woman and two girls. Already, a man lay badly wounded on account of him and now he was placing them all in danger.

Jobe stood, finished with his inspection of the canoe. "Damn boats trashed. Skin's torn below the waterline."

The grimness of Jobe's look left no one in any doubt about who he blamed. Renco signed awkwardly but Jobe ignored him and moved instead to his injured companion. "How is he?"

Amos looked up, "Not good, but it could be worse. His arm and leathers took the brunt, but the arrowhead is still buried. Blood's clean though, don't think it's hit anything vital."

A gasp of pain rose from Jerkze, "Bloody feels vital."

Jobe gave a hopeful look at Junip and wished he hadn't.

"I told you already. I'm no damn physiker." The mage glowered.

"He'll be alright, Junip." Annabelle laid a comforting hand on her shoulder. Her young voice trembled though, and her hazel eyes fixed imploringly on Amos.

"It needs to come out," Amos said, "Belle, fetch my pack." His words sent the young girl scrambling. Amos removed his gloves whilst he waited and blew on his hands, rubbing them vigorously until Annabelle returned.

"Sit and bite on this," he instructed Jerkze, helping him upright and placing a leather shaving strap between his teeth. Amos glanced up.

Without words, Jobe settled behind his friend, clasping him tight around the chest and pinning his uninjured arm. He forced a grin to his face. "This'll hurt to seven hells. Try not to swear, eh. Think'a the little girls."

"Sku uw," Jerkze retorted.

There was a sudden crack. Jerkze threw his head back and screamed.

Amos worked quickly, trimming loose splinters off the snapped shaft. Satisfied, he gave a curt nod to Jobe and pulled Jerkze's arm up and off the broken arrow.

Jerkze bucked in pain, biting hard on the leather strap, muffled swearing leaking past bared teeth.

Afterwards, the arrowhead was removed. The point was un-barbed, meant for piercing armour rather than snagging flesh. And whilst the wound was tidy because of it, it bled profusely and Jerkze lapsed into unconsciousness. Amos staunched the blood with a wadding cloth before smearing the wounds with salve then dressing and binding them. By this time, both girls were sobbing quietly and Junip was awkward in her comfort of them.

Renco spared a glance for Lett who had barely said a word since their rescue. Her face was a complex mask of emotions, her deep blue eyes fixed intently on the girls. She moved hesitantly towards them speaking gently. But it was Jobe's rough voice that he heard.

"So who in the hells are you?" Jobe asked as he left Jerkze's side and stalked forward.

Renco didn't answer. His head throbbed with a dull ache.

"Hey. I asked you a question."

"Softly, Jobe," Amos murmured. He had moved to the boat and didn't look around. "The lad can't talk."

"Kildare's hairy ballsack! Are you pissing me? Those Red Cloaks ain't gonna let this go and this… boy can't even tell us why." Jobe spun, eyes fixing on Lett.

"You got no trouble talking. Now what the…" He stopped himself. Belle and Lady Constance stared up at him, wide-eyed at his temper. Jobe grimaced, then started again. "Who are you and why did Red Cloaks stick an arrow in my friend?"

Standing, Lett squared her shoulders and faced him. Her voice, when she spoke though, was contrite.

"His name is Renco, and the fault is mine. I am Letizia Goodwill, daughter of Luke Goodwill a sanctioned bard of good standing. The Red Cloaks caught us in Fallston, murdered my father, and brought us south. We escaped in the storm, and you rescued us, for which you have my eternal thanks." Lett could feel Renco's dark eyes on her. "We didn't mean for any of this to happen. We're sorry about your friend."

"And the boat?" Jobe kicked it, "You sorry for that too I suppose?"

Lett swallowed and nodded her head.

"Why?" Amos had finished his scrutiny of the boat and his question was as crisp as the snow on the ground. "Why would Red Cloaks kill a bard and take you?"

Renco gestured, awkward with his broken fingers.

"What's he doing?" Amos asked, looking across.

Lett shrugged, "He talks with his hands, but I only know a few signs."

"Fascinating, like the ilfanum." The voice was Junip's. At Amos's piercing gaze she shrugged. "Master Lutico's study has a book on the ilfanum, an Order book. It is written that the ilf can talk with their hands faster than a man can speak."

Amos frowned, it made no sense. He glared at Lett. "We need to get gone. But not before you tell me what this is all about. If you tell me false I'll drag you back to the Red Cloaks myself."

Lett looked at Renco who gave a resigned nod.

"My father and I met Renco, his master, Hiro and their companion Maohong on the North Road. We travelled together for a time. Only, it seems Hiro was an Order man. The Red Cloaks came for him at Fallston only to find him gone. It was just before the town fell to urak and they had not the time to hunt him. Renco was taken by a Red Priest named Zoller in the hope of trapping Hiro when he came for him. Zoller murdered my father then took me hostage." Lett swiped at a tear that had escaped down her cheek. "We'll not go back, either of us."

"Lady's will," Jobe cursed, "Bloody ass end of nowhere and still she tests us." He looked accusingly at the clear sky and the small crescent moon of Nihmrodel hanging in the dawn mist. No remnant of the previous day's storm remained. They would get no help from the gods in covering their trail.

"Will they come?" Junip asked.

"Oh, they'll come," Jobe answered, "Blood has been spilt and the bastards will want back what was taken. Question is, what to do with them?" He indicated Renco and Lett.

There was a dry cough followed by a groan. Jerkze was awake. "Lady Constance and Belle, you must keep them safe." He gritted his teeth. "There were ten Red Cloaks, too many to fight. You must leave me and go."

"No, I'll not leave you." Annabelle ran to Jerkze and hugged him, drawing a wince of pain. "I've lost my Ma. I won't lose you too. Jobe, tell him. Amos?"

"There's a lot more of them than ten," Lett interrupted.

"How many more?" Amos asked.

Wearing a look of frustration, Renco signed, the fingers on his good hand clicking and snapping in quick succession.

Lett answered for them. "Thousands and led by Jon Whent, Archbishop of Killenhess."

Amos shook his head, "Lord Commander of the Faith Militant, you don't do things by half." He paced in thought, then, regarded Renco. "I have heard of this Master Hiro. My father has spoken of him on occasion, though I do not recall him myself. Are you of the Order?"

Renco shrugged his shoulders.

"Well, no matter. Facts is facts and we are where we're at." Amos frowned. "Nearest bridge is at the Defile giving us a little more than half a day by my reckoning."

He glanced across at Jobe who gave a shake of his head. "If we followed a road, mayhap. More likely a day in this country. Maybe longer with Jerkze injured as he is."

Amos nodded reluctant acceptance. Once the storm had moved away the imposing fortress had appeared in the south as if a veil had been lifted. Tantalisingly close but still too far it seemed. "He'll have trouble walking, there are no two ways about that."

Renco pointed at the boat then Jerkze and mimed putting something into it.

"Ai lad, that's well thought but I'm thinking we must meet these Red Cloaks. Jerkze needs a physiker and the girls need safety. I've heard it said Archbishop Whent is honourable. I will intervene on your behalf."

Renco looked at Lett, pointed then held his hand flat.

"No," Lett argued. "I'll not stay. I'm with you."

Frustrated, Renco shook his head, no. Then knuckled his temple at the ache it caused.

"Yes, I am. I'd sooner die than go back. I swear it, Renco. They might have broken your fingers and stripped your back, but they murdered my Da and…" Lett paused, suddenly mindful that the girls were listening avidly. She hissed, "…used me."

"I will not let them harm you," Constance declared suddenly, standing. "You can be one of my Ladies. Then you will be under my protection."

Returning a broken smile, Lett took the young girl's hand. "That is very generous, Lady Constance. But the only 'right' they see is their own. I would not willingly put you in danger." Warmth filled her chest; she'd barely known the girl five minutes so why did her eyes water so? Bending, Lett hugged both girls tight. "But thank you. Stay safe both of you and look after each other." Giving a nod to the frumpy nanny, Lett turned and strode from camp.

Renco gave a short, sharp whistle and waited until Lett turned to face him. With a tight grin, he pointed to the southwest.

"I knew that," Lett muttered, changing direction.

Having no words, Renco gave a short bow to Amos. He repeated the gesture to Jerkze then to the woman and each of the girls and finally Jobe.

"They'll catch you by sundown," Jobe offered. Renco shrugged his shoulders then followed Lett.

"Hey, kid," Jobe called out.

Turning, Renco was just in time to catch the pack hefted at him, his broken hand smarting at the sudden motion.

"Think you'll need that more than me."

* * *

"There's something behind us," Annabelle called out. She walked at the back of the group, following the deep rift left in the snow by the others. Her muscles ached with fatigue and her feet would have hurt if they weren't already numb with cold. They had walked most of the light out of the day and the Defile had edged ever nearer but all too slowly.

Amos called a halt from the front, where he and Jobe dragged the canoe by its lanyard over the snow. They left a flush faced Junip to watch over Jerkze and joined Lady Constance and Annabelle at the back. Annabelle pointed out a flash of red through beams of trees and snow-covered bushes.

"Red Cloaks," Jobe confirmed. Now they had stopped, they could hear the faint sound of horse and harness on the breeze.

"Must have missed us going north then hit our trail," Amos said. "We'll await them here."

A score of Red Cloaks cleared the woodland, riding single file as they followed the tracks in the snow. A cry rang out at spotting their quarry and they broke into a canter, quickly closing the distance. As they neared, the column split, horses high stepping through the snow to surround them.

They were heavily armed with shield and spear and Amos saw that several carried the mid-length flat bows favoured by the middle kingdoms.

Picking out a burly, sour-faced sergeant, Amos stepped forward. "Hail, Brothers, may fortune shine upon you."

The riders shifted, horses snorting plumes in the air. The sergeant sneered. "And Kildare's judgement on you; now, unfasten your sword belts and keep your hands where I can see them."

"There's no need. I'm Lord Amos Duncan and on my honour, I will not raise my hand against you. Now, take me to Lord Commander Whent.

The sergeant gave a terse laugh. "If you're a Duncan then I'm High Cardinal Lannik." He signalled and spears were levelled, and several bows raised and drawn.

"If I have to ask again, the first arrow will be through your man there." He indicated Jobe.

Amos looked at Jobe. Together, they slowly unbuckled their sword belts, letting them slip to the ground.

"Now, before I string you up. Where are they?"

Amos opened his mouth to answer when a voice trilled.

"That's not very clever. If you're going to string us up why should we tell you anything?"

Amos gaped at Constance.

"And who might you be, child?" The sergeant smirked, "Lady Duncan perhaps or a princess maybe?"

"I am Lady Constance Bouchemeax of Thorsten and Lord Amos is escorting me to Rivercross at my father's behest."

The sergeant laughed again but there was something in the girl's demeanour that rang true. Her blue eyes flashed, and her chin came up and now that he looked, all their clothing and cloaks were of good quality. These were not peasants.

Amos raised his eyebrows at Constance. "The two you hunt left us back at the river. They are ill-prepared and will likely freeze to death by morning. Why not leave them to their fate?"

The sergeant didn't reply, his horse pawing the ground impatiently. Finally, he twisted in his saddle. "Brother Jekka, bind them. Take them to Captain Warwick. I'll go for the boy."

"And the girl?" Jekka asked.

"Lord Commander said nothing about her." With a touch of knee and rein, his horse wheeled about. The sergeant shouted orders over his shoulder and half the Red Cloaks peeled away, following as he took the trail back north.

* * *

Renco looked up at the sun and closed his eyes, letting sunspots play across his eyelids and feeling the warmth caress his skin. Though his head hurt still he felt energised. The fingers on his left hand ached terribly but it was a good ache. Healing pain Mao would say. Something he was familiar with. He rolled his shoulders to ease the muscles where the straps of his pack dug in and was pleased; the skin on his back was tight where it knit together but it hadn't torn anew.

His belly rumbled, adding its unwelcome voice to the litany of sensations he was feeling. He ignored it, concentrating instead on the crunch of snow that grew steadily louder. When he judged it close enough, Renco opened his eyes and set off once more.

"We've been walking for hours," Lett panted. She scowled at Renco's back, then, not wanting to lag behind again, trudged wearily after, grumbling to herself. How could she feel so hot, yet at the same time her hands and feet be numb with cold? Even the skin on her face was sharp and sensitive. She glowered at the watery sun then stopped with a puzzled expression on her face.

"Hey, we're going north?"

Renco gave no sign he'd heard and Lett raised her voice. "I said we're headed north." Temper rising, she increased her pace, catching him. As she reached a hand toward him, Renco twisted to face her. It was so sudden that Lett stumbled to avoid running into him and fell.

Renco caught her easily in his arms, leaning his head away to avoid contact with hers.

She gasped face flushing and pushed away. "Damn fool." Her heart was beating wildly. "You're going the wrong way. Did you not hear me?"

Renco signed, 'I hear you.' He held an exaggerated finger to his lips, turned away and continued walking.

Glaring, Lett stalked after, muttering under her breath. His warning was clear though, so she kept it just loud enough he would hear without carrying further. Before, she had followed along blindly, but his terse command had her scanning the trees and surrounding bushes. Their tracks snaked out behind, obvious in the snow. They would be easy to follow and there was no way around it. Now she looked though, there were other tracks in the snow made by creatures smaller than they. Disgruntled and with a growing sense of trepidation she toiled after him.

As the day advanced, their path slowly curved back to the east and with every step, Lett's frustration grew. Only Renco's unflagging certainty stopped her from venting it. The sky had changed from blue to a darkening emerald when they entered a tight thicket of laurus shrub, startling a flight of whitetails from its ever-green canopy. The thick foliage, close above their heads, formed a natural barrier and the ground beneath its roof was a carpet of fallen leaves that was blessedly free of snow. Signalling they would rest, Renco eased the pack from his back and propped it against a thin trunk.

Sinking onto the bed of leaves, Lett hugged her cloak tight around, pleased to be out of the chill wind. Shoulders slumped, she watched as Renco ducked low beneath the overhang. Parting branches and bushes he stared out into the descending twilight.

She sighed heavily. That Renco seemed unfazed by the cold and untroubled by fatigue both intrigued and annoyed her. As if sensing her scrutiny, his head bent and his eyes fastened on hers. Hooded and dark in the half-light, Lett couldn't hold them, the accusation in them was too much. Glancing away, she fell back and closed her eyes.

Unfastening his cloak, Renco silently crossed the space between them and swirled it so the cape flared and settled over her prone form. It caused Lett to startle, eyes snapping open. He signed for her to rest before moving back to his watching post.

Lett didn't know, he suspected, but they had come full circle. To his left, no more than sixty paces away and hidden by a border of dense trees and brush, was the River Oust. The quiet sound of water barely discernible beneath the flutter of wind touched leaves. To the south, open ground extended a hundred yards before turning to bushes and a stand of eldas. The trees were the same ones from this morning. He couldn't see the remains of Amos's camp but he knew it was there. Crouching on his haunches, he settled in and waited.

The wait turned out to be both short and long. As the sun was shedding its final light, a sound intruded. Indistinct at first, it was nevertheless incongruent. It did not belong. Renco phased.

A myriad of indistinct images exploded in his mind; a swirling kaleidoscope of purple and violets and indigo with clumps of colours from across the spectrum weaving through it. Around and above it all, the gold of the heavens, mellowed by the retreating sun. Tae'al, aether, the energy that binds all things; Renco marvelled at it.

Focusing, Renco moved his consciousness, shifting through the purple and violets of the open ground to the indigo and blues of the trees. The further his mind passed however, the more opaque the colours became and the harder it was to untangle and discern the weave of what lay beyond.

There.

A distortion in the aether.

White swirls, faint but distinct with yellows and browns threading it and the smaller yet clearer tell-tale of greens and browns. Horses and riders approached. Renco let go of his sense, a wave of nausea rinsing through him in punishment and his already tender head pulsed in pain. He retched.

"Renco," Lett called softly. "Are you alright?"

Renco spat to clear the taste of bile from his mouth. Moving to his pack, he took a swig from his waterskin and swilled it.

"What is it? Are you ill?" Lett was on her feet, brow wrinkled.

Renco waved he was okay. Stoppering the waterskin he offered it to her. Lett shook her head and he re-tied it to his pack. He signed, aware she would not understand what he said but conveying enough that she knew they were no longer alone.

She moved to his watching post and peered out through the bushy leaves and Renco joined her. "I don't see anything," she husked.

Renco pointed out the direction then signed to wait and listen. They had spent much time together, close, huddled for warmth underneath blankets and beneath the canvas tents of the Red Cloaks. It was strange then, that at that moment, he felt so aware of her. How their hips touched, and her leg brushed against his; the way her breath caressed the air in a soft cloud. He could feel his blood, heating, pulsating in his chest.

"There, I saw something," Lett whispered.

Her words broke the spell and Renco looked to the far trees and glimpsed a splash of red. He glanced at Lett and her eyes met his, her look hard to discern; shy, uncertain, fearful? The blue of them was so loud against the red of her cloak and hood. Renco's eyes went wide. Signing urgently for her to follow, he moved back, deeper undercover. Lett didn't hesitate, a wrinkle of a question tugging at her mouth. Touching her cloak, Renco pointed with his broken fingers in the general direction of their sighting and was thankful when Lett's expression changed to one of understanding. Unclasping the red cloak, she deftly rolled and folded it, laying it neatly on top of their pack.

"I didn't even think," Lett said, moving back to observe the far trees.

Renco followed, settling again beside her, though keeping a small gap so that they did not touch. He didn't need the distraction. Renco could hear the occasional snicker of horses and the vague sound of men.

"There, you see that red through the trees and there." Lett pointed them out. "Red cloaks for sure. What do we do now?"

'Wait', Renco signed. And they did, as the last of the light slowly faded. They watched as two shadows stepped out of the treeline and made their way slowly east until they disappeared in the thick bush and shrubs that lined the river. When they returned to view a while later they walked, unhurried it seemed, back to the stand of eldas.

"Do you think they will camp the night?" Lett whispered.

Renco peered at the sky. It was clear of cloud and the night promised to be a sharp, cold one. The moons were out. Nihmrodel, who had graced the day, was moving below the horizon. Ankor was rising in the west and Kildare high and to the south. Together, they provided a witching light to see by. More than enough for the hunters to track them by through snow that was quick to give up the secret of their passage. Renco shrugged and returned to his vigil.

After a time, Lett grew tired and moved away shivering with cold. Wrapping herself in her cloak once again, she curled up on a bed of leaves. Dragging Renco's cloak over herself, she fell into a fitful sleep.

Renco waited, listening until Lett's breathing was deep and even. He could taste the sting in his throat from his earlier venture reading aether. Reluctantly, and, resolving not to overextend himself again, he phased once more into ki'tae. The purple and violets of the grasslands were tinged with the pink of snow cover and dotted and clustered with specs of white like the stars in the heavens. With a thought, his mind swept over the meadow grass until he reached the whorls of blue, indigo and aquamarine, all laced with browns and golds and yellows. It was beautiful and tranquil, sensing the life all around. Trees were always so vibrant, each thread of colour pulsating like veins. Something he always found soothing.

Beyond it though, was what he looked for. Faint knuckles of white bloomed; life of a different nature. His consciousness hovered. He was near the limits of his ability, pushing further would bring back his nausea from before. This will be enough, he told himself.

Obscure through the clouds of aether, he could nevertheless count the horses, gathered in a cluster together, and the men. There were ten. Fewer than expected but more than he wanted.

After a time, the swirls moved, merging and gathering and instinctively, Renco knew they were preparing to depart. A flare of white glimmered then faded, like lightning on a distant thunderhead.

Something else was out there.

With a thought, Renco pushed deeper. The men and horses brightened, and he could see the strands of colour weaving a lattice through the white, each unique and distinctive.

He moved past, the aether seeming to fade into a haze that occluded his mind until he could move no further. The faint bloom of white could barely be discerned, as if looking through thin gauze. It was enough though to see that the white was bound in wires of deep purple and dark reds.

Renco lurched, retching violently. Rolling forward onto his knees, he vomited bile onto the leafy carpet. His head pounded mercilessly and he groaned.

"Renco? What's wrong?" Lett was by his side though he'd not heard her approach. Hands gripped his shoulders and pulled, insistent, and Renco shuffled backwards. He felt weak and slipped over onto his side. The ground was cold against his head, and he was grateful for it.

"What is it? What can I do?"

Renco rolled onto his back, hands splayed out, digging beneath the carpet of leaves to the earth below. His palms and fingers brushed against the soil and it eased him. Grounding him somehow, though he knew not how.

"You're worrying me." Lett's whisper sounded loud in the darkness.

Reaching up for her with his good hand, Renco patted her shoulder to ease her worry, then, touched fingers to her lips to still her words. He could not answer her questions and she couldn't see him in the darkness even if she could understand his signing.

Abruptly, Lett lay beside him. Drawing his cloak over them both like a blanket, she snuggled her warmth next to his. They laid there a while, taking comfort in each other's nearness. After a time, Lett spoke, her voice soft.

"If we ever get out of this, I don't know what to do or where to go. I have family in Midshire, aunts and uncles in Harker, but I don't want to go there. Maybe for a time, it might be alrig…"

A howl broke the night and Lett sat bolt upright. A distant clamour rose up with her. Iron on iron, shouts and the squealing screech of panicked horses.

"Renco, I think they're fighting. You don't think Lord Amos…" Lett's voice trailed off. "Urak. It's urak isn't it? You knew. Somehow you knew."

Renco dragged himself upright beside her, his head still sore, the pain persisting. He laid a calming hand on Lett's shoulder and stilled her.

Sinking back down, Renco lay with his good hand behind his head and listened to the orchestra of battle.

Chapter 6: Death Road

Northeast of Upper Rippleton, The Rivers

They rode northward, moving in single file, following an old path that stretched across the snow-covered grasslands. Stama led the way. As promised, Lord Idris Inigo had provisioned them with horses, unloading them from one of the barges. They were fine animals from his stable with strong temperaments.

Nihm rode at the back, Ash and Snow bounding along at her side. The snow was not so deep that it hindered the wolfdogs who revelled in it with the exuberant excitement of youth. The adrenalin from her earlier confrontation with Ironside had slowly worn off as they rode and was replaced with apprehension at the enormity of their task. Somewhere out there was Renco, Amos and the others too and the golden-haired woman, Lett. Finding them would be difficult.

The company maintained a steady, ground-eating pace interspersing walks with trots and canters. Grey clouds, discarded remnants of the earlier storm, dappled the blue sky but they were high and the riders found themselves in sun more often than cloud shadow.

As fresh as it was, Nihm enjoyed the coolness on her face and the way the breeze plucked playfully at the hair tufting from the bottom of her wool hat. It was invigorating. She glanced at Morten riding just ahead and smirked. His bay roan was frisky and headstrong, and he was all arms and legs trying to control her. Morten was usually good with horses, just maybe not to ride them.

<*I detect you find Morten's discomfort amusing. Why?*> Sai asked. <*If he cannot ride well, he is a hindrance. A hindrance is a danger. You should instruct him.*>

<*His thighs are gonna be chaffed red-raw by tonight. He'll be walking bow-legged for days. Tell me that's not a little funny, Sai,*> Nihm replied, <*Besides, he'll learn quick enough.*>

As they stopped to rest, Nihm watched Lucky approach a miserable-looking Morten. He spoke quietly, his voice low so the others wouldn't hear but not low enough to escape her hearing. With only a hint of shame, Nihm listened in.

"You ride like you're sitting atop a log. Your mare knows what she's doing better than you, lad. She can feel your tension and sawing on the reins as you do is not helping. It's sending the wrong signals."

"I'm trying, Lucky, but I've never straddled more than a pony before. She won't do what I want."

"Look Red, imagine you've got a hunk of metal in your mouth and some idiot is yanking on it every second. How'd you like it? Try relaxing into the saddle. Keep your posture firm, reins still and in the name of all that's holy, try and rise to her rhythm. It'll go a lot better for your ass and be a damn sight easier on your horse. For now, until you learn, let her have her head. She'll follow the others, don't you worry."

He gave Morten a good-natured slap on the arm, got up, and moved off towards his horse.

Morten saw her watching him and Nihm turned away, red-faced, guilty for being caught out but also a little ashamed that Lucky had looked out for him. Morton was meant to be her friend and she should have done better by him.

<I did advise you,> Sai lectured.

<Yes, alright!>

They set off again soon after, the foothills on the far horizon drawing nearer as the day grew longer. As the ground started to rise, the ancient fortress of the Defile could be discerned between hill crests, obscure pennants flapping above its battlements, only to be lost completely as trees and dense bush sprang up around the path and blocked their view.

It was a nervous time. On the plains, urak could be easily spotted, any trails they chanced upon an easy tell. Here in the wooded hillside, it was the opposite. Urak could be lurking anywhere, waiting in ambush.

Nihm sent Ash and Snow ranging ahead. Although their training had not extended to this, both dogs seemed to understand what was needed and they soon vanished in the undergrowth.

As daylight began to fade, their path ran into another and Stama signalled a halt. This road was wider than the one they were on but unlike their own, its carpet of snow was churned to a dirty mush. Stama called Nihm forward.

"Marron told me you could track. My own skill is okay, but I'd like to know what you see?"

The casual mention of her mother was like Stama had reached out and clenched a fist around her heart. Nihm trembled.

<Tell me what you see?>

The memory was of her father, the sound of his voice so distinct it was like he stood beside her. Annoyance overrode her pang of grief, which she supposed was entirely Sai's intention.

Her eyes travelled to the road and she crouched down to examine it.

"Horse and wagons," Nihm said.

Stama gave a withering look. "Maybe Marron oversold your ability. Red could have told me that."

"Hey," exclaimed Morten.

Stama ignored him and Nihm was too busy glaring to take note. "Stop talking about my Ma," she hissed, voice tremoring. Frowning, she held Stama's gaze until he gave a sharp nod. She turned back to the road.

"If you must know, I'd say at least a score of wagons, probably more, with riders in escort. It's hard to tell exact numbers, there are so many tracks that each spoils another. An armed caravan most likely and I'd say they passed this way late last night or early this morning."

"How so?" Stama knelt on his haunches beside her.

"Look here." Nihm pointed out a wheel rut in the compressed snow. "There's a crust on it but it's not clean. The tread from the wheel is rumpled; snow fell after this wagon passed by, but not much, else it would be covered."

Stama stared at her a while, his mouth twitched. "Thorsten market seems such a long time ago."

He glanced past her, eyes tracking the road east. "They'll be headed for the Defile. Question is, are we? Any more insight as to where Lord Amos might be?"

Sai had assessed with Nihm what they knew and drawn up various probabilities, all of them were low. They just didn't have enough information. Her last dream walk placed Renco and Amos north of the Defile and on the west bank of the River Oust. Nothing new from what she'd told them earlier.

"We must assume Amos will try to head south. If we follow the road towards the Defile, I can search the verge for signs they have crossed. If I don't see any by the time we reach the Oust we can turn and follow the river north until we find their camp."

Stama rubbed a hand over the stubble on his chin. "Too many ifs for my liking. Still, it's the best we got. At worst it'll put us a day or two behind them; if we can find their camp and if'n it don't snow again to cover their trail and if'n we don't run into any urak. Like I say, too many damn ifs."

Rising, he rested a hand briefly on Nihm's shoulder, then turning, he walked back to his horse, mounted and led them east.

* * *

The sun was gone and the night had settled its mantle between the avenue of trees with Ankor the only moon high enough to cast a baleful eye down upon them. Travelling at night held risk. With the temperature dropping, the snow on the road turned hard and crunched with each tread of the horses' hooves, the sound loud in the night air. They could see no more than twenty, grainy paces ahead when Ankor was out and only five when the moon was obscured by cloud.

Not so, Nihm. For her, the surroundings took on a grey-green aspect that was crisp and clear and she had no trouble seeing the way. Strange fluorescent glows would sometimes manifest where the bush encroached upon the road and again, deeper in the woods. Fungal growths and plants, Sai informed her, not normally visible to the human eye and of no concern. His matter-of-fact statement left her unsettled; what were her eyes if not human?

Her hearing too had changed, enhanced. Even through the nighttime sounds of the forest, Nihm could hear the others walking their horses, despite the fact they were a way down the road and around a bend or two. Following behind, whilst she scouted the way ahead. It was something Mercy had grudgingly agreed to and the thought made Nihm tetchy. Despite everything they'd been through together, the mage seemed reluctant to put faith in her tracking abilities. It was only Stama's endorsement that swayed her in the end.

<She sees me as a child still of seventeen summers,> Nihm moaned.

<Mercy has seen you at death's door. When you were weak and needed care. It was she who kept you safe. It must be hard for her to shuck that responsibility and suddenly be reliant upon you.>

Ash and Snow suddenly crouched low and still. Their tails flat, heads up, ears erect and forward. Nihm dropped to her heels beside them. Senses outstretching, she listened for anything out of place. Her eyes shifted without thought through several spectrums, only to reveal nothing untoward.

The faintest scent carried to her on the breeze. She found herself stripping away the smells of the forest; tree bark and leaf, the earthy underlay of soil and plant litter, the churned mud of the road with the cleanliness of snow adding its unique fragrance to it all; and found what bothered the dogs.

The rusty smell of blood, with a seam running through it that was both sweet and bitter, which Sai identified as faeces and urine?

<Faeces and urine?>

<In baser terms, shit and piss,> Sai answered.

Death. She'd smelled its like before, many times; on the hunt and with the urak in the fields both north and south of the Grimwolds. This though was less clean, more like the tainted stench of the dead bear and urak back in the old forest.

Nihm ran a hand each over Ash and Snow, letting her gloved fingers trail through the ruff of their fur, taking comfort from it as she used to do with Bindu. She could feel the tension in them, their muscles quivering, ready for the hunt.

"Let's go see then." With a pat, she stood up and Sai interjected.

<It would be prudent to warn Mercy and the others first.>

Her lips were dry and Nihm moistened them with a swig from her water skin. She felt reluctant. Mercy might insist on sending Stama in her stead. But as skilled as he might be, he was no hunter and did not possess her unique abilities.

She stoppered her water skin, <And say what? That I smelt something dead? It could be a deer or anything.>

When Sai didn't respond she felt a twitch of self-reproach. What was worse, she didn't know if it was from Sai or herself.

The dead, when she found them, were around a curl in the road. A broken wagon was the first sign. It lay on its side, a wheel missing.

Nihm gestured at the dogs and clicked her tongue, sending Ash scampering into the forest to the north and Snow away to the south. As they disappeared in the undergrowth, Nihm followed Ash through the bushes and shrubs and moved through the tree line where she could observe the road from cover.

The snow beneath the trees was much shallower than on the roadside. Thinned by the branches above, it rippled in frozen waves, white caps glinting with errant starlight. Moving noiselessly was impossible and whilst careful placement of her feet limited the sound of her passing, it was proving too slow and she was mindful that the others would not be far behind. She felt an 'I told you so' coming. But Sai, for now, remained blessedly silent.

Ki'tae. The word formed in her mind. Master Hiro was not here to tell her no, so why not. Suddenly, eager to try, Nihm crouched on her heels. Concentrating, she felt the shift as she phased, opening the way to her hidden sight. Colours blossomed in her mind. Tae'al swirls of indigo, blue and aquamarine tinged with purples and violets. Extending her sense above, the sky became a mottled shade of burnt gold. As ever, it was awe-inspiring. Orienting forwards again, she sent her awareness out and clouds of tae'al drifted past her. They became thinner, predominantly shades of purple and violets but much more opaque and less vibrant in hue. The road, she assumed.

Nihm followed it, looking for the tell-tale white splashes of life, and found… lots of it. Like the sky on a cloudless night, tiny swirls spun all around. But like the stars in the heavens, they appeared tiny, insignificant. Not the larger, bolder swirls threaded with the green and brown of humans, or the purple and red of urak. She detected something through the fog of colour. It drew her like a lure and she followed it. Zoning in, it expanded in her mind and she felt herself grin, as a white flare bloomed, the green and gold filaments instantly familiar. It was Ash.

With a thought Nihm phased back, feeling a rush of awareness as her other senses came crowding back. A rinse of pain ached behind her eyes but it did not seem so bad as that time on the plains and faded within seconds. Standing, she moved confidently back to the road and crunched towards the upturned wagon.

<*This is hardly discrete.*>

<*It's okay. Other than the dogs, I sense nothing bigger than a buck rabbit.*>

The rut marks in the road grew deeper, the snow and mud more churned as she approached the wagon. Much of its cargo lay strewn across the road from crates that had smashed open.

It looked like the wagon had lost its wheel, dragged on its axle, flipped, and rolled before ending on its side. It must have been moving quickly to have done so.

Despite her insistence that there was nothing nearby, she held her bow in hand with an arrow loose upon its string. The sharp, cloying smell grew as Nihm drew level with the wreck. Her eyes were drawn to the still form of two horses, dead in their traces, bodies stiff and stinking with morbidity. A snapped arrow shaft protruded from the flank of one.

Pinned beneath the front of the wagon, Nihm found a man. His face was planted in the mud and snow. The back of his head was crushed and brain matter splattered in a demonic halo around him. Only two limbs were on view and both splayed at obtuse angles. Other than his head wound, there was very little blood. In the grey-green light of her night vision, he looked more like a broken doll than a man.

Nihm knew it should bother her, the death and the stink of it all, but the thought was obscure as the cool analytics of her mind took over. The overpowering smell became a stimulus to evaluate rather than something to retch over.

Further along the road, Nihm spotted a humped shape lying on the verge. A light dusting of snow covered it and an arrow, complete with its fletching, stood upright, pointing accusingly at Ankor above.

Moving to it, Nihm knelt and checked the body. Another man. The arrow that pinned his cloak to his back was thick shafted and longer than her own and confirmed what she suspected. Urak.

With a grunt of effort, Nihm turned him onto his side and brushed the frosting off his chest. He wore chain mail over a dark gambeson with a green tunic on top. The tunic was embroidered with a tower.

<This is no caravan guard.> Nihm recognised the emblem from her Ma's lessons. Rising, she moved further down the road, kneeling now and then to examine the ground. Each time was the same, a mired mess of wheel ruts and horse marks. On the fringes, she found a clear set of hoof prints and measured the pace off with her eyes. *Running.*

A gust of wind and the smell grew more pungent in her nostrils.

<What has gone before was merely an apéritif.> Sai intoned ominously.

Nihm didn't know what that meant but assumed it was nothing good and found herself testing the tension on her bowstring.

The scene as she rounded the next bend was one of carnage. Bodies of men and horses were spread across the road with three more wagons rising like islands among it all. Nihm walked through the dead. It looked more like a slaughter than a battle. She found no urak, but there were signs that bodies had been dragged off, judging by the scuff marks. Some patches were darker than others and when she dipped a gloved finger to one of them and sniffed it, the smell was headier, more metallic than she expected.

<Urak.> Sai confirmed. Needlessly, for the odour was becoming familiar.

Nihm followed the blood trails into the forest to the north of the road and spent several minutes examining the ground, trying to piece together what had happened.

The remote background noise of harness and clump of hoof stopped. It told Nihm the others had found the first body and she wandered back towards them. Rounding the bend in the road she spied them by the upturned wagon. It wasn't until she was thirty paces away though that Stama suddenly tensed and raised his bow.

"It's me, Nihm."

"Fool, I coulda stuck you with an arrow," Stama growled.

"I doubt it." Nihm smirked, "Maybe a tree."

"It's not a game girl. This isn't one of your hunts," Stama said. "Men have died here."

"Thirty-two men, eight women, and eighteen horses," Nihm said, surprising herself. She hadn't really been counting.

"What?" Mercy stepped forward, staff thrust out, runes pulsating faintly along its length.

"This was no merchant caravan or people fleeing in convoy. The dead are guards from Greentower," Nihm said.

"What?" Mercy repeated.

"They wear Duke Brant's colours and crest," Nihm explained not entirely sure if that was the question. "The urak ambushed them here. Only a few I suspect. Hit them from inside the treeline, enough to set them running. The main attack happened around the next bend. From the track marks, I'd say there was no more than a score of urak. In the panic and darkness, it probably seemed like a lot more."

"I can hardly see. How? We can't have been more 'an ten minutes behind." Nihm could see the scar on Mercy's face pucker as she spoke.

"You know I'm different now. And this, this is what Da trained me for."

She saw Morten peering myopically from the back of the wagon and Lucky anxiously trying to survey the surrounding forest.

"The urak are gone," Nihm reassured them. "Their tracks lead away to the north and the dogs will let us know if they return. They have the scent." She wasn't ready to tell them everything.

"What now?" Morten asked. "We're going north too. What if they find us?"

"Nothing's changed." Mercy's tone was brusque.

"The only decision is, stop for the night or carry on?" Lucky said.

"Carry on," Stama said. "I'll not stay here among the dead and another hour should see us to the Oust. Besides, the urak may return yet to scavenge what they can."

"As long as we don't miss any sign of Amos," Mercy said.

"I'll lead off," Nihm answered, "If there is I will see it."

"This time, if you find anything, like, oh I don't know, say like dead bodies. You come back and tell us, eh," Stama said.

"Sure, wouldn't want you tripping over anything in the dark and hurting yourself," Nihm smirked.

* * *

Nihm stared at the distant lights. They stood a handsbreadth above the treetops to the east. Yellow rents carved in a background darker than the night in which no stars glittered. The lights from the Defile were not what had made her stop though. Something deeper tickled her spine.

The night was young. Barely an hour had passed since she'd left the dead behind. Occasionally dropping into ki'tae, Nihm would search for life beyond normal sight. Always she would locate Ash and Snow patrolling on her flanks and each time she did she would breathe a little easier.

She'd found no tracks that might indicate Amos had crossed or any further sign of urak. But still, something nagged at her and Da always said to heed her instincts.

A faint shiver set the small hairs on her body tingling.

<I can feel something,> Nihm said. <It's almost like that time Mercy cast in the Broken Axe.>

<It is not dissimilar to the energy I absorbed when I was first awoken, though much less substantial,> Sai agreed. <It is emitting on a bearing 18 degrees from magnetic north.>

A vertical line appeared in Nihm's sight, a marker pointing the direction. She didn't even question it, simply adjusted her head to centre it. <A magus maybe? It must be.>

<Mercy is a mage, perhaps she will know,> Sai prompted.

<Yeah okay, I was going to say that.>

A query of scepticism coloured her mind.

<I was damn it.>

They waited for the others to draw nearer. When they were close, Nihm called out.

"What is it? Have you found a sign?" Mercy asked.

"I'm not sure. Something," Nihm was vague. The minute pulses of tae'al had slowly ebbed until now they had faded altogether. A few months ago she would have felt foolish and not mentioned it. Put it down to her imagination. Not now. Now, Sai gave certainty to everything she did.

Mercy squinted into the darkness to the northeast. Coincidence, Nihm wondered, or maybe she had felt something too?

"Well? Spit it out." Mercy's abrasive voice answered her unspoken question.

"I felt a touch against my skin. Like when you cast that spell in the inn that day."

"Aether touched? That is strange, I felt nothing." The mage appeared thoughtful though rather than dismissive.

"It could be urak, or maybe it's Amos?" Nihm queried.

"Amos is no wielder of magic, nor Jobe or Jerkze. Renco?" Mercy mused.

Nihm recalled the lesson's Hiro taught her and the ease of his instruction. "Master Hiro never said and I never asked, but I think it's possible."

Mercy closed her eyes in quiet contemplation. Horses snorted, impatiently shuffling and Morten led his and Nihm's to the verge to forage. The rest stood in silent regard.

"It's no good. I sense nothing," Mercy announced finally. "Are you sure?"

"I'm sure," Nihm answered. Lining up her waymark she pointed out the direction, before realising they couldn't see her clearly in the night. "I have a bearing."

"Well, let's go take a look then," Mercy said.

"Think it's Amos?" Stama asked.

"If Nihm's right it could be. If not, then someone has wielded magic and whether it's Amos or no, they must be in trouble to have done so," Mercy replied.

"The Oust must be near. Let's hope it's this side of the river," Stama said.

"If it isn't Amos and this Renco boy, let's hope it's not," Lucky replied. Then, disgruntled, he addressed Mercy, "This is a bad idea. The horses are tired. Hells I'm tired. We can hardly see our way now and won't see for shit in the woods."

<*Master Lucson is correct. The safest and most efficient course would be to make camp south of the road and rest till morning. The Defile is in easy reach but we have insufficient information to ascertain in whose possession it resides,*> Sai said.

<*What if morning's too late? What if it's Renco and Amos and they need our help now? What then?*> Nihm argued.

<*As Master Stama would say, there are too many ifs. The risk is too high that we stumble upon urak. The horses are weary and cannot be ridden at speed, in the dark, through trees. At best we would all be separated, at worst caught and killed. What use is our mission if everyone is dead?*>

Their discussion had lasted but a second and Nihm knew Sai was right. Her Da would agree and Master Hiro. She listened as Mercy raised the same objection to Lucky that she had used.

"If Amos is in trouble I'll not sit quietly around a campfire eating beans." Her voice was stressed.

"I love your brother as much as you do," Lucky returned. "But he'd agree with me. You know it. He'll not thank us for getting ourselves killed fumbling around in the dark all cos Nihm got a chill in her bones. Fuck knows I got a chill in mine."

Nihm could understand Mercy's angst. Amos was her brother. It dawned on her then, that as much as her father might agree with Sai there wasn't a shadow of doubt in her mind that were it she that was missing her father would not rest, nor Master Hiro for Renco.

"Sound carries at night. Why don't you all talk a little louder?" Nihm said. Morten's eyes went round at her words and she tightened her lips to hide the smile. Not that any could see it. "Lucky is right. Make camp in the woods to the south. The horses are about spent. I'll take Ash and Snow and see if I can find this 'chill in my bones'."

At her words, everyone turned, peering at the hooded shadow obscured by the darkness. She could read their faces like they could not. Lucky painted a scowl, Morten wide-eyed and fearful, Stama with lips pursed in quiet regard, and Mercy. Mercy looked wild, angry. The mage opened her mouth.

"I'll com…"

"No, you won't," Nihm interrupted. Then, not unkindly. "You need to rest more than any of us. You've been riding your nerves all day. Besides, you'd only slow me down. Make too much noise stumbling around."

"I can't…"

"Trust me, it's better that I go alone. I'll see any urak long before they see me."

<We will?>

Nihm ignored Sai, peering instead up at Ankor. The clouds were thicker than before and the moon was half obscured.

"Clouds are gathering. It'll snow again tomorrow I think. I'll be back before then." Nihm walked to her horse as she addressed them. Opening her pack she fumbled around inside, taking a rind of dried meat and a knuckle of stale bread out.

As Nihm retied the flap, she felt a hand on hers and looked up into hazel green eyes. Eyes full of concern. "Don't go, Nihm." Morten's voice was barely a whisper.

She scoured his face, observing the worry lines creasing the skin around his eyes. He'd not shaved for days and coarse whiskers covered his cheeks. It was a handsome face and the look suited him, Nihm thought. Made him look older, more rugged but it had come at a price. He'd lost something of himself since Thorsten. She felt a prickle of guilt. That she had some part to play in its losing.

<We are all changed.>

Fervently, she hoped he'd find it again.

"I'll be alright. I'll be back," Nihm said, squeezing his hand in reassurance. "You'll see."

Pulling her hand free, she turned back to the others.

"It will be cold tonight. A small hollow would be best, to mask any fire."

"This is not our first time," Stama muttered irritably. He looked to say something more but instead gave the old travellers' blessing. "The Trinity watch your way and guide your path."

Nihm shrugged. "There is no Trinity. I will find my own way." With that, she slipped into the darkness.

Chapter 7: Leave The Dead Behind

Northwest of the Defile, The Rivers

The horses are tired, Amos thought, observing their sweat-lathered flanks and steaming breath. The Red Cloaks had ridden them hard and trekking through snow took a toll as his own weary body could attest. At least the girls were out of it, both Constance and Annabelle were seated behind a rider. As for Junip, she was given a horse; a high-minded Red Cloak giving up his mount as she struggled to keep the pace.

No such luck for Jobe and him but at least they no longer had to drag the canoe. Instead, they walked beside it, nudging it to keep it upright whilst another Red Cloak pulled it behind his horse. He glanced inside the boat at Jerkze's pinched face and pallid skin. His friend had lapsed into a fitful sleep and it worried him. His wounds needed attending and the bandages on his arm and side changing. They weren't life-threatening but Amos knew that could soon change without proper attention.

Amos gave a distracted glance to the Defile. The ancient fortress had drawn closer as the day ebbed but all too slowly. It was the price paid for having to forge a new path through virgin snow in uneven terrain. *The winter days are short and there isn't much light left in this one*, he mused.

He trudged on.

As the sky deepened, the pale disk of Ankor brightened in divergence and a spattering of stars began to sprinkle the eastern horizon, spreading like a rash as the light slowly bled from the firmament.

The Red Cloak corporal, Jekka, gave no sign of stopping or of making camp for the night, seemingly intent on making the Defile. Amos didn't blame him. There was a tension riding with them. He could feel it. It was enough to keep the monotony of the trek at bay and his limbs moving, one fatigued step after the other. Just the thought of his legs turned them leaden, and Amos groaned inwardly as they started up another incline.

He'd half ascended the slope when a cry went up and his head snapped to the brow of the low hill. The lead rider had crested it and was twisted in his saddle looking back the way they'd come.

Amos found himself turning and following the line of the man's arm, but it was no good, his elevation was insufficient to see over the scant trees at what was coming. His heart sank. It didn't matter. It was clear from the call they were discovered. It lent him a sudden spur of energy that gave brief respite to his weary bones. By the time Amos reached the brow of the rise, it was spent and he was panting from the exertion.

Jekka talked in urgent tones with his Red Cloaks. Amos ignored him, looking about instead to see their pursuers. In the fading light, they were hard to pick out at first, but their movement drew his eye.

"At least a score," Jobe muttered beside him. "They'll be on us quick; thirty, forty minutes behind. No more than that."

Amos grunted acknowledgement and both men turned to survey their surroundings. From the crown of the hill, they could make out the glimmering ribbon of the river Oust and to the south a thickening band of wood that seemed to run east to west. Jobe pointed out the fortress, sitting like a wart on top of the Defile, then ran his hand down towards the river and then to the dark stain of trees.

"The West Road Bridge sits between us and the fortress, an hour on a fresh horse, two maybe three hours on foot." He didn't state the obvious; that their horses were about spent and too few to carry them all. Or that they'd already broken the trail for the urak and would be caught well before the bridge was ever reached.

Amos clapped Jobe on the shoulder before turning towards the huddle of Red Cloaks. As he approached them, one leapt upon his horse and, in a cascading rush of snow, set off down the far embankment.

"They'll be on us in half an hour," Amos said. "What are your intentions?"

"My orders are to bring you to Captain Warwick. But we'll none of us make it as we are." Jekka scowled. "You and Lady Constance will ride for the Defile with two of my men in escort. The rest of us will hold the hill and buy the time needed."

Amos nodded downslope at the retreating Red Cloak. "And him?"

Jekka turned and looked. "Brother Rashud is the smallest and his horse the least spent. If we're still standing by morning, my brothers will come for us."

He spoke loudly and Amos knew it was as much to reassure his men as it was him. Lowering his head, Amos spoke so only the Red Cloak corporal would hear. "You'll all die here. You know that. My man counted a score of urak and they move faster than the wind. Trust me, I've ridden before them and barely escaped.

"So, here's what we'll do corporal. You will send Lady Constance as stated but with the woman and girl in my stead. I'll not abandon my men. Then we need to look to our defences. This hill gives us a strong defensive position and there is little enough else I see between here and the Defile that would suit us better."

Jekka stared, annoyance flitted across his face at Lord Amos's tone but a part of him felt relief too. Here was a man used to command and someone prepared to die with his men. He could respect that, but his Lordship was also wrong. "The woman and the girl are no riders. The woman can barely sit her saddle without groaning. I'll not sacrifice my men in vain."

Grudgingly, Amos conceded his point, but he was damned if he'd let Belle perish here. "The girl then, else Lady Constance will not go."

"She'll go, even if I have to truss her up," Jekka said, though inwardly he relented. The girl was a waif, his saddlebag weighed more; he shook his head exasperated. They didn't have time for this. Spinning on his heels he snapped out orders.

"Canting, Welling. Escort the Lady Constance to the Defile. Oh, and Canting. Take the little one with you."

The Red Cloaks acknowledged their orders, but a brief argument ensued, "I'll not leave you." Constance wailed at Amos.

"You will and you must. We can hold out till morning but not if we have you and Belle underfoot," Amos said, the lie slipping easily from his tongue. "Now go. You're the Lady of Thorsten. Your survival is paramount. Nothing else matters."

Kneeling, he clasped Constance to him. "Take care of Belle for me. She has nothing and no one," he whispered in her ear.

"I will." Tears tickled his neck.

When Constance stepped away, she wiped a gloved hand over scared eyes. Then, face tight, she turned away. "Come on, Belle."

A cloaked bundle flew past her and into Amos, clasping him tight around the neck. "I don't want to leave you. Not Jobe nor Jerkze and not Junip," Belle sobbed.

"I know little one." Amos ran a hand over her hair. His heart lurched, threatening to unman him. "We'll come for you, Belle, my oath on it. But right now, you must be strong for Lady Constance. She's not as street savvy as you are and will need you. Will you look after her?"

"I will," she cried, unknowingly repeating the promise made by her friend only moments ago.

"I know you will. Now dry your eyes and wipe your nose." He ticked her chin with his finger then cupped a hand to her cheek and stared into hazel eyes. "Go on, off with you now," he said gruffly. Then he rose to his feet and walked away.

"Come on girl, grab my hand," a voice called out.

Amos didn't turn to look until he heard the creak of harness and clatter of horses moving off. When he did, they were already thirty yards downslope and hazy in the glooming light.

* * *

As the sun disappeared the land was submerged in a rising tide of darkness. It was lightened only by the moon, Ankor and the kaleidoscope of stars which slow wheeled in the heavens; a phantasmagoria of light.

The defenders atop the hill heard the urak long before they saw them. The crunch of compacting snow gave away the first strained sounds of their passage. Quickly it grew in volume until laboured breathing could be heard as well, underlying it. The urak were on the hill, climbing its slope; the night proving no barrier to the hunters when the snow gave such an easy tale of the hunted.

The defenders were nine all told, seven Red Cloaks, Jobe and Amos. They'd left Jerkze and the horses in a bush rimmed hollow on the far downslope, with Junip to watch over them. The mage apprentice had looked wretched when Amos left her. Pale, shivering with fear and the cold, she would prove no use in a fight. Much as he might wish it otherwise, Junip was no battlemage.

I have my weapons returned at least, Amos reflected, I will die with a sword in my hand. The thought though wasn't the comfort he'd hoped. He didn't want to die at all and laying there thinking about it wasn't helping any. Pushing the knot of fear in his belly deeper, Amos willed strength into his numb arms and weary legs and felt his blood responding, a burning energy spreading through his body at the impending fight.

The sound of crushed snow grew; so close now that Amos thought they must surely see the urak. To his sides, he could sense the Red Cloaks waiting in hiding. 'Surprise and the high ground is our only advantage', Jekka had extolled earlier, instructing everyone to await his signal before breaking it; and Amos had to concede the Red Cloaks were disciplined and well drilled.

His eyes strained downhill fixing towards the noise. Amos detected the faintest shift in the darkness. A shape emerged, indistinct, blurring and merging with the night so that it was hard to tell where its form started but there was no denying what it was.

Urak.

Another haze of darkness materialised behind the first, then a third. What is Jekka waiting for, they're almost upon us? Amos sensed movement at his side, the snow squeaking as it compressed, and he found himself rising to his knees in unison with the men around him.

A guttural command and the blocky shapes all stopped. The strain of a bow drawing whispered in the air, followed immediately by a half dozen more.

A bark of warning shattered the night. At the same time, seven arrows sped downslope. It was too dark to see them strike but the smack of flesh rippled out amid howls of agony to say that some at least had found their mark.

The shapes vanished and a wail sounded from somewhere nearby.

"Hold fire," Amos's voice rattled along the ridge. Several Red Cloaks had already loosed a second time but were blind firing at nothing. "Conserve your arrows."

A moan of pain from down the hill covered the sound of movement, as the wounded were dragged or shuffled back into the safety of the night.

"They'll not be gone for long. Stay alert," Jekka ordered. "Darding and Jesmon cover left. Smit and Ricar take the right. They'll try to flank us."

It seemed loud as the men relocated. Jekka moved past Jobe and knelt beside Amos just below the rim of the hill.

"They know we're here now. It'll not go so easily next time."

"We're well-armed but lightly armoured. If they close to melee we'll stand little chance," Amos replied.

"Bit late for second thoughts," Jekka said. "We're committed. Besides, you said yourself this is our best defensive position."

"Ai, I did. But tired men make tired mistakes. I thought they'd charge as soon as we attacked, not retreat," Amos said. "There's so much we don't understand about them."

Jekka snorted. "They're savages, hardly more an' wild beasts. If you're a believer you should have no fear, Lord Duncan."

"Ai, well I'm both," Amos replied. Feeling the weight of Jekka's gaze, he turned to study the Red Cloak, but his face was unreadable in the dark.

"The Protector guides our arms. We'll kill as many of the bastards as we can. And if this night is to be our last then our Lord, Kildare will welcome us to his embrace," Jekka intoned.

"Yeah. Sure," Amos said drily.

Reaching out, Jekka clasped a hand to Amos's shoulder. "Keep your faith strong, Brother. It will shield you."

Amos fought the urge to punch the Red Cloak in the face.

"Nice words but I can't hear shit with you two babbling on," Jobe interrupted. A crunch of snow sounded at that moment from behind, making a lie of his words. All three men spun towards it, Jobe and Amos raising bows and Jekka placing a hand on his sword.

"It's us," Junip's voice called out. She sounded apologetic. "I couldn't stop him."

"Damn fool," Amos blurted, but couldn't keep the tug of a grin from forming.

"I'll be damned dying on my ass listening to you lot mess it all up," Jerkze grunted, unable to disguise the weakness in his voice. "Besides, you shouldn't underestimate Junip. She can help."

"Fighting is a man's duty," Jekka replied.

A howl rose, undulating, shattering the calm of night. It ended all conversation and the defenders on the hill strained their senses downhill.

Junip forgotten, Jekka called out, "Be ready."

Another howl lifted into the night, this one away to their left, answered moments later by another on their right. It sent a cold shiver down Amos's spine. "Jerkze, keep an eye out behind." It was the only place they hadn't heard anything, and he didn't trust it.

The sound of movement drew their ears and Jobe and Amos nocked arrows, ready, eyes straining against the night.

"Lumousim arctum," Junip's voice tremored, and a ball of light immediately gathered at the tip of her staff. It lit up the brow of the hill and blinded the men upon it.

"Lorim." The ball of luminescence swirled then shot into the air, low over the hill so that it barely cleared the heads of the defenders.

It illuminated the far slope and brought into relief the urak crouched low at its base creeping uphill, their own bows were drawn and ready. The harsh glare of light dazzled them, a sun flare in the night that ruined their vision.

Jobe sent an arrow, skimming over the snow. It narrowly missed his target, flying just over the shoulder of an urak, who'd instinctively dropped to the ground as the light floated lower.

Amos and another Red Cloak released their arrows. The other bowmen though, covering the flanks, had no shot. The light did not extend to their fields of fire. The urak retreated from view.

"Too soon, lass," Jobe muttered angrily. If Junip had waited till they were closer the targets would have been more compelling, whether they hugged the ground or not.

A shout came from the left followed by the low thrum of bowstrings. Shouldering his bow and drawing his sword, Jekka ordered one of his Brothers to follow and loped off in support, leaving Amos command of the hill.

A cry of pain and a warning call sounded from the right flank. "Watch the front," Amos ordered the remaining Red Cloak, "Jobe on me."

They set off, following the ridgeline to a small thicket of brushwood. Pushing through it they came out behind a Red Cloak kneeling beside a tree for cover. He was leant out, his bow focused downslope, bowstring pulled back to his ear. On the high ground nearby sat a fellow Brother, back propped against a small boulder. A sob escaped him as he plucked weakly at a thick shaft that protruded from his shoulder.

A chirr, barely audible over the simpering, sped the arrow out of sight.

A mass appeared. A roar of challenge crashed out as it charged. The Red Cloak dropped his bow, drew his sword and stood to meet it.

Jobe cursed roundly, calling out. The man blocked his aim. If he heard though, the Red Cloak gave no sign as he raised his sword, feet moving, turning his body in a defensive guard.

The on-rushing shape resolved in shades of grey. The urak was broad-shouldered and stood a head taller than the man. Its blade swung in an overhead cut and was met, in a grate of steel, which staggered the man, who gasped at the impact. He did enough though to deflect the blow wide and slashed his sword up in a counter move. It cracked against the wooden block of a shield and was batted aside.

Off-balance, the Red Cloak took a pace backwards. The urak followed, stepping in. An arcing blade struck the man below his left armpit shearing into his body, parting armour and flesh, snapping ribs and lodging deep in his side.

The Red Cloak gave a grunt, a final bloody sigh then collapsed in the snow.

The urak bellowed in triumph. Placing a foot on its victim it tugged, working its blade free then lurched as two arrows struck, so close together, the thud of impact sounded as one.

Another urak appeared behind the first. It fastened a beefy arm around its brethren and pulled it back into the night.

Amos waited, the only sound the two urak as they retreated. Taking a careful step towards the wounded Red Cloak, Smit or Ricar, he didn't know which, a distracting thought wormed its way into his mind. Only two?

"This was a feint," Jobe hissed, reaching the same conclusion. "Come-on. We've no time for the wounded, this is far from done." Placing a stern hand on his Lord's arm he pulled Amos back just as a shout went up behind.

"Damn it." Turning, Jobe disappeared back into the brushwood.

Amos followed. Fear clutched at his heart. The urak were savage, Jekka was right, but they were also so much more. *They are warriors who understand the art of warfare perhaps better than we*, Amos thought, disturbed by the notion.

Brightness suddenly flared against the brushwood and bloomed in the air. It was accompanied by a crackling snap-hiss of energy that set Amos's skin tingling in warning.

Jobe abruptly stopped. Using the last bush for cover, he peered out. Joining him, Amos stared, eyes pinched against the glare.

Jerkze stood not ten paces away, stance favouring his right side, sword drawn but held low, as though its weight was too much to bear. It was not this, however, that drew the eye but Junip. She stood on the high ground behind Jerkze. Raised up, she looked taller than she was, her skin fairly glowing and eyes glinting with fervour. There was no fear to look at her now, loose strands of hair danced in the energy that coalesced at the tip of her staff. It lent her a maniacal look.

Her gaze was rigidly fixed down the slope and Amos followed it and spotted half a dozen urak transfixed on the embankment. They looked fierce, covered in animal hide and straps of leather banding. Several carried bows with swords tied across their backs, the rest bore shields with weapons drawn.

The urak archers raised their bows, taking aim and Amos shouted out in warning. At his cry, a ball of energy launched from Junip's staff, burning a path across his retinas as it streaked downhill. It forked, like lightning, each tine striking an urak, so quick it was hard to comprehend. The urak all jerked violently, their furs burning where the lightning touched. Then, as one, they toppled to the ground.

"Fuck my days," Jobe exclaimed.

Junip collapsed and the light, paltry now above her staff, snuffed out in a blink and darkness rushed in to fill the void.

Amos lurched past Jobe, racing towards Junip but Jerkze was already there, kneeling at her side. He laid a hand to her brow then placed his ear above her mouth and listened.

"She's breathing easy. I think she's just passed out is all."

"Never seen anything like it," Amos said. "I didn't know she had it in her."

"Don't think Junip did either," Jerkze said. His voice sounded pained but Amos could tell, despite the dark, his friend was smiling.

There was a creak of movement and Jobe strode past, bowstring pulled tight against his cheek, an arrow nocked and ready. It came from the far side of the hill and was followed by a hiss of pain.

"Jekka?" Jobe called.

"In Kildare's embrace," answered a voice.

"Guess he'll be happy with that at least," Jobe muttered under his breath. Then louder so that all could hear, "What's the status on the flank?"

"Clear for now but the attack was a feint, never saw no more than two urak. Brother Jesmon took an arrow to the gut and Brother Jekka fell in battle. Just me and Brother Darding here is left and we came soon as we heard the commotion."

"Okay, gather the horses we're leaving. Darding, go help Ricar on the right, he took an arrow to his shoulder and will need a hand. Smit is gone," Jobe commanded.

The lone watchman guarding the hill's brow called out. "I think they're gathering again. I can hear them."

"Let us know if they approach and be ready to move when I say," Jobe replied.

Junip moaned and Amos checked quickly to see she was okay. Satisfied, Amos rose and moved to stand beside Jobe.

"We'll not likely outrun them," Amos said.

"Odds are against it," Jobe agreed. "Still, Junip took out six of the bastards and we know some at least are wounded. Maybe they'll be more cautious, wary of an ambush. If we stay here, we're dead for sure. So, I'll take those odds. How's she doin' by the way?"

"Weak as a kitten but she'll be fine with a bit of rest. Think Junip about blew herself out. I don't think we can rely on her saving our asses again any time soon," Amos said.

"Well, look at the bright side. At least there are enough horses to go around now," Jobe said, earning a shake of the head from Amos.

They wandered towards the hollow as they spoke, the soft nicker and smell of horses a comfort to both men.

They quickly helped gather the mounts, then lifted and strapped Junip onto one and helped Jerkze onto another who grunted as his leg swung over the saddle. Breathing heavily, he told them to tie him on. It would be a long ride and each step would be a trial of pain for him, they all knew it.

"Try not to cry like a bairn," Jobe said, cinching the final strap tight.

"Ai, an' you try not ta lead us in a big circle. If'n I see this hill again I'll be pissed," Jerkze hissed through gritted teeth.

In short order, they were mounted and ready. With no further talk, they moved off shuffling downhill. The horses were tired but eager, it seemed, to leave the dead behind.

Chapter 8: Hunters Hunt

West of the Defile, The Rivers

Walking through the woods at night in the snow was reminiscent of many walks Nihm had taken before. Above her, through the cracked canopy, the stars were the same. The constellations familiar friends that watched over her, which was a comfort in its way, for despite everything that had happened, they, at least, were a constant. Even without the snow to tell her it was winter, she would have known it. The heavens gave so much to those who could read them and nothing to those who couldn't.

The walk may have been similar but it was not the same. She was not the same. The land was strange, the woods unfamiliar and lacking the comfort of the old forest of her childhood. The thought made Nihm smile. Childhood was that time from before the hunt. She could remember the feeling of anger and frustration boiling inside at being treated as such by her parents. Unjustified emotions she realised now, for in truth she had been a child still, much as she hated to admit it. Strange then that now, only a few months later, she was a child no longer, the transition passing without acknowledgement or awareness. That her father had let her forge her own path was the final proof of it.

But Nihm's smile was a melancholic one. Thoughts of her Ma and those childhood times were crystal clear in her mind and oh, how she wished she could go back to them.

<*The universe is chaos and we an infinitesimal part of its whole. The only constant is the past. Those stars in the heavens are not unchanged but roil in ever-evolving motion and energy. It is just that your viewpoint is so far removed you cannot see it. Perspective shapes so much of life. The past guides the future just as each step along the way informs the next. But always remember, the future is uncertain and unknowable. Chaos rules all things.*>

"I was having a moment," Nihm said, "Why'd you have to go ruin it."

<*I am sorry. I was trying to enhance your knowledge and improve your disposition,*> Sai replied.

"Yeah, well there's a time and place and it wasn't now."

<*I disagree. Your attention was not fully on the task at hand. I was trying to help.*>

"Yeah, I know Sai. But a girl's got to have time for her moods. Ma always said that reflection is good for the soul. Still, it's done now."

A sudden patter of snow crystals dusted her shoulders and brushed against her cheeks. The wind had picked up, hardly noticeable beneath the shelter of the woods but enough to make the branches sigh. The air was crisp against her skin as the temperature continued to drop.

It turned out the woods were not so deep. Barely a half-hour and she had reached its broken limits, where the tree line gave way to snow-covered sedge grass and pockets of brushwood. In the near distance, several hills rose like black pimples on the landscape.

Focusing, Nihm made the shift to ki'tae, the transition becoming easier, more effortless with every use. Colours expanded in her mind. The honey gold of the heavens giving the impression of warmth but her body told her it was false. The violets and purples of the grasslands billowed like fog before her. Her mind sorted out the nuances of colour, their tones and depths of opaqueness, almost without thought. Her awareness translated, gliding past the polychromatic clouds.

There was so much life. Life unseen ordinarily by the naked eye, pinpricks of whiteness that gave a static discontinuity to everything. Larger splashes resolved, haphazardly strung out. Nihm's heart rate quickened. Then, as they expanded in her mind, she released the breath she was holding. Not horses and definitely not human or urak. Deer, Nihm decided. Somehow knowing that they were not big enough or numerous enough to be one of the bison herds that roamed the north.

With a thought, Nihm's consciousness returned to the mundane. She blinked, the sharp grey-green images of the landscape seeming almost routine to her now.

All was as it was before. The compass mark from earlier, that Sai had imposed upon her vision, aligned neatly with one of the hills.

Waypoint marker, a point of reference used for location and navigation. The knowledge from Sai was attained without effort or request and Nihm did not query it. She had bigger questions to ask, the foremost of which was what to do next?

The grasslands appeared flat and uniform beneath its blanket of snow. Ankor still rode high in the sky and the red crescent of Kildare was rising in the east. Urak were here. The ambushed dead on the road told her that much, but where and how well can they see in the dark? How far?

It went against all Nihm's instincts to blindly walk out upon the plain. Its grasses were not the same as the tall marsh grasses south of the Grim and would provide no cover. The thickets of brushwood might provide some protection, but each was an island and moving from one to the next would leave her dangerously exposed.

Ash loped in, tongue lolling, and brushed up against her legs. Crouching, Nihm gave the wolfdog an idle pat, running her glove along his flank. "What do you suggest, Ash, eh? Should we risk it?"

Ash turned his golden eyes to hers. He whined then yawned, his warm breath telling Nihm that he'd done more than just guard her flank. It carried the scent of fresh blood and, now she looked, she could detect traces of it on his black snout.

"At least we've both eaten," Nihm told him. "I hope yours was more filling than mine you rascal."

Ash sniffed, tongue licking his chops as if to say he was still hungry, then his head lifted and swung around towards the east. Ears twitched and fixed forward.

"You hear something, boy?" Nihm turned her body, following the treeline and concentrated. Her hearing was much improved but still no match it seemed for the wolfdog.

All she heard were the sounds of the forest and… she spun, anxious, just as Snow padded out from behind a bush.

The white wolfdog's head was also fixed to the east. Whatever it was, she heard it too.

"Well, guess that's decided then." Rising, keeping just inside the treeline, Nihm set off at an easy jog.

* * *

The riders passed into the forest before Nihm had a chance to intercept them. There were eight all told and the way some sat in the saddle told her a few were carrying injuries. She might have tried calling out to them, but she was too far away, and half wore red cloaks which, in her night vision, appeared a deeper hue of green. But somehow, Sai could ascertain their true colour and the knowledge flowed to her as if it was her own certainty.

As she watched them disappear beneath the trees, one of the horses stumbled to its knee's spilling its rider, a Red Cloak, into the snow. The horse regained its feet and stood, head low, breath billowing the air in thick clouds. The rider seemed stunned and was slow to rise but the horse waited while he regathered the reins and pulled himself up again into the saddle. With a weary trot, the horse disappeared.

It didn't add up, four Red Cloaks and four others. Where were the two children she'd seen through Renco's eyes? From what she knew of Lord Duncan and having spent so much time with Mercy, his sister, he would not have abandoned them. As well, somehow, she knew Renco was not one of the riders.

<It's not them.>

<There is no certainty one way or the other. In your vision, Renco and Letizia were both wearing Red Cloaks,> Sai replied.

<I just feel it. He is not there.>

<They are pursued.>

Nihm's head twisted to the north. She'd been so fixated on the rider's she had lost herself for a moment.

Urak.

As she watched she counted sixteen as they came into view over a small undulation in the landscape. They were so close, how had she missed them?

<The trees will make riding impossible in the dark. The urak will catch them in the forest. If you are certain Renco is not among them, we should return to Mercy and consider our next step.>

<What? And just leave them to their fate. I can't do that.>

<It is not logical to take on sixteen urak. The chance of surviving an encounter is…>

<Sai! Don't give me numbers. I know it's dumb and I'm scared as hell, but I can't just leave them. The Trinity knows I'd love to run away but I'm not sure I could live with myself. It's not how I was raised.>

<I have set a new waypoint; a path of interception based on current distance and the expected terrain, given our experience of the forest. I suggest you hurry, or you will not be able to affect the outcome.>

Without further discussion, Nihm set off at a steady lope, the tangled roots and forest debris proving no hindrance with her enhanced sight. Ash and Snow ran by her side, tense and alert. Nihm's body language was enough to tell them that they hunted.

Following the waypoint marker in her vision, Nihm closed perpendicular to the hunters. Numbers appeared alongside the marker, counting down.

<I have projected an estimate of the distance to potential contact. An indicator only, nothing is certain,> Sai informed her.

Time merged, seconds turning to minutes as the numbers fell away. The sound of her breathing and the noise of her passage seemed loud to her ears as she wove a path through the trees. It did not concern her. The uraks' own pursuit would deafen them to what small noise she made.

Snow was the first to detect them. The wolfdog adjusted her path, her brother following seamlessly with Nihm trying to keep pace. In her vision, the counter ticked inexorably down into double digits. Then they jumped, as she heard movement ahead.

<Corrected for contact.>

Nihm slowed, pulling the bow from her back. She ran gloved fingers along the bowstring to warm it and took the tension. Satisfied, she shed her gloves and fitted an arrow.

The noise ahead was louder and getting closer. Nihm stopped as a shape cut through the trees and both wolfdogs slunk low to the ground, shivering with excitement.

More figures emerged, easily spotted by their movement. They were large, appearing brutish in the green hue of night and moving in single file following an unseen trail.

The number and way marker in her vision disappeared, replaced instead by lines that marked each urak with numbers beside them. Instinctively, Nihm knew the digits denoted distance to target.

Drawing the arrow back to her ear, Nihm slowed her breathing, letting her quickened heart calm. As the last urak came into view, Nihm sighted. The arrow's projected line of flight curved across her vision and she adjusted, aligning until it painted the urak's upper body. Her Da would have called it a bold shot in the dark against a moving target but Nihm knew she would not miss. With a slow exhale the arrow sped into the night, bisecting trees and branches. The urak stumbled and crashed to the ground with a loud cry. An arrow shaft jutting from its back.

Nihm was already moving, changing position, her silent guardians following.

Cries barked out, echoing beneath the shroud of trees and the urak hunting party stopped. The fallen urak gave an agonised call and Nihm watched whilst two urak stalked back, wary, scanning the forest surroundings.

They don't know where the shot came from, Nihm realised. Knowing that movement drew the eye, she took cover behind a tree that afforded a relatively clear path to the wounded urak. She nocked another arrow and aimed as she pulled it back, drawing a new line.

The thrum of release hummed in her ear. This time, she watched dispassionately, as the arrow's fletch spun before striking its target. Already, her hand was fitting another arrow and as the urak groaned and fell, Nihm drew, sighted and launched on the remaining urak.

It missed, kind of. At the moment of release, the urak was moving, ducking away, too late for Nihm to adjust her aim.

The arrow struck the urak in the hand, passing through the meat of its palm, and shattering the small bones. Rearing its head, the urak roared in agony and Nihm's next arrow found its throat, silencing it.

Multiple bellows shattered the night. Nihm could see the crouched forms of urak, keeping to the cover of the trees. They moved randomly, one or two at a time. It was like a choreographed dance making it hard for Nihm to target any single one before they were back in cover.

<*We have their attention, but we also only have five arrows left. I do not need to tell you that the arithmetic is not good.*>

<*I told you, Sai. No numbers.*> Nihm blew a slow breath through her nose. The nervous energy of her pursuit had evaporated at first contact. In its place lay a cold, analytics. <*They know our approximate location. They're also making enough noise to awaken the dead. It's time to move.*>

Slipping back, Nihm moved cautiously from tree to tree. She knew that each second kept the urak from their original quarry and that, ultimately, was her goal. That she was their new focus was somewhat disturbing.

After a while, it became obvious to Nihm that the urak could not see as well in the dark as she could. With growing confidence, she angled away from their path and manoeuvred to the south.

Taking up a position behind a fallen tree, Nihm waited. The urak swept the wood, the closest fifty paces from her post. Ash and Snow fidgeted, eager to make their mark, but Nihm would not release them. Not yet. Only if she had to would she risk them against so many.

The urak moved by. Setting an arrow to her bow, Nihm silently rose, drew, paused whilst her target turned to manoeuvre around a tree trunk, then released. The arrow whispered as it parted the air, striking centre chest. The urak grunted then collapsed to the ground like a bag of bones.

<Twelve.>

<Numbers!>

Nihm froze, profile low to the fallen trunk. A cry. An urak calling out that another had fallen. That she could understand it surprised her. They spoke common?

<Most unusual,> Sai echoed.

The urak seemed nervous now, their movements more furtive. <The hunters are hunted and they like it not.> Nihm grinned, listening in to their talk.

"There is a Qu'ri in these woods," a voice grumbled.

"You show your fear, Bortog. Are you a chala still? Cowering in the dark at what you cannot see?"

"I know a Qu'ri's tracks when I see one, Mar'kik. And I see the markings of a warl and human moving as one. There is a spirit in this forest, and we are its prey."

"Superstition. Humans are pitiful. Their souls are weak and disdained by the gods. Why would they bind one as a Qu'ri?" Mar'kik hissed.

"I do not answer for the gods. Only the shamans know their ways and speak their words," Bortog said.

There was a discordant murmur. A thick brogue, Nihm could not easily discern when the others spoke out at once.

"Quiet fools," Mar'kik hissed. Whatever he'd heard though seemed to decide him. "Chu'chuk, Bortog, gather the wounded. We will move north and join up again with Tarsik-Dur. We will let him decide if there is a Qu'ri in this wood."

Nihm waited, watching whilst the urak moved off. Once she was sure of it, she rose. Turning to the south-east she set off once more at a steady jog.

She picked up the trail the urak had been on and followed the hoof marks and boot prints, which curved away south and then south-west. Nihm allowed herself a smirk. It was easy to get disoriented in the woods, doubly so at night.

She caught them just as they reached the road. They looked weary, their horses walking with stooped necks. As the party prepared to remount, Nihm recognised Lord Amos and Jobe, who were helping a man and woman into their saddles. The man was injured, and the woman just plain awkward. Their backs turned as they settled themselves and Nihm knew them as well, Jerkze and the woman was the frumpy one from her dream walk with Renco. Where were the children and where were Renco and Lett?

She watched, as Jobe and Amos pulled themselves up onto their horses, eyes nervously searching the treeline to the north. Neither detected her presence until she called out.

Hands went to swords and bows were raised.

"Who goes there? Show yourself," Amos called. Two of the Red Cloaks circled, their horse agitated, trying to fix on her location.

Nihm raised her voice again. "The urak lost your trail in the forest. You are safe for now."

"How do you know? We heard their war cries. Who are you?" Amos said.

"Mercy sent me. She is camped nearby with Lucky and Stama. I can take you to them."

Nihm stepped out of the woods, bow held loosely in her left hand. She moved slowly across the narrow verge and onto the road, aware that two of the Red Cloaks and Jobe had their bows nocked and ready. As Nihm walked closer, she circled, placing Amos and his horse between her and the Red Cloaks. She didn't trust them.

At twenty paces, the cloud partially obscuring Ankor cleared and Nihm saw Amos Duncan's eyes flare in recognition. "Jobe, Jerkze. You both look like hell," Nihm called out.

"Ai, well its bin a rough few weeks." Jobe grinned. "You're looking better than when last I saw you at least."

Nihm didn't say anything at first. The last she remembered of Jobe was sitting around a bar table watching him spin his knives. "I guess we've all had it tough since we last saw each other. Come. Mercy is this way."

"Hold." The call rang out, overly loud. "Lord Amos, our orders are to take you to Captain Warwick. You'll be coming with us."

"Of course I will, I have business with your Lord Commander and I must reclaim my charges," Amos replied. With a flick of his reins, he guided his horse towards Nihm.

"But first I will see my sister." He gave a nod to Nihm and grinned.

Nihm mirrored it. Turning away, she set off down the road. She listened to the Red Cloaks bluster and curse then the squeak of saddle and tack as they followed Amos and the others.

Giving a low whistle, she heard a gasp from behind as Ash and Snow padded out of the bushes and to her side. She was listening for it over the sound of the horses and amazed herself when she detected the taut strain of a bow being drawn.

Tilting her head, Nihm called over her shoulder, her voice taking on a false cheer. "If you shoot at my dogs, I will kill you." Bloody Red Cloaks.

* * *

Finding where Mercy and the rest were camped proved easier than Nihm expected. She tracked the southern verge for signs of their passage, but it was Ash and Snow that found them first.

Their camp was well chosen with dense bush screening the small gully they were in and shielding the light from the fire they had started.

She detected Stama on sentry duty first. He was well hidden using an asper tree for cover, but she picked him out easily enough. His bow had an arrow fitted and the tension in his stance told Nihm he knew they were coming.

"Ho, Stama, it's me and I've got company."

"I know it. I could smell 'em before I heard 'em." His face broke into a grin as he relaxed his bow. "Besides, caught a glimpse of summat earlier and thought it might be Snow. How many you got?"

"Stama you reprobate. Stop you're yammering and go roust my sister," Amos called out.

The reunion was both short and subdued. Alerted by Stama, Mercy and the others were already awake. That it was Amos, a wounded Jerkze and Jobe was unexpected and there was much joy. The Red Cloaks seemed uncomfortable at first but were ushered in close to the campfire to chase the chill from their bones and they spoke quietly together, accepting a broth Morten had warming over the flames.

Amos spoke in earnest with Mercy. "Lady Constance Bouchemeaux is at the Defile. I gave the Black Crow my oath to see her safely to Hawke Hold with the offer of sanctuary. And there is another I have…"

"We have," Jerkze interjected.

Amos smiled at the correction. "There is another we have taken into our care. A waif called, Annabelle. It's a long story… well it's not actually but I'll explain later. But both are at the Defile with the Red Cloaks, and I must go for them. Besides, Jerkze here got in the way of an arrow and his wound needs a physiker."

"It's just a scratch," Jobe said. "He's milking it."

Nihm left them talking, the dogs settling by the fire with Morten, and made her way back to Stama on lookout still. "Why don't you go join the others, I'll take watch."

"Sure? Ya must be…"

"Yeah, a bit, but I need time to think, Stama. Can't do that down there, thought I may as well take watch. You must have plenty to catch up on with Amos and the others."

Stama laid a thoughtful hand on her shoulder. "I know you came for Renco. Don't worry, Nihm. We'll find him. Wake me for the next watch." With that, he wandered down into camp.

Settling in the spot Stama had just vacated, Nihm crouched. Her muscles ached but it was in a good way she decided. The excitement of the past hours had left her feeling drained. I will just rest a bit, she told herself.

<How will you do it?>

<Not going to try and reason me out of it?>

<The parameters of our mission have not changed. You came for Renco, and he is still out there. Besides, the Red Cloaks hold the Defile and Lord Amos has made it clear that is his destination. Clearly, it is not ours. So, no.>

Tuning out the sounds of the forest, she listened to the soft murmur of voices below. They seemed merry but soon enough the voices grew fewer and quieter until the camp fell silent. She was tired. Her eyes felt gritty, and a dull ache throbbed behind them.

A hole in the tree cover showed the stars above and she picked out the bear constellation and spent some time studying it, whiling away the time and letting her mind drift aimlessly.

<Wake…it is time.>

Nihm blinked her eyes. Horror covered her face. How could she have fallen asleep and for how long? It was still dark. She glanced up through the canopy again, but the bear had moved on.

<You needed rest. Your serotonin levels were dropping. Do not worry. I undertook surveillance of our immediate surroundings.>

"That's not…"

<That's not the point. I fell asleep.>

<I induced your vessel to produce more melatonin to encourage sleep. You need it for now, whilst I do not.>

Nihm chewed her lip, digesting what she had learned. <What are serotonin and melatonin? They sound nasty.>

<They are hormones, two of a multitude produced by your vessel. They are chemical messengers released into your bloodstream. Each exerts different functions and processes on different aspects of your machine… your body, if you will.>

<So glad I asked.>

<If we intend to leave, we should do so now,> Sai observed.

Nihm rose, she was cold, and her joints were stiff and aching. She shook her arms and legs to loosen them and get the blood circulating. <You could have moved me a bit. I feel like I've run into a tree.>

<Motor control of your vessel is limited by my protocols to emergency use only.>

Nihm made her way down the gully, skirting the camp and the low burning fire that enticed her chilled bones. She could feel the subtle heat even from where she was.

She could hear and smell the horses and found them, corralled behind a screen of bushes, herded together for warmth.

Nihm found her mare and rubbed a gloved hand over her neck. She scowled.

"I can hear you breathing, Morten. I heard you the moment you rose from your bedroll. Go back to it, it is early still."

The snow gave a soft crunch as he walked towards her until he stood by her side. Reaching a hand up, he stroked the horse's withers.

"I don't think I will." His tone was hushed, barely a whisper. "I think I will come with you instead."

"What? No!"

Morten made a shushing motion, bringing his hand to his lips. "Not so loud. We don't have much time. We should go now unless you want me to wake the others?"

Nihm hissed, her blood rising. "Are you threatening me Morten Stenhause? You can't come. You're too noisy for a start and will slow me down. Besides, it's dangerous. I've not the time to nursemaid you."

"I can hear your lips flapping. But I'm coming whether you like it or not. So, if you wanna go we should go. I'll not leave you, Nihm."

His face was earnest in the dark. His eyes stern and his jaw set. She'd seen it before, on her father, and arguing with her Da like that was always pointless. Stubborn, thick-headed…

Nihm shoved him, surprised when he stumbled back. It only served to underline her concern. He was a taverner's son and would be next to useless where she was going.

<We could subdue and render him silent, but any overt noise will likely wake the others.>

Angrily, Nihm found his saddle. Lifting it, she shoved it at him, and Morten yelped in surprise, before snatching at it. He hadn't seen it coming, as blind as a newborn cub in the dark. She pushed the needle of guilt to the back of her mind with a scowl. His uselessness was already showing itself.

Nihm bent for her saddle and was surprised to find a dozen arrows propped against it. Nihm shook her head with a rueful smile and placed them in her quiver. Then, with a grunt of effort, lifted and settled the saddle on her horse before swiftly cinching the girth straps. Slipping the bridle, noseband and bit, over the horse's muzzle she fastened the straps. Then turned and helped Morten, who was struggling still in the dark.

<Stama is watching from the bushes.>

<I know. If he was going to say anything though, he would've by now. Besides, who do you think left the arrows?> Nihm led her horse away from camp and Morten duly followed.

They walked the horses for ten minutes, circling around and then back up towards the road. They didn't speak.

Amongst the trees and undergrowth, just out of vision, Nihm felt as much as sensed, Snow and Ash. They were pack, always guarding and protecting her and as faithful and dependable as the sun rising. She loved them unreservedly. They were the only warmth in the chill night.

Chapter 9: Fallen Cardinal, Fallen King

Anglemere, Kingsholme, The Holme

The flesh of his face was pallid and coated in a thin sheen of sweat. Up close, tiny capillaries covered his cheeks and nose in a red lattice. His breath was shallow, and its scent was sweet.

Her nose wrinkled. Tortuga reeked of death. Sinking slowly into her chair, Princess Matrice released the breath she'd been holding. They were alone in his room in the South Tower of Anglemere Castle where she had sequestered him the day before. As far as she could tell, Tortuga had not moved. A carcass of meat, except for the diaphoresis coating his skin, and the slow rise and fall of his chest.

Matrice had only met him four long days past. Back then he was a Cardinal of Kildare and an oddity at that. Kildare being a martial god, Tortuga hardly fit the mould, immense and bloated as he was. Now though, he was the new High Cardinal and proclaimed Voice of Kildare. As much as it grated her to admit it, she needed him.

She had hoped for more time but her father's Lord Chamberlain, Malcolm Riebeck, had pre-empted matters and released a bird to Lord Henry Blackstar. With the family estates just outside of Ramelo, a day's fast horse ride to the north, Matrice had little chance to strengthen her position before her uncle arrived.

Her brow furrowed; nothing had quite worked out as expected. Herald should have been with her father. Drank the same wine, suffered the same fate, and the blame laid squarely at the door of Lord Renix and the Order. Instead, her fool brother had escaped and was loose in the city somewhere. How? He was completely incompetent. Someone must be helping him. Lord Renix certainly would, if wasn't dead already.

Her mouth quirked into a smile at the thought of the Order ambassador; her tongue darted, moistening her lips as she recalled the euphoria of the day before. It had been liberating and intoxicating. First, witnessing her father's poisoning, then the sweet delight as she thrust her blade into Renix. The feeling as it first pierced then parted flesh, of his blood on her skin staining her dress crimson. The final ecstasy as the light faded from his eyes and death claimed him. *'By my hand'*, she shivered.

Stirring, Matrice rose from the chair. Tortuga's instructions from their only meeting had been precise and portentous and resounded in her now.

'Whatever happens in the Red Conclave let no priest or physiker attend me. I have foreseen it. If it is otherwise, you will never become the Red Queen. Promise me, Highness. Let it be as Kildare ordains.'

And so she had, but looking at him now, Matrice was anxious. What use was he if he were dead? It was not too late to call the royal physiker. Turning for the door, Matrice resolved to check on him again later.

Outside the room, Sir Gart Vannen, her first sword, was waiting along with seven Kingsguard, all from her personal detail. Two stood watch on either side of the door, the remaining hand fell in behind her and Vannen.

Leaving the south tower, Matrice crossed the parade grounds towards the central keep. It was busy, filled with the royal gold and red of Kingsguard. The priest when he found her, blended well with them in his red cassock.

"Highness. May I speak with you?" He fell into uncomfortable step as she swirled by.

Matrice recognised Father Manning from her meeting with Tortuga. "Make it quick. I'm busy."

"Thank you. I seek Cardinal Tortuga and was told he was given into your care. That he was in a parlous condition."

"You mean High Cardinal Tortuga, surely? It's not my calling but I remember my religious studies well enough. Better than you it seems." Matrice sneered. "Nine shall enter one will be chosen and I saw with my own eyes, eight dead cardinals, one alive. Unfortunately for you, High Cardinal Tortuga has ordered that no one attend him, not even for food or water."

Father Manning peered anxiously at Matrice. "But I must see him. The bishops have tasked me to report on his health and well-being. Highness, we have suffered a grievous loss. Our entire senior hierarchy has been wiped out."

Matrice stopped suddenly, turned and glared at the priest.

"Not entire. High Cardinal Tortuga survives. Did you know he foretold that this would pass? Worsten Lannik, your former Voice, did not heed him and now lies dead for his arrogance. Maybe the Cardinals were purged by Kildare, struck down by his hand."

"He never told me, Highness." Manning's hands twitched nervously as he spoke.

"Well, tell your brethren so all may know it. And tell them the Voice of Kildare will speak to them soon. That the High Cardinal is recovering in holy retreat, communing with Kildare, who will sustain him, if he is worthy." Matrice started walking again, the audience concluded. Her Kingsguard brushed past Manning, leaving him standing, watching as her diminutive form disappeared behind their bulk.

* * *

The High King's war chamber was clean but for the marked bloodstain on the floor near the high end of the map table. Lifting her eyes, Matrice regarded the room.

It was filled with the same Lords and High Lady, the same councillors as the day before but with several notable additions. Their High Holinesses, Rand Luxurs head of the Church of Ankor, and Maris Jenah, High Priestess of the church of Nihmrodel, were sat in quiet discussion. John Taran, First Magus of the Council of Mages stood silent, framed in bright light by the large window that overlooked the turquoise waters of the Deeping Rift.

And finally, reclining listlessly in her father's chair, her chair, was Queen Margot Blackstar, her stepmother. Matrice returned her weak smile, enjoying the pain she saw in the Queen's powder blue eyes. That the queen loved her father, she had no doubt. As far as Matrice was concerned it was her only redeeming feature.

"How is father?" Matrice asked in genuine interest.

The queen did not reply immediately, and the room hushed as they waited to hear her response. "He lives," she murmured, looked to say more but then clamped her mouth shut.

"I will see him after," Matrice said.

Margot's eyes squinted. "The physikers say he needs to rest and should receive no visitors."

"I'm not a visitor. I'm his only daughter and now his only child after my brother's betrayal," Matrice said. "As painful as it might be for me, I need to see him."

"Of course, my dear. We can discuss it later. I still can't quite believe Herald is involved in all of this. He revered your father. I just can't see it," Margot replied.

Matrice shook her head. "None of us did, mother. Though I for different reasons. He was my brother. We fought all the time, as siblings are wont to do, but I knew him better than anyone. He despised our father and me but most of all, you. He was cunning, petulant, and ambitious. But shrewd enough to only show the side he wanted people to see."

As she spoke, Matrice looked about the room, gauging the impact of her words. High Lord Zacorik wore a relaxed expression, his eyes bright. The other Lords and High Lady were harder to read. They had played this game longer than she.

"Besides, the proof is overwhelming. Most in this room heard father say that the wine he drank was from Herald. Herrick and Lord Valenta, who you know and trust, can attest to that. As well, an innocent would not run from the truth. Not unless he was guilty of it."

She turned again to the Queen. "If the wine had been shared, most in this room would now be dead or laid low. Did it not occur to you that father could just have easily shared that wine with you rather than his council?"

With a sharp intake of breath, Margot's hands clutched at her stomach.

"Clearly not," Matrice scowled, hiding her gratification.

A voice interjected. "Still, tis a shame you took it upon yourself to execute Lord Renix. He could have told us much, I am sure."

Matrice speared Malcolm Riebeck with a look. The Lord Chamberlain was ancient but prestigious and had been a permanent fixture at Anglemere for over fifty years. His hair, what was left of it, was thin, white, and short. It framed a lined, pale-skinned face dotted with pigmentation spots that stained it like inkblots. Ancient he might be, but his eyes were shrewd and alert and the old bastard knew her better than most.

"An Order Knight would tell only what he wanted, lies. The Tankrit Red was his. I know he and my brother spent a lot of time together recently. Herald even flaunted the bottle in front of me before gifting it. I'm afraid the only truth we'll get will be from Herald, speaking of which; Lord Harkul."

Stood unobtrusively near the door, Magnus Harkul, Lord Commander of the Kingsguard strode forward, "Your Highness."

"Commander, what actions have you taken and what is the latest on my brother?" Matrice asked.

"Kingsholme is sealed. The Gates have been locked as ordered. The Kingsguard and City Watch scour the streets and are conducting house searches. It will take time but if he is here, we will find the Crown Prince."

Eyes flashing, Matrice all but snarled, "He is a traitor and Crown Prince no longer. He is stripped of all title; remember that. Tell the Kingsguard and City Watch I want him alive."

Magnus Harkul dipped his head, "Of course, Highness."

A new voice called out, High Lady Elizabeth Hardcastle. "As interesting as all this is, perhaps you could tell me why the Lord Chamberlain has summoned us here at your behest. This is a matter for the Crown, not the Kingdoms."

Finally, pleased at the change in direction, Matrice faced the High Lords and Lady. "I seek to do what my father intended when he summoned you all here. He is High King and ruler of these Nine Kingdoms and in his absence, I will honour his purpose."

Amusement lit Elizabeth Hardcastle's face. She was forty-eight and had ruled Midshire for over a decade. She had eight children all of them older than the young girl who stood before her. "What are you, fourteen, barely in your blood? Hardly old enough or experienced enough to assume your father's mantle while he recovers, if he recovers. Queen Margot is surely better placed."

The room erupted in noise as her words brought a torrent of indignation. Irritated, Matrice picked up a marker and rapped it hard against the tabletop before raising her voice.

"Your niece, my stepmother, is very capable and I value her counsel as much as I do yours. However, she is a Blackstar by marriage, not blood, and only blood rules here," Matrice announced.

It brought Queen Margot from her chair. "You're a girl still, Matrice and I would not rule. Your father is king but it's only right, as his queen, that I convey his will while he recovers. Please, this bickering is unseemly."

"Royce the First, Regal the Third and Eighth, Jorin Blackstar, my great grandfather, and many others should I care to go on. All High Kings, all younger than my fifteen years when they were crowned." Matrice glowered at Elizabeth Hardcastle. The old hag knew her age was not fourteen. "You slight me because you think me young, less capable. Well, have a care High Lady for in this your opinion matters not a whit."

"Matrice," Queen Margot gasped, "apologise at once."

"Attend my father. That is your place, mother. It is not here," Matrice said. Turning dismissively, she raised her voice to the room.

"Master Wendell has reviewed the Royal Protocols and issued copies of the appropriate legal texts which underwrite my position. They are on the table. Take one before you leave. However, first to business.

"Lord Henry Blackstar will be here in a day, two at the most. All of you know my uncle. I need not tell you he can be a difficult man. He will demand an accounting for my father but also for the war in the north for which you have done nothing."

"Hardly fair, your Highness," Dumac, High Lord of Westlands said. "We came at the High King's behest and but for this unfortunate incident, I am sure agreement would already have been reached."

"Unfortunate!" Matrice retorted, "It is treason and who knows how far it extends or who else is involved. Questions my uncle will want answers to as do I."

High Lord Derek Trevenon surged forward. "My oath is to the High King, whilst he lives. I'll not take orders from a child, even his. You have my notice. I leave for Eosland in the morning. Tell your uncle to come see me if he wishes to discuss my 'treason' or anything else for that matter."

The blond-haired, Lord of Eosland was renowned for a surly temperament but this was the first time Matrice had experienced it. She was mildly disappointed. "I'm afraid that will not be possible. The city gates remain barred whilst my traitor brother is loose. Besides, you were summoned to attend a war council. One we will have, once Lord Henry Blackstar is here."

Derek Trevenon exploded, "I will not be held prisoner!"

"Hardly, High Lord, more a valued guest," Matrice demurred. She held a hand up to still him, her eyes scanning the others in the room.

"I remind all of you we are at war. It may not have arrived at your doorstep yet, but it will. I have read the reports sent to my father. The urak have taken much of the Rivers and move on the Norderlands. If we are not careful, the enemy will roll us up, one kingdom at a time. Unless we make a stand. This is not a time for the Game of Lords. Our situation is dire, and I will not stand for any politicking. And let me assure you, as uncomfortable as you might be dealing with me, you will find it a lot more palatable than dealing with my uncle.

"Now, when he arrives we'll reconvene here. At that time, I expect a firm commitment from all of you for supplies, materials, and men-at-arms. Winter is upon us and while it may slow us down it should also buy us time in the north."

Derek Trevenon ground his jaw but the remaining High Lords and even High Lady Hardcastle looked more guarded and reflective. Leaving them no time to raise any further complaint, Matrice swung her gaze to John Taran.

"First Magus, the council agreed with my father to send a hundred mages north for an anticipated spring offensive. I expect that to be honoured. It would be useful if you could give a disposition of your contingent in writing and who will be leading them, before our council."

John Taran was a shrew of a man who nonetheless drew the eye, his persona confident and self-assured. "Of course, Highness, the council serves the Nine. Your earlier assessment aligns with our own. We must act together to address this threat in the north. If I could, I would be interested to know how the Trinity will support our efforts, especially given the attack on the Red Cardinals."

Maris Jenah replied, her face serene and unwrinkled, the few grey strands in her hair giving the only truth to her age. "The Lady will send what she can. Our Church Knights are few but what we do have will be sent to assist our Holy Fathers and Sacred Mothers. We will provide support, both spiritual and physical to your armies; our healers and physikers are as good as any in the Kingdoms."

"Likewise, Ankor the Giver will make similar endeavour." Rand Luxurs offered. Unlike his companion, Luxurs looked aged, his body thick around its girth, shoulders stooped, and face creased like the rings of a fallen oak. "As regards the Church of Kildare, they are in disarray at present. That is to be expected until the condition of High Cardinal Tortuga is known. I believe, in that respect, your Highness is more in tune with his ailment. Perhaps you could advise on his well-being?"

Matrice gave a slight bow to both eminences. Her position would be far more secure with both churches backing her. "Thank you, your Holinesses. If there is anything the Churches need, the Crown will help, just let me know. As to High Cardinal Tortuga, his condition remains stable but perilous. It is by his order that he remains undisturbed. He considers himself in holy retreat and, against my better judgement, I have agreed to honour his wish. His eminence communes with Kildare and believes he will be delivered of his sickness."

"You sound unconvinced, child," Maris Jenah replied.

Matrice frowned. "Just uncomfortable, it seems an extraordinary act of faith to hope Kildare will cleanse him, as he says. I just… don't understand it."

"I see," Jenah hummed, her face thoughtful. "Yet, what is life without faith? Perhaps, Kildare will find him worthy. One can only hope."

* * *

Afterwards, with the room empty, Matrice stood where John Taran had and gazed out at the white-capped waters of the sea below. The light that had illuminated the Magus now fell upon her and she basked in its warmth. She heard the soft crease of leather behind her.

"Are we alone?" Matrice asked.

"Yes, my queen," Gart Vannen replied.

"I've asked you not to call me that." She turned. The stone dais around the window was a step above the chamber floor and, stood as he was below her, their eyes were on a level.

"Bortillo Targus is called the king of thieves, or so they say. Legend has it that he has been king almost as long as the city is old. Do you believe that?"

"No," Vannen said, "At least, no to one man ruling for all those lifetimes. There is a Bortillo Targus though and he is the thief king, at least until he is murdered and replaced by another Targus."

"How disappointingly ordinary," Matrice muttered, "I want you to find him."

"Can you not send another? I would not be from your side," Vannen replied.

"You are the only one I trust. It must be you," Matrice replied, gracing him with a smile. "Find him and talk to him in person. Offer him my brother's weight in gold if he delivers Herald's head before the Kingsguard find him, double if it's before my uncle arrives."

Gart bowed. "It will be difficult, but I'll try, princess."

Matrice stamped her foot, "I don't want try. Anyone can try. Just do it. I want him dead, Gart. I want Herald's head at my feet."

Gart bowed his head, "As you wish." Turning, he strode crisply away. As he reached the door, he spared a final glance at his queen. She had returned and gazed once more out of the window; an unearthly vision of beauty encompassed in golden sunlight. Heart clenching, he pulled the door wide and left.

* * *

Her father was not dissimilar to Tortuga, Matrice decided. He had the same ashen hue to his skin and was clammy with sweat. Dark shadows ringed his eyes and a dribble of saliva followed the line of his jaw. He looked dead. Gathering his hand in hers it was surprisingly warm.

"What does Loren Cripps have to say?"

Her question hung in the air, unanswered. Twisting in her chair, Matrice glanced over her shoulder.

Queen Margot stood silently by the door, hand covering her mouth. Her eyes were watery and large and full of sadness.

"Mother?" Matrice prompted, her voice gentle.

Margot shook her head, left then right. Gathering herself she took a sharp breath that turned into a loud sniff. Her hand dropped listlessly to her side. "That he may never regain consciousness and if he does his mind might be broken. That it is only the intervention of Ankor that he still breathes."

"May, might... father is stronger than that. He'll recover. He has to," Matrice countered.

"Cripps said... he said... the chance was small. That... if Edward regains consciousness and his mind, he may live but he'll not be the same. His organs are weakened by the poison; heart and lungs, liver, and kidney." A sob leaked out. "And he will never walk."

Rising, Matrice went to her stepmother. Felt her shuddering cries as she clasped and held the older woman close. Biting a lip to stop her smile, Matrice waited. She felt no sadness for her father; no sorrow at what she had done, only elation. Was it so wrong? She knew she should feel something for him, but she didn't. No empathy, no guilt. But then where was he when mother had died? She was a young child, ignored and left to suffer in grief, alone. Her father gave no comfort, offered no solace. It was she who witnessed the burden of his loss as well as carrying her own. He never once helped her to understand the pain or make her feel whole. Who was there to mend the rift in her heart? Not he and certainly not her stepmother the queen.

"Edward did not deserve this. He is a good man. Why? Why would Herald do this to his own father?" Margot cried.

Matrice tasted iron in her mouth and licked the salty blood off her lip. This was getting tedious and the whining annoying.

"I'm pregnant," Margot sobbed.

Her heart stopped. A cold shiver ran down her spine but Matrice did not say anything.

"Ouch, you're hurting me, dear," Margot pulled away. "I'm sorry, I shouldn't have told you like that. It's just, your father and I have been trying for years and now he might never get to see his son."

"A son?" Though it was her voice, to Matrice it seemed as if the words were spoken by another.

"Yes, you're going to have a baby brother. Loren read the weaving and confirmed it three days ago. I didn't want to say, it's early yet and bad luck but I had to tell you." Margot wiped the tears from her cheeks and gave a small, tight smile. "I know we've never been close, though The Lady knows I've tried, but we both love your father, and we will need each other to get through this."

"A brother, a baby brother," Matrice muttered.

The Queen clasped a hand to each side of her stepdaughter's face. "Yes, a baby brother."

Matrice hugged the queen again, holding her tight. "That's… wonderful news. I'm going to have a brother!"

"Yes." Margot squeezed her back, pleased at the reaction. She'd been nervous about telling the princess. That it had just popped out like that, well, the response couldn't have been better.

"I would like to sit with father for a while if that is alright?" Matrice murmured.

"Of course, dear. I'm sure he'd love you to keep him company." Margot broke their clinch, gave a warm smile then turned for the door.

"Mother," Matrice called out and waited while the queen looked back. "It would be good to talk. Before my uncle gets here."

"You can always talk to me. I'm always here, my dear."

Matrice returned a weak smile and waited while the door closed before sitting once more and holding her father's hand. She raised it to her lips and kissed the back leaving a smudge of blood upon it. She leaned in close and laid her head next to his. Eyes watching the slow rise and fall of his chest, she spoke softly.

"So, father, a new son and heir. You must be happy. Only, if you die now, he'll never take the throne, Uncle Henry will seize that for himself unless I stop him and I'm not ready." Matrice kissed his cheek.

"So don't die, father. Not until I say."

Chapter 10: The Abyss

Highwatch, Norderland

Krol stood at the edge of the precipice gazing into a yawning maw of jagged rocks and hard edges. He felt the pull of the abyss drag on his body, calling to him like a siren's song. It exerted a subtle gravity on his limbs making them leaden and unresponsive.

One step was all. One step to end his torment and he yearned to take it. The wind gusted. Strong and insistent, it pushed against his back, urging. But Krol stood unmoved.

Not so his Hurak-hin. He could feel his warriors bristling with nervousness. It was their duty to protect him, but none would approach or say anything. They believed him touched by the gods. It was a convenient untruth, for much of what he did, was not urakakule. Volatile and unpredictable, they feared him as much as they revered him.

Darkness swirled in his eyes and his feet shuffled until the toe ends of his boots touched air. The shade of the Morhudrim lapped up his misery and drank in the angst of the Hurak-hin.

Eyes suddenly clearing, Krol rocked forwards then backwards and took a step to safety, then another. Leery, he turned from temptation and fixed his gaze upon the rockslide blocking the pass.

"Damn fool."

The path over the broken mountain provided the only route for his people to cross and reach the lands beyond. The rockfall presented a barrier that needed to be breached, and urgently. Mar-Dur and his White Hand were at their backs.

Whilst he held an accord with Mar-Dur he knew he'd be a fool to trust in it. His precipitous actions in destroying Redford and sacking everything east of the human settlements of Marston and Fallston arguably broke their pact. At the very least it fostered no goodwill between them.

Krol bared his teeth. Warring was in their blood. Even at the best of times the tribes were fractious; it was the nature of urakakule. Mar-Dur should have known better than to sit idle, waiting for the Bite to pass. Waiting for the renewal of the Return.

Still, it placed the Blood Skull in a perilous position. Krol, as warchief, had been forced to array over half the tribes defensively to guard against the White Hand. His war host now stretched from the mines of Kagauld and Chortonwood in the south all the way to the headwaters of the Ous'trak five days to the north. They were wedged against the mountains with nowhere else to cross but this one pass. If he were Mar-Dur, accord or no, he would strike. Seize this opportunity and crush his rival.

All this was as nothing though. As precarious and concerning as it might be for Krol, it paled into insignificance against the yearning, incessant will of The Taker. The Morhudrim drove him eastward with a pathological imperative that could not be resisted and now, his Master placed upon him another.

He turned to Tar-Tukh, first of his Hurak-hin. "Fetch Nuupik-tarn. Carry him if you must. Then ask the Circle of Shamans to join me."

Tar-Tukh clenched his right fist to left breast in acknowledgement, before turning to do as bid.

Krol cast a disdainful look at Jekis-Dol, Chieftain of the Muritoome. It was their honour to assault the fort guarding the broken mountain and now it was their shame.

"Damn fool," Krol repeated the words of a moment before this time directed at the chieftain.

Bridling, fighting back his rage, Jekis-Dol glared in return. "I lost many warriors, most to the gods when they brought the mountain down upon us. They have spoken. This is not our path."

Krol hissed. "Our path is what I say it is. Humans brought the mountain down. Not the gods." His arm extended, pointing past Jekis-Dol at the rockslide and the chieftain turned to look.

"An avalanche of rock and you run, hiding your fear behind the mighty." In a blur of motion, Krol thrust his spear, so sudden and so violent that it impaled Jekis-Dol through his lower back, its tip bursting from his gut.

Jekis-Dol's teeth clenched shearing into his tongue, lips contorting in a rictus of agony. The strength left his legs, and he would have collapsed had Krol not stepped in close and held him upright on the spear.

If Jekis-Dol were able to feel shame and humiliation, there was no time for it. Krol pivoted, lifting the spear and launching him out, spinning, over the abyss. To his credit, the chieftain of the Muritoome didn't cry out.

Krol turned back and stared at the hand of warriors not his own. Jekis-Dol's Hurak-hin looked ready to rush him. It would be their death, as was right. He was unarmed and they would seek to take him with them to Varis-tuk's Hall. But Krol held them with his eyes. Like a snake holds a mouse they stood frozen. And like that, the moment was lost, his own Hurak-hin were at his side, ready. Krol held his arm up and waved them back.

"Your Chieftain falsely invoked the gods. Now, he has gone to meet them. They will judge his worth." Krol held his hands wide. "As Warchief it was my right. If any feel aggrieved strike me down. My Hurak-hin will not interfere."

Two of the five needed no further invitation. With a battle cry, they raised their weapons and charged, closing the small space in a moment.

Krol was ready. The burning taint of the Morhudrim pulsed through his veins, filling his limbs with energy and power. At the last instant he moved, leaping inside the swing of the first warrior's blow. His hand blocked against an arm, deadening muscles, the descending sword sent spinning from nerveless fingers. His other hand gripped the warrior's throat, fingers and nails digging into his windpipe. Krol turned him into the path of the second warrior who stumbled, pulling his strike.

The held warrior struck Krol in the face, but it only brought a sneer of contempt. He lurched as his eyes locked with the warchief's. They swirled like blood in water. Black blood. Before he had the chance to wonder at it or cry out, he was grappled, spun and thrown, staggering towards the cliff edge. Arms pin-wheeling, the warrior teetered on the brink. The wind gusted and he fell, plummeting with a shriek.

Sensing movement, Krol twisted. His hand snapped out, nonchalant it seemed to the watching Hurak-hin, and pushed against the flat edge of the thrusting blade. The warrior stumbled, his sword not meeting the expected resistance of flesh, and Krol struck. His fist crunched into the side of the warrior's head sending him to the ground. Krol followed with a kick to the ribcage that spun the fallen urak over onto his back. Looking down, Krol saw defiance in the warrior's eyes. No fear. It pleased him.

"You have honour," Krol said, "Not so these others."

Cocking his head, he called over his shoulder. "Take them. Give them no warrior's death. Let them join Jekis-Dol. Maybe they will guard him better in the Never."

There was a surge of bodies as his Hurak-hin rushed by. The three remaining warriors all fought but against so many it was futile. After a brief skirmish all were wounded, one mortally, then disarmed. Cursing, spitting hostility, they were dragged unceremoniously and heaved out into the abyss, their cries turning to screams.

"What is your name?" Krol asked the urak at his feet.

"I am dishonoured. My name is dust. A Hurak-hin dies with their chieftain. End me."

"No. The Blood Skull and Muritoome have need of you and Varis'tuk does not call you. Not yet." Krol could see the troubled look on the warrior's face, the doubt in his eyes.

"I will do what your chieftain could not. I will take the wall, alone and with only Nos'varg to bear witness. Now, tell me your name," Krol demanded.

The urak gazed back. His face a war of shame and anger. "Varg-warl."

"Warl," Krol mused with a wry chuckle, "A cunning and clever hunter, but you have lost your pack, Varg-warl. Rise, and claim a new one. The eye of Naris-Krol sees you."

Varg-warl rose slowly to his feet, his emotions high but confused. He should be dead. It was his right. But there was something intangible about Krol, something other. A power that was both compelling and otherworldly. He was called mad by some and by others gods touched. Was it a coincidence then that the blood moon hung above him? Were the gods bearing witness? He could feel the omnipotence of their gaze.

Hand clenching into a fist, Varg-warl clasped it to his chest and bared his throat. "Your will, warchief." Turning, he pushed against the knot of Hurak-hin, feeling their enmity. The scent of blood percolating the air enticed violence. But death would be a reward, Varg-warl did not fear them.

Reluctantly they moved aside for him, and Varg-warl walked through them. His tribe would decide his fate.

* * *

The sun was lowering and despite the gusting wind, the cloud and mist had returned. It was unwelcome but not untoward. Johanus Ulrikson the Barle of Highwatch, glared at the fading slopes of Eracus to his left. Of the ten men sent to trigger the rockslide from her flanks only six had returned. Always, the mountains asked a toll and Eracus had taken her due.

The avalanche of stone shed by the mountain straddled the pass and brought a premature end to the urak attack on Highwatch but Johanus was not fooled thinking them safe. It had bought them a day, maybe even a couple but the urak would be back. Unless more warriors arrived from Skaag and Helg, he had little hope of holding the walls. They had barely survived the last onslaught and Eracus would not repeat her favour. The Order man, Tannon Crick had told him the High Barle was two days away with thousands of men. If they had two days it would be enough, he grunted to himself. Two days.

He was weary and Johanus knew he should be resting. With the sudden return of the cloud-mist, he'd already set sentries every ten paces along the wall. Moved the three surviving mangonels, placing the nags so they would provide a staggered, spread of cover along the line of approach. Then had the facing walls slicked again with water. There was nothing further to be done but wait, gather his strength and prepare his weapons and armour. But something held him there, a foreboding deep in his bones that urged his vigil. It would not release him.

No one knew these mountains like him. No one was better placed to watch than he. The air carried a diversity of alpine scents that gave a tale hard for most to discern. The stone beneath his feet was Brikka's stone and he felt connected to the mountain in ways he could not explain and few, who were not Highwatchers, would understand.

The wind was from the north, something an outsider would not know. The giant sentinels of Eracus and Ocanik funnelled and channelled it so that the wind eddied and swirled in a vortex giving a counter current that gusted from the west. It chaffed against the exposed skin on his face. No, an outsider could not understand the ways of the mountain.

The mist had grown steadily thicker until abruptly, Johanus realised the slopes of Eracus had vanished. Looking to his left and right the sentries had become vague outlines and soon were gone from sight altogether. He was stood alone in a sea of grey-white murk that was darkening rapidly as the sun fled the sky.

It was unnatural. Johanus knew this intuitively. Conditions could change in an instant on the mountains, but the density of the fog was unlike any he had experienced. Holding his arm out he could barely discern his gloved hand. The wind shrilled and beneath it came the muffled crunch of snow and grit as the sentries on each side of him shuffled, trying to keep warm. The urak could be ten paces away and they'd not see them.

'Ai, but we'll hear them, and the wind will bring the smell of the bastards if they come,' Johanus told himself, stamping his own feet; the reassuring firmness of Brikka's stone the only comfort in this nothingness.

A muffled sound. A moan of complaint to his left that was taken by the wind. Gods damned Riekason. It irked Johanus that he had not enough men to rotate watchers. It had been a mistake allowing Riekason and his low-landers onto the wall. They were Barle Janis's men and what did they know of mountains outside of boar hunting the low passes? Nothing.

Moments later it came again. Lower, harder to discern, but still, it irked Johanus who slapped his arms in anger. Riekason and his men bitching like boys on their first hunt. Only this was not their first hunt, they should know better. Awkwardly, Johanus followed the wall he could not see, the touch of his boots against Brikka's stone guiding him. It was enough. He had walked its length many times.

The cloaked form of Kuviksson materialised and the two Highwatchers clasped arms briefly.

"Fucking low-landers," Kuviksson muttered, his bush of beard crackling with frost as he spoke.

Johanus's eyes glinted his agreement before he moved by and walked further along the wall. He passed Mairlik, then Steigson but then nothing. The next guard in place should have been one of Riekason's men. He could hear talking. A low voice that undulated with the wind and was answered by another.

He placed a hand on his sword when his other senses caught up with him. The vague shape of a person emerged, accompanied by the smell of rosebay and crocus which steeped the air and filled his nostrils despite the wind. It stopped him in his tracks.

His wife scented herself with rosebay and crocus. A highlander through and through, she was harder than most men he knew. The perfume was one of her few vanities. So odd to smell it now in the bite of winter. It brought an ache to his heart that had long been buried. A yearning pain for the woman who had died in childbirth three winters ago.

The figure moved and he groaned. It was she. As impossible as it was, he had known it somehow even before she turned. The way she stood, the tilt of her head and shoulders, it resonated deep inside on a level he barely understood but that his body and mind recognised and responded to. Her broad face lit up at seeing him. It warmed his heart. The bright eyes and easy smile were just as he remembered.

His hand dropped from his sword hilt and he sighed. All the pensive despair and emotion at her loss, suppressed and brewed inside him these past three years, were released in that breath. The next felt like the first clean air he had taken in all that time and it was a balm to his soul.

"Arnika?"

She moved towards him, her heavy cloak parting as her arms lifted to encompass him.

It wasn't right. She was dead. He had held her lifeless body in his arms. But the rosebay and crocus swirled about them, soothing his mind. Maybe he had died without knowing it. Maybe this mist was a pathway to the gods and she had come to greet him.

Then she was kissing him, his urgency rising to match hers. His head tilted upwards to meet her hunger as he tried to encircle her in his arms. His hands could barely reach, her body seeming uncommonly large. It did not match what his eyes told him or the lie of her scent.

This is wrong. Johanus struggled to break their clench, but it was already too late. A vapour of decay slid down his throat and pooled in his lungs. In an instant, his blood circulated the contaminant, its foul taint sinking into his flesh and seeping into his bones.

He screamed only for the sound to be swallowed by his dead wife. Then silence. His will crushed, fled to the back of his mind and he could only watch in mute horror as his Arnika shimmered and twisted into a monster.

* * *

For Krol, it had been a long night at Highwatch. The circle of shamans had worked the wisps of mist and fog and shaped it, making it dense and impenetrable past a few feet. It had made Krol's work possible but far from easy despite his heightened senses and the life he could feel upon the walls.

Approaching, with Nuupik-tarn in toe, had been gratingly slow going. The Sartantak's former shaman being both blind and frail, made him something of an oddity to the tribe, despite the reverence and esteem shamans were held in. To the urakakule, either condition should have precipitated the long walk. The tribe expected it. Instead, Nuupik-tarn persisted. An outcast for his infirmity, he was only suffered because of Krol's intervention.

Not now. With the mist dissipating in the freshening wind and Marq'suk the life-giver renewing in the east, the shaman lay dead at his feet. To Krol, he looked shrunken and wizened his skin pale rather than the healthy grey it should have been. A cloth strip was bound across Nuupik-tarn's eyes. A symbolic gesture rather than for any natural reason.

Bending, Krol lifted the body in his arms. The old shaman's purpose was complete. The Morhudrim essence he had borne cast anew and his life force was spent with each casting until he was no more. Krol wondered if the gods would accept Nuupik-tarn's spirit and allow it to pass Nos'varqs Gate or whether even in death the Morhudrim would claim one final victory.

Krol could feel the humans gather behind, following him silently as he walked towards the cliff's edge. Standing upon the abyss, he cast the dead urak into its depths and watched the body spin and flop into the void until it left his sight. A part of him felt sadness and shame, that Nuupik-tarn's life should end so at his hands, from a self-conceit started ten cycles in the past.

"Varis'tuk take you."

Turning about, Krol surveyed the humans arrayed before him. They were pallid, pasty-looking creatures, ugly to look upon, their features soft and weak. Yet, despite this and their relatively diminutive size, they looked compact and dangerous. Even the warg fears a pack of hounds, thought Krol, as their black, soulless eyes regarded him in return.

Nothing was said. No words were needed. The Morhudrim laid claim to each man and woman and regarded Krol through forty pairs of eyes. As one they turned away and Krol watched as they walked past the dead and gathered their horses. Mounting, they rode for the east gate, unmindful of the bodies they trampled on the way.

The Morhudrim essence inside of Krol swirled and he could taste its impatience. Giving a final, forlorn glance at the abyss he walked to the west gate. Unbarring it, he pushed the gates wide then climbed the walls and waited. As Marq'suk warmed his back, urak appeared and at their forefront was his Hurak-hin.

A howl went up when they spied him up on the wall and as one, they broke into a run, chanting his name so that the sound crashed against the side of the mountain.

Baring his teeth, Krol threw his head back and roared.

Chapter 11: Connections

Northwest of the Defile, The Rivers

Lett seemed upset and sulky and Renco didn't know why. They were alone the two of them in the wilderness and far from safety. He assumed it was that, though a nagging doubt had him questioning and wondering if he'd done something wrong.

The night before, they had both listened as a battle raged in the forest to the south. The fight had been short and fierce, the sounds eliciting brutal scenes in Renco's imagination. The Red Cloaks had been attacked just after night had fallen and the churchmen, seemingly surprised, had stood little chance. Shortly afterwards the light of a fire had coloured the far treeline with enticing yellows and golds. The uraks' guttural barking, reaching against the breeze, harsh and alien.

Maybe it was that which accounted for Lett's sombre mood. It must be so, he decided. Her back was to him, but Renco could tell she was awake just from her breathing. Leaving the warmth of their cloaks he rummaged through the pack Jobe had given them. The rations were minimal. Some hard cheese, dried meat and hardtack. Two days, three at a stretch if they were careful. Unsheathing his knife, he cut a meagre portion for them both, his stomach grumbling its complaint in anticipation.

Nibbling on his breakfast, Renco moved to the edge of the laurus shrubs and peered out between the evergreen leaves towards the far treeline. The camp lay hidden from view, but his ears could hear what his eyes could not see. The urak were there still. He had hoped they would move off in the night, either following the tracks south or, since they likely came from the south, the trail in the snow he and Lett had left, heading westward.

There was a rustle from behind. "Is this all? I'm starving."

Twisting around, Renco gave a stern look that went ignored. Annoyed, he shuffled over and touched Lett's shoulder waiting until she glanced up at him. His admonition died as she did so, his anger fading as her haunted eyes regarded his. Lett's mouth twisted into a wilted pout, her breathing was shallow and fast, nostrils flexing at each intake and exhale.

Whatever she saw in his face, Lett was suddenly kneeling and hugging him, arms clasped tight, worrying the cuts and stitches still healing on his back. Renco ignored the stabbing pain as she sobbed against his shoulder. He was unsure quite what he should do. Master Hiro and Mao had not prepared him for this type of interaction. So, he held her and endured until Lett's sobbing slowly abated and she slumped back on her heels.

Peering at him through damp lashes, Lett sniffed and gave an awkward smile. "Sorry. Ever since Fallston, I seem to step from one hell into another. I'm so scared all the time and so bloody cold."

Renco heard her words, understood her fear and enjoyed giving her comfort, really he did. But urak were camped in the woods nearby, she was talking far too loudly and his head still pulsed with a throbbing regularity. Bringing a finger to his lips, Renco pointed to the south and almost like magic, Lett's mood flipped as if he'd poked her with a stick. Like a static discharge, the air felt suddenly tense.

"You're impossible and such a boy!" Picking up the slither of hard cheese cut for her breakfast Lett shoved it whole into her mouth and chewed on it as if she were grinding rocks.

Renco blinked, confused and feeling mildly unsettled. After a moment, he decided it might be best to go back to his observation post. The danger posed by the urak was real and so much easier to understand.

Screened by the shrubs, he settled again to his watch. There was a frigid iciness in the air, but Renco did not mind it and though the leaves above rustled in gentle song, no wind reached through the dense foliage to settle its chill upon him. In the sky, grey-white clouds skudded south and across the moat of meadowgrass, sunlight glinted, fracturing off the ice crystals in the snow.

He could hear Lett behind, fidgeting as she pulled her boots on and laced them, then a rummaging. She said nothing further but the atmosphere between them felt decidedly colder than the frosty air.

A sudden clamour shattered the morning, drawing his attention forward again. It startled a band of wood pigeons into flight; their sluggish wings lifting them out of the trees and over the meadow.

Though Renco was too far-removed to make anything out clearly, many voices were raised at once and the urak sounded riled, their gruff tones urgent. Without thought, Renco dropped into ki'tae.

The bloom of life energy exploded in his mind. The former red cloak camp had been on the edge of his ability and it remained so, though this time the splashes of white he found were distinctive for the lattices of purple and reds that ran through them, rather than the green and browns associated as human.

Urak, last night there had been a score of them. Now, he counted a score and twelve. More had arrived. The realisation was unsettling. Perhaps they would move off together. Or, maybe they were expanding the camp with more urak on the way. Maybe this was to be a staging post for their invasion? Renco blew a cloud of breath. No point second-guessing, time would tell. Still, it was obvious that the longer they lingered the greater the risk of discovery. The urak, if they stayed, would forage and the hideaway was entirely too close to their campsite for comfort. The painted memory of the fight from the night before cluttered his mind and Renco shook his head to clear his thoughts. *'We'll wait an hour, then if they remain, head north and work around'*, he told himself.

A muffled squawk came from Lett.

With an audible sigh, Renco turned to see what she wanted and startled, his hand snatching at the knife on his belt.

Lett was seated on the cloaks, eyes wide with fright. Behind, knelt a hooded figure with one hand clamped firmly over her mouth and the other reaching towards him. It was empty, with two fingers extended as if about to bestow a blessing. On the ground beside them was a staff, elaborately carved with runes and gilded sigils.

The stranger seemed untroubled by Lett's struggles and held her fast. Renco could see nothing beneath the hooded cowl of the cloak other than an ominous gleam, but it was the hands that drew his eyes. Long-fingered and delicate, he thought at first, they must be gloved for they were mottled green, tarnished with hard reds and soft golds with strange crescent-shaped hints of blue that reminded Renco of autumnal leaves.

The hand moved, signing for Renco to lower his knife and he did, though he held it ready by his side. The voice that whispered from inside the hood was sonorous.

"No harm is meant. Hunters are near. When I release you, make no sound."

Not waiting for acknowledgement, the stranger removed his hand and Lett scrambled across the soft loam, rasping fearfully until she reached Renco's side. Twisting about, she gasped. "Who are you?"

Renco signed to lower her voice, the splinted fingers on his left hand aching as he flexed them. They were healing quickly.

Immediately, the stranger signed back and to his amazement, Renco found he understood it. All this time, he'd thought his sign language was created for him by Master Hiro and Mao. Junip, the young woman from yesterday-morn had mentioned the ilfanum using sign and he found himself looking in expectation at the hooded stranger with the mottled, leaf-skinned hands. He gestured.

'I understand you.'

"What are you saying?" Lett hissed. "Who is he?"

Finding her tone mildly accusatory, Renco clenched his jaw and wondered how to answer when he barely knew himself. The stranger resolved his dilemma.

"I am ilfanum. Your companion, I think, was surprised I knew his signing. It is wise of him to use it with the urakakule camped so close."

"An ilf?" Lett's face changed, shifting from fear to undisguised curiosity as the stranger raised his hands and lowered his hood.

The face revealed was male and human-shaped in contour but with eyes that were larger and slightly canted and with tiny ridges of skin wrinkling his nose. The ears were hard to distinguish, lying flat against his head and the soft brown, vine-like tresses that sprang from his crown, were pulled back and gathered at his nape. The dark orbs staring back showed no white and lent an other-worldly aspect that had Lett holding her breath and which sent flutters through her chest.

"Your cover is well chosen. The urak will soon move off. Until then we should remain silent. Their hearing exceeds your own and it would not do to attract unwanted attention."

"I'm Letizia Goodwill, Lett, and this is Renco." Leaning forward, Lett extended her hand uncertainly. "He doesn't speak but we are pleased to meet you."

The ilf glanced at the proffered hand but made no move to take it, until, with cheeks reddening, Lett withdrew it.

"He speaks. That you do not understand him does not make it any less so," the ilf replied. "You may call me, Nesta. Now," in a parody of Renco earlier, the ilf raised a finger to his lips, gesturing for silence.

Biting her tongue at his mild rebuke did nothing to stifle Lett's curiosity and she examined the ilf in fascinated silence. The ilf for his part seemed transfixed by Renco and his slender fingers danced a weave, to which Renco replied, his signing less elegant, encumbered by the splint binding two of his fingers and the cloth that covered the cut on his hand. Lett watched in growing frustration as the two conversed, then, feeling a strange mixture of riled and bored, set about tidying their shelter, repacking the backpack and shaking out their cloaks, huffing at the dirt that coated the red fabric and picking off the leaf debris.

Her task was over all too soon. Settling her cloak around her shoulders she drew it close for warmth and sat on Renco's. She longed to ask what they spoke of but the ilf seemed terse and Lett was scared to draw his ire. Instead, as the morning light grew, she made a note in her mind of the ilf and worked it into words to add to her story. Words that could be shaped into the cadence of a poem or song, just as her Da had taught her.

At the thought of her Da, a pang of sadness and guilt gripped Lett, the former for his death and the latter for her part in it. Long, she had dwelt on her actions that day and suffered much remorse and misery because of it. His death and her heart-wound were too fresh to open anew.

Renco was aware of Lett fussing in the background even as he spoke to the ilf. Saw a flicker of distress cross her face and wondered at it, only for it to fade just as quickly as it arrived. Lett caught his eye and scowled before pulling her cloak tight. *She looks freezing.* The thought was banal, for Renco knew there was nothing to be done.

'I am intrigued. The markings on your face? How did you get them?' Nesta signed.

The question caught Renco off-guard, and he raised a hand to his cheek. 'Is it obvious? I'm not sure. It was only mentioned to me a few days ago.'

The ilf nodded and looked to say more but the gestures when he made them imparted a more mundane message than Renco was expecting.

'I will observe the urak. Do not disturb me.' Nesta said and with that, the conversation was over.

It left Renco with much to ponder. With nothing left to do, he glanced at Lett, then back to the ilf before returning to his watch-post with only a headache for company.

They had not been waiting long when Nesta roused himself and announced, in hushed tones, that the urak were on the move. Renco strained to listen, but the sounds were indistinct. He contemplated phasing into ki'tae but was stopped by a nagging intuition that Nesta had already done so. The ilf held an aura, a mysticism, that brushed against his mind and spoke of magic. It was subtle but not unlike the energy his master exuded when casting. Or, as Master Hiro liked to call it, manipulating aether. It was an ability he lacked. He could quicken his senses and had awakened his ki'tae, but much to Renco's chagrin, he did not possess the art to wield aether.

Staring at the far trees, Renco was aware of Lett as she settled beside him. She had remembered the lesson from before and shed her red cloak. Her hand found and gripped his.

A flicker of movement drew the eye, fleeting shadows obscured by the trees, and Renco followed them until he was sure before squeezing Lett's hand in reassurance. They moved west.

The urak broke clear of the woods and into view and Renco counted them out as they did so. Twenty. Where were the twelve?

The answer presented itself almost immediately. The dozen breaking from the trees to the south and into the meadow. They carved a single path in the snow as they crossed, moving in a loping gait that covered the ground quickly.

Assessing each of them, Renco noted that three urak moved awkwardly and bore fresh signs of injury. His thought's touched briefly on Lord Amos, wondering if perhaps they had clashed and met their end before his mind shifted back to the now. The urak were fast approaching and it was as if they made a beeline for their position. Sinking further into the foliage, his fingers curled about his sword grip.

"Move deeper into the shrubs and lay still." Nesta's voice was so low it barely reached their ears, yet despite this it conveyed clear warning. Lett scrabbled backwards and reluctantly, Renco followed, leaving the ilf as their lone observer.

Raising a hand, Nesta pulled the hood of his cloak up and Lett took a sharp breath, nudging Renco needlessly. The black fabric shimmered and rippled, the colour changing to a broken pattern of browns and greens. The green a perfect match for the laurus leaf.

In moments, the first urak rushed by, panting as it broke a trail north. Then the next. Each passed within feet of their hideaway, their shape obscured but enough to convey size and mass. A heady musk reached them, worming its way on the air and Renco's nostrils flared at the unfamiliar tang.

Counting them as they went by, Renco held his breath when the last but one stopped. A sharp snort sounded.

"Come, Bortog. We fall behind," a gruff voice urged.

"Thought I caught a scent of summat." The prompt though seemed enough and the one named Bortog lumbered away followed by its companion.

The sound of the urak receded before fading altogether. Nesta gestured at the humans to remain silent and watched until the urak were out of sight, then waited some more until he was satisfied.

"It is safe," Nesta announced. Picking his staff up, he pushed through the shrubs and followed the newly created path across the meadow.

Shrugging the pack onto his back and donning his cloak, Renco followed, then Lett, both hurrying to catch the ilf.

"How did you find us? Why are you helping?" Lett called out.

The ilf stopped and looked back, head tilted as if he had not considered the matter properly until that moment.

"It seemed to me that you needed help, and our paths align." Turning, he resumed his march, long strides bearing him towards the wood opposite.

Renco made to walk after, but a hand on his arm held him back.

"I don't trust him," Lett hissed.

Renco pursed his lips. If the ilf meant to betray them surely he would have done so. Maybe the urak warred on the ilfanum or maybe he was gathering information for his own kind. He shrugged, either way, as Nesta said, their paths aligned and he for one was more than a little curious about their new travel companion.

"What is the sign for, watch?" Lett asked. Renco obliged and she observed as he extended two fingers and carved a circle in the air.

"Watch him." Lett mimicked the sign and waited until Renco gave a curt nod of agreement. Returning a tight-lipped smile, she grabbed his hand and set off after the ilf.

The urak campsite, when they entered it, was well-ordered but gruesome and unrecognisable from the one Amos and the others had set up. From the branches above hung the bodies of six Red Cloaks; naked, tied feet high and creaking like grim marionettes. The cadavers of four others lay nearby, limbs missing and flesh butchered. There was no sign of their horses except for the saddles which were stacked to one side near the discarded clothing of the dead.

The ground in and around the camp was punctuated with bloodstains, corrupting the snow like spilt claret, pink where it had diluted, deep red where it lay in more abundance. In one place, near the butchered, the ground was saturated crimson, and the sour miasma of the dead polluted the air.

Looking at it all, breathing it in, Lett felt sick, her mouth sharp with the taste of cheese as her stomach threatened to expel its contents. Retching, she staggered towards the remnants of a fire which smouldered in the camp's centre, the comfort of its radial heat a lodestone that sang to her chilled flesh. Kneeling before its warmth, she gasped deep breaths, the woodsmoke cleansing the smell of slaughter from her nostrils. She groaned, revelling in the heat, body aching as the cold slowly chased from her bones.

Renco too felt sickened. This was a place of death and only the ilf seemed unperturbed by it. As terrible as it might be though, he knew it was also a place of opportunity.

"The urak will return. The hanging bodies say as much." Nesta commented.

It rattled Renco, who thought the ilf's tone approving but recognised as well the warning it held. The sooner they were gone from here the better. Distasteful as it was, Renco rummaged through the pile of discarded clothing and packs for anything that might be of use.

His haul, in the end, was respectable. The urak had plundered the weapons but had no use it seemed for hardtack and he filled half a bag with the bland-tasting biscuit. And, whilst most of the clothing had been cut or torn from the bodies and were of no use, he did find a spare undertunic and shirt in one of the packs that were of a size to fit Lett. Added to that some mittens and a scarf and she would be better attired for the winter conditions. It would only get colder.

For himself, he found a pair of boots, sturdy and better quality than his own that fit him well enough. He worked quickly, eager to be done but paused when one of the bodies twisted on the vine, revealing the frozen face of Sergeant Comter. The sightless eyes were open and accusing. With a sad shrug, Renco returned to his task, pocketing a coin purse before moving on to the next pack.

After he was done, they did not linger. Eager to leave the camp behind they followed the now well-worn tracks left in the snow towards the foothills in the south. Little more than a day had passed since Amos and the others had first beaten this trail. A trail followed by the Red Cloaks and the Trinity knew how many urak. There was a message to be had in that, Renco knew but following it was the only sure means of not leaving fresh tracks of their own.

As the day wore on the clouds thickened and lowered, deepening to a drab, uniform greyness that threatened more snow. The sun became a muted ball of light that struggled to penetrate the cover and a sombre bleakness prevailed.

Grimacing at the sky, Renco felt the first flakes of snow strike his face and with it, the temperature seemed to plummet. Pulling the hood of his cloak up, he trudged on, widening his stride to close up again with the others. Lett was just ahead and thirty paces further on, Nesta.

The light faded early, the sun giving up its fight and, encouraged, the wind picked up, driving against their backs. After a while the trail became hard to follow, the snow flurries drifting and covering the way ahead. It was both a boon and a bane thought Renco. The inclement weather would hide their tracks but hinder their travel.

"It'll be dark soon. I can't go much further," Lett complained. Of all of them, she struggled the most. Renco had lived a life of walking and the ilf seemed tireless.

Nesta stopped and waited whilst they caught up. "I know you are weary." He gestured to the small hill ahead, a blur, hardly distinguishable through the swirling snowfall. "We will make camp on the leeward side. It will provide respite from the wind at least and there is a place of shelter. If it remains."

Without awaiting an answer, Nesta turned and continued his trek. Grumbling, Lett hurried after, muttering about lees and what was wrong with the copse they were in and tugging her newly acquired scarf tighter.

The low hill when they reached it was only a short climb but Renco's thighs burned at the effort. Ahead, Lett's ragged breath billowed, whipped away by the wind, only to be replaced by another plume. He could tell she was nearing the end of her endurance.

Reaching the hill's crest gave momentary respite to aching muscles before they continued on the more precarious journey downslope, bringing a whole different set of struggles. The wind at least abated, and the snow swirled from above rather than at their backs.

In contrast to the hill's north face, its southern decline was covered with tall shrubs and dense bush, and they had to pick their way around them. They had not gone far however when Nesta led them to a large, dense thicket that sat in a wrinkle on the hillside.

To Renco, the ilf seemed to meld into the foliage, his strange cloak blending seamlessly. Lett was far more ungainly, snagging on branches until finally managing to bull her way through. When Renco joined them, he was surprised to find the thicket was hollow at its core, with leafy branches arching above forming a roof of sorts. It was unusual, but Renco didn't waste time wondering about it. Instead, he removed his cloak and laid it on the frozen detritus and bid Lett sit. Up close, her face was grey with exhaustion. Mumbling thanks, she slumped wearily onto it.

Sitting beside her, Renco pulled her close, trying to share his warmth. The elements did not bother him so much it seemed and other than a slightly pounding head, the familiar ache of worked muscles and a rumble of hunger, he felt fine. As Lett shivered next to him, Renco returned his attention to the ilf.

Kneeling in the middle of the shrouded glade, Nesta was scraping and pulling at the leaf litter, tearing at wiry strands of groundvane until a circular bed of rocks was revealed. Bundling the vines into a tight ball, the ilf placed it between the rocks and held his hands out over it.

"Ignatituum forus arctum."

The groundvane gave a sibilant hiss then burst into flame. Nesta quickly dressed the fire with the leaf scrappings, then added twigs and deadwood until it settled into a steady blaze.

"I will scout the area then gather more substantial fuel. Until I return, keep the fire fed." Gathering his staff, the ilf rose and disappeared back the way they had come.

The heat from the fire settled around them like a warm blanket and Lett shuffled forward until her boots almost touched the ring of stone. Leaf litter and deadwood were plentiful but damp, hissing when Lett placed any on the fire. Renco signed at her to go slowly which earned a sharp reprimand.

"I know what I'm doing."

Sitting back, Renco shrugged and left her to it. Crossing his legs, he enjoyed the sensation of tingling skin as his body warmed. Clearing his thoughts, he let his mind drift.

The presence, when he felt it, was unexpected and so slight he could easily have missed it. But he'd sensed it before, and knew its touch and, strangely enough, it eased the ache behind his eyes. It was her. Turning his mind inwards, he directed his thoughts at the consciousness hovering behind his eyes.

<Dog girl?>

Like a rope pulled suddenly taut, a connection snapped into place. Anchored now at both ends his mind linked with another's. It felt immediately familiar but instantly strange. After all, he mind-spoke with master all the time. Only, this was not his master.

<Dog girl!> Echoed back, only this echo was amused.

<Sorry. Nihm. Your name is Nihm.> Colouring, Renco projected thoughts of that time when he had seen her, the only time. Standing on the road leading into Fallston, bent against her staff as if it were a crutch and at her side, two of the biggest dogs he'd ever seen. Unlooked for, unexpected, a bond had woven into being that day. He had asked her to look to Mao, unsure why even now. Except that they had connected, somehow.

<Yes, and you are Renco,> Nihm responded. A swathe of images and thoughts swirled across the link. Images of Master Hiro and Mao. <They both live. Though not without injury, they are fine. I have come for you and will take you to them.>

Renco's shoulders slumped in relief. They were alive. Why then had master not come for him? Why Nihm and why alone and how? She could barely walk last he saw her. Who was she?

<Questions for later,> Nihm said. <Lord Amos and the others you met are safe too. I've followed the trail they left but it is covered now by snow. Where are you? I feel you are near.>

Again, Renco projected images. This time of his trek south, the hill they climbed and the thicket of shrubs they sheltered in. It conveyed much and quickly but not their position.

A doleful howl, eerie and long, wailed into the night.

<That was Ash. Do you hear him?> Nihm seemed distracted as she asked.

<Half the Rivers heard.> Renco grinned. <Hard to pinpoint but we are to the north at least.>

<Something comes.>

The link abruptly terminated, leaving Renco disoriented, his mind flailing like a tattered cloth in the wind and the doleful ache returning.

"Renco!" A hand gripped his knee.

"I said, did you hear that wolf?" Lett looked concerned. "You alright? You seem… elsewhere."

Patting her hand reassuringly, Renco gave a sharp nod. His thoughts though crashed like thunderheads at what had just happened. It was… momentous… and made no sense. The sudden vitality suffusing his body vibrated, humming as if a bell had been struck, so low and so profound it was overwhelming. It was as if a missing piece had slotted into place inside him. A piece of what? His mind grasped at the thought like a falling man a rope.

'Something comes.' Nihm's last projection worried at him. She was troubled. Extending his mind down the remnant of the severed link yielded nothing. Nihm was gone.

"Do you think there are more wolves? What if they are hunting?" Lett prodded. "Renco? You're not listening. Again. What's wrong with you?"

Renco signed back. 'I'm fine.' But immediately stood, pacing in agitation. At a loss for what to do, but feeling the need to do something, anything. He felt suddenly hot, his skin prickling with heat and a harsh pain pulsing in his skull.

Abandoning the fire, Lett rose and grasped Renco's arm to still him. "You're troubling me. Is it Nesta? I admit I had some doubt about him but the ilf has led us true and found us shelter. If you can call it that."

Renco grimaced, his head pounding.

Lett gasped. "Renco. Your face. The markings." Raising a hand she brushed his cheek, "So vivid they look raised only they're not."

Feeling nauseous, Renco groaned in blessed relief as the coldness of her fingertips caressed his skin. Concern clouded Lett's face and she guided him to the cloak where he promptly sat, finding the effort exhausting.

"It'll be alright. I'm with you," Lett whispered giving him a brief hug. Pulling away she felt his brow. "You don't have a temperature, but you do feel clammy."

The palm of her hand soothed where it touched, easing the pain from his face. Then, as sudden as it beset him the pounding in his head dissipated into a dull ache and the heat in his body left him.

"The markings are fading. I can barely see them now."

Renco could hear her wonderment. Lett's hand slipped down to cup his cheek, her sky-blue eyes piercing his. He felt a different heat suffuse his body and leaned forward, unable to stop himself. The force of her a magnet. But then her hand dropped and she withdrew.

"You look better. Maybe we should eat," she prompted, turning away. "I don't know about you, but I could chew through a log right about now."

Renco's traitorous stomach rumbled its agreement. Sitting back to distance himself, he watched Lett drag the pack over and take out some of the plundered hardtack. Together, they sat and ate and watched the flames, Lett speaking to fill the awkwardness.

She told a tale. Falteringly, to begin with. The memory of the telling reluctant at first to be recalled, for it evoked images in her mind of her Da. But once begun a tale must be told, as is the way of the bard. Besides, it was one of her favourites. The poetic story of William Regal the Third, the child-king who at fifteen conquered the Splintered Isles in the western seas, but in the doing lost his heart to a slave girl.

Afterwards, with no sign of Nesta and the night deepening, Renco gestured for Lett to sleep, indicating he would keep watch and attend the fire.

Fatigue sapped and with heavy eyes, Lett offered no argument. Curling up on his cloak by the fire and dragging her own on top as a blanket, she was asleep in moments.

Time lumbered, indolent. Renco gathered deadwood and fed the flames. The fire though was safely established, with a glowing bed of smouldering ash that took little care to attend.

Sitting back, warmth suffusing him, Renco allowed his mind to wander. His thoughts blended, shuffling through a haze of emotions; the intenseness of his connection with Nihm and his cursed feelings for Lett. His clumsy attempt to kiss Lett brought a wry grin to his face. What a fool. Several snowflakes escaped the canopy above and he watched their lazy meander towards the flames then oblivion and felt a union with them.

A crunch drew him to his feet and had him reaching for his sword. Hilt gripped in one hand and sheath in the other, Renco slid the steel blade smoothly out. Its unfamiliar weight unbalanced and cumbersome to his hand.

A soft nicker. Snow scrunched growing louder. More than one approached. Renco toyed with extinguishing the fire, its light would not be entirely hidden, no matter how dense the branches of their hideaway but he resisted the idea. Instead, closing his eyes, Renco dropped into ki'tae. Liquid white splashes painted his mind, stark against the indigo swirls denoting plant life and the pink fog of snow. His heart thundered painfully, chest suddenly tight. Horses, humans, dogs and another he did not recognise but guessed at. The white spiral of life of this last had weaves of ochre and gold, themselves veined with indigo and emerald.

The tall shrubs rustled, and Renco opened his eyes and levelled the tip of his sword just as the branches parted and Nesta appeared. With an economy of motion that took but a heartbeat, the ilf's gaze swept over the fire, took in Lett's still form, then returned to Renco. Raising his hand, Nesta placed a slender finger on the sword point and guided the blade aside.

"I bring friends."

The voice was enough to rouse Lett, who rolled and cracked a bleary eye before startling and sitting up.

"What's going on? Why is your sword drawn?"

Stepping back, Renco sheathed his blade just as the branches swished and another appeared. A woman he barely knew, yet whose face was etched so clear in his mind. A face that was smudged. Auburn hair, black in the reflected firelight, was pulled back against her nape and bound. Dirt stained, cloak ripped at mid-calf, he could smell her sweat and grime.

She leant upon an ash-hewn staff, little better than a straight-cut branch, the same one as that day on the road, only now she stood tall and straight, the stave no longer a support for a crooked body.

Dark eyes glinting, she smiled.

"It's good to finally meet you."

Renco shivered. The look and tone when she spoke seemed to reverberate in the air. It penetrated his bones, harmonising in pulsing synchronicity with his core. His body roiled, flesh and blood rising, so hot, Renco thought he burned. His head fell back, spine arching and teeth bared as an unbridled scream ripped from his throat. Beams of golden light burst from his eyes and mouth, lighting the small space like a sun flare and shrivelling leaf and branch where it touched.

Frozen momentarily in shock, the ilf was the first to react. Dancing forward, Nesta jabbed fingers into Renco's chest.

"Secora optim," the ilf whispered words of power and as quickly as it appeared the blaze of light extinguished.

Renco's face contorted, then relaxed before his eyes rolled white and he collapsed, dropping as if his bones had turned to water.

Chapter 12: Blood Money

Kingsholme, The Holme

The inn was loud and pipe smoke hung in a smog around its beams, suckling at the candlelight and hemming in the scent of warm bodies and stale straw. It was not unlike most taverns Gart Vannen had been in.

It was late evening and he listened as a bard tuned his lute, the melodious strings a counterpoint that threaded the din of noise. Gart had been waiting an hour already and he was sat, back to a wall, at a table where he could observe both the entrance and bar to some degree. He was incognito; his steel-mesh shirt hidden beneath a plain tunic with dark trousers, brown boots and a black cloak completing his ensemble. The ale in the tankard he'd been nursing was lukewarm, flat and tasted like piss.

A pretty harlot with a goblet in hand slipped through the press of people. His eyes had flicked over her at first but returned. It was obvious from her direction and the way her gaze strayed to his corner that she'd singled him out. Laughing, as hands groped for her, the woman batted them aside or twisted away, leaving behind a disparaging stare or artful comment that left men either scowling or howling with laughter.

Gart's jaw clenched. His patience was already paper-thin. But for his queen, he'd have left a long time past. The image of Matrice's diminutive frame and pale yet beautiful face filled his mind, and the surroundings faded into the background until he could see nothing else. 'I don't want try. Anyone can try. Just do it. I want him dead, Gart. I want Herald's head at my feet.' The way her mouth moved, her lips, the green intensity of her eyes; they pierced his very soul.

The woman swayed in front of the table, breaking his reverie. She was black-haired with skin darker and more vibrant than any touch the sun might have made. She wore a dress the colour of straw with a red sash tied around her waist that clashed in high contrast. Loosely buttoned at the front, the dress lapels peeled away from her neckline and chest in a vee, revealing soft skin and enticing cleavage. Her brown eyes sparkled with mischief.

Gart glared. Whatever beauty she thought she was, it did not move him. But equally, his look did not seem to bother her. The bitch didn't so much as flinch.

"Move along. I'm not buying what you're selling." Gart took a dismissive sip from his tankard and wished he hadn't bothered.

"And what do you think it is I'm selling?" The woman hooked a foot around a stool leg, grating it against the floorboards as she dragged it out, before promptly sitting. Her goblet clacked on the tabletop as she set it down, before giving a white smile that revealed a set of teeth that were both complete and straight.

Unusual enough for Old Town, thought Gart, but especially so Gloamingate. His eyes were drawn to a small tattoo on her neck. It was of an upright cross in a circle, a slavers mark. A mark he'd seen many times. It told him she was from the western isles or the

Morass, maybe even Blue City. As if feeling his eyes on her skin, the woman pulled the collar of her dress up. Her smile did not falter.

"Whatever it is; whores, bit of knorcha, even your own skank arse, I couldn't give two shits. Now fuck off. I'm busy."

The woman made a show of glancing around before her mirthful eyes returned to his. "I can see that. Been watching and you've been busy a whole hour already. Maybe your honey's not coming. I can't see why though. You're such a ray of sunlight with all your sweet talk and all."

Instantly wary, Gart looked past her shoulder, eyes searching the room. Something stank and not just the sweaty bodies and spilt ale. He saw nothing, yet instinct still crawled its warning across his skin. Dipping a hand beneath the table he leant forward. "Who are you?"

"Don't do that." The woman cocked her head. "Pull that blade and you'll be dead before it clears the table."

Lifting the goblet to her mouth she took a sip before returning it to the wooden top. Wearing a wry look, she waited.

Gart shrugged, released the knife and settled one hand over the other where they could be seen.

"Good. You're not a complete ass-head," the woman said. "Now, as for who I am? Well, let's just say it's none of your gods cursed business. It's enough I know who you are, Sir Vannen. Chief shit-kisser to that pretty little princess up on the hill."

Gart's jaw clenched and his eyes glinted dangerously. It brought an amused chuckle from across the table.

"Stop with the come fuck-me eyes, you're not my type." She leant on the table, just a woman talking to a man in quiet transaction; her jovial face though did not disguise the sudden hard temper in her eyes.

"You bore me, Vannen. I've told my friend it's a mistake for him to meet with you. You're dangerous but then again so is he, and he does so love a bit of intrigue." She pursed her lips. "Slide a coin across the table so all can see it, then come with me. No copper though. I'm not a cheap whore from the back alleys."

Masking his rising fury, Gart did as instructed; slipping a silver kern from his purse, he scraped it, with a nonchalance he didn't feel, across the stained wood. It was enough to buy ten gutter whores or two from a brothel of middling repute but damned if he'd baulk at the price. It was the crown's coin after all.

The woman chuckled, snatching the coin as soon as his finger released it. She stood. "Follow."

She led him across the room, bumping and brushing through the knot of men in its centre. A few gave Gart long stares but when he returned them, none would hold his eye.

His nerves thrummed, his previous impatience evaporating with it. Something was off. He could taste the threat.

The woman too was more than he'd assumed. She weaved through the crowd with a lithe seduction that reminded Gart more of a fencer than the prostitute he'd mistaken her for. They passed the bar counter and innkeeper, who studiously looked the other way, then through a door and up a flight of stairs to the second floor.

Gart stopped on the landing. Six men filled the corridor. Hard faced and armed with long knives, their violence sang to him and his hands twitched in anticipation.

"Come on, lover," the woman taunted.

"Murder," One of the men grinned, stepping aside as she nudged his shoulder.

"Leave your weapons with Rooq here. You'll get them back when you're done." She paused at the third door and winked at the giant guarding it.

The hulk scowled, unamused, and knocked a rhyme against the wood frame. Moments later a 'shunk' sounded as a bar was slid back from inside. Grasping the door-latch in a meaty paw, he lifted it and pulled the door wide.

Gart followed his guide through into the room beyond, feeling naked without his weapons. The man, Rooq, had found the shiv in his boot and the stiletto sheathed in the small of his back, taking them as well as his sword and long knife.

A man stood just past the entrance and another by the shuttered window on the far wall. Both wore hemp tunics and long breeches, much like the men in the common room below, but Gart could make out the dark leathers worn beneath and it took but a blink to note their weapons and recognise the coiled wariness in their stances. He dismissed them; bodyguards both to the third man, who sat with languid ease in the centre of the room, smoking a long pipe. The chair he sat upon was the only furnishing in the room.

He was nondescript to look at and Gart judged him to be around fifty years of age. His brown hair and trimmed beard were greying and the skin on his face was creased around the eyes, which in the candlelit room were shadowed.

Removing his pipe, the man spewed a stream of smoke into the air before tamping the bowl with practised ease against his palm, sending a wedge of smouldering tabacc to the floorboards which he ground his boot over.

"There are five watching the inn. You were told to come alone," the man admonished, his voice measured and even. He raised his eyes. Brown and mocking, Gart felt their intensity.

"My men are out of sight and await my return. After all, Gloamingate at night can be dangerous to walk," Gart replied. "I'm here with you and alone now. Are you the Targus?"

The man inclined his head, disappointment rolling off him. "Merca here counselled against meeting with you and I'm beginning to wish I had listened to her."

Gart shook his head, "I…"

"I, always I, I, I." The Targus rose, forestalling Gart. "Surely what you mean is she. Let's not pretend you're anything but a messenger boy. I already know what your mistress wants Kingsman. Or should I call you Queensman? Make her offer then you can take her mine."

"It's better if we talk alone," Gart muttered.

The Targus laughed. "Merca here told me what a dour fellow you were but, Murder my dear, I think you are mistaken."

The floorboard flexed beneath Gart's foot as the woman at his back shifted her weight.

"A fool and a jester should not be confused, Bortillo," she murmured, acerbically, "By your leave?"

The Targus waved a dismissive hand and Gart tensed, ready to turn. Instead, he felt her presence move away, heard the door open then close, aware all the while of the Targus studying him. *Bloody filth and scum the lot of them.*

As if hearing his thoughts, Bortillo raised an eyebrow. "You think us egregious and abhorrent. You disguise it well Queensman but I sense it in you. Yet we are merely the tails to your heads. Whilst your coin operates in the plight of day, by rules and laws created by the 'just' and powerful to serve themselves, our coin subsists in the darkness. Living off the filth and scraps left to us. Have a care, Sir Vannen, for one day that coin will flip."

Gart gave a wry shake of his head. "Horse shit. You're nothing but leeches suckling at the city's armpit, slithering and hiding under your rocks. Don't pretend otherwise. Your whore said it was unwise to meet with me, well I offered the same advice to her highness. Now let's get this over with so I can go wash the stink out of my clothes."

Bortillo's eyes narrowed. "I offer insight and you return insult. You're too easily riled, Sir Vannen. What use would you be to her highness without a tongue I wonder? Perhaps you might give better counsel?"

"I am here under parlay. I will leave here whole or dead. It's your choice, Targus but if it's to be whole let us conclude our business. This endless talk does not suit me."

"I see you're a lover of irony and danger both, to rely so upon the word of a leech for safe passage. Very well, what is Matrice offering?"

"His bodyweight in gold," Gart murmured. The Targus smiled and he heard the doorman behind, take a breath. It was a staggering sum.

"The High King lies on his deathbed. Black Henry, his brother, rides to Anglemere and will be here on the morrow and your pretty little princess wants me to find her brother. I know what she wants else she would not have approached me. But it does beg the question; does his body weight in gold include head-on or off?"

"On, for the gold. Off, for the job."

"I want to hear the words. I want to hear her name and offer in its entirety from your mouth, Sir Vannen. For clarity and so that I can see just how much more honourable your princess is than I."

Gart scowled, hand gripping the fabric of his breeches. "I'll not sully her name here. The commission is for the death of the traitor prince, Herald Blackstar. His body left outside the main gate of Anglemere castle. It must be recognisable. In recompense, you will receive the prince's weight in gold."

"Better fatten him up before we murder him then, eh!" Bortillo smirked, drawing a laugh from the man by the door. "But I think the Queen or Black Henry might match that or better it."

"Henry Blackstar would cut your balls off and feed you them before ever he'd give you a copper bit," Gart argued.

"True enough." Bortillo sank back down onto the chair. Taking his pipe out, he started packing it with tabacc from a pouch on his belt, humming gently.

Gart shuffled uncomfortably, his temper rising as he waited. "Is that it then?" Feeling the air shift and floorboards creak, Gart glanced around. The doorman stood blocking the exit, hand on his blade.

"Yes, I think it is," the Targus said. "Tell the little princess I already hunt for her brother. What I do when I find him though… well that's to be determined. My counter to your mistress is this; said 'gold on offer', but in addition, a Royal Charter."

"For what? Only the High King can sign a Royal Charter," Gart said.

"The Haven Pier in Skelside; as for the signing of it? My birds tell me the princess plans to rule for her father-in-absentee. There is of course the small matter of her uncle to overcome but that is Matrice's challenge to face not mine. If she passes it, then I want that charter. Until then, if I find the prince, I will keep him safe and feed him well."

The Targus signed and the shutter man took a candle from its sconce on the wall and held it out. Keeping the pipe side on to the flame, Bortillo drew on the stem until the tabacc flared and a cloud of smoke puffed into the air. Satisfied it had taken, he glanced up at Gart.

"Well. Piss off then. Maybe next time come alone, eh."

* * *

Gart stepped out of the inn, the door thumping shut behind, and was hit by the stink of Old Town. It had been over a week since the last rains and the ripe bite of street waste tainted his nostrils and tasted on his tongue. Looking at the night sky, he sighted the lodestar near the pale orb of Ankor. Taking a frigid breath, he watched the plume of his exhale rise like the smoke from the Thief King's pipe, fracturing and obscuring the moonlight.

Leaning back against the door, waiting for his eyes to adjust, Gart pondered something that had troubled him on his way out. The inn's common room had been noticeably different. It was less crowded for one thing and there seemed more women. Partners, wives whatever, but the whole vibe of the place had changed. The bard played a quiet tune in the background and the noise was altogether more comfortable, less raucous. If he hadn't known better, he'd have said it was a different tavern. His mind wandered back to the woman, Merca and the easy banter with some of the men as she crossed the room to meet him. They knew her. That seemed clear now and Gart drew the uncomfortable but obvious conclusion.

Eyes acclimatised, they travelled to the shop front opposite. Pushing off, Gart strode confidently across the lane towards it. A dark shade stood in its doorway, barely discernible unless looked for.

"O'Keev?"

No reply. The inky blot eerily still.

His knife was instantly in hand. Laughter and music from the inn seemed suddenly loud as he scoured the lane and surrounding buildings for any hint of something out of place. Futile, the different hues of darkness were impossible to penetrate.

Apprehension growing, blood pounding, Gart moved to the shop's entrance. His hand shot forward and struck the shade, a tap, nothing more. It met with fabric and the soft yield of flesh. His fist came away moist. A sniff was enough to tell Gart it was blood and from the stillness of the body that O'Keev was dead.

Fuck, Gart scanned his surroundings again. Tensed, at the sound of movement and raised his knife. The blocky outline of a couple came into contrast as they passed the cracked light from a shuttered window; turning off, they disappeared down an adjoining lane.

"Bit jumpy, Butcher," a voice called from the night.

His nostrils flared in irritation. He'd not heard that name in a while, not since coming to the capital. The voice had come from opposite and up high. His head tilted to the tavern's roof but saw nothing. No silhouette against the skyline and no shadow in the dark. The voice though… the voice he knew. He gritted his teeth, feeling exposed and vulnerable. It rankled.

Gart took a step away from O'Keev then stopped as a light flared. It wasn't much but dazzled his eyes as it blazed towards him in a streak.

He was too slow, but the flame was not meant for him. The fire arrow thudded into the ground by his boot and middled the doorway.

"If your fate this night was to die it would have happened already, Butcher," Merca called from the darkness.

Gart could tell from her voice she had shifted position but bright dots from the flames ruined his eyes and shattered what little night vision he had. Instead, he was drawn to the arrow; its fire paltry but harsh enough to flick fingers of light across the shop's entrance. It illuminated O'Keev, revealing a garish scene.

O'Keev's throat had been slit and what looked like a blacksmith's poker protruded from his chest pinning him to the door. His front was covered in a cascade of blood though none pulsed now from the yawn of the cut.

"There was no need for this," Gart called out.

"You created the need, Butcher. The lesson is yours to learn. Old Town is our domain. You'd do well to remember that next time."

A glint of silver by the poker handle drew his attention. Reaching a bloodied hand to it, Gart grasped it, knowing what it was.

"Keep your blood money," Merca cried. "Use it for your man there. Consider it a gift from the Targus but don't bother looking for the others."

"I don't know you, Merca or how you know me but when this is done with, I will kill you," Gart shouted, only to be met with that annoying laugh of hers.

"Berins-Low. Berins-Low is where we met. A condemned man ought to know what he's dying for. And make no mistake. I've marked you, Butcher, and for that, you may call me Murder. Look to the shadows you vile fuck, cause that's where I'll be, waiting."

"Berins-Low… can't say as I recall it. Must be one of those pissant towns out in the Hook?" Gart called back. His voice trailed off into the night, unanswered.

Merca was gone.

Chapter 13: A View From A Hill

The Defile, The Rivers

The parchment crumpled in Father Henrik Zoller's fist. His already sour mood stirred like disturbed sediment. He was still awaiting the five hundred Red Cloaks promised by Cardinal Tortuga and now this.

"Holt, prepare the carriage."

The hulking protector dipped his head. "Yes, Father. Are we leaving?" Not even his dog could hide the hopeful expectation in his voice and it grated, reflecting Zoller's own desperate need to escape this place. His reply was terse.

"No. I've been summoned. Leave a hand of men to hold the chapel else Duke Brant will no doubt fill it with worthless heirlooms whilst I am gone. Brother Patrice will command them."

Holt's one good eye blinked, his misshapen head tilted, looking inexplicably thoughtful. An uncommon enough occurrence that it caused Zoller to raise an eyebrow.

"Yes?"

"Brother Sebastien thinks he saw Tuko. Just thought ya should know, Father." The cyclopean eye blinked. The look questioning.

"Barrack gossip?" Zoller rankled. "If Brother Sebastien has seen Tuko he should come to me, directly. Have the fool stand double watch at the chapel. I'll see him when I return."

"Yes, Father," Holt rumbled.

After the door had closed, Zoller paced. The summons from Lord Commander Jon Whent, Archbishop of Killenhess had been concise and polite but gave no hint as to its reason. The mere brevity of it though felt portentous and left his mind agitated. The Lord Commander had returned, unscathed it seemed from his brief foray in the north. His army of five thousand Red Cloaks bivouacked in the valley below. What could the Archbishop want that he hadn't already imparted almost a ten-day ago? Maybe he could convince Whent to return the boy. He sipped his watered wine and picked at the platter on the side table, his mind awhirl over possibilities.

Holt was soon back and escorted his charge to the stable block and the awaiting carriage. The dozen Red Cloaks in Zoller's entourage had shrunk to ten with the unfortunate demise of Brother Perrick and the missing Tuko and it was noticeable. With five held back on guard at the chapel and one driving the carriage, it left a paltry two Red Cloaks to ride front and two back.

The sound of hooves and wheels boomed, echoing off the stone walls of the barbican as the carriage crossed beneath the portcullis and onto the high road.

The ride down proved uncomfortable, the rocky path tight with winding switchbacks. As they descended, Zoller surveyed the landscape. The first snows of winter had fallen a few days ago coating everything in a cleansing, pristine white. Only the river as it wound its way south and the strips of forest east and west held any colour. The Oust a grey-blue ribbon, the woods a dappled patchwork of evergreen and shaded jade.

It was a serene and quite breath-taking panorama but as the carriage rounded a sharp bend, Zoller dragged his eyes lower and closer to the valley below and the only blemish in his viewing. The Red Cloak encampment sat like a canker on the land. Campfires drifted lazy fingers of smoke into the sky, a taint that was whisked into a bleary veil by the breeze. Beneath its haze huddled row upon row of brown canvas surrounded by an earthen dyke. Large horse corrals spattered the camp, with wagons and large pavilions standing like warts amongst it all.

It was to the largest of these pavilions that Zoller's entourage was directed. Leaving his men outside with the carriage, he followed a guard through the canvas flap, then a horsehide inner flap leading to the interior. It was spartan. A wax candle waved cheerily over a trestle table with two low-standing braziers adding both heat and light. A single camp bed was to the side with a large trunk at its foot. By the entrance, as if to guard it, a coat of armour hung on a frame. Red lacquered and gold gilded.

Zoller barely registered it, his eyes fixating instead on the pavilion's occupants. There were four all told. Whent and two travel-stained commoners sat on the most basic of camp stools, whilst the fourth, a Red Cloak Captain from his insignia, stood behind and to the side of the Lord Commander.

"Ah, Father. Thank you for attending so quickly." Rising smoothly, Lord Commander Whent extended an arm.

Dropping to a knee, Zoller took the proffered hand and kissed the back of it. "Your Grace."

"Rise, Father. I have news and, as you can see, esteemed guests. Lord Amos Duncan, Lady Mercy Duncan, this is Father Henrik Zoller."

Zoller could feel the heat of their gaze. Regaining his feet, he turned and inclined his head towards them. The man seemed stern, his bristled face hard to read. She, on the other hand, was more animated. The defiling scar that marred her left cheek from ear to jowl was twisted in disapproval and bookended dark eyes that gleamed, hard and flat. A Lord and Lady; initially dismissive of the pair, Zoller's eyes roved the two anew, noting that their attire, whilst bemired, was quality.

"You are far from home, Lord Duncan, my Lady." Unable to resist, he inflected a challenge in his cordiality.

"And you far from your congregation in Thorsten, Father," The woman replied, her tone sharp and the words quickly spoken.

Lord Amos laid a hand on her arm and she leaned away, lips drawing thin and tight, her knuckles whitening where she gripped the staff nestled against her right shoulder.

She knew him or of him. Interesting and foolish to convey as much. Zoller spread his arms wide. "You're mistaken, my Lady. Father Mortim ministers to the faithful in Thorsten. My visit there was a fleeting one. My parish is this pile of rock we stand beneath."

"Indeed." Amusement tugged at the corners of Whent's mouth. "Lord Duncan tells me the Black Keep still stood when he escaped Thorsten and left in concealment. The urak, it appears, have no interest in attacking it or indeed occupying the town now that they deem it no longer a threat. Using it as a blooding ground for their younger warriors to hunt."

Zoller nodded. "That seems to bear out other testimonies I have heard. The urak come for our land it seems, they do not care for our bricks and mortar."

"They're nomadic warriors and our constructions an antipathy to them," Whent agreed. "But we digress. Captain Warwick, some wine if you will."

The heavyset Red Cloak moved to the table and filled four wooden tumblers from an earthenware vessel.

"It's honeyed wine from the vineyards at Killenhess and I'm rather proud of it," Whent said as Captain Warwick distributed the mugs, receiving his last as was proper.

"A messenger has arrived from Rivercross bearing dire news from the capital. It seems we face rebellion within as well as the horde without. High King Edward Blackstar has been attacked and lies in serious illness. Poisoned in a vile and heinous act."

"How? Do we know who?" Amos Duncan leaned forward on his stool. "The succession is unequivocal. It makes no sense to attack him, unless; Olme!"

"The missive from High Lord Twyford lacked detail. Either the news travelled to Rivercross by bird or, I surmise, conveyed by the council of mages. The mages are ever reticent to say much unless it suits them." Whent paused, turning sanguine he continued. "It was not Olme, though. In addition to the High Lord's note, I received letters from the church. Respectfully, I cannot divulge all they contain, church business you understand. But I can tell you that Crown Prince Herald stands accused and that Order Ambassador Renix died in the attempt on the High King."

Amos Duncan exploded from his stool, startling Zoller and causing Captain Warwick to take a protective step forward. "I don't believe it. Can't. The Order would not dare, I know Lord Renix as an honourable man. It can't be."

Dismissively, hand out, Whent signalled the captain back. "Throughout the history of these Nine Kingdoms, the Order has always interfered. They stand in light but work in shadow. It is an old saying but one I believe. It would be naïve to think otherwise. As for any coup, to be successful it must remain hidden and unthinkable until enacted else be destined to fail. That you do not believe it makes my point and highlights how well the Order manipulates. Now, as for the Crown Prince; he is ambitious, entitled and young and the young are always prone to impatience. It is not beyond doubt that such a man might be influenced or inveigled so by another, more malign influence. Do you not agree?"

"To the one maybe but not the other," Amos replied. "It makes no sense. Herald is the heir, and the throne will be his in time."

"It was said the High King was in good fettle and had many years of rule still ahead. It has also been whispered that the Queen Consort is pregnant and carries his son. Both reasons enough some might say. But forgive me. This is hearsay which I abhor. I deal in truth. No doubt as we march south things will become clearer."

Zoller's eyes flared at this last, but he held his tongue. This news was momentous but unlikely to change his current predicament. His eyes swivelled expectantly to Lord Amos, who turned and paced, a sombre mood about him as he spoke.

"You hold a strong position. The river guards your western flank, the Defile your back with the Abannas to the east creating a natural draw. Easily defensible. The urak can only attack in any great number through the north vale. Yet you march away and Twyford hides with his armies at Rivercross. So quickly you abandon the Rivers."

Whent's calm riposte was in steady contrast. "I am a priest of Kildare, Lord Amos. But I am a soldier too, a commander of men and defender of the faithful. The church has ordered my return to Killenhess but even had they not, still I would retreat. We cannot win here, merely hold them for a time. If the Kingsguard and the armies of the Nine Kingdoms were converging at our backs it would be tenable, strategically speaking, but they are not. High Lord Twyford understood this. The Rivers is all but gone to the horde and we must pick our battles carefully whilst gathering our strength if we are to have any hope of victory."

Amos rubbed a hand over whiskered jowls before giving a reluctant nod to Whent. "You said, we?"

"Indeed. You offered sanctuary, and the Black Crow gave you wardship of the Lady Constance. It stands to reason you convey her to Hawke Hold. No doubt you'll have a report to make to The Duncan. I offer passage, at least to Killenhess. We leave at first light on the morrow."

Mercy Duncan rose from her stool. "It seems we share a path. We thank you for your offer, Lord Commander."

Zoller watched the byplay as the Lady slipped a hand into the crook of the Lord's arm whose look turned from pensive to bemused before he bowed. "Indeed, very generous. Tomorrow then."

"Until then," Whent replied.

With a shuffle, Zoller stood aside as Lady Duncan steered towards the exit. The crackle-snap of smouldering coals a backdrop to the sudden silence in the tent. It was broken with an observation.

"They barely touched their wine." Whent sounded rueful before turning towards the Red Cloak. "Have someone fetch Father Milgorin for me, Captain. But do not send him in until I call. Then wait outside and make sure I am not disturbed."

"Lord Commander." Warwick bowed, gave a curt nod to Zoller and left.

"Sit Father. Come, tell me the wine is not all bad." Whent seated himself before taking a sip from his beaker as if to assure himself of its integrity.

Zoller did as instructed and found the wine a tad too tart for his liking. "I have tried the Killenhess blend before, Your Grace. It's as I recall and warming for these inclement conditions."

"Bah," Whent thumped his wooden mug on the table which creaked and shivered at the impact.

"You will be returning with me to Rivercross and onwards to Killenhess. It's too sharp, isn't it?"

Zoller rocked on the stool. Thoughts swirling like the vinegar in his cup as he tried to buy time for them to settle. "There is a wine for every occasion and this lights a fire in the chest. A perfect match for Our Lord, Kildare."

Whent harrumphed, knowingly. "Well?"

"Killenhess, Your Grace? Cardinal Tortuga volunteered my pastoral care and, er, military expertise here. Has he sent new orders?"

"No, no, he hasn't." Whent sighed rubbing a weary hand across his eyes and face as he considered his next words. "But you and I both know you're no military man, despite that rather impressive dissertation you made to the ministry college, all those years ago. And yes, I did read it but damn it, Henrik you don't even have your armour with you. It's probably closeted away in Rivercross gathering rust. So no, you're no holy knight and I'll not allow five hundred of my brothers to be wasted on this lost cause, nor lose your talents when they can be better employed elsewhere."

"I was always good at studying and understanding things," Zoller agreed. "But as an acolyte, I barely scraped through military training. My strength has always lain in another direction." Zoller mirrored his superior's relaxed tone. But there was more to this than sudden altruism.

"What has happened?"

With a curl of his lip, Whent took a sip of wine, eyes regarding Zoller with uncomfortable intensity.

"I first met Cardinal Tortuga at his ordination ceremony. A stout man they told me and he was, but I found him so much more. Sharp, both in wit and intellect, and compassionate." Whent huffed. "Compassion. An oft-overlooked virtue frowned upon as a weakness by our church, but the Cardinal showed me the opposite, taught me its strength. I confess that I liked and much admired him at the time."

"I had not seen him for many years but by chance, he stopped at Killenhess on his way to the Red Conclave. I barely recognised him. He was a bloated, darker version of the man I knew. That wit I sensed was gone, replaced it seemed to me with cunning. And the compassion… well, that was like dust on the wind for he had none. Abrupt, direct and pleasantly manipulative. My admiration was much diminished. He was not who he was."

Zoller was stunned into astonishment. That the Archbishop would open his mind so and convey his thoughts aloud. No wonder he'd sent Captain Warwick away. "Has something happened, Your Grace?"

"Yes, yes it has. You might need some more of that wine you're not so fond of, for this news is dire."

"Worse than the High King's attempted assassination?" Zoller blurted, unable to help himself. It drew a steel-eyed look from Whent.

"The Red Conclave is concluded. Eight of the nine cardinals are dead including High Cardinal Worsten Lannik. The Book of Faith is clear, nine shall enter one shall pass and be anointed. There resides a new High Cardinal in the Church of Kildare. Your mouth is open, Father."

Zoller snapped his jaw shut.

"In case you are wondering, Tortuga was the lone survivor. He was borne out on a stretcher and is said to be balanced between life and death. If he recovers, we will have a High Cardinal like none before. Kildare has spoken."

Whent's tone made it clear he was uncomfortable at the prospect. Pragmatic and honest, Zoller wondered how the man had risen so high. Still, Whent was wise not to share his obvious scepticism of events, it was blasphemous. *What is my role in all this?* He asked himself. The answer framed itself slowly, obvious but incomplete. Not until Whent confirmed it would he acknowledge his burgeoning hope.

"I see," Zoller replied.

"I am sure you do. These are dangerous times, Henrik, and the church stands in crisis. I would have you accompany me to Rivercross and, depending on the news we find there, onwards to Killenhess. You were Tortuga's under-study, his protégé until recent times. You know his Holiness better than anyone and I would seek your insight if you will give it."

And there it was. Was his revoked assignment at the Defile incumbent on his answer? Yes or no, did it matter? Zoller felt euphoric, destiny called, he could see it stretching before him in his mind's eye, beckoning him onward, begging him to step upon the path.

"Of course, Your Grace. Turmoil abounds, we must ensure the Church navigates its turbulent waters and emerges the stronger for it. I'll help however I can."

"Father Milgorin." Whent's voice boomed loudly and moments later the horse-hide curtain was pushed aside and a man entered. A priest in red robes but wearing an embossed steel cuirass on top in matching colour. The clunk of his tread and the way his skirts bloomed, intimated at boots, greaves and cuisses beneath.

"Your Grace." Milgorin took a knee and kissed Whent's proffered hand.

"Take a squad to the Defile and relieve the brothers at the chapel there. They are to rejoin and attend Father Zoller as soon as they are able."

"And my orders, Lord Commander?"

Opening his robe, Whent withdrew a sealed scroll and handed it over. "You're to represent the Red Church and our interests at the Defile. Offer counsel to Duke Brant in the art of war and holy service to the soldiers in his command. Take a loft of pigeons and report to me as matters dictate."

Rising, Milgorin's eyes slid to Zoller, who nodded at the look, which elicited a scowl from the armoured priest who turned and departed.

"A proper Holy Knight. To each task the right tool," Whent stated.

Zoller didn't care. Not for the condescending look of superiority the priest gave nor that Whent sought to use him. *Be careful the blade you wield*, he internalised, *for this one cuts both ways.*

Chapter 14: The Conduit

Northwest of the Defile, The Rivers

"What just happened?" Nihm pushed past the ilf toward Renco's inert form.

"Do not touch him," Nesta counselled.

The tone in the ilf's voice was enough to stop Nihm short. Not so the woman, whose long blonde hair, tawny in the firelight, was scattered and tangled, whipping about her face as she dropped to her knees and lifted Renco's head onto her lap.

"What did you do to him?" Lett's look conveyed her accusation every bit as much as her words.

Nesta's answer was matter of fact. "I interrupted the flow of tae'al in his body. He was open and it was necessary. He was burning pure energy." Then, seeing Lett's scowling countenance he simplified, "I made him sleep."

The bushes rustled and Lett twisted to the noise as a man appeared. He was gangly and tall, with skin a marbled blue-white and with red hair poking from the fringe of an oversized, brown woollen cap.

"Thank the Three, a fire," he chattered. Sidling past the ilf, he pulled his mittens off and stepped quickly to its warmth. Hunkering down, he held his hands as close to the flames as possible. "Quite a light show back there. That him then, this Renco?"

Dark rimmed, bloodshot eyes regarded Lett as he spoke and she glowered back, nerves all ajangle and on edge. Her hand moved to the hilt of her knife. "Who are they?" she demanded.

The ilf replied. "As I said, they are friends. This male human, availing himself of our fire, is named Morten Stenhause, the female is Nihmrodel Castell. They have been searching for Renco and therefore you, and remarkably have found you both, with only a little assistance from me at the end. Now, gather your things. It is time to leave."

"Leave! I'm shattered. We've only been here a few hours. I need to rest and in case you haven't noticed, he's out cold, no thanks to you." Lifting Renco's head, Lett dropped it onto her lap again to illustrate her point.

"Nihmrodel and Morten brought horses. We will tie Renco to one. You may ride the other."

"Whoa, what?" Morten exclaimed. "The horses' have bin pushed hard an' need rest every bit as much as we do. Besides, it's black and cold as a murderer's heart out there. That wind may have died down but the snow ain't letting up none."

"No choice," Nihm interjected. "That burst of power from Renco could have been seen by urak and worse. Master Hiro says things hunt in the aether. Told me that they can sense my unguarded presence. By extrapolation, Renco just rang the proverbial town bell."

Morten cussed.

"Master Hiro sent you?" Lett murmured her subdued voice barely a whisper.

Nihm heard her anyway. "He was injured else he would be here. He awaits us at Wooliston. Come, we should leave."

Nesta crouched beside Renco and passed a hand over the slackened face then lower, over his chest and body. "He will not wake till morning. Come, child, let me bear him."

Lett wetted dry lips, her face pinched. Reluctantly, she nodded.

Nesta slipped his arms around Renco before easing him up and then over his shoulder. Rising, he marched to the break in the bushes before disappearing through them to the outside.

"Wrap up as best you can, it will be cold," Nihm offered before following after Nesta.

Lett's gaze flickered to the man by the fire, still warming himself. It annoyed her for some reason as if the heat he stole was hers. "You have any 'state the obvious' pearls of wisdom to offer too?" she asked, her voice muffled as she rewrapped her scarf.

The man stood and dragged the woollen hat from his head. It was as if he peeled a husk from his scalp for it revealed another cap beneath. With a wry grin, he lobbed it at her. "Here. You can thank me later." Turning, he left, pulling his mittens on as he went.

There was another surprise awaiting Lett once she joined them that made her startle and drop the pack she lugged into the snow. Two wolves stood, tense but immobile, amber coals regarding her intently as if she were a rabbit they were eying for dinner. The first was a scruffy white that toned well with the snow, the other was black enough to blend with the night.

Morten chuckled. "Don't mind them. That's Snow and Ash. I'll leave you to figure out which is which." He clucked his tongue at them and the dogs loped over and nuzzled his hand. "Go on away. I've nothing for you." He tussled them playfully before turning and asking. "It's my horse ya be riding. You need a hand getting into the saddle?"

Heart still hammering, Lett scowled. "I know how to ride." She moved to the bay roan and strapped the pack to the saddle-back before moving up the mare's flank and running a gloved hand along her neck. "We'll get along just fine won't we, lady," she whispered. The horse's ears quivered and pivoted to her voice.

They left as soon as Lett was mounted. Nihm led the way with the dogs ranging on either side. Morten followed, guiding the horse with Renco tied across its saddle. Then Lett with Nesta bringing up the rear. The ilf was content, it seemed, for Nihm to guide them into the snow-dappled night.

The pace was arduously slow. The track they followed was the same as that forged by Nihm and Morten on their way northward, but as the night deepened fresh snow filled the tenuous trail until it was indiscernible from the surrounding cover. It didn't bother

Nihm who pushed on undaunted, arrow straight. They cleared the low foothills and crossed a snowdrift-covered plain, punctuated intermittently by solitary manakas, whose thick trunks extended thirty paces into the air before topping in clusters of bulbous, purple-green cauli-heads crowned with a mantel of snow.

By the time the orange rays of daybreak bloomed in the eastern sky, they had entered the forest straddling the east-west road to Karston Abbey where Nihm had hunted urak. The horses were exhausted and showing clear signs of distress and they were forced to make camp. Here, Nesta took over and lead them to a bush lined gully with an overhang that disguised the dark mouth of a cave. Its entrance was narrow but once breached the interior widened into a bowl-like cavern.

Nesta conjured a ball of light that pushed the darkness away. Its radiance left pools of shadow in the rocky nooks and an ominous pitch where the cave disappeared deeper beneath the earth.

"This cave has been used before," Nihm said, taking in the relative smoothness of the floor and the worn surface of the rocks around the centre. "Do the ilfanum come here?"

"Once maybe, in another time," Nesta replied, peering at the walls as if searching for something.

"Strange that no beast has laid claim to it. It would make a fine lair," Nihm observed.

Leaning a hand against a craggy protrusion, Nesta murmured arcane words and a faint surge washed out. It prickled the hairs on Nihm's arms making her startle.

"What's wrong?" Morten asked.

"You didn't feel that?" Nihm shuddered.

"Feel what?" Morten's eyes darted about, looking for whatever it was that had unsettled Nihm. His gaze fixed on the black maw at the back. He didn't like it. The cave was different somehow to the caverns at Fallston. The smell for a start was more earthy and the air danker. The ceiling was lower and the walls closer, more claustrophobic.

Faint lines of light suddenly loomed into being, jigsaw cracks that spread up and around the walls and ceiling, the glow growing steadily stronger.

Morten gaped. "What magic is this?"

"Arcidu Cerafloris," Nesta replied. "Not magic. Not really. Just thousands of lichenous plants, each casting spindle arms to gather their sustenance. I merely imparted more energy to them than is needed. The excess is bled off in the form of light." With a word, the orb snapped out of being and the ambience dipped to the dreary yellow and green emissions from the lichen. It was enough to see by.

The cavern was sufficiently large to accommodate the horses and they were settled near the entrance and a makeshift camp organised. The still form of Renco was laid out on Morten's bedroll with Lett assuming his care. The newcomers seemed friendly enough to her, but Lett was leery all the same. Sure, the old monk had sent them, but the woman,

Nihm, was too young and self-assured for her liking. So she watched guardedly as they worked and she nursed.

Soon a small fire was established. There was a natural draw in the ceiling that funnelled the smoke into a craggy rift to disappear who knew where. Water was set to boil whilst Morten took care of the horses and Nihm disappeared with the dogs and her bow. She returned a short while later with a brace of white-furred jackrabbits.

"Renco is burning up?" Lett announced, "and I can't wake him." She held a hand against his fevered brow. "What's wrong with him?"

Nihm came over to look, hands bloody from preparing the hare. Nesta, who had sat in quiet contemplation since starting the fire, stirred himself and wandered across.

"What are those markings on his face?" Nihm asked. Her sight had shifted through several lenses, and in numerous spectrums, and the motif of swirls and lines were clear to see and in one echelon, they fairly glowed.

"You've good eyes," Lett said, "I can barely make them out in this light. He's had them since our imprisonment at the Defile but they are often faded so you can't see them. Well, most of the time. I don't know what they are or what it means."

"Rune marks, from a time when others lived in amity with the world. They are ancient even to me," Nesta said. He phased, dropping into ki'tae and examined the youth. The aura of his lifeforce was different. Changed. He had sensed it earlier when he had touched Renco's tae'al. But the energy emitted at the time was so extreme, so pure it had precluded proper inspection. He had not had a chance to examine Renco again, until now. What he sensed sent a shiver of foreboding through his body, something that he had not felt since the Tower of Iskinnis. Despite his trepidation, Nesta observed with an abstract certitude, as the equilibrium of the human's lifeforce whorled out of balance. Its filaments twisted and knotted, the strands tightening. Renco was dying.

"Something is wrong." Nihm had also used her hidden sight and made a similar observation. Though not proficient enough in reading tae'al to understand what she saw in detail it was clear to her that Renco suffered some malady.

Sai intruded on Nihm's worry. *<The ilfanum are difficult to read but I detect in Nesta a hesitancy.>*

<Maybe he is unsure of the affliction?> Nihm countered. To her, the ilf looked stolid, his black eyes emotionless pits. He was different somehow to M'rika and even the surly R'ell but she could not say in what way, they were so alien. But, as annoying as Sai could be with his analytics, subtle readings and calculations, she had learned to trust him. Sai was rarely wrong. So she pushed.

"If you are able, why would you not help him?"

Nihm's challenge caused the ilf to shift his regard to her. "Your question is subjective. Every action has a consequence, a price that must be paid. Saving Renco may have a higher cost than not. I have yet to decide."

Lett screeched. "He's dying? And you're gonna just let him."

Nihm raised a bloody finger to the ilf. His words and Lett's accusation thrummed through her body. Her chest ached, like a fist tightening, her heart constricted. Her voice quivered, low and dangerous, so incongruous she did not recognise it as her own.

"Renco is meant to live. I feel it here." Nihm thumped her chest, soiling it red with jackrabbit juice. "I know who you are, De'Nestarin, ilf-mage. My Da told me of you not four days past in Fastain. How he saved your life a ten-year ago. When he did, he did not think about the price. He helped because he could, and it was right."

Nesta gave a rueful shake of his head. "Humanity is a plague for precisely that reason. To act without consideration or foresight is ignorance. You do what is right for you in the now without regard for the wider implications. So is the way of the human. It is why you are doomed to repeat the mistakes of your forebears."

"Why are you here, Nesta? It is not fate that brought you," Nihm growled.

"No indeed child, it was you and him. I am one of those… hunters in the aether that you spoke of. I felt your presence explode like a star only for it to vanish days later. You have learned to shield yourself well, child, and quickly."

Nihm snorted. "This is all well and good, but it isn't helping Renco. Why won't you save him, or can you not?"

In answer, the ilf dipped his head as if in deep contemplation. The silence stretched until it became unbearable. Lett looked askance at Nihm and opened her mouth to speak but snapped it shut again when the she-ranger held a hand up to forestall her. Lett's jaw clenched in frustration, her hand subconsciously brushing the unruly mop of hair from Renco's brow.

Finally, Nesta opened his eyes and spoke. "Temptation is a part of life, even for the ilfanum. But we are creatures of the Nu'Rakauma and they guide us in all things. In this, I cannot save him. However, a debt is owed. If you wish it, Nihmrodel Castell, I will tell you how you may save him."

"Tell me," Lett blurted. Then with a hint of petulance. "He's my friend and this is my fault. He'd not be here if it weren't for me. Please, let me save him, not her."

Nesta replied, "Your wish is well-intentioned but misplaced Letizia Goodwill. Your emotional bond is strong, forged in the crucible of shared ordeals, but like iron untempered it is brittle, tenuous. Even were it not so, still, it would not be enough. Only those attuned and able to manipulate tae'al may hope to save him and Nihm has already… ah, but I say too much."

Lett's face fell at his words, her shoulders slumping.

"I'll do it. Just tell me how," Nihm said unmindful of Lett's distress.

"And the price, are you willing to pay it?" Nesta asked.

Nihm didn't hesitate. "Yes."

Sai chimed up. <It would be prudent to ask about the cost first.>

<What matters the cost if it will save him. I must. I feel like this is mine to fix. I can't explain it, Sai.>

<You do not know this Renco. Your thought process is illogical, emotional,> complained Sai.

<My Ma would argue it is what makes us human.>

"So tell me? What do I need to do?" Nihm asked of Nesta.

"The aura shield you project is very good. There is a cadence, an order to it that hints of ilfanum influence. Given that I know you were not trained by the ilf-mages in Antén-Wahr, it tells me you consumed a knowledge seed. Who gave it to you?"

Nihm gave a nonchalant shrug. "M'rika dul Da'Mari. She travels with my Da to the Order Halls on Tankrit. She said my shielding was flawed. I think she owed my father a life debt, so I guess she wanted to help."

The ilf's face contorted, mouth twisting. "M'rika, an old friend but young still for one into her fourth seeding. We must talk later. There is much I would know. For now, tell me, will you accept another knowledge seed? This one will convey all you need to know. Including the cost. If so hold out your hand."

<I would stress caution...>

Ignoring Sai, Nihm extended her right arm, hand flat. Nesta placed a hand over hers and a tingle of sensation tickled the bowl of her palm. When he withdrew, a single fibrous, fingernail-sized shell remained.

"Swallow the kernel whole and the knowledge will subsume as the seed breaks down, you will barely notice it. Chew it first and the knowledge will hit you at once, but it will be uncomfortable. You have time for either so you may choose."

Nihm picked the nut up and examined it. Green and hairy it was ugly to look at and completely unappetising. M'rika's seed, in contrast, had been tiny and smooth as a pip and it had slipped easily down her throat. Three pairs of eyes watched, each reflecting a different light but only two could Nihm discern. Morten's concern was self-evident, whilst Lett's regard was disquieted and reticent. Nesta remained an emotionless enigma.

Popping the nut into her mouth, Nihm cracked it and retched. Her taste buds exploded in complaint as a bilious coating smothered them, leaving her thick-tongued and a rising numbness climbing the walls of her cheeks to the roof of her mouth.

"Uggh, 'atsch vile," Nihm gagged. She forced herself to grind and then swallow the nutty pith, the numb creep following the seed debris down her throat.

<I can't breathe.> Nihm's eyes flared.

<You can,> Sai replied, <Breathing function remains unimpaired. Nerve receptors have been blunted imparting a sensation of swelling and suffocation. Adjusting.> The choking feeling faded and a lungful of air relieved Nihm's momentary panic. She directed a fierce scowl at Nesta and imagined a hint of amusement on his face.

"Could'a warned me," Nihm accused, yawning and working her jaw as if it would relieve the rancid flavour. Morten nudged her shoulder with a waterskin and she glared at him as she took it. The ilf's amusement might be imagined but the wide grin on Morten's was not.

After swilling her mouth out, Nihm handed the skin back and focused once again on Renco, aware all the while of Lett watching hawkishly.

Closing her eyes Nihm dropped into ki'tae. The blazing brightness of energies swirled in her mind's eye, so much more than it should have been. It was like staring into the nucleus of the sun, all white light with flares and ripples of colour coruscating the whole.

Sai interjected, seeming awed. <I can sense the energy imprint of Renco in your cerebrum. It is unlike anything stored in my memory or that my rand-exp routines can expound or classify.>

<I don't understand what any of that means,> Nihm complained.

<It means that I can read your sixth sense, this new sense you speak of where before I could not. It is most fascinating. As it imprints in your hippocampus I can analyse it and, if I can write a new subroutine to process the information within a centisecond or faster, I will witness what you witness within the same quaginsphere. It will be very beneficial.>

The thought exchange had lasted less than a second, but Nihm's attention was already fixated on Renco. Sai's uncharacteristic awe and excitement would have to wait along with whatever in hells a hippocampus and quaginsphere was.

Somehow, Nihm knew to move her awareness into the energy. Riding the maelstrom of white and colour she perceived Renco's core. His aura was strong but not without blemish. He had been damaged but instinctively she knew it was not by the energy buffeting him now. He was flawed, scarred and Nihm wondered, now that she knew to sense it, whether, if she examined herself, she would bear her own wounds.

Withdrawing a little, she dampened the brilliance not knowing how she did, just that the thought was enough to make it so. Minute details previously hidden took shape. Tendrils of tae'al, his aura, frayed and swam in the soup of churning energy. Her focus expanded on a single, diaphanous filament until it grew large in her mind and as she observed it knowledge blossomed. She knew in that instant what he was. That he was dying and how. Knew also the cost to save him and it rocked her.

Nihm gasped, eyes wide as if coming up for air after a deep dive.

"What is it?"

"What's wrong?"

Lett and Morten's concern tumbled over each other. Morten placed a hand on Nihm's shoulder to steady her and proffered the water skin again. She clutched it, her mind in turmoil and took a slug, letting the coolness of the water ease down her throat.

"Well, did you fix him?" Lett asked, trying and failing to mask her concern.

"Not yet. I…," Nihm stammered to a halt, head hanging as she tried to sort through what she had witnessed. The seed consumed had given her the knowledge needed but not the time to process it all. Annoyingly, Lett was intent on not giving it to her either.

"You said you'd save him. I should have had the seed. I would have tried harder."

Morten rushed to Nihm's defence. "Hush now, Nihm will do what she can. You carryin' on so ain't helpin' none."

Nihm ignored them both, lifting her eyes to Nesta she said. "He's a tae'alénn-vos. Rune marked, a conduit. How is that possible."

"It is extremely rare but not unheard of," Nesta replied.

"What in hells is a talenvoss?" Morten asked.

Nesta thumped his staff down thrice on the ground which startled them all. Markings blazed up its length in an intricate and detailed network of runes. A burst of light belched from the staff's tip and washed against the cave ceiling before dissipating impotently.

"My staff is tae'alénn-vos. Attuned to me, it accumulates and stores tae'al, life-energy, from the surrounding environment and acts as a conduit, so that I may call upon that energy without disrupting the harmony and balance of the world around me."

Nihm reflected in silence, her mind working through the implications of what she now knew, Nesta's calm disposition helping to cement her understanding of what she faced.

"So ya sayin' this 'ere laddie is soaking up magic only I'm guessing he don't know it or how to use it and it's killing him?" Morten reasoned. "Just give him one'a ya seeds, like you did Nihm."

Lett stirred and looked across at Nesta, bitterness marring her features. "Renco can't can he? He's like that dead bit of wood in your hand. He cannot call forth the magic he holds no more than that staff and it's killing him. Tell me, Nesta, what happens to your staff if you should die? I'm guessing it's the same as for the magi whose staves are said to burst into flame upon their demise. Tell me I'm wrong?" A tear dripped off Lett's cheek and splashed against Renco's brow.

"Oh, this wood is not dead." Nesta tamped his staff again on the ground. "But you are correct. Once unbound, the tae'alénn-vos consumes itself. However, Renco is more than a simple énn-vos. He is a Runewalker. A unique one in my experience, for the rune marks on his face and body are ancient and unknown to me. Unless his attunement is completed, he will die but I cannot say with any certitude when or how except that it will be violent."

Lett spat, "You're scared of him. That's why you wouldn't save him, isn't it?" The tears flowed freely down her cheeks. "It would be better if he died. He'd never want to be your weapon. Another staff for you to wield."

"Shut up! Just, shut up," Nihm shouted, angst and guilt boiling over at Lett's haranguing discourse. "He can't save Renco, okay. No one can… no one but me." She said this last softly, her eyes reflecting the anguish she felt.

Lett's glare twisted to Nihm then faltered. She stuttered. "Why… why you? Who the fuck are you?"

"I don't know the why or how or any of it except that somehow he connected with me in Fallston and I to him." Nihm shook her head. "Only… I can fix him. I just don't know if I should, if it is right. It will not be the same, he'll be different than he was before. I will be changed. I… I… don't know what to do."

The slap when it came shocked Nihm as much as it hurt. She saw it coming, was aware of the flex and draw of Lett's arm before it had barely moved, she could easily have avoided the blow. Instead, her body locked rigid and tight, waiting for the strike to land. The sting of pain lingered long afterwards. That too she could have ended… yet it seemed right to feel it.

"You do what it takes." Lett rocked back, Renco's head settling once again on her lap. "Cause if you don't, he dies and dead is worse than different. You hear me?"

"There's more to it than that. More than I imagined…" Nihm started. Then, as Lett's face turned ugly and she raised her fist again, Nihm snapped. "Don't even try it… I'm trying to do what's right… I need to talk to him… see if it is what he wants."

Lett lowered her hand, but her tongue had not given up the fight. "Stupid bitch. He can't talk. Not to me, not to you, not to anyone." As she spoke her eyes slid to Nesta. "Maybe him. If Renco will awaken."

Nesta replied. "I cannot reach him and there is no certainty Renco will regain himself. He is in a downward spiral to non-being. Nihm, you must make a choice but know this. If you cannot bind him, Renco will remain here. The cave will not contain the ensuing energy release, but it might muddy the air a little, for the Morhudrim will surely sense the discharge and his dark agency will come looking."

Nihm's gaze shifted back to Renco, the keenness of Nesta's speech hanging in her mind. The ilf had answered her unspoken question.

"You have everything you need. Decide." Nesta walked off. Not far, but enough to imply he had done with talking. With a supple elegance, legs folding, he knelt comfortably.

Nihm watched the ilf close his black eyes but knew that he watched still, his awareness no doubt riding the swirling currents of aether. With a deep breath, Nihm set her mind once again to Renco, aware of Lett in her periphery following her every movement. Nihm blocked her out and dropped once more into ki'tae. This time she focused on the central core of Renco's aura and understood what was needed.

Nihm wavered, whatever knowledge subsumed from the seed was spontaneous but discordant. To learn something without knowing the how or why of a thing gave her nothing to anchor it to, giving a false, almost ethereal feel to it, as if it had been dreamt. She didn't want to trust knowledge that had not been earned. Do or do not, her Da would tell her and so she chose.

A peaceful clarity settled upon Nihm. After all, in the end, the choice was life or death and what kind of choice was that for him. Renco was not made to die here.

Nihm studied the ragged edges of his core which churned against the tae'al he'd absorbed, tearing and mixing only to recoil violently. With a thought, Nihm teased tae'al from her aura and willed it to nestle around Renco's. Instantly the raging energies ceased their combat, retreating to either side of Nihm's intervention, but buffeting wildly, eager to rejoin the fray.

Nihm's aura brushed against Renco's which held a hint of familiarity to it that resonated. As if drawn from deep waters tae'al rose to the surface of his aura, sending tendril feelers twining with hers. The tae'al was his but its design had changed to align with her own. 'This was me,' the thought trickled in the background of her consciousness, and she knew it was so. The motif strands coiled and merged and Nihm felt an electric jolt of energy roll through her as Renco's own body reciprocated.

Nihm withdrew, observing as the tae'al bound together, merging into one and, like thick oil settling over water, formed a barrier as the rushing maelstrom surged against it. The shield held. Renco's aura was protected, safe like a seed in its shell. He would live and Nihm was pleased but couldn't stop the wash of bitter irony that came with it.

Drawing her will back inside her body, Nihm phased back to the mundane, her eyes snapping open. As she blinked in the low light, she could perceive the weight of him still along the tether of their binding. Could sense him stirring, his consciousness slowly returning and she feared for what she had done and how he might feel about it on waking. She felt sick.

"Did you do it? Will he live?" Lett intruded. Her hand grasped Nihm's shoulder and pulled her around.

Water glistened in the corners of her eyes as Nihm fought tears and her rising gorge. Shoving free of Lett she rushed out of the cavern and moments later could be heard retching.

Morten went to go to her aid, but Nesta stopped him. "Leave her be. It was a difficult thing Nihmrodel Castell has done. But she is in no danger, and I suspect would not thank you for your concern. Give her space."

"Well, is he saved or not?" Lett demanded. Her hand on Renco's brow felt clammy but the heat from his fever seemed lesser. Hope sprung inside but she would not concede it until she knew. Until she heard it.

Nesta answered. "He will live. He sleeps now a proper sleep and when he awakes... well, we shall see."

Chapter 15: Eastern Promise

Wooliston, The Rivers

The journey to Wooliston had been an uncomfortable one, though for none of the reasons Darion associated with travel for the roads winding through the Maag foothills were well-used and maintained. No, the discomfort was in the company he rode with.

The altercation at Lower Rippleton, between Ironside and Master Hiro, had left both men nursing injury, and a surly atmosphere pervaded between the two; though most notably from the Order Knight. Master Hiro's feigned indifference seemed only to exacerbate the tension.

That first day on the road, saw both antagonists repair in separate wagons. Ironside; suffering a broken nose with accompanying black eyes, bruised body and a foul temper; staged a remarkable recovery and by the following day was well enough to ride again. He spent most of it alongside his fellow Order Knight, Lyra Castigan, talking quietly when he talked at all.

Master Hiro offered no better companionship. Nursing cracked ribs, he rode the back of a wagon and as much as Darion would have liked to have spoken with him, the old monk spent most of his time meditating, sleeping or conversing with Mao and Father Melbroth who rode in the same wagon along with the ilfanum, M'rika and R'ell, who were still dressed in their guise of White Priests.

It was left to Darion to lead them south with the ever-faithful Bindu at his side and, high above, the gliding outline of Bezal, R'ell's raven. That first day out he was oft joined by Lyra Castigan but their conversations, whilst friendly enough, were all perfunctory and mostly of Tankrit and the goings on at the Order Halls which Darion had not seen in over fifteen years.

Despite the snow dumped across the land by the first of the winter storms, they made good time with the volume decreasing noticeably the further south they went. Where it settled upon the road the snow was churned a dirt-grey and compressed by the hundreds that had gone before them and the horses pulled the wagons easily enough along its meandering length.

At the start of their third day out, they left the rolling hills of the Maag behind and joined the lakeside road leading south to Morport. A major route, it was wide enough to accommodate two carriages riding abreast and was busy with traffic, most scurrying south, though several times they were passed by columns of armsmen with shield and spear tramping and stamping as they marched to Rivercross, and once a troop of riders.

The road hugged the shoreline and the villages and hamlets they passed bustled with people escaping the urak invasion. On approach, many of them were blighted with the patchwork bruises of impromptu camps, most abandoned only to fill again with the dispossessed as the day extended.

To their left stretched the cold, dull waters of the Emerald Lake, reflecting the grey overcast. Its far shore was unseeable making the lake seem more a sea, with waves grinding against pebbled beaches. Boats rode its plain, small fishers with larger merchant vessels plying north and south, most with sails unfurled but a few with masts bare, rowing against the headwind.

By the time they rolled into the small township of Wooliston the sun was faded and the moon, Ankor, had risen, its sullen yellow glow threatening to break through the cloud cover. The streets were full despite the late hour and Lyra and her grey knight, Ansel, took point following the main thoroughfare to the town square before turning off towards the lakeshore. Down a narrow side street, they pulled up outside a large brick and timber building where a darkened sign proclaimed, Eastlight Traders.

Dismounting, Ansel approached the wide double doors and thumped twice against the oaken panels. A brief delay, then a bar sounded, chunking in its blocks. With a scuff of wood on cobbles, the doors swung wide revealing a swarthy barrel of a man wearing a peaked cap and a beaming smile. "You're late, Ansel."

Ansel grunted, "Master Gúl." He walked his horse inside, the wagons rumbling behind. The gateway opened up through an internal arch to a flame-lit courtyard with boxes and goods stacked around its periphery.

Gúl watched them pass, his cheery demeanour changing as he counted them in, before pulling the doors closed and sliding the lock bars in place. "Trouble on the road, I see." He called to Ironside and Castigan. "Get y'urselves and your holy guests inside and warmed up. Molpa will get some warm food in you."

Giving four loud claps, Gúl raised his voice. "Erna, Marj, Hoik, Bikna. Get ya lazy good fer nothin' butt's out here'en help."

Four youths appeared, three young men and a girl, siblings by their shared features, each with the same brown eyes, snub nose and wide mouths that proclaimed them children of Master Gúl, though each was tall and thin in comparison to their father.

Waving his arms, Gúl berated the four. "You make me shout. 'Be ready' I say, and you tell me, 'yes, papa' but you are not! You punish my indulgence with slackness. If idle children are a god's curse for a bad life, I must be a very bad man indeed. Now, hurry, hurry."

The four took the reins of the horses, smiling and unperturbed by their father's ranting. Gatzinger and Regus stayed to help whilst the rest followed Master Gúl inside the largest of the annexed buildings.

"A difficult journey. I can see by the wound in your eyes and the empty saddles that you have lost much," Gúl proclaimed as he bid them sit around a long hardwood table.

A tall reedy woman, dark-skinned and fine-featured entered, the wafted scent of warm food following behind. "Ertu, please. You forget yourself, again! No business. First, our guests must refresh themselves and then eat. They will be travel-weary and hungry.

There will be plenty of time to swap news later." The lilt of her voice was as comforting as the promise of food.

"Molpa, it warms me to see you again." Lyra Castigan crossed the room, taking her hand.

"And you, Lyra Castigan." Molpa saw in an instant the stress lines creasing the knight's face, read the forced smile and the deep well of sadness in her eyes and wrapped her arms about the woman. "I'm so sorry for your loss." The words were whispered.

Closing her eyes, Lyra hugged back but said nothing. Not trusting herself to speak but thankful for the comfort offered.

Molpa stood away and brushed a hand at the corner of her eye. "Look what you've done. I'm going to have to change my pinny, it's all dirty. We'll talk later, you and I." Turning away, she breezed from the room leaving an awkward silence which Ertu Gúl was quick to fill.

"The water is cold but clean and I have soap and drying cloths. Follow me." He watched as one of the cowled priests whispered to the tall broad-shouldered man he did not know, before retiring to the far side of the room with another of the priests. Gúl raised an eyebrow in query.

The tall man answered it, "Their needs are few and they will attend themselves."

Gúl shrugged, "As they wish." Something was off about the Holy Fathers, but he would know what before the end of the night, of that he was sure.

Afterwards, clean and sated, Gúl opened a bottle and poured a ruby-rich port for each of them, barring the two silent priests who had touched nothing all night.

Mao clutched and downed his almost before the last drop was poured then held it out for another measure.

"This drink should be savoured not quaffed like water," Gúl admonished, but refilled Mao's tumbler all the same. Erna, his eldest boy stoked the fire whilst Marj, his second, offered the tabacc pouch around and the pleasant smell of spiced goulash was replaced with pipe smoke and burning wood bark.

"The *Eastern Star* left late afternoon," Ertu Gúl started. "I could not hold her any longer without raising questions from the Dockmaster. However, the *Eastern Promise* is due early tomorrow. In anticipation, I've filed papers for her to Lakeside, as was agreed. Though for fifteen not twelve, plus horses and wagons?"

Ironside ground his teeth. "Well, it seems we've no choice but to wait. But we are ten, not twelve. Hiro and Mao are not coming with us. I trust that's not an inconvenience and will not cause any problems with your paperwork. Rest assured the price will be paid in full."

Gúl ducked his head. "My home is yours. As for the paperwork, trivial it may seem to you, Sir, but taking care of the little details prevents bigger problems later on."

Castigan chuckled. "That your family motto, Ertu."

"If it were, I would not be displeased," Gúl retorted with an easy grin.

Darion watched and listened. The ease at the table and friendly banter throughout the meal and now, made it clear the Gúls were old acquaintances. They never spoke of Keeper or the Order though, except in the abstract, which set Darion to wondering about the Gúls agency. Did they belong to the Order or were they merchants sympathetic to the cause?

"You are eight fewer than when you left here. Some I knew better than others. I am sorry for your loss, my friends," Ertu Gúl was saying. "Might I ask, for my family's sake, should I expect trouble at my door?"

Ironside shook his head, but it was Castigan who spoke.

"Not the trouble you hint at. It's urak we ran into, not the Red Church or Realmsmen. It did not go well for us, but it went even worse for the urak. So yes, trouble is coming. For once the urak cross the Fossa in numbers they'll have free reign to the Sindhow Plains and beyond. Make sure you are not here when they do."

"This is most troubling." Ertu Gúl wrung his hands. "Lord Rakoman has levied most of the young and able-bodied and marched them north to Rivercross. The High Lord intends to hold the urak at bay there until the spring when the High King will come. My agents in Morport report that a contingent of mages set sail a week past for Rivercross and will rain down powerful magics upon the beasts."

Hiro responded. "Master Gúl, the urakakule do not covet as we might. It is the land they seek and our towns and cities a convenient place to hold us to. They care not for our bricks and mortar."

"Twyford steals our young and hides behind his walls then?" Gúl spat. "Leaves us like lambs to be sacrificed."

Hiro shrugged. "Twyford does what he must to safeguard Rivercross. He has too few spears to challenge the urakakule in open battle and win."

Unconsoled, Gúl's temper was raised. "Lord Rakoman might be old and a fool, but he would not leave us without warning if this were known to him. The High Lord has left us to die."

"If Twyford told his Lords the truth they would turn up with fewer armsmen. Besides, you know as well as I, Ertu Gúl, that the refugees pouring through Wooliston are warning enough and none have the luxury of boarding a ship and sailing to safety as you do."

Ertu went to rise but Molpa placed her hand on his shoulder. "Your words are deeply disturbing, Master Hiro, but I thank you for speaking them, and you Lyra. We will think on what has been spoken. Now, you must rest. We will all be better for a good sleep and you will be weary after such an arduous journey." She clapped her hands and a door opened. "Hoik and Bikna here, have prepared your bedding. If you will follow them."

Gathering his feet, Darion rose with the others. Molpa's tone had been friendly enough, but it did not disguise the fact she had dismissed them. It was an abrupt end to a pleasant evening. He trailed behind as they followed Hoik and Bikna, who led them outside and across the yard to an extension next to a stable block. Inside, a hearth fire crackled sending out an inviting warmth. The room itself was devoid of furnishings with only a few crated goods stacked at the back. Bedrolls had been laid for each of them on a mattress of fresh straw.

"We break our fast at sixth bell, the hour of the cockerel," Bikna said, her voice a young facsimile of her mother's. "Hoik or I will return for you then."

Darion followed her outside and she glanced nervously over her shoulder at him. "I would check on Bindu, my wolfdog."

Bikna nodded and walked on but Hoik turned. "She's a beauty. Fierce. I bet she could hold her own in the fight pits."

"Pits?" Darion raised a quizzical eyebrow. "You have fight pits here?"

"Yes, but we don't go. Mama says they're brutal and a filthy reflection of a bad soul. It's just that my friends talk about them after every contest. I bet she'd show them, eh!"

"Bindu is not for fighting. Not for sport," Darion growled. "Listen to your Ma boy, for she's right."

The lad flinched at his tone. "Yes, Sir. I meant no offence." At Darion's unblinking gaze, he turned and hurried away.

"Before now, my last interaction with humans was in my second seeding." M'rika's words reached him and Darion spun for he had not heard her approach. R'ell stood silent guard at her back. "I recall attending a dog fight. It was presented to me as a great spectacle. I killed four dog handlers before my brethren interceded. I was disappointed not to have killed them all. I was recalled to the forest after that, and I was pleased. For there was much about your forebears that I found barbarous and distasteful. It seems not a lot has changed in the intervening cycle of time."

Darion's shoulders dropped. "I know many people that would agree with you. I am one of them. But not all humans are so, M'rika dul Da'Mari."

"And yet still it happens. The ilfanum have a saying 'a bad seed will taint the pod unless it is removed'. Humanity has too many bad seeds. I wonder why it is your people have never learned this lesson."

"Maybe we learn it but slowly. Come, I must check on Bindu." Darion led off. M'rika, accepting the deflection, followed closely with R'ell gliding silently behind.

Bindu was overjoyed to see Darion and whined from behind the stable door until Darion released the bolt. Bounding out, she urinated her vengeance against the door frame before brushing against Darion's legs and then M'rika's, hunting for attention.

"Come on, ya mutt." Darion roughed her playfully before leading them back across the courtyard.

A gust of air and the descending flap of wings announced Bezal's arrival on R'ell's shoulder; the clash of her black plumage a stark contrast against the ilf's white cassock. R'ell stroked the raven beneath her beak and produced a morsel which Bezal snatched before flicking it up and into her gullet.

"You've been quiet these last few days," Darion intruded on the reunion, "even for you, R'ell."

"We talk, M'rika and I." R'ell waggled his fingers. "It is difficult. To pretend to be human when I am not and rely on the same for safe passage. The sooner my task is done and I am returned to Da'Mari and the Rohelinewaald the better." The ilf clicked his tongue at Bezal and with a shrug of his shoulder, launched the raven back into the air. She vanished in a moment into the deepness of night.

"There is much good in us," Darion announced suddenly. "We are not all bad. Most folks live with good intent. Do not think poorly of us for the actions of a few." With that, he pulled the door wide to their accommodation and disappeared inside. He did not see the silent exchange between the ilfanum.

R'ell's fingers talked. "It is more than a few. Is he blind?"

M'rika gestured back. "No, not blind. He wishes to see the best in his people and there is strength in his words. Even so, wishing a thing does not make it a truth. I am sorry my seed brother asked you to come."

R'ell replied without hesitation. "D'ukastille del Da'Mari may have asked it of me, but it was Da'Mari's will. You know this. My purpose is whatever Da'Mari demands it to be and I do it humbly and with honour."

M'rika signed. "You are a worthy companion. Darion too is worthy."

R'ell snorted a breath. "If you say it, it must be so."

"Da'Mari says it. The Great Mother named him ilf-friend, not I." With that, M'rika dul Da'Mari followed after the human.

* * *

The hour of the cockerel came and the only bell to toll its hour was Bikna's knock on the door. She entered to find her papa's guests already awake and dressed. She led them to breakfast across a pitch-dark courtyard while sleet fell gently from the sky and melted the instant it struck the cobbles. Cracked light from a shuttered window and door edge guided the way. Pulling the door wide, Bikna bid them enter and the company found themselves in the same room as the evening before.

The long table was adorned with freshly baked bread, cold cuts and cheese, and a variety of bright-coloured fruits and nuts. Molpa appeared from the kitchen clasping a steaming kettle in a gloved hand.

"Happy morn to you all. I trust you slept well. Sit, eat. I have hot cha and porridge if any desire it."

Darion sat with the others and forced himself to eat. His usually formidable appetite blunted. His talk with M'rika and R'ell still troubled him but it was thoughts of Nihm that weighed most heavily on his mind. He lifted his eyes across the table to distract himself.

Master Hiro sat with Maohong at his side. Mao had been old the first time Darion had set eyes on him and showed remarkable tenacity and vigour for a man so ancient. The intervening decade and more hadn't appeared to have slowed him down any for he attacked his food with gusto, untroubled by the mottled bruising that stained his face. A reminder of the brutal beating he had taken and somehow survived.

Resilient old fart, there is more to you, Darion thought. It had not been talked of, but he knew Mao had done something at Lower Rippleton. He alone stood whilst others had faltered and Ironside was beaten and flung overboard. *How?* Darion wondered, picking at some ommi berries and finding the tart fruit suited his mood.

He could feel Hiro's eyes watching back, mouth chewing slowly. When his old Master spoke, his voice was low but reached across the table, against the background hubbub of noise, to ring in his ears.

"It is hard having lost so much to let go of what remains."

Disgruntled at being read so easily, Darion bit down on a berry, the citrus tang sharp and cleansing. "Ai, that it is."

Hiro sipped cha then broke some bread and chewed on it, he could wait and after a time Darion spoke what troubled him.

"It feels final. That when I board this ship today, I'm closing a door behind me an' opening one ahead. I should ne'er have let her go. Not without me. What was I thinking?"

Hiro set his cup down. "I will speak a wisdom you know already but you will hear it because sometimes a thing must be said. It will not console you. It will offer no comfort and ease no pain. But it is a truth."

"I'm no longer a child, Hiro, ta listen so ta your sermons."

"We are all children, Darion. Is that not so, M'rika dul Da'Mari." A smile played at the corners of Hiro's mouth as he turned to the ilf, hidden beneath her cowl.

"It is so. Nonetheless, tread carefully, Hiro," M'rika warned.

"Always," Hiro replied. It elicited a guffaw from Mao that drew several gazes. Unperturbed, Mao distracted himself with a piece of cheese. With a slight shake of his head, Hiro continued.

"We do not own our children, Darion. You know this. You did the brave thing, the right thing in letting her choose her path as you have chosen yours and Marron hers."

"Marron did not choose to die," Darion hissed. "If I had…"

"Ai, ai, ai, ai," Hiro admonished. "That way lies madness and grief. It will aid you not. Few get to choose the hour and time of their death. All any of us can influence is how we live, and Marron lived well, so well. Remember that and try to honour it. Clear this morbid slant from your mind. It helps no one, least of all Nihm."

"You're a harsh bastard, you know that," Darion growled. "I'll do my duty but when Nihm turns up here you better guard her with your life. Tell her…tell her…"

"She knows already, my friend." Hiro reached across the table and gripped Darion's forearm. "Do not confuse duty with honour or right. You will find they are not mutually exclusive. Do what is true for you." He released Darion's arm with a pat. "Now, when your 'duty' is done, look for Nihm at Hawke Hold for once my business is concluded in Kingsholme I intend to visit the Duncan."

Darion nodded understanding. Hiro was right, though his sagacious advice had been no comfort and Darion's mind twisted at the thought of Nihm out there without him. Helping himself to a handful of cold cuts, he rose and headed for the door knowing one certainty. Bindu would be hungry, her appetite unabated by the vagaries of men.

* * *

The morning dragged by. The air felt heavy and damp, the sun struggling to make its presence felt. Hiro and Ironside avoided each other but in the enclosed space the undercurrent of tension between the two sullied the mood of the group.

For Ironside, the incident on the *River Arrow* replayed in his head time and again and forced him to reevaluate Maohong. To his eternal shame, he had relayed everything to Keeper and been admonished for his handling of matters. It only served to strengthen his dislike and distrust of Mao but much as he might wish it otherwise, Keeper had been clear in his instruction. Mao was not to be touched.

At mid-morning, the hitherto absent Ertu Gúl appeared and announced that the *Eastern Promise* had docked and was being unloaded. He bid them wait with Molpa out of sight whilst goods were shifted to and fro. "The fewer people that see you here the fewer tongues to wag and the safer we will all be."

Molpa kept them well fed, with a legume soup of beans and leek and chunked potato, lightly spiced and this time Darion managed a double helping. When it came time for the loading of their horses and wagons, Ertu Gul agreed to the help of Regus and Gatzinger but refused any others on the grounds they would get in the way. It wasn't until afternoon's second bell that the Trader finally returned for them.

Darion enfolded Mao in a bear hug. "Try and stay out of trouble you old scoundrel." Which earned a grunt in response.

He clasped arms with Master Hiro. "Look after her, Hiro."

"I will do my best and just you mind yourself on Tankrit. Stay true, Darion Castell." On that sombre note, they parted.

The walk to the dockside was a short one with Ertu Gúl's home and compound situated only fifty paces away. Three long wooden piers jutted into the waters of the Emerald Lake and it was on the furthest of these that the *Eastern Promise* was berthed.

Darion had not been aboard an open water vessel since leaving Tankrit fifteen years earlier. Then, he had spent the entire trip in a hot-cold sweat, nauseously puking into a bucket. Despite the calm look to the Emerald Lake, he didn't much care to revisit the experience.

From the quayside, the *Eastern Promise* looked wide beamed and large. She was twin masted with a single row of banked oars situated below her main deck. As Darion walked the boarding plank, he saw the familiar figures of Gatzinger and Regus near the foredeck with the horses. The company's two wagons were lashed down, facing each other and straddling the centre-ship between fore and mainmast.

Ertu Gúl was speaking quietly to a thick-set man with a bush of a beard who, from his attire and bearing, Darion took to be the Captain. After a brief discussion, they shook hands and Gúl turned to address them but stared pointedly at Father Melbroth and the two cowled priests at his shoulder.

"Holy Fathers, Captain Maveison here is a devout man and asks if you would bless this ship and all aboard her?"

The wizened priest smiled in return. "Of course, I would be honoured to do so. My brothers however are in their vows, observing a period of abstinence and silence until Nihmrodel's cycle returns to fullness. May I ask, were you able to secure with the master of this vessel, a private berth for our contemplations?"

Gúl's thick brows knit together. "The ship may look large, Father, but she is built for cargo, not passengers. There is barely room for such luxury," Gúl said. "However, I do own the ship and it is merely a day and night to traverse to Lakeside. The captain has agreed you may use his quarters for your prayer and respite."

Gúl lifted his eyes and gave a rakish glare. "The rest of you I'm afraid will have to rough it with the crew. I wish you luck with the hammock."

"Now, I will bid you all farewell. May a strong breeze and calm waters follow you." Clasping his hands together in prayer, Gúl bowed before moving toward the gangplank.

Darion watched silently as Rutigard and Ansel each shook hands with Gúl as he left. He was unsettled, his opinion unformed, for Darion found the man a strange mix of honourable and roguish. The Trader paused for a quiet word with Lyra Castigan then Ironside, who slipped a purse to Gúl as they clasped arms.

"May the Gods watch over you, my friend," Gúl blessed.

"There are no gods," Ironside replied.

Darion felt himself smile, for it seemed a ritual between the two and eased his mind a little over the Trader. He watched Gúl alight the boarding plank with an unexpected grace for a man as well-fed and stocky as he, before descending to the dockside with a nonchalance that told Darion the man was as much at ease on the water as off it.

Captain Maveison crossed the deck casting a leery eye over the massive wolfdog which sat quietly at the feet of a large man whose black beard was tangled and a match for his own.

"I'm Yonah Maveison, master of the *Eastern Promise*. Whilst aboard, you will address me as Captain. There'll be time enough later for pleasantries. It ain't now. Casting off is a hectic time and I'll not 'ave ya underfoot gettin' in the crews' way. Watch from the bow or aft deck else get ya'selv's below. Fathers, my cabin is yours for the duration. After ya blessin' I'll get a swabbie to show ya the way. Gentlemen, Fathers, ma Lady. That is all." With a tap of his hat, Maveison turned away, bellowing orders.

The sailors aboard busied themselves, a dozen more boiling up from below decks, like ants out of a mound, and forming up on the main deck. Father Melbroth needed no encouragement to step forward. The White Lady, Nihmrodel, called by some the Traveller, was particularly venerated by sailors. All bowed respectfully as Melbroth offered a prayer and blessing for their safe passage.

No sooner was he done than Captain Maveison was shouting commands and the crew scattered like leaves in high wind as they prepared the ship for departure. Twin boats were lowered over the clean rail and into the slight chop of the lake before men scrambled to fill them.

Ironside, Castigan and what remained of their company moved to the bow and watched as long ropes were played out to the rowboats and tied off.

"Release the bitter," bellowed a man stood beside Captain Maveison. Onshore, mooring lines were released and men scurried up the side of the *Eastern Promise* like rats. The gangplank was withdrawn and with a creak of cordage and grinding of the hull, the ship eased away from the dock. The small boats strained and dragged her out, away from shore to deeper water.

All the while, the Captain stood on the aft deck, scanning the rigging and gauging the wind and ride of the ship. With a nod to his first mate, who hollered a command, the topsail on the foremast unfurled. It was enough to hold way. The tenders were taken back on board before another shouted order released the mainsails. Heeling against the wind the boat was underway.

Darion watched in fascination. His belly rolled with the ship and a burp of nausea rolled up his throat. Looking back, he was surprised to see they were three hundred yards from shore, Wooliston growing smaller with every moment. Unbidden, the words he spoke to Hiro earlier echoed in his mind.

"*It feels final. That when I board this ship today, I'm closing a door behind me and opening one ahead.*"

Darion's gaze drifted to the north, his hand resting on Bindu's head, with an all too familiar ache in his chest. He fretted over Nihm, unable to shake the sense that he had let her down, abandoned her. Marron would never have left her. His face twisted into a grimace, for he knew it to be true and it shamed him.

Chapter 16: A Small Matter Of The Succession

Anglemere, Kingsholme, The Holme

High King Edward Blackstar, her father, was dead. Matrice wanted to be there. Wanted to watch the light fade from his eyes. To see her father's body convulse in the final throes of agony before surrendering to the toxins that coursed through his veins. She wanted her face to be the last thing he saw, knowing it was she who had killed him.

But death was cruel. Death danced a moribund song, taking life according to its own, twisted, enigmatic whim. And so it was that her father shucked his mortal coil in the black of night, alone at the end.

Instead, she witnessed a deflated corpse, shrunken and stinking of shit despite the incense sticks that burned. The experience was a poor substitute. Worse though was enduring the tear-streaked face of her stepmother, Queen Margot and her whining lies that her father had passed peacefully. It only took one look at the contorted grimace on his face to reveal that untruth, *bitch*.

Bitch she may be, but Matrice needed the Queen, for now. So Matrice hugged her stepmother, patted her back and sobbed into her shoulder. Afterwards, she retired with the Queen to her solar. For nothing bonded so much as shared loss. Or so it was said.

"A pity father could not have fought a little longer," Matrice said.

"A lesser man would have succumbed days ago." Margot's shoulders went back, her face tightening.

"Of course. Father was the strongest man I know." A sad smile played across Matrice's lips. "I only meant that it leaves us in a precarious position, that is all."

Margot slumped, bloodshot eyes glistening with the residue of tears. She daubed a handkerchief at them.

She is weak, Matrice thought. "Lord Henry could and should have been here two days ago. Then he would have seen his brother king before he passed. Uncle, as you well know, does not possess the kindness or wisdom of my father and does not yet know about my brother. It makes me suspicious of why he tarries so."

The Queen scowled. "The whole city talks of Herald. He'll know soon enough."

"No, mother," leaning forwards, Matrice reached out and touched a palm to the Queen's midriff. "I meant this brother."

"Oh," Margot folded her hands over her stepdaughter's.

Matrice tilted her head. "We have suffered a grievous loss and are at our weakest when we need to be strongest."

"Whatever are you talking about, dear. Mourning a loved one is not a weakness." Margot sniffed and gave a broken smile.

Matrice mirrored it. "They call uncle, Black Henry. He acquired the honorific during the Reavin Rebellion where he massacred whole villages. Thousands died; men, women, children, it mattered not. He opened their veins and let their blood feed the soil."

The queen frowned, her tears momentarily forgotten. "Henry crushed the rebellion. Was hailed a hero, though I recall your father refused to acknowledge him for it. It was the start of the bad blood between them."

Discomforted by their touch, Matrice withdrew her hand. "It is said history is written by the victor. I know, as did father, that the price of uncle's victory was the blood of innocents. He is ruthless. And now, with father gone and Herald named traitor for his murder…"

Matrice poured some wine into a goblet and passed it across. "Drink, but not too much." She waited whilst the queen sipped before continuing.

"My uncle will move to claim the Kingdom Throne. If he succeeds, I fear my unborn brother will never take his first breath. Both our lives will be forfeit. Black Henry will leave no one to contest the crown."

Margot splashed her wine setting it down, then clutched at her belly. "I don't believe it. He wouldn't dare."

"As his Queen, my father shielded you. But talk to your aunt, Lady Elizabeth. As High Lady of Midshire, she'll know well my uncle's reputation, his nature, his… politics. Call for her. Seek her counsel if you do not trust mine." Matrice stood. "Our hearts are filled with grief, mother. But we do not have the luxury to mourn. Not yet. You must do what needs to be done to protect my brother."

"Where do you go?"

Matrice walked to the door, turning as she reached it. "Place no faith in the Lord Chamberlain. Riebeck messaged my uncle precipitating this matter. Maybe he told my uncle more than that my father was dying. If you trust your maids, send one to Lady Elizabeth. If not, one of your Ladies-in-waiting if you own their loyalty."

"Matrice!"

"Your aunt does not know me, nor trust me. I am a Blackstar after all." A delayed pause, as if she considered whether to say more. "I go to speak with the High Lords and to consult Luxurs and Jenah. I would see where they and the Churches stand in this matter." Without awaiting a reply, Matrice pulled the door wide and left.

Outside in the corridor, Captain Loris was waiting along with her escort. "The meetings are arranged, Highness."

"Did any seem reluctant?"

"With the Lord Commander, it is hard to tell. The rest seem accommodating enough. They assume it to be about the High King."

"And so it is." It was not safe to talk openly in the corridors of Anglemere. Information was the richest currency and more than she had eyes and ears placed to gather it. She pondered their earlier conversation, in the privacy of her chambers.

"Will the Lord Commander support me, Captain?" she had asked. The reply was as expected but still unsatisfactory.

"I don't know, Highness. He is rooted in honour. If he does swear an oath to you, the Kingsguard will be yours," Loris said.

"And if not?"

"Then he must die and quickly."

Now, striding the corridor with a confidence she did not feel, she turned intense, green eyes to Loris. He was thirty-something, young to be a Captain, he had overseen her protection since she was twelve. He met her gaze and held it but was the first to look away.

"You have news, Captain Loris?"

"The guards posted in the Seawatch Tower have heard movement inside. You ordered none to enter." Loris left the rest unsaid, as mindful as the Princess of where they were.

"Good, take me. We have time before the meeting."

Loris frowned. "That red priest, Manning, has been hanging about and asked to see you. Persistent devil."

She smirked. "The bishops push for answers. Let them wait a little longer."

* * *

The heady musk of sweat and stale piss assaulted Matrice as soon as the door was opened. High Cardinal Maxim Tortuga was perched on the edge of the bed that Matrice fully expected him to die in. Pallid skin hung against his jowls and gathered in folds beneath his chin, the flesh consumed by his body as it fought the poison that should have claimed him. He seemed half the size of before and looked all the more grotesque for it. To Matrice, he was a wonder.

Beady eyes, red-rimmed and blood-filled, seeming almost black, peered out in demonic aspect from sunken sockets. With gravitas, they watched her as she closed the door and crossed the room.

"Highness…"

A coughing bout overtook Tortuga and he clasped a hand to his face until the fit subsided. His hand, when he lowered it was speckled with blood.

Matrice moved to the centre table and poured water from a jug into a cup, before carrying it to his side and holding it out.

"It is a miracle you are up. For many days I thought death would claim you. You look…"

"Better than dead but not by much," Tortuga chuckled, then broke into another fit of coughing. He raised a heavy hand and clutched at the cup, gulping a mouthful of water that spilt down his unshaven chin. When he looked up again, he seemed more composed.

"Every bone in my overburdened body aches with a passion and my head feels ready to burst. But I am alive and if Kildare has not claimed me then it is for a purpose. I must lay back and rest a while. But first I must know, how long?"

Matrice took the cup from his hand and placed it on the sideboard beside the bed, watching whilst he rolled onto his back and closed his eyes.

"Four nights have passed since the Conclave."

"I have no memory that is not an agony. Tell me, child, what has transpired since? Spare me nothing."

* * *

Harris Benvora watched with a growing sense of unease. She was not alone in that. Others in the room looked equally apprehensive. Most of the Close Council were present and so too their eminences, Rand Luxurs of the Brown and Maris Jenah of the White. The imposing figure of Magnus Harkul, Lord Commander of the Kingsguard stood near the map table and, sat unobtrusively in the grand arch of the seaward window, John Taran, Prime Magus of the Council of Mages.

Rudy Valenta, Chancellor and Master of Coin, was speaking, "I do not wish to be disputatious, your Highness. If the Lord Chamberlain were here, he would tell you himself that the forms are clear. Your brother is still the Crown Prince, appointed heir by the High King before his untimely death. Should Herald be found guilty of regicide then his position, his life, would be forfeit. However, we must observe due process and until this matter is tried and concluded one way or another we cannot move forward as I see it."

"As you see it?" Princess Matrice sat in her father's chair in his recently repurposed War Chamber. The dark stain on the map table was still visible from that night.

The Princess appeared delicate, yet despite her diminutive stature possessed a wild, robust nature. To Harris, who had known her since birth, Matrice was hardly recognisable from the impudent, wilful child of a few weeks before. Indeed, she seemed hardly a child at all. Now there was a hawkish set to her shoulders and a predatory look in her eyes that reminded Benvora of Kenning Blackstar, her grandfather, or dare she say it, Lord Henry her uncle. Matrice had killed, and it had been easy to see the pleasure the princess derived as she slid her blade beneath the chin of Lord Renix. This was no child to be trifled with. Something Rudy Valenta seemed oblivious to.

"I will tell you how it is and forms be damned," the princess declared. "Urak assail our lands, our Nine Kingdoms. And, in our hour of need, the Order perpetrates a great betrayal, turns my brother's head with whispered treachery who then murders my father. Why? Always the Order championed themselves as protectors of the realms. Not just these Nine Kingdoms but all realms. Now it is clear they work toward an unknown agenda. One we will all pay the price for if we sit here pontificating. Direct action is needed and that means crowning a new High King, or… High Queen."

"And you petition for the position, your Highness? There has never been a High Queen," Valenta replied. It was the wrong thing to say, the glacial arrows Matrice threw from her eyes said as much.

Despite herself, Harris Benvora couldn't help but smirk as the usually unflappable Master of Coin looked suddenly flustered.

Matrice gave a clap of her hands. "I petition nothing. I am next in line by birth and rightful heir, gender be damned. As the gods bear witness, I will be the first Queen of these Nine Kingdoms."

The chamber doors opened. The room turned to watch, as first, Captain Loris and Master Wendell entered, then four Kingsguard bearing a stretcher with a red cowled body heaped upon it.

Silent until then, the heads of the churches of Ankor and Nihmrodel were first to react. Rand Luxurs exclaimed in wonder. "High Cardinal Tortuga, can it be so?"

As the stretcher was set down, both Holinesses rushed to Tortuga's side. He gave a pained moan as he tried to rise.

"You should be resting, Brother," the High Priestess admonished, astonished at his morbid appearance and wrinkling her nose at his strong odour. She glanced at Luxurs who nodded and together they helped Tortuga gain his feet.

Tortuga groaned. "Four days I have fought death and it would have come had not Kildare stood by my side. Trust me, I would like nothing more than to feel the kiss of my bed covers but there is much that must be done. I do not speak rhetorically when I say Kildare was with me."

Luxurs' worried eyes reached to Jenah who raised her eyebrows in response. "Captain, a seat for the High Cardinal."

But Tortuga waved it away. "I will stand and say my piece, Sister, if her Highness will allow me?" At Matrice's assured consent he gave a grimaced smile.

"Thank you, Your Highness. I am deathly tired, but my Lord Kildare has lent me the strength to convey his words." Tortuga coughed in counter to his words and rubbed a hand over his mouth and unshaven cheeks before recovering himself.

"As my mind wandered in delirium, My Lord came to me, cleansed the poison that should have claimed me and spoke to me. He showed me things no mortal man could have seen. Of what has been and what might come to be."

Tortuga licked dry lips; his throat rough as a sanding block. Jenah whispered and one of the Kingsguard fetched water from the table and proffered it. Clutching it gratefully, Tortuga gulped a mouthful whilst the room waited in silence.

"Bless you, my son," Tortuga said once his thirst was slaked. He looked up again.

"My God showed me the Nine Kingdoms, poised on the brink, blindly walking towards its doom. Two urak clans war upon us and contest against each other. Rivers has all but fallen, with the tribes of the White Hand claiming everything north of the Fossa. Rivercross is the last bastion of defiance before the way south to the heartlands is opened. The other clan, the Red Skull, have breached the fortress at Highwatch and descend upon Norderland. The Norders too are destined to fall.

"We are wounded, haemorrhaging the blood of our people, yet instead of standing together, Kildare has warned of a divided nation. Even now internal conflict threatens to strip away the strength of the union. Some, like Great Olme, would seize this opportunity to secede, renouncing the Nine. My Lord showed me many things, many possibilities of what might come to pass. That to survive, the path we must tread is a narrow one. And, the only visions where we triumphed and navigated to safety, were with a Queen at our helm."

Tortuga's arm swung like a pendulum transcribing an arc and pointed at Matrice. "That Queen."

An agitated murmur circled the room. "I am the voice of Kildare and My Lord has spoken through me. The Red Church stands beside High Queen Matrice." Spent, Tortuga slumped back and the two Holinesses lowered his still prodigious weight onto the stretcher.

Rudy Valenta was the first to venture an opinion. "The Lord Chamberlain should be here, yet he is not. In his stead, Your Eminence, Your Majesty, I feel it incumbent upon me to point out that the churches of the Trinity have no influence or bearing on the succession. That has always been so."

Master Piert Wendell cleared his throat. "Indeed, Lord Valenta. That is first and foremost the purview of his Royal Majesty. However, precedents have been established in crown law whereby if no heir has been named…"

"Master Wendell, you have no purpose here. You are an academic, a teacher. If I need consultation on issues of law or protocol, I have a host of clerks happy to lecture on it. Is there not some Lordling you should be instructing?"

Matrice rose like a dervish from her chair. "I called this meeting, Lord Valenta. I invited Master Wendell for his knowledge and insight and because I trust him. Not an opinion I hold for some in this room."

Valenta's neck reddened and his mouth opened, only to close again when Harris Benvora placed a hand upon his arm and, leaning close, whispered. "Be careful of your next words, Rudy. Once spoken they cannot be unsaid."

Valenta went to speak again but Harris squeezed his arm, and her eyes beseeched him to silence. Blessedly, he listened. Harris turned to the room but paused when the chamber door opened and a harried-looking guardsman entered.

"Your Royal Highness, Her Majesty The Queen Consort and the High Lady Hardcastle."

The two women breezed in at the pronouncement. Queen Margot, dressed in a black mourning gown, trailed the stern-faced countenance of the High Lady who waved for them to continue. "Don't mind us, by all means, do carry on."

Harris Benvora spared a glance at Matrice who seemed unperturbed, amused if anything.

The Princess spoke. "In your grief, I did not wish to trouble you, mother. But you are both welcome." She shifted her eyes. "Harris, I believe you were about to say something?"

Benvora felt decidedly unsettled. She was witnessing part of some machination she had no say in but understood well enough. Powers were shifting, realigning. Sides would be taken and none in this room could be trusted. It made no difference. Her decision, her choice, had been made thirty years before. She inclined her head to Matrice, who sat once again in haughty regard upon her father's seat. Heart pulsing with a vibrancy not felt in years, Harris turned to address the room.

"This situation none could have foreseen or wished for. I am honour-bound to Edward Blackstar and his line. He was a great man and a good friend, but he is dead and Herald is gone, and my duty lies with her Royal Highness. Protocol and precedent are not fixed in stone. Whosoever sits upon the Kingdom Throne will decide it. You all know as well as I, there are two principal candidates. Edward's daughter, Princess Matrice and his brother, Lord Henry Blackstar who, even as we speak, marches upon Kingsholme with an army of Blackcoats at his back."

An excited murmur bustled the room.

Lord Lowenstow seemed most agitated, but it was High Lady Hardcastle that was first to give voice. "The city has been locked down for four days. A magus is oath-bound to their House or the Enclave and the Enclave is infamously neutral. How do you claim to know this?"

It was not Harris Benvora that answered but John Taran, the Prime Magus disengaging himself from his position at the seaward window.

"To walk the keen knife-edge of impartiality is difficult and, as one might imagine, deeply discomforting." A small grin teased his face. "Let me just say that some of our mages are more neutral than others. The information was mine, though I confess I did not expect Harris to announce it to the world."

He raised a tawny eyebrow. "We live in perilous times as expertly conveyed by High Cardinal Tortuga and my fellow magus Harris Benvora, who makes her intent plain. Her simplicity of purpose is something to be applauded, I think. Would that my fellow mages were so clear-minded, but the truth of the matter is rather more complicated. It is fair to say that the Enclave is divided following the High King's death. One thing we agree upon, however, is that a successionist war cannot be allowed."

John Taran turned to the princess. "Some call your uncle a renowned general, others notorious. In either case, he is experienced and has only known victory. The argument will be, that Henry is the King the Kingdoms need to fight this war we are in. Not an unseasoned, fifteen-year-old Queen."

Matrice sprang from her chair, and in the space following Taran's words, moved to the giant map table. She trailed fingers over the lands depicted upon its surface and slowly walked the circumference.

"My uncle is divisive at best. The Reavin and Doran Islanders loath him as do half of western Branikshire. The Southlands of Olme will not tolerate him and we will need their strength in the north. Were my uncle, Black Henry to gain the throne he will rule with the iron fist of fear. Whereas I would rule with the steel of hope. Only through me can we truly unite the Kingdoms. For if we do not come together as one, we will succumb to the darkness. Like sheep separated from the flock and picked off one at a time by the wolf, so would the Kingdoms fall."

Matrice pushed the sleeves of her gown up and held her arms wide. "The Blackstar's blood runs in my veins but also the blood of my mother's people, possessed of the fire of Sumar and the Southlands. Great Olme will see themselves in me. I will settle their discontent and bring them back into the fold; something my uncle could never do without violence."

Rigard Lowenstow pushed his portly frame past Rudy Valenta to the centre of the room where all could see him.

"Pretty words but if any here think Lord Henry will allow a girl to sit upon the throne you are sadly mistaken. He will seize it for himself and any that defy him will be impaled and left to rot outside Highgate, their families taken and slaughtered. All for the whim of a fifteen-year-old girl." His gaze circled the room. "You know I speak the truth."

Harris Benvora saw the Princess give a barely perceptible shake of her head and opposite, Captain Loris relaxed, his hand leaving the sword hilt he grasped.

"Thank you for being so candid, Lord Lowenstow. It is strange though, whenever someone professes truth my mind runs to the complete opposite. Maybe I am just contrary," Matrice shrugged slender shoulders. "Maybe I should spike you and stick your body outside of Highgate. Then you would no longer call me girl. Then you would not disparage me in front of this council and in my father's chambers."

Matrice sighed. "But I am not my uncle. You have made your position plain, Lord Lowenstow and I respect it. You fear my uncle's retribution should you not support his claim. Does anyone else here have anything to say about the succession? If so, speak it."

"The Queen is pregnant. With a son." High Lady Elizabeth Hardcastle's high voice lifted to the rafters and rang around the room. "It was Edward's dying wish that he ascend the throne upon reaching his majority at fifteen."

"Meaning what exactly?" Rudy Valenta could not contain himself. "That the Nine Kingdoms must wait for his birth and I presume the Queen consort sit as Regent until his majority? Where is the document with the High King's hand upon it? You do not even look pregnant."

A hushed exclaim followed this last. Realising that he skirted the bounds of impropriety, Valenta's face paled, and his eyes darted between the Queen and Matrice, unsure whose wrath he would incur first.

What has possessed you, Rudy? Harris Benvora thought. Her friend was known for his quiet words and soft speaking. He was not himself this day.

The delayed acrimony from Elizabeth Hardcastle, when it came, was tangible as if she'd drawn breath like an archer did a bow before release. "How dare you impugn by implication her Majesty's honour."

Reaching out, the Queen placed a hand upon her aunt's arm and stilled her. "I have known Lord Valenta for many years and consider him a close friend. I know he did not mean to speak out of turn. Should any have doubts about my unborn child, Loren Cripps, the Royal Physiker will verify my condition."

The Queen's cheeks flushed. "As to my ambition. I have none other than honouring my husband's wishes. Before he succumbed, he instructed me that our son be named after him and that Matrice should rule until Edward's majority. High Lady Hardcastle was giving me comfort at the time and witnessed his instruction."

"Let us hope the Nine Kingdoms still stands when he reaches age," Matrice murmured, then beamed. "It is decided then and I accept unless anyone else wishes to dispute the Queen's testimony? Lord Lowenstow perhaps?"

Lowenstow snorted. "I find it unconscionable. How an unborn child can be named heir apparent is beyond the pale. It is unheard of and against all tradition. It will not stand and I cannot support it." With an indignant huff, he turned his back and walked for the door.

Matrice called out. "Lord Commander, please have Lord Lowenstow escorted to his apartments. He is to remain there until further notice."

The room watched, as Magnus Harkul, with barely a pause, issued instructions and two guardsmen moved each side of Lord Lowenstow who spluttered in protest.

Oh, you clever girl, Harris Benvora thought, as the increasingly incensed Lord was bustled from the room. Few knew it, but Harris had spent enough time around both the princess and Harkul to know he was enamoured of her. Loyal and honourable to a fault the former Norderman would never act upon his feelings. Seven hells, Harris wouldn't be surprised if he didn't even acknowledge he had any. Men could be dense like that, especially the honour-bound ones. It stood to reason that Harkul would act to protect her. But that Matrice had known of it too was telling and, with a single command, she'd neatly manoeuvred the Lord Commander into supporting her claim for the throne. It was artfully done.

"Very well then, it is settled," Matrice was saying. "I will be ordained this afternoon. Master Wendell has drawn up an order of proceedings. Every Lord and Lady in Kingsholme will be expected to attend and offer their fealty."

Rudy Valenta shuffled in agitation and the princess turned on him.

"Never fear to speak to me, Lord Valenta. My father trusted you implicitly. As do I." The distant clamour of protest from Lord Lowenstow reached out from the corridor and through the doors.

Matrice wore a look of understanding. "I know your complaint. That proclamation should go to each of these Nine Kingdoms and the High Lords and Ladies gathered for the coronation. But most of them are here and those that aren't have not the time nor the inclination with urak at their doors. We do not have the luxury to adhere to tradition, it would brook too much delay and if it is not this day then it will likely not be any day. Not until the Kingdoms lie in ruin for there are many that would support Black Henry."

Tortuga coughed, his debilitated voice calling out from the stretcher. "The Red Church stands with you, your Majesty."

"And I am grateful High Cardinal. But it is not enough. I cannot do this alone. I need the blessing of the Churches of Ankor and Nihmrodel, of the Magi and from this Royal Council. If I do not have it, then I fear darkness will reside in these Nine Kingdoms. I am asking you to be brave. To do what is best and right for our people."

* * *

The light of a new day sparkled diamonds upon the waters of lake Cud when Henry Blackstar, Lord of Ramelo, marched his Blackcoats down the King's Road, filling it like an inked vein only to burst and spill upon the fields before the walls of Kingsholme. They displaced the merchant caravaners, traders, travellers and farmers that had been forced to encamp there whilst the city gates remained barred.

Matrice stood in surveyance atop the immense barbican that guarded Highgate. Despite the Blackcoats' saturation of the plains below, she couldn't help thinking they looked small. Bugs upon the ground that she could crush with a slippered heel.

"How many do you think they are?"

"Eight thousand, maybe…" Gart Vannen's answer trailed off at the petulant, flash of annoyance directed his way.

"I did not ask it of you," Matrice hissed, turning instead to Captain Loris.

"Sir Vannen's assessment is accurate, your Majesty. Though, not all are Blackcoats." Loris stretched out an arm and pointed. "I see banners for Lords Jentis of Bazal, Collis of Portisil and half a dozen more besides."

"They seem hardly enough to trouble these walls," Matrice suggested. "They have no siege engines that I can see and the Kingsguard and City Watch overmatch them. Uncle is posturing." Her voice though was uncertain, and her eyes sought confirmation of her words.

Loris's brow wrinkled. "They have camped outside the range of our long weapons as if prepared for a siege. If they war upon us they will not need to attack the walls, merely starve us into submission. We have a city of two hundred thousand to feed."

Vannen called out, directing them to the fields below. "Guess we'll find out soon enough."

Three riders had cleared the Blackcoat encampment and were ambling down the road towards Highgate. One held a golden pennant emblazoned with a black star that fluttered and snapped in the breeze.

"Captain, it's time. Ask Lord Commander Harkul to join me below then gather the others as arranged. Let us see how my uncle wants to play this."

"Your Majesty." Captain Loris gave a formal bow, before turning and marching away. Matrice headed for the steps, a silent Gart Vannen at her back.

It was cold in the deep shadows of the gatehouse and by the time she reached the cobbled stones her breath steamed the air from her exertion. Sir Elwin Wolsten, Master of Horse, awaited with a company of grooms and a score of horses, all saddled and wearing the red and gold caparison of the Royal Guard. Mounted upon one was the dark cloaked figure of a glowering Harris Benvora.

"You should have asked for me, your Majesty," the mage said. "I'm both your counsel and protector until you appoint another in my stead. I'll be coming with you."

Matrice smiled. "There is no other I would trust, Harris. Only you."

Harris returned a curt bow, only slightly mollified.

Matrice spied Lady Marta and several of her maids waiting in the wings and her smile gave way to a sigh. Marta, beaming at her, clapped hands and ushered the maids forward.

Resigned, Matrice lifted her arms, waiting whilst the maids buckled a golden breastplate over her favoured black riding leathers, tolerating them as they struggled with the unfamiliar bindings and heavy buckles. They finished with a red cape, embroidered and edged in gold silk, that looped over her shoulders and fastened to a bevelled notch on her armour.

Once they were done, feeling stiff and a little top-heavy, Matrice walked to her horse where Sir Elwin himself boosted her into the saddle with little effort. Marta appeared at her stirrup and passed up a golden helm with a red plume, exclaiming all the while how heroic she looked.

Heroics be damned. Matrice scowled at the thought. The armour was uncomfortably tight and along with the fit of her helm, she felt restricted. The sombre face of Gart Vannen staring back didn't help matters either. He sat astride his horse with languid ease as though his armour was a familiar friend rather than an inconvenience.

"Your Majesty," Lord Magnus Harkul boomed as he clunked into view with a dozen Kingsguard at his back. With the aid of the grooms, the knights all mounted and formed a guard around her.

"If you are ready, Lord Commander, take us out."

Harkul managed to bow in his saddle before giving a bellowed order that echoed against the walls. They waited as with a metallic clack, then crank of chain, the portcullis was raised. The outer gates groaned before grinding slowly open. Light from the new day split the tunnel, affording a growing view of the plains beyond.

With a clatter of hooves, Lord Harkul led them in a clipped trot beneath the ominous teeth of the portcullis, through the maw of the gate-arch and out upon the King's road. They broke into a canter that Matrice found more comfortable, easing the blunt edges where her armour pinched. It fit her well enough but needed some small adjustment and she made a painful note to summon the armour fitter when time permitted.

The parley of three outriders had stopped upon the road and as they closed to within two hundred paces, Harkul slowed them to a walk. "I believe that is Lord Henry at the front, Your Majesty."

"The cowled one will be Greta Kunning, his magus and the standard-bearer, Victor Horn, first sword," Harris offered. "Both are dangerous, Your Majesty."

Matrice had not seen her uncle in four years but she recognised him still. His hair looked more grey than the black she recalled and, never one to follow the fashions of court, he was clean-shaven.

"Have your Second wait here with the Kingsguard," Matrice ordered Harkul. "Harris, Sir Vannen on me."

They walked their horses forward, Harkul joining them moments later. Four riders to her uncle's three. At one hundred paces Matrice reigned in her mount.

"Stay here." At their incredulous looks, she glared at each of them. "I command it. Sir Vannen, I will take it from here."

Vannen untied a stained, burlap sack from his saddle horn. Manoeuvring his mount close, he leaned across and handed it over without a word.

It was heavier than Matrice expected but it looped easily enough onto her saddle. With a squeeze of her knee, her horse stepped out and she left them standing, feeling their eyes heating her back.

Her uncle's all-black charger matched hers, Lord Henry leaving his two companions behind and closing until they met equidistant.

"You look over small for a messenger. You wear Royal armour that has not seen daylight in a hundred years unless I'm mistaken. Take off that helm and let me see your face." Lord Henry was helmless, his dark hair, long and flecked with grey, was tied back in a simple ponytail. His angular face looked stern with a robust jaw and sharp, brown eyes.

With exaggerated slowness, Matrice removed her helm, which slipped from sweaty palms and rang as it struck the road. Matrice fumed, at her clumsiness, and her hair that had caught in the helms padding and pulled loose but mostly at her uncle's order that she had been all too quick to follow.

"Matrice?" Lord Henry exclaimed. "That is you? It has been so long. You must have been eleven, twelve when last I saw you. Did that miserable goat Reibeck send you to greet me?"

"No one sent me," Matrice rasped. This was not going how she imagined. Her uncle was leading the conversation and it grated.

"Well, I am pleased to see you, child. Tell me, how is your father, my brother? Reibeck sent a grim account of what happened."

"He died two nights ago, uncle. You could have seen him if you had not dallied bringing an army to the capital. But you did, and now you have missed the coronation."

The black stallion stamped and danced on the spot, sensing his master's agitation. "Reibeck told me Herald had been implicated in the High King's poisoning. I will not bow to the man who murdered my brother," Henry rasped.

Matrice smiled. "No, you will not. But you will bow to me uncle. I was crowned yesterday. First High Queen of these Nine Kingdoms. As my blood, as family, I do you a courtesy coming to meet with you."

Henry threw his head back and roared with laughter and Matrice fidgeted in her saddle as she watched and waited for his dramatics to abate.

"That is once, I have saved your life," Matrice continued. "It is why I rode to meet you alone, for if our exchange had been witnessed, I would have had to take your head, family or not. And I need you, uncle."

Henry sneered. "You're a child, playing in a man's world. This is no game. The Southlands of Olme will look for any weakness to break away and you have not the strength nor wit to prevent them. Urak invade the north and you have not the experience nor talent to defeat them. Step aside, Matrice." The threat was unspoken but clear in his voice.

In answer, Matrice pulled open the burlap sack, reached inside it and pulled out a head, the skin rigid and mottled from the lack of blood. "This is Lord Rigard Lowenstow. He too looks a little different from when last you saw him. He was the last man to call me child." Gripped by the scalp she held his head high until her arm tremored, then dropped it with a thump upon the ground.

Henry stared at Rigard's head as it rolled then settled, his eyes shrewd, recalculating. "You are not as soft as your father was, or an imbecile like your brother. But your self-proclaimed coronation is not valid, niece. I am surprised Lord Reibeck entertained it. He is a stickler for protocol."

Matrice reached inside her bag again. This time she struggled, needing two hands, for this head had no hair with which to hold it. Drawing it out, Matrice threw it so that it hit the ground and rolled towards the hooves of the black charger, her uncle leaning out to follow its course until it came to a rest in the dirt.

The age spots, wrinkled face and balding head told Henry who it was but still he stared at it a while. When he next spoke it was with quiet regard.

"Reibeck taught your father and me when we were boys. He was a hard taskmaster and I confess there were times I hated him with a passion. A cantankerous old bastard but loyal to a fault. He deserved better."

Matrice laughed. "Don't talk to me of better, uncle. My father deserved better, my mother better, but they are dead and gone. I will state my position, then you will state yours and we will proceed from there. Agreed?"

Lord Henry lifted brown eyes that smouldered with intent. "You will not find it so easy to take my head, child. But I will hear you."

A pert smile lit her face. "When my father summoned the High Lords and Ladies of the realm to Anglemere, he invoked the Articles of War to do so. Amongst other things, the Articles allow in times of war for a new King or Queen to be consecrated without the need of a civil coronation and all the forms and traditions that would duly be invoked.

"Consequently, a service was held yesterday at Saints Light Cathedral. The High Cardinals of the Trinity blessed and sanctified my ascension to the Kingdom Throne. There I gave an oath and took one of allegiance in return, from Lord Commander Harkul of the Kingsguard."

Matrice flicked her head to the side and gestured with her hand. "Behind me, upon the walls of Kingsholme, are the banners for Midshire, Westlands, Eosland and Branikshire. All have sworn fealty to me. Even the Council of Mages have endorsed my claim, John Taran himself watches from those self-same walls. That means not only am I High Queen but I am High Lady of the Holme. I will have your sworn oath before we part or I will order you stripped of your title. I have already signed the papers to make it so, should you decide to strike me down."

As she spoke, she watched her uncle closely. He masked his anger well but the lines about his eyes tightened, his lips pinched and severe, a slight flush to his neck.

"I have lost much already. My mother, my father and my brother. I do not wish to lose you too, uncle. I want you. You're our greatest field commander and I need you to fight this war for me."

Henry barked a laugh. "Save the idle flattery, niece. You named four banners. Four great houses that each see a different opportunity. They will seek to use you to their advantage, knowing they would not get the same leeway from me. You've been played, Matrice, your ego stroked. And, what of the four High Lords and Lady unaccounted for? They'd rather my strength of arm than your pretty face. Apart from Zakoris, where is that dog? I know he was here in the capital."

"He broke the harbour blockade three days ago," Matrice admitted.

"Hah, he may be a treacherous heathen, but he is no one's fool." Henry snorted. "That you could not keep him in Kingsholme tells me you are not ready. Relinquish the crown to me or we'll be facing war in the south by summer."

"Yanik Zakoris is my cousin thrice removed on my mother's side. We share blood. I understand him better than you. He faces sedition in the Southlands, seceding from the Kingdoms is a distraction he wields to control his people. It will not come to pass but he needs help to defeat these rebels and we will need his Defosi riders if we are to defeat the urak. I will bring him to heel with the promises he wants to hear."

Henry's horse stomped, sending Reibecks head spinning into the grass. "You were a sulky, conniving little fox when you were small, but I did not know your ambition was aimed so high."

"No higher than your own," Matrice said.

"I do not trust you. Nor believe for a minute that cretin brother of yours murdered Edward. He was too craven for one, for another he loved his father. Herald was the Crown Prince and heir to the throne; it makes no sense. If it makes no sense, it is a lie."

Smiling, Matrice chuckled. "You have been gone too long, uncle. Father never said it, but he despised Herald for the same reasons you do. Did you know? Margot is pregnant with a son. Reason enough many would say."

With a soft heel to her horse's flank, Matrice closed the small space between them until they were abreast. "It's good that you do not trust me, uncle. That way we share an understanding. Trust must be earned or won and I will win yours. Now take my hand. Kiss it and swear me fealty. Or strike me down and face oblivion."

Lifting her arm, Matrice held out her hand and waited. Incrementally slowly, Henry's hand rose, taking her delicate fingers in his callused palm. He stared at her soft, unblemished skin then lifted his eyes to meet hers, staring as if to burn a hole through her skull. Lowering his head, Henry brushed warm lips against her flesh.

Matrice withdrew her hand. "Say the words."

Black Henry sneered. "I, Henry Cavil Blackstar, Lord of Ramelo, promise upon my faith that I will honour her Royal Majesty, High Queen Matrice Suran Blackstar, never to cause her harm, to observe my homage to her completely against all persons in good faith and without deceit."

Matrice beamed a smile. "Excellent. You will, of course, repeat your oath in witness later today in the throne room but for now, I am satisfied. Attend me this evening. I'll leave orders that you be allowed to pass Highgate with an honour guard of five. Please bring Lords Collis and Jentris and any others you have with you. I will take their oath at the same time. Then we will discuss your new position as Lord Marshall."

Using legs and rein, Matrice spun her horse about and high-stepped down the road. Twisting her head, she called back over her shoulder. "Be a dear, uncle. Fetch my helm with you when you come. Do what you will with the heads."

With a cry, she eased the reins and her horse leapt into a gallop.

Chapter 17: The Prince and the Mouse

Kingsholme, The Holme

A familiar despondency filled Tomas. They had changed safe house three times, each move nerve-edged and full of danger but it was the in-between times that proved the problem. Too much time spent with nothing to do but think.

Tasso Marn had informed him the morning after their escape, of Lord Renix's demise. With the news, that seed of self-worth, of belonging, planted inside of him by his benefactor had gone. How strange that he was only aware of it now that it was no longer there.

Before all this, he'd had nothing and no one except himself and Sparrow and that was just the way it was. Each day a fight to survive in a city that didn't care. Why should it? He'd gotten pretty damn good at surviving too. But not anymore. Now everything was dead. First Sparrow then Renix, a man he'd known barely a month, but who, despite this, had marked him profoundly. It left him with a yearning ache he couldn't comprehend and a fist-sized hole in his chest that refused to go away.

He touched his fingers to his neck and trailed them lower, pressing through his clothing to the token that rested against his skin. It had been given to him by Renix and Tomas had studied the medal many times. It bore the Lord's house crest, of a bird in flight. Artfully crafted, if Tomas should hold it between his fingers, he would feel the birds finely raised edges.

The voice of Lord Renix sounded in his mind in that annoyingly passive, knowing way of his. A memory.

"It is a falcon. A lone hunter that soars high in the skies and sees all things."

"It looks expensive," he'd replied. "Bet I could get five kerns for it." A fortune to his young mind. He smiled at the recollection. Renix had stared so intently at him.

"It is not for selling, Tomas. It means freedom. Something money will not buy you. With this token, I have accepted you into my house. On Tankrit, you will grow and learn."

"Learn what, milord? I learned most'a what I need ta get by already."

"The world is bigger than you can imagine, my boy. Tankrit will teach you the most important thing in life." Then at his quizzical expression. "How to become the best of yourself."

The memory faded and his fingers dropped from where they pressed the token against his heart. "I don't feel free, nor the best of meself," he murmured.

"Will you stop that infernal muttering, boy? You are driving me insane." Rald was propped on his bed against the opposite wall.

Tomas eyed him. The prince looked rough. His hair had been shorn and was patchy, sticking up in places and bare in others. His cheeks held a soft fuzz of growth and his skin looked red and blotchy. He wore coarse clothing to blend in. Worn brown hose and a frieze wool tunic the colour of sand which irritated from the way Rald constantly pulled at it.

"Don't much like it down here in the dirt with the rest of us, eh!" Tomas smirked, unable to resist antagonising him. Five days in hiding with Rald's constant sniping had eroded his instinct to curb his tongue around the bigs.

Tasso Marn looked up from the knife she was slowly running over a whetstone. "You're both getting tiresome, niggling each other at every opportunity. As I have said, the one needs the other, so try to get along."

"He scorns me. Constantly." Rald moaned.

Marn's eyes hardened. "You provoke the boy and he mocks you in return. You're a man grown, not a child, Rald. Change your behaviour and he may change his."

An ugly fury filled Rald's face. With a gentle shake of her head, Marn returned to her task and the room fell silent but for the soft rasp of steel against stone. Outside, the noise from the streets filtered up to them.

Tomas moved to the shutters. Tasso Marn was right, it was something Renix would say, though he would have used twice as many words saying it. He smiled at the thought as he inched the board open and stared down at the lane below.

It was busy but not as it ought to be. The sealing of the city gates was slowly throttling commerce. It was the first time Tomas had ever known it to happen and it could not continue, the city was a voracious beast, that like its citizens, needed constant feeding. Already, according to Tasso Chiguar, food prices had started to soar as stocks diminished. Another couple of days, he'd said, and there would be riots on the streets.

Rald expelled a heavy sigh and in a moment of clarity, Tomas realised that as lost as he was feeling the prince must be infinitely worse. Tomas had nothing of worth in his life before all this, whereas Herald had had everything. Crown Prince, heir to the throne, riches beyond belief, servants, enough food in a day to feed him for a week. Two. And in a night it had all gone, taken from him, even his name. The only thing Rald had left to lose, Tomas mused, was his life.

Yestereve, as if to punctuate the prince's misfortune, all the bells in the city had tolled. Not in alarm but in pealing, harmonious proclamation. A final nail, as if one had been needed, that the Nine Kingdoms had a new High Queen, its first-ever. Queen Matrice.

Tomas was aware of Marn rising and shifted from his observations outside to watch her. She had set the whetstone down but not the blade and moved to the door. A floorboard squeaked from the corridor outside then a knock and a subdued voice.

Unbarring the door, Marn swung it wide and Chiguar entered, the stooping figure of Horyk Andersun following behind.

"Word is rife on the streets," Chiguar said without preamble. "Lord Henry Blackstar has come with an army of Blackcoats and camps upon the Shorune Plain."

"Trinity save me, thank the One," Rald cried, rocking to his feet, his face animated. "Uncle will not believe nor stand for this nonsense. He will sort this unholy mess out. Matrice is behind everything, he'll see that."

Horyk placed a consoling hand on Rald's shoulder. "I'm sorry. Rumour says Lord Henry has already bent the knee to your sister."

"You do not know my uncle. He would not. Never." Rald shook his head in disbelief. "Get me to him, Horyk. Chiguar. Once I speak with him, Lord Henry will see through whatever lies Matrice has spun."

"No more of that talk, you are Rald now. Nothing else." Marn's voice was stern. "Did you think your uncle came for you? He brought his Blackcoats to stake his claim for the Kingdom Throne. Only it seems he underestimated Matrice, as we all have. Present yourself to Lord Henry and you'll seal your death, else become a pawn for him to use. No, I will get you to the Duncan as I was charged by Lord Renix. The Duncan at least is a man of honour; your best path lies with him."

"How? You can't even get me out of Kingsholme." Rald's voice grated.

Chiguar's brow furrowed. "The three gates might be closed but there are other ways. Clandestine ways. Unfortunately, all are watched and our escape needs meticulous planning if we are to avoid the watchers."

"The Gates will open soon enough," Marn said. "Else the streets will erupt in violence. Then will be our best chance."

Tomas returned to his vigil by the window. This was not the first such conversation on this topic.

"They will get you killed if you're not careful." O'si's voice whispered in his ear making him shiver. Tomas scowled, the sháadretarch's words echoed his thoughts but he was unable to respond without drawing attention.

"It's only a matter of time. Thrice you have moved. The noose tightens each time," O'si hissed.

Something caught his eye on the street. A man. He ambled slowly in the traffic, head scanning left and right. He looked for something, a shop maybe or a person. It was not unusual in and of itself but there was a belligerence in the way he walked; as if he owned the street, reinforced by the way people flowed around him. Most telling of all though were the street rats. He'd spied a few. Having been one himself the young hustlers were easy enough to spot. Only now they'd vanished, melting down alleyways or hiding in the shadows. The man was acozi, a made man, no doubt about it.

O'si left off his needling, "Trouble? I sense no gifted. I will go look."

The man's back was to him, thirty yards up the lane but Tomas fancied he knew him. The acozi turned suddenly and in two strides made the far side where a blind beggar sat propped against a wall. The beggar nodded and the man twisted and peered back and up. Tomas resisted the urge to move, movement drew the eye. Hidden from view by the shutter, barring an arrow strip of light, the man could not possibly see him. Despite that, the acozi's gaze paused for the briefest of moments before brushing past. A cold dread settled in Tomas's chest and trickled down his spine to his bladder. He needed a piss.

The man dropped a copper into the begging pot, then rose and stalked off. His head no longer searching, he had found what he sought.

The blind man jumped suddenly and gave a strangled screech immediately shaking his head as if to clear it.

Bloody, O'si. Tomas inched the shutter closed and turned to the room.

"Who is O'si?" Marn demanded.

Bloody hells and damnation, had he spoken the name out loud?

"No one. It's just an expression," Tomas said, then rushed. "We have to go. We've been made."

Chiguar brushed by Tomas, cracked the shutter and peered at the street below. "We weren't followed. Are you sure, lad?"

The faintest of drafts fluttered the back of Tomas's neck. It was no breeze from the window, O'si was back. "I'm sure."

"The blind man can see," O'si's whispered in his ear and Tomas rolled his eyes.

Chiguar misconstrued the gesture. "It may be obvious to you, but I see nothing untoward."

"See the blind man thirty strides up on the left?" Tomas said, waiting for Chiguar to find him.

"Yes, I have him."

"Well, he's no more blind than Rald is mute. He's an Eye for the syndicate. Knows who belongs on the street and who don't. He sees you once, maybe you're passing through, twice you'll have his interest, three times you're marked. He just fingered us ta Rooq, an acozi."

"This Rooq, one of your crim friends?" Rald taunted. "And what in hells is a cosy?"

"A-co-zi, an enforcer for the syndicate, a made man. So yeah, he's a criminal but no friend. Trust me, on the streets, ya don't want no acozi knowin' ya. I see'd him afore but only ta avoid."

Chiguar cursed, then glanced at Marn. "We're running out of safe houses. Each time we move it's a risk."

Marn shrugged, "Can't be helped. I have Arran scouting for more, but I don't know when he'll be back. There's Red Lotus?"

"That's Mornside, a long walk with people hunting you," Chiguar said.

"We've no choice," Marn argued.

"I know a place, maybe," Tomas interjected. "These are my streets, knows 'em betta than my own face. It'll be tricky though and we're best gone when it's dark."

"No doubt some rat-infested cellar," Rald said. "Think I'd rather die." The room ignored him.

"Night falls in an hour. You reckon we've time to wait?" Chiguar asked.

Tomas nodded. "They'll be lotsa Eyes informing, all wanting to make a kern or two. Bet there's a dozen like that 'blind' man all spinning Rooq and the other acozis a yarn. He'll tell the Targus and they'll check it out but it might be we're safe a bit yet."

"You've no idea have you, boy?" Rald snapped. "They could be coming for us as we speak, and you want us to sit here and wait."

"You'd rather die, so what's it to you? Go, for all I care." Tomas was sick of the whining fuck.

"He will get you killed."

"Rald, hush now." Chiguar's words were softly spoken but his tone made it clear it was an order. He turned to Tomas. "There's a curfew. Moving so many at night is too dangerous, we can't risk it."

"Need ta. This place is close but the best way in is by rooftop. I'll take Marn and Rald one at a time. But not Horyk nor you. At least not from here, yaz too big."

"How close?" Chiguar didn't flinch at the exclusion.

"Eeling Lane off Skel Street. Look fer a burnt tenement. It was took by fire last winter and boarded up but it's still standing, mostly. People with nought to their name live there."

Chiguar lifted an eyebrow in question. "Hardly secure, don't you think?"

Tomas shrugged. "There ain't time fer this Red Lotus place if'n it's in Mornside. Besides, most 'a the second floor is gone, stairs up too. But half the third floor remains, mostly. We take the roof, slip in from above none'll be the wiser, if'n we stay quiet." His eyes travelled to Rald then back before continuing.

"Those with nought get in round the back, loose board on one of the shutters. Reckon you and Horyk will be just another pair'a down and outs. No one's looking fer a black man or a pale giant."

"If that Eye made us they'll be looking," Chiguar said. He looked across at Marn and some silent interchange passed between them for after a time she gave a nod.

Chiguar turned back to Tomas. "Let's talk."

* * *

Luck for once was with them. The broken cloud in the night sky curtailed the light of the moons but allowed enough through for Tomas to see by. Almost perfect for thieving.

He could hear Marn breathing beside him. She had a wiry strength to her that he recognised but running the thieves' highway required a different kind of fitness and exacted a different toll on the mind and body. As he had struggled to spar with Herald, so Marn struggled to sneak. Still, she had managed at least to keep up, he doubted Rald would prove as proficient.

Tomas closed his eyes and listened, tuning out Marn's laboured breaths to the sounds of the city. It was so familiar; Kingsholme was like a beast with a heartbeat all its own. The beast slumbered but even in sleep, it spoke to him.

The breeze sighed its melancholy as it channelled between buildings and swirled at street corners, as erratic as a raindrop drifting on a pane of glass. It carried sound with it and the malodorous, everyday city stink that settled unnoticed in his psyche. Nothing untoward.

He opened his eyes and stared across the narrow gap at the soot smoked roof opposite. It was only three paces wide and the distance of no concern. What was though, was the landing. The roof was charred and broken in parts. How solid was it? Could it support his weight should he leap? The night offered no chance to survey it in detail and now faced with it, he felt his unspoken bravado sitting heavy on his shoulders.

"Want me to go first?" Marn whispered.

Tomas jumped, soaring over the space, cushioning his landing with instinctive ease on tiles that crackled underfoot but did not break.

"Wait," Tomas hissed over his shoulder, before shuffling along the roof to a chimney stack, testing the roof tension underfoot as he went, searching for weakness.

At the chimney, he turned and whispered to the night. "Clear."

The thump as Marn landed seemed overtly loud to Tomas. He held his breath, eyes searching the darkness, ears tuned for any discordance. Her flustered pant was almost as loud as the scrabble of her feet as she moved towards him.

"Shh."

Tomas didn't wait for her acknowledgement looping a rope around the stack and cinching it tight before tracking carefully along the roof to a blackened hole.

A loose tile broke and fell into the rent and crashed to the level below. Tomas grimaced at the sound but at least there was a floor. He lowered the rope over the edge and waited until Marn pressed up behind him.

"Take the rope, climb down and wait." His whispered command barely carried but she leaned in close until her breath tickled his ear.

"Give this to Chiguar before you return with Rald." Marn pressed something into his hand, a piece of cloth. He shrugged and tucked it into his belt.

Grabbing the rope, Marn inched by, then reversed and using the spur the fallen tile had rested upon to brace against, lifted herself over the yawn before swinging down, submerging into the inky depths of the building.

The rope twined as it swung back and forth until it stopped abruptly and went slack. Straining, Tomas could hear movement. Marn was safely down. Without a word, he headed back the way they had come. The air was turning colder and care was needed to place his feet correctly before jumping the gap.

"Do we have to go back for that annoying little Garumbat?" O'si's voice whispered from the night. "I have spoken to P'uk and he agrees with me. We should leave, that whiny puke is gonna get you all killed."

"Tell P'uk ta tell me hisself, if he ever deigns ta show his face." Tomas touched a hand to his chest and the hidden falcon. "Nah. I'll get his precious Highness out if I can. It's what Lord Renix wanted. Besides, Chiguar has my pack and the book."

"Renix is dead and wants for nothing," O'si growled. "That token you touch is our ticket to Tankrit. Get the book with the prince. Should he happen to 'fall' to his doom that would be tragic but hardly your fault."

"As appealin' as it sounds, I ain't never murderized no one afore. I ain't startin' now."

O'si rumbled his displeasure. "The prince is a liability. To us and your Nine Kingdoms. Killing him would save many lives."

"Like our own ya mean."

O'si snorted. "Your death might prove annoying, but I will survive whatever befalls you, human. Just remember our pact. The book will open a way to Sházarch but we need aether, lots of it to power the portal, and symbols of power to control and stabilise it. These are best found in Tankrit or the Enclave. Choose one."

"You and P'uk have been trapped hundreds of years in this ring and bracer." Tomas held up his left arm as he spoke. By some magic, only he appeared able to see them. "You keen ta return and face hundreds more? Not me, the Enclave means certain death. Told ya, I ain't goin' there."

O'si swirled before him, an insubstantial veil in a clouded night. "Time and space have a different meaning in our world, Tomas. Two hundred years is but a blink of an eye. If it must be Tankrit then we do not need the prince. He is a burden. Cut him loose or I will find a way."

Tomas leapt another chasm, his feet finding silent purchase. "I was a burden. To Lord Renix. He saved me. So, help me or go hide in your dimensal ring."

"It's dimensional, fool. But fine. When this bites your arse don't come moaning to me about it. I've got a hundred ways of telling you I told you so and I will use all of them."

The veil swirled and was gone leaving blessed silence.

Tomas moved quickly, revelling in the freedom of the rooftops. Above stretched the vastness of the cosmos; impossible, unknowable, pure and he an inconsequential speck. And below lay the noise and filth of the city. That he, Tomas, strode this purgatory was a balm he didn't understand. Didn't need to. Up here, treading that space between worlds he just was.

He landed on the roof and scuttled to the tiles dislodged earlier. They had been loosely returned and he pulled them easily aside before sliding through the rafters and struts to the loft space below. He crawled the short distance to the hole created in the ceiling boards and called softly. "It is I."

"It is I," Tasso Chiguar echoed the all-clear.

Tomas waited. There was silence below when there should not be. Rald was meant to get boosted through the hole to join him. He laid a hand on the knife Renix had gifted him.

"Do you have something, Tomas?" Chiguar prompted.

Tomas scrunched his face at what he could mean, then recalled and reached for the cloth on his belt given by Marn. He dropped it through the hole. Clever, he mused, the Tassos did not trust him. First, Chiguars insistence the book remain behind, now Marn with her little tell.

A grunt of exclamation, then voices. Horyk whispering so loud he may as well have just spoken the words. "Stay safe, my prince. I will be right below."

Tomas could tell from Rald's muffled response he was nervous. Moments later the prince's head appeared, hands grasping at the tie beam as he pulled himself up and through.

"Now my book." Tomas lent through the hole and reached out. Horyk, loomed beneath, face creased with worry. He held a pack out but did not release it when Tomas gripped it.

"See him safe, Tomas, or I will see to you."

With a jerk, the bag was released, and Tomas snatched it through the gap. He felt his book through the material, its weight and dimensions familiar. He gave a satisfied grunt before swinging the pack over his shoulders and beneath the cloak he wore. In his life, only Sparrow and Renix had believed in him. Maybe the others were right to distrust him, for both were dead and gone. Disgruntled at his turn of thought, he looked at Rald.

"Do not speak. Step where I step. Jump where I jump an' ya might live." Tomas spun away, crawled to the hole in the roof and adroitly disappeared through it.

Rald followed, making rather less noise than expected. *Bet he's pissin' hisself*, Tomas consoled himself, moving along to the jump point for the neighbouring building. He took a fast pace and leapt, landing in a deadened crouch. He moved away before twisting to watch Rald.

He seemed to wait an age. The huddled lump of the prince was as still as the stone stack of the chimney behind until eventually, Tomas's patience ran out. With a step he jumped back, landing beside Rald who jolted in fright and promptly sat back against the roof.

"Ain't got all night. What's wrong with ya?" Tomas breathed.

Rald stared back, then, in muted tones. "Can't see shit but that drop. Don't think I can do it."

Tomas had heard of this. Sparrow, for all he'd named her after a bird, didn't like the rooftops, it scared her silly. But she was younger than him and Rald a grown man. He sniffed.

"You jumped puddles afore?"

"What?"

"When ya was young? Ya jumped puddles?" Tomas asked. "Just thinka that drop like a puddle only it's four paces wide. Steady ya feet, take a step back, a quicken forward and jump. Don't land in the puddle. Watch."

Rald squinted at the umbrous shape beside him as it swayed back then surged forward and sprang into the night. It was followed by a soft chink as the boy landed on the roof opposite. Fear coursed his veins and he shivered as it warred with his resolve.

"Want me ta comes an hold yer 'and." The words ghosted out of the night. *Cheeky little gobshite*. But Herald's indignation was enough to bolster his pride and before it could fade, he swung back then forwards, planted his foot and soared. His breath exploded as he landed with a loud, jarring crunch. His knees buckled and cracked against the tiles as he fell to his hands. He'd made it. A heady blend of triumph and exhilaration filled him. He'd never done anything so reckless.

"Ya cleared it easy. Next time, try not ta make such a damn racket, eh." Tomas moved off, following the line of the roof ridge.

The journey across the rooftops took far too long for Tomas's liking. At each jump, the prince had to bolster his courage and 'his Highness' made far too much noise. The final leap to the fire-ravaged tenement brought a sense of relief. So focused was he on Rald getting across and to safety that Tomas didn't sense the ghost as it glided out from behind the chimney stack. Nor did he hear the snick as the rope tied earlier was cut.

Rald landed with a grunt. A tile snapped from beneath his right foot and skittered into darkness, sending him scrambling and clutching in fear as his leg went with it. He felt a steadying hand grip his cloak then heave, helping to drag him to safety.

The roof groaned and trembled beneath him and Rald shuffled in fright toward the chimney stack, unmindful of the dark shade that stood immobile beside it. Not until it moved did he start, but by then it was too late.

His head snapped back, light exploding behind his eyes. Rald swayed, then collapsed to all fours as the light flares faded to black. Ears humming, face throbbing with a numb pain, he choked on blood which gushed from somewhere but his mind was a fugue. Then, eyes shivering, he passed out.

The shade stepped over the inert body and paused, glancing down in study before its head swivelled and fixated on the boy.

Tomas rolled to the side, gained his feet and shuffled around, moving higher up the roof, closer to the hole Marn had descended earlier. If the Order woman was still alive, maybe she could help, though she would be easy prey for the shadow should she try to climb the rope.

As if reading his intent, the silhouette slid, just two steps but enough to block him. Ankor appeared through a gap in the clouds, lifting the night. The figure it revealed was dark and slender and moved with an oily smoothness that reminded Tomas of the snakes in the dockside gaming dens, great hooded things that swayed as if to mesmerise their prey.

Tomas sensed the strike too late but slid his head enough that the blow glanced off the side of his skull. It sent him reeling back and to his knees.

"The Prince and the Mouse. Two little rodents when hunting one. Lucky me. The Targus will shit his britches when I bring you both in."

Her words bought time for his head to clear. The shadow was a woman, the accent that of the western isles. A dread feeling knotted his stomach, a nauseous suspicion of who she might be. He had heard the stories.

Tomas lurched to his right, instinctively knowing he had little but speed and his small size to his advantage. If he could lure her to where the roof was tenuous, maybe it would unbalance her. Else he could run and escape, there was no one faster than him on the thieves highway. He had the book. It was him or the prince, she could not chase both.

"*Yes, go.*"

A stinging slap sent Tomas tumbling to his back, leaving the side of his face smarting and eyes watering. He hadn't seen her move.

"We were having a conversation. That's a teeny bit rude don't you think, little Mouse."

"*Schyostrakor. Concentrate on your bracer and say it.*" O'si's hiss was desperate. Without thinking twice, Tomas responded.

"Schyostrakor."

The ghost leant in. "You say summat? Can't keep up with all that street lingo you kids use, swear it changes every week, but it sounded like you were cussing me. I don't much like folk cussing me."

"Moan, Tomas." The voice was different somehow. It was not O'si that spoke. That commanded.

"P'uk?"

"Fuck indeed. See that one I know." The shadow chuckled and waggled her blade at him. "You know, you've been a bad little Mouse. Bortillo is very put out fer you not dying when ya should, and, leading him a merry dance to boot."

Her voice lowered conspiratorially. "Secretly, between you and me and despite everything, I think he was rather impressed by you, Mouse. Still, orders is orders and dead is dead. As my old slaver was wont to say, there's no use crying over spilt blood. But I want you to know, your death will pay the debt I owe so I'm grateful. An' for that, I'll make it quick."

A glint of moonbeam struck steel as she stepped in close.

"Moan, or die." Came the voice. A sense of something other manifested before him. He could not see nor feel it but it was there.

"Ugghh." It was pathetic but as the sound passed his lips the air shimmered and vibrated before him.

The snake paused.

"Again. Louder."

"Arrgh." The vibration rose so that his hair tousled and skin prickled.

In a blink, the assassin sprang away but a pulse of something rushed out and struck, propelling the shadow woman up and away, tumbling her like a leaf in a storm. It sent her clattering against the tiles before the rent in the roof swallowed her whole. As if the building cleared its throat, there was a crump of impact from below.

In the city, dogs yowled, an echoing cacophony followed by the bark of their owners. Tomas gathered his feet and, stumbling to the edge of the hole, glanced down. He could see nothing but sensed movement.

"Tomas?" Marn called. "Bless Keeper you're alive. The rope was cut. I couldn't get up."

"Is she dead?" Tomas whispered.

"She breathes but is unresponsive. I'm using the rope to secure her, but I think it better I should kill her."

A groan from behind set his nerves jangling and he spun. The prince lay flat out on the roof, a hand to his head. Tomas quickly moved to his side. They needed to get undercover, one hunter could mean more.

"U'm bleedin. 'Ed's kullun. Argghh, Saunt's suk," Rald moaned then howled as Tomas gathered a handful of tunic and pulled him upright.

"Shh," Tomas hissed. "Might be more a them devils out here."

Rald held his head, then touched fingers to his nose and whimpered. "Whut 'appun?"

Tomas thought furiously. How could he account for events, none would think him capable of defeating a hunter. Especially if the said hunter was who he thought she was. "Don't cha remember the assassin? Ya saved me. Saved us I mean."

"Noo, jus a gost. Paun t'en nuddin'."

"Well, that ghost hit you good then turned on me. I was a goner. Only ya rose like a kami as if Kildare's wrath was burning inside ya. Ne'er see'd nought like it. Her blade was reaching fer me throat when ya sent her spinning down below. Saved me life."

"Good, but too much elaboration. A lie is best kept short and simple." O'si whispered.

"Oy dud?"

"Yeah, ya did." Reaching out, Tomas patted him on the arm. "I owes ya one. Now let's get off this roof, eh? Before any more assassins show up."

The talk of assassins proved more than sufficient to get Rald moving. Marn tied the woman with the rope and what was left of it after was insufficient to reach the chimney works as it had before. Instead, with Rald holding his legs, Tomas leant over the hole and tied a hitching knot to a roof strut.

It was like descending into the pitch-black maw of the nether hells, Tomas thought as he lowered himself down. The charred smell grew strong in the enclosed space, the air filled with it. Above him, was the grey disk of the rent and in it, a single star from the heavens beckoned to him.

"There are no windows. We are in some sort of storage room far as I can tell," Marn whispered. "The floorboards stink of smoke but are untouched by flame damage."

"A door?" Tomas asked.

"There's a trap in the floor but it has warped and is stuck in its frame. It would be safe to light a candle I think?"

Tomas nodded, "I guess."

But for a soft moaning, Rald was silent. Sparks blinked into being as Marn struck a flint but died as quickly as they appeared. She struck again, then again until one of the sparks settled and smouldered on a piece of lighting cloth. Blowing on it, the glow turned to flame from which a candle was lit.

The light was harsh in the darkness and Tomas blinked his eyes to adjust. The candle's radiance was weak but extended enough to reveal the greyed walls of their cell.

Rald was a beaten mess. His nose looked broken and blood coated his mouth and chin and blotched the front of his tunic. The prince stared at the blood on his hands, as if traumatized by it, eyes sparkling in the candlelight. *It's not as bad as it looks*, Tomas thought, switching his attention to the ghost.

Marn had moved to the body and was checking the bindings. Satisfied it seemed, Tomas watched as she rolled the woman over onto her back and lowered the hood of her cloak. It revealed black hair and dark skin which only added further to his unease. He found he couldn't take his eyes from her. She was younger than he imagined from the tales he'd heard. Prettier too than she ought to be for someone in her trade.

"You look uncomfortable. You know her?" Marn asked.

"Not exactly. She's a hunter for the Targus. There are a few assassins that are women but only one from the Western Isles. It's said if she hunts you, you don't know it until she whispers her name as she slits ya throat." Tomas glanced up from his study, sure of it. A chill tingled his skin.

"That's Murder."

Chapter 18: We Are The Grim

The Grim Marsh, The Rivers

It was dark and surprisingly warm in the witch's drying shed. Airing plants hung suspended from wooden beams and were tied to hemp lines that crisscrossed the small space. It left precious little room for Tom but he liked it well enough. It smelled of wildflowers and herbs of a hundred varieties; the potpourri much more pleasant than the waft of swamp and the close press of grimmers that he'd grown accustomed to over the years. So much so that he'd become inured to it, only now, with his sense of smell liberated, the ripeness of the Grimhold assaulted his nostrils afresh each time he left the shed.

The witch had even provided a cot with blankets and a stuffed sackcloth for a pillow. At night, alone but for the perfume of the shed and stridulation of the marsh crickets, Tom felt as much at peace as he ever had.

As usual, his thoughts drifted to Wraith. Since coming to Hett's cottage and finding Wraith sitting and responsive, three days had passed. Each had seen a marked change in her bearing. She lived still with Hett who attended to her basic needs, but twice daily he was called upon to feed her aether and she hungered for it, always greedy for more.

The only word she spoke was his name and only when he was there. Wraith could now walk unaided and followed Hett and Tom whenever they were in the cottage, watching every action, black eyes constantly roving. She was smart, Tom knew she was learning, taking everything in and working it out for herself. Strong too. Last evening, he'd split a harknut with a cracker and popped the salty nut-meat into his mouth. When Wraith had picked another out of the bowl, he had proffered the cracker but instead, she squeezed the fibrous shell between finger and thumb, cracking it and mashing the kernel to a pulp. He remembered laughing when she licked her fingers clean of the mulch, only to screw her face up and stick her tongue out at the taste, wiping at it in disgust. He couldn't recall the last time he'd laughed so freely and when Wraith had stared at him strangely with her head canted to one side, it had only made him laugh all the harder.

A rapping battered the door to the shed jerking Tom from his thoughts. Usually, he could hear someone approaching.

Hett's deep croak was muffled by the wall. "You're late. Black Jack sent word he'll be coming so get up and feed Wraith, she's unsettled and buggin' the seven hells outta me. No doubt that dark-hearted bastard'll want to see her." The crunch of footsteps signalled Hett wasn't waiting around.

Tom's heart sank at the news and a shiver tremored his whole body. Since his almost-death, Tom had avoided Jackson Tullock, Lord of the Grimhold. His father. A task made easy since Black Jack had been gone these past three days. Now, it seemed, he was back.

Dressing quickly, Tom pulled his boots on and laced them tight. Hitching his cloak about his shoulders he left his sanctuary. A quick dunk of his head in the water butt to wake himself up, wash his face and slick his hair back left him gasping and hopping from one foot to another.

The guards stationed outside the Apothecary watched him in amusement. Egg's teeth gleamed and his bald crown glinted in the sunlight. The other, Sunny Mordrunski, was a dour fellow whose sad bent was cracked in a momentary scowl of pleasure.

Tom wiped the water from his eyes. The two guarded Lord Sandford. Tom had not seen it himself but he'd heard enough about what had happened to Millie Grainne. How her tiny, blood-spilt body was found draped over Sandford who lay asleep as if resting after a fulsome meal. She was a child, an innocent and what she'd endured consumed him whenever his mind strayed to either of them.

As with previous mornings, Tom called out. "How's his Lordship doin'?" To his eternal disappointment, the answer was the same.

"Alive and happy as Sunny here." Egg cocked a thumb at Mordrunski who frowned.

Tom nodded and gave a short smile as if amused. Egg had made the same jest yester-morn but it didn't seem to bother the man. Walking the path to Hett's cottage, Tom rapped his knuckles against the door and waited for the muffled 'enter' before pulling it wide.

Wraith awaited on the other side, her body quivering with excitement. She pawed at him and growled his name, "Toom."

"Good morn, Wraith." Tom captured her hand and led her back across the room to sit by the fire. "You're eager today. I hope you've been behaving yaself." He looked around for Hett but she was gone from the room.

"Hett!"

A terse response rattled from the backroom. "I'll be out."

Tom grinned at Wraith, "She sounds mad. You bin winding her up again?"

Wraith leered a smile that twisted her mouth, deforming the black stain of her lips and rippling the moko'd tendrils on her face so that they seemed almost alive. The first time she attempted to smile, Tom had about wet himself in fear but he'd grown accustomed to it. Sort of. The hand gripping his was tight and starting to pinch.

"Ow, just relax your grip a little," Tom instructed, but instead it tightened and the pain intensified.

"I said stop it," Tom hissed and pulled his hand free. He shook it vigorously flexing his fingers. Wraith's distorted face snapped to its neutral, lifeless position.

"I'm trying to help and you need to learn, fast. So please listen. I know you understand me." A lie, Tom didn't know any such thing but what else could he do? "This is a bad place for people like us. You need to understand that and how things work around here or you will get hurt and I don't want you to get hurt."

He stretched his hand out again, captured hers and gave it a gentle squeeze. "See, that is how you do it. That is good." Wraith's soulless eyes peered back, her thoughts unfathomable.

"People like us?" Hett rumbled from behind.

Tom startled, the old witch had a habit of sneaking up on him. "I meant different, we're both oddities. People pick on what's different, that's all."

Hett dumped something at his feet making him jump again. He looked at it unsure at first what it was. Then sat abruptly back. Knowing but asking anyway. "What the hells are they?"

"Rats my boy. Desiccated rats. Nought but skin, bone and tail. Seems Wraith here has been snacking on them."

Tom looked closely. The rats appeared wrung out and dried up but whole. "They don't look chewed on?" Tom challenged. He yelped as the back of his head was clipped. Wraith's head swivelled and fixated on Hett, black eyes unblinking.

"Don't be a fool. The sustenance she craves is aether. Wraith here has suckled the life force out of them. A damn hard thing to do to a living creature, with a mind and a will all its own. Damn hard, yet there they lie."

"Maybe I need to feed her more?" Tom rubbed his scalp.

Hett's jowls wobbled. "Don't think it matters. Wraith craves aether like a Knorcha addict does weed. Still, best you do so before Black Jack gets here, eh. We'll have ta figure this out later."

At Hett's gesture, Tom cupped his hands. As soon as he did so, Wraith's gaze settled back on him.

"Close your eyes, Wraith," Tom prompted. He smiled when she complied, the darkened shells of her eyelids hiding her soulless gaze. Reciprocating, Tom pulled on the energy around him. The cloud-like aether was a riot of colour and ebbed all around. He could sense white blooms and knew them for life. Hett's large and close; then hazier, further away what he presumed were Egg and Sunny Mordrunski and another, the splash of this last tainted by shadow. Lord Sandford, Tom thought, in no doubt that the taint was his stained soul.

Concentrating once more on the clouds of aether, Tom willed energy into his cupped palms and it came, slowly gathering and coalescing. It was so much easier than before, his control almost without effort. In his mind's eye, a ball crackled and pulsed in his cupped palms. Then, with a snap-hiss it was gone, accompanied by an ecstatic moan.

Opening his eyes, Tom found Wraith rocking backwards and forwards. Her eyes were open and fastened on his and Tom was drawn to them. It was like staring into an abyss and he felt himself leaning inwards.

"I hear voices outside." Hett broke the spell. "Come on, let's meet them. Bring Wraith. I don't want that fucker sullying my doorstep."

Rising, Tom urged Wraith to follow. Outside, Black Jack was talking boisterously with Egg and Sunny but stopped as soon as they appeared. He waved them forward, his face eager.

"You fixed her, Hett? She's walking," Black Jack said. "I knew you could do it."

"Not completely," Hett grumbled. "She can walk but not talk and is havin' ta learn everything like a newborn. I'm not even sure she is all there. I need more time."

Black Jack scowled, "Don't push it, witch. You've had time enough. I'll teach her what needs to be taught."

Tom felt his hands balling.

"An' what's my bastard doin' here? Bit young for your wrinkled old cunt." Black Jack laughed then stopped, the mirth in his eyes draining as they darted to Wraith then Tom. His lips pursed.

Hett ignored the slight. "I'm tired Jackson. I gave the lad a roof when Sayzan kicked him out. Seemed right since he already gathers the herbs and plants I need, only now he sorts out my woodpile and does the chores these knarled hands and tired feet struggle with. I'm keeping him else ya ken find yourself another physiker."

Black Jack barked. "Think I give two shits? He's tougher than he looks but he is weak," he tapped a hard finger to his skull, "up here where it counts, he's soft as curd. So you keep him. But she's coming with me. Now."

Tom could see Hett's shoulders go back, her face wrinkling in disapproval and feared she would say something. Black Jack looked calm but Tom had taken enough beatings to recognise the gleam of eye and twitch of frame that promised violence. But then, he couldn't just let Wraith go. If she left he would not see her. At least not like this, not like he had been. She would become Black Jack's toy, a plaything. The memory of that night out in the marsh. The things Black Jack had done to her. Tom had blocked it from his mind but they were not forgotten, merely repressed and they came screaming to the fore. She had been near death then, what would she have to endure now that she was whole?

"You look like you want to say something. Do you want to say something?"

Tom blinked, the menace unmistakable but Black Jack's question was directed elsewhere and the pounding in his chest eased a fraction.

Hett stepped back. "Take her. But don't say as I didn't warn you, Jackson Tullock."

"Age and wisdom. You've got them both ya old sow. Cause I know you'd defy me if ya could. Well, don't you worry none. I'll take good care of her." Walking forwards, he grasped Wraith by the arm who looked at Tom.

Tom's heart sank like a stone into his stomach. He panted, his breath clipped and short as though the air he dragged into his lungs was sucked through a blanket. He could do nothing. Knew if a word was said that Black Jack would end him for real. The coward in him quaked and trembled. The only defiance he could muster was to say nothing. Tom averted his gaze, not wanting Wraith to read the shame in his eyes.

It didn't matter. Wraith's look had not gone unnoticed and Black Jack stepped in and balled a fist into Tom's gut dropping him to the dirt. "I don't want you looking at her. Got me, boy?"

Tom gaped like a landed fish struggling for air. Eyes watering, he coughed and gave a tiny nod in return, aware all the while of Wraith stood watching. Her tongue darted out, moistening black lips before slithering out of sight. Then she was gone. Black Jack dragging her pliantly behind him.

With a groan, Tom drew a ragged breath, slowly gathered his feet and stood. "I hate…"

Hett stamped hard on Tom's foot and he yelped, "Shut ya damn trap. Go wait inside."

Tom loathed her. The witch was no better than the rest and he glared his hatred at her.

With a sniff of disdain and shake of her head, Hett walked away leaving Tom stood alone with his hate and anger and shame.

* * *

Black Jack was pleased with his prize. His body was charged with an ecstasy he'd never felt before. There was a bestial wildness to her that sang to his soul and his loins stirred every time he looked at her.

Wraith, her name whispered in his mind. It was right. The witch had chosen well for it matched her perfectly.

She was sat in his room on a chair by the fire, head pivoting to follow his every movement, black eyes absorbing her new surroundings. She had tried to wander off when first he had released her, shuffling for the door and ignoring his commands when he called her back. Now, a chain snaked on the floor between ankle and wall, chinking whenever she moved, which was infrequent.

Wraith would learn soon enough, he thought.

Earlier, walking her back to the Grimhold, people had stopped and stared, whispering behind their hands and he'd been filled with a blinding rage. Wraith had been dressed in one of the witches old shift's which was barely adequate. It hung from one shoulder, too wide for her shapely frame but also too short, exposing thigh and knee and revealing pale flesh marbled with black veins.

"What the fuck you looking at," He'd snarled when Jessop made no effort to hide his intrigue. At his simmering threat, Jessop sneered but held his hands up and backed away.

"Just looking, chief."

Torn between gutting Jessop and covering Wraith up, he'd eventually dragged his cloak off and slung it about her shoulders, wrapping her tightly and hiding what he could.

Weak gets ya dead, his Da's words came to him like an omen. Staring at Wraith as she sat, silent but watchful, Black Jack knew she was his weakness. A weakness others would seek to abuse, he didn't need a stone-reader to tell him that. Torgrid and Jessop, deviant shits that they were, would be ruthless enough to exploit anything if they could. That they loathed one another had always mitigated their threat to an extent and it had been something he'd fomented over the years. But this. This changed things. Like wild dogs tracking wounded prey, they would sniff that weakness on him.

After a while, Black Jack rose and crossed to Wraith and stood a moment looking down at her. Cupping her cheek in a callused hand, he tilted her head and stared into the blacks of her eyes and felt complete. "I'll be back soon, my love. And I'll bring ya something better to wear than these rags, eh."

He left her, locking the door behind and made his way down the ruined staircase to the ground floor. He crossed the open space of the central keep, scattered with the refuse of the men who made it their home. He called for them to follow.

Outside, he issued orders for a gathering then sent a dozen men to the Holes and a further hand to the Apothecary. Black Jack waited, steel-blue eyes reading his people as they slowly assembled. On one side of the impromptu gathering stood Torgrid and his lackeys with Jessop occupying the opposite. Both watching with guarded interest to see what was up.

A distant clack of chains echoed, accompanied by a pitiful moaning which grew louder, rising it seemed to meet the murmur of the crowd. Black Jack turned as the shambling wreck that was Lord Jacob Bouchemeax appeared from the Keep. Ashen-skinned, eyes glassy with fatigue he was bent double, limbs seizing with cramp. Black Jack sneered. A broken man. A mere shadow of the one he was when first he set foot upon the Grimhold. Well, he was a Lord no more. Just a wretch.

His eyes moved past Bouchemeax to the remnant of the man that followed. Black Jack could not recall his name if he had ever known it. It was enough that he was a Black Crow. Tall and rangy when he went into the Hole, he'd left it stumbling and crooked, no taller than the witch.

Black Jack's face creased, his mouth twisting in contempt. Ten days in the Hole was all it had taken to reduce them to this, to half men.

The third man shuffled into view and Black Jack felt his jaw clench and the sneer leech from his face. Ned Tullock, his half brother, who had forsaken their father's name for Wynter. The play on the name was not lost on him either. Winter being a cursed name from ancient days given to the unwanted. Days, when ice and snow took their toll and surviving the wilds was a trial of heart and bone. It was a time when brutal choices had to be made and cruel decisions taken. Where Winter's children were left abandoned so the rest might survive. Hard days in a harsh land from an unforgiving time. It was an apt name for his brother.

Like the two that came before him, Ned Wynter was a mess. Crooked as a hark tree he moved with arthritic precision, each step carefully placed. It must have pained him greatly, yet his face held a dogged determination. Bowed maybe but he was unbroken.

Returning his attention to the gathering, Black Jack scanned the crowd, his eyes drawn to a ripple of disturbance as it parted for the five he'd sent to the Apothecary. They escorted Egg and Sunny who in turn each lead a man, roped and bound. The squat troll-like Hett followed after with Sofia Grainne at her side, slack faced and moving with limp indifference. Behind them, his bastard.

Black Jack felt his blood thicken, malice pulsing behind his eyes. The boy's blonde hair did not match his dark; was weak where he was strong, soft to his hard. To have produced something so... pitiful. Surely Sayzan must have lain with another. Tom could be no son of his. Of course, she denied it and in his heart he knew it was so however he might pretend it otherwise. Not for the first time, he wished he'd ended the boy. He was unwanted, a Winter's child. The thought inflamed him and his mind whirred in sudden cogitation. Then, he smiled.

Holding his hands high, Black Jack waited whilst the murmur of the crowd settled, the sounds of the never-silent marsh seemingly loud in their stillness. They were not many, his people. Three hundred and fifty souls give or take of which little more than two hundred stood before him now. The rest were foraging or away patrolling their borders.

"We are the Grim and the Grim is us." His voice carried easily the familiar maxim. "Each day the Grim seeks our death yet always we triumph, taking instead what we need to survive. The Grim is a hard master but it has taught us, tempered us. Made us resilient. Made us who we are. We are the Grim and the Grim is us."

The words hung heavy in the air and Black Jack knew if he hadn't their full attention before that he had it now.

"I have kept you safe, kept us strong all these years but times have changed and we must change with it. It is not enough any more to merely survive. War is here and the lands around us burn. Urak, foul beasts that hunger for our flesh, roam the Rivers. They will seek us out. Not now nor tomorrow but soon enough. When they do we must be ready. We must learn how best to kill them. How best to take from them that which we need to make ourselves stronger. We must make them fear us. Fear the Grim."

The large belching cry of a boamer echoed in the empty-space his voice vacated and was answered by another.

Black Jacks teeth flashed "See. The Grim agrees with me." His quip drew a ripple of laughter from his audience but it was nervous, a release for the pent-up dread that settled like a shroud over many of them. Black Jack raised his voice again.

"I know many of you fear me, think me brutal and well you should, for I am that and much worse. But it is not without purpose. In the Grim, only the hard survive. In the Grim weakness means death and I will not allow it. I am Lord here. I am life and I am death."

The ringing of his voice faded away and he walked a slow circuit on the ground, his men scattering from his path like fallen leaves in a sudden gust. An agitated murmur rose then hushed when the Grimlord's rabid eyes swept them. Held them.

"Any who would gainsay me threatens all." The words were softly spoken but the intimidation no less for the volume. "It creates division and what divides us makes us weak. Weakness, I will not tolerate. So I will ask, here and now. If any wish to defy me stake your claim and let's be done with it. We will decide this the old way. With knife and rope."

Black Jack paused, his head navigating the crowd so that all might feel his gaze. He lingered over Torgrid, shaggy-maned and bull-like who stood a head taller than most men, and whose eyes were bright for the fight. But Torgrid remained unmoved and eventually returned a nod, his fleshy lips drawing a mirthless line across his face.

Black Jack sneered, knowing if any would challenge it would have been Torgrid. Jessop was smaller, the wolf to Torgrid's bull. His challenge when it came would be in the night and when least expected not in the open against a man faster and stronger than he, and so it proved. Jessop scowling and turning away when their eyes crossed.

"I will challenge you, brother," the voice was hoarse and barely carried but enough heard it.

Turning, Black Jack regarded Wynter, the brother as unwanted as the son. "Once maybe, when we were kin, I would take your challenge but you are no brother of mine. Take him."

Two guards seized Wynter and with a cry of pain dragged him upright, feet twisting as his legs tried to straighten.

Jackson 'Black Jack' Tullock watched, contempt and longing mixing with disappointment. They had been inseparable as children, their father proving more dangerous to survive than the Grim ever had. Neither would have made it without the other. Then came his betrayal and now this. The knife grew heavy on his hip and he longed to draw it. To take his time, peeling the skin from Ned's flesh. To slice knuckle from bone, one at a time and ask him, why?

"You should never have come back, Ned. But you did and now, I need you this last time." Spinning, Black Jack raised his hands once again to the crowd.

"The Lords of this realm hunt us. Hang us when they catch us for no reason excepting we refuse to bend a knee to their High Lord." Black Jack stabbed a finger at his brother.

"This man is not our man. He forsook us long ago, abandoned the Grimhold and all who live here and swore fealty to the Black Crow. The worst, dark-hearted bastard fucker of the lot. No brother of ours and no kin of mine. Our laws are simple but clear. As the Grim is our judge, what is the punishment for treason?"

"The sallies," cried a voice, the words were taken up by another, then more until it seemed the whole crowd chanted it. Black Jack let the words wash against him then held his hand up for silence. Almost instantly they stilled.

"The Sallies it is. But he'll not be going alone." The Grimlord signed and the nameless Black Crow was dragged until he knelt in the dirt at his feet.

"Ordinarily I'd sooner slit your throat as waste spit on you." Those at the back of the gathering pressed forward, straining to hear what was said. "But times have changed and circumstance makes beggars of us all. What was done to us rests with your Lord and you just followin' orders. I need men who can fight. What is your name soldier? Swear it to my blade and you'll see the sun tomorrow."

The man raised bloodshot eyes and wiped a parched tongue over dry lips. His body shivered, the chill air seeming like ice against his skin after the warmth of his hole.

"Thornhill," he croaked. "Water?"

At a nod, a waterskin was raised splashing mouth and chin until he spluttered, choking.

Black Jack waited while the Black Crow recovered then asked. "Well, Thornhill?"

Thornhill ran his tongue briefly over his lips and worked his jaw before answering. If anything the cold dowsing charged every ache and pain in his body so that he felt them anew. His teeth were loose and he tasted blood. "Thank you, but I'm already a sworn man." The words sounded weak to his ears but it was as if he'd slapped the Grimlord. The small victory brought him a smile. "Besides, ya talk too much, been listenin' now and…huu."

The knife pierced the soft flesh beneath Thornhill's jaw, parting hair and skin and sinking deep. Black Jack pulled the blade free and a patter of blood stuttered from the wound and leaked from his mouth. As if his body deflated, the Black Crow sunk back against his heels, eyes glazed in death. Then keeled onto his side in the dirt and slush.

"NOOO… NOOO…" The scream rang out from the crowd, only to be silenced with a sickening thump. Black Jack did not need to look to know that the other Black Crow had been struck down. If Sunny had killed him, he would be mad.

"He made his choice," Black Jack announced. "And I have made mine. I have two Lords of the Rivers and they're not worth the shit I had this morning. Their families are gone their lands taken. If a blood ransom cannot be paid then a blood price will be taken. This is MY sentence.

"In two days, Lord Jacob and Lord Sandford will be taken together with our traitor brother to Morqhill in the Stench. By our laws, they will be chained to the madstone. The Grim will be their judge and the sallies their executioners. So it has always been."

His people roared. Across the crowd, he sought his son and their eyes met. Flinching, Tom turned away and Black Jack's stare hardened, his brows meeting as his face furrowed into a scowl.

"Don't worry my son. You'll be coming too."

Chapter 19: Death Comes In Darkness

The Skárpe, Norderlands

The high steppes of the Skárpe were vast, touching the highlands of Torannog in the east and the Torn Spur mountains in the west. A tall-rider in the heights of summer riding hard could make the one hundred league crossing from Jarlsheim, which sat at the foot of Mount Herna-Var and known by most as 'Giant's Reach', to Highwatch in four days.

But it was not summer and the Nordáas possessed few of the tall beasts used by the rest of the kingdoms, preferring instead the hardy steppe ponies. For what they lacked in size they made up for in robustness; perfectly acclimated to the mild summers and cold winters of the Nordáalund and able to forage on the scrag grasses and bushes of the highlands and heath.

The warriors of High Barle Justin Janis, numbered three thousand and with the new snow and the half-days of winter growing ever shorter, it was nine days before the broken tooth of Mount Brikka appeared in the Torn Spurs. Upon Brikka's back stood Highwatch and whilst it seemed close, experience told them it was two days distant still.

A weather front cycled from the north bringing snow flurries and as the temperature dropped they made camp in the lee of a tumbledown bluff. The shag-furred ponies were herded and corralled where they could share the warmth of the herd whilst the Nordáas sheltered beneath oiled, bison-hide tents.

Tannon Crick and what remained of his Hand lagged behind the High Barle and his army. The campfires beckoned them on, promising light and warmth, food and shelter.

What a lop-sided creature I am, Tannon Crick observed. His body was bruised and his bones ached with a dull throb but it was his left arm and leg to which he referred. Both were strapped and splinted and pained him greatly. Thankfully, the headaches had left him the day before and the mental exercises he employed helped to manage the pain, though not it seemed with the infernal itching. It could have been worse, Crick reflected, he was luckier than most. Not just in the manner of injury but in being an Order Knight. Not many survived the Trial of Ascendance, but those that did were blessed with long life, fast healing and an unnatural resilience of both mind and body.

He rubbed the fingers of his good hand at the binding atop his leg, wishing he could stretch lower to his calf before giving in and reaching for his itching stick.

"You do your leg no favours scratching so," Marus Banff chided. "Leave it be."

The man had eyes in the back of his head. Crick gave a defiant itch with his stick before his steward's scowl had him slip it like a sword into his belt. The wagon bumped and rattled, the beaten trail they followed little more than rut marks in the trampled snow. Over his friend's shoulder loomed the Torn Spurs, their shadowed peaks renting a dark sky dammed with clouds. They had left Highwatch three days before, though Crick could only recall the last two. Now they were returning.

Crick's eyes travelled lower, to the firefly spark of campfires and his hackles rose. Speed was crucial, yet Janis insisted on travelling en masse and with his supply wagons; humping everything up at the start of each day, lugging it slowly across the Skárpe Steppes only to set it down, unpack it all, then do the same the following. The High Barle could have been at Highwatch two days since if he'd taken his Karls ahead and not stopped till after dark. But they had not and unless the Helg and Skaag had sent more warriors he feared the worst for Highwatch.

"Bloody fool," Crick muttered.

"Pardon, My Lord?"

Crick waved Banff's query aside. "Just an old man muttering."

Well known to the watchers on duty, they rumbled unchallenged into camp. Scanning ahead, Marus Banff picked out the large pavilion belonging to Janis and steered a path for it through the avenues of tents. Horses nickered, wagon oxen bellowed and the laughter of men drifted on the wind; carried with it was the heavy musk of beast and man, spliced with the more pleasant aroma of wood smoke and hot food. His stomach rumbled.

"Ser,"

Banff's tone was enough to cause Crick to raise himself off his bed in the wagon, stifling a groan as his right half dragged his left upright.

A crowd of warriors milled outside the High Barle's tent and a hand of horses, Redford light draughts by their conformation, graceful and nimble despite their size. Not unlike our own, Crick observed. The horses stomped, pulling at their bridles and tossing their heads, nostrils belching steam.

An unease settled over him. The horses' covers were the High Barle's red and green. The few horses Janis possessed had gone west with him to Highwatch, ridden by Marlik Riekason and his veterans. Were they returned? Had Highwatch fallen then?

No, Riekason would not abandon Highwatch unless it had been overrun. But if that were so there would have been little time to saddle horses and mount an escape. Something was off, and the flickering torchlight did little to shed any light on what that might be.

The wagon drew to a halt, Banff unable to drive it further. The thick brogue of Nordáamen filled the air, loud and questioning, calling out to the lone man who held the horses but who stood unresponsive, eyes lowered.

A roar and flare of light blazed the night, painting the walls of the bluff in gold and black. It was accompanied by the frightened exclamation of ponies and the low bellow of oxen. As one, the Karls turned and stared, Crick and Banff with them, as a harrumph of flame erupted to momentarily drown the panic of the herd.

Underlying the sudden clamour of noise, Crick's skin prickled with magic and his head snapped towards its source. The pavilion. Janis.

With a sudden dread, Crick shouted. "Beware, the High Barle. To arms." Many of the Karls had already charged towards the flames and did not hear him. Those few that did, turned at his call.

"Marus, help me up. And get my sword, this will not do." Brandishing his scratcher, Crick flipped it into the wagon back.

"Hand, on me."

Katal Zakpikt, Karl Hubert and Merin Somar surged forward. The three surviving grey knights were dressed for travel, wearing leathers and furs rather than the slate grey armour of battle but all were armed and their weapons were drawn.

In that instant, the hide-flap to Janis' tent was thrown back and three warriors strode out.

"Marlik?" There was no mistaking the tall, wide-shouldered frame of his friend. But as the bearded head pivoted and aligned with Crick's the smoke-black eyes that stared back were not those of Marlik Riekason. The eyes of both men flared in mutual recognition.

"Hold," Crick bellowed. Then, with a sideways glare at his steward, hissed. "Marus, my sword, curse you."

"You can barely walk with a crutch, my Lord. Do you plan on hopping to battle?" The smouldering return could have melted ice, but Banff remained unmoved.

The seconds of distraction was all it took for Marlik, who was not Marlik, to mount his horse.

Crick thrust an arm at Riekason. "Seize him,"

The Karls nearest looked confused, Riekason was a kinsman. But Crick, an Order Knight, was counsellor to the High Barle and much respected. At another, insistent cry, the warriors leapt to obey.

The horses wheeled and swords swept out, slicing into those that reached for rein and bridle. Blood flew and the screams of the injured met the cries of the outraged. Steel was drawn and rang as blade meet blade but in the madness of the melee and the stilted light from torch and fire, the horses broke free and vanished into the murk of night.

In a towering rage, Tannon Crick raised his hand to Karl, Merin and Katal, ready to loose them after the Taken only for Banff to lay his hand upon his arm.

"We've lost much already. Would you lose more, my Lord?"

"Damn it, Marus. They were not men."

"Your eyesight is better than mine, Sir, but that was Marlik Riekason, I swear it," Banff replied, his tone measured. He had never seen his Lord so incensed.

Crick's eyes simmered. He wobbled trying to manoeuvre his splinted leg. "Gods damn it, help me down. Merin, Kat look to the High Barle."

The crowd had thinned. Karls had left to attend the blaze oblivious to the turmoil left behind and many of the warriors that remained pursued Riekason into the starless night. Merin Somar and Katal drove their horses through the milling remnants before drawing up outside the pavilion. In a rushing dismount, they vanished inside.

Tannon Crick grunted with effort as Karl and Marus helped him to the ground. *Gods-cursed splint.* Instead of his sword, Marus handed him the piece of long wood, cut and padded for his crutch. Disgruntled at having to use it and anxious for what he might find, he hobbled after Merin and Kat.

Along the way, he snapped out orders. A horn was raised and wailed a forlorn note that echoed off the bluff.

Utarr Gant appeared from between a line of tents, his war axe clenched in one thick, gnarled hand and his shield slung across his back. A dozen warriors followed behind.

"Ser Tannon?" A man of few words, his deep inflexion made a question of the name.

Crick's face turned grim. "Highwatch has fallen. Look to your cousin, Utarr. But first, send out scouts, secure the heights of the bluff and prepare for battle."

Without breaking stride and in his usual, gruff manner, Utarr issued instructions. Half his warriors vanished to carry out his bidding, the rest rushed ahead to secure the ground about Janis's pavilion. Utarr nodded his bearded head at the Order Knight, the blue of his eyes seeming yellow in the reflected torchlight. He moved past, reaching the tent just as Merin Somar appeared from beneath its hide entrance.

Somar's face was wrapped against the cold, but the tanned skin around brown-flecked eyes marked him as a southerner, an Olmesman. Utarr only knew of one. "Merin?"

Somar shook his head, unwilling to speak aloud what lay beyond, aware of the warriors gathered around.

With a loud grunt to hide his growing fear, Utarr brushed the hide flap aside and stepped within, the sound of Tannon Crick's crutch tamping behind.

The smell hit first. The bitter, iron-tang of blood overlaid that of voided bowel and piss, and beneath it all the char of burnt leather and cooked flesh. A brazier waxed pale light against the interior. Barely adequate, it was nevertheless enough to display the dead. There were four, three lying in pools of blood and the last a smouldering ruin.

Crick hobbled past Utarr, his eyes, adjusted to the low light, drinking in every detail.

Hans Steilmenn lay on his back, glazed eyes staring upwards. Blood soaked his abdomen and pooled beneath his body. A jagged tear stretching from gut to chest still dribbled fluid. The High Barle's first sword had not had time to draw his blade.

Utarr brushed past and knelt beside Janis, knees turning red with blood. A gash rent a garish smile across his cousin's throat. Stretching out, Utarr closed a hand over dead eyes giving a low moan. It rose to an anguished cry until he threw his head back then stopped, eyes screwed shut. Utarr's nostrils flared as he rasped air in and out of his lungs.

Ignoring the Norder's distress, Crick moved around his large frame and glanced at Janis, taking in his wound with a seemingly analytic indifference. Yet beneath it, a deep sadness filled him. He'd watched Janis grow from a babe to a man. Had taught him his books and history, read poetry and taught governance. Skilled him in different fight techniques, not just the Nordáa ones. He was a good student and a better Barle. Crick suppressed the pang in his chest. Now was not a time for emotion. Janis would be missed but dead was dead. There was nothing to be done about it.

Crick turned his attention to the magus. Borik Shan was as dead as the rest, a single sword thrust to his chest had seen to that. He lay in a rumpled heap on the ground, blood turning his black robe a deeper shade.

Old he might be, but the mage was the only one to strike in retaliation. Borik's staff fair thrummed with magical discharge despite having rolled from his grasp to lie against the wall of the tent.

Crick hunkered down beside the last of the dead and screwed his nose up at the stench. Borik's magics had engulfed the woman, singeing her hair, blistering and melting the skin on her face and turning her lidless eyes into aqueous pools of gloop. She was unrecognisable. Only the bear claw charm about her neck gave clue to her identity along with the etched pattern on her bracers. The motif was that of the Ead. Ebba Darjhalen wore such a thing. Ebba was one of Riekason's Karls, all of whom were sworn to the High Barle. If she were a Taken, then the magus had seared the Morhudrim's essence from her body.

Crick turned for the entrance. "Come Utarr. If there was ever any doubt there is none now, war is joined. There is no time to mourn."

* * *

Pyres were built and the bodies laid to rest but not without some discourse.

"I'll nae send this treacherous bitch onward," Utarr declared. "I'd rather leave her for the wolves."

"Ebba Darjhalen was ever faithful. But she was Taken, like Marlik and the rest of his warriors are Taken. It was not their will but the Morhudrim's that murdered the High Barle," Crick argued.

"Argh, so ya keep sayin'. Tales ta scare children, Order man," Utarr raged.

"No Utarr. Not tales. I saw the black in Marlik's eyes and knew it then. I have never told you false, nor the High Barle. I have fought with you and bled beside you and as brothers in blood I am true in my word." Crick raised his voice to the gathered warriors. "If the Nordáas are to survive what has come you must accept that the Tainted One has returned. Already we have felt the wrath of the Morhudrim's Taken."

In the cold light of morning, the black-scarred face of the bluff hung above them, a reminder of the blaze from the night before, an ominous backdrop that echoed the Order Knight's words.

In the end, Crick swayed them. He had lived so long among them that not a warrior there did not know and respect him. And so it was that four pyres were lit, sending smokey black plumes into the overcast.

As a final act, Crick planted Borik Shan's staff at the head of his pyre. Made of White Merl, a living wood, its attunement with Shan lay broken and without it, the staff would accumulate aether uncontrolled. Its only destiny now was an explosive self-combustion, though how long that would take Crick could not say.

A council was convened by Utarr with the Jarls where they pondered the night's events and listened to Crick's words, mostly in silence.

Utarr spoke. "Kaygó Janis, son of Justin is the new High Barle. A Grand-Moot is needed and each Barle called ta swear fealty."

Crick interjected. "Kaygó is seven. A boy still and we are at war. There is no time for a Grand-Moot. If, as I suspect, the urakakule have breached Highwatch, their tribes will be pouring into your Heartlands even as we speak. If we sit here much longer, we will feel their fury."

"It's our way," Utarr grumbled tugging at his plaited beard. He wrinkled his nose, sniffed deeply and hoicked a wedge of phlegm onto the snow hardened ground. Then grudgingly, "I've sent scouts ahead ta look for signs of what ya say. I'll listen ta y'on counsel."

Crick's head turned, surveying the assembled Jarls, including them with his look and his words. "The High Barle sounded the horns of war before we left Jarlsheim. The Clans will answer his call and warriors will gather but they need to be led and you need to lead them Utarr. Have the Barles that come swear to Kaygó but you must be made Warmaster."

The Jarls grunted their approval, but Utarr's face clouded.

"Ya could say all this on't road. Which means yar nae coming with us. If'n urak make war on us and Taken are truly here among us then ya'll be needed. The Order is needed."

Crick frowned and gave a shake of his head. "I travel north to Skaág and Helg and Helvenin. They are isolated and face the gravest, most immediate threat and I will be more useful there. Besides, the Taken saw me as surely as I did him. The Morhudrim knows me now and will hunt me. It will assume I return to Jarlsheim and I would be a fool to go where the Morhudrim expects."

Utarr blew a cloud of breath into the air as he considered, then nodded to himself. "These urak, do ya know of them? When the heavy snows fall will it hold'em till the thaw?"

"Urak live in the harsh lands of the Norde-Targkish. They are used to hard winters. I fear not, Warmaster."

Utarr shook his head at the title, "I can smell the snows coming, nae these paltry droppings," he scuffed his boot against the ground, "but thick. Our wagons will be hard-pressed ta move when it does. Skaag is two days hard travel to the north. I'll give ya the wagons an' five hundred warriors."

He peered at the few Barles and gathered Jarls and Frode of Lonn stood forward. "I have kin in Helvenin and Skaag. I'll take my Karls and accompany Ser Tannon."

"T'is agreed then." Utarr slapped Lonn on the back.

"It may take a full cycle of Kildare's moon but Keeper will send others in my stead to advise you, Utarr," Crick said.

"Bah, they'll nae understand our ways like ya' do, my friend. Just try not ta get yaself killed, eh. Be a pain in my arse ta break another of ya in," Utarr grumped.

They clasped arms then embraced. Behind them, the flaming pyres spluttered and spat. A fitting backdrop.

* * *

<Janis dead, and by a Taken no less. That is grave news indeed and the Taken here sooner than expected. It means at the very least the Red Skull is compromised,> Keeper mused. <This Utarr, he does not possess the head of a High Barle.>

<He is a respected warrior. The Jarls accept him and the Barles will too. He says little but is shrewd and well suited to Warmaster, if for no other reason than he does not covet it. Do not underestimate him,> Crick replied. <The Nordáa will need help. I know the High King promised aid to the Rivers but this war has captured the entire north. Renix must inform the High King.>

A squirt of memories and information pulsed across their mind-link and as each packet unfolded it rocked Crick to his core. Renix lay murdered, the memory of his passing conveyed by Renix himself. The High King poisoned, and whether he lived or died was unknown. Worse, the Order stood accused.

Crick could not speak. It had been decades since he had last seen Renix but he had known him all his life. They had grown as boys together in the Order Halls all those many years ago, more years than he cared to remember.

<Four hundred and twenty-eight,> Keeper supplied. <Renix is sorely missed and I share your heartbreak, brother. I will send Rhool Dhunn to Jarlsheim and a score of Greys.>

There was a fractional delay. <You hoped for more. I sense it in you Tannon. Maybe Chivalry and a thousand of our brethren?> A mental shrug wormed its way across the link.

<You know I cannot risk more than what is offered. The Kingdoms must respond but they see the Order as their enemy as much as the urakakule. The Morhudrim has played its hand well and we have been found wanting. The Kingdoms will not listen to our warnings of the Taken or Morhudrim even if we had the means to deliver it. I will endeavour to make private representation to each of the High Lords, but it will take time and until then our presence is not welcome. It cannot be guaranteed even in Nordáalund now that Justin Janis is dead. Tread carefully, my friend.>

Crick grimaced. Keeper's news was bitter and his insight did not sit well with him even if it was the truth. <*We've had a thousand years to prepare and yet it appears it was all for nothing. Have you nothing good to tell me?*>

<*Some.*> A sense of warmth. <*Ironside and Castigan escort an ilfanum ambassador to Tankrit. I hope to rebuild our ties with Da'Mari. Also, there is a new power in play. Hiro is mixed up with it and it is too early to say for certain but if things transpire as I would like then this power could prove a decisive ally in the war to come. Pivotal even in the downfall of the Morhudrim.*>

Hope flared against the loss that seized his chest and Crick let it fill him. <*I have not heard Hiro's name in a ten-year. That is good to know. I was beginning to think he'd crossed the Great Expanse again.*> He asked a dozen questions, each one triggering in his mind one after the other, each acknowledged and dismissed; Keeper would tell him what was needed, not what was asked for.

Another wash of warmth crossed the link and Tannon knew Keeper smiled.

<*Your injuries heal well, Tannon. Travel in haste but go with care, for the road you have chosen is a perilous one.*>

Like a door closing the link chinked softly as it terminated.

Opening his eyes, Crick squinted in the light of day, grey and muted as it was. The sound of the wagon as it rattled across the high steppes seemed loud, accompanied by the rhythmic clomp of two thousand hooves against the tundra. In the far distance, the towering skyscape of the Torns dominated the horizon and a thick, dark smudge sat between where the mountains met the land. The forests of Helg.

Chapter 20: Hot Rocks and Ice

West of the Defile, The Rivers

Renco stirred, awareness returning as if rising from the depths of a deep lake. The burning heat suffusing his body receded with it, mellowing to a warmth that tingled his skin and steeped his bones. He felt energised.

"Nesta, I think he wakes." A palm pressed against his forehead. It was cool, the touch comforting, the voice familiar.

The hand moved, cupped his cheek and he sensed a presence hovering above him, breath brushing his face. "Renco? Can you hear me?"

The voice resolved in his head. Lett. They lived then. But what had happened to him, to them? He recalled the thicket they were in, then the dog girl appearing and a soaring energy building inside until it became all-consuming, unbearable. Then nothing.

His thoughts grew erratic. Nihm. The dog girl was called Nihm. Just thinking of her pulsed an electric line of energy through his core. A connection. He could feel her through it, knew without opening his eyes that she stood nearby. That he could trace that contact right to her.

He cracked his eyelids and found Lett staring down at him, eyes as blue as a summer sky. The faintest of freckles ghosted her cheeks, with yellow-gold hair framing an alluring face marred with concern but which transformed almost instantly to joy. With a squeal she bent and hugged him, tucking her head against his. "I was so worried."

She felt soft and pleasant, the scent of her acquainted and reassuring. As well as energised, he felt inexplicably whole. The headaches that had plagued him these past ten days and which had grown steadily worse were noticeable by their absence. He made to rise only for Lett to sit up and press him back down with a firm hand.

"You just lie there, Mister. Let Nesta check you over first." With a mock pout, she shuffled to the side making room.

At first, Renco wondered at the ilf that settled beside him, thinking him a vision from a dream. It took a moment for his memories to catch up and reassert themselves.

"You are most intriguing." Nesta passed a hand up and down the length of Renco's body. "Your resilience is quite remarkable. I judge you fit to travel though there is a problem."

Nesta lifted his eyes and Renco twisted and followed his gaze which settled upon Nihm. His body thrummed in recognition, vibrating like a plucked chord on a lute. Despite barely knowing her, Nihm's face was etched in his mind and like the jaded memory of his long-dead parents, she gave off that same sense of kinship. He shifted uneasily, unable to explain his feelings, just that he was drawn to her. Dark-haired, brown-eyed, she had a wide mouth with a curious quirk to it as if she were amused.

"Renco's aura is recovered, but the tae'al he has subsumed is staggering. It lights him like a beacon for those with the gift to see such things." The ilf's eyes fixed on Renco again and he signed.

'Tell me, do you possess the hidden sense, ki'tae?' Then for added clarification. *'Can you read tae'al, aether as humans are wont to call it?'*

Renco nodded his head.

'Can you manipulate it like your Master, Hiro?'

Renco's eyes narrowed and his hands and fingers moved. *'How do you know about Hiro? I never told you of him.'*

The ilf was silent, his chin dipping as he waited for an answer. Finally, Renco conceded. *'No, Master taught me to sense it, but I can't call it as he can. I do not possess that talent.'*

"You know, talking your secret hand language might be considered rude by some." Lett intruded.

Nesta grunted in response, coughed then choked. Sweeping a hand to his mouth he plucked something from between his teeth and held it out. Pinched between thumb and forefinger was what looked like a nut.

"Take this seed, swallow it. It will adapt your mind, enabling you to create a simulacrum that will allow your tae'al to project through it. The tae'al you have absorbed, however, will be hidden, shielded. It will protect you from observation," Nesta bobbed his head from side to side. "Mostly."

"I took a similar one." Nihm raised a disgruntled eyebrow. "I did not realise at the time it was regurgitated but it has helped me and done me no harm. Besides, Nesta is right, you are glowing like a house on fire in the aether."

Fighting his reluctance, Renco reached out and plucked the seed from Nesta's fingers. Everyone was looking at him, even the lanky, red-haired strip of a man hanging in the back. Closing his eyes, Renco popped the nut in his mouth before he could change his mind, then grabbed the waterskin proffered by Lett and took a quick swig to wash it down.

Abruptly, Nesta stood and swept the room with black eyes. "Now everyone is rested and Renco recovered we need to move, quickly. Pack and prepare the horses, we depart immediately."

* * *

Their disparate band reached the road to the Defile and turned away, following it westward towards Karston Abbey. They passed the broken carriages and the dead, disturbing flocks of black-winged scavengers who took flight and circled the skies or watched from the surrounding woods, waiting to return with eager dispassion.

Nihm scowled, it had only been a few nights since she had found the dead but so much had happened it seemed much longer than that. It was worse, she decided, seeing the fallen in the light of day. Like mottled bruising, blood stained the snow-packed ground and despite the cold some of the bodies had started to bloat or leak a bloody foam from empty eyes and open mouth.

For some it was too much and Nihm turned at the sound of gagging in time to see Lett retch and throw up. Renco moved to assist her and Nihm turned away. At least Sai had dampened the stink of putrefaction, the others had no such luxury. Sai could do nothing though for the scene. The agony of the dead was locked in fearful grimace upon many faces and gaping wounds evidenced the violence as much as their dead eyes proclaimed it. It was harrowing to look.

They left the dead behind and later found the track that Nihm and Morten had taken north and followed it back, stopping only to rest the two horses. There were no signs of urak and with the wind from the north, north-east, Nihm knew that Ash and Snow would smell or hear any pursuit if it came. Nesta too, often walked in a daze like trance, observing the flow of tae'al, reading the currents.

Nightfall found them still upon the road. Nesta pushed them onward regardless of their weary limbs and none complained, for the broken dead were fresh still in their minds. By the time they reached the banks of the Fossa the night was mostly gone and a new dawn beckoned. They took shelter in a copse of elda and wilabarks that bordered the river.

"Light no fire," Nesta instructed. "It would not do to attract unwanted attention."

"We're frozen. A little one would hardly be a risk," Morten complained. "The wood'll hide any smoke. Besides, we need it fer water and summat hot ta eat wouldn't go amiss."

Nesta stared back, head slightly canted in thought. The surrounding trees were mostly bare of leaf and would provide no hindrance to any smoke. He glanced at Nihm who shrugged, then Renco. "No fire. But there is another way."

The ilf walked off, brushing past wilted ferns and the still green shojo bushes that cared not that it was the Bite, their spikey leaves and red berries colourful and bright.

The others watched as Nesta moved between the trunks, looking for something. He stopped suddenly then raised his arm and signalled.

"Come on." Nihm set off through the trees, pulling on the reins of her horse which reluctantly followed.

"Me feet are killin' me," Morten grumbled as he trailed after them, dragging his bay roan behind him. The horse plodded, neck lowered exuding the weariness he felt.

They joined the ilf in a small clearing by an outcropping of rocks encrusted with moss and lichen. "This rock is not ideal, but it will do," he told them.

"Do fer what, sittin' on?" Morten dabbed a hand at the damp surface and scrunched his face up then yelped, jumping away as Nesta tumbled a loose boulder that must have weighed a hundred pounds. It clattered against its neighbours before rolling onto the snow-covered leaf litter.

"Now," Nesta said, regarding Nihm and Renco. "Your first lesson. Heating a rock."

Renco looked puzzled and signed. *'Told you, I can't use aether.'*

"No, Nihm will."

"What?" Nihm exclaimed. "I can't heat a rock. Unless you mean for me to start a fire and warm it?"

"I will explain. First, give your reins to Lett." Nesta waited until it was done before continuing.

"I gather you have received no training in how to call tae'al?" Nihm shook her head, curious despite her reservations.

"To heat a rock requires energy. Tae'al in its simplest form is energy. If you can call tae'al it means simply that you can draw upon it. Both your own and the tae'al that surrounds you, allowing you to use it in all manner of ways and manifestations." Nesta saw that he had their attention, only the wolfdogs were disinterested, sniffing and exploring the glade.

"Doing so is not always easy. Living things, particularly sentients, have a natural resilience that makes this extremely difficult, though not impossible to do. Plants are less so but still can be troublesome. Care is needed too, lest you take too much. It can weaken, even kill a thing and what right or warrant do any of us have to harm another living being in that way?"

Nihm shrugged her shoulders. "Master Hiro explained some of this to me. But I've done nothing other than read the currents. I can't use tae'al in the way you speak of even if I understood how."

"But you can and have already," Nesta said. He indicated Renco. "Tae'al exists not just in living things but in all things, even the air and earth, though in those it is so weak as to appear inconsequential. Though the circumstance of it is a mystery to me, Renco is rune-marked. As he walks and even as he sleeps, he has been absorbing unchecked the tae'al that surrounds him, unaware he was doing so. A trickle here and a drop there but as we ilfanum say, raindrops will fill a river and a river will feed a lake." Nesta thumped his stave against the ground and addressed Renco directly.

"You are as much to Nihm as my staff is to me; a source or conduit. It is what attracted my interest and drew me to you. When we met you glowed like the sun on the horizon. Others too will have seen it. But I digress." The ilf turned to include Nihm.

"A conduit is normally created and attuned to its maker. You though, Renco, are an anomaly, for you are rune-marked but unbonded. Left unchecked you would have gathered tae'al until you could hold no more. The outcome would have been catastrophic."

'Were. Would. What are you telling me?' Renco signed.

Nihm sighed and a worried look crossed her face as though she had already surmised the conclusion.

"I am saying that you and Nihm already share some kind of bond from before. Something I would seek to understand, but maybe later." Nesta muttered this last to himself. "If Nihm had not attuned herself to you, you would be dead. Now, you are paired, much as I am with my staff. As I might call upon the tae'al gathered within it, so Nihm might call upon the tae'al you have absorbed.

'You're saying I'm a gods-damned piece of wood?' Renco shook his head violently, his fingers dancing in anger. *'I'm no conduit. I don't even know her. We've hardly met, and I don't need some girl using me like… like… some tool. I don't want this, and sure as the seven hells below didn't ask for it. Take it away. Please.'* His eyes pleaded in anguish.

Nihm choked in shock as Sai spontaneously interpreted Renco's silent outburst. Did he blame her? Before she knew it her temper flared. "This 'girl' has a name you ungrateful shit. I did what I had to, to save you. Think I asked for any of this? That I did it to use you somehow? How? I don't get it. I don't understand it, but I want to. I need to. We both need to because this is where we're at."

Her outrage battered Renco. Emotion thrummed through their link clearer than the anger in her voice. She was scared and uncertain, just like him. He felt overwhelmed and was not sure if the sense was his or hers, maybe it was both of theirs. She was close to tears, but he knew somehow she would not shed them. He did not know her but nonetheless, he knew that.

<*I didn't know you could read my signing.*> His thoughts projected to her without effort. Though he had tried many times before, this was the first he had been successful. <*I owe you my life. I know it, but I feel like my soul has been twisted out of shape. I don't know what is happening to me or who I am anymore. But know this, I did not mean to cause you upset.*>

<*Nor I, you.*> Nihm's eyes fixed on his and she grinned. <*I kinda wanna know how to heat a rock though. Don't You?*>

To Renco, Nihm had seemed so serious, older than her sixteen or seventeen years but that smirk and the curiosity in that last statement eroded the impression in an instant. As intrigued by Nihm as he had been, she was never more compelling to him than she was then. He sniffed loudly and gave a nonchalant shrug of his shoulders. <*Sure.*>

As if he had eavesdropped on their mind link, Nesta clapped his hands. "Very good. Now pay attention. You should find this straightforward enough." He directed them to stand near the rock on the ground.

"Direct contact is best. For my curiosity would you mind removing your upper garments, Renco?" At his quizzical look, Nesta clicked his fingers. "Come, come, don't be shy. It is cold but this will not take long."

'The cold does not bother me,' Renco signed. He stared at Lett who returned a scowl, then Morten who towered beside her wearing a serious, unblinking expression. And finally, at Nihm who shifted uncomfortably beside him. All three were kind of how he felt.

Lifting a hand, Renco unclasped his red cloak and let it slip to the ground. He pulled the woollen smock over his head and followed it with his black linen shirt and undervest until he stood naked from the waist up.

"Nihm, as you did in the cave I want you to sense Renco's aura, connect to it as you did before. If you hold his hand or touch him directly in any way it will make your link unbreakable."

Nesta frowned, why did she dither so? Her eyes glistened strangely, the brown of them changing tone. Curious. Then, as if making some momentous decision he watched her turn, lift a hand and clasp Renco's wrist.

Humans, so full of drama when there was none. "Good. The barrier you attuned and created before will protect Renco and allow you to call upon that tae'al that he absorbed and holds. It will be manifestly different from his own. Sense it, hold it in your mind that which is not his. Can you feel it, child?"

"I can." Nihm's face a mask of concentration.

"Hold your hand out to the rock." It was not necessary but Nesta knew from experience an outward physical sign of action helped enact the metaphysical one. "Reach out to it with your mind, sense it. Its barrier is weak for the rock's aura is tenuous. Tell me when you have it."

Nihm's head twisted and turned, weaving as though to some tune only she could hear. "I think I have it."

"Do not think it. Know it." Nesta tsk'd. "When you are ready, call the tae'al from Renco and project it through you into the rock."

Nihm's forehead wrinkled in concentration and then she jumped as if startled. There was nothing tangible to see at first. Then the rock hissed in anger as a cloud of moisture evaporated from its surface. The lichen and moss dried and shrivelled. The air shivered and a waft of heat radiated outwards.

Phasing into ki'tae, Nesta observed on a different plane, the energies pouring into the rock. It was the simplest of manipulations. The transfer of tae'al increased and the warmth brushed against his leaf-scale skin.

"Step back both of you else the heat will mark you. I sense no moisture inside the rock but if there is any it could crack or explode it." Nesta phased back to the mundane and watched as Nihm and Renco walked backwards, away from the rock which started to glow. His eyes fastened in wonder upon the male human.

There was an audible gasp from Lett, and Morten swore as rune marks traced into definition on Renco's face and emblazoned across his chest. Strange markings that were unknown to Nesta but carried a sense of something familiar.

Distracted, Nesta whispered. "I think that is more than sufficient."

Staring down at his body in wonder, Renco didn't hear him.

Nihm did though and phased back, releasing her grip on Renco's wrist. She blinked her eyes, mouth open at the runes and symbols etched boldly across his body and face. They were the same ones she had seen through a different lens but now it was as if they had come to life. Without thought, she raised a finger and traced a swirling loop on his chest then snatched her hand back when she realised what she did.

Renco expelled the breath he'd been holding, deeply uncomfortable. Everyone was staring at him and he could still feel Nihm's silken touch against his skin. With a huff, he bent, gathered his clothing and stalked off, as unsettled as they were by what he had seen.

* * *

"'Cross the river', he says," Morten moaned. "We could just follow the road east to Rivercross and be there by evening." His boots were off and his feet were held out to the rock which was still hot even after the sun had risen. He picked at some loose skin on a toe. The remnants of a blister.

Lett smacked his shoulder. "Leave that be or you'll make it raw. Then I'll have to listen to you whining all day as well as all night."

"I ain't whined none." Morten massaged his foot as if that had been his intent all along and her words unreasonable. Lett was a sticky one. Walked around like she had a burr up her butt. She didn't like him, that was easy to tell, but that was better than Nihm. From the sideways glances Lett gave and the way she avoided Nihm, she liked her not a jot. Nihm, who was the nicest most honest person he knew.

He looked toward the far side of the glade and felt a pang of jealousy. Nihm was training with Renco. Both performing an exercise, weaving slow shapes and patterns in the air, then holding a pose before gliding into another. It was strangely soothing to watch.

They did not perform it together, he reassured himself. Renco had started first, something Lett told them he did all the time. Some martial discipline taught by Master Hiro, the same it seemed the monk had shown to Nihm but not to him. When Nihm had risen to perform her own version of Renco's dance, Lett's face had looked like she'd bitten a lemon. He would have laughed at it had he not felt the bitter ache in his own breast.

Morten knew he should practise his stave but felt self-conscious doing so on his own, aware his movements would look clumsy next to the grace already on display. And he couldn't exactly ask Lett, much as she needed a good thwacking. So he watched as Lett watched, their only sparing restricted to unsatisfying, verbal jousts.

Snow lifted her head from where she lay basking by the rock, white-furred ears coming erect. Whatever she heard it was no threat for she didn't bother to get up and laid her head back down.

Moments later Nesta appeared, making enough noise that they could hear his approach. The ilf observed Renco and Nihm practising their forms, each moving to a different rhythm. He wondered if they realised that their movements were perfectly juxtaposed. As one spun left the other right, Renco high form, Nihm low. They both stopped when he entered the clearing each with an awkward glance at the other before wandering to join him by the radiating boulder. Humans, endlessly complicated, morbidly fascinating.

"I have found a vessel large enough to bear us across the river. We will leave now."

"You said we'd stay 'til nightfall. We're hardly rested." Morten complained. "Me eyes are so gritty I think they've sand in 'em."

"Put on your boots. You may rest when we reach the other side of the slow water." Nesta waited whilst the others packed what few belongings they had and Morten pulled on stockings and boots, wincing as he laced them tight.

"Whiner," Lett whispered before moving to the horses, which earned her a glare from Morten.

Nesta led them out of the copse. On the horizon, the risen sun was little more than a sullen imprint in an overcast and leaden sky. They headed east, across a field that bordered the banks of the Fossa. Tracks in the snow had already been laid by Nesta and Morten bit back on why they traipsed through a field when there was a perfectly good road fifty yards to their left.

They crossed through a hedgerow to another field and several buildings appeared. A farmhouse and barn and by the river, a squat structure with one end suspended out into the water. As they approached, Morten could see a large stationary wheel attached to the building, part-submerged in the river. A waterwheel. They were not used much in the north; most of the rivers were too unruly and wild. This was the first time he had seen one and he longed for a closer look to see how it worked and understand what it did but Nesta led them past it and across the yard.

There was no sign of life. Whoever lived here had left a while ago and taken whatever livestock they had with them. The dogs explored, sniffing every corner and disappeared around the back of the farmhouse.

On the far side of the watermill, they found a wooden quay that ran twenty paces alongside the river. There were no boats moored to it but just past it lay a barge with one end dragged up the river bank and the other extending into the water. Nesta stopped before it and pointed.

"Here."

Lett, who was closest, glanced down critically. "That has a hole in it. It's not going anywhere except down."

Nesta was undeterred. "I have inspected the vessel. It will suffice. We will use the horses to raise the holed end and I will then make it watertight."

Morten peered over the edge of the quay and the others followed suit. They all saw what he saw. A hole the size of an ale cask. The boat would need to be landed and several boards replaced then sealed with black tar to make it river worthy. He shivered. The water looked cold, implacable despite its gentle meander.

Nihm spoke. "It's large enough if you can do it." Her eyes flickered to Morten and away again. "Those who can't swim can get tied to the horses just in case."

Morten's cheeks coloured at the reference and Lett didn't miss it. "Oh ho…" she started but never got to finish.

"Enough." Nesta spun, whatever semblance of tolerance he'd shown before was gone. "You talk too much when action is needed. Morten, Renco look for rope. Nihm, Lett unload the horses and prepare them."

By the time the two men returned, the horses were positioned ready. Taking the ends of two ropes, Nesta leapt nimbly onto the sloped rim of the barge, the wet wood and inclination proving no effort to the ilf. The ropes were fastened, each to a stanchion whilst the other ends were harnessed to the two horses.

"Okay, Morten, slowly does it."

The horses took the strain as Morten whispered and clicked his tongue, urging them forward several steps. Gradually the partly sunken stern lifted, half floating and supported by the ropes.

Nesta watched the barge as the hole in its bottom let the water out until the weight of it settled and it would raise no more. A good bit of water sloshed still in the bilge.

"My staff please."

Nihm gathered it from the quayside, marvelling at the bone-white merl wood and the intricate runes carved along its length. They were different but still reminiscent of the markings that had flared to life on Renco's face and torso. It was the first time she'd had a chance to touch or study it and it fair hummed with power beneath her hand. It was unpleasant and it was with a sense of relief that she tossed it to the ilf who snatched it without effort from the air.

Balancing on the stern rail, Nesta held his staff in his left hand and extended his right. With a frown of concentration, his lips moved but he spoke no words, at least none that could be heard.

Nihm watched in fascination. The water inside the boat shimmered and the air abruptly warmed only to be swept away on the breeze then replaced by another waft of heat. The water in the hull stilled and grew sluggish, its hue changed from clear and dark to an opaque whiteness. The timber groaned as if it were alive.

Like an acrobat on a high rope, Nesta walked the rail post, hand weaving. The boat's moaning followed everywhere he trod as if his touch were torture, the white ice followed him.

"How did you do that? I've never seen anything like it." Nihm could not keep the awe from her voice.

Nesta looked up at them. All, barring Morten who was with the horses still, stared at him in amazement.

"I already told you that tae'al in its simplest form is energy. This was a simple trick, easier than the one you performed warming the rock. There you willed energy into it from your source. So much so that it became superheated. That took far more effort than this affair. Here I merely took energy from the water which cooled it. When cooled sufficiently water turns to ice and ice as all know, floats. Ice is also watertight until it warms and loses its integrity."

"But the water was already cold and the air grew warm…." Nihm stopped and the look of puzzlement on her face suddenly cleared. "Oh, I think I understand."

"You do? Explain it to me then," Lett said.

"Later," Nesta said. "The ice shell I have built around this vessel will seek equilibrium, to return to the natural order of the water that surrounds it. Even now it fights a battle it will eventually lose. I suggest we board and depart whilst it still holds."

With some direction from Nesta, the rest of them pushed against the bow post and the barge creaked, groaned, then slowly slid back into the water.

Embarking the horses proved tricky at first but the ilf had a calming way of talking to them and with a few whispered words they clattered over the hastily erected boarding planks.

Releasing the bowline, Renco was the last to board and the barge slowly twisted in the current as it released from the muddy side. The river was wide, its waters slow-moving and placid. Using broken planks as paddles they swept furiously for the far side, doing little more than drifting the vessel across.

The land to the south of the Fossa was interspersed with farms and around a bend in the river, a road suddenly swung into view, pinched between woodland and a rising landscape of snow-frosted hills.

The road was not empty.

Brightly coloured wagons filled it pulled by horses decorated with ties of greens and yellows and reds. The people were as garishly attired as their horses and wagons. They spied them upon the river, and a small group assembled at their likely landing point.

Dragging his cloak tight around him, Nesta grunted in displeasure at the sight. A cowl sprang into being that he pulled up high to cover his head.

"Don't think that'll do it," Morten muttered.

Nesta murmured and the air about him seemed to oscillate and shift. The autumnal leaf scale of his body and limbs roiled and mutated. When it settled, he was no longer an ilf but a man dressed in plain brown garb and a black cloak.

"Okay, that might do it," Morten conceded, unable to keep the wonderment from his voice. He gave a lopsided grin. "Still. Chances are they'll slit our throats and rob us anyway."

"Why would they do that?" Nesta asked.

"Who are they?" Nihm said, startled at the ilf's transformation, her gaze alternating between Nesta and the colourful people on the bankside.

Morten scowled.

"Wylders. They're gods-damned, Wylders."

Chapter 21: The Road to Thorn Nook

Lakeside, Cumbrenan

The *Eastern Promise* docked in the early pre-dawn. Darion did not know by what witchery the crew had navigated, for clouds obscured the night sky leaving no markers for Captain Maveison to steer by. However it was done, the lights of the town of Lakeside had appeared like fallen stars, growing steadily brighter as the ship approached.

During the crossing they had rested as best they could, knowing that a day of hard travel awaited them, but it proved an uncomfortable night. The Captain offered them hammocks below decks but Ironside and Castigan had refused and with nothing but the deck to sleep upon and Bindu warming one side, Darion awoke half-frozen, stiff and feeling worse than when he'd lain down.

When they disembarked and Darion set his feet on solid ground again it was with a sense of relief, open water was not for him. Father Melbroth joined them shortly afterwards with M'rika and R'ell, attired still in their white vestments. They gathered on an already bustling quayside whilst the crew unloaded their horses and wagons with noisy efficiency.

Captain Maveison joined them briefly. He did not speak of their business. Indeed, he had exchanged few words with them when they were aboard, but he offered some now.

"T'is a strange air about the place. Like a tinderbox near an open flame. Might just be 'cause of the war in the north but have a care, leave Lakeside soon as ya can. I don't need ta tell 'e that Killenhess is only a day south." The captain bowed to Father Melbroth and gave a doff of his peaked hat to the rest before striding back up the ship's gangway.

Regus and Rutigard hitched one of the wagons and Gatzinger and Ansel the other. They drew many curses from the carters and dockworkers that had to move around them. It attracted unwanted attention, and an officious-looking man turned up with two guardsmen in tow.

"I'll need to see your landing papers. Who is in charge?"

Father Melbroth nudged past Ironside and Darion. "I guess that would be me, my son. As for our papers. Captain Maveison, Master of the *Eastern Promise* will file the correct paperwork at the harbourmaster's office."

The official wet his lips nervously and glanced at the men and woman that accompanied the three priests. They looked hard-bitten and seemed unimpressed by his status. "Forgive me, Father. I'm not from the harbourmaster's office. I'm charged with securing goods and, ah, the enlistment of any able-bodied man or woman. For the war effort. Might I enquire…."

"No. You may not," Melbroth interrupted. "This is church business. The Church of Nihmrodel does not have such a militant arm as Kildare. No luxury of White Cloaks to escort us, so these men and this woman, devout in their faith, have been charged with our safe conduct. The why and the what for is none of your concern. Now, before we depart would you like a blessing?"

The man stuttered. "What? Er, no. I'm still. I must...."

"We are all children of the One, The Trinity answers to no man or woman. No Lord nor King. You have no right here. Now stand aside lest you incur my ire." Melbroth turned as if the matter were concluded.

"Lyra. Help the good Fathers onto the wagons if you please. Darion, would you assist."

Ironside stepped close to the official, forcing his eyes away from the priests as they made to board the wagons. "The roads are filled with the desperate fleeing the north, people who have lost everything. Tell me, what does your Lord do for them?"

The official leaned away. The man's face was battered, yellow bruising ringed his eyes and his nose looked red and swollen.

"High Lady Montreau has decreed safe haven be given to all Riversfolk. Those savages they run from, these urak, they will follow. Only we'll not run. We Cumbrenans will fight. My Lord Vandis of Lakeside has ordered the enlistment of every able-bodied man and woman to help drive them back. You are fortunate to have the White Fathers skirts to hide behind else you'd be joining us. Now, get out of my face before I change my mind, White Fathers or no."

There was a rattle as the wagons moved out and Ironside stepped back. Taking the reins of his horse from a waiting Rutigard, he mounted. His horse danced as his weight settled, sending the official and both guards scrambling backwards. Ironside leered. "Well, I wish you luck with that. I hear the urakakule like to wash their meat down with a Cumbrenan white, try not to leave them any, it would be a waste of good wine."

Laying reins against his horse's neck and with a little heel, Ironside followed the wagons, Rutigard falling in behind.

The official watched them go, angered by the exchange and uneasy. There was something off about it all. White Priests were not normally so brusque, and their escort seemed wrong. The large, bearded man had been dressed in plain, hardy garb, but with a cloak that seemed to shimmer and shift in the light and with what looked like a giant wolf at his side. The others wore riding leathers and clothing that was expensive and of the highest quality. Not the sort a mere guard might afford. He turned to his men.

"Get your horses and follow them. Discretely. I would see where they're headed."

* * *

Lakeside was bustling with activity and Darion saw guards dressed in three different liveries. On their way out of town they were stopped and questioned twice, and each time Father Melbroth took the lead and deflected any enquiry.

He has his uses, Darion conceded. Without him, escorting the ilfanum undetected would have been nigh on impossible. *I wouldn't have gone through any towns though,* he told himself.

They took the eastern road out of Lakeside and just outside its bounds they passed through a ramshackle camp of bivouacs and tents that stretched away to the north. It was filled with the wretched, Darion had never seen anything like it. His nose wrinkled. The reek of humanity, carried on the wind, was repugnant. The refugee camps in the north had been transitory, fleeting places. Somewhere to stay before people moved on. Whereas this camp had a sense of permanence about it. As if most of its inhabitants had been here for days if not weeks and with no sign of any leaving.

He forced himself to look. To witness their plight. Most were children and their mothers, else were old and frail. *Where are the fathers and the older sons and daughters?*

"The High Lady has conscripted the able-bodied," Ironside observed from behind as if reading Darion's mind. "But it seems she does not wish to inflict the dispossessed upon the rest of Cumbrenan."

Darion rode on in silence. What was there to say? That it was barbaric, inhuman? Those were words, all just empty words. Words that would not help these people. Marron would have been distraught. She would have tried to help, to do something, anything, but he knew not what and he felt weak, impotent by his lack.

Bindu loped in the verge, head lowered, reflecting her master's mood. Some of the children ran alongside the road enthralled by the wolfdog and Darion watched as she let them pat her and run hands through her fur. She too was silent when normally she would growl warning at such attention.

They passed a waymarker for Thorn Nook and shortly after it the children fell away, returning to the squalor of camp and Darion was ashamed to feel a sense of relief.

The road east was flat and straight and unusually quiet of traffic. It took them through farmlands, with fallow fields covered in pristine snow and orchards that were bare of leaf and fruit. The small villages that they passed were subdued, its residents watching in silent regard from open doorways and street corners.

In the summer months, they would have reached Thorn Nook in a day, but the winter sun was soon descending toward the western horizon and the light started to falter.

Lyra Casitigan, who rode lead with Gatzinger, called out. "There is a farm ahead and I know the farmer. I'm sure he'll put us up for the night in his barn."

Ironside trotted his horse forward from the rear. "We should ride through to Thorn Nook. The clouds are breaking and the moons will light the roads, enough at least to see by."

Lyra shook her head. "With what has happened we can't chance it. If Thorn Nook is anything like Lakeside it's too risky. We'll overnight here, bypass Thorn Nook on the morrow then strike east for Waterdale."

"What do you mean by what has happened?" Father Melbroth called out.

Lyra looked at Ironside who gave a reluctant nod before she answered. "The High King was poisoned and lies dead or close enough to it as to make no difference. Crown Prince Herald stands accused of high treason and the Order is falsely implicated. Lord Renix, who was our ambassador to the High King, has been murdered without trial by Princess Matrice. The Order Accords were already rescinded by the Rivers and Cumbrenan but suffice it to say our stock has fallen even lower. We are hunted openly now and not just by the Red Church."

"When?" Darion asked. "How long have you known?"

Ironside twisted in his saddle to stare at him. "Six days, Keeper informed us at Lower Rippleton."

"And you only seek to tell us this now?" Father Melbroth rejoined.

"Save your anger, Priest. You are lucky we told you at all. Now there's a risk you'll act differently. Fearfully. If we must deal with any patrols or checkpoints that fear can be smelt or seen and acted upon. So no, we did not tell you sooner. It did not suit our purpose. Still doesn't." He aimed this last at Castigan who shrugged indifferently.

There was a flutter of wings as Bezal glided in, flapped and stalled to alight upon the white-clad shoulder of R'ell, interrupting their discourse. R'ell bowed his hooded head low as if the raven whispered to him.

"We are followed. Two men on horseback."

"How does the bird know this?" Castigan asked. "Any may travel the road to Thorn Nook."

The shadowed hood yawed toward the Order woman. "They stop when we stop, as a hunter might that stalks its prey. They observe us from afar."

"Do not stare, Father," Castigan ordered Melbroth, who squinted into the failing sun.

"Sorry," The priest muttered, contrite.

"Come. Let's find this farmer," Ironside said. "We will do as you suggest, Lyra."

It was said a little too easily, Darion thought. He watched the two Order Knights, aware that some unspoken exchange occurred between them, for they held each other's gaze overlong before Lyra abruptly turned and led them on.

She took them down a beaten, rutted track to a squat farmhouse that licked a lazy ribbon of smoke into the air from a lone chimney stack.

As the wagons rolled into the courtyard, dogs barked wildly to announce their arrival and Bindu's hackles rose at the challenge. Darion called out to settle her just as a trio of hounds belted around the side of a large barn.

The horses pulling the lead wagon shied at the clamour and R'ell leapt down from the box seat where he rode beside Gatzinger and confronted the dogs. Holding his hands out flat, he called to them and the dogs immediately fell silent and lowered themselves to the ground. The dogs watched the ilf avidly until he was next to them, then rolled over as his hands rubbed at their ruffs and then their bellies.

The door to the farmhouse creaked open and a tall man limped out, bearing a hardwood staff in his right hand and wearing a sour expression. An expression that lifted a little when he spied Castigan.

"Lady Merrin? T'is late," the man said. He glanced at the party in one easy sweep, eyes widening at sighting the White Priests.

"Rollo," Castigan replied, "I'm sorry for the lateness of the hour. How is your good wife and family?"

"Ai, Marley's fine considering. Rest 'ave gone. Lord Ferec's men took 'em almost a ten-day back. Din't offer no choice. Just stuck'em aboard a wagon for this 'ere war ah theirs. So if ya've come looking ya'selves, ya too late."

"I'm sorry, Rollo. I didn't know. I assure you conscription is not our purpose. We're escorting the White Fathers here to the Monastery at Borin. I was hoping…."

"I know what ya's hopin', Lady Merrin." Rollo sniffed, then regarded them in sombre silence for a few seconds. "Guess you better put the wagons in the barn. There are spare stalls for your horses. You know where."

The farmer turned to go but paused in the doorway. "I'll tell Marley to make some more stew." Then he disappeared inside.

"He doesn't seem none too pleased to see you, Lady Merrin," Ironside remarked. "He always this dour?"

"Oh, he likes me well enough. It's the rest of you he's not so sure of. Let's get these wagons in and the horses settled whilst there is still some light."

Afterwards, with the wagons unhitched and the horses rubbed down, watered and fed, they assembled near the front of the barn.

"Rollo is a good and simple man, but he knows not who I am," Lyra began. "It goes without saying, M'rika and R'ell must remain here. We cannot risk revealing their identity. The less he and his wife know the safer it will be."

"Safer for us you mean," Darion answered.

"For all of us. A man cannot tell what he does not know," Lyra replied.

"Then I will remain too. With Bindu," Darion said. "I'll not take a man's food under false pretence."

Ironside shook his head. "Ai, but you'll take his shelter. Thought we taught you better than that, man. Save your self-righteousness, come, eat."

But Darion would not be moved on it and the others soon left, Father Melbroth having been persuaded by Ironside. "It'll look suspicious if no White Fathers attend," he'd argued.

Darion was relieved once they were gone. He felt much like he had aboard the *Eastern Promise*, adrift, his life's path at the mercy of events and those others around him. He twisted the ring on his finger, as was his habit when he took to self-reflection. The warmth that had made it seem almost alive was long gone and the metal lay cold against his skin. *Marron is dead and Nihm has gone, what in hells am I doing? I am alone.*

Bindu's wet nose nudged against his hand and he dropped to his haunches and ruffed her neck affectionately. "You know what I mean, girl," he murmured, staring into her soulful, amber eyes. "Come on, best keep busy."

Grabbing his waterskin, he moved to the well and refilled it before beginning a slow patrol of the courtyard, familiarising himself with what there was and the layout. The stables around the back housed their horses along with an old, rangy mare of the farmers that seemed indifferent to her guests.

Back in the barn, M'rika and R'ell were stood, eating something. Darion's stomach ached, reminding him he'd barely eaten all day. He ignored its complaint, cured jerky and hardtack was all he had, and he couldn't face it right then.

"You seem troubled, ilf-friend."

To Darion, M'rika's all-dark eyes seemed soft somehow as she spoke.

"Worried, that's all."

M'rika nodded understanding. "You fear for Nihm. I see that."

"Do you? Do the ilfanum know what it is like to have a family? To love and then lose that which makes them whole?" Darion asked.

"We all know loss. I would die for Da'Mari, would have for Grold as he did for me. What greater love is there than that, friend Darion?" M'rika's voice was steady but Darion couldn't help but notice that the vibrancy of her leaf scale had dimmed a little on her face, it was the only part of her that he could see from the robes that covered her, it was as if a shadow had passed across her.

"That was careless. I was not thinking. I did not mean to cause you pain."

M'rika smiled. "I remember all of Groldtigkah, not just the ending of him. It is as it should be. Pain after all is part of life. Without it, we would feel nothing."

R'ell shook his head, "I do not understand humans."

"How so?" Darion asked, it was rare that R'ell spoke or offered an opinion. "All most want are simple things. A family, a good home with food and friends, a means to live and forge our own lives."

"The words you speak do not match the actions I see," R'ell complained. "You live on top of each other in your cities and your towns which reek as a seven-day carcass reeks, of corruption and poison. You covet more than what is needed and to the detriment of others, creating few with much and much with few. You do not act as a herd might, nor with the ordered structure other species exhibit. You take from the land but do not give back. There is an imbalance in humans that makes no sense to me."

It was the most Darion had ever heard R'ell say and he found his words disquieting. "It is our nature to seek more. To be more, to better ourselves. Without it, we would still be living beneath animal hides, roaming the land and foraging, surviving rather than living. We would have no written word, or books or great places of learning. We have made many mistakes, but we have also accomplished much as a people."

R'ell shrugged. "I saw a thing today that troubled me greatly. The human elders and the younglings discarded outside the settlement you call Lakeside, it was, disturbing."

M'rika laid a hand on R'ell's arm. "You are Umphathi and have only known the forests of the Rohelinewaald. You have limited contact with the wider world of which there is much to understand, even by me whose purpose it is to know. Not all ravens are the same as your Bezal and not all humans are the same as friend Darion. We fulfil a different purpose for Da'Mari but in the end, we are both gardeners are we not?"

"We are," R'ell said.

"Then do not judge. Observe, listen and seek understanding. In the end, Da'Mari will decide on all things."

R'ell inclined his head and shoulders toward M'rika. "Forgive me K'raal. I did not mean to speak out of turn."

"Nonsense." Darion clapped R'ell on the back. "Never fear to speak to me or ask your questions. You have made me think on things I took for granted without consideration. And that is a good thing."

Bindu's head lifted toward the barn entrance, ears trained forward. Both ilfanum were immediately wary and Darion turned to look. There was nothing but the night outside. R'ell moved swiftly to the barn door and peered unobtrusively through a crack in its wood. He stayed transfixed for a dozen heartbeats then signed to M'rika.

"It is the one called Ironside. He has left the farmhouse and moves in stealth back toward the road," M'rika reported.

"Alone?" Darion asked.

The ilf nodded confirmation. Then placed a hand on Darion's shoulder as he went to move past. "No good will come of following him."

"He means to do murder." Darion pushed by and Bindu fell into step alongside. Picking his sword up on the way out, he left, taking the track back toward the road.

The way was dark, the tri-moons hidden in cloud, their orbs sullen imprints in the sky. Darion sent Bindu ranging ahead, the hunt familiar to both. Reaching the main road, they turned back towards Lakeside and followed the way up the smallest of inclines. At its apex a blossom of light could be seen to his right, yellow fingers dancing against trunk and tree branch.

Bindu waited, low and alert, pointing the way. Darion found boot prints in the snow stretching toward the firelight. He patted her and immediately she sloped off in a hunter's crouch, paws punching almost soundlessly through the snow crust.

Stepping in the broken footprints, Darion stalked toward the fire. A growl in the night sounded to his left, Bindu had found something, something that was aware of her presence else she would have remained silent.

Darion drew his sword and sprang forward, speed more important than stealth. A black shape stepped out in front of him, silhouetted by the campfire behind.

"It is done. Put your sword up, Darion." Ironside's voice was precise and calm.

"What is done?" Though Darion knew, had guessed already back at the barn. He rose to his full height and brushed past the Order Knight to the camp beyond.

A canvas hung over a low branch and a man lay sheltered beneath, asleep on a bedroll. The blood from the gash in his throat gave the lie to that, it stained his neck and chest and soaked the covers, looking brown and corrupt in the grey-light. The man hadn't awakened, didn't see his death coming or the blade that claimed it.

"Why?" Darion asked, he faced Ironside. "Why? He was someone's father, a son. A man murdered for following orders."

Ironside laughed. "The Wylds are meant to harden a man, not make him soft."

"What, ya think this amusing? Ya killed a man." Darion squared his shoulders.

Ironside's humour vanished. "Lower your tone. You weep for this piece of shit who would turn you in to people who would burn you alive at a stake. So yeah, my fucking arse I killed him. You got no idea do you?"

"No, but I'm starting ta see the light now." Darion's voice lowered.

Ironside stepped in and grabbed a fistful of tunic and pulled the bigger man to him. It elicited a full-throated growl from Bindu that rattled in ominous warning.

"Back, girl," Darion commanded.

Through clenched teeth, Ironside hissed. "Good, cause if she takes a bite, I will end her in a heartbeat."

"And then we'd have an accounting," Darion replied.

Ironside pushed him away. "We're at war, fool, have been for centuries only now it's out in the open. There's no sitting on the fence. No pretending it is otherwise. My mission is to get the ilfanum to Keeper. Pray you do not get in my way."

Ironside spun, sword hissing as it left its scabbard, so fast that Darion barely had time to startle. He was aware of movement. A dark mass in the night that was not there before. That Bindu gave no warning was strange until the darkness spoke.

"You talk so loudly, I heard you from the roadside." M'rika stepped out from the night and into the flicker of firelight. Her hands were empty. "Lower your sword and step away from Darion. He is ilf-friend and Da'Mari's chosen, you may not threaten him without consequence."

"You think an ilf is a match for me?" Ironside growled.

M'rika's eyes blinked in slow regard. Ironside moved but not before an arrow thumped, embedding itself into the trunk of the nearest tree, sending splintered wood bark pattering against the knight.

"Let's not find out," M'rika said. "Even should you best me, you would fail your mission would you not?"

Ironside gave a sudden grin and slid his sword back into its sheath. "You have a point."

"I have another," M'rika said. "Friend Darion is correct. Your actions were precipitous and illogical. You killed one man when two followed. The other no doubt returns to report on our direction of travel. Before, we were a curiosity. Now, you have told them we are not. In future, do nothing without discussing it with me, else we will go our separate ways to this Isle of yours."

M'rika held her hand out and gestured to Darion. "Come, we will return. Ironside of the Order will clean this mess up." She turned to the Knight. "The body must be hidden, the blood and all trace of this camp removed as if it never was."

* * *

The incident was not spoken of again. The only reference made was by Lyra Castigan, who calmly informed Ironside that he had blood upon his cheek.

In the morning they left before the sun had risen and though a light shone through the shutters of the farmhouse they never stopped to offer thanks or say goodbye. 'Lady Merrin' had offered both the night before.

As a final act, Lyra left two tarnished silver kerns in a pouch then placed it on the porch by the door. She would have left more but knew if Lord Vandis of Lakeside or Lord Ferec of Thorn Nook came looking for their man and called on Rollo and Marley, that if any more were discovered it would be out of place. The two had lost their children, taken for the war. They had lost enough already.

Chapter 22: River City

Rivercross, The Rivers

Rivercross sat at the northernmost tip of the Emerald Lake at the confluence of three mighty rivers, the Fossa, the Oust and the Plago. The River City, as it was oft known, was built on four tracts of land that had been carved and fashioned by the rivers. Along their wide, open flanks, immense walls towered above the flood plains, protected by deep moats that were fed by the great rivers. It painted an illusion that the city floated upon the Emerald Lake.

"It looks so big. I bet it smells bad," Belle announced. The street orphan sat upon a wagon next to Jerkze. It had been given to them, albeit temporarily, by Captain Maesons, the commander in charge of the Red Cloak auxiliaries.

"Thorsten stinks worse," Jerkze replied.

"Does not," Belle spluttered.

"Does too." He glanced at her and laughed at her expression. Jerkze passed the reins from his good hand to the other, his wounded arm trussed up still in a sling, then pointed across the flood plains at the wide ribbon of the Oust and traced its flow to the city.

"See, the rivers bring fresh water in and wash the muck and filth out." He grinned. "So, for a big city, Rivercross smells not too bad." He passed the reins back from his weak hand.

Belle looked thoughtfully at the tall walls and the wide, mirror sharp waters of the moat. There were boats upon it, punting around the city's girth. "I'd like to see inside. Do you think Lord Amos will take us?"

"I don't expect so, Belle." He ruffled her hair drawing a glare for his trouble. "Our journey lies south."

"With these Red Cloaks?"

"Ai, as far as Killenhess at least." His comments drew another scowl from the girl. "They lent us a wagon; else you'd be riding double with me on horseback. You didn't like that much the last time as I recall," he chided.

"I can ride by myself," Belle said with the bravado of a ten-year-old, believing her lie even if only for a minute. Her eyes shifted to Lady Constance Bouchemeax riding just ahead with Jobe and the big man everyone called Lucky. Her friend was only a year older than her, yet she sat the saddle as if melded to it. How hard could it be?

Conn giggled at something the giant said and Belle felt her teeth grind.

Glancing across, Jerkze saw the pinched expression on the girl's face and followed the line of her sight.

"I'll teach ya when we've time," he assured her. "Lady Constance has been astride a horse since she could walk. I'll have ya riding just as good soon enough."

Belle pouted. "Tell me something funny?"

Scratching his chin, Jerkze thought for a while, then gave a short nod and smiled. "When I was a boy, nought much older'n you, I knew this man, old man Barley, mean as a cuss. Blind, with one leg. Use ta clatter about on a crutch."

"What's 'mean as a cuss'?" Belle asked.

"Jus' grumpy, cranky, I guess."

Belle's nose wrinkled. "Doesn't sound funny."

"I've not told it yet," Jerkze complained. Then, at her raised eyebrow, he snapped. "You wanna hear it or not?"

The girl shrugged. "Sure, I guess."

"Alright then," Jerkze composed himself, sniffed a sharp breath and began. "Bitter Barley we called him."

"Cause he was mean as a cuss?" Belle queried.

"Exactly, now you wanna ask twenty questions or ya gonna listen?" His brow furrowed when Belle mimed stitching her lip. Chary, he started again.

"Bitter Barley might be blind but 'e prided himself on knowin' his way around everywhere. Lived in or around town see, since afore he was blind." Jerkze held a finger up in warning to Belle, who looked about to interrupt. She refrained and an increasingly disgruntled Jerkze continued.

"One day walkin' ta town, he decides to take a shortcut across a wheat field. It was the funniest thing, weren't found till the next day, exhausted and madder than a snared weasel." Jerkze tapped his thigh at the memory and chortled. "See, with one leg and no eyes, Bitter Barley never trod a straight line. With no path ta follow he'd walked a circle neat as can be. Musta gone five leagues or more and never left that damn field. The farmer was fit to bust when 'e found him."

Belle's nose wrinkled. "That's horrible."

"Eh?" Jerkze laughed, wiping a hand to an eye. "Na, it's hilarious. See he kept walkin'. In a circle."

"Maybe Barley was bitter because you were all mean to him. Mean as a cuss."

"What, no. You don't get it? That's not how it was." His reply was cut short when a mounted Amos and Mercy trotted up alongside their wagon.

Amos stared between the pair. Jerkze vexed and Belle serious. "All okay?"

"He told me a joke about Bitter Barley," Belle announced.

"Saint alive," Mercy cursed with a laugh. "You still telling that tale. It's not even an amusing anecdote."

"What's an anecdote?"

"Don't answer that else we'll be here till nightfall," Jerkze warned. Then, at Belle's cross look, he relented. "I'll explain it later."

Up ahead, rising above the ordered column of Red Cloaks was the tall spire of a tower and Amos pointed it out. "That's High Praise. Lord Commander Whent intends to clear the tower hamlet and set up camp past Dunning."

Jerkze glanced at the cotton clouds, judging the height of the watery sun. "There's more 'n enough light left in the day to reach further south. To East Rising at least."

Shaking her head, Mercy disagreed. "Road will be full past Dunning and on the Plago Bridge. Bullish as the Red Cloaks are at clearing the way it'd be dark before we reached East Rising."

Jerkze glanced about for any Red Cloaks in earshot. "Let's thank the Lord Commander and take our leave then. We can travel further and faster than an army of Red Cloaks."

"No," Amos said. "At least, not yet. There are conflicting reports of urakakule to the east, crossing the Plago out near Charncross."

"You think them true?" Jerkze asked.

"Who knows? Probably more risk of getting ourselves conscripted. There's an aggressive drive for recruits. I think slow and safe with Whent is our best call for now." With that, Amos spurred his horse on, Mercy by his side.

Belle watched them pull alongside the others, Amos gesticulating as he explained. They were Duncans, brother and sister, Lord and Lady. She'd been wary of Mercy at first. She was a mage for one thing, for another the scar that marred her features lent a stern look Belle found intimidating. But having ridden with Lady Mercy for a day, Belle had come to realise that although more serious than her brother, she was just as kindly.

Mercy's forecast proved prophetic, the small hamlet of High Praise was packed with people, bannermen and refugees alike and it took a while to clear it and reach the snow-crusted fields beyond. To the north, rows upon rows of neatly ordered tents were arrayed, flying the pennants of a dozen Lords. To the south, more camps, these of the dispossessed, a patchwork quilt of browns and greys with thick ribbons of smoke rising between them.

The village of Dunning lay ahead and the roads became congested. The army of Red Cloaks snaked south to avoid it, churning the hard ground and snow into a pliant sludge under their procession. Rivercross sat away on their right, the walls formidable, the Margate barbican imposing. Crossing the Dunning Road, they turned east again toward the Plago

Bridge where the lead elements had already encamped in the same regimented order as they always did.

Belle found herself watching as the others set up their tents. Conn was busy, tending to the horses with Jerkze, limping on a crutch, and Junip. The young mage seemed eager to help out even though she wasn't much better than her with the beasts. Belle caught a snippet of conversation. Jerkze was retelling his tale of Bitter Barley to Junip. With a groan of disdain, she moved away, any thoughts of lending a hand vanished.

She wandered around the wagon pleased to stretch her legs, knowing she should be doing something to help only no one had told her what. Bored and curious to explore, she waited for her moment before slipping away unobserved. She'd be back before anyone noticed.

Walking between avenues of tents, dodging stern and busy looking Red Cloaks, Belle reached a wider path. Drawn by a rowdy chorus of jeers and laughter she turned and followed the noise, skirting wagons on her right and tents on her left. A thrill of fear and daring fluttered in her chest, for she should not be here. Only nobody seemed to bother. The sounds rose and with it her curiosity. Some sport from the heckling banter.

Passing a food wagon her stomach growled in hunger. It was unguarded, so Belle helped herself to a hard loaf and an apple, tucking the latter in her pocket for later. Tearing a chunk of bread off with her teeth she chewed it, moving along before she was discovered.

The noise grew close and drew her between two wagons where Belle was confronted by a wall of men, all with their backs to her. Scared to push through and draw unwanted attention but eager to see what occurred, she clambered aboard the nearest wagon and hunkered unobtrusively behind the riding board.

There were a dozen red cloaks making noise enough for twice that number. Over the tops of their heads, Belle spied what had their attention. Another wagon, this one bearing a cage and inside it the blocky, bulk of an urak.

The urak sat immobile. It had been marked, a rivulet of blood, dark against grey skin, ran down its arm. The Red Cloaks taunted it. The butt of a spear weaved outside the bars to draw the urak's attention. With a snarling rush, it spun, swiping at a spear shaft that suddenly thrust from the opposite side of its cage. It was quick, got a hand to it but the Red Cloak holding the spear wrenched it free before it could grip it properly. The back of its head was struck by the first enticer, short and sharp. It growled, swiping backhanded but too late to strike its antagonist.

A man ran past her wagon, startling Belle who ducked behind the seat. She'd been too slow, the guard must have seen her.

Then came a whispered shout, a name. "HENREECE."

Boots mulched and armour creaked. Belle risked a peek above the riding board in time to see the Red Cloaks dispersing between the wagons, moving in all directions but the one the lookout had come from. Until only one remained.

Unhurried, this Red Cloak glanced around then walked to the back of the cage wagon unhitching his belt and trousers on the way. Belle saw him fumble down below, her eyes widening when a pale stream arced out and into a bucket, tinkling a tune on its way. He was soon done, shook himself off then tucked himself in before buttoning up and cinching his belt again. "See how ya like the flavour of your water now, eh." He banged his palm against the bars of the cage.

This time, without the noise of the spectacle, Belle heard the steady tread from behind and ducked lower in the wagon as a man marched right past her.

"Sir."

"There is meant to be two here. At all times. Where is our Brother?" The voice was soft to Belle's ears, friendly almost but the guard sounded nervous. Belle risked a peek.

"Mehrtens got the shits, 'e won't be long, sir."

The new man was red-cloaked like the rest but wore a black, quilted top that looked heavy and warm. He didn't say anything for a bit and the guard shifted, the bluster leeching out of him with every passing second.

"Did Brother Mehrtens complain of fever or nausea? Belly cramps, maybe?" Blacktop asked.

"I'm not sure, sir."

"Tell me, why is there fresh blood on my urak?" Blacktop stepped closer to the cage. "And bruising on its head?"

He was slight, half a hand shorter than the guard, but all the threat emanated from him as he swung to face the bigger man, "A Brother died capturing this urak, yet you think it alright to have your sport with it. Do you think this is a game? That this creature is here for your amusement?"

"No, Sir."

Belle grinned at the guard's discomfort.

"No, Sir," Blacktop repeated, so softly Belle had to strain to catch the words. A knife appeared in his hand. "If I believe you, Brother, then I am forced to conclude that you betrayed your orders. Else, I must assume you just lied to me. Which is it I wonder?"

The guard said nothing, but Belle could see that his face had drained of colour.

Blacktop casually raised the knife and rested its tip against the man's left cheekbone near the outside corner of his eye. "Do not move."

The knife slash was sudden and the Red Cloak was unable to stop from flinching. Skin parted from eye to jaw, blood sluicing from the wound to sheet his face.

"It smarts like a bastard, doesn't it?" Blacktop smiled. "I will arrange new guards, ones I can trust. Now go, leave the wound unattended. Seek me out before morning prayer and I will heal it for you. Until then, consider your actions, accept your penance."

Groaning, the guard clasped a hand to his cheek and moaned a response before shuffling, hurriedly away.

"Oh, and tell brother Mehrtens I would like to see him when he has finished shitting," Blacktop called after him. Arms outstretched, he turned a slow pirouette and raised his voice.

"I trust this has been a valuable lesson to you all. This is my beast. If there is a next time, know that I will not be so tolerant."

Belle didn't know to whom he spoke, there was no one here but him and the urak. She felt her heart trip, and me, she realised.

Blacktop returned to the cage as if suddenly recalled to the urak it contained. "Your kind tortured and murdered our brethren. Hung their mutilated corpses outside our camp. So you see, my Brothers are rightly riled."

The urak remained silent.

"I am sorry they attacked you. Not for the pain they caused, that you deserve, but at their loss of discipline. Because discipline is important, yes? Without it, we are no better than animals. Ruled by need and desire."

Blacktop shook his head. "I know you understand my words. I can read it in your face, see it in your eyes. You will talk to me." Spinning on his heel, Belle ducked low, listening as he marched by her wagon until his steps vanished in the hubbub of camp life.

Scrambling down, Belle knew she should get back to Amos and the others, but something compelled her and she found herself standing by the cage.

The grey-skinned urak regarded her back, eyes set wide and intelligent. Belle was fascinated. Its face was flat and broad with a large mouth, squat nose and a ridged and bony forehead creased by a puckered scar that looked newly healed. Short, dark hair slicked into spikes gave it an unexpected flamboyance.

The urak leered suddenly, flashing a mouthful of blocky teeth and she jumped, a gasp escaping her. It rumbled and in sudden intuition, Belle realised it was laughing. It made the urak less scary, that a beast could laugh so.

She remembered the guard from earlier, pissing in the bucket and his words afterwards. Moving to the pail, she knocked it over, spilling the water.

"You can't drink that. It's dirty," Belle announced moving back to the cage.

"I'm Annabelle, but my friends call me Belle."

The urak blinked then slowly turned away.

"I'm sorry they beat you. They shouldn't be mean like that." Belle sighed, she should get back. What was she even doing talking to it? She slipped the remains of her loaf through the bars and reached inside her pocket.

The urak lunged and, too slow to escape, Belle gave a startled squeal. Grasping a fistful of clothing like so much loose skin it hoisted her high, dragging her against the bars until their eyes were only inches apart.

Too scared to speak, Belle held her hand out. In it was the apple she'd stolen earlier. The urak sniffed her face as tears leaked down her cheeks.

Its gaze flickered to the apple, snatched it from her hand then raised it to its nose. Belle screwed her eyes shut, fear pounding off her only to feel herself being lowered and then released.

Cracking an eye open, she was in time to see the urak lick the apple. She took a step back, then another, out of reach. "You bite it, not lick it." Belle turned to go. She had pushed her luck enough for one day.

"Belle."

The name was barked like a cough. She glanced back over her shoulder at the cage. The beast touched a fist to its chest. "Bartuk."

"Bartuk." She tried the name several times, then smiled. "You called me Belle. That means we're friends. I have to go but I'll try and see you again, promise. I'll bring some proper food."

She fled, pleased to get away but also, feeling strangely euphoric. The urak could have killed her but hadn't. Instead, it had spoken her name and given his. That had to mean something, didn't it?

Bartuk. She rolled the name around in her mind and grinned.

* * *

It was safe to say that Belle's absence had not gone unnoticed. On her way back she soon got turned around, one tent looking much the same as the next. She had wandered up and down the camp lost until she spied the tall frame of Lucky who spotted her in the same instant.

"Fool of a girl, it's lucky I found you," he said as they came together. The words, though, held no bite and his grin told of his relief.

"I got lost," Belle tried.

"Ai, we gathered that. But here's the thing." Lucky crouched so that he could look her in the eyes. "You're one of us now. We watch out for each other, see. So you can't just take off without letting anyone know. Otherwise, it don't work."

"I thought you'd be angry," Belle confessed only for Lucky to laugh.

"Ai, well, you have a point and I'm sure you'll feel some heat from Amos and Lady Constance. Mercy and Junip too if I'm not mistaken. The way I figure it that's more 'n enough telling for one young adventurer that you don't need none from me." Lucky stood and was surprised when a little hand slipped inside his. Awkward, he set off for their tents.

In the end, it wasn't nearly so bad as Belle thought it might be. Conn was first to spot her and cried out in relief before rushing and clasping her tight. She felt guilty at the worry she'd caused but at the same time warm inside. She was a street kid from the westside and Conn a noble and yet her friend's emotion was real, Belle could feel her trembling as they hugged. "Next time, take me with you," Conn had whispered, drawing a smile.

As for Amos, he berated her soundly for running off and made her swear not to do it again but that was all. She wasn't even thrashed for her misadventure or starved. The worst punishment came from Junip. The apprentice mage lectured her endlessly until inflicting the worst of ordeals upon her.

"Lady Constance tells me you cannot read. Since you have time on your hands to run off and get up to mischief, I will teach you your letters."

The next morning, the Red Cloaks were up before first light. They broke camp and by the time the sun cleared the eastern horizon, they were on the march again.

Belle rode with Jerkze on the wagon but this time Conn joined them and sat beside her, her horse tied to the backboard. The two girls chatted ceaselessly.

Conn pointed out the battlements at Rivercross and then switched to the people camped outside the walls, both fascinated and worried by their plight. Belle felt bad, having never considered what it might be like for them. The way she saw it they were no different from her. However, Conn's concern even after having lost everything, including her whole family, was genuine and it made Belle feel small.

Keeping the village of Dunning to their left, they passed camps of soldiers and Conn further impressed her by naming each flag of every House they passed and their Lords. It left Belle wondering how she could remember such things.

The front of the column started across the Plago Bridge and it was as they approached it that Conn suddenly stopped talking, midsentence and stared.

"What is it, Conn? What's wrong?" Belle asked. Her friend's eyes were transfixed ahead but she did not answer. Instead, it was Jerkze that spoke but not to her.

"Amos, Mercy," he called out. By the time the two rode forward and joined them the bridge was twenty paces away.

"What is it?" Amos asked reining his horse in.

"Those guards on the bridge. The tabards they wear."

Now she knew to look, Belle noticed instantly. The soldiers wore the Black Crow of Thorsten.

Amos whistled and signalled ahead to the others and together they pulled themselves out of the column of Red Cloaks. Conn jumped down before the wagon had stopped and was running. Stopping in front of a giant, bear of a man, bigger even than Lucky. She did not know him, though his size seemed familiar to her.

"Who are you to wear my house colours?" Her voice was high and shrill, and her face flushed, though not from the cold air.

The Red Cloak wagons rumbled past, the flat steel tires loud against the worn cobbles. The giant Black Crow detached himself from the rest of the guards and stepped forward. His eyes glanced at the woman behind, mounted but dressed in fine leathers and a thick cloak of high quality. He knew her. Had left her not five days gone on the banks of the Fossa. Lady Mercy Duncan.

The girl before him repeated her demand and he turned back to her. "How can this be?" he asked. His face was earnest, struggling to believe who this child must be but knowing it was true. It was proven beyond doubt when Junip Jorgstein suddenly appeared. He knew her well enough to recognise, even though they had never spoken before.

He dropped to his knee and bowed his head. "Forgive me, my Lady. I am Sergeant Mal Kronke. My commander was Captain Anders Forstandt who died fighting urak near the Old Forest. My Lord is Richard Bouchemeax of Thorsten."

Kronke glanced behind and gave a sharp twitch of his head, and the four guardsmen, three in Black Crow livery and one without, dropped to a knee.

"I am Lady Constance Bouchemeax, daughter of Richard. You have a story to tell and one to hear, but that will be for later," Conn said. "How many?"

"Just what you see here, My Lady. The rest perished in the north."

"Rise, please. All of you." Conn signed for them to get up. "Sergeant, how is it you come to be guarding this bridge?"

Kronke looked down at the girl. Diminutive she might be, but the Black Crow's daughter carried herself as a Lady, not the child she was.

"That is a long story best told in private. Lady Mercy there knows most of it."

Conn glanced at Mercy, who nodded, then back at the moustachioed giant as he spoke again.

"The short of it is that Lord Idris Inigo of Confluence has taken us in. He supports our cause and has been willing to provide us with food and supplies. In return, we pay with service. Lord Inigo has been tasked with guarding the Plago Bridge and by happy circumstance, you caught us on duty."

"Your duty is in the north, to my father," Conn snapped. "Not hiding down here with Lord Twyford and his lackeys. A man who has forsaken the north. A man…."

Amos placed a hand on her shoulder. She flinched unaware he had dismounted.

"Words spoken in the wrong place can be dangerous, My Lady. The Red Cloaks will not wait, we need to leave, now."

"I will not leave without my Crows," Conn declared.

Amos cast a doubtful eye over them. The big man seemed formidable, but size was not an indicator of ability. The rest were motley, one of them not even in uniform. He looked down at Lady Constance and could see the determination on her face.

"Mercy, take Lucky and Stama and inform Lord Commander Whent we will be delayed. Tell him we will catch them on the road."

He waited while they rode off, rejoining the flow of Red Cloaks as they crossed the bridge, then he faced Lady Constance once more.

"Well then. Guess we'd best go find this Lord Inigo."

Chapter 23: Lady White Crow

The winds of war blow in the north, the embers of strife fanning into flame between Westlands and Rivers.

Its locus is the Wesling Rumbles which marks their border. It is a hilly moorland that no Lord would want were it not for the iron and copper lying buried beneath its black loam. And, at the heart of this contestation sits the town of Ganz. For it is known that whosoever controls Ganz controls the Rumbles.

My Lord knew that with both kingdoms maintaining sovereignty, confrontation was only a matter of time. With that expectation, he sent his third son and third daughter north to take stock of its Lords and Ladies and measure the character of its peoples. To assess their resolve and gauge the possible magnitude of the coming conflict.

Only now war is here. Thrust upon us in soonisity by a different antagonist and upon a different field. Not some low-scale, disingenuous play for metal waged by greedy High Lords but an abrupt and brutal invasion by a long-forgotten foe.

Urakakule.

Taken from the Journal of Remus Fitch, Steward to Atticus Duncan of Hawke Hold, The Duncan (1017c 4A)

Rivercross, The Rivers

Nothing ever quite works out the way it's meant to, thought Amos. Coming north, he'd hoped to see the Old Forest and gaze upon ilfanum lands. To behold the mighty peaks of the Torns, called in ancient scrolls 'Teeth of the World' and, heroically, the 'Dragon's Spine' in even older vellums.

Alas, it wasn't to be and his desire to explore remained unfulfilled, for, at Thorsten, everything had changed. There had died Silver and Seb, one an old friend the other a young one. Then had come urak and bloody war joined. A war which the Kingdoms were hopelessly unprepared for.

Safety lay south, as did his charge, given to Lord Richard Bouchemeax the Black Crow, to remove his daughter to the sanctuary of Hawke Hold. However, for someone who had only seen eleven summers, the young lady was proving hopelessly difficult. Jaw tightening, Amos glanced toward the grey-haired, liver-spotted Osirus Smee who was talking in droll overtones.

"Lady Bouchemeax, your father lives still. The magus, Lutico, possesses a wizarding orb and has been reporting to the magisterium. Thorsten lies in ruin but the Black Keep holds."

Amos gave a hard stare to the mage from Confluence. The news, whilst good, would do little to help his cause, for the Lady Constance was already wavering. He watched her place her head in her hands and sob, and little mousy-haired Annabelle wrap arms around her in comfort.

A street urchin and a lady, it should have made Amos smile but not today. "That news is blessedly welcome," Amos said drily. He turned to the boy that was trying so hard to be a man.

"Lord Inigo, the Lady Constance politely seeks discharge of her Black Crows from their service to you. If we are to catch up to the Red Cloaks we travel with we will need to leave soonest."

Idris Inigo wore a solemn expression that seemed misplaced for one so young. "Of course. I will arrange for a replacement guard at the Plago Bridge. Si Manko will see to it."

"My Lord," acknowledged the lean-framed man sitting on the camp stool to Inigo's left, his brown eyes sharp and intense despite his relaxed posture.

"You should make haste," continued Lord Inigo, "It is said the Cumbrenans hold our peoples at the border, in camps. For processing supposedly. The Red Cloaks at least will get you through that cordon. I mean no disrespect Lord Amos, Lady Mercy when I say that your appearance does not lend itself to your status."

"It has been a hard road," Amos admitted, dusting at his clothes as if it might improve their condition.

Constance rubbed the tears from her face leaving smudge stains on her cheeks. "No. I won't go."

Amos frowned. "My Lady, we have spoken about this. Your father…"

"…sent me away because he expects to die. Would have my mother too, if she were not so frail and stubborn. Now that I am here, I will not run any further. The Black Crow is my father and I know he would not tuck tail and run. Nor leave our peoples stranded on the plains like chaff from the harvest. If you say otherwise, I will call you a liar and meet you outside this pavilion with my sword."

The Lady Constance did not possess a sword. Amos stared down at the little girl who glared defiantly back. "I gave your Lord Father my oath."

With an exasperated huff, Mercy stepped forward, her face twisted in stern reproach. "It is to secure your future Lady Constance and that of Thorsten. When this war is done it will be up to you to rebuild what has been lost."

"With what?" Constance Bouchemeaux trilled. "They are just empty words to make me leave. How in the name of the One can I, in all good conscious abandon the very people you would have me rebuild for. No, I will not go. And I will not debate it further. Captain Kronke."

"It's a, Sergeant Kronke, My Lady," rumbled the immense Black Crow, moustachioed ends quivering as he spoke.

"I have a mage advisor in Junip and 'Your Lady' requires a Captain of her guard, which is you until I say otherwise." Constance talked with proficient quickness, afraid to leave space for someone, anyone to fill. She had never been so bold before, had not the need, but now she had started on this path she could not leave it. She shifted her attention to Lord Inigo.

"I cannot begin to repay you, My Lord, for the worthiness you have shown towards my Black Crows. Know that if I can repay you or you have need of me, you may rely upon my goodwill. I'm afraid that is all the currency I have to offer at present."

Lord Inigo's sudden grin made him look even more boyish than his fourteen years. "I was reminded recently of that which I already knew but had forgotten. That a Lord without his people is no Lord at all. I am considered a child still by many, as you are and will be. But I have faithful advisors, loyal friends that I trust whose knowledge I can use. If you surround yourself with the right people, then those who underestimate you will come to regret it. Welcome to the game, Lady Black Crow."

"By all that's holy," Amos hissed under his breath.

Mercy clapped her brother on the shoulder. "I'll take the borrowed horses and wagon back to the Red Cloaks." She bowed to Lord Inigo and with a flick of brown eyes, Stama and Lucky followed her from the tented pavilion.

"There is a council of Lords. If you are staying, Lord Amos, perhaps you should attend." Idris Inigo rose from his camp stool.

"Perhaps I will," Amos muttered, scratching at his whiskers, disgruntled at being out-manoeuvred by a child.

"I would represent my father and Thorsten if you would vouchsafe me?" Constance asked gazing up at the furrow-browed Lord Amos.

"Of course you would. But a Lord's Council is no…" Amos hung his head and shook it in resignation. "Fine, but try not to talk, eh, nor draw attention to yourself. Lord Inigo called it a game before but trust me, it is one you are better off not playing. And Belle, don't even think about asking."

Young Annabelle pulled a face and stuck her tongue out. Amos turned to Jobe and Jerkze and the hovering Junip Jorgstein. "Try and keep an eye on Belle this time, eh. See she doesn't wander."

* * *

"Fallenfaire in the east has fallen, meaning urak have crossed the Plago, and we've seen no boats on the Fossa nor refugees from the west for over a day. As you know, Sire, the last bird from the Defile was yester-morn, Duke Brant reporting they were encircled. Nothing since." Sir George Flik, Knight-Captain wore the blue tabard of Rivercross, a wolf's head emblem emblazoned over trident rivers that merged into one. His leathered face looked tired and he rubbed a callused hand over eyes bruised with fatigue.

"Thank you, Sir George." High Lord Trenton Twyford considered briefly whether to order Flik to rest. His captain was of no use dead on his feet but Twyford knew it would fall upon deaf ears.

The High Lord turned to the room. It was filled with serious men with stern faces and anxious eyes. He knew many by name and most by sight and those he did not were minor names with no influence and therefore of no regard, except that he needed their arms. To his right stood a quartet of mages, magisterium from the Enclave, their eyes judging the room.

Twyford's gaze settled upon Aric Nesto who stood toward the front, shoulders slumped, seeming small despite standing a hand taller than his neighbours. The arrogance the young Lord normally displayed was absent, replaced by weary despondence. Nesto had returned not two days gone, bloodied and with only half the horses and men he had left with. His report had been sobering.

"Lord Aric," Nesto's eyes rose from the floor to meet Twyfords. "Why is there only one Lord of Charncross here? Where is Lord Victor?"

Aric pushed to the fore. "My Lord Father remains at Charncross with fifteen hundred of our Burning Cross. Sir Lucspar, as I'm sure you must know, arrived this morning with the bulk of our forces."

"Victor thinks to hold Charn Castle? He will fail and that is fifteen hundred less to defend Rivercross." Twyford thumped a fist to his gut. "May Kildare curse him, I'll not countenance disobedience, Lord Aric. Your father was ordered here. Damned fool."

The High Lord glowered at the son, who bristled, some of the arrogance and vigour returning to his face and, inwardly, Twyford was pleased by it.

"My father maintains he can hold till spring. He has enough supplies to last."

"AND WHAT!" Twyford's shout stilled the room. "Sally forth and rout them. If he keeps horses they will be fit for nothing come spring and if he doesn't the urak will swallow his meagre forces and thank him for the fodder."

Twyford took a calming breath and when next he spoke it was in a more reasoned tone. "I have tens of thousands of civilians camped outside my walls, from the Korbanning Floods to East Rising, none of whom I can accommodate in this city. I've a good mind to place them in your charge to move them south. It is fortunate for you that I need your Burning Cross and that there are others more suited to the task."

Trenton Twyford strolled back toward his throne-like chair and, lifting a goblet from its side table, took a sip of wine. Sir Manus, his Lord Chamberlain, stood close and whispered in his ear. His eyes scanned the room, searching the crowd.

"Lord Inigo, step forward. Your companions too if you will." Raising an arm, Twyford waved them on.

"Sire." Idris Inigo gave a perfunctory bow but remained otherwise silent.

"A child lord brings a girl-child to my council chamber. Pray tell, is it to announce your betrothal? If so it is ill-timed." The room erupted into laughter. Twyford leered, "And you, sir. State your name and purpose."

The man addressed stood with easy confidence behind the girl and Twyford noted in his eye corner two of the elder mages of the magisterium with their heads together, whispering. He knew then Manus was right even before the man confirmed himself.

"I am Lord Amos Duncan of Hawke Hold." A murmur swept the room at the announcement. "This girl-child, as you call her, is the Lady Constance Bouchemeax. Given as my ward by her father, Lord Richard."

"I can speak for myself, Amos," the little girl hissed, her whisper loud enough to reach many at the front of the room.

Lord Twyford frowned. "You surprise me, Lord Amos. You travel my realm without the courtesy of a visit. I expected better of the Duncan."

"My father is guilty of indulging a son's whim to explore and travel the kingdoms. If there is any fault it is mine, for I wished to be discreet. Forgive me if I have caused offence. It was not my intent, High Lord."

"Intent? No indeed, I suspect it was not." Twyford's piercing blue eyes tightened, then softened as he turned them onto the child. "The Black Crow lives. Did you know that, girl?"

"Yes, Lord Inigo told me," Constance replied. The High Lord's stare became intense, brows knitting together into a frown. Amos nudged her gently. "Lord," she added, blushing as another smattering of laughter rippled around the room.

"And how many Black Crows have you brought me, Lady?"

Constance licked dry lips, her mouth parched as a stone. She had never seen let alone spoken in front of so many Lords before and was beginning to regret her decision to come. Amos placed a comforting hand upon her shoulder and, when she looked up at him, received a nod of encouragement. "Five," she muttered, then, lifting her chin said louder. "I bring five Black Crows."

An amused murmur stole through the room and her blush deepened, only Lord Twyford was not smiling.

"You are fierce like your father, Lady Black Crow, I can see it in you. I would like to hear the story of your escape, but time is pressing, urak close in on this city as we speak. It could be a matter of days before they are here." Raising his voice, Twyford swung his gaze wide to encompass the room.

"Lord Inigo, the people camped outside these walls cannot remain. I charge you with moving them to safety. Liaise with my shipmaster, Rodasun. Board as many as you can upon departing vessels, the rest will have to go by road to Lakeside or Wooliston then onwards. Seek out Sir Manus my Lord Chamberlain later this morning and he will give you my warrant. Perhaps the Lady Black Crow and her five can assist you."

"Lord," Idris and Constance mirrored the other in response. When neither made to move, Twyford clapped his hands twice.

"Did you not hear me? Go. I have given you a task and time is paramount."

Lord Inigo gave a bow and Constance a curtsy before both turned to leave the room.

"Lord Amos, you're welcome to remain. Perhaps you have some Southron insight to impart?" Twyford called out.

Drawing back, Amos considered the room, eyes flitting over the many Lords then briefly over the huddle of mages before returning to Trenton Twyford with his council arranged like shojek pieces behind him.

"It seems to me you have an abundance of consultants already. Your purpose is known, action is needed not words. That is my insight, for what it is worth. Good day, my Lords." Amos marched from the room, the guards closing the heavy oaken doors behind him with a boom.

As they walked the wide corridors of the Palace of Versen, Idris Inigo gave a glance towards Amos, unable to keep the humour from his face. "The Duncans are renowned for diplomacy, or so I hear tell. I did not expect you would be so blunt. I confess I enjoyed it very much."

"I've faced siege and battled urak. I know what's coming and how fast the urak can advance." Amos was fuming. "The High Lord has given you both an impossible duty with no time to do it in. Considering all things, I think I was very tactful."

They descended a wide, sweeping staircase to an entrance hall, where bold frescoes lined the walls, ceiling to floor, each depicting a scene from the Rivers' turbulent history. In intervals around its edges stood imperious statues, inert guardians that separated each giant piece of artwork. Above, golden chandeliers hung from gilded chains, their fat candles fluttering a rich aroma and casting everything in sombre yellow illumination.

There was little time though to admire the garish splendour, for the hall bustled with activity and waiting at the fringes of the scrum of people were Osirus Smee and Junip Jorgstein, sheltering in the lee of a pillared statue of Richard Varthenon, 7th King of the Rivers. Amos forged a path towards the double doors that heralded the exit and the two mages hurried through the crowd to catch up.

Outside, they passed between a row of mighty columns, whose intricately carved stone bowers supported a balcony that ran almost the width of the Palace. They descended a cascade of white marble steps towards a flagstoned road that bisected a large courtyard thick with soldiers and equipment. It led straight north to ponderous black-steel gates set in the high walls guarding the palace.

Constance rushed to keep pace, her mind full of teeming thoughts.

When first they'd arrived in the city, she had gazed in wonderment as they passed beneath the Margate barbican. The crowded streets beyond were so wide that walkways bordered them, and they were clean, just like Jerkze had said. Three and four-storey buildings had risen like canyons on either side, casting them in perpetual shadow apart from when the crossways aligned and the low winter sun reached through.

On their way to the Palace of Versen, they crossed two canals over magnificent arching bridges, scullers with long poles plying their waterways with goods and passengers alike. The houses after that first crossing had been grander than before but they were as nothing compared to those after the second. Here, sumptuous estates stood in walled gardens with guardsmen stationed outside the gates of each, watching in lazy boredom as they passed.

The road took them through the estates and into a park where the city faded behind its veil as if it was never there. Once they emerged from its greenery, palace walls loomed above a rocky rise. As the road ascended to meet it, Constance looked out upon her left where the River Plago flowed, then to her right to the Fossa and Oust which merged into one. Across this wider expanse of water stood the domed majesty of the Divinity Cathedral. It had been apparent, even from a distance, that its size dwarfed that of the Red Church in Thorston and it was gracefully constructed, a blessing on the eye.

Now, as they left the palace grounds, Constance got to experience it all in reverse, only her mind would not settle on the grandeur of it all, consumed instead with the thoughts of those people trapped outside the city walls along with a singular, guilty, memory. It was from just after Thorsten had fallen. Back then, she had stolen to the top of the Black Keep to stare down in dismay at the people, her people, trapped in the square below. She had felt sorrow for them and deep despair but also a relief. That she was not down there suffering with them, nor worrying whether this night the urak might come and steal her away. It shamed her.

Saint help me, she prayed. *How can I save them?*

* * *

James Encoma scratched at his arse then rubbed his hands together and blew on them, his fingers were numb with cold.

"Stop fidgeting," Jess Crawley growled. "You're always bloody moving. It's distracting as fuck and annoying as a priest on Tenday."

"Sorry." James tucked his hands beneath his armpits and looked at her. Jess was comely he guessed, a bit small and sinewy perhaps but her brown eyes were bright and alluring and her raven hair soft, he could tell, even tied up as it was in a ponytail. Only her mouth was as filthy as a gutter and her temper seemed never far away. It could turn her pretty face into an ugly mask in an eye-blink. Jess glared at him, and he shrugged, *what?*

Jess's tongue darted out, moistening chapped lips, her face screwing up as if she tasted something vile upon them. "See that white cloth pinned to me tit?" She waited.

James' eyes travelled to her chest and the dirty thumb of linen sown to the left breast of her leather tunic, as did the eyes of the two guardsmen who stood to attention outside the pavilion of their Lord.

"Erm, yeah."

Reaching up, Jess patted his cheek with calloused fingers making him flinch. "What does it tell you, greenhead?"

"That you're a sergeant?" James said carefully.

"That's right, a fucking sergeant. I'm not your ma and I'm not your friend. So, when you address me, I want to hear the word sergeant come out ya mouth, either first or last. If I don't. If I have to remind you again, you'll be talking so high the dogs are gonna bark from a half league away."

James shook his head. "What?"

A driving pain exploded between his legs doubling him over, sending breath and spit retching from his mouth. His strength fled and unable to stand, James dropped to his knees before toppling onto his side in the mulched snow. A warm, excruciating agony spread from his groin to his lower abdomen.

"What, sergeant?" Jess prompted, leaning over. "You better wise up, weasel-dick, else your pebbles will be taking up permanent residence somewhere between your neck and yar arse."

The cloth flap of the pavilion swished and the diminutive Lady Constance Bouchemeaux stepped through it, followed immediately by the hulking shape of Kronke, Amos Duncan and the mage Junip Jorgstein. Jess blessed herself, head, heart and stomach. She wasn't overly fond of mages, they were unnatural.

"What occurs here, sergeant?" asked Constance Bouchemeaux glancing at the prone man and seeing it was her ununiformed Black Crow.

"Bit a training, bit a discipline, My Lady," Jess pressed her lips tight, it would not do to smile she decided, something which wasn't helped by the grinning Lord Amos. *Bet he's a good hump.*

Constance craned her neck up at the former sergeant, now captain and Kronke returned her the barest of nods. Adolescent eyes swung onto the still writhing James then back to Jess Crawley, noting that the dark livery of her Black Crows uniform was stained and torn. "Try not to break anyone, Sergeant, I've only five of you as it is."

"Yes, My Lady." Jess couldn't suppress her grin any longer as Lord Amos led the mage and Lady Constance away.

"Where's Zon and Morpete?" Kronke's voice sifted like gravel.

"Foraging, Captain. We need supplies of, well everything really and Zon, he ain't good for much but this."

"In that case, bring James," Kronke rumbled. "He's your mess. Carry him if you have to."

With a spluttered curse, Jess tried to pull James to his feet. "Get up, man."

She dragged on his arm, hauling him to his knees then dug a shoulder into his armpit and hefted, grunting at the effort.

"Fuck, get ya feet under and help or you'll be talking like a girl the rest'a ya miserable life." James draped against her like a cloak half removed and Jess staggered under his weight.

The two guards from Confluence smirked all the while, chuckling, and she resolved to carve them new assholes, only James was heavy and Kronke's back was fast retreating. Committing the men's faces to memory, Jess lurched after Kronke and her Lady, thankful that they moved at the girl's pace and not the captain's.

With every passing step, the greenhead recovered and, eager it seemed to stand on his own two feet, was soon limping along unaided. Jess didn't need to turn to feel the heat coming off him. Anger or wounded pride, she didn't give a godsdamn, just so long as he learned. The shrill voice of Lady Constance rose from up ahead.

"I don't understand why Lord Manus has not issued a warrant. It has been two days. He was present at the High Lord's council and heard his command. How can we evacuate using the ships in the harbour if we can't get people through the city gates."

"Every Lord in that room heard Twyford's order but none will hear your complaint," came Lord Amos's reply. "I suspect you will not see a writ until Lord Manus has overseen the evacuation of non-combatants in Rivercross. Likely, that means not at all."

"I don't understand?" Conn's face scrunched. "The High Lord can't just abandon his people."

"Oh, but he hasn't." Amos gave a terse grin. "Twyford has entrusted them to your supervision and that of Lord Inigo's. The Riverlords all heard him. The High Lord's problem is now your problem. The question is, what can you both do to resolve it? Twyford expects you both to fail and I suspect he cares not if you do."

"That cannot be true, Amos. These are all our people. No Lord would be so uncaring," Constance said.

"Not all nobles are as altruistic as you, My Lady," Amos replied. "When we ride to see the people look closely and you will find that most are elders or younglings dependant on their mothers. Most have travelled far with only what they could carry. To the High Lord, they are a burden in hard times and with nothing to be spared are more easily cast aside. It is a harsh and inconvenient truth but a truth nonetheless."

"It's vile," Constance snapped before lapsing into stony silence. *Had father not made similar choices. Barred the gates of the Black Keep when no more could be accommodated and left them outside at the mercy of urak. Sacrificed them so that others might have a chance to survive.*

She walked the rest of the way to their camp in sullen contemplation, unmindful of the guards that acknowledged her as she passed from the Confluence encampment into their own. Their horses nickered and whinnied where they stood corralled and she breathed in the scent of them finding it soothed her troubled mind.

Their small enclave consisted of half a dozen campaign tents given to them by Lord Inigo. In its midst, huddled on top of a paltry campfire, sat Stama, Jobe and Jerkze sipping from mugs.

"Saddle the horses," Amos called.

The three men rose to their feet to comply. A tent flap threw open and Mercy emerged. Then, an instant later in the next tent along, the large frame of Lucky Lucson appeared pulling on a fur shrug.

"Amos, Constance. Where do we go?" The scar on Mercy's face stood out, unsoftened against the livid coldness of her skin.

"The writ from the High Lord is still not received." Amos didn't elaborate, the look on his sister's face told him it was unnecessary. "We can delay no longer and must speak to the people. Try and get them moving to Lakeside and Cumbrenan. Lord Inigo will undertake the same for those on the Korbanning Floods, only to Wooliston."

"We will need to leave a guard in camp, two at least, else we'll have nothing to come back to," Mercy said.

In the end, they left Jobe and Lucky and the still delicate James Encoma, whose face visibly blanched at the prospect of getting on a horse, and finally, Annabelle who protested loudly at being left behind.

"It's cold with nought ta do but shiver. Why can't I come?"

Amos, though, was having none of it.

"It's no jaunt we go on, Belle, and there's plenty to do around camp. Maybe if you're good and help out, Jobe or Lucky will show you how to sit on a horse properly. You know, teach which is the front end and which the back." At Belle's glower, Amos laughed and roughed her hair.

Mercy's eyebrows pinched. "I sometimes wonder which of you is the child." Her brother usually showed only polite interest in children, including his nieces and nephews. This side of him, with the girl, was different, new. Impatient to be gone Mercy squeezed her knees and her horse moved off.

The eight riding out headed north until they reached the busy Margate Road which they followed towards Rivercross, passing row upon row of neatly ordered tents flying banners for a hand of different Lords. They turned north again before the city walls, passing guards in Rivercross livery stationed along the carriageway, then into the squalor of the refugee camp. The hotchpotch of lean-tos and tents were crowded together and stretched across the plain as far as could be seen from horseback.

They turned onto an avenue of sorts, the snow and mud a frothy churn that squelched and sucked at hooves and hocks. With every step, people stared at them. Old-timers with bushy brows and hooded eyes, and women with babes on hips or young ones gathered around their skirts. They looked half-frozen and some were sickly, with red-rimmed eyes and hacking coughs. A few of the older children followed, running between the tents parallel to their course, the braver ones calling out for food.

Conn felt deeply troubled by what she saw. The wretchedness was disturbing and the stench rancid. She had smelt it from their own camp, that cloying sewer-sweet filth born on the breeze, but there it had been bearable and her nose dulled to it after a time. Here, at its source, it was more pervasive and malign and over-powered her sense. *How can people be left to live like this?* She looked at Mercy riding beside her.

"This is inhuman."

Mercy returned an uneasy stare and, after a moment gathering her thoughts, she spoke.

"This is a mass exodus the likes of which has never been seen, Conn. Darkness resides in us all, but it is in desperate times like these it is most oft seen. And, when dark choices are made it is always the old, the weak and the young that pay the deepest price."

Constance spluttered in outrage. "That's not right. These people should be helped not abandoned."

"I agree, but all choices bear a consequence. In war, a First Lord or First Lady must determine the best course, even if it would be abhorrent in normal times. A festering wound on a limb that cannot be healed will eventually kill but if it can be cut away and the body saved then you would do this thing would you not?" Mercy said.

"These people are NOT a festering wound, Lady Mercy." Conn's argument though died on her lips at the thought of her Da. Thoughts that had already plagued her mind. *Father killed people with the choices he made but he is a good man, god-fearing and caring of his people. Was he wrong?*

"A bad analogy perhaps." Mercy leaned over and held a gloved hand out to the young girl who looked so doleful. Conn's small hand took it and Mercy gave a squeeze.

"Not all is lost, Conn. These people are not entirely forsaken. They have us." Mercy gave a lopsided grin. "And I see over there the white-robes of Nihmrodel and the brown of Ankor doing what they can."

Releasing her hand, Mercy indicated past her right shoulder and Conn turned to look. Not fifty paces away people gathered, swirling and undulating like jetsam caught in a current. In amongst the writhing mass she saw flashes of crisp white, earthy browns and blood reds. Priests in their cassocks. *Servants of the Trinity.* It buoyed her spirits to see them, even the red priests.

Their horses started to climb as Amos led them up the gentlest of inclines to a flat top that elevated them enough that they could gaze out upon the fields of Dunning. The tented township swept wide and followed the land as it curved around the city walls and moat.

"This will have to do," Amos announced, finding a clear space around an old campfire, its ashes cold. He circled his horse. "Conn, beside me if you will. Mercy if you would."

Taking a block from her saddlebag, Mercy threw it onto the dead fire sending a puff of ash into the air.

Nudging her white stallion with knee and rein, Constance moved alongside Amos until they were almost touching.

"Ignatituum forus arctum." Mercy chanted, gesticulating at the fire which burst into unearthly emerald flames. It sent plumes of luminous green smoke into the air.

"You should have their attention, brother. Speak and they will hear you." Mercy laid reins against her horse's neck and coaxed the beast alongside Lady Constance, who startled when Amos spoke, for his voice seemed to thrum in the air.

"RIVERS HEAR ME."

Amos held his arms on high and waited what seemed an age to Conn but was likely only a handful of seconds.

"I AM AMOS DUNCAN OF HAWKE HOLD.

THESE ARE DESPERATE TIMES. YOU HAVE LOST MUCH AND TRAVELLED FAR. ENDURED MANY HARDSHIPS AND HAVE MORE TO FOLLOW. FOR WINTER IS COME AND BRINGS WITH IT URAK.

THIS CITY HAS BECOME A FORTRESS, A BULWARK AGAINST THE HORDE. IT. WILL. NOT. ACCOMMODATE. YOU."

A palpable silence became the backdrop to his words which seemed to reflect off the city walls, like a receding wave washing into an oncoming one. Conn knew that through some arcane means, the people heard every word spoken. Could see the faces of those closest turned and watching. She cast an eye at Mercy as the mage worked her craft and wondered how it was done and how far Amos's voice was projected but then he was speaking again and her thoughts were lost.

"BESIDE ME SITS THE LADY CONSTANCE BOUCHEMEAX. ONE OF YOUR OWN. SHE TOO HAS SUFFERED LOSS. TOMORROW WE WOULD TAKE YOU SOUTH TO CUMBRENAN FOR IF YOU STAY HERE YOU WILL LOSE EVERYTHING. FOR THE URAK WILL COME."

Amos paused, trying to gauge the mood of those he addressed but failed. Those closest that he could make out looked weary and hungry and those behind a broken, incomprehensible assembly. A lone voice called out, an aged voice that creaked and cracked like dry tinder.

"Lord, we are old and frail. Young and weak. Many have taken sickness." The ranks closest rippled at these words and then, to Amos' left, parted. An elderly man leaning on a staff hobbled forward until he stood clear. "We have little food, man of the south, and only water from the moat to drink. The High Lord must help us for we can go no further."

Constance swallowed, tears forming unbidden in her eyes. The elder's words were the truth and it dawned on her that Amos too had spoken true. That her task was indeed impossible. She could not save them. Not all.

The fear and pity and grief she felt was overcome by a sudden, cold, outrage and another, deeper something. It was unrecognised at first, for Conn had never experienced it to this degree before. Hate, loathing. *Twyford is no Lord of mine.*

Conn touched heels to the flanks of her horse and nudged forward. "Assist me, Lady Mercy."

She waited, not knowing if the mage would heed her or not. Gathering her breath and her courage, Conn began.

"MY FATHER IS THE BLACK CROW OF THORSTEN AND HE STILL FIGHTS IN THE NORTH. HE COULD HAVE SAVED HIMSELF BUT INSTEAD, HE STAYED. SENT OUR YOUNG AND OLD SOUTH. SENT ME SOUTH. MANY SIT IN THIS VERY CAMP." If Conn wasn't so keyed up she would have wondered at hearing her voice resonate so.

"MY DA EXPECTS TO DIE AS DO MY PEOPLE, OUR PEOPLE, THAT ARE WITH HIM. FOR US." Conn twisted in her saddle and pointed a finger at the walls of Rivercross. "OUR HIGH LORD WILL FIGHT. BUT NOT FOR YOU. NOT FOR ANY ONE OF YOU. HE HAS NOT THE MEANS TO SAVE YOU ALL AND NEITHER DO I. BUT STILL…

…IT MIGHT BE I CAN SAVE SOME. THOSE THAT ARE ABLE I BESEECH YOU, WALK BESIDE ME. MAYBE WE SHALL LIVE BUT IF THE ONE DEEMS IT OTHERWISE, THEN AT LEAST OUR DEATH WILL NOT BE AS LAMBS WAITING FOR SLAUGHTER.

WE ARE RIVERS.

WE CARVE OUR OWN FATE."

She paused, heart hammering as if she had run a quarter league.

"I WILL COME AT FIRST LIGHT. THOSE THAT WOULD FOLLOW ME, BE READY."

Silence settled as the last of her words faded. No sound was uttered but for coughs and a baby's cry. Conn too cried, tears unashamedly running down her cheeks. Pulling on her reins she turned the white stallion back the way they had come.

Junip Jorgstein swung her horse protectively in beside her Lady's, a fierce pride coursing through her blood. In a moment of epiphany, she knew that Constance was more than the child she had perceived her to be. That this was her mistress, her Lady and she would devote her life unto her.

The ride back to camp proved a less sombre one. The people that gathered and crowded the path along their way looked as destitute and unkempt as before only Conn felt a subtle sea change of difference in them. Some at the front reached hands out to brush fingertips against her horse and leg, and many called and shouted, their words merging into a low babble that followed them like a bow wave did a ship.

That night, back in camp, Lord Idris Inigo arrived with a delegation of priests in tow.

"This is Mother Erwain of the White and Father Larson of the Brown. They would speak with you Lord Amos, Lady Constance."

Their small group stood gathered around the campfire and each one of them knelt before the priests. Mother Erwain gave a perfunctory blessing then bid them rise.

"The ground is cold and wet and there is no need for discomfort on our behalf." Mother Erwain seemed young for a priest, her face unblemished by age and her cheeks rosy with the cold. Her bright eyes held a warmth that when focused upon a person drew them in.

"Thank you, Mother," Amos said, offering a camp stool for her to sit upon and another to Father Larson. "What can we do for you? You did not traipse out here in the dark to bestow blessings I am sure."

"Amos," Mercy admonished, slapping a hand to her brother's arm. "Your Holinesses, forgive his directness."

Father Larson smiled, "Bluntness in times such as these is welcome, my child." An older man, the deep mahogany of his face was lined and bags hung beneath rheumy eyes. His bulbous nose sat atop a wide mouth which was framed by an unkempt beard. *If not for his brown priest robe he would look like a beggar*, thought Amos.

"We too shall be direct," Mother Erwain continued. "Both Father Larson and I were there today. We heard your words and have witnessed the truth of them every day in the fields. The task that you have undertaken is both worthy and … monumental. Most shall not go with you, however, because they are scared or they are unable or they hope."

"Hope, Mother? Hope for what?" Amos raised a singular eyebrow.

"Hope that you are wrong."

Amos' shoulders sagged and his face turned grim. "We can only help those that can be and want to be."

Father Larson took out a pipe from a pocket in his brown robe and packed it with tabacc. As he listened, he tamped the end then clicked his fingers over the bowl and applied his will. It sparked into a glow.

"Many will still follow and you are few." Larson slipped the pipe stem between his teeth and took a long draw, puffing a cloud of smoke.

"The road will be hard and you will lose some along the way. Both to the season and hunger." His eyebrows twitched like hairy caterpillars. "To urak as well if they catch you."

"I expect so," Amos replied, his tone noncommittal, wondering where this was leading.

Larson took another tote on his pipe and Mother Erwain took over.

"We brought your words, Lord Amos and Lady Constance, to our churches. After much prayer and contemplation, Primate Hennim of Our Lady and Primate Korring of Our Saint wish to assist you in your endeavour."

Amos glanced at Mercy, then Constance before returning to the priests. "I take it you are the assistance?"

"We are," Mother Erwain beamed, "Though we are not by any means all. The churches of Nihmrodel and Ankor will provide twenty wagons with priests and acolytes to drive them. Half will bear food and supplies, and half will be empty, used for those least able to walk. It is far from enough I know but it is what we have. Also, whilst the Church of Kildare have yet to appoint a new Cardinal, I have been told that fifty Red Cloaks will be riding with us for Killenhess."

"That is most generous," said Amos, "More than we could have hoped for. Thank you."

"No thanks is required. We are all servants of the Trinity who serve the One." Mother Marr, blessed herself, touching the fingers of her right hand to her head, then heart and stomach.

Everyone there gathered did the same, apart from Father Larson who took a final puff of his tabacc. Removing the pipe from between his lips he tipped the bowl and tapped it against his palm, emptying the contents into the snow before climbing to his feet. "There is much to do for the morrow. We will be on the Dunning Road at first light."

Lord Idris spoke up. "I've half my forces on the Korbanning plain and will be away early tomorrow with the rest. There will be no time for farewells, so, I will bid you all a safe journey." He clasped forearms with each man and bowed to the ladies but as he turned to lead the priests away Mother Erwain instead approached Constance.

"For one so young you spoke well, child. You made a favourable impression with the people."

"Thank you, Mother," Conn replied, flushing at the praise and watching as the priest swung a bag from off her shoulder.

"They have a name for you. Do you know that?" Mother Erwain said, cheeks dimpling as she smiled. She proffered the pack.

Conn reached a tentative hand out and took it. "No, I did not."

"They call you, Lady White Crow," Mother Erwain said. "Wear what you find inside, my child so that in the days to come, when the forgotten look for hope, they may more easily find it."

The priests left, following Lord Idris into the night, vanishing in a moment as they left the arc of the firelight.

Setting the pack down, Conn opened the ties and pulled out its contents, her girlish curiosity irresistible. A fabric of pure-white ermine unfolded in her hands, her fingers revelling at the silken softness of the fur.

It was a cloak of the Traveller, the White Lady Nihmrodel. It was worn only by the holiest of the White Church. Her mouth agog she held it out. "What does it mean?"

A chortling Jerkze clapped her on the back. "Look fer hope the priest said. Rather Lady, don't fall in the snow else we may ne'er find you."

Chapter 24: The Morqhill Sallies

The Grim Marsh, The Rivers

Lord Jacob Bouchemeax laid his head back and closed his eyes; a picture of calm. But beneath his exterior, the turbulent currents of grief, rage and anxiety coursed through him. The turmoil of his emotions contrasted with the beguiling warmth of the hot pool he lay within, its gentle heat seeping through skin and flesh, soothing his aching body but not his soul.

Thornhill's death percolated his mind like a canker. The casualness of his friend's dispatch, the memory of it, wormed through every thought. He'd seen death, why did this one trouble him so? To distract himself he spoke.

"Why did Black Jack give us two days?" Jacob did not raise his head nor open his eyes. "Why not kill us like he did John?"

"John Thornhill." Wynter's voice was rough, quizzical. "I ne'er knew his first name."

The ranger sat up, sending hot water lapping against the sides of the pool. "They feed us and bathe us so that we might recover some strength. Not much, but enough to make a show of it."

"A show of what? What is this Morqhill your brother spoke of."

Wynter grimaced, "We share blood, but he is no brother o' mine." He settled back against the basalt sides of the pool. "Morqhill is an island. A mound of rock and bone that sits like a giant turd in the Stench. Nothing grows on it and nothing lives there but the sallies, who bask and fuck and spawn on it."

"Sallies?" Jacob queried.

"Skáalbáakers in the old tongue, Razorback Salamanders in the new. A kinda water dragon only they don't have wings nor breathe fire. They're bigger 'an a horse, their bite is venomous, their spit poison. They hunt the Stench, where the waters are warm and the air reeks of the seven hells."

A door grated open and both men turned at the sound to see a burly, gnarl-faced man enter. "Sunny," he called out.

In one of the many recesses of the room, a shadow moved in the darkness. "Busk."

"Give ya any trouble?" Busk asked.

The man chuckled. "Naw. The Betrayer 'ere just educatin' Lord Crow on his future."

"Ai, well, it's time. Black Jack is waitin'. Get 'em out," Busk said.

Four more shapes moved, stepping into the torchlight, two with hands on their knife handles, one bearing a cudgel and the other a billhook.

Jacob and Wynter were urged from the waters, where they dried themselves on coarse sackcloth that roughed the skin before dressing in their still filthy clothes, though minus their leather harness, their armour having been appropriated before their descent into the Holes. Lastly, they were manacled and chained.

Busk led them from the humid warmth of the room. Escorted by Sunny and the other guards they made their way through the cellar corridors of the dilapidated keep and up into the sharp, crisp air of a new day.

A crowd had gathered. It seemed the entire Hold had turned out, and a murmur rippled through them as Jacob and Wynter appeared.

Black Jack stood at the raised entrance to the keep and Jacob bristled. The Grimlord was wearing his leather cuirass and steel-forged sword on his hip. Predatory eyes regarded them both as he and Wynter were ushered to the side. As unnerving as Jacob found it though, it was the repellant gaze of the pale-skinned figure next to the Grimlord that discomforted Jacob more. Dark tendrils tattooed her face lending a wild, inhuman aspect to the woman whose all-black eyes sent a shiver of revulsion through him. A she-demon, Jacob thought, but one that triggered a faint recognition in him that he struggled to understand. It was as if he knew her from somewhere, yet he was certain that he did not, for once seen she would not be forgotten. Unless in a nightmare.

The Grimmers on the steps made way and any thoughts of the Grimlord and his devil cycled to the back of Jacob's mind when he spied Sand. His cousin looked unrecognisable from the man he knew. As gaunt and pallid skinned as the black-eyed woman, he wore a stubble of patchy regrowth on his skull and his blue eyes were sunken, black-ringed and haunted. Still, a vast improvement, a miraculous one in fact, from the burnt-skinned, black-scabbed man they had found a breath from death on the banks of the Oust.

"'Tis good to see you cousin," he murmured and received a knife pummel to his ribs for his trouble. The pain took his breath and dropped him to a knee.

"No talkin'," Busk grunted.

Black Jack raised his arms and waited for the murmur of the crowd to grow quiet before he spoke.

"It is time. For those that wish it, you may watch from the Horing Bank. The fires 'ave been lit and the Sallies cleared by my Murkhawks." He turned, eyes sweeping to those he cast judgment upon. "Jacob Bouchemeax, son of Lord Black Crow; Sandford Bouchemeax, son of Mad Bill Lord of Redford; and Ned Wynter, our brother the Betrayer. You will be chained to the madstone on Morqhill. As is our way, if you survive till sunrise tomorrow you may go free. Bring him forward."

The Grimmers arrayed on the side opposite Jacob shuffled apart and Mahan appeared, his arms were bound before him and he hobbled like an old man. His wide-eyed terror from the Holes was replaced by a hazed, unfocused stare.

Black Jack a leering grin. "You've had time ta think, Mahan. Will you join me at the Grimhold or stand the judgement of the madstone?"

Jacob watched, waiting for the Black Crow's answer as avidly as the Grimmers, unable to keep the worry from his face. Mahan was his man, his friend. They'd sparred since Jacob was a boy. Had served together, got soused together. Indeed, he'd been carried home by Mahan the first time he'd drunk himself into a stupor. The man who stood opposite though was not one he recognised. His friend had suffered in the Holes, it had broken him.

Mahan did not respond at first. He heard the words but it was as if he did not understand them. Then, his eyes cleared and he moved. Dropping to his knees, Mahan held his hands out.

"I'm oath sworn to Lord Jacob," the words were whispered, hoarse.

"Loyalty is to be admired when it is to me, else I don't give a good fuck. Die then with your Lord." Black Jack nodded and the guards on each side of Mahan roughly grasped his arms.

"Wait, WAIT." Mahan's head rose, his eyes wild. "I will. White Lady forgive me. I will."

Black Jack signalled and the guards stopped, holding Mahan in place. "Will what, exactly? Swear to me?"

A tear leaked from Mahan's eyes and snot dribbled from his nose into the whiskers atop his lip. "When Lord Jacob dies, it will release me from my oath. Then I will swear my name to yours. I promise."

Black Jack stared, a smile playing across his face. Survival trumped honour in most men. For all that people followed the Trinity and believed in The One, few seemed eager to rush to meet them. The instinct to live, he found, crushed most other needs. For Mahan, all it had taken was a constant beating, no sleep and threat of the Holes to crack an already fragile man.

Wraith's hand latched on to his arm and Black Jack could feel the tremor of her excitement through their touch. Could almost feel her purr of pleasure. In a rare sign of affection, he patted her hand. She was made for him. He sniffed disdainfully, tiring of the matter.

"Take him to the Horing Bank. Make him watch."

* * *

The journey to Morqhill was further than Jacob expected. A flotilla of boats joined theirs each packed with as many grimmers as could fit. A thick line of craft stretched ahead and to their sides with more behind.

Their boat was paddled by two grimmers who Wynter knew, for he addressed them both by name, the man at the stern as Nils and then, more guardedly, the woman at the prow as Varla. Neither answered Wynter but Jacob got the impression both were conflicted.

He did not sense in them the hostility many of the other grimmers had and he wondered at that.

Jacob shivered. The cold air and icy wind that had at first been invigorating now sapped at his already depleted strength. Mahan's betrayal had rocked him badly but now the shock had settled a little, Jacob couldn't help but feel a slither of relief. Did he want Mahan to die at his side? What purpose would that serve? Unbroken, Mahan would never have folded like that, would have died first. But the Holes had snapped something inside his friend and with time to dwell on it, Jacob's outrage had ebbed, replaced with pity and sadness. He was Mahan's Lord and yet had done nothing to aid him in his need. "*We have failed each other.*"

"What?" Wynter asked.

Jacob turned and looked back at the ranger in confusion, the boat rocking gently at the motion.

"You spoke," Wynter clarified.

"To myself. I did not mean to share my thoughts nor intrude upon yours," Jacob replied.

Wynter chuckled. "They say darkness resides in all men's hearts. You hide yours well, milord."

"Maybe so," Jacob conceded. "My father told me life is but a trial for the soul. That light cannot exist without the dark, nor the dark without the light. That the balance of a man is in how he manages the two. I think, for Lord Grim, I might show a little more of the dark would fate permit me the chance."

The sound of paddles sculling was soft in the muddy waters; a rhythmic beat. After a time, Wynter answered.

"Grew up in this shit-stained, curse of a swamp. Life 'ere is a battle just to survive. Humanity at its rawest, wildest extreme. But I reckon your Da had the right of it. I see'd things you'd ne'er believe. Done things ta stain my soul, black deeds that shame me even now just thinkin' on 'em. But I done good things too. Your Da saw that in me when I didnae see it in meself."

"Some things are clearer to see when looking in rather than out," Jacob said.

"Your Da tell ya that wisdom too?"

Jacob's lip curled into the semblance of a smile. "Lutico. My old Master had a thousand sayings just like it. Annoyed the seven hells out of me at the time but mostly because he was right more oft than not."

"Pity he's not here," Wynter observed, "A mage would be right useful about now."

They didn't talk much the rest of the journey. The marsh changed the deeper they went, through fields of yellow lilies and tall reeds, past earthen mounds crammed with foliage of greens and violets and blues. The brown-silted waters were still and the air was filled with the wet decay of plant matter shot through with the aroma of the various flowers and fauna they passed.

The waters slowly changed colour from brown to grey to blue and became clearer with each gradation. The plants grew brighter, more effervescent, the air warmer and more soiled, becoming pungent and sulphurous. Ahead, a low-lying island emerged, long and narrow with stunted trees crowning its top and spindle-armed bushes with pink blossoms scattered in between. Torches burned around its circumference and grimmers patrolled the shoreline attending each one.

"The Horing Bank; a grandstand for the masses," Wynter declared. The boats of the Grimhold made for it, many had already beached and been dragged higher up its lower slope to make room for the next.

Jacob watched as several of the boats immediately ahead of them swung wide of the embankment. The Grimlord and his devil rode in one, Sand another and Varla and Baka paddled in their wake, following their lead.

As they rounded the island end, the air grew warmer and more fetid still. A light mist hovered in patches over the water which had turned an unnatural, milky blue. Seventy yards on, in the centre of the cerulean lake, stood another island, this one little more than a raised sandbar with a mound of melted rock at its heart. Round and squat, black and tan, it looked every bit the giant turd Wynter had described it as earlier.

Morqhill.

At the centre of the rock stood a large, grey monolithic stone with a lopsided lean to it but after a cursory glance, it was the foreshore and slopes that drew the eye. Giant logs, orange and brown in patina, lay as if washed ashore. As unnatural as this place was, Jacob found these the strangest of all. Then they moved.

Jacob blanched. The Grimmers though whooped and yelled from the lead boats and two more sculled past. Lids were removed from buckets, and arrows their tips blackened with pitch, were thrust in and immediately ignited.

Soon, burning shafts began peppering the island, thudding in between the great beasts which hissed and snorted before retreating, with surprising agility, to the safety of the water, submerging into its cloudy depths.

The skiffs ground ashore and Black Jack's Murkhawks pulled the boats up and out of the water. The coal buckets were quickly lifted from their cradles using long poles and arranged in a deep semi-circle around the boats. A nugget of agent was tossed into each causing them to flame into life with a roar.

"Up," Varla commanded. "And don't loiter as ya get out. The sallies are fearsome quick in the water and will snatch a man before he's time to know it."

It was awkward to rise, manacled and chained as he was, and the red bandanaed Varla didn't help. Jumping clear of the boat, she held its bowline taunt and waited whilst

Jacob grasped the plank seat in front to lever himself upright. He stumbled with his footing, his legs cramping, then stepped over the bow and onto the gritty black-sand surface of Morqhill.

The smell was as bad as his fear. The sulphurous odour he'd become somewhat acclimated to but not so the reeking stink of the Razorbacks. Moulted skin hung in clumps on the rock and dung smeared the ground, the beasts unmindful of where they lay, rubbing it like some evil marinade into the rock.

"T'is a wicked place ta die," Wynter muttered as he moved past.

Black Jack and his devil waited for them atop the sludge of flat rock by the tall monolith. Jacob counted a dozen of his so-called Murkhawks arranged around him, turned outwards with spears in hand. He could hear more following behind.

The Grimlord stepped forward. "I ain't much for last words, yours or mine, brother." He glared at Jacob. "And I sure as shit don't give a copper bit fer anything you gotta say."

"Just get it done," growled Wynter. "Fucking peacock."

Laughing, Black Jack beckoned. "Tom."

Jacob turned to see a man push forward. It was the same man that had seen to them that first day in the Holes. Young, not much more than a boy, he wore a passive expression. It was a mask, for Jacob could read the uncertainty behind his eyes.

Wynter swore. "You've a devil's heart, Jackson Tullock." He raised his arms as Tom stepped close and, shackled as he was, managed to cup a hand to the lad's cheek. "Do what ya gotta do, boy. This only ends one way whether you chain me to the stone or no."

"I'm sorry, Ned. You shouldna come back." Tom's voice broke and he wiped a hand to his eye.

Wynter pulled him close and whispered in his ear. "We both know it. I'm sorry I left ya, lad. It were me biggest regret. Now. Dry ya eyes. Don't give 'em no weakness else they'll beat ya down with it."

Tom pulled away and sniffed. "Ai, well come on then." Grabbing the chain linked to Wynter's manacles, Tom led him forward, dragging him past Black Jack who wore a knowing sneer upon his face.

With a snap, Tom locked the chain to a rusted loop set in the madstone, then, without a word waved Jacob forward and repeated the process. Finally, Lord Sandford was pushed towards him and Tom fumbled for his chain. Sandford's pale face and deep blue eyes regarded him, the look penetrating. The eyes darkened as if a cloud passed across them, then cleared again.

"To my shame, I have committed atrocities. But I did not murder the girl." The voice was surprisingly warm, kindly even. Tom locked the chain in place and stepped backwards.

Troubled, he surveyed his handiwork. His chest hurt as if a fist had battered him. This judgment was his, Black Jack might have decided their fate but he had bound the accused. He was the executioner and the final arbiter. Their death, Ned's blood, was on his hands and it would forever stain him and bind him to his father.

Wraith's eyes were on his back. Tom could feel the intensity of her gaze, sense through his burgeoning abilities that she fed like a leech off his angst and shame, his bitter regret.

Lord Sandford's words echoed in Tom's mind. He spoke the truth, didn't he? Isn't that what a dying man did? For the first time, Tom felt doubt about Wraith, for if Lord Sandford had not murdered Millie that only left one other.

A metallic rattle and clump sounded behind startling Tom from his self-doubt. With a creeping dread, he turned and saw a set of manacles and chains on the ground. Above them, a cruel lilt upon his face, stood his father.

"I think you misunderstand me, Tom." Without turning, Black Jack signalled behind. "It's time to face ya own judgement, boy." Varla stepped out and passed the other Grimmers, her eyes downcast.

"Bind him. Chain him to the madstone."

Varla's tongue moistened her lips. "What about Hett? The witch won't be pleased. She's come to rely upon the boy for gathering and such."

Black Jack struck and Varla barely had time to move her head. The blow collided with her cheek and sent her reeling to the ground.

Varla shook her head, face thick and numb, ears ringing. She rubbed a hand against an aching jaw, then touched fingers to her bloody lip. Black Jack had pulled his punch else she would not be getting up. Nonetheless, it was a struggle to suppress the urge to take her knife and bury it in his gut. Instead, she grunted. "Just askin'."

Gathering the manacles and chain, Varla wandered across to Tom. "Arms out."

Stunned into silence, fear crippling him, Tom did as instructed. The manacles were locked in place, then he was dragged around and fastened to the madstone.

"Your own son!" Wynter shook his head in disgust. "There is only hate and bitterness in you, Jackson."

Black Jack sneered. "He is here because of you, brother. You twisted him against me. Turned him into a weak, spineless fool. Stole him from me."

"No." Wynter shook his head. "No. This is on you. You gave him nought but fear and hatred."

"It was to make him strong. Like father made us strong. Instead, you twisted him into some mewling worm. I could almost forgive your betrayal, but I can't forgive you that."

A stunned silence settled over Morqhill. An uneasy calm. A calm that Wynter filled.

"Tom needed you. I gave him what was missing because you could not. Da was an evil cunt an' we killed him, only you're just like him. Hold a mirror up Jackson and you'll see father staring right back. Take the boy with you. Prove me wrong, make it right."

Black Jack gave a low chuckle that rose louder. "Fuck you, Ned. The boy was born weak. I've given him more chances than 'e deserves. Time ta see if he'll die like a man."

Tom glared at his father. His legs still trembled with weakness but a stiff resolve filled him. "I hate you. I've always hated you." He cringed when Black Jack strode close, shrinking away until his back brushed up hard against the madstone.

"Words boy. All ya are is wind and fear. Look at you. Ne'er a scratch nor scar on ya, untouched by the Grim in all these years. You're a gutless craven. I don't hate ya, that requires a strength of feelin' I don't have, but I do despise ya." A blade flashed in Black Jack's hand. His other clamped Tom's jaw in a vice-like grip.

Tom's eyes darted to the knife, fear leeching at him so that he would have fallen were it not for his father's hold and the madstone behind. His Da's words stung worse than the fear though and somewhere, deep inside, something began to stir and suddenly the fear held no sway.

"I've scars, father. You can't see them but each one was etched by you."

Black Jack's knife dipped, slicing a line across Tom's brow above his left eye. "Well, here's one you can see." Releasing his hold, he stepped away, expecting Tom to collapse but his son stood, then straightened.

Turning, Black Jack grabbed Wraith's hand and led her away. His raiders raised the spears they'd levelled at the chained and followed.

Wraith pulled free suddenly and before any could stop her, skipped to the madstone and stood before Tom, head tilted in quizzical regard.

A spike of jealousy coursed through Black Jack, only for him to grin as Wraith reached up, pulled Tom low and licked at the blood flowing from his wound. Tom whispered as if in reply to something, only Wraith never spoke, did she?

"Come here, Wraith."

Tom felt torn, conflicted when Wraith responded to his father's command, returning to his side as if she were a well-trained dog. He watched as they left, taking the coal buckets with them and leaving in their place a sack covered bundle, its strong smell vying with that of Morqhill and the Stench. The last of the Murkhawks to leave ripped the sackcloth free and he heard the sudden intake of breath from Lord Jacob. The soiled body was that of the Black Crow, murdered by his father and it lay stiff upon the ground, bait for the sallies.

The skiffs paddled swiftly towards the Horing Bank which was crowded with hundreds of Grimmers. Tom knew them all. His Ma would be one of them and he wondered briefly what she thought and felt seeing him chained to the madstone.

"What did that thing say?" asked Jacob, testing the chain and steel loop against the madstone.

"That my blood is strong, whatever the hells that means. Does it matter?" Tom replied.

"Not really." Jacob tore a strip off his shirt and held the tattered cloth out. "Here, let's bind that wound."

"What's the point?" Tom said but shuffled nearer. As the rag was cinched tight and knotted, he grimaced, wiping at the blood in his eye. "Been stood on that bank afore. Watching like the rest of them as the sallies tore some luckless bastard to shreds and fought over the remains. It's what they come ta see. The beasts fighting over the spoils. Far enough that they're safe, close enough to enjoy the spectacle."

As if summoned by Tom's words the milky waters of the Stench stirred and a large, arrow-shaped head broke the surface. Orange and brown mottled the creature's skin and a long tongue snaked from its mouth, flickering and tasting the air. Around it, dark shapes moved in the depths growing more pronounced until several more heads appeared.

A cry went up, the jeer of the crowd, as the first razorback lumbered out of the water. A black, spiny ridge ran down its long, squat body giving reason to its name. It extended further, down a tapering tail that ended in a spiked barb. It was quadrupedal and moved in a rhythmic, alternating, left, right gait as it zoned in on the human remains.

"By the One," Jacob gasped. It was as long as a horse and cart.

The water exploded in a sudden frenzy as more sallies scrambled onto land and a ferocious battle ensued over the carcass. Tails whipped, and jaws opened, hissing to reveal row upon row of tiny, serrated teeth. Two of the larger beasts clashed in fearsome combat, tails and bodies entwining, heads snapping. Their grunting bellows were loud enough to drown out the distant cheering of the crowd.

Blood flew from lacerated flesh from both razorbacks until at some unknown signal they unwound themselves and one limped away in defeat. The victor barked its triumph then snarled at a smaller creature that had snaffled Thornhill's body. Grabbing its bounty, the lesser razorback scampered into the water pursued by several of the quicker salamanders.

"Ankor, preserve us," Jacob murmured, touching a clenched fist to his heart. He crouched, searching the ground for a stone or rock, anything that might be of use but there was nothing. Morqhill seemed to be one giant piece of melted rock.

"Hush," Wynter whispered. "The beasts are near blind but their hearing is exceptional. T'is said they taste the air with their tongues as well. Let's not make it easy for 'em, eh."

"They'll smell my blood, Ned. It's why he cut me," said Tom. "It's a couple of hours till sundown, we'll never see it let alone survive the long night till dawn. You know it."

"Aye, well it might be I can buy us some time. Fire's not the only thing the sallies don't like." Wynter fumbled in his clothing and pulled a flax-leafed parcel out. It was folded into a square.

Tom gawped, the packet was so like the ones Hett prepared, how had he acquired it and what did it contain?

Crouching low, Wynter unwrapped the leaves revealing a cake of yellow powder. "Not entirely sure what the hells this is," he confessed. "Nils slipped it to me in the boat. It's from the witch I'm guessing, said it might help? Not sure if we eat it or rub it on our skin. Any ideas, Tom?"

There was enough give in his chain to allow Tom to kneel beside Wynter. "Can't see how ingesting it would help. More like to poison ourselves."

Tom touched a finger to the powder then sniffed it. "Smell's of nought."

There was a rattling bark and a hiss. "Decide quick, that big bastard is climbing the slope," Jacob urged. He moved and his chains clacked together, ringing out. The razorback stopped at the noise, its head swinging wide, side to side. Its tongue flickered from between its jaws then disappeared. It took an unerring step towards them.

Tom's mouth was dry and he sucked his cheeks trying to generate some saliva. He spat in his hand, then, wetting his finger pressed it into the cake of powder before rubbing it into a paste in his palm. An aroma immediately filled the air. It was an earthy, nutty smell, one that seemed familiar but that he could not place, and he knew more than most about the plants and smells of the Grim.

"You rub it in I think?" Tom hissed and spat in his palm. But as he reached for the powder again a hand clamped his.

"T'is poison. Ingested it will kill, painfully. Absorbed through the skin it will do the same, just slower." Sand released his hand. "It's ariqksen, we use it for killing nests of rats. Not sure what use it will be against these beasts."

Wynter looked up at the leaden sky, judging the breeze, then grabbing the leaf wrap he moved to the downwind side of the madstone. Finding a depression in the rock floor he set it down. "Piss on it ta release the smell. Maybe that will keep the sallies away. If not they'll give us a quicker, more painless death than this stuff will."

Tom looked hesitant. "I don't think so. It don't feel right. It's shaped like the peat blocks we burn."

The scrambling clack of clawed nails on rock grew louder.

In a hushed tone, Wynter swore. "Unless ya got a firestarter on ya I suggest we piss on it." Standing upright, he started to unlace his britches.

"I can try," Tom said. Shuffling around he crouched low over the block of ariqksen and cupped his hands over it.

"What are ya…"

"Just shield me from the Horing," Tom urged.

Something in his tone caused Wynter to stop and cinch his drawstring tight. Without speaking, Jacob and Sand gathered close.

"Whatever you're doing, Tom. Do it quick, lad," Wynter muttered. He turned to observe the sallies, they were close, the big one no more than seconds away. Fear coursed up his spine. There was no time.

With a howling battle cry, Wynter lurched towards the giant amphibians and was almost dragged from his feet, the manacles biting into his wrists as the chain binding him to the madstone arrested his charge.

The sallies stopped at the bellowed challenge, tongues flickering madly. His cry rolled out from Morqhill and echoed across the stench. It was met by a roar from the crowd.

Then, of all things, the sallies wavered. The biggest of them was no more than a lunge from taking him. So close, Wynter could smell the sour reek of its breath and the fetid tang of its body. One of the beasts backed away. Then, in a sudden, mad rush, they all retreated.

Throwing his head back, Wynter opened his mouth and bayed like a wolf in triumph, screaming his victory at the people, his people, watching upon the Horing Bank. His skin felt charged, the hairs on his arms standing on end, fuelled by his fear and elation. He'd stared death in the jaws and death had run.

The smell registered first, the earthen, piquant tang of the ariqksen spreading like incense did in a church. However, it wasn't until Wynter turned and saw the smoke trickle in the air that realisation struck. His eyes locked onto a writhing, maelstrom of fire that hovered above Tom's hands, a fire which, with a snap-hiss, disappeared. "What in hells."

"I'll explain later." Tom stood and looked past Ned's shoulder. "It seems to have worked. For now."

Reaching across, Sand gripped Tom's arm. "Piss on your hand."

"You what?"

"The ariqksen. You need to wash it off your skin."

With a grimace of distaste, Tom obliged, stepping near the madstone, he unhitched his trousers.

"They've not gone far," Jacob observed as Tom scoured the yellow stain from his palm.

The giant razorback waited on the black grit at the base of Morqhill, its tongue flickering out in an agitated fashion. Its slightly smaller brethren were scattered nearby, careful not to get too close to each other so that soon Morqhill was ringed by the creatures.

"Now what?" asked Tom, wiping his hands against the madstone to dry them. "That block will not burn more than an hour or two."

A touch of moisture struck his cheek, then his nose. He glanced upwards. It was snowing, the warmth of the stench enough to turn the flakes into slush.

Wynter cursed.

"Let's pray it stops. Else it'll be minutes." Jacob glanced in concern at the ariqksen but even as he spoke the sleet came faster and heavier. The smoke plume spluttered and fragmented.

A vibrating hiss rolled over Morqhill and cries from the crowd on the Horing Bank resounded in their ears.

"Fuck," said Tom.

Chapter 25: Everything Is Soup

The Grim Marsh, The Rivers

"SMOKE." Varla hollered and pointed. It rose low in the west, a dark stain against a slate sky.

The Grimmers closest to her turned at her cry, but those further away were too transfixed by the sport playing out at the madstone to bother. Others, though, took up the call and a slow wave of panic rolled over the Horing Bank as more and more realised what it meant.

The Grimhold burned.

Black Jack shouted for attention and his Murkhawks fanned out around him, prickling with menace. Some luckless raiders had been left to guard the Black Keep and a few Grimmers had chosen not to attend the spectacle at Morqhill but Black Jack knew they would not be enough to protect the keep should it come under a sustained assault. But from who? The Grimhold had long been guarded by the mysteries of the marsh, its ever-shifting waterways and bogs made it a perilous maze, impossible to navigate without the knowledge. It is why his brother's betrayal cut so deep, for Ned had it. But Ned was dead on Morqhill or would be soon enough. None escaped once chained to the madstone.

Sleet started to patter from the sky, at first in drops then in ever-increasing volume.

"Jessop, take a hand and scout the Grimhold. If it's under attack report back, by who and numbers."

Black Jack did not say it. Didn't need to. In his lifetime and in every tale he'd ever heard tell, the Grimhold had never been attacked. The Lords of the Rivers could not fight what they could not find. The outlaw settlements in the wilds of the Grimwolds, however, never fared as well. He hoped if the Grimhold had been discovered it was by them and not the urak that infested the land all about. Men, they could deal with.

"Torgrid, take your band and circle to the north of the hold. Await my word."

Immediately, the two men moved off calling out as they went. Both were rivals, both coveted his mantle as Lord of the Grim but instinct told him neither would make a move, the protection of the Grimhold would take precedence over treachery but in the mayhem and uncertainty anything could happen, he would be ready for it if it did.

He shouted orders, quickly organising the Grimmers into groups and appointed his most trusted lieutenants, Busk and Egg, Rogar Sanning and Sunny Mordrunski to lead each one, with a hand of his Murkhawks to help each of them. The rest of the raiders he kept for himself.

The black-bearded Nils Baka pushed to the fore, face stern, his tone vehement. "What of Morqhill. Judgement must be witnessed."

Black Jack considered the words and the man. He knew Baka's history, that he'd been close once to his brother. But Ned had burnt him when he left. Betrayal always hurt those closest and Baka wanted his pound of flesh almost as bad as he did.

"Very well, take a hand and bear witness. Once it's done, join me at the hold." He clapped Baka on the shoulder. "Oh, and take Varla. I want her ta watch both Tom and Ned. I know you're friends, Nils, but if she refuses to look or turns away, leave her there. Understand me?"

Baka paused, a sour expression upon his face. Then he grunted and gave a curt nod. "Ai."

Black Jack walked away, organising his men. Listening with a cruel twist to his lips when, moments later, Varla's mewling wail resounded. "Aousa's there, I won't stay. I don't give a godsdamn shit about witnessing."

Baka answered her. "Ya stayin' if'n I have ta tie ya to a tree. Now quit bitchin'. Sooner this is done, sooner we go, and on my life, I'll help ya find Aousa."

What else was said was lost to the wind and sleet as Black Jack grabbed Wraith's arm and guided her down the slope of the embankment to his boat. Grimmers had started embarking their craft and some had already paddled away, following the smoke trail in the sky.

A knuckle of fear lodged in his gut. As much as he wanted to watch Ned and Tom perish, especially Tom, not to mention those 'better than thee' Lordlings, that desire paled into insignificance against the thought of losing the Black Keep. It was the seat of all power in the Grim and he'd fought too hard, sacrificed too much to lose it.

He settled Wraith in the skiff. Of them all, she alone seemed happy, wearing a glazed look of contentment upon her face that contrasted sharply with the mantle of fear that hung like a pestilence upon every other man and woman present.

Climbing in behind her, he grabbed the paddle and edged them away from the bank. Without a word, the frontman pulled deep and the light boat surged across the water, Black Jack steering the prow for home.

* * *

Nils Baka watched as the boats vanished one by one in the drizzle of sleet and snow, before turning back to Morqhill.

Curiously, the great orange-bodied Razorbacks were spread around the base of the island. Above them, huddled around the monolithic madstone at Morqhill's crown and still very much alive, were the four judged. Hard to distinguish now the weather had moved in.

Baka hadn't known what was in the packet he'd slipped Ned Wynter, he'd not had the opportunity to speak with him. Hadn't wanted to in truth. Forgiveness was a currency with little value in the Grim and his former friend's return had torn open old wounds that had scabbed over but never fully healed.

He moved towards Varla who stood, shoulders sloped in weary despondence, staring in the opposite direction as if she could read the distant tale of the smoke. Her weight shifted imperceptibly to her right side. Nils had sparred with her enough to know she was aware of his approach and more than familiar with her short fuse. His hand dropped to his knife hilt.

"You're looking the wrong way, Nade. Black Jack says ya has ta watch."

She spun, eyes flashing. "I'll look where I want."

The other raiders were drawn to the brewing argument, Baka could sense them gather behind him. It made him uncomfortable. Nip Rokan and Sis Lafferty were old comrades but the other two he didn't trust a spit. Seth Crombie and Mallory Lorcini were both Black Jack's men and Nils was under no illusion that they'd been left to keep an eye on things and see the Grimlord's orders were carried out. A pity really, for it left him no choice.

He drew his knife. "Black Jack's orders, Nade. Ya hasta watch both Ned and Tom."

Varla's eyes travelled to the knife. "I'll not play his game, Nils. Not when my Aousa is at the hold and it's aflame. I'm taking one of the boats." She took a step backwards, eyes darting like a bird between them all.

"Bin friends a long time, girl. Don't make me do this," Baka said as Seth Crombie came alongside.

The raider smirked. "You bicker like an old woman, Baka. Talkin's done." He reached for his sword.

With a surge, Baka spun, driving his blade upwards. Crombie shifted, flinching away and the knife tip missed his throat, grazing instead the side of his neck. Skin parted and blood fountained as the carotid artery severed.

Crombie's eyes flared in fear and the raider's hand clamped to his neck, rich blood pulsing between his fingers. There was a scuffle of movement from behind and Baka grabbed a fistful of tunic and swung the bleeding man like a shield towards Mallory Lorcini.

The air hummed as a sliver of metal passed Baka's ear and buried itself into an already dying Mallory. Sis Lafferty stood behind the Murkhawk raider, tall and lean she had one hand extended around his neck. The other grasped the hilt of her knife, its blade buried deep into Mallory's back.

"Kildare's hairy fuckin' balls are you both insane?" Nip Rokan swore as he backed away. He drew his sword pointing it tip first at Sis then Nils.

"Put it away, Nip. We ain't got time to mess about," Baka growled. He stared into Seth Crombie's eyes as they glazed over then released him to slump bonelessly onto the ground.

"Black Jack will peel our skin then murderize us. What the fuck?" Nip Rokan was wild-eyed.

"Yeah, what the fuck's goin' on, Nils?" Varla cried.

"I'm busting Ned out. Tom and the others too, I guess."

"Fucking idiot! And go where?" Varla screeched. "Ned left us. Abandoned us like we meant nothing and you want to save him?" She stopped suddenly, a dawning realisation hitting her.

"Oh Gods, he'll kill Aousa." She started to back away, her head shaking wildly, eyes burning with anger. "If any harm comes to her, I'll kill you, Nils. Wherever you go I will find you and murder your sorry arse."

"Hett has her."

The words stopped Varla dead.

"I don't know about the fire, but I suspect that was Hett too. A distraction. She asked me if the chance presented itself would I save Ned. I didn't say yes but damn me fer a bastard I didn't say no either."

"And you didn't tell me." Varla's head throbbed, her emotions changing from dread to rage to hope all in an instant.

"Told only Sis. The Black Crow over there I don't know nor trust." Baka indicated the silent Mahan, bound to a tree and all but forgotten in the ruckus. "As fer you, ya temper gets in the way sometimes Nade and I knew you'd fret about Aousa. It'd make ya act different and Black Jack notices shit like that. Besides, I didnae know if I would or not."

"Fucking aye, what about me?" Rokan hissed. "You didn't think ta tell me any a this."

"Ya talk, Nip."

"Lyin' sack a shit, I do not." Rokan bristled. "I thought we was mates. Watched out for each other and shit, only ya've gone and stiffed me, Nils. And you…" His eyes blazed at Sis Lafferty.

"Quit bitchin', 'e means in ya sleep," the woman chided, wiping her blade clean on Mallory's cloak. "Every night ya yabber about some such or other. It's enough ta give a girl a headache." She grinned.

"Where?" Varla demanded of Nils. "Where has Hett taken Aousa?"

Nils sheathed his knife then bent and slipped his hands beneath Seth Crombie's inert frame. He glanced up.

"No time ta explain. Whatever's keepin' those sallies at bay ain't gonna last long. Now, grab the other end, we'll take these with us. I'll talk on the way."

* * *

Jacob was drenched, they all were and whilst the rock was surprisingly warm underfoot it wasn't enough to counter the sniping wind or the icy spikes of sleet.

He shivered and huddled with the others against the massive bulk of the monolith, its lee giving some small respite from the elements. His eyes travelled downslope to what awaited them. The Razorbacks were on the move again, growing bolder now the powder block had washed out.

"Tom," he called, waiting until the young man's head swung around, hair plastered to his scalp. "You some kind of mage? Can you call fire like before? They don't like fire. Or break these chains at least?"

"Don't rightly know what I am. I see aether, can draw on it only I'm not very good," Tom replied. "Not like I had anyone ta teach me."

Jacob pulled sharply on his manacles, the chain binding him to the madstone clinking as it pulled tight. "Well, we ain't going anywhere and those things aren't going to wait for you to learn. What can you do?" he challenged.

"What can I do?" Tom's voice rose hysterically. "What can I do, he says. I can blow blue fucking flames out my ass and incinerate those bastards. Then call angels from the heavens to carry us to safety. If only you'd asked sooner." He held his shaking hands out and focused on them as if they held some treasure.

A yellow-red ball of fire grew almost at once. It spluttered and hissed as it spun. Drawing his arms back, Tom launched the flaming orb towards the stalking sallies only for it to arc and drop, dashing against the rock with a sizzle of steam.

"That's what I can do. Any more requests?" Tom muttered, slumping with his back to the madstone.

"It's something we didn't have afore, lad," Wynter said. "Seems to me ya done the hard bit, ya're just doin' that last bit wrong."

Tom returned a withering glare but didn't answer, uncertain how to vocalise how he felt to the one man that had ever cared for him. Until he hadn't. Until he'd left.

With a rattle of steel link, Sand pushed off from the madstone and walked two paces, the furthest extent his chains would allow. "It's metaphysical." Low spoken, the words were hard to hear against the staccato beat of the sleet.

"What do you mean?" Tom asked.

Beyond Lord Sandford, a long, flat snout appeared and Tom lurched to his feet. Abstractly, in the distance, three lights burned out on the lake, diffuse and flickering. Tom ignored them, for the razorback would be on them in moments, its rhythmic gait swaying its body side to side as it zeroed in on its prey. Claws scratching at the igneous rock it gathered momentum.

Lord Sandford looked back at Tom with eyes black as obsidian. "I mean, that aether is controlled by the mind. Something, to my eternal damnation, I learned to do only recently."

"Sand?" Jacob called. A rush of static rippled through the air and brushed Jacob's skin. He watched in disbelief as his cousin held his hands up and dark whorls of liquid energy began to form around each. Two, coalescing maelstroms that grew large in the space of a heartbeat.

The giant razorback lunged forward. In the same instant, one of the spinning shadow-orbs shot like a rock from a sling and splattered against its head.

The great beast skidded, legs back-peddling. It clashed its jaws in pain, emitting an agonising wail that rumbled against the monolith, deafening the condemned before a percussive boom knocked them from their feet as its head exploded in a shower of bone shards and gore.

Sand alone stood, unmoved. Watching as the remaining sallies scuttled away, retreating to the safety of the lake's waters. Above his hands, the writhing energy of the remaining orb fizzled and spat as it dissipated. With a weary sigh, Sand leaned over and collapsed.

Jacob was first to react. He caught his cousin before his head cracked against the unyielding ground and lowered him the rest of the way.

Ned Wynter stood tall over them both, peering intently downslope and across the water looking for any sign of the razorbacks. "Lord Sandford alive?"

"Yes, he's out cold but his breathing is steady." Jacob glanced up. The sleet stung where it struck exposed skin, the bad weather seemed to be intensifying.

"There are lights on the water. Three of them," Ned replied. He turned to Tom. "Can ya do anything with these chains, lad?"

"With what, how?" Tom snapped, unable to contain his exasperation. "There's so much aether in the Grim I need hardly reach for it. I can summon energy, but don't know how to fashion it or use it to defeat these locks. I can thicken air somehow, don't ask me how, so that I can keep the marsh flies off and smells out, like a barrier, but nothing more than that. I'm sorry, Ned."

He followed Wynter's gaze, immediately spying the lights from before only this time they were brighter and distinct. Tom's heart sank. "Good old Da returning to finish the job."

Ned scratched at his chin. "Why only three boats? He brought a dozen to chain us and keep the sallies off."

Jacob joined the discussion. "We'll find out soon enough. Even if we could break our chains, where would we go? We need those boats, they're our only chance. Just be ready."

The three of them watched as the lights became less fractured until out of the mist and sleet the prow of a boat appeared, followed line astern by two more.

They watched as the boats ground ashore and as their cloaked and hooded occupants leapt out and dragged them with haste out of the water.

"That's Mahan," Jacob exclaimed, he knew it beyond doubt for alone of the new arrivals, he wore his hood down, wet hair plastered to his scalp. Two bodies were lifted from the boats and intrigued, they watched as they were carried to the base of the rock and laid just as it started to rise.

They were five including Mahan and two of the hooded returned to the boats where shortly after a burst of flame sissed from the fire buckets as fuel was added.

"Be ready," Jacob growled. He checked Sand again but found no change in his condition. He grimaced. Three against four, four against four if Mahan was himself.

The four grimmers and Mahan climbed the slope to the madstone, giving a wide birth to the headless Razorback and standing just beyond the reach of the chained. In the growing gloom and sleet, their faces were shadowed within their cowls.

Ned Wynter grinned. "Nadine Varla. Din'nae think I'd see ya again. Nor you, Nils. Can't blame ya fer wanting to finish the job ya'selves, but not Tom 'ere, eh."

"Shut the fuck up." A woman's voice. "Tom, on ya knees, hands on the ground." Reaching up, she lowered her hood revealing a bush of wiry black hair and the infamous red bandana that failed to contain it. "You're first, Tom, in case I change me mind 'ere on Ned," Varla said.

Tom knelt in disbelief. "What are ya doing, Var? What about Black Jack?"

"Cocksucker's gone. We're 'ere ta rescue you ya idiot. Nils!" Varla called.

Baka crouched beside Tom. "Alright, Tom?" He pulled a metal hammer from a knapsack and a large spike. "Don't move," he ordered. Placing the point of the piton against the keylock on Tom's manacles, Baka raised the hammer and gave the spike a sharp blow, pounding the prong through the mechanism. The manacles cracked open and Tom pried them wide and slipped his hands out, immediately rubbing his chaffed wrists.

"Now you," Varla ordered Jacob.

"Thank you," Jacob said once Baka had freed him. The man grunted in response then backed away. "And my cousin?" he asked.

"He stays," Varla said, her voice tight.

"What? No. You must free him," Jacob insisted.

"We ain't gotta do shit. You're only free cause of Tom here." Varla sniffed. "And him." She nodded at Ned Wynter.

"I ain't leaving without him," Jacob replied.

Varla shrugged. "He murdered the girl. Prick stays."

"It wasn't him, Var. It was Wraith," Tom said.

Varla shook her head, suddenly angry. "First ya tell me she wouldn't hurt a fly, next ya tellin' me the bitch butchered little Millie." She glanced at Ned and then cursed inwardly for doing so. As if she needed his approval. Need or not, he gave it.

"He saved our lives." Ned raised his manacled hands and pointed at the hulking body of the razorback. "Fer what it's worth I don't think Lord Sandford did it either."

Baka had moved across to the prone man. "Nils!" Varla snapped.

"Don't fucking Nils me," Baka said. "Damn his soul, I came fer Ned. All this jabbering is wasting time. Now, let's get gone, you can always slit Lord Lah-di-dah's throat later if you want. Thought you wanted to get Aousa?"

That last comment stung Varla to silence but only for a second. "You're a shithead."

"Yeah." Baka grinned. With an expert swing of the hammer, he freed the unconscious man from his manacles and chains and then looked at Ned. He was soaked through, his long dark hair tight against his head, yet somehow he still managed to convey an air of unflappability. *Smug bastard.*

Reluctantly, as if battling his own intentions, Baka gave a curt nod and waited whilst Wynter knelt and placed his hands against the rock floor so that the lock on his manacles was facing up. "I'm sorry, Nils."

Baka didn't reply but struck through the lock with a little more force than needed.

"Good. We all done?" Sis Lafferty said. Not waiting for an answer, she stalked around the stinking carcass and down the slope towards the boats.

Nip Rokan was first to follow, leaving Baka and Varla to escort Ned and the others. He stopped by the grey-skinned bodies of Crombie and Lorcini. They had been stripped already of anything useful, weapons, boots, belts, cloaks and tunics, nothing was wasted in the grim. It left them in nothing but their small clothes.

Gritting his teeth, Rokan pulled his knife and thrust it into Crombie's belly and sawed. There was a squelch of blood and a putrid stench filled the air as his blade pierced bowel and intestine. It added to the already unwholesome flavour of Morqhill.

"What the hells, Nip." Tom spluttered as he passed, watching as Rokan moved over to Mallory Lorcini.

Ned clamped him on the shoulder. "It's alright, Tom. It's ta draw the sallies attention 'stead of us. Those fires are about out."

Tom looked at the boats, one of the coal buckets steamed madly, its flames already extinguished, another spluttered, hissed and died as he watched. He stared at the water. A thick fog hung over its surface but he imagined he saw a shadow of movement.

"I'm not good for much but I think I can help." Tom advanced towards the boats his arms held wide and called aether to him. Immediately balls of swirling fire gathered above his hands. He waited whilst the inert form of Lord Sandford was dumped unceremoniously into one of the boats, the others spread out to balance the load, the bloody-handed Rokan last but him to board.

They kept the boats together as Tom slushed through the shallow water and quickly clambered into the middle skiff, where he stood, weaving his hands in the air unsure if he was attracting attention or warding it away. Ned grabbed a hand to his belt then gave a sharp command and they paddled away.

There was a mad splash as first one Razorback then another surged from the water. They scuttled ashore and made a beeline for the butchered bodies.

Morqhill and the sallies faded into the mist and sleet. *I'm still alive*. Tom wondered at that, he could not return to the Grim, the only home he had known, but at least he wasn't alone.

* * *

The boats headed northeast, Baka and Sis Lafferty leading the way, though it was hard to tell direction with the overcast sky and night settling in. The mist soon vanished and the sulphurous air with it as they left the warmer waters of the stench behind, the marsh smelling sweet in comparison. To compensate the cold returned with a vengeance and the sleet changed to snow.

They paddled with dogged determination, no one speaking as they followed Baka's lead. Time lost meaning to many of them until suddenly, steering through a forest of tall reeds they broke through into the clear waters of the Reach.

Snow still fell but the intensity slackened as Baka turned his boat west and followed the border of the lake.

"Longstretch is the other way," Wynter said.

"Think Nils don't know his way, Betrayer?" Varla growled.

"Gods I'm sicka that name," Wynter muttered before lifting his voice enough to be heard. "So where are we goin'? I need ta get Lord Jacob south, ta Rivercross."

"Fuck you, Ned, and fuck him." Varla glowered. "Hett has my Aousa. Once I get her you can do whatever the seven hells ya like."

Baka chuckled. "Didnae think anyone would hate ya as much as me or that cockshitter brother of your'n but I reckon Nade might just have it. A woman's ire, Ned."

Wynter ignored Baka's jibe. "Aousa? Ya have a child, Nade? Didn't take ya for the motherin' kind."

"Speak her name again and I will cut your throat," Varla snarled.

"Best no one speaks anything," Baka said, trying to ease the tension in the boats. That Varla and Ned rode in the same one didn't help matters any. Bad planning that. He gave a rattling snort and hoicked a wedge of snot over the side of the boat.

"This 'ere is life after death fer you, Ned, you and your precious Lordlings," Baka stated. "Everything is soup from here on out. But let me say this. Everywhere that ain't the Grim is full of urak. I'll take ya far as the cliffs, then it's up ta you whatcha do."

Dipping his paddle, Baka pulled deep speeding the skiff into the snow-laden night. The other boats followed, the water swishing a gentle lullaby as they sculled.

In the last of the boats, Jacob shivered at the cold. He looked at Mahan, the back of his head anyway. Life after death, he mused, finding the words strangely apt. Maybe for both Mahan and he, this was a second chance. He grinned inadvertently, 'everything is soup', Jacob thought, what in seven hells did that even mean?

Chapter 26: Of Mouse and Murder

Kingsholme, The Holme

Whispering Death, Shadow Blade, Black Bitch, Dark Slayer, Dead Heart and a half dozen more names besides sprang to Tomas's mind. Merca Landré might only have appeared in the city four years before but as her kills accumulated and her notoriety grew so did her monikers. Most on the streets though knew her by one. Murder. Merca 'Murder' Landré. As handles went it didn't get much better than that. Better than Mouse, anyway. He took a deep breath and held it before exhaling slowly.

Murder sat propped against a soot-stained dividing wall, trussed up and as silent as the death she dealt. At first glance, she didn't look like much. More exotic than dangerous, a sheen to her black skin giving her an alluring vibrancy. Slight, and of average height, she was hardly the picture of a killer.

Tomas shifted awkwardly, for she was reminiscent of O'si's princess manifestation, as lithe and shapely but not as full-breasted. His face coloured at the thought of breasts for despite having seen whores displaying their wares, this was different. This was a legend.

Murder sneered as if she could read his mind and Tomas felt his blush deepen as he stared into her eyes. Eyes that told a different tale if one cared to observe them. They were brown, green flecked and intelligent. Hard though, unforgiving and calculating, they were completely and utterly devoid of emotion.

Tomas shuffled, feeling awkward under her scrutiny. In some strange way, her gaze was as discerning as Lord Renix's. Thoughts of the Order ambassador brought a crooked smile to his face.

"You're a bold one, Mouse." Murder's voice was deeper than he expected, huskier than it ought to be and it drawled with the musical lilt of the western isles. "Do you like what you see?" Her leathers were close-fitting and like her cloak, variegated shades of night. Everything about her was dark, everything but her summer eyes.

"Did you kill Sparrow?" Tomas answered, surprising himself with his audacity. The floorboards shivered beneath his feet as Murder adjusted her weight. He found himself holding his breath waiting for her reply.

Merca's eyes glinted but she remained silent.

Outside, the faint hubbub of the city reached Tomas, a background to the laboured breathing of Herald. Tasso Marn had plied the prince with poppy seeds to manage the pain of his broken nose and it had the added benefit of knocking him out cold. His highness would not awaken for a while judging from the ragged wheezing.

As for Marn, she was gone. She had removed Murder's small arsenal of weapons the night before and at first light, after re-checking the assassin's bindings and gag, the Order woman had left to meet with Tasso Chiguar, her husband.

"Keep away from her, Tomas. Even restrained she is dangerous. Do not engage her in conversation." They were Marn's final instructions. Instructions Tomas had already broken. He needed answers.

His resolve hardened at Murder's continued silence and, frustrated, Tomas drew the blue-tinged dagger from the sheath strapped to the small of his back. "I asked you a question."

The summer eyes flitted to the knife then returned to Tomas's face. They danced with amusement. "It's a pretty blade, little Mouse. But you have played it too soon. Now you have given yourself two choices. To use it or not. If not, then your power to question is gone." Merca tilted her head upwards. "If so, then I would offer the throat as an easy kill. The flesh is soft with no bone except the spine leaving only cartilage and muscle to penetrate."

Her movement exposed a tattoo on her neck of an inverted cross, a slavers mark.

"Think I won't use it, Acozi," Tomas threatened, inching closer only for her to laugh.

"Acozi." Merca jeered. "There are no women Acozi, fool. Only men. The Targus is always a man. His inner council, men. So it has always been."

Tomas blinked in surprise. A street thief avoided the Acozi but he knew she was right and wondered why he'd not noticed it before. He sniffed, feigning disdain and waggled his blade at her. "Think I care? Now tell me. Did you torture and murder Sparrow?"

"A falcon does not answer to the mouse. Use your knife or do not."

The words jarred Tomas whose hand moved, perforce, to the token beneath his tunic. Its etched symbol was a falcon. What did it mean?

"You're no falcon. A falcon is a noble bird that hunts the skies," Tomas spat.

Murder smiled, showing a glint of white teeth. "You've lived a hard life, Tomas the thief. You're a survivor but in the end still just a child with a child's warped perspective." She took a long breath, then expelled it.

"A falcon is noble only so long as it is free, if it can be broken to the fist then it can be wielded like any weapon." Merca slammed back suddenly, head striking the sooted wall behind, teeth bared in pain. The black cross on her neck emblazoned, turning silver-white.

"Interesting," O'si murmured appearing at Tomas's shoulder.

"What is it? What's wrong with her?" Murder's groans of pain were rising, getting louder, yet Tomas held back from replacing the gag. Both arm and leg bindings looked secure, but he was wary as a startled cat, unsure if it was some ploy to draw him close.

"An enchantment marks her neck. A binding. It appears someone has called upon it. The call fades," O'si declared.

Merca's head slumped forwards, eyes closed. Sweat beaded her brow and her breathing came shallow and fast.

Tomas waited. "Can it be broken?" He glanced askance at O'si who had manifested in his imp form.

O'si gave an incongruous, all too human, shrug of his shoulders. "It is a rudimentary casting at best. So simple that for one such as I, with the sight and the ability, it would be like unlacing a bow. One merely needs to find the end to unravel it."

Murder's eyes cracked open and she lifted her head. "They say talking to one's self is madness, Mouse. Yet your words intrigue me. What do you mean by them? What do you know?"

"Answer my questions and I might answer yours," Tomas replied.

"I do not torture nor murder children," Merca stated, bluntly. "Now, what did you mean by 'can it be broken?'. Tell me what you saw?"

"I haven't finished asking," Tomas replied.

"A question for a question, little Mouse."

"Except you are bound and at my mercy." Tomas brandished his knife only for Murder to laugh at him, again.

"You're not the only one to bind me and I fear my owner more than I fear you. So answer my question or make your choice." Merca lifted her head, inviting his blade to her throat for a second time.

Tomas chewed his lip, feeling disgruntled. His mood not helped by O'si's muttered statement of the blindingly obvious. "She manipulates you."

"A firm thrust upwards under the flesh of my chin would be the quickest, most humane way," Merca prompted. "A slice to the windpipe if you want to watch me suffer and fade away slowly. Or the side of the neck. Cut the vein or artery and I will lose consciousness in seconds and die in minutes. That last can get messy though, the blood spray from the wound is a sight to behold and one not easily forgotten."

Tomas glared. "I saw that you are bound by magic, but not who holds your tether?" he lied. "Now tell me, who killed Sparrow? Who tortured and mutilated her body? Did you have any part in it? Speak, I will know if you lie."

"A blatant lie is a worthless lie for it is seen," O'si hissed irritably. "I thought we spoke about this."

Merca shook her head and smiled, oblivious to the secondary conversation. "You know your answers already, little Mouse. But I will spell it out if you are too afraid to look inside for them." She leaned forward.

"You, little Mouse and Bortillo Targus. Your question starts with you and ends with the Thief King." At his crushed look a distant emotion prickled her flesh. Long forgotten, Merca smothered it before it could take root.

"Now it is my turn. You used magic before to defeat me. So tell me, if you see the sorcery that binds me can you break it? Because Bortillo just summoned me for the third time. This last he was most insistent as you witnessed. If I do not return, he will trace me here else kill me through my bond if he thinks I abscond. Either way, time is pressing."

"Haha," O'si gloated. "We've got her. Do it. Make her swear to protect you if her warding is removed. She will agree but with treachery in her heart thinking to betray you. She treats you as a child and will either kill you or take you to this thief king. I would guess the former."

Uncertain, Tomas hesitated. But O'si was persistent and the Sháadretarch's words mirrored his own reckoning. He knew Merca Landré could not be trusted but neither could he kill her, and the thought that Bortillo was somehow wending his way to their hideout filled him with a dread terror.

Sensing his acceptance and pre-empting his questions, O'si spoke again. "Ask her to place her hands in yours. I will insinuate myself between them. In exchange for removing her bond of entrapment ask her to swear her life to protect yours. As soon as the words are said, she will be marked with my brand and bound to honour her oath, however much she might wish it otherwise."

Tomas shook his head. It would make him no better than Bortillo Targus to enslave her so, but what choice did he have? He could not kill her, and he could not set her free.

"Your bond can be broken," Tomas said finally. "But there is a price."

Merca gave a mirthless smile. "There is always a price. Name yours?"

"Swear your life to mine. That you will protect me above all things and your bond will be removed."

"Swap Bortillo for a street rat," Merca mused. "I think I'll let him find me. My reputation might suffer but really, I don't give a good godsdamn about that. Think I'll stick little Mouse."

"She thinks to play you like one of those screeching, wooden instruments you humans pluck," O'si mused, much to Tomas's annoyance. *Always stating the bleedin' obvious.*

Tomas turned his voice pleading and whined. "Please, I just want to get out of the City. Once I'm out I'll release you from your oath. On Ankor's heart, I swear it."

Murder's brown flecked eyes regarded the boy thoughtfully as if considering his offer. A groan sounded. Herald was stirring and it seemed to make her mind up.

"Fine, I agree. What now?"

Tomas grinned and Murder's face tightened in suspicion until he nodded his head towards the restless prince. "Just in time, huh," he said.

Sheathing his dagger, Tomas shuffled closer to the assassin, uncomfortable despite knowing she was secured. He held his hands out and reluctantly she placed her bound ones in his.

"Your hands are cold," Merca stated flatly.

"Say the words," Tomas urged and watched whilst she took a deep breath as if what she was about to say was momentous. He could see though, the calculated gleam in her eyes and was not fooled by her show. It wouldn't matter, just so long as she gave her oath. He'd travelled this road himself and made the same mistake.

"I swear by my life to protect you above all things," Merca intoned. "There. Good enough?"

The boy gripped her hands tight and a sudden searing pinprick of pain stabbed through Merca's palms and ran through them to the back of each hand. Involuntarily, she clenched his fingers before trying to pull herself free, but his grip was like iron until suddenly she was released. Two identical runes, golden-red like a dying sun, tarnished her skin, one upon the back of each hand. She watched as they faded to nothingness.

Of a sudden, Merca clutched at her throat. It felt like a garote choked her but even as it drew tight and she struggled for breath it gave a little, then slipped and loosened as if unravelling until suddenly it was gone.

"What the fuck did you do?"

Tomas shrugged, matter of fact. "The Targus's enchantment has been broken. Replaced by a stronger warding. You are bound to me now."

"I gave you my oath and you enslave me with it?" Merca hissed.

"Who's the child now?" Tomas retorted. "It's the nature of an oath is it not? Besides, we both know without it you would be gone to the wind. Probably with me dead and you claiming a nice bounty on Rald over there. So spare me your indignation. At least this way we both get to live a little longer."

Chapter 27: Fire Flight

Kingsholme, The Holme

Merca 'Murder' Landré sat quietly watching the exchange with feigned disinterest.

"Are you insane?" Tasso Marn declared. "You cannot trust her. I've spoken to Chiguar and we are in agreement, she must die. It is the only way. She knows too much and is too dangerous to leave behind."

"She can do what you can't," Tomas stated.

Rald interjected, his voice pained and nasally. "I amw a pwince an she bwoke my nowes. She bust die. I commant it."

"Shut up," Marn and Tomas spoke in unison.

Marn looked askance at the boy from the Stacks and, not for the first time, wondered at Renix's charge. Her eyes narrowed. "Explain yourself?"

Tomas flushed under her scrutiny but was defiant. "I mean that you've had seven days to get me and Rald out of Kingsholme and yet we're still here. We move because staying too long in one place is too risky, yet each time we do it brings more danger."

"You will get caught," Merca Landré purred. "The Targus sits like a spider waiting for you to trip his web. Some already have fallen prey to him have they not?"

Marn took two strides, gripped the woman by the throat and slammed her back against the wall. "You do not speak unless I say you speak." A knife appeared in her hand and she flourished it, holding the cold edge just beneath Merca's left eye.

The two women eyeballed each other, neither looking away. Tomas noted, somewhat peevishly, that Murder did not offer her throat to the Order woman.

"What did she mean, some have fallen?" he asked, trying to defuse the tension. It was as if he hadn't spoken.

"Your breath is foul," Merca observed. "I'm surprised they have not found you by it." The blade dipped and threatened to break her skin. "I have carmigar seeds if you would like to refresh your mouth."

"Stop, both of you." Tomas astounded himself when he crossed the room and laid a hand on Marn's knife arm and was surprised at the corded tautness he felt beneath his fingers. Both women were more than they appeared.

"This is not helping," Tomas urged.

Reluctantly, Marn stepped back and released her hold, taking several calming breaths.

"Look," Tomas began. "Murder...urm, Merca here was warded with an enchantment. A slave to it if you will. But I kinda broke it and she is free from that now."

"Care to explain that?" Marn drawled, neck flushed. Her blood still seething.

"I can't really, except to say it appears I have some ability," Tomas said.

"You can't say?" Marn murmured, her plain face scrunching into a frown.

"Before, at Lord Renix's apartment, when Rald ordered you to leave me behind you didn't. And again, at that first place you took us to, you threatened to take me and leave Rald behind. So I gots to figuring that means something.

"See, Renix gave me his token, took me in and not just cause I was some stray. He saw something in me and ordered you ta keep me safe and to take me to Tankrit, didn't he?"

Marn didn't reply, her lips tight, brow furrowed.

Tomas rushed on. "I can do things, things I don't understand, not yet. But he trusted me. From the very first Renix believed in me, and I don't know why and now he is gone and he cannot tell me what I need to know."

"He was a great man and my dear friend." Marn sniffed. "The dead always have questions to answer for those they leave behind."

"Oh please. Get a godsdamned hanky and go boohoo somewhere else. We ain't got time for this horseshit," Merca said harshly.

Tomas threw Merca a glare which she returned with a feral grin. Ignoring her, he turned back to Marn. "I know she is vile and that you do not trust her, but I am asking you to trust me. She can get us out. Then she is free and clear herself to go her own way."

"You're not telling me anything, Tomas," Marn said, dourly.

Tomas shrugged. "I'm twelve or thirteen, I think. I don't got nothin' to tell, not really. Now, what did Merca mean before when she said some had fallen."

Marn closed her eyes briefly, head bowed. "Arran and two others failed to turn up as arranged. Chiguar thinks they have been compromised, taken."

Tomas scowled, "If Bortillo has them they will give up what they know. Don't matter how strong they are. Your safe houses are no longer safe. We need to get out. Now."

"Mouse is right. We need to get gone," Merca said.

Marn pointed the knife back at her and glowered.

"I dowt twust 'er," Rald stated.

"Yeah, you and me both," Marn muttered. Finally, she relented, lowering her blade. "Speak. Tell me how."

* * *

It was late, the last of the daylight was soon to fade and when it did, curfew would fall. In the maze-like streets of Old Town, in the poorest district of Kingsholme, it made little difference. To the denizens of Gloamingate the City Watch were a rarity, patrolling only the main thoroughfares, never the back lanes and alleyways, something they knew and exploited. With curfew unenforced, life continued unimpeded for the most part.

A sea-fret ghosted the streets, as winter air from the north clashed with the warmer waters of the Deeping Rift, its icy touch spreading like an incoming tide from Kings Harbour and Skelside up the rising ground to Gloamingate.

The fog was a canvas for the despondency and anger that lay heavy over the streets. The city-wide lockdown had been in force for seven days and food had grown scarce as those with the means bought up everything they could, leaving little for those without.

Three cloaked figures, cowls pulled high, trudged down Knockback Lane, keeping to its middle to avoid the filth and squalor in the gutters. The three walked with a purpose that had most scrambling from their path, not least because the leader stood taller and broader than anyone else and oozed menace.

Approaching an alleyway, they slowed to take stock of where they were. A broken half-plaque with the word 'Skit' hung from the side of a building, whatever else it was meant to say was gone. The three entered the alley's narrow confines and found it ominously devoid of life.

The mist seemed to thin, but the close sides and failing light cast a deep gloom as they moved with ever more caution down its corridor. The giant at the front stepped over a pile of refuse then tripped, catching himself as he stumbled, biting back the curse on his lips.

A boot. He'd tripped over a gods-damned boot. Only the boot was attached to a leg, the leg to a body, one that lay buried in the litter. His hand slipped from his sword hilt to his long knife.

"You make enough noise to wake the dead," a voice admonished. "And you're late."

The giant spun, and with a hiss of steel one of his companions drew his sword. Three pairs of eyes searched the half-dark and were drawn to a shade that rose above the eaves of the building opposite. The shade jumped, spinning in a swirl of cloak to land with a damp thud on the cobbles.

Horyk Andersun lowered his hood. The voice had been a woman's in the sing-song lilt of the Western Isles and it was easy on the ear. It did not belong to any woman he knew.

"Merca?" he asked in his thick, northern brogue only for her to tsk.

"Names in the night are poison on the lips. Utter mine again and I may have to kill you."

The phantom stood no higher than his chest but there was a pomposity, a hubris to her and he couldn't decide whether to be intrigued or annoyed by it.

Tasso Chiguar moved up from behind, his tread uncommonly light for such a solid-built man. He navigated the dead body, slipped past Horyk and gave a patterned knock on the battered wooden door of the building.

Immediately there was a chunk and slide of a bolt and the door creaked open to a darkened room. With a click of his tongue, Chiguar waved their third companion forward and ushered him through it.

"Whit Ludy, wat is dhat schtink? I didn' fink it poshible to schmell worsche." Herald, former Crown Prince of the Nine Kingdoms, lowered his hood, wincing when his arm brushed against his broken nose as he tried to ward against the smell.

He was rudely jostled by Chiguar who pushed in behind, forcing him to stumble deeper into whatever cesspit this was. He could sense the weight of bodies in the darkness, their breathing filled the air. The door banged shut and Herald jerked, heart tripping like a hammer on an anvil. A bolt slid home and a light flared so that he had to shield his eyes from the glare.

The boy stood holding a lantern aloft, an evil smirk on his face, a face Herald felt like punching, only two dead bodies lay between them. He lurched. By the One, he was stood in the blood of the nearest. His feet danced to get out of it.

"Quiet oaf," the phantom hissed from behind.

Marn stepped into the light and spoke. "Be still, Rald. If we are to succeed you need to be brave and silent."

Herald's eyes fixated on the dead and he gave a mute nod. They were men, throats slashed, claret soaking each torso. Their open gaze stared blankly at nothing, and a metallic miasma of filth and ichor shrouded their bodies.

He'd never been this close to death before and felt uncommonly hot. His stomach roiled and nausea rippled through him, each wave stronger than the last. Unable to resist, he bent double and with a strangled retch, threw up over the dead.

Lifting the prince, Horyk coaxed him to the back of the room talking to him in subdued but soothing tones.

Chiguar stepped around the blood and vomit. The room must have been a workshop at one time. It was long and narrow, and the shattered remnants of a bench cluttered the far wall. On the long side, crates were stacked, and burlap sacks were piled high.

"Once…"

"No names, I said," growled Merca. "No talking except me. Ya'll do what I say and maybe we get through this."

Chiguar stepped close to the woman and stooped so that his face was an inch from hers. "I don't trust you. You are not in charge here."

Merca's eyes wrinkled with mirth. "Oh, but I am. Until I get Ratboy out of the city, I am."

"Hey, it's Mouse," Tomas exclaimed.

Merca sneered. "I'm bound to the boy but not any of you. So if ya'll wanna tag along you do things my way. After we're out, I don't give a gods-damn fuck what ya do because Ratboy here promised to release me from my… oath. Ain't that so, Ratboy."

"Yeah." Tomas mumbled.

Merca placed a hand on Chiguar's chest and pushed him away. "Besides, if'n I wanted ya dead, we wouldn't be havin' this conversation."

Merca pushed past the Order man, feet clipping a staccato beat on the floorboards. She stopped near the back of the room and with a flourish, spun to face them.

"Now listen up. The city walls are fifty paces away and on the other side is the Stacks. Below this room is a sewer that runs to the Iron Cliffs and discharges into the bay. The Syndicate have fashioned a tunnel from that sewer, through the foundations of the walls to a storehouse in the Stacks. Simple."

"Simple," Chiguar grumbled. "How many guard the way?"

Merca gave a nonchalant shrug. "The sewers? None. If ya think it smells bad in here, wait till we get below then ya'll understand."

She leered at Chiguar. "You're with me, you look the part. You," she hissed at Horyk. "Stay at the back, cover our rear."

With that, Merca knelt and dusted her fingers over the floorboards. She stooped and pried at a loose block then slipped her fingers into the gap it left and heaved upwards. Dust and debris sloughed off onto the floor as the trap swung open. A stagnant belch of corrupt air issued from the hole. Standing, she took a lantern off a nearby crate and opened its shutters. More light filled the room. Lifting it high, Merca moved back to the trap. Reversing, she clambered one-handed into its depths.

It was like descending into a latrine, the air below rancid and foul. Chiguar was down before she'd hardly cleared the ladder, wearing a look upon his face like rumpled sackcloth. The wait for the others was interminable. The Mouse scurried down quickly enough but Merca watched with disdain as Marn had to coax an ashen-faced Rald down the ladder. The prince gagging and threatening to throw up all over again.

Horyk was last down, pulling the trap over with a sullen thump that felt ominously like a cell door closing.

The sewer was wide and the ceiling high and it needed to be, for a thick sludge of effluent and refuse occupied the centre channel. The blackness sucked the light from the lanterns, reflecting grimy, brown-tarred walls that were moist and stained in a verdigris of mould.

A raised walkway extended along one side of the sewer and Merca led them down it, sending a horde of rats scurrying from her path, claws scratching and skittering against the stone.

A cavernous mouth yawned on her right, an earthy-smelling dead space where the air did not move. Without hesitation, Merca climbed a small mound of crumbled stone into a timber-framed tunnel, her face tearing at the cobwebs that laced the entrance. Grimacing, she pulled her cowl up and trudged on, Chiguar, like a shadow, one step behind.

It was a mistake to be so close, Merca thought. It would take but a moment to spin and bury a knife in his gut, leaving barely any time to react or counter her. Maybe Chiguar thought he was that good for it was clear he was no fool. She grinned, fool or not, nobody was as fast as her. She could be gone before they knew it with no chance they would catch her.

The mere thought burned a line of fire through her skull that made her stumble and miss a step. She hadn't been thinking of harming the boy, why had her magical fetters hurt her so? It must be more artfully crafted than Bortillo's enchantment had been, less open to circumvent. Disturbed by the revelation, she sniffed a lungful of air and wished she hadn't, her sense of smell might have dulled but it soured her lungs.

Regaining her balance, Merca walked deeper into the tunnel, her mind writhing as it always did with thoughts of bloody vengeance. Fortune had taken an abrupt turn, but she couldn't yet decide if it was for the better. The boy was something else. She didn't know quite what but he was no Bortillo.

The ground dipped and sloped before levelling off again. The timber supports gave way to rock and hard-packed stone and the roof of the tunnel dropped so that Merca had to duck her head to move forward. The ominous weight of the walls seemed to press from above and an irrational relief flooded her once she'd crossed beneath them.

The floor of the tunnel gently inclined, beams and supports taking up their duty again as the passage straightened. After a minute of silent trudging, the light from Merca's lantern flickered and the walls opened out onto a wide area stacked with contraband. An oaken, iron-bound door was set in the facing wall.

"Close the shutters on that lantern. Stay out of sight. Say nothing," Merca ordered, then waited until the light diminished leaving a single pool of radiance from her own.

Like a prowling cat, she stalked to the door and tried the latch. Barred. Setting the lantern down she thumped a fist loudly against the oak. Lowering her cowl, Merca pressed an ear to the timber and listened.

Nothing.

Glowering, she pulled a dagger from her hip and struck the pommel harshly against the wood, sending out a booming peel. She listened again.

Movement. Her mind sorted through it. Three… no two approached, by their tread, men, their steps tentative, wary. Merca's nose wrinkled in thought, no one was expected so they would likely have weapons drawn. She straightened and rotated her head to release the tightness in her shoulders and neck.

"A light in the darkness," mumbled a thick voice.

They would be on edge, any delay would only add to it. Merca waited, the curl of a smile tugging at her lips.

The man spoke again, his voice rising, insistent. "A light in the darkness."

"Bring's shadows and death," Merca finally replied.

There was a pause. "Weren't expectin' no one till tha' morrow."

"Lucky fer you I ain't no one," growled Merca. "The Targus sent me, so open this godsdamned door else ya'll wear my knife up your ass."

"That you, Murder?" the man returned, his voice held a note of question. A hint of panic. There weren't many wester-isles in the city that worked for the Syndicate. Why would the Targus send his pet assassin? He turned and glowered into the shadows by the stairwell. If Greik had been skimming off the top again it wouldn't be just his life on the line.

"Don't you fucking move," he hissed into the darkness just as another bang rattled the door. "Yeah, yeah, keep ya skirt on," he murmured, trying to keep the fear from his voice. He glanced at Rimul alongside, who gripped a long knife and gave a nervous nod.

"You got summat ta hide in there?" Merca growled.

"Can't be too careful is all," the man said.

The bar scraped against its blocks, then, with a chunk, the latch lifted and the door swung wide. Merca immediately saw two men, one stood behind and to the side of the other. Both were armed, holding knives in their right hands.

"You look as happy ta see me as I am ta be here," Merca teased. She gave a lopsided grin. "Ya gonna invite a girl in or keep her waitin' at the door all night?"

"Weren't expectin' no-one," the man repeated. He was tall and lean as a pole so that Merca barely reached his chin. The red blotch of a birthmark covered one side of his face.

Birthmark frowned. "Who's that'n ya got with ya?"

Merca pushed forwards and the man took a quick step back as if afraid they might touch. She sneered.

"Just some hack from the Trades, here ta take an inventory." Merca raised her eyebrows theatrically. "I'm a fucking babysitter now. Me. Can ya believe that?"

Her head tilted a fraction. The faintest of noises issued from the darkness behind. A puff of sound, which, amplified by the tunnel, grew like a strengthening wind. Fuck and damnation.

Birthmark's eyes narrowed as he too heard the hollow echo. "What…"

There was no time for finesse. Like a snake striking, Merca stepped inside his knife arm and stabbed Birthmark, once, twice, thrice, twisting the blade in his gut with each thrust. As his belly tore open, she levered him into his companion.

An arm crashed into her back sending her tumbling to the floor. As Merca rolled, cat-like, to her feet she registered a snap-hum and in the same breath a thud.

Beyond thought, Merca's body moved of its own volition. Her left hand grasped a throwing blade from her right hip and she spun, whipping her arm violently to send it spinning into the shadows. In the same motion, Merca twisted towards the second man whose long knife was already thirsting for her. As she brought her blade up to deflect it, he staggered. Stumbling, the man's tongue lolled, mouth gaping like a landed fish, before he dropped, knees cracking, to the stone floor of the cellar. His jaw clamped shut, shearing a chunk of flesh from his tongue, then, with a deflating sigh, he folded, face first, onto the ground.

Stood behind was Herald, eyes so wide the whites of them encompassed the hazel-brown of his irises. He clutched a bloody dagger in one fist.

Merca winked. "Thanks, pet, but I had it covered." In the flickering half-light of the cellar, the prince looked more pallid than ever and she found herself grinning, how was that possible? A speck of dried vomit sat, wart-like, on Herald's chin and she noted with contempt that he trembled like a leaf in a storm. Fucking great.

Even as she made the observation, Merca felt a tremor take hold of her muscles as the rush left her. A familiar, low ache throbbed through her skull. She spied Tasso Chiguar, kneeling just inside the doorway. A feathered bolt sat lodged in his chest and, from the bubble of pink froth on his lips, it had pierced a lung.

Tasso Marn rushed to his side emitting a warble of denial. "No… no… no… no…." Her hands fluttered over the shaft, afraid to touch it, afraid she might cause him pain until, with a low-pitched groan, Chiguar captured them in his own. He coughed, spraying bloody phlegm.

As Chiguar gasped for air, Tomas slipped through the door, eyes taking in the scene and how it must have played out. Alighting on the Order man and a shaken Marn, he edged away from them towards the unnaturally quiet Herald. He was followed into the room by Horyk.

The Norderman gave a grim frown. "We are pursued through the tunnels. We've minutes before they are upon us."

"Love," Chiguar gasped. His voice was weak but still deep so that it seemed to vibrate as he spoke. "There's… no time… you… must go. Leave… me."

"No, no, I won't. We can find a physiker. Fix you up." A tear leaked from Marn's eye and dripped unnoticed down her cheek.

"It's... mortal. Both... know it." Chiguar panted, "Go. Remember... our... charge. You must... see... it through... love." Every suckle of breath rattled his chest. "We... meet again... in the stars."

"I love you." Marn cupped a soiled hand to his cheek.

"And I... you. Now, go...let... these be... our... last words," Chiguar coughed blood.

Leaning forward, Marn bent and kissed him tenderly on the forehead, then cheek. Her limbs felt heavy as she dragged herself to her feet.

"Horyk..." Chiguar huffed, blood rimmed his lips and speckled his chin. "Crossbow... take...." He slumped as the Norderman crossed to his side.

Horyk glanced at Tasso Marn who gave a sharp nod, hand wiping at her face. He grasped Chiguar beneath the arms and with a grunt of effort, half-lifted, half-dragged the Order man across the room into the dark of the stairwell and propped him against the wall next to a dead man. A dead man with a knife protruding from his eye and a crossbow resting on his gut still gripped in one hand.

Horyk broke the man's death grip on the weapon then cranked and loaded it with a bolt. He glanced at the darkened outline of Chiguar and placed a gentle hand on his shoulder before laying the crossbow on the Order man's lap. Once their pursuers broke through the cellar door Chiguar would get one shot. They both knew he would not have the time nor the strength to load another bolt.

As an afterthought, Horyk pulled the knife from the dead man's eye and wiped the bloody mucus off the blade before turning back to the others.

Merca was hissing orders. Crates and sacks and anything else they could lift was being barricaded against the door. Of a sudden, the assassin crowed with joy and began rolling a barrel across the cellar floor.

"Tear me a strip of cloth," she commanded. Setting the barrel into position, she pounded the pommel of her dagger at a bung then fed the material Tomas gave her into the opening.

"Best ya'll clear out. There'll be one maybe two on watch outside so wait for me upstairs." Merca didn't stop to see if they complied. Didn't see the final, forlorn look the Tassos gave each other, Marn the last to leave. A boom shivered the door rattling the bar in its cradle.

Merca ignored it. The pungent smell of naptha-oil permeated the air making her gag. Feeding the other end of the taper into her lantern it sputtered and caught flame. Panicked, Merca sprinted for the stairwell. The rush took her again, everything seeming to slow as she moved. In the flare of firelight, Chiguar's eyes danced in reflected glory, then she was past him and up the stairs.

The explosion when it came was larger than anticipated. Much larger. A concussive roar crushed her eardrums sending a compressive pain through her skull. Fingers of flame surged through the floorboards moments before they splintered and cracked as a raging inferno blasted upwards. By some miracle, Merca found herself propelled, tumbling, into an oasis of calm.

The boy, Mouse, stood at the centre of it, the others gathered at his feet like fallen dolls. By some art, a coruscating sphere rippled around them all, the wildfire buffeting against it harmlessly.

Tomas was terrified, Merca saw, the boy's face ashen and eyes wild with fear. His hands were held out wide and shook uncontrollably and, of all the things, he was humming, in one, long, sonorous tone that evoked memories of the night before.

As if all seven hells vented their rage another belch of flame erupted. A plank of wood, torn loose, shot toward Tomas but in a blink, it was gone, repelled across the room as if launched by a giant to smash through a wall.

Merca had forsaken the gods a long time ago but found herself touching a hand to her head, heart and stomach in bewildered supplication before berating herself for her lapse. She coughed, the room was filling with smoke, the barrier that protected them from the heat and flames was pervious to it.

An external door, set in the wall furthest from the devastation and largely unscathed, wrenched open and a man and woman surged into the room. A look of fearful awe lit their faces at the destruction. Smoked gusted, parting briefly to show that the far wall was gone, a jagged hole venting flame to the outside world. A cross beam gave way with a crash and whoosh of cinders and both lurched back towards the door.

Through the billowing smoke, a shadow moved, and another.

"Greik? Rimul?" the woman cried. "Run, the whole place is coming down." She turned, intent on following her own advice when something smacked her in the back. Her legs gave way tumbling her to the floor.

"Murder?" Her companion stumbled with an agonised cry and his blood splattered the ground and in her hair. A sharpness pierced the woman's shoulder but she gave it no heed. Arms flailing, her fingers scratched at the floorboards for purchase, a blind panic overtaking her as the building groaned its death throes. She knew a moment of pure terror when a weight pressed her down, a boot on her back. A stab to the base of her skull chased the pain away and her life with it.

Rising from the dead woman everything screamed at Merca to be gone. To just run. But her head pounded louder still and a compulsion held her rooted to the spot.

"Ratboy, out, now." She took a tremulous step back into the inferno and the pressure in her head eased. Horyk passed her, shielding the prince with his body in a mad dash for freedom. Then Marn appeared, pushing a soot-faced Tomas before her. Merca grabbed his arm and pulled him towards the door. Then they were out, coughing and dragging in deep lungfuls of air.

The Stacks has never smelled so sweet, Merca thought, hands resting on her knees as a raking hack threatened to bring up a lung. The heat through her leathers was harsh and, as she turned to regard the fiery holocaust, it forced her back several paces.

The adjacent building was compromised, flames already licked at its sides and Merca could see some stabbing from its roof. A bell sounded somewhere in the night, its urgent toll matching her racing heart.

People started to gather, drawn like moths. Fires were a rare but ever-present danger in the Stacks, for the houses and tenements were made of cheap lumber and built atop each other. Answering the ringing call to arms, more and more came to battle the fire, knowing if it wasn't arrested half the Stacks could be lost.

The crackle and roar of flames grew louder. *We need to go,* Merca looked about for the others. Marn had a vacant, faraway look on her face, oblivious it seemed to all around.

"This way." Merca grabbed Tomas and propelled him towards an alley, away from the towering walls of Kingsholme and the destruction she had set in motion. She heard footfalls behind, and a quick glance told her the others followed. Good, she might be bound to the boy for now but if she could break free, as was promised, the prince was worth his literal weight in gold, it would be a shame not to claim it.

Merca led them out the far side of the alley, across a street then down the night-blackened maw of another. Tearing around a corner she stuttered to a halt, Tomas running into her back. A dark mass had detached from the wall not ten paces ahead and blocked the way. Her knife leapt to her hand. She sensed another shade behind the first.

A startled exclamation issued from Marn who spoke in a tongue Merca had not heard before. It made the small hairs on the back of her neck tingle.

"Tskgoten, bik naden."

Merca's head ached, twice she had quickened already, a third time in such quick order would make the comedown, if she survived, debilitating. Still, it was not like she had any choice.

"Time for you to try out that fancy dagger of yours, Ratboy," she murmured.

"Stop. Put up your weapons." The command came from the darkness, powerful yet gently spoken.

Murder laughed as the rush filled her veins. She couldn't see shit but then, neither could they. With a surge of speed, she jumped at the wall then kicked and propelled herself up and over, body twisting, arm extending. Everything became instinctive, the sounds in the alley marrying with her blunted sight. Made up of inconstant shades of darkness, the night ebbed and flowed, its varying degrees subliminally guiding her blade.

But her strike did not bite and the surprise barely had time to register when a touch feathered against her legs as she arched past. It was enough that her landing was put off, sending her crashing to the ground.

Agony ruptured from her knee as it struck the dirt of the alleyway, only the soft yield of the mud saved her from more serious injury. The flaring pain obfuscated to the back of her mind as Murder rolled to her feet and into something hard that snapped her head back.

White light exploded and her mind went blank.

Chapter 28: The Wylders

The Maag Hills, The Rivers

It's beautiful, Nihm thought, studying the valley. The road they were on curved around a hill with bare trees scattering its slope, their skeletal branches dark against the snow. In the vale below a brook tumbled along, its waters sounding a sweet murmur that was hard to hear over the crunch of wagon wheels and the rattle of horse harness. But not for Nihm. She heard everything with perfect clarity and, with Sai's help, it was easy to focus on the sounds she wanted and ignore those she did not.

Since setting off earlier that morning, Nihm had spotted deer and spied various tracks by the roadside where they had crossed. Not all spoor were deer though, there were wolf tracks and fox trails and once a boar, a sow judging by the adolescent hoof prints that followed it.

Releasing a contented sigh, Nihm watched her breath plume the air. The sights and the sounds combined to set her mind at peace, reminding her of better times. Of hunting with her Da and gathering with her Ma and walking the old forest. Almost, for an instant, she could forget the pang in her heart, ignore the hole her Ma's death had left inside her. Dismiss too that she was hunted and that urakakule invaded the Rivers.

In moments like these, she could just be.

That completeness never lasted though. Often it was as fleeting as a breath of wind against her cheek as inexorably her head and heart would drag her back. She sighed again, this time a weary one.

<*Your eyes are leaking. You are sad, again,*> Sai observed.

Nihm dabbed a finger to her cheek and it came away wet. Self-consciously she glanced to her right. Mama Besom sat beside her, steering the wagon with a click of tongue or word as much as by rein. To Nihm she seemed old but spry, the natural frizz of grey hair holding hints of the black it once was. It was pulled tight and bound at the back in bright yellow strips of cloth to lay halfway down her back. Mama's rich, mahogany skin was wrinkled like aged leather though the crow's feet around her deep, brown eyes revealed them to be clear and astute. At the Encoma Holdstead, Nihm found that the older women liked to chatter and always had something to say but Mama Besom spoke rarely, something for which Nihm was grateful. The old lady glanced across then turned her eyes forward again.

Nihm wondered why she rode with Mama Besom. There were one score and twelve Wylder wagons in all and, according to Sai, one hundred and eighty-two Wylders, all brightly attired in spring colours of browns and greens and yellows. And every one of them deferred to Mama Besom, even Kafelie Dax, the leader of the Wylders, who had offered them fire and food the night before and later invited them to travel south.

"We ride to the Forest of Arden. Away from this trouble in the north. You are welcome to join us," Dax had offered to Nesta. The ilf in his guise looked as human as any of them but the Wylders still seemed fascinated by him. Deferential even, though to Nihm it was not clear why.

<He must possess powerful magic to transform so,> Nihm projected at Sai. <I have never heard of such a thing.>

<In Lower Rippleton, your father spoke of the ilfanum. That he was told there were many different types and that each served a different purpose for Da'Mari. Maybe Nesta is different again from M'rika or R'ell. My logic and perception routines hypothesise that his skin morphed to simulate the texture and colouration of a human. An ability that has been documented before in nature.>

Nihm shrugged. <And the clothes as well?>

<A complex pattern but entirely possible,> Sai responded, somewhat haughtily, Nihm thought, only he was wrong, she knew it in her bones.

<Hiro taught me how to construct an aura shield to both contain and reflect my tae'al, my essence, and make it appear less. To guard against those with ki'tae. I think Nesta does the same but with his appearance. Projecting that which he wishes others to see.>

Sai's reply was instant. <Tae'al, aether, essence, auras, call it what you will but they hold no validity according to my databases. To say that we have witnessed magic would be a misnomer. It is merely a term ascribed to something not yet scientifically understood.>

Nihm laughed. <And you think I'm stubborn. Open your mind, Sai. I have done things that defy any explanation you have given and Nesta turned water to ice, we both saw that.>

<Energy transference.> If Sai had eyebrows, Nihm was sure they would be raised. <An exothermic reaction. In the case specified, the transfer of heat from water to air caused a state change from liquid to solid. I do not understand how it was achieved but the principle is well understood. The matter requires further analysis.>

"You are strange, child," Mama Besom murmured. Her words brought Nihm back from her internal discourse. She glanced at the old woman whose eyes followed the road ahead.

Mama spoke again. "We Wylders are friendly enough but oft misunderstood. It means we keep to ourselves for the most part. But we experience things on our travels most of you Holders never do."

"Holders?" Nihm asked.

One of Mama Besom's bushy grey eyebrows arched in her direction and Nihm grinned. For some reason it made her think of Sai.

Mama said, "It means anyone who is not Wylder. Wylders are travellers whereas Holders set roots down, build houses and live in one place most all their lives."

"I know of Wylders but you are the first I have met," Nihm confessed.

Mama Besom gave an indignant grunt as if to say her point had been perfectly made but gave no reply. After an uncomfortable while, Nihm asked another question.

"Why do you think me strange?"

Mama Besom gave a shrewd look. "I might be old, but I see clearly enough. I see conflict in your eyes that tells of suffering, that much is true. But I also see an aura that reflects none of that turmoil, as neat and tidy as a laced bow, that much is false. Would you not find it strange? That, and having two tame wolves, revealed in the manifestations of Jarekicar and Noimenor."

Nihm was taken aback at Mama Besom's reply and glanced at Ash and Snow who trotted alongside the wagon, but she was intrigued as well, and her words slipped out before she could call them back. "Jarekicar and Noimenor, who are they?"

At first, Nihm thought Mama Besom would not answer for she turned away with a pinched expression.

"The One and his Trinity were revealed little more than a thousand years ago, yet we have been here far longer than that," Mama finally answered. "Whilst the old gods have been forsaken by you Holders, they have not been forgotten by us Wylder. Jarekicar is Lord of Light and Noimenor Lord of Dark, just two of the many gods."

"Now, leave me be child," Mama huffed. "I'm not your mother to bother with endless questions. Any Wylder will gladly educate you as to our ways and the true gods. For myself, I prefer the solitude and contemplation of my mind to that of idle chatter. So, unless you would like to tell me what you truly are I will return to it."

A numb silence settled over Nihm, her jaw clenching at the mention of her mother. Casting her eyes back to the valley and hillsides she sought the calm found earlier but it eluded her. Her mind was a jumbled mix of longing, melancholy, and hunger, a desire to know more. That last sat unappeased for Mama Besom exuded a surly countenance, one Nihm was scared to intrude upon.

The rest of the day was spent travelling through the foothills and valleys of the Maag. Blue skies extended overhead with tufts of white cotton cloud tumbling south in a strengthening breeze that chilled where it touched the skin.

Nihm often found herself wondering about the others. They had been dispersed between the Wylder, each riding in one of the large, gaudy wagons that were home to a family. When the curve of the road allowed, she would catch a glimpse of Nesta and Renco, who rode on horseback alongside Kafelie Dax at the head of the caravan. It aggrieved her no end that Renco was riding her mare, it should be him sat here not her. After all, she thought bitterly, he'd make the perfect travel companion for Mama Besom.

She felt a tug against her mind.

<*What's wrong?*> Renco asked.

Something else to feel aggrieved about, she thought sourly. Their bonding meant she could sense where Renco was, sometimes feel his mood and it seemed he could read hers in return. Nihm's jaw tightened as she ground her teeth. All she wanted was to be left alone with her own thoughts in her own mind, but now, not only did she have Sai intruding on her every waking moment, she had her link to Renco to contend with.

<Nothing,> Nihm projected down their link.

<I've enough 'nothings' of my own to worry about without feeling yours,> Renco replied before abruptly ending the conversation.

Nihm fumed. Ungrateful, thankless, selfish… and he stole my horse. Mama Besom clucked her tongue and Nihm got the distinct impression it was at her rather than the horses, even though Mama's head never strayed from the road.

By late afternoon the cotton clouds gave way to rolling grey pillars and the air turned colder still with the promise of new snow. The Maag gradually transformed from low hills to flatlands and the turgid waters of the Emerald Lake appeared on the near horizon.

The Wylders seemed to know the land well and Kafelie Dax led them to camp in a snow meadow that bordered a copse of elda trees and wilabarks, these last lining the banks of a creek that ran towards the lake.

There was a well-trodden orderliness, Nihm found, in the Wylders. There was no discussion on the placement of the wagons, yet soon a small hamlet had sprung up, with a thoroughfare running through its middle. The older children and some of the adults attended to the cattle and the horses, towering shires, two each to a wagon and a score of the more elegant morabs for riding. The master of each wagon checked them for damage or wear and the busy sounds of their labour soon filled the air.

Mama Besom steered her wagon to a clear space near the centre and no sooner had she stopped than a boy appeared, black-haired, dark-complexioned, no older than twelve, Nihm guessed.

"Isha, Mama, isha," the boy hollered in cheery greeting, reaching up to scratch the neck of the nearest horse before his nimble fingers started on the buckles of the harness.

"What can I do?" Nihm asked.

"We leave at first light." Mama Besom groused. "Do not be late." Clambering down, she hobbled to the back of her wagon where a woman awaited with a babe on her hip.

"Isha, Marla, come in," Mama said, climbing the steps at the back and unlatching the door. "How is little Venzella? Red cheeks and a runny nose I see."

"Isha, Mama. Teething and telling the whole world about it." Marla followed the old lady into her wagon and the rest of their conversation was muted as the door closed.

Nihm heard her name called and turned to find Morten striding towards her, a huge grin on his face. His head was bare, his woolly cap clenched in a ball in one fist. The wind tugged at his red hair which was getting long and unruly. The stubble on his face was turning into a beard. He looks older, Nihm thought, a man. Ash and Snow brushed against her hips demanding attention and she balled her fists in their fur.

"These Wylder don't want no help," Morten declared, "Which is fine by me. Wanna walk? I could do with a stretch out."

Nihm fell into step beside him, and they trod the makeshift street, watching the Wylders go about their work, laughing and bantering with each other, several even called out greetings to them and they waved and smiled in return.

"Isha, Moreg," Morten called out to one young woman with hair as red as his own.

"Thought you didn't like Wylders. That they'd slit our throats and rob us." Nihm arched a teasing eyebrow.

"Sshhh, not so loud." Morten hissed, glancing about. He sniffed and wiped a finger under his nose. "It's just what folks say. I ain't never spoken to any afore and I reckon these 'uns seem decent enough. Friendly at least and the kids like me tales."

"Is that all it takes Morten Stenhause, someone to like your stories?" Nihm laughed.

"Who knew I was so shallow, eh?" Morten chuckled. "Mind you, they tell some tall 'uns of their own and it seems ta me they're hungry for new ones."

They walked in idle chatter for a while leaving the tall wagons behind them. The light was failing and Ash and Snow loped off into the surrounding bushes to explore.

"What are we doing, Nihm?" Morten asked in sudden seriousness.

"What do you mean? We're going to Wooliston, you know that," Nihm said. "To meet with Master Hiro."

Morten stopped and turned, a hand reaching out to clasp Nihm's arm. "But why? This Renco seems to have some hold over you, Hiro, too. I don't like it. We've barely known the lad five days yet even before that you dragged us halfway through the Ramiras looking for him."

"I didn't drag you anywhere. I didn't force you to come." Nihm pulled her arm free and pushed past him. The cheeriness of their walk a tattered ruin, though she couldn't say why his questioning riled her so.

"I've got nowhere else."

Morten's words stopped Nihm in her tracks, her body suddenly heavy and unresponsive. She didn't look back. She couldn't.

"Everyone I know or care about, 'ceptin you, are in Thorsten. Probably dead. My Ma and my Da..." Morten choked. "...I ain't got no way of getting back to 'em. So don't tell me I had a choice. You're all I've got. I need to know, Nihm. You owe me that much at least."

She didn't have any answers. Not for him. Not for her. What was she doing? Feet furrowing the snow where she dragged them, Nihm walked away.

***

The campfire was a communal affair. The Wylders built it at the camp's centre, and it was large enough that several racks stood across it with kettles and pots artfully suspended above the flames. A handful of attendants tended to them with long-handled poles and heavy clothes. Music played whilst the food was cooked, on slim-bodied, short-necked lyres the Wylders called fiddles which were clamped beneath the chin and played with a bow. They were higher pitched in tone than their larger cousins and played at a great tempo, accompanied by piping flutes that lent a merry atmosphere.

As ever, Renco observed it all in silence. Lett had eaten her meal next to him and, surprisingly, so too had Morten. The tall man he'd first glimpsed at Fallston was always with Nihm, but she sat apart, near Mama Besom, whose sour face rivalled Maohong's. He smiled at the thought of his friend, the tight lump in his chest was gone now that he knew Mao lived. The old man was tough as old boots, but he'd feared for Mao after the awful beating he'd taken at the hands of the giant Red Cloak, Holt.

"Lovers tiff?"

Renco glanced at Lett whose blonde hair was golden-red in the firelight. Her blue eyes twinkled with mischief, but her words were not directed at him, and his gaze settled on Morten who had been unusually quiet and aloof.

"Stare at Nihm any harder and you'll set her on fire," Lett teased.

Morten's glower twisted to Lett. He scraped at his bowl, neck flushing red as he spooned it in.

"Want my advice, go say you're sorry," Lett pressed. "Whatever she did, or you did, I don't care but I'm safe for the first time in an age and your face is bringing the mood down."

"What do you know?" Morten snapped, "About me or Nihm? Nothing. That's what."

"I know what I see," Lett fired back. "A love-struck boy pretending to be something he's not. You're a taverner's son. What are you even doing here?"

Renco watched the red tide creep up Morten's neck to his cheeks. People were noticing, eyes following the argument as it escalated, and many of the observers wore terse looks on their faces.

Morten rose to tower over Lett. "What are any of us doing here? We barely escaped with our lives. The urak have moved south as quickly as we have run and you think we are safe, here? With these people?"

Renco set his bowl down and stood. This had gone too far. Many Wylders were watching now even Kafalie Dax their headman and, beside him, Nesta, his human face placid, showing no emotion. Had it ever?

He raised a hand to Morten's shoulder only for it to be slapped away. Renco saw the wild look in Morten's eyes but pain too before he barged past, stomping into the night.

Renco watched him go then turned to look at Lett.

"What?" Lett hissed. "What'd I do?"

He held her gaze and shook his head wishing he had words.

"Fine. I'll go talk to him," Lett sulked. Gathering her feet she got up, then, seeing Renco's sceptical look gave a sharp smile. "I'll be nice. Promise."

<What was that about?> Nihm's thought hovered in his mind. He could sense more than words though. He could feel the worry in them as well.

<You. Me maybe. The here and the now.> Crouching, Renco gathered the bowls and spoons abandoned by Lett and Morten and neatly stacked them. He could sense Nihm's confusion through their link, and the lingering uncertainty.

Marj appeared by his side, the matriarch of the Rojcha family with whom he was staying, and she emptied his hands. "A guest is welcome so long as they do not break the harmony of the group."

Her message couldn't be clearer. Renco bowed his thanks then turned and left. He needed to find his centre, his own harmony. 'To think without thought' as Master Hiro would say.

He walked out past the wagons to the edges of the brook. It was ink-black and cold away from the fire but neither bothered him as he disrobed down to his britches. He dropped into a stance. Clearing his mind, he let his body move, feet sweeping the snow as he glided from one position to the next.

Since their bonding, Renco and Nihm shared awareness, the one for the other. Nihm's mind was unguarded and cluttered with thoughts. So it was, that Renco was cognizant of her approach and could sense confusion and anger in her still.

Taking station on his right, Nihm unfastened her cloak and stripped off her jacket and over-vest to just her tunic and trousers, hanging them on a tree branch next to Renco's discarded apparel, before assuming a pose and moving gracefully through her own dance.

"What did you mean before? About Morten. You, me, the here and the now? Do you like spouting horseshit?" Nihm spoke into the darkness.

Renco paused, his body slowly unwinding until he stood upright. <You are angry but do not understand why and so you seek to take your ire out on me.>

<You think to read my mind. Know my thoughts?> Nihm retorted, whirling to a new stance, arms weaving into a blocking position.

<I can't help but know them. You bellow them unguarded at me. It's like asking someone not to listen as you shout in their face. You need to learn control.>

What is wrong with me? Nihm asked herself but found she couldn't stop, her momentum too great to halt.

"Like that night in Fallston when you screamed at Lett like a puppy for its master. Control like that you mean?"

<*You're being irrational and foolish. See, I thought that before you intruded on my exercise, but you are only knowing it now that I am directing the thought at you. That is the control I speak of. Believe me, after today I do not want to be privy to your every imagining. Frankly, it is draining.*>

<*This is a bad idea,*> Suggested Sai as Nihm stopped and turned to Renco. She struck a pose. "Let's spar."

<*Tomorrow.*> Renco began to gather his hung clothes and cloak, for there was no harmony to be found in his forms this night.

"Coward." Nihm knew she was making a fool of herself but couldn't help it. Ever since Morten had pressed her, her mind had been a mess. What was she doing? What was her purpose?

Renco laughed, like he hadn't since before Longstretch, since before Lett's betrayal. It was the wrong thing to do. He could sense Nihm's anger rachet up another level.

He bowed to her. <*Tomorrow, if you still wish it, we will spar.*>

* * *

The snows came during the night and the following morning in the pre-light before dawn the Wylders left, leaving no sign they had been there except for the remnants of their bonfire, the compressed snow where each wagon had hitched and their footprints. Signs that the falling snow would soon conceal.

Kafelie Dax led them south through farmland, meandering down country lanes until, like a stream merging into a river, they joined the main road to Morport. On their left, the sullen waters of the Emerald Lake loomed dismal and grey, a mirror to the skies above.

The roads were quiet of fellow travellers but the few groups they did meet were all headed south. Dax and the other Wylders would call out in greeting as they passed but were always met with surly indifference.

The scattered villages and hamlets, normally so vibrant, lay mostly abandoned and it felt eerily strange to rumble through them, feeling eyes watching them from behind closed shutters.

At one point, not far outside Wooliston, the caravan ground to a halt when they were stopped by a detachment of bannermen on horseback. They wore green tabards trimmed in gold with a leaping white unicorn upon its front that was unfamiliar to Nihm. Their leader spoke briefly with Kafelie Dax before they filed past the wagons wearing a look of grim countenance upon their faces. None of the riders called out in greeting to the Wylders and more than a few glared in open hostility. It troubled Nihm, for she could see no reason for it, though Mama Besom, unperturbed, answered her troubled look.

"They do not know us Wylder. The lack of knowing a thing oft ferments fear and breeds distrust," she said, before flicking the reins to get the horses moving again.

A short while later, on the approach to Wooliston, Renco, riding near the front of the caravan behind Dax and Nesta, spied two figures in the distance. They were stood by the roadside, their horses tied to a leafless tree. With a whoop, Renco spurred his horse into a canter. His heart hammered and his blood surged as the cloaked figures both lowered their hoods, the silver-queued hair of one and the bald head of the other instantly familiar.

<Renco?> Nihm probed.

<Master Hiro and Mao are here,> Renco returned, joy washing through every word.

Renco's exuberance buoyed Nihm despite their fallout and she found her spirits lifting with his. Only, she was stuck on a wagon with Mama Besom not riding free on a horse, her horse. She considered dismounting and running, it would be faster than the measured rumble of the wagon but the thought of it seemed foolish. Besides, she'd known Master Hiro and Mao little more than a cycle of Kildare's moon. Barely anytime at all. So, reeling back her eagerness and anticipation, she sat instead fidgeting on the wooden bench seat.

"You will be with your companions soon enough, child. Patience is a valuable lesson," Mama Besom stated.

Nihm turned. "Do you read minds now?"

The old woman smiled, showing yellow-stained teeth. "Of a sort. The body has its own language and, for the observant, it speaks more honestly than words."

Mama Besom had been no better company today than the day before and this had been their longest discourse since. Nihm turned back, straining her neck to see past the wagons and riders ahead. "It sounds a useful skill to learn," she muttered.

It drew a wry chuckle from Mama Besom, mirth that seemed at odds and out of place given their last two days of travel together. "What?" Nihm asked.

"You do not need to placate me with empty words, child," Mama said. "My humour is at myself. For I am old enough to know that asking the young to have patience is like asking the wind to stop blowing." She cackled, pleased with herself.

For some reason, it made Nihm grin. Whether it was the sudden lifting of her mood or the plain incongruity of Mama Besom's laughter she didn't know or care and her smile rose to touch her cheeks. For the first time in, she couldn't remember how long, Nihm felt relaxed. She found herself talking.

"Da used to tell me the same when we hunted. 'Patience, Nihm. A hunter must have it to be successful.' Ma as well, teaching me to spar. I can hear her voice even now telling me. 'Strike when there is an opening. An opening you can wait for or make. The first requires patience, for your opponent must make a mistake. The second requires speed and skill to create the opportunity.'"

Mama Besom stared. "I find you interesting as well as strange. If times were other than they are, I think I would like to have met your parents. Between you and me, that is not something I have oft said about Holders."

It pleased Nihm, both Mama Besom's words, for she heard the truth in them, and her memories. For the remembrance did not bring its usual pain for her Ma, nor the worry for her Da and it felt good not to bear the burden of them, even if it was just for this time.

The wagon rumbled on, loud in the silence that followed their words. The snow, which had relented in the afternoon, started to fall again. The flakes coming small and fast in the blustering wind.

Nihm looked at Mama Besom whose ancient eyes were dull beneath her cowl. "Patience is all well and good," Nihm grinned then vaulted from her seat to the roadside. "But the wind is not the wind unless it blows."

Setting off, she ran towards the front of the caravan, feet crunching the snow. Ash and Snow bounded to her side, yipping like puppies, excited that Nihm had come to play. They brushed against her, threatening to knock her from her feet, before spinning into the deeper drift off the verge and then back again. Laughing, Nihm was unmindful of the stares of the Wylder as she tore by. She slowed as she passed the last wagon, or was it the first, her mind teased.

<It is both,> Sai answered, <depending on which perspective you wish to apply.>

Kafelie Dax cursed, his grey morab dancing skittishly as Nihm ran past with the two wolfdogs, then crooned to settle the horse which stilled almost immediately. Beside him, Nesta rode without reins and whispered a word to his mount whose nostrils flared in alarm but otherwise walked on evenly.

Ahead of Nihm, no more than fifty paces, Renco had dismounted and was signing at Mao and Master Hiro. All three turned at her approach, Renco having to tighten the hold on the reins as the horse nickered and tugged.

Nihm slowed and came to a standstill five paces from them, suddenly unsure what to say now that she had gotten there.

"I found him," she said at last.

Master Hiro flicked a thumb beneath his nose. "Renco has changed, and it would appear so have you."

Nihm's eyes widened at Hiro's accusing tone and Renco looked almost sheepish, like a child who had been found out from some misdeed.

"Much has happened, and I cannot explain all of it," Nihm began, her voice rising defensively. "But I did what I needed to save him."

"It is plain that you both have much to tell," Hiro said. "But now there is no time, you have chosen unusual travel companions and they will be with us in moments. Let us wait for them together." Hiro folded his hands, each one into the opposing sleeve of his robe, then tilted his head to look past Nihm's shoulder.

"What? Not even a thank you," Nihm blurted. "I risked my life looking for Renco and we barely made it here."

Hiro cast a steely eye back on Nihm. "I am more than grateful that Renco is returned and for your part in it. But tell me, did you do it for me? Renco perhaps? Or maybe it was your own need that you fulfilled."

<Bloody ass.> Thought Nihm, only it was directed to Renco, not Sai and she bit her lip in horror at her mistake.

Renco pinched his lips, fighting a grin. <Sometimes I think so too. But Master is almost always right, which can be just as annoying.>

Hiro cleared his throat. "The world is full of surprises. You are Wylder, Dax by your colours if my mind recalls rightly." He called loudly as the column of riders and wagons lumbered to a stop.

The lead rider inclined his head, though his eyes remained on Hiro. He smiled. "Your mind is sound. I am Kafelie Dax, leader of this caravan and you must be Master Hiro."

"I am." Hiro's eyes narrowed briefly as they strayed to the man riding beside Dax. He was not Wylder and there was something other about him that tugged at his memory. "I must thank you for Nihm and Renco's safe passage and that of their companions."

Nihm glared. *So he could say it*, she thought.

Kafelie Dax lifted his chin, his hazel eyes bright with good humour. "We need no thanks. We would be poor Wylders not to give a hand when all that was needed was to extend it. They have proven interesting company."

"I have no doubt," Hiro said agreeably. He looked up at the slate grey sky in judgement. "It will be dark soon and this snow looks set in. There's an encampment of Jorin bannermen outside of Wooliston and you would do well to set camp south of them."

Dax nodded his thanks for the warning. "Then let us ride and talk."

"My presence might be dangerous for you," Hiro said.

"A claim we Wylders could make in return. Let us chance fate together, eh." Dax grinned. "Besides, you have four horses and seven people. It would be a miserable journey for those walking would it not."

Hiro smiled, "Agreed, I accept your hospitality."

Turning, he and Mao trudged to their horses and unlashed the reins from the tree and mounted. Renco did likewise, leaving Nihm alone on her feet.

"Mama Besom will be along shortly. I think she has enjoyed your company," Dax said. "Rarely have I seen her so happy." He laid the reins against his horse's neck and the dappled-grey mare gave a snort of frosted air before marching on, Nesta silent beside him.

Nihm watched as Hiro, Mao and Renco fell in behind the Wylder leader feeling left behind and despondent at the thought of Mama Besom's stagnant company. Snow and Ash brushed up against her, one on each side warming her flanks.

"It's alright for you two," she grumbled. "You get to run and play. I get Mama's silent judgement and an occasional lecture."

The first of the wagons rattled by. Several children waved at her from the back, hanging half out of the open doorway.

"Isha, Nihm," they called out, their jolly faces a stark counterpoint to her mood.

"Isha," Nihm replied, raising her hand and forcing her face to smile. Her effort was rewarded by a fit of giggling before the children all disappeared back inside the wagon.

She groaned, there were another eight wagons before Mama Besom's.

Chapter 29: To Spar or Not To Spar

Wooliston, The Rivers

Kafelie Dax led the Wylders past the township of Wooliston, skirting the Jorin bannermen that were camped outside its walls. They were five hundred strong, Master Hiro proclaimed, though, with the poor light and swirling snow, Dax found it hard to see the emerald-green flags the Jorin flew, let alone make out tents and estimate numbers.

Heavily armed sentries watched their progress on the approach road, regarding them with stern looks and spears clasped ready. But when the Wylders turned away to follow the road south they were content to let them go, reluctant to leave the warmth of their braziers.

The caravan managed a further half-league when Kafelie Dax spied a wood of evergreens. They offered shelter he could not turn down and soon the hamlet of wagons was set up on the fringes of the forest.

Eager to test her bow and her skill, and with Ash and Snow prowling by her side, Nihm joined a hand of Wylder hunting for fresh game.

<You seem in better spirits.> Renco's thoughts intruded on hers as Nihm slipped away, unseen by her companions. Unseen, but not unnoticed, not by Renco at least.

She blew her cheeks out and watched her breath steam the air. <I'm hunting. I'll be back soon.>

Nihm didn't know a grunt could be thought, but Renco managed it. Her face twitched, lips cracking into a half-smile as she followed the hunters. Slipping between the wooden beams the Wylder camp vanished within moments.

Renco felt her leave, sensed her nearness diminish. It was a weird feeling. With a shrug, he turned to help the Rojcha family whose turn it was to gather wood. He was joined a short time later by Morten with three children trailing after him, begging for stories only to be hushed and chased away by a young woman with fiery red hair.

"This is time for work, not stories. If you have none, I will find you some," she threatened, lunging at the nearest.

The boy dodged with a laugh and the three ran off, disappearing back between the wagons.

The woman turned to Morten. Her face was as pale as the snow, but her sea-green eyes were bright and full of mirth. "You've told them tales and now they'll pester you to death unless you show a firm hand. There's a time and a place for such things."

"Isha, Moreg Hass," Morten grinned, running a hand through his unruly hair. "A teller of stories never chases away his audience. Else there would be no one to listen."

"Oh, a storyteller you say?" Moreg teased. "And here I thought you were just a vagabond rescued from winter's bite."

"I canna deny either claim," Morten laughed, the wind whipping his hair into his eyes in a sudden gust.

"This wood ain't gathering itself," grumbled a voice from nearby. It belonged to a young woman, who held a trimming axe in one hand and a branch in the other. "Maybe save your courting till later, Moreg."

Moreg leaned in towards Morten. "Don't mind Erin," she said in a loud but conspiratorial tone. "She's just raw cause her beloved is off with that Lett of yours looking for snowberries and knotwort. A pretty girl with golden hair and I hear tell a golden voice to match." Bending, she lifted a fallen branch and shook the snow from it.

"Lett's not mine," Morten stammered.

"Is that all ya can do, Moreg Hass, foment trouble," the young woman called Erin hissed. "There's a dozen folk gathering, not just Kaid Dax."

"If ya say so." Moreg arched an eyebrow, winked at Morten, and then snapped the branch she was holding, folding its ends together.

Erin pursed her lips and cast an eye between the Holder and Moreg. "I trust Kaid. Besides, I saw Lett walking after Morten just last night after their tiff and they were gone a good while. Hard words, as we Wylder say, make the blood hot and passions high."

Morten felt the colour rise on his cheeks when a hand tugged on his arm and he turned to find Renco behind him. As the two Wylder women continued to argue, he signed for Morten to follow and they cut out the other way, quickly fading out of sight in the murky thickness of the wood.

"Thanks," Morten said, "These Wylder seem hot-tempered and passionate. I don't know whether ta look left or right sometimes." Then, remembering Renco couldn't talk, he lapsed into silence.

They wandered deeper, the sounds of the two women growing distant. Morten thought he heard his name called but Renco didn't stop and Morten felt compelled to follow.

Beneath the boughs, the forest seemed almost to talk, creaking and groaning in complaint at the weight of its winter coat. The snow underfoot was sparse with occasional flurries tumbling free of the branches above to sprinkle the ground.

They reached a break in the canopy where one of the giants had split itself, one of its mighty limbs sheared and lying in ruin on the forest floor.

Renco pulled the basket from his back and set it onto the ground and started gathering the debris, trimming smaller branches off the fallen bough with an axe. Morten didn't have an axe nor a basket but he rummaged for loose branches and kindling and between them they soon had the basket filled.

Done, Morten rubbed his sleeve at the sweat on his brow and could feel its clammy touch on the nape of his neck as it cooled. He grinned, his muscles ached with the satisfaction that came from hard, physical work and it felt good after riding in a wagon all day.

His grin faltered when Renco signed he should carry the basket. Casting an accusing glare, Morten shrugged reluctantly into the straps. With a grunt, he took the weight as Renco helped to pull him upright.

His sourness at having to lug the basket back to the caravan slid from Morten's face when he saw Renco lift a log end upright. It looked too heavy to bear. Morten tugged at the straps of the basket that were already digging into his shoulders and waited with a wry look on his face.

Turning, Renco slid his back against the length of the log then crouched letting the weight drop onto his shoulder before clasping it and driving upwards with his legs. He took a staggering step until he found the centre point of balance.

Bloody show-off, thought Morten, impressed despite himself.

They made their way back to the caravan with slow but steady purpose, Renco stopping twice to change shoulders. By the time they left the overhang of the evergreens, Morten couldn't feel the cold anymore, only the heat of his body and the sweat on his neck which had now travelled down his back. As they walked down the boulevard of wagons the children were back, five of them now, pestering Morten for stories despite his burden. He spied Moreg and Erin walking towards them.

"Glad to see you boys didn't bunk off," Erin beamed. There was no such banter from Moreg, no chasing the children away this time, just tight lips and a scowl.

"Never," gasped Morten, which was all he could muster, his breathing coming deep and fast, the basket seeming heavier with every step. Nevertheless, he straightened his back, standing a little taller as he passed the women, Erin tittering behind her hand, Moreg's sea-green eyes feigning indifference.

It was with great relief that Morten slipped the straps from his shoulders and dropped the basket by the woodpile. Two Wylders preparing food helped, exclaiming at the weight and size of the load, which pleased Morten more than he wanted to admit.

Twisting, Morten turned to watch as Renco lowered the log he carried into the mush at the edge of the bonfire. The fire-tenderer was a pot-bellied man with a round face, retreating hairline and a ponytail. He clapped Renco effusively on the back before taking and expertly manoeuvring the log into position. Satisfied, pot-belly dropped the beam into the middle of the flames, sending a whoosh of hot cinders into the air like angry fireflies, drawing a hoot of excitement from the children.

Renco joined Morten and they stared back at the spluttering fire, both of them arching their backs and rotating their shoulders, working out the kinks and aches.

A cry went up and they turned at the noise.

A hand of Wylder walked the lane between the wagons. Two pairs each carried a deer strung between poles. The last Wylder, a burly woman with a happy face, held a brace of rabbits and three pheasants and next to her strode Nihm, with Snow and Ash ambling one to each side, the wolf dogs glancing uneasily at the growing crowd.

"Looks a fine hunt, Lob," Kafelie Dax called out. His voice, louder than any others, stilled those gathered.

The woman carrying the small game grinned. "Ai, we'll not starve with Nihm. She bagged both deer, from forty paces no less and through thick forest. I've never seen shooting like it."

Kafelie Dax turned to Nihm and regarded her in cool appraisal. She was young, older than sixteen summers but less than twenty, he judged. Taller than average but not much, with raven hair and dark eyes that gave her a hawkish look in the evening light. There was a sureness in the way she moved and no sign of weariness from the hunt. She was neither plain nor pretty, unlike Lett, her golden-haired companion. Still, there was a vitality about her that Dax found alluring and he knew that if he found Nihm so, then so too would all the young men in the caravan. He sniffed and pinched his nose, both women could be a problem, young Wylder men were prone to foolishness and would need watching. He resolved to talk later to the mothers.

"That sounds mighty impressive, I would like to have seen it," Dax said focusing once more on Lob, who was not yet finished in her praise.

"Those wolves of hers corralled the deer towards us else we'd never have had the chance. They were downwind and jittery from our scent," Lob explained, reaching a hand out to the black-furred wolf who sniffed at it, saw it held nothing and, disinterested, turned away.

Dax nodded his head. "That's all well and good but you can regale us with the hunt when we eat. Let's get the deer prepared and on the spit. The rabbit and pheasant too will make a fine addition to tonight's stew."

He clapped his hands loudly. "Night is soon upon us. Get your work done."

The gathering broke up and Nihm wandered over to join Renco and Morten her cheeks dimpling as she grinned. "It seems an age since I've done a proper hunt."

"Ya seem ta have made quite the impression," Morten said.

"It was just a hunt." Nihm shrugged. "We got lucky is all. If we'd come back without the deer, they would no doubt think differently of me."

She spied Master Hiro climbing down the small steps from the back of Mama Besom's wagon and frowned, watching as first Mao then Nesta followed him. She gave Renco a nudge and nodded towards them. "What have they been chit-chatting about I wonder."

<Maybe the path ahead,> Renco replied.

"Julan Haas says the old woman is their mystic," Morten said. "Their physiker. Maybe it's Mao. I swear he ain't right after that beating he took. Sometimes, when he looks at me his eyes seem different. Ancient."

"He is ancient you idiot," Nihm laughed.

"Ai, but it's like someone else is looking outta them. I can't explain it, but it creeps me out."

A look of alarm flashed across Renco's face and with wide strides he marched towards Master Hiro.

Nihm shook her head at Morten.

"What?"

"Mao is his friend and they have only just found each other," Nihm said, "Now you've got him worrying all over again."

"Well, it's true." Morten crossed his arms. "Mao ain't all there. You told me yourself he blasted Ironside right off that boat. He ain't what he seems."

Nihm took a breath and held it. Morten was right, even if his observation was bluntly delivered. Unsure how to respond, Nihm let her mind drift.

The snow was starting to fall more heavily, settling on her hood and sticking to her cloak. It was an odd sensation, the warmth of the fire on her front and the cold of winter on her back. She found it oddly soothing.

Wylders moved around them and she watched with distracted interest as they strung ropes between the wagons closest to the centre. Then they unfurled awning cloth and pulled them tight over the lines to create a sloped shelter beneath.

"Clever," Morten gave his assessment.

More awnings were raised until a large semicircular tent had been erected, with a hole at its centre and open on the downwind side to draw away the smoke from the fire.

The aroma of meat cooking filled the air and Morten's stomach growled, drawing a hooded glance from Nihm.

"Sorry," he muttered. "But I'm starved."

* * *

The Dax-Wylders ate well that night and despite the inclement weather the fiddles played, and the flutes trilled, and songs were sung. Nihm and Morten sat together, the previous night's altercation left unspoken. After they had eaten the children gathered and pleaded with Morten for a story.

With a solemn face and grave tone, Morten bid them sit. When they had settled, his face turned animated as he began the tale of the Green Knight of Annandale.

Face creasing, Nihm smiled knowing what was to follow. But she had read the Green Knight many times and heard it told by a bard. So instead, her curiosity had her rising and wandering the camp, drawn by the playful tune of the fiddlers and the harmonised sounds of the folk songs. Fingers tapping against her thighs, Nihm mumbled at the lyrics.

A flash of golden hair drew Nihm's eye. Lett was with the singers, her lyrical voice weaving around theirs, her cadence adding a haunting, melodic tone.

Making her way through the knots of people, absorbing the music and the quiet buzz of conversation, Nihm could feel the communal spirit. It was not unlike that of the Encoma Holdstead only this felt much deeper, richer somehow. Certainly, it was merrier.

Nihm crossed to the far side of the gathering and found Renco sitting with Mao on the edge of the shelter and wondered fleetingly if she had been seeking him all along. She shook her head, no, where else was there to explore? It was just circumstance.

Renco turned and their eyes met. Nihm felt a flush of guilt as if she had been caught out. It immediately annoyed her but for some reason, she stuck her tongue out at him. He looked startled, his eyes widening and brows marching up his forehead. *Very mature Nihm*, she berated herself. Embarrassed, she turned away and walked right into a Wylder woman sending them both sprawling.

"For someone so artful in the forest, Nihm, you're clumsy as a spring lamb at a gathering," Lob laughed, picking herself up and brushing herself down. "I was coming to ask ya ta join us. We got the blood and heart from one of the deer. It's a hunter's right and Wylder tradition ta drink the one and eat the other. It honours the beast and the kill and, it is said by Goroga, God of the woods, that its essence and strength will pass across and be forever part of the hunter."

Nihm found herself being led away, a waft of amusement emanating from Renco behind.

<I've not forgotten our sparring,> she directed at him.

<Tomorrow.>

Smug bastard.

<I heard that as well. I do not believe I am either of those things. Tomorrow then.>

But they did not spar the next day nor the day after that.

* * *

It took the caravan three days to travel from Wooliston to Dalby Mead, a day more than it should have, for the weather had been vile. The southern road was eerily deserted, and the snow had taken some effort to plough through with the lead wagon breaking the trail being changed out every league or so to spell the horses.

It was not just wearying for the horses, however. The Wylder struggled in the ice and snow with setting camp each evening, the stormy weather making everything that much harder. Hunting had been poor and gathering had proven laborious and care of the horses had taken many more Wylder than usual to attend to, their welfare being paramount. For a Wylder without a horse was no Wylder at all.

"Normally we would shelter in a forest and wait things out," Kafelie Dax explained to Nesta and Master Hiro on the first day out from Wooliston. "Only Mama Besom says there are worse dangers should we tarry. So we'll not rest till we reach the Arden."

Dalby Mead, when they passed it, was a walled town of similar construction and size to Wooliston. Through the falling snow, though, it had been difficult to make out anything other than the smudged outline of its walls, the battlements punctuated by firelight which winked and flickered like errant will-ó-the-wisps. If any of the guards between its crenels spied them, none sallied forth to challenge them.

A league south of Dalby Mead, Kafelie Dax led them down an old ranger path to a forest of dormant elda and sycamore trees, their skeletal limbs crowned with snow instead of leaves. The trees towered above a skirt of green, snow-coated shrubs and wilted, rust coloured ferns.

There the Dax-Wylders set up camp. Once the horses were sheltered and snuffling hungrily for the coarse grass hidden beneath the snow, the Wylders turned to their own needs. Parties were sent out foraging and the hunt returned triumphantly with a boar but also with an injured Wylder that Mama Besom ordered to her wagon.

"It's nought but a love bite, Jaxsa," Lob pronounced, patting the injured Wylder on the shoulder. "A scar ya can impress the girls with."

A pale Jaxsa winced, the leg of his trousers was torn and stained with blood. "Piss off, Lob," he gasped.

"Don't get rich with me," Lob laughed. "Weren't me trying to dance with the beast. Next time get out of the way or better yet stick your spear in it."

"Enough," growled Mama Besom. She cast a beady eye at Nihm, who had returned with the hunt. "Bravado is what'll kill ya, Jaxsa Morgson, not a boar. I'll have words with your mother later."

Jaxsa clenched his teeth as his gored leg and buttock spasmed in pain. "You mean father," he gasped.

Mama Besom scowled. "That boar raked your ass, did it addle your brain as well? Don't tell me what I mean," she huffed.

Turning her back, Mother strode for her wagon, an agonised cry following her as Jaxsa was lifted and carried behind.

* * *

Snow fell in thick clumps though the wind was still and the weather clearing. The thwack of wood on wood had drawn a crowd of onlookers, intrigued by the torch-lit space the Holders had cleared and curious as to the strangers' doings.

Renco had stripped out of everything but his boots and trousers, the sight drawing an excited murmur from those gathered, both for the frigid temperature and the welter of scars that crisscrossed his back. He stood in the guard position, with a basic, wooden stave held lightly in one hand and extended toward his opponent. His free hand he flexed, working the fingers that, until recently, had been bound and splinted. They were stiff and sore.

Opposed, stood Nihm, turning him slowly. She had borrowed Morten's war staff and whirled it in a lazy arc, eyes fixated on her target. Like Renco, she had discarded her cloak and outer jacket but still wore her outer vest, shirt and undervest. Her cheeks were red, and her breath misted the air.

She lunged. The steel-shod tip of her staff was a blur of motion that defied the eye.

With a clack, Renco guided the blow high over his shoulder, turned, then pivoted to avoid the follow through before stepping in close, the air whistling as it was parted by the war staff.

She was fast, almost as fast as Master Hiro but Nihm's moves were basic and obvious. With every strike blocked, Renco learned, reading the incremental tells around her eyes and in her stance that gave warning of her intent, enough to anticipate and avoid each blow a fraction before it was delivered.

As she twisted to follow his movements, so did he, in a strange choreography that was graceful, fluid and lightning quick. Their shoulders brushed as they parted and each resumed their position, Renco holding the centre-ground, staff forward, Nihm twirling hers and pacing around him like a prowling wolf.

Both were aware but unmindful of the crowd, whose exuberant exclamations had grown louder with every clash. It seemed the Wylders loved a good spectacle and bets were being called out.

On one side of the makeshift arena, perched upon a tree stump, sat Master Hiro and Nesta, observing in silence. The human with an alert glint in his eyes and the ilf-man wearing a passive expression. Near to them, standing, watching with the crowd were Morten and Lett following every move and every attack.

"Come on Nihm. Sit him on his arse," crowed a round-faced woman with a wide, beaming look on her face.

Morten recognised her as one of the hunters. "I'm with her," he said, raising his voice to Lett and waggling his thumb at the Wylder. "Reckon, Nihm's got his number. It's all he can do to block."

Lett sneered. "He's toying with her. I saw him take out three full-grown men with his bare hands in Greenholme." Her words were a lie, but they assuaged the worry in her chest, and it pleased her to see the doubt it cast in tavern-boy's eyes. How was Nihm so fast?

Morten's concern washed away almost immediately, his voice forceful and overloud. "Nihm's killed urak. She's a cat playing with a mouse I tell ya."

As if spurred by his words, Nihm darted forward. Like a snake strike, her staff snapped out, feet gliding in behind her attack so that as Renco knocked the blow away, she was close, rendering any counter impotent.

Her body crashed into his and in a single frame of time, she smelled the sweat on his skin. Felt his breath on her face. Counted the snow in his hair and spotted his shoulders. Saw her reflection in russet eyes that were a mirror to her own.

Whatever Nihm felt, so did he. Sensing in Renco a momentary hesitancy, Nihm planted a hand in the middle of his chest. The rhythm of his heart pulsed through her fingertips.

She pushed. Hard. Sending him reeling.

A single step away and Nihm pulled her staff back, spun it around her neck and grasped it with her off-hand in a complex motion that took Renco by surprise. She brought it down with more force than she intended.

CRACK.

The blow would have split Renco's skull had he not blocked it. There was a snap of splintering wood as his stave was sundered, and the steel-shod staff broke through his guard, narrowly missing him as he spun away.

Nihm sucked a lungful of air. Shocked to stillness at her violence. She could have killed him. She sensed the motion before she saw it and whipped her staff up.

Sweeping in, Renco wielded a broken staff end in each hand like two skinny billy clubs. She beat his first strike away sending a stinging vibration up his arm. The other half of his ruined weapon, he swung against the steel tip she battered toward his head, and he held it with a grunt of effort. She was strong.

Renco slid the broken haft down the wood of the war staff and skinned Nihm's knuckles. With a yelp, she leapt backwards, only to trip as Renco hooked her leg with his own sending her tumbling to the ground.

Unsighted, Nihm rolled onto her back, raising her staff to block the expected follow-up only for Renco to fall on top of her. The impact crushed the wind from her lungs. She gasped as he wrestled for the staff, writhing beneath him, struggling to throw him off. But Renco held the upper hand, his knees pressing tight against her hips and his weight bearing down, levering the staff they grappled closer to her chest and throat. As strong as she was, so was he. Her eyes flared.

Years of training with Master Hiro had refined Renco's awareness and his finely honed reflexes sent him rolling off Nihm as a snarling, flash of fur and teeth leapt for his throat.

The wolfdog struck a glancing blow, its teeth snapping inches from Renco's face. Tumbling out of reach and onto his feet, Renco sucked a deep breath in through his nose.

His shoulder gave a flare of pain and the treacle touch of blood slithered down his back from a wound he could not recall receiving.

The staff had been won in his tussle with Nihm and Renco swung it defensively towards the dirt-white wolf. Snow growled, baring her fangs at him, amber eyes pinning him in place.

"Beware," Hiro cried in warning.

Snow was a diversion, a distraction.

Renco ducked to the side, a mass of black passing above him as Ash pounced from behind. Rolling to his feet, Renco brought the staff to the ready, placing Nihm between him and the furious wolfdogs.

"STOP." Hiro stepped in front of Renco, holding his own staff in the horizontal.

"Ash, Snow, down. NOW," Nihm commanded, swiftly rising. She glared at the wolfdogs until they whined, sinking to their bellies in the trodden snow.

Nesta glided from his log seat to the middle of the makeshift arena and cocked his head to one side at the animals.

"You should not chastise them," Nesta admonished, "You call them wolfdogs because you think them tame but the wild spirit of their kin flows in their blood. They do not understand the games you play but they know a blood fight when they see one. If there is any blame here it is yours, Nihmrodel Castell. Your *tame* wolves were simply doing what they must to protect the pack."

The man-ilf knelt before Ash and Snow as he spoke and stared at them with such intensity it was as if he could perceive their minds. When his speech was over, Nesta reached a hand out to each wolf and allowed them to take his scent before they lowered their heads and he scratched them between their ears. Nesta stood and without any further words walked out of the clearing, the silent crowd parting before him.

A growing murmur of conversation rose once Nesta had gone as if the ilf had broken some spell that held them enthralled.

"Go about your business. This sport is done," Master Hiro growled, silencing the crowd once more, stern eyes glaring until the Wylders, reluctant at first, started to wander back to camp. He waited until they were gone from sight then turned back with a glower.

"What part of defensive stance only did you not understand," he berated Renco.

"I am sorry, Master." Renco signed and then bowed his head. The quickening had faded from his blood and its aftermath left the stinging aftertaste of bile in the back of his throat.

"It was my fault. I took things too far," Nihm interjected. "I could have killed him."

"Your lack of control was obvious and disappointing," Hiro stated, turning on Nihm. "Your attack had intent, as it should, but you hesitated. Hesitation is what kills. You are a child still."

"But you," Hiro refixed Renco with cold eyes and shook his head, stroking his hand over a whiskered chin. "A few weeks apart yet your discipline failed you completely. Even the simplest of instructions, neh!"

Hiro sniffed loudly, then, reaching inside his cloak he brought out a wooden cup the size of his fist. He held it out and Renco took it.

"Fill it with water."

Renco nodded acceptance and turned towards camp.

Hiro tsked loudly, bringing Renco to a stop.

"Did I ask you for Wylder water?" Hiro raised his arm into the tar of night. The stars were not out but Renco knew his Master pointed to the east. "The water I want is from the Emerald Lake."

Nodding his understanding, Renco reached for his discarded clothing, tucked beneath his cloak and hung over a bush.

Hiro tsked loudly a second time and gave a thin shake of his head.

Renco swept a hand through sweat-brown hair, dislodging the snow that had collected in it. It was bitter-cold and a long slog through snow ladened fields to the lake. Resigned, he bowed to Master Hiro then turned and set off.

"You crazy old man? He'll freeze out there," Lett said grasping out to stop Renco, only for him to shake free. Renco cupped a hand to her cheek then was gone in the night.

Lett turned with a look of fury on her face. Her blue eyes flashed in temper.

Hiro regarded her solemnly, unfazed by her anger. "The last time you interfered between me and my student you got your father killed, neh. He was a good man, though a touch pretentious if I may say."

In the stunned silence that followed, Hiro moved to one of the torches stuck upright in the ground. Waggling it free he lifted it high and wandered off towards camp calling a final instruction over his shoulder.

"Do not tarry overlong. As Miss Letizia has already pointed out. It is very cold."

Morten waited till the old man was out of sight, grateful now that Hiro had turned him down back in the caverns. "He's a hard bastard," he muttered. "What are you doing?"

Nihm had shrugged into her outer jacket and fastened her cloak and stepped out into the night.

"I'm going after Renco."

"That's crazy. It's pitch black. You'll freeze," Morten argued.

But Nihm didn't answer. Already she could sense Renco growing distant. She would have to move fast to catch up. She disappeared into the inky blackness, Snow and Ash looping behind.

"You'll get lost," Morten called hands wringing in concern.

"I thought it was just men who were fools," Lett said. "But I swear I don't know which is the bigger, her or him." She bent and picked up the remaining torch.

"My feet are frozen. I'm heading back and so are you unless you're a fool as well." Lett tramped off, following the crushed path back towards camp, a disgruntled scowl marring her features.

A crunch of snow sounded as Morten followed.

Chapter 30: Redwood Sunset

Skaag Lak, Norderland

The village of Telvenn stood eerily silent.

Like shells scattered upon a white sand beach, the long, wood-beam and stone dwellings stretched from the midnight blue waters of Skaag Lak to the rising ground just to the west.

A frost-coated jetty extended into the lake but there were no boats moored to it and none pulled high upon the pebbled beach.

No one walked the streets and no beast foraged upon the sloping meadows. There were no dogs, no smoke and no noise but for the gusting of the wind and the quiet, rhythmic grinding of shingle as the Skaag's waters washed against the shore.

Two riders appeared from the direction of the Skárpe Steppes to the southeast. One sat upon a hardy, shag furred steppe pony, the other on a tall ranger dressed in a grey quilt to protect it from the elements. The riders had watched the village for an hour before moving down from the bush-lined crag of their observation post.

They walked empty streets, adding the crunch of snow and hoof to the sound of wind and the grate of pebble until they reached the longhouse at the centre of the village. It was three times the size of any other building and was the hub from which everything else radiated.

Leaving their mounts tied to a hitching rail, they approached the tall, weathered beams of the longhouse and found its doors cracked and broken, scarred by axe blows.

The pony rider, tallest of the two men, leant his weight against one of the doors and pushed it wide with a reluctant scrape of wood, allowing daylight to pierce the gloomy interior. The shaft of light though did not extend far before it was picked apart and swallowed by the dank penumbra inside.

His companion stepped through the entrance and pulled the mittens from his hands before taking a torch from a wall bracket. Holding a hand to it, he muttered a word of power and watched the torch flare into life.

"Didnae know ya had the talent, Katal." The first man spoke with the brusque accent of the Nordáa and as he lowered his cowl it revealed a blonde-haired man in his middle years with a braided beard and weather-beaten face. He turned his pale-blue eyes away from the flare of brightness and squinted into the room.

"Some, Orik of Lonn. Some." Katal Zakpikt, Grey Knight of the Order, pulled his own hood down and dragged the white woollen scarf that covered his mouth and nose, low around his neck. Moving into the longhouse he held the flambeau aloft.

A hardwood pillar loomed and Katal lit the sconce that angled away from the beam with his torch, adding its spluttering light to his own and revealing more of the room.

Wooden benches and tables emerged in the inky darkness, arranged around a large firepit that occupied the centre. Any fire it had held though had long since burnt out, its coals lying grey and dormant.

Kneeling on the stone hearth bordering the pit, Katal held his arm out to it. His brow wrinkled and he touched a hand to the charred and ashen embers before sinking his fingers deeper into the ash.

"There is some residual warmth, though barely. I would say a day at least since this fire was fed."

Orik of Lonn heard but gave no reply. He had lit a second torch and moved deeper into the longhouse. The earth-beaten floor was dark in patches and a strong odour of rust pervaded. It mixed with that of ash and smoke and another, more malodourous undertone. Most of the benches and tables, Orik found, were out of place and showed signs of damage; chipped boards and splintered edges and their tops stained a rich umber as if wine had been spilt and left to seep into the wood. It was not wine though.

"The people of Telvenn died here. If any survive they are long gone," Orik said. He turned to Katal. "We should go. Tis clear ta me, urak have reached Skaag Lak and the Helg."

The grey knight shrugged in response. "I would know more before we leave." He rose from the firepit and advanced into the longhouse. He too could smell blood and worse. He clapped the tall Nordáa on the shoulder as he passed him.

Orik puffed his cheeks out, unhappy at the prospect of staying longer. A death shroud covered Telvenn, it was in the air and he could taste it on his tongue. "I'll fetch our mounts inside. Nae use leavin' the beasties on show," he grumbled and moved back towards the entrance.

Katal grunted, his torch flickered and spat as he held it to another sconce. The light deepened, chasing fingers of black down the walls and revealing in the semi-darkness the outline of a raised wooden platform upon which were two solid-carved chairs. Something sat upon each, an object. He moved closer, the arc of light dispelling the deeper shade encasing the thrones.

Two frozen heads sat, bloodless and morbidly white, the skin jagged and loose where their necks should be. One was a man, the other a woman and both leered in death, starring with blank, glassy eyes at their lost domain.

Passing the gruesome spectacle, the Order man moved to a darkened doorway at the back of the platform, his boots clomping softly against the wooden boards. A leather curtain lay crumpled on the floor where it had been torn down. Stepping over it he crossed the threshold into the room beyond.

Katal heard the Nordáa, leading his pony inside but his mind was already fixated on the room. It was spacious and sectioned off with more hide curtains. He was in a living area with a low table surrounded by rugs and flat cushions. There were several braziers but each was as lifeless as the firepit. Katal shivered, a deep-seated chill filled the air which was still but for his breathing.

Nestled within the brittle coldness was the taint from the central hall, only stronger.

Katal inhaled a slow breath through his nostrils, like he might when taking the scent from a glass of Tankrit red. His face creased, he did not much care for this bouquet, it was cadaverine and laced with decay. Moving about the room, the odour grew stronger until he stood in front of a curtain. Steeling himself, Katal swished it back.

Nothing.

Not nothing, there was a wooden trap in the floor leading to a cellar. Kneeling, Katal grasped the rope handle and pulled it abruptly upwards.

A waft of soiled death struck his face. It set him gagging and Katal clasped a hand over mouth and nose before reeling back from the hole. He spat to clear the cloying taste from his throat then coughed again for good measure.

"By 't gods! That stinks worsen 'en Mirna's cooking." gasped Orik from behind.

"Remind me never to eat at your place," Katal muttered, the humour though was thin and stale and neither man laughed. Pulling at his scarf, Katal dragged it over his mouth and nose. It made little difference to the stench but he felt better for it as he advanced once more on the hole.

Crouching, Katal extended the torch over the trap and lower, into the maw. His eyes flared wide and his stomach roiled. He forced himself to look, levering his shoulders into the hole and studying what the light revealed.

He lurched upright and turned to Orik of Lonn.

"I've found the villagers."

Orik looked at the trapdoor to the cellar and edged over to it. He waved his torch low enough to see the marble eyed reflection of the dead, their grey-white flesh riddled with veins of blue, their carved faces bland, inhuman.

"I dinna understand." Orik levered the trap up with his foot until it reached the tipping point and crashed closed with a dull boom. He'd seen enough. "Why?"

Katal grimaced. "It's a cold space, and this a long winter to come. The urak will be back I think." He said no more. No more was needed.

The two men left. Katal's thoroughbred, a dark bay and Orik's piebald steppe pony were both impatient to be gone, neither liking the stink of the longhouse.

Katal rubbed a hand over his mare's nose. "I don't like it much either, Blue." He pulled his mittens on before leading her back outside.

"We shad burn it," Orik of Lonn called out. "It's the least we can do for 'em."

The Order man glanced at the sky. It was clear blue above but clouds gathered around the Torns, obscuring the jagged teeth of the mountain range. There would be no new snow to cover their trail this day. "They are dead, Orik. All it will do is give us away."

Lonn argued. "It's our way. You Order folk burn ya dead as well, so ya do."

Katal sighed. "I'm not your Barle, Orik. Do what you will. But we were tasked to scout and report. Your cousin will not thank us if we trail a horde of urak after us."

"Bad ká not ta. Frode would do the same," Orik stated.

Lifting his foot into a stirrup, Katal clasped the saddle horn and pulled himself up. Blue stamped her feet as his weight settled. He glanced back.

"Do what you must, Orik, but my horse is weary and not up for a long chase through snow. I will await you at the crag. If you're followed, I'll ride for Skaag and your cousin. I mean no slight but one of us must get back."

Lonn nodded. "Ai, brother. I understand right enough, so I do." Walking over, he held his sword arm out.

The grey knight leaned over and the two men grasped forearms in a warriors grip.

"Don't stay to see it burn, Orik of Lonn. It'd be a shame if they find you and realise you're all they've got left ta eat."

"Yar a cheery bastard, soya are," Orik laughed, he slapped Katal's mare on her rump to send her on her way.

"If they do," The Nordáa called after. "I'll be sure ta make 'em choke on me."

* * *

By the time Katal reached the craggy spire of their lookout, a liquorice pillar of smoke cut the air above Telvenn, slanting away in the breeze until it tattered and broke apart.

Watching from his hidden vantage, the grey knight thumped his mittens together to get the blood flowing to his fingers then rubbed at his face, which was numb despite his scarf. *Fuck, but I hate this cold.* He longed for the warmth he'd known as a child, of Morna, in the Sunset Isles where he was raised. *I'm about as far away from there as a man can get.* He shook his head, clearing his mind of such thoughts and gazed back towards Telvenn. He spied the speckled dot of Orik of Lonn and his pony.

It had been a mistake, he knew, letting Orik burn the Longhouse but Norders were known for their stubbornness and pride. Once Orik raised the matter it was done and nothing short of an order from his Barle would have stopped him. Foolish, but gods he loved them for it; for their simple honour and uncomplicated way of looking at the world. When a Norder said a thing it was meant, even if, half the time it was unreasoned.

Squinting against the glare of the lowering sun, Katal scanned the foothills to the west. They'd be hard-pressed to see any pursuit with the sun at their backs and the translucent mist that clung to the hilltops shrouded what lay beneath. But it cut both ways, the mist on the hills might hide the smoke some, he reasoned, and beyond that, the smudged outline that was the Forest of Helg should shield the dark plume from casual observation. Unless any urak were close they should be in the clear.

He looked once again to Telvenn. But for the finger of smoke that billowed and the memory of what he had seen, the village would have looked peaceful, nestled against the shores of Skaag Lak.

Turning away, Katal removed his mittens and made the short climb down the rocky, ice-encrusted outcrop before retracing the path crumpled in the snow from earlier. It led downhill to a bush lined clearing. Blue snorted and shook her head at him, her brown eyes admonishing.

"Yeah, I know girl. I know," He crooned, rubbing her nose then patting her neck with one hand whilst reaching his other into a belt pouch for the biscuits she was so fond of. As bland and tasteless as they were, Blue's nostrils flared as they caught the scent and she nuzzled his hand greedily when he held the treat out.

Taking her reins, Katal led his horse out of the glade and followed the trail they had laid to Telvenn. A barking cough carried on the wind, followed by a low, hollow grunt. He sniffed, the faintest of musks touched the air. A herd of elk was nearby.

Orik joined him a short while later and Katal made to lead them north, towards the lake and the elk.

"If they chase eastwards their tracks will cover our own," Katal said.

"Wishful thinking my black friend," Orik scoffed. "But elk'll lead us a merry dance if ya plan ta follo 'um and it won't be ta Skaag."

"Maybe. But they'll stay close to the water I think. The bushes are thick by the lake and there is plenty to forage. If not, we follow the lakeside round to Skaag." Katal indicated the clear sky above and the mauve disk that hung above the horizon. "The moons of Ankor and Kildare will be out tonight, enough to see by. Ride hard till sunset, rest the horses a few hours, then ride through the night and we should see Skaag by day end tomorrow. If the elk go our way, so much the better."

Orik gave a shake of his head. "This is my country, outlander. That bush ya speakin' of ain't no fun dragging a horse through, not with me on its back, moons or no. Nah, we'll cut across ta the Skárpe, might be longer but it'll be quicker, trust me."

The Nordáa turned his pony east and Katal had no choice but to follow. They travelled through tall shrubs and bushes which grew sparser the further east they went until fading altogether, the land transforming into a stretch of heathland. Orik's hardy steppe pony had a knack for finding the best path. It seemed to know where the snow was thinnest and was content enough to barrel a path for her taller sister.

They reached a shallow stream slippery with ice and followed it for a league until they reached a grove of redwoods. The towering sentinels were indifferent to the wintery conditions and their trunks stretched imperiously high, their coats of coarse, feather-like leaves unruffled by the snow covering them. From high up in the branches, birds chattered, hidden in the shadows, band-tails and jays and some Katal did not recognise.

Just inside the treeline they rested and fed the horses. Both men cast shaded eyes back the way they had come, looking for signs of pursuit but they saw nothing.

"T'is god's own country, so it is," muttered Orik. A corona of golds and reds captured the sky, the setting sun spreading its plumage like a peacock, vibrant and vivid, as it was slowly consumed by the purpled peaks of the Torn Spurs.

Katal couldn't deny him. It was breathtakingly beautiful. Enough, almost, to make him believe in the One. It was utterly still. The birds had fallen silent and even the breeze seemed to hold its breath in wonder. Only the nearby stream was impervious it seemed, bubbling its merry way.

Blue snorted and stomped a hoof behind him. It broke the moment and Katal tore his gaze from the majesty and walked to his horse.

"Always so impatient, girl, eh." He took her reins and held a treat out for her to nibble but she knocked it from his hand in a temper and whinnied.

Katal bent to recover the tidbit from the snow. There was a snap of a twig and the arrow aimed at his body, narrowly passed where he had stood. The Order man felt the air shift and was startled by the crack of the arrowhead as it shattered against a boulder but it took a moment to register before he rolled to the side with a cry of warning.

A blurred, hint of motion, too fast to see properly or avoid. A sledgehammer struck Katal, mid-thigh and took his leg from under him sending him careening to the ground.

A numb intensity radiated from his groin up into his body that took his breath. Gasping for air, Katal rolled onto his back. A thick shaft protruded from his leg, though he couldn't feel it.

Brown, wild eyes stared down at him. His mare tossed her head in agitation and pawed the ground with an iron-shod hoof, nostrils flaring at the scent of blood.

"Fly, Blue," Katal grunted, gritting his teeth against the flaring pain. "Fly, damn you."

Orik's steppe pony bolted and with a final toss of her head, Blue followed.

Guttural cries rang out from deeper in the grove and more arrows flew, hissing like angry hornets as they fizzed overhead.

Tangled in his cloak, Katal unclasped it with a hand then sat and dragged himself on his arse to the wide bowl of a tree, growling at every jerk of movement. The trunk of the redwood was solid and rough against his back, immoveable and prestigious it towered above him.

Unsheathing his sword, Katal stuck its point into the frozen earth and then levered himself upright, using the giant's bulk for support. He cried out, the motion causing an explosion of pain through his leg. Whatever anaesthetic his body had employed was gone, used up.

Tearing the white scarf from his face, Katal gulped ragged breaths. His head pounded, temples throbbing. He felt over-hot and sweat beaded his brow as he tried frantically to clear his mind and take stock.

Reaching out with his shield hand, he gripped the finger-thick shaft in his leg thinking to snap it off but doubled up as the arrowhead sawed against his thigh bone. His world went white for a moment but he caught himself and leaned back into the tactile comfort of the redwood. If he'd fallen, Katal wasn't sure he'd get up again, his body was a riot of agonies and fatigue wearied every limb.

It felt as if an age had passed but it must only have been moments. The heavenly skies, now turning pink and purple, calmed his mind. He spied the still form of Orik of Lonn at the edge of the wood, two arrows speared his chest. Katal had not heard the arrows strike nor his companion fall.

Lifting his sword, Katal pushed away from the trunk and staggered two steps before a jarring agony threatened to send him to oblivion. *I will die on my feet with a sword in my hand.*

Stumbling about, he faced the deep wood and waited for death to come.

A shape moved in the depths, then several more. Hulking shadows that resolved into urakakule, a head taller and half again as broad as a man. They looked savage, heads smeared in red as if dipped in blood. They approached him.

The pounding in Katal's head faded, the pain receding to a dull nag as a calmness overcame him. In the back of his mind, in some nebulous recess, it pleased him. Always he had feared death. That when it came it would find him wanting, that it would unman him. But he was resolute. His blood would water the soil, his flesh and bone feed the earth. It was the way of all things.

He thought of Orik of Lonn lying dead behind him. *We shared a glorious sunset, brother.*

Katal raised his sword, looping it out of habit, into a longpoint guard, the blade extending straight out. He said no words, his mouth was too dry and what was there to be said.

The urak talked amongst each other, and as deep and inflected as their tone was, Katal understood each word. Once uttered though, they would not stick in his mind. A kaleidoscope of sound they were like shards from a shattered mirror.

Katal watched an urak hand his bow to another then reach back and draw a sword from over its shoulder. A slow hum was building in Katal's ears, enough to drown out their fractured language. The urak swung its sword and stepped out into the light of the fading sun.

Long braids hung past the urak's back, with large, bright eyes set too far apart below a heavy, ridged brow. Their blue colour was incongruous and dramatic against the red-painted skin.

He was a she. The revelation etched the barest hint of a smile on Katal's face and he would have laughed at the inanity of his prejudice had his mouth not felt like sand. He jerked his sword again to beckon her on.

The urak tossed her braids and flexed her shoulders. She circled to his left then back to his right eying him, gauging his motion and reaction.

She lunged, sweeping her wide blade towards his head. It was all Katal could do to raise his sword and block it with a loud clash of scraping metal. The blow staggered him and Katal stumbled on his one good leg. His sword was driven low and sent twisting out of his hands.

Grimacing, snarling at the pain, Katal could do nothing but wait for the return strike to end him, but it did not come. Instead, the urak stepped in and his head snapped back. Blackness exploded through his skull, bright spots sizzling in the deep like firebugs. And as they burned out so too did he.

* * *

"End him. We have no time for your foolishness, Por."

Porpor-pok stood over the human and glared back at the grumbling Mognatuk. She scoffed, "You bitch worse than a chala."

Crouching low over the prone body, Porpor-pok rubbed a finger across the man's forehead in fascination. She froze, head cocked to the side like a bird. Her shoulders shuddered and like ink dropped in water, her eyes clouded and filled until there was no more blue, only black.

She felt Mognatuk arrive by her left side and stare over her shoulder at the human. Porpor-pok murmured darkly as the other urakakule gathered around. "This is no white skin like the rest but it bleeds the same. A curiosity, don't you think?"

Mognatuk hissed his response, hating her all the more for her irreverent tone. She was favoured by Karth-Dur else he would have removed Por's head from her shoulders a long time past. The grizzled veteran indicated the setting sun.

"Karth-Dur ordered our return before Marq-suk renews. Gut it, harvest it if you must but be quick. We leave before Marq'suk fades."

Porpor-pok rose slowly. Movement caught her attention out past the stream. The two carvathe, the big and the small, had not run far and regarded them guardedly from a safe distance. As minor a thing as that was, it decided matters.

Stepping away from the human, Porpor-pok turned almost casually into Mognatuk. Her knife thrust was sudden and unseen. It parted leather, skin and flesh, its tip angled up beneath the sternum to pierce the heart. So sudden and so unexpected was her attack that the old warrior had no time to react. He slumped against her shoulder with a grunt and a look of utter disbelief as the strength in his limbs fled in an instant.

Mouth agape, Mognatuk's grunt changed to an agonised wheeze as if air escaped his punctured body. With a last great effort of will, the urak raised his head to gaze into the swirling maelstrom of Por's eyes.

Porpor-pok shoved roughly, sending Mognatuk sprawling onto the ground. He didn't move and she swivelled her head to the remaining two urak.

Startled, one dropped his bow and fumbled at his shoulder, reaching for his sword only to shudder and tremble as the other stepped behind him. A viscous glob of blood spewed over his lips and down his chin, a deeper, browner red than his warpaint. He slipped to his knees with a frothy gurgle then lurched to his side, gasping blood into the snow like a landed fish.

The two urak still standing did not acknowledge each other. There was no need. Porpor-pok returned to the black-skinned human and knelt by his side. Leaning in, she lowered her face over his and breathed new life into him.

Afterwards, Porpor-pok wrestled the arrow from the man's thigh. By chance, it had missed any major arteries but it still bled profusely as she pried and cut the arrowhead from his flesh. The man thrashed in delirium, dark eyes fluttering at the pain. Pain, she knew the Taker relished, pain that in return would sustain the man and make him strong.

She licked the blood and torn tissue from the arrowhead before inspecting it for damage. Satisfied, she slipped it back into her quiver. Next, she washed the wound clean with snow before stitching the ragged entry-point closed with a fishbone needle and garkgut from her pack. To finish, she washed the congealed blood away a final time before binding it with hemp cloth.

When she was done, Porpor-pok rose and the jet of her eyes cleared back to blue. Night had fallen and the blood moon, Naris-Krol was overhead with Jud'pur'tak above the eastern mountains.

"Come, Tihmon-chuk. We'd best not keep Karth-Dur waiting." Without giving the human a backward glance, Porpor-pok set off at a loping run, into the light cast by Jud'pur'tak.

Chapter 31: The Rider

Skaag, Norderland

Two thousand souls lived in Skaag and many more than that in the surrounding holdsteads and, like a kicked-in termite mound, the town bustled with activity. Forge fires burned hot and the pounding of metal rang loud, a heartbeat to the busy sounds of Skaag preparing for war. Brash, dark-furred warriors strutted the frost-hardened ground between longhouses. Loud and bellicose they were full of bravado.

We'll see how long that lasts, thought Tannon Crick from his vantage point atop the fortified stone of the carn. Built high upon a butte the carn overlooked both the township and the dark waters of Skaag Lak to the west, with the Skárpe Steppes to the south and the Forest of Helg stretching away north and west, backdropped by the Torn Mountains. It was as beautiful a sight as a man could wish for.

Crick tensed with a silent groan before crutching back to the room and tapping his way to the map table and the wooden cup that held his wine. He took a swig of the tart liquid despite the discontent glared his way by Marus Banff, or maybe it was because of it, for he was in an irascible mood.

His leg healed fast, Order Knights always did, but it had been a bad break and whilst Marus agreed his injury was much recovered his steward insisted he not put weight through it. Well, no argument there for it hurt like a bitch when he did but two days cooped up with Marus was beginning to rankle. Apart from stating the bloody obvious, his steward fussed and clucked as bad as his wives ever had. *Well, apart maybe from Mara,* Crick thought, a smile ghosted his lips, *she would have filled his cup and one for herself and ribbed him endlessly about his leg...* his thoughts trailed away. Gods but he missed her, missed them all. It had been forty years since Mara had died but he could recall her, all of them, so vividly still. It only added to his surly disposition.

Returning his steward's stare, Crick raised his cup in a mock toast. "Stop frowning, Marus. Pour yourself a cup and unwind that stiff neck of yours."

Marus narrowed his eyes and lowered his chin. "I think you consume enough for the both of us, Sir."

"I can drink as much as I like, it never impairs me. You know that." Crick took a swig as if to prove the matter.

"I do, sir. That is hardly the point."

"The point? You mean there is one to all your mothering and glowering. I would like to hear it?" Crick stated.

Marus glanced at the two others that were in the room. Karl Hubert grinned at him as if to dare him to speak his mind whilst Merin Somar paid no heed at all, running a sharpening block over his sword edge and testing the cut with his thumb.

"Well, sir, your excessive drinking just for the sake of it is bad form. You do it because you are irritated by your injury, bored by your enforced recuperation and worried for Katal who is a day late. Also, I suspect, because it bothers me which gives you some perverse joy."

Tannon Crick thumped his wine down on the table. "Are you saying I'm vindictive, Marus?"

"You did ask, sir. I'm just saying there are better ways to occupy your time than drinking and looking at the same map all day long. The Barle of Skaag is preparing to face urak in battle and he could do with your advice."

"My advice to Magner is the same as before. To leave here and move his people to Lonn or better yet Helvenin," Crick replied, somewhat testily. "That grizzled fool is as stubborn as any Nordáa I ever met but I swear he's grown even more intractable with age. For two days I've tried and it's like talking to a stone wall. No, Magner of Skaag will not listen to any wisdom but his own."

"I know the feeling well, Sir," Banff replied.

Crick shook his head at his steward but couldn't stop a grin tugging at the corners of his mouth.

"Guess I deserved that. Come then. Let's walk the streets, gauge the mood and see if I can't talk that old bastard round some. Hopefully, Kat will show."

"But your leg, sir. You really must rest it," Marus insisted.

Crick waved off the concern. "It's splinted is it not and I have my crutches. Besides," he gave a wolfish grin, "if I tire the three of you can always carry me back."

At Karl Hubert's scowling head shake and impending retort, Crick added. "Don't sass me on it, Karl, or I'll put my armour on before we go, then you'll be sorry."

They left the chambers, the guards outside the doors closing them behind with a bang, as Crick led them, clacking, down a wide corridor. Various tapestries, faded and dull, covered the walls and they passed a goat of all things which was tied up outside a solid oaken door and bleating its unhappiness.

They descended a narrow stairwell to a central hall that was filled with long tables and benches most of which were occupied by warriors, eating and drinking their fill and talking overloud. Many of them called out to Tannon Crick but he waved their enquiry and goodwill away as he clomped around the outside of the hall towards its open end.

On the walls, pinned in brackets, they passed armaments of every description, from halberds and poleaxes to ancient claymores and warhammers. The four men neared an immense, thick-framed painting and as ever their eyes were drawn to it, for it depicted a tornbear fighting an equally ferocious-looking, hrultha. Every Barle of Skaag that had ever been, boasted that the painting was to scale, and Crick knew it for no idle brag for the pelts of both beasts lay in the Barle's chambers.

The artisan who had worked the oils had rendered something special. So life-like was it that Crick felt more an observer than an admirer. The black-furred tornbear towered over the bristling, thick shouldered mountain cat, which was itself the size of a steppe pony. It sat upon haunches ready to spring at the bear, its slightly longer, more heavily muscled front legs lifted with claws extending like giant thorns. Locked in a snarl, the hrultha bared faintly curved canines that were as long as a child's forearm and just as thick at the base.

Crick pushed himself past the imagery, grateful to leave it behind. Artfully made it might be, but there was something eternally sad about it. His attention twisted back to the hall, to the raucous noise and the familiar, redolent smells of sweat and leather-oil, cooked meat and wood smoke, the latter creeping from two open hearths which were set in opposite corners at the front of the hall and which radiated a salubrious warmth.

The four of them passed into a busy hallway that had two tall doors at its far end, leading to the outside, one of which was ajar allowing a waft of cool breeze into the carn. A pair of guards stood indolent, one on each side of the open entrance. At seeing the Order Knight approach, one eased his head past the door frame and called out something to the guards beyond and the trickle of people entering the carn stopped.

"Tis cold and slippy as an eel in butter, Ser Tannon. If'n ya want, I can get a cart brought round fer ya ta ride." The guard's voice trailed away as Crick barged past. Marus Banff gave an apologetic lift of his shoulders and followed his Lord outside.

It had been three days of blue skies with no new snow and what lay upon the ground had been trudged into a hardpack of mud, ice and straw, the straw having been laid down to provide some traction. Even so, it was a precarious journey down the hill for a man on crutches and after crossing beneath the gatehouse in the curtain wall, Tannon Crick struggled doggedly not to lose his balance or his pride.

Eventually, after reaching more even ground, they turned south and followed the lake edge, walking the thoroughfares between longhouses and past stalls, the barrel-chested Karl Hubert clearing a path through the mill of people. Children followed them, pointing and calling out, drawn like bear cubs to a honey pot, for outlanders were rare in these parts and they were an oddity, particularly Merin Somar, whose olive-skinned complexion and neatly trimmed and oiled beard marked him as different again.

They passed into what was, in normal times, a market square. But the market stalls and traders were gone. In their place, at its centre, stood a timber frame. From it, dangling like meat on display hung three urakakule, limp and bloodless, their skin the colour of granite. Nordáas, Skaagens, stacked four and five deep around the urak, prodding and poking them so that each swayed, creaking the wood beams as they spun.

A lecturing voice rose over the gathering, and a rank smell wafted to the order men on a gust of breeze.

"…is bigger 'en stronger 'en any warrior. But they bleed like us and die like us just the same." There was barely a pause for breath as the man continued, "They'n blood is blacker 'en ours as ya can see and look 'ere."

A murmur rippled the crowd. "They'n guts and insides are the same, more or less, only they'n hearts is bigger 'un ours and lies mid-chest, guarded by this 'ere thick bone. Hard ta penetrate, ya need ta angle ya blade up, under the rib cage ta reach it. En' see 'ere. They'n got two lungs like a man but they's split, one each side of the heart like angel wings. Now, the best killin' points…"

Crick led them past the demonstration, Karl Hubert turning to look back as they edged around the end to glimpse the bloody remains of a carcass lying on a butcher's block. His eyes touched briefly on the watchers and whilst all were dressed and armed for battle, it was clear to Karl that not many were warriors.

They left the square behind and soon a large earthen embankment appeared. It extended eastward from the lakeshore and curved around towards Carnhill and the distant forest. It marked where early Skaag's palisade had once stood. But Skaag had outgrown that boundary and once the carn had been constructed there was no further need for the wooden walls and they had long since disappeared.

Now though, the earthwork was the focus of defensive efforts once again. Heavy wood beams and stone had been hauled up with block and pulley by teams of mules and steppe ponies and an army of Skaagens. There, with the ground too frozen to dig out, they were laid flat along the top of the mound, as a makeshift barrier. It would provide a semblance of cover for any defender but it would not stand much. Crick frowned; thick poles protruded horizontally from the new defences, pointing like lowering spears not out, but back towards town and he wondered as to their purpose.

He spied Magner, Barle of Skaag, standing at a break in the earth wall near a barricade of stone and timber. With a listless sigh, Crick crutched inelegantly towards him.

Frode of Lonn was with the Barle. The two were deep in discussion with a black-robed man who stood a head taller than both. Despite his attire, it was clear that he too was a Nordáa, with long yellow hair riddled with white and which fell down his back in an elaborate plait and bound with black ties.

The tall man spotted Crick's approach and broke off the conversation, leaning on a white merl staff to wait. Crick could sense the power the staff held like static from a thundercloud. If he didn't know it already, it would have told him that its owner, Jonah Terik, was a mage.

The magus glowered. He possessed a wizarding orb, one of the few in the north, and news of the High King's death had reached Skaag well before Tannon Crick's arrival. That Crick also brought word of High Barle, Justin Janis' murder and its circumstance caused a huge furore.

Jonah Terik had demanded his incarceration. An Order Knight stood accused of killing the High King and for another to be present at Janis' demise could be no coincidence, he argued. If not for Frode of Lonn's testimony, and no doubt the five hundred warriors at his back, things could have turned ugly for him.

It was Magner of Skaag who had had the final word though. He and Janis were distant kin and Crick was a well-known and trusted advisor and friend to the now-dead High Barle. As well, Magner's father, Morgrar and his grandfather before, Mordant, always held the Order man in high esteem and that was something no Skaagen gave lightly, especially to an outlander. So the Barle had overruled his mage. "Urak are on ma step, seeking the blood of ma people. Whether this dark Lord, this Morhudrim, this taker of souls is returned makes nae difference ta me. I'll fight an' take every bit a help I can, Jonah."

What Magner had really meant, Crick thought, as the Barle's bearish gaze settled upon him, *was I'll take those hundred hands you bring to defend my walls.*

"Didnae 'spect ta see ya out here on that leg a y'orn." Frode of Lonn beamed. "How is it?"

Crick returned the Nordáa's cheer with a billow of expelled air. "Healing," he replied somewhat acerbically. The Lonn man had taken no convincing to stay and fight. The damn idiot was eager for it.

"Go back, Ser Tannon." Magner was darker-haired than most Nordáas and it showed streaks of grey as he shook his head at Crick. "Yar no use ta me on crutches and I'll nae hear more on running ta Lonn or that cock-fingered, Runé of Helvenin."

Karl Hubert gave a snort. Crick ignored him. "I've wasted enough breath on that, I'll not waste more. Though it's a mistake not to move the less able east, to safety. The mothers and the children. The old, the infirm. They will only be in the way."

The Barle laughed. "Tis irony. Ya've bin in our land longer 'en any Nordáa livin' but still, nae understand us. They'n what makes us strong, Ser Tannon. They'n puts the iron in our spine and death in our arms. A warrior fights all the harder knowing what's ta lose is more'n just they'n lives."

Crick's cloak snapped in the breeze and he shifted on his crutch, "I know it, but this is no skirmish between clans, of Skaag butting heads with Helvenin. This is whether there will be any Skaagens left at the end of it all and if you… bah," the Order Knight huffed in exasperation. "You've made a liar of me already. Tell me, what can I do? What do you need from me?"

"Nae 'athing," Magner leered, grey eyes like granite. "Ya told what ya can of what we face. Think ya should heed ya own words and leave while ya can. If ya canna fight with that leg of y'on then ya nae use ta me."

Crick nodded. The Barle spoke a harsh truth, but his words were fair. If not for Katal he would have left first thing that morning. Should still have left only the bond between an Order Knight and their Hand went both ways. *Tomorrow. I will leave tomorrow come what may.*

"Rider!" The cry came from the embankment.

It sent an anxious Frode of Lonn scrambling up the side to see for himself. He squinted his eyes to the south. "It's your man I think," he called to Tannon Crick, before stumbling and sliding back down. Grim-faced, Frode didn't wait to explain further but instead ran to a gap left in the barricade.

They followed, Magner bellowing to his warriors who had already stopped work. Hefting weapons, a dozen of them jogged after their Barle.

The space beyond the barricade was a jumbled mess of snow and rubble. The longhouses had been torn down, their beams and stone, taken for the makeshift defences and their thatch used to feed the fires.

Crick surveyed the ruin, *Skaag already bears the blight of war before ever an urak has been sighted,* the thought was fleeting though as he craned his neck looking for the rider.

The Skaagen warriors spread out to the sides, twisting axes and longswords in their hands to keep them warm and the blood flowing to their fingers. No sooner had they settled when a rider came into view and the blunted clop of hooves reached out against the wind.

There were two mounts but only one man who sat, listless, as if about to topple and roll from his saddle. The horse he was on was a tall ranger, a dark bay thoroughbred that walked with lowered head and weary steps. Behind trotted a pony, a shag-furred piebald steppe with a body slumped like a roll of sackcloth over its fur-lined saddle.

With a wailing bellow, Frode of Lonn started running.

A nod from Tannon Crick sent Merin Somar and Karl Hubert pounding after, the horse was as familiar to them as the man who rode upon its back.

Katal Zakpikt slumped over Blue's neck and the horse lifted her feet and pranced to the side trying to keep her rider's boneless weight centred.

Merin caught Katal as he fell and lowered his friend to the ground. The fool wore no cloak, and his dark skin was waxen and cold to the touch. Blood saturated his left leg and a crusted binding, dark with old blood showed beneath. Katal gave no response when Merin called to him or when his eyelids were pried open and peered into. Only the white mist of his breath gave any sign he still lived.

"He's like ice. We need to get him inside and quick," Merin shouted. Unclasping his cloak, he swished it over Katal's inert body.

Karl panted, catching his breath. "Let's lift him onto Blue. She's carried him this far she'll carry him the rest of the way."

As the two men bent to the task, Magner bellowed out orders calling for a wagon whilst a sombre-faced Frode of Lonn walked by leading the steppe pony with his cousin's lifeless body still draped over the saddle.

Frode's face was fierce and the warriors parted to let him through, none speaking, respecting the Jarl's loss and his silence. It was the first death but each of them knew it would not be the last.

* * *

Marus Banff took control of matters once Katal was safely ensconced back at the Carn. The injured man stirred into wakefulness long enough to give a wan smile from his bed before Banff began ushering everyone from the room. The steward was well versed in many things and war wounds were no exception, but he was no physiker. He was unable to pry into the substance of a man and coerce sickness from their essence and expel disease from their flesh.

"I'll dress Kat's wound and bathe him but not with you lot gawping and asking a hundred questions. You can wait till I'm done. Oh, and send for a physiker," he commanded, before slamming the door in their faces.

The physiker arrived a short while later but had only been in the room moments when he came huffing back out tugging on his beard and muttering about god-cursed outlanders wasting his time.

When Banff finally appeared an hour had passed and Tannon Crick raised a quizzical eyebrow at him. "I take it from the medico's grumbling retreat that Kat is fine and well?"

Karl and Merin gathered around Banff who sighed. "For someone who was frozen to the bone like he was and with a hole in their thigh as thick as my finger I would say remarkably so."

"So what's eating you?" Crick asked, knowing Marus well enough that something bothered him. His steward glanced sharply at him and then gave a shake of his head.

"Agh, it's probably nothing. He's been through a lot. In truth, I don't know how he made it."

Karl Hubert grinned. "Tough as ten-year boot leather. That's how."

Tannon Crick held a hand up to silence Hubert and waited for Banff to continue.

"Kat's a good man, we all know it, but he grabbed that physiker by the beard when he got too close. Thought he was gonna chew the man's face off. That ain't like Kat, pain or no. I had to pry him off. He was feral." Banff glanced with unease at each man in turn.

"There's more?" Crick asked.

"The wound. It's neatly sutured. Almost as good as I could do myself." Banff shrugged. "I don't know, maybe it's nothing but I don't see a man stitching his own leg that well and using some kind of gutstring. If I had to guess, I'd say it's from an urak bow given its thickness. Don't know, just, something doesn't sit right."

Crick clapped a hand on Banff's shoulder. "You asked him about any of it?"

"Nah, he ain't said much of anything. Asked about Orik and that damn horse of his but nothing much else. I got some hot broth in him and the man should be sleeping, he's exhausted, but he's not. Eyes are dilated like he's on something. I know you need to talk to him, just…." Banff didn't finish but turned back to the door and pulled it wide. The three men filed past him into the chamber beyond.

Katal Zakpikt lay on the bed where they had dumped him barely an hour past, only now he looked a whole lot better. Washed and wearing clean clothes, he sat propped up with his wounded leg outside of the covers. A fresh binding strapped his upper thigh which was clean but for a target splotch of red wine in the middle. Katal did not call out in greeting, nor smile at them, instead, he regarded each man with haunted eyes as they arranged themselves around the bed.

"You're looking better." Karl Hubert placed a hand of comfort on his friend's shoulder and smiled broadly. "Fer a black man, I ain't never seen ya so white. Ya gave us a scare so ya did."

Katal glanced at the hand, eyes following the arm and travelling to Hubert's face. He didn't say anything, his expression flat.

Karl pulled his hand back. "Ya can speak can't ya? Be a cryin' shame if some urak got your tongue." His cracked smile though robbed the banter from his words.

"Need to ask what happened, Kat," Tannon Crick said. "I need your report. Preferably before Frode of Lonn comes barging in asking the same questions. You brought his cousin back dead and he'll want answers."

Katal's head swivelled slowly from Hubert to Crick. A sudden spark kindled behind his eyes and like a drowning man coming up for air, he gasped a sudden and deep breath.

"What's wrong with him?" Karl asked making way for Marus Banff who held a hand to Katal's forehead which was clammy with sweat.

"Get off. Stop fussing damn you," Kat growled. "I just… where's my damn horse."

"I told you before, don't you remember?" Banff spoke softly. "Blue is stabled and is being looked after."

Kat pressed his head back against the pillows and seemed to deflate in on himself. "Agh, fuck. Orik."

The grey knight rarely swore and the expletive sounded alien coming from his mouth.

"Fuck indeed. Can you tell us what happened?" Crick asked.

Closing his eyes, Katal took several breaths before opening them again and beginning.

"We reached Telvenn and found it empty, the people gone, or so we thought." He paused, taking a sip of water from a cup Banff offered him.

"The moot hall showed signs of violence. We searched it and there we found them. Dead. Stored in the cellar, food for the winter." Katal rubbed a calloused hand across his face.

"Not all," Tannon Crick said in consolation. "Boats from Telvenn turned up the day we arrived, carrying some. Not many."

Katal blinked but it was as if he didn't hear. "I left but Orik stayed. He burnt the hall down, a pyre to commend their bodies to Kildare and release their heart-souls to Ankor for judgement. You know how they are."

"I watched from afar, he wasn't followed so we met and travelled east heading for the steppes. I don't recall much after that, it's all a bit vague. I remember a sunset and a grove of redwoods. A hammer blow of agony. The rest is a fog in my mind, one I can't seem to penetrate." Katal took another sip of water and composed himself.

"When I awoke it was with a bloodied blade, two dead urak and my leg bound and feeling twice the size it should. I have no recollection of how I killed them or if I did. Certainly, I have no memory of stitching and binding my leg wound. It hurt real bad to move but the cold took the edge off some and the pain probably kept me alive. Otherwise, I think I would have just lain down and let winter take me."

Tannon Crick nodded. "You did well, Kat. As well as a man might in that circumstance. And Orik?"

"Dead. Probably before he knew it. Found him by the stream, stiff as a plank. Took two arrows in the chest. Blue came back and that little steppe pony of his, else I'd be laid out there with him I guess."

Marus Banff stepped in. "That'll do for now. Kat needs rest. You can talk again in the morning."

They left, Merin, giving a curt nod as he did and Crick clasping Katal's hand briefly in farewell.

"I'll slip ya some whiskey if I can find some," Karl Hubert promised, slapping his fellow grey knight on the shoulder.

"You'll do no such thing," Banff admonished, shooing him away like a disgruntled parent.

Outside the room, once the door had closed again, Crick turned to Merin Somar and lifted an eyebrow in question. Somar gave a noncommital shrug in response. Disquieted, the Order Knight addressed Marus. "We move out in the morning."

"If that leg takes infection with no physiker on hand, he could lose it," Banff warned.

"It'll be four days maybe five till we reach Lonn. Gather what you need but say nothing to Kat for now. In the meantime, I'll talk to Frode, explain what I can and see if I can't get him to change his mind about staying. Karl you're with me," Crick called.

The crutches tapped a tattoo against the stone as Tannon Crick made his way out, Hubert at his back.

Chapter 32: A Thousand Barbed Thorns

The Road to Ramelo, The Holme

From the blackness of no thought, Merca Landré lurched upright, gasped a breath then promptly heaved, retching and snorting over the side of the wagon.

She panted, sweat beading her forehead before a groan rumbled up her throat followed by another explosion of stomach bile, the acid scouring the soft tissues of her gullet and nostrils on its way out.

After a moment her nausea subsided, lodging in vague threat at the bottom of her gut. Clutching at the wagon's sideboard, Merca released a hand to wipe her chin clean then hacked and spat to clear the debris from her mouth and nose. Then again. In riposte, Merca's head gave a pang that blossomed with brutal immediacy into a raging headache that forced a pained cry from her lips.

"Fuucccckk."

The expletive hissed out, long and slow, and with it, Merca flopped, exhausted to the wagon bed.

Normally, in her experience, immobility was best when confronted with such a bad head and laying flat took no effort and no energy which suited her just fine for she had none. Unfortunately, the jostling of the wagon as it rumbled along negated, somewhat, the medicinal benefits of lying down and did nothing at all for the vinegar coating her mouth.

With a grimace, Merca pressed a palm to each temple as if her hands could contain and ease the strobing ache in her head, but an involuntary moan creaked out underlining the futility of that ambition.

Where am I? What happened? Her mind was woolly, a fugue of broken images that were slow to surface through the fog of her hangover.

"You're in a wagon," squeaked a voice. "You a… took a knock. To the head. It's good your awake. Grema wasn't sure you would or if you did that you'd be the same."

Who the fuck is Grema? Merca wondered. Too tired to articulate the thought she didn't say anything for a bit, trying instead to process what she'd heard and that voice. It was familiar, she knew it from somewhere. *Seven hells my head*, Merca sucked air through her teeth, tasting the sourness at the back of her throat, before wheezing a polluted breath out. She tried to open her eyes but her lids were heavy and refused to budge.

* * *

When next Merca was aware, she felt blessedly better which was not to say, well. Her head was tender and ached in the dull aftermath of whatever had ailed her, but it was no longer all-consuming. She could think, and Merca's first thought was that her illness wasn't from a drunken night out and a tumble with Rooq, that was for gods damned sure.

Her body was battered, something that was not helped by the hard board beneath which juddered and shook. Laying there, eyes closed, nostrils flaring at the sour stink of vomit, it became plain to Merca that she was in a wagon. The gritty crunch of metal on stone and the clop of hooves left no doubt. She had a strange sense that she'd been here before, her thoughts an imprint of an earlier memory. One that was hazy and slipped away when she tried to grasp it.

Her weapons were gone, Merca didn't need to reach for them to know that. Clothed she might be but the subtle pressure of straps and sheathing against her skin was missing. It left her feeling naked and on edge. Another ghost memory fluttered inside her skull.

Sunlit warmth caressed her face and a patina of light played across her eyelids. It told Merca it was day and that the sun was high. More accustomed to darkened alleyways and night shadows it was, nevertheless, a familiar sensation, a distant friend from another time. She basked in its rays, letting the heat chase through weary limbs.

Unfamiliar voices called out and the vibrating rattle of the wagon subsided. Cracking her eyelids, Merca peered through long lashes but could see nothing but the glare of the sun above. Not without moving her head.

"You're awake. What is your name?" The voice was gruff and a woman's but the accent was nondescript. Merca could not place it.

"I'm not here to play games, girl. I will not ask again." The tone was lower, more abrasive.

Threat and intimidation, Merca applied it in her every day, had experienced and performed it herself too, many times, and with a deep-rooted certainty, she knew the woman's words were absolute. The unanswered question was one of consequence should she not heed them.

Merca opened her eyes wide, deciding now was not the time to find out. She knew too little and in any case, she needed answers of her own. Still, Merca couldn't help herself.

"I'm no mainlander ta give my name so freely." She meant it to sound provocative, to gauge reaction but her voice cracked like an old woman's and ruined the effect. She sat up, muscles protesting, head fuzzing.

"Your name is known already. Just answer the question." The voice rasped.

Merca glanced at the woman. She was kneeling, yet despite this, Merca could tell she was tall, and a strange dichotomy of shape and size. Her arms were overlong, shoulders broad like a man's. Winter-grey eyes that were pretty but too small for her face. Hook-nosed, mouth soft and wide, skin pale as a morning mist with hair a scraggy tangle of black bangs.

Merca fidgeted, the woman's discontinuity of features was awkward to look upon and her returning evaluation was hard and unblinking until a noise drew both women to the wagon's backboard where a sandy mop of dishevelled hair appeared framing a pair of dark brown eyes.

"Oh good, you're awake," Tomas said. He gripped the backboard with one hand and slung a waterskin over the side with the other.

"I see you've met Grema," Tomas said cheerfully. "She was worried about you."

Merca cast a doubtful glance at the steel-eyed woman who looked anything but, then swung back to watch as the boy clambered gingerly up onto the wagon, his oversized brown tunic billowing as the breeze caught it. Something about him tugged at her mind and in a flash of cognizance fresh memories crashed to the fore like waves breaking against a cliff face. Her face contorted into a scowl.

"I got you out of Kingsholme, little Mouse, as agreed. Yet I see you're armed still with that pretty little prick sticker whilst I am disarmed. We had an agreement."

She wanted to say more, to demand her release, for, light as its touch might be, Merca could still feel the little asswipe's binding upon her. It wound through her psyche; a thin mesh yet one she could not break. Merca's eyes flashed dangerously when the Mouse had the gall to beam his response at her.

"It's not like we've had the chance for any of that. You…um attacked Kal and Grema and, well, you took a bad knock and here we are." Tomas shrugged, deciding it best not to mention that Tasso Marn wanted to slip a knife between Murder's ribs or that Kal Meyar and Grema Bergrun were happy to let her. Only his objection and oddly enough the intervention of Herald and Horyk had forestalled Marn.

Merca listened to the soft nicker of horses and the jocular banter of men. It filled the silence between the boy's words. Words that elicited more by what the Mouse didn't say as did. As well, the fact the boy thief walked free and armed meant he'd been found by the right people, not the wrong. *Order Knights then? Or agents of the Order,* thought Merca, no other scenario seemed to fit.

Merca gave a dissatisfied grunt both at his answer and to hide her alarm at how quickly things had turned to shit. She'd been on the cusp of freedom with Bortillo Targus, if she had delivered the prince. But that was all ashes in the wind now. She'd gambled on the boy only to rid herself of one master and tie herself to another. She'd badly underestimated 'Tomas the Mouse' as indeed had Bortillo. Merca tugged her lips into the semblance of a grin, she'd not make the same mistake again.

"And where is here exactly? I can hardly protect you if I don't know anything. A job made more difficult without my weapons I might add," Merca said, her tone reasonable and calm.

The woman, Grema, laughed; a strangely feminine, merry sound that to Merca, did not fit with the rest of her.

"You're a hired killer," Grema said. "An assassin. A murderer. I think I will keep your blades for now."

Merca flinched. She couldn't deny it of course but Grema's tone dripped with contempt and it irked somewhat.

"You're no better. You drugged me with summat then abducted me. Probably woulda slit my throat if you thought it suited. Peel it all away an' ya stink just the same as me," Merca hissed.

Annoyingly, Grema laughed, again.

"Your ailment is quickening sickness, I know the comedown well enough to know it even if your acrobatics back in the alley hadn't told me so. My guess is you quickened too long, too hard or too much. Three, maybe four times? There's no one to blame for that but yourself, girl. You should know, there is always a price to pay."

"What's… a quickening then?" Tomas asked, only for both women to ignore him.

"In answer to your other question," Grema continued. "We're on the road to Ramelo. We passed the Blackcoat cordon this morning and we're half a day north of Kingsholme. Now, I would ask some questions of my own, but you'll only lie. I don't know what you're running from, girl, but you will tell me when you're ready. For now, you're safe."

With beguiling fluidity, Grema rose and vaulted over the side of the wagon, her long legs striding with purpose towards a group of warriors dressed in brown livery and black cloaks.

"I ain't running from anything," Merca called after. "And stop calling me girl."

Abruptly, Grema turned and fixed granite-eyes upon Merca. "Until you say your name, I will call you nothing but." Like a flax unwinding, Grema twisted forward again and continued her journey.

"Bitch." Merca spat her contempt though it was uttered so that only the Mouse heard it. She swivelled and fixed her eyes on the boy who held up the waterskin.

"Drink?" Tomas offered, "Ya might want ta wash that carrot off ya cheek too." He swizzled a finger by his face to indicate the offending location.

With a glower, Merca snatched the proffered skin, unstoppered it and gave the bunghole a quick sniff. Satisfied it was only water she swigged a mouthful, swirling it between her cheeks before ejecting the rinse over the side of the wagon. Merca splashed more onto her hand and rubbed it over her face then took several deep glugs, the cool liquid a tonic for the roughness of her throat. Replacing the bung she slung the skin behind her, checking as she did that nobody was close before fixing the boy with a stare.

"Thought an Order Knight would look more… imposing," Merca said. "Why've they got such a hard-on for you though? A little street rat nobody."

"You're imposing but they took you out in a second," Tomas retorted.

Ballsy little fucker, Merca's smile was soft and unpleasant. In deflecting her question the boy had confirmed what she suspected. She wagged a finger at him and chuckled.

"You've talent. Seen you use it, not least on this magical fetter you enslaved me with." Tomas flinched at her words but Merca pressed on. "Thing I don't get is, that hardly makes you special. Mages are rare but hardly unique yet Marn treats you like you are. I watched her earlier and she was more concerned for you than that idiot prince. You some kind of prodigy?"

"What's a prodgee?" Tomas shifted, uncomfortable. Murder was fishing that much was obvious. No one spoke to him this long unless they wanted something from him. Except for Sparrow and maybe Renix. *Both dead,* the thought whispered in his head.

"Pro-di-gy," Merca enunciated. "It means someone gifted or exceptionally talented. In your case magically or so I'm inclined ta guess."

Merca wafted a hand at her face and chest. "I mean untrained you worked this… binding. I'm thinking that's some complicated shit and you did it without breaking a sweat. Speaking of which. You swore to remove it once I got you out of Kingsholme. So, if you wouldn't mind obliging."

"Pro-di-gy. It sounds like a title," Tomas stalled, inching back, his voice distracted. "About that other thing. I will. Course I will. Only, I can't right now."

Ready for it as he was, Tomas still startled and barely rolled away in time as Murder lunged, hands reaching for his throat. With a clatter, Tomas struck the wagon's backboard, the top edge sharp against his back. There wasn't time to feel pain as dark eyes, glinting with malice, descended upon him. His own held only fear, he didn't even think to reach for his dagger.

In the space between thoughts, the string wrapped around Merca's core flared. It was like a thousand barbed thorns ripping into her soul. Her eyes lost focus, rolled up and she crumpled, head cracking against the boards.

Tomas edged away, heart tripping like a blacksmith's hammer. The urge to bolt was burning and deep-seated, yet something held him there watching Murder writhe. The water just consumed gushed from her nose and mouth and pooled before gravity sucked it through the cracks in the planking.

With an ionising churr, O'si materialised. Absent since before his rescue in the Stacks, the sháadretarch was in his imp form and huddled against the sideboard as if hiding.

"You're a fool. I will not release her so don't even ask it," the imp hissed before Tomas had said a word. *"This creature will protect you more ably than P'uk or I, at least without revealing ourselves. Remember, Tomas, you are a Vox Léchtar Fai-ber. Bend her to your will. Assert your dominion over her. Say nothing of us."*

O'si vanished so suddenly the air seemed to pop. The tall figure of Grema Bergrun was there by the wagon with the slightly shorter, thick-bodied Kal Meyar at her side.

Where in the hells did they spring from so quick? Tomas wondered. They had arrived almost as fast as O'si vanished. The two Order Knights peered into the wagon, the barrel-chested Kal Meyar moving around it with a grace that belied his bulk. Both gave only a cursory glance at Merca Landré. Whatever they looked for it was not her.

They're looking for O'si, instinctively Tomas knew it. Knew they must have sensed the Sháadretarch, only now he was gone, hidden in the vessel that was his ring.

"There was a disturbance. What occurred here?" Kal Meyar asked, his voice commanding.

"She just started choking," Tomas said. Merca's thrashing had abated to a slow body-rock and was accompanied by soft moaning.

Kal Meyar returned a stare that was unequivocal. It was not the answer to his question.

Tomas squirmed beneath the Order Knight's scrutiny but pressed his lips firmly together and kept his eyes fixated on Murder.

"You might not be used to trusting anybody, Tomas, but we are here to see you safe." Meyar rubbed a hand over a bald pate and down his neck, tugging in obvious affection at his warrior's queue which fell halfway down his back.

"As I told you before," Meyar continued gruffly, "You wear our brother's token and that makes you our brother now. There's no need for lies or subterfuge between us. As we journey together, I hope you will see that."

With a final glance about the wagon, Kal Meyar turned and walked away. Grema Bergrun made to follow but stopped at the last moment.

"There was much to Lord Renix and more to the Order than you could possibly imagine, Tomas of Kingsholme." Grema's winter-grey eyes flickered to Merca Landré, "Her too for that matter. The world is full of endless wonder and mystery, some can be right in front of you and not even be noticed."

Tomas fidgeted, knees aching against the boards. He stood, as Grema sauntered after Kal Meyar who had rejoined the huddle of warriors. As they parted to make room for Grema, Tomas spied the mysterious Lady Mori, whose entourage, he had learned, this was. The brown clad warriors were hers and each wore an emblem above their left breast of a golden sun with a black hawk in its centre, talons extending.

He had seen the Lady Mori once before, earlier that morning with the sun barely risen. Back then her hood had been raised and he had not seen her face. She had alighted from a gilded and elaborately appointed carriage to remonstrate, loudly and vociferously with the Blackcoats whose army had taken station on the Shorune Plain outside Kingsholme and whose warrant was needed to pass north or south.

From her waspish tirade and the deferential, almost beleaguered looks the Blackcoats returned her, it was apparent to Tomas that the Lady Mori was already known to them. Diminutive against the guards she might have stood but her tongue more than made up for her size and the Blackcoat Captain on duty had waved them through with his apology at the delay and a writ to speed their passage through any further checkpoints.

But seeing her again now, Tomas's eyes bulged. The Lady Mori looked younger than he imagined, svelte and elegant, completely opposing the shrew-faced conjurings of his mind. There was a resonance that struck him, a familiarity in line and looks yet he knew beyond doubt he had never seen her before.

"Close your mouth Tomas or you'll catch a fly."

Startled, Tomas jumped, turned and shinned himself. He would have toppled off the side of the wagon had Tasso Marn not reached a steadying hand up to brace him.

"What's with everyone sneaking?" Tomas scowled, cheeks colouring as he regained his balance.

"Says the thief," Marn replied.

She looks old and tired, Tomas thought. Bruised rings encircled Marn's eyes and a melancholic air settled about her. *The loss of Chiguar has hit her hard and no mistake,* Tomas's heart lurched in empathy, the scars from his own grief still fresh, still raw. Sparrow had been his only friend and Renix, for lack of any real familial understanding, a father. For, despite the shortness of their time together Renix had changed his life beyond measure. Tomas shook his head, a father, what did he know of such things, it was nothing but a boy's daydreaming, Chiguar had been Marn's husband.

"I'm sorry," Tomas blurted and although he didn't articulate what for, the sudden glisten in Marn's eyes showed that she understood his meaning.

"Ai, everyone's sorry." Marn dragged in a breath and closed her eyes. Then, as she expelled it, she papered on a smile. "Come, let me introduce you to Lady Mori."

"Introduce?" Tomas's voice held a note of horror. More used to going unobserved, walking into a bunch of steel-clad warriors and meeting a real Lady filled him with terror. *I've met a princess before,* he reassured himself, *ai,* he argued, *one that murderised Lord Renix, her own father and if chance happened it, Herald and me too.* But, instead of the not-right-now ready on his lips, his bastard mouth betrayed him.

"Sure."

His traitorous body then clambered awkwardly over the backboard to the ground. His butt and thighs ached so bad he almost fell, *it would serve damn right,* he cursed inwardly.

As they started towards the gathering, Marn raised a speculative eyebrow. "What's wrong with you? If you need to relieve yourself, do it now, we'll be heading out again soon."

Tomas glowered, "Never ridden no horse. Didn't know it hurt so much. My legs are rubbed raw."

Marn pinched her lips as she tried and failed to suppress her mirth.

"I got a crick in my neck. It ain't funny," Tomas moaned. "I've been pressed up against Grema most of the morning and seen nought but her cloak. Feels like my spine is coming out my ass. It's been hell. Rald got to go in a carriage and he can ride. That ain't fair."

Marn stopped and placed a hand on Tomas's shoulder. "Rald was a necessity. Face beat up as it is we couldn't risk him being recognised. However," Marn sniffed, "I have been remiss with your wellbeing, my mind has been elsewhere. I'll arrange for you to ride in one of the wagons. You'll still get a sore arse but the rest of you should be fine."

Tomas shrugged. "Grema already sorted that. Said I wriggled worse than a worm on a hook, whatever that means. Why would anyone stick a worm on a hook?"

"Well, that's good." Marn gave a distracted look. "I'm thinking now maybe isn't the best time for introductions after all. Up close you stink of smoke and ash and less pleasant things besides and you're filthy to boot. I suspect I'm no better. Tonight, after we're cleaned up." With that, the Order woman turned and left him standing alone.

* * *

The Lady Mori's retinue numbered eighty-three with sixty-two riders, escorting four wagons and two carriages. It made for quite the procession, but for an escape, it was hardly subtle. Tomas glanced from his wagon seat to the driver, a short, rotund man with a long, waxed moustache that, quite frankly, looked ridiculous.

The man's name, jovially offered, was Mordan Mordignus and he was quite the chatterbox. *Perfect,* Tomas had thought, only now after several hours in his company, he couldn't quite decide who was fleecing who for information. Mord, as he insisted on being called, had an easy manner and a way with words that had Tomas spilling more than he wanted to even when it was him asking the questions.

He stared at Mord's brown tabard which was stretched tight against the paunch of his belly and Tomas wondered, not for the first time, how he managed to squeeze into it. The emblem of the hawk strained as if it would break its stitching and ping off his breast at any moment.

"Couldn't they find you a bigger tunic?" Tomas said. "It hardly fits you." He added this last hastily when Mord stared at him.

"It shows my shapely curves, unlike y'on which looks like a dress," Mord retorted, the twinkling gleam of his eye teasing. "Maybe we should swap garments."

Tomas tugged at his voluminous tabard which hung, loose, from his shoulders and he pulled it tight through his belt for the umpteenth time that day. "I mean no offence but mine will fit you no better."

"Never start a sentence with 'I mean no offence', Tomas ma boy, it indicates the complete opposite intent," Mord replied good-naturedly. "For example, if you were to say to the Lady Mori, 'I mean no offence milady but that dress you wear is too tight' I would wager a silver kern, nay a gold mark, she would not thank you for the say so."

It brought an airy smile to Tomas's face and a bit of colour high up on his cheekbones. Something Mord did not miss despite his eyes not straying from the way ahead.

"Lady Mori will want to meet you tonight I expect. She's a bright wee thing. Inquisitive and quick-witted, generous too like her mother but with a temper to match so they say. Not someone to be trifled with so watch you don't go 'meaning no offence' young Tomas." Mord chuckled and ruffled the boy's hair.

Scowling, Tomas pulled his head away and asked somewhat sulkily. "So who is she? I know Kal and Grema are Order Knights 'cause Horyk told me earlier, but you can't all be Order else we never would have made it past that first guard post."

"Indeed, young master, you are correct. Lady Mori is the youngest daughter of the Duncan and all in her party wear the tabard of Hawke Hold. Though some of us, like my good self, wear it better than most." Mord winked, cracking a lopsided grin that tilted one end of his moustache up at a jaunty angle.

The road ahead forked and Tomas was happy to let the sign marking the way ahead distract him. Because for all his jocularity, Mord was too insightful, too easy to talk to and that was anathema to Tomas. In his experience, people talked like Mord right before they robbed you, beat you or worse. Besides, all this chat of Lady Mori was uncomfortable for she played constantly upon his mind. Tomas gazed at the wooden board, the jumble of markings resolving sharply in his mind. Ramelo, it announced was straight on, Portisil the righthand branch. The lead riders took the right.

"We go to Portisil then not Ramelo," Tomas murmured, though neither place meant anything to him.

"We follow the road at least," Mord replied, his expression thoughtful.

"And from there?" Tomas asked.

Mord gave a nonchalant shrug. "I am but a humble servant, master Tomas, duty-bound to follow. However, I would posit that the only way from Portisil is north."

The rest of that day passed quickly. Mord had stories to tell and someone to hear them and, in his way, he told Tomas what he needed to know about Hawke Hold and the Duncans and even some of the history of the Nine Kingdoms. Something that a bored Tomas consumed like a thirsty man a drink.

Late afternoon a crisp wind picked up scouring them, and bringing with it a brief slurry that melted as soon as it landed. The black cloak Tomas had been given was enough to shield him from the worst of it and, for someone used to the Stacks in winter with only rags and mouldy blankets to stave off the cold, it proved more than sufficient to keep him, if not warm and dry exactly, then at least moist and only mildly chilled.

The roads they travelled were wide and well-maintained and they passed many people going both ways. Mord told Tomas about the war in the north against the strange beast-men called urak. He seemed to judge himself quite knowledgeable in such things and gave gruesome detail in more horror than Tomas had ever heard from Lord Renix. Yet as dreadful as Mord's tales were, at the same time Tomas found his blood quickening and his mind wandering, conjuring images of worthy champions riding into battle on noble steeds.

"TOMAS!"

"What, yes?" he blurted.

"You've nay heard a word I've said," Mord accused with a frown.

An urgent clatter of hooves forestalled any apology Tomas might have made. Man and boy twisted in their seats to watch a rider approaching from the rear. Angry curses trailed after as people were forced, scurrying from the horseman's path. Reaching the back of the column, the rider reined in and as he trotted by, Tomas could see that he was breathless, his horse lathered in sweat and frothing at the bit like some rabid animal.

Kal Meyar and Grema Bergrun, leading at the front, spoke with the rider, their trenchant demeanour and clipped tones enough to convey the seriousness of whatever message was imparted. In short order, Grema dropped back, manoeuvring her horse next to the Lady Mori's carriage.

"What do you think is going on?" Tomas asked Mord.

"Nothing good I wager," Mord replied. "But we'll know soon enough."

Whatever conversation Grema had was brief before she moved back to the front of the column. Shortly afterwards they left the main stretch to Portisil turning more directly north, taking a smaller road that wound its way through farmlands. They followed it for a time before taking yet another road that led towards a hump of low-slung hills crowned with trees.

The bump and rattle of the wagon became more pronounced as the way became pitted and Tomas felt every uncomfortable jolt through his seat. They passed a weathered sign with a one league marker etched beside the name Paulsen and an hour later, as the sun began to fade in the west, they entered a picturesque village that nestled against the foothills, a tinkling brook anchoring its eastern border.

For Paulsen, a retinue this size was unusual and the whole village turned out to see them. The gilded carriages garnered much attention for only rich merchants or a named house could afford such opulence. The look on many of the villagers' faces was comfortingly familiar to Tomas, for it was the same a stall-holder or trader in Kingsholme might wear when money walked in. For someone who had never set foot outside the city and who found the open roads and countryside all too strange, it was somehow grounding to know some things at least were the same.

Instinctively, Tomas's eyes roved in calculation over the neatly ordered stone and timber houses, assessing barriers and entry points and he liked what he saw. *Amateurs, the lot of them,* he smirked. For of the few open shutters he could see, all were simple latch affairs and the doors didn't look any more secure. *I've never burgled a house through the front door before*, he smiled.

A horse drew alongside Tomas, its rider blocking his view and dislodging him from his criminal musings.

"The Lady Mori will be staying at the tavern. Most of the rest of us will be setting up camp outside of Paulsen," Marn sounded as tired as she looked. "Stay with Mord until I return. Oh, and try and stay out of trouble. Make yourself useful, aye."

Tomas rolled his shoulders, feeling guilty, as if she had somehow intuited his turn of thought. Seeing Marn reminded Tomas of Lord Renix. She was the last connection, tenuous as it was, to his life before and a witness to his metamorphosis from street urchin to… what exactly? Tomas wasn't sure, even now. He'd only ever known thieving. Take that away and what was he? *Vox Léchtar Fai-ber* echoed in his mind. That thought was even more disturbing.

"Sure," Tomas muttered.

There was only one inn and the two carriages and a contingent of twenty riders made for it whilst the wagons and remaining warriors continued until they passed out of the village and reached an open field where a camp was established next to the burbling brook which snaked its way out of the hills.

Dismounting, Tomas arched his back, stretching the crick from his lower spine. His legs were sore, thighs still tender but better than they were. Everyone seemed busy doing something or other, but Tomas felt unnoticed and unheeded until a hand clamped him on the shoulder making him jump.

"Wax in your ears, Tomas? I said, lend a hand 'ere." Mord spoke loudly to be heard above the rattle of horses and harness and the bantering talk of the riders who attended them.

An hour later it was a different kind of ache that he experienced but, strangely enough, it felt kind of good. He'd never laboured before, and his arms felt sapped and his shoulders sloped in weariness. At first, he'd felt small, a child among men as he worked besides Mord. But the fat little man kept him busy and there was no time to feel out of place. Exhausted, Tomas slumped onto the sleeping roll Mord said was his, beneath a canvas lean-to he'd helped erect and closed his eyes.

Someone kicked his boot and Tomas woke with a jolt.

"Bah, you haven't even washed. Get up," Marn growled. "Mordan!"

Mord handed the ladle he was holding to a fellow and wandered over from the cooking fire he attended. He glanced at the boy rubbing his face to wake himself then the scowling Marn.

"From what I've heard the young master's been through a lot. You should leave him be till it's time to eat," Mord rumbled affably but Marn only glared in response and with a grumble of complaint, he rummaged through a pack and brought out a soap block and drying cloth and handed them over.

Tomas had washed before, course he had, he wasn't no animal. But not like this. Marn had him strip naked and wade into the brook till his balls shrivelled at the water's touch. Under her critical eye, he washed with a cleaning cloth and a soap block that was abrasive and roughed his skin so that it felt like he was peeling layers off. There was no pain though, the ice-cold water numbed his whole body. It set him shivering so much his lips quivered.

Then, just when Tomas thought it could get no worse, the evil bitch insisted that he dunk his head and lather what little soap residue he could get off the block and massage it into his scalp. By the time he emerged, Tomas's whole body was a palpitating riddle of mottled blue veins and his teeth were chattering.

Marn wrapped a drying blanket around him and rubbed vigorously until the warmth started to seep back into Tomas's bones. It drew more than one bawdy comment from some of the on-looking warriors but they fell silent when Marn's gaze swept over them.

When she reached for a pile of clothes that sat neatly folded upon a tree stump, Tomas wished the ground would open up and swallow him. "I ca-ca-can dreessss myselff."

"Course you can, I'm not your mother. Just be quick. We're late as it is." Marn turned her back and wandered over to the nearest campfire and promptly threw his old clothes onto it before holding her hands out to the flaring warmth.

It took Tomas longer to dress than normal. His body still shook but sensation was returning, and his skin felt sharp and sensitive. He didn't know where Marn had acquired the clothes from, but they were good quality and fit his slight body surprisingly well.

"Tomas, come. We've dawdled enough," Marn said as the boy laced his boots. Not waiting to see if he followed or not, she marched towards town calling into the dusk tarnished sky. "Merca Landré!"

A shadow figure appeared from behind a wagon and fell into step without uttering a sound.

Tomas had given no mind to Murder since their altercation earlier and a nervous anxiety filled him as he rushed to catch them up. He stopped only to swing his pack onto his back, the familiar weight of 'Sházáik Douné Táak', the Book of Demons settling between his shoulder blades.

A board outside the inn announced it as the 'Horse and Harvest' and when they entered it smelled of straw, beer and bodies. A large hearth fire crackled to one side and a comfortable heat brushed the chill from Tomas's cheeks. The room was packed, the locals squeezed in amongst the soldiers from Hawke. Ale was flowing, orders being called out at the bar and a solitary barmaid bulled her way through the crowd, expertly wielding a tray ladened with tankards.

The atmosphere was convivial and full of good-natured laughter which to Tomas was strange enough, but this wasn't what struck him most, it was more that this was the cleanest tavern he had ever seen. In the Gloaming part of Old Town that was his usual haunt, the taverns were low slung and seedy. They were places where people drank with one hand whilst keeping the other on their coin purse or dagger handle.

Marn manoeuvred them through the crowd and towards a doorway, giving a nod to the barmaid who angled to let them pass. The room they entered on the other side was comparatively empty with barely more than a handful of people present. There were several large tables arranged around a fireplace that was a match for the one in the main lounge.

Sat behind a table, nearest the warmth, was Lady Mori. She looked a child, sandwiched as she was between the wide-girth of Kal Meyar, who was seated on her left, and the bruise-faced, red-eyed Herald on her right with the ever-present Horyk Andersun's towering frame stood behind.

A beatific smile lit upon Lady Mori's face, though whether it was for Marn, Murder or him, Tomas didn't know. Certainly, the glower from the former Crown Prince of the Nine Kingdoms was all his and Tomas couldn't help winking at him knowing it would infuriate the pompous princeling. Sure enough, 'Rald's neck reddened but Tomas fought his own blushes when Lady Mori's head tilted fractionally towards him, smiling as if the wink had been intended for her.

"Fool," Merca murmured. Her mouth barely moved, and the word was uttered so softly it hardly reached Tomas' ear.

"Welcome, Tomas. Welcome Merca Landré. I am Lady Mori Duncan. Forgive me, I have been remiss in not greeting you earlier." The lady's eyes flickered to Kal Meyar and then Grema Bergrun who stood on the opposite side of the hearth. "My companions asked for your safe conveyance from Kingsholme and I agreed, somewhat reluctantly I have to admit, but here we are. Please, avail yourselves of any refreshment."

Lady Mori indicated a table behind them and to the side. Tomas stared at it, the waft of bread, cold cuts and cheeses reached his brain a fraction after his eyes registered the food. His stomach rumbled its desire and Tomas needed no second invitation; hunger trumped all. He moved to the table and shoved a slice of ham-hock into his mouth and chewed it around, bliss exploding in his mouth. He felt slightly anxious when Murder moved alongside him, but it was only to take a plate and start loading it up.

Lady Mori raised her voice. "Lord Meyar, Lady Bergrun, Tasso Marn. If you could leave us please."

"The woman is an assassin," Kal Meyar began. "She is dangerous, and the boy is our ward."

Lady Mori stared at the dark-skinned woman with raven hair who had paused in her efforts at the buffet table and returned her look, eyes brown and still like a hunting cat. A killer's eyes.

"Do you have a contract for my murder?" asked Lady Mori.

Merca Landré's nostrils flared at the word murder, her moniker used like that made the question seem intimate, personal. Merca sneered.

"Before today I'd never heard of you."

"Hurtful," Lady Mori held a hand to her breast as if wounded but the skin about her eyes creased in good humour. She turned to the Order Knight at her side.

"See, Kal, perfectly safe, she's never heard of me. Assassins, professional ones, and she strikes me as a professional, kill only when there is need or money. So I must ask for your indulgence. Rogan and Milak will be attending as ever and there is Horyk of course."

Kal Meyar opened his mouth to argue but then shut it. He scraped his chair back and rose following after Grema who already moved towards the door. Marn held a finger up to Merca Landré but then curled it back into her fist before stomping out after the Order Knights.

After the latch clicked back into place the Lady Mori sat quietly whilst the killer and the thief, if she believed Herald, sated themselves. The prince's patience however expired well before the thief's hunger.

"Stop stuffing your faces and attend us," Herald wheezed, his swollen nose making the words deep and nasal.

Tomas licked his fingers, snatched a bread roll into the pocket of his tunic, then, turning away from the table of delights to face the Lady Mori and the pompous prig that sat beside her, discreetly lifted a wedge of cheese.

Murder brushed past his shoulder, her elbow dislodging the cheese to thud upon the floor. She stalked toward the long table, a plate of food still in her hand.

Godsdamnit, cursed Tomas, bending to pick up his loot, *why didn't I get a plate?* He picked off a bit of something stuck to the cheese skin and wandered over, then, self-conscious that everyone was looking at him, he stuffed it hurriedly in with the bread roll.

"For later," he said to no one in particular, then sat.

"I find myself in somewhat of a quandary," Lady Mori began, folding her hands in her lap, "for it occurs to me that I have taken you under my care without having spoken to either of you or knowing if indeed you wanted my help to begin with. I have the word of Lord Meyar and the Lady Bergrun, of course, but that is not to say I should accept matters without having discussed things first with you."

Tomas fidgeted. Merca sat still as stone. Neither said a word.

This close to Lady Mori, that overriding sense of knowingness, returned to Tomas in full force, the haunting familiarity of her, and it suddenly struck him why. She was older certainly, a woman, and her blonde hair immaculately coifed whilst Sparrow was but a slip of a girl with tawny hair all a tangle, but that aside their faces held a symmetry. Noses pert, mouths slightly too wide, lips of a thinness, their cheekbones high and chins elegantly pointed, but it was the eyes that sealed it. They were the same. The same shade of swirling blue, emitting the same warmth so that as Lady Mori's gaze met his own it was as if she saw him and only him. Her words, though warmly spoken, did not match the turmoil of emotion that seized his chest and took his breath.

"I have agreed, at his request, to take 'Rald' to see my father the Duncan. I understand that you will be travelling with me as far as Hawke Hold. However, before I agree to that I need to be sure it is what you want. I do not condone holding people against their will nor who I feel are being coerced."

Tomas risked a glance at Murder. The Lady Mori talked of free will and coercion and whilst he wasn't entirely sure what that last one meant it had the ring of what O'si had done, binding the assassin to him. All Murder need do was speak up, and then he wasn't sure what would happen. Whatever it was, Tomas had the sense that the Lady Mori would not be pleased.

Murder's head inclined and she looked down upon him through narrowed eyes. Cold eyes. Tomas felt his heartbeat slow to a ponderous thud. Then her gaze slid away, to Herald where it lingered.

"You use a lot of words when a few would do," Merca said. "I wonder if you had no money and no name. If you had to muck around in the filth and squalor like the rest of us, if you would feel quite so altruistic."

The prince's face purpled and looked set to rupture like a blister but as he made to rise, Lady Mori placed a calming hand over his.

"Please 'Rald. Sit, be at ease." She waited till Herald had settled then addressed Merca once more.

"We are all creatures of circumstance and chance. I can no more answer that question than you could should you sit in my chair and hold my experiences for your own. I can only be what I am. So tell me, what is your wish, Merca, for truly I mean you no ill."

Merca muttered under her breath and chewed her bottom lip before answering somewhat angrily. "My wish, eh. My wish is ta take my blade and…." Her voice trailed away and she pinched fingers to her nose. "Wishes are for assholes… I go where the boy goes."

"Very well, Tomas?"

"What? Me?" Tomas belched the words and put a hand to his mouth, embarrassed.

"Yes," Lady Mori smiled. "You."

The intensity of her eyes was every bit as warm as the heat from the fire. Tomas swallowed then blabbed. "Marn says she's taking me to Tankrit. For Lord Renix. I got nowhere else. The Targus wants me dead so I can't go back there."

Merca shook her head once, so slight yet dripping with meaning. *She thinks me a fool*, Tomas thought and a memory popped into his head, of old Benny Four Fingers. *'Information is currency, every bit as much as a silver kern or a copper bit. Do not be quick to give it away and never for free.'* Merca was right, he had said too much. Tomas clamped his mouth shut.

"Well then. That is settled," Lady Mori declared.

"Is it?" Merca said, "You asked what we want when we don't know shit. That rider today? The one with the bad news. What did he say?"

Lady Mori gave a wistful sigh. "It is pertinent in its way," she said as if to herself. "The rider was a grey knight, Salu Kimer, one of Grema's to be precise, left to watch the crossroads. A royal decree was posted on the waymarker confirming what was already coming."

"Which is what exactly?" Merca asked.

"The Order Accords, the ancient charter signed so long ago has been rescinded, officially, by Her Royal Majesty, Queen Matrice, the First of her name. Counter-signed and sealed by the three Holy Churches and the Council of Mages."

Merca shrugged, "So what? Like you said, it was coming."

"The Order Accords are ancient and each of the Nine Kingdoms signed their own, as did my own house. It is something outside of royal remit. This means it is up to each signatory to resign and break from the Accord as some already have. However, it cannot be ordained by the Royal House and remains one of the few freedoms outside of royal purview."

Tomas yawned, something Merca felt some sympathy with. "Said afore, ya use too many words. Spit it out, sister."

"The decree posted states that any signatory that does not revoke their own article of accord by Dreadnigh will be in direct conflict with her Royal Majesty. In essence, on the first ten-day of Dreadnigh, any signatory that still holds with the accord will be at war with the Crown."

"So what?" Merca said. "Soon as the High King died and the Order and Prince La-di-da over there took the fall it's been coming. That it?"

"No, Lord Henry Blackstar is announced as Lord Marshall, the first in over two hundred years, and a state of war declared. The urak in the north are cited as the reason but my feeling is there is more at play. Black Henry will have the power to call upon any High Lord or High Lady to provide men-at-arms and to use them as he sees fit. Salu Kimer also reported that a contingent of two hundred Blackcoats followed shortly afterwards, taking the road to Ramelo in some haste. The road I told the watch captain I would be taking. If it is me they seek then it will not take them long to realise I am no longer upon it. Now you know what I know.

"Master Milak," Lady Mori gave a curt nod to a brown-clad man with sallow skin and brooding eyes who stood unobtrusively by the door. He ducked his head in acknowledgement, then, unlatching the door disappeared through it. He returned moments later with Kal Meyar, Grema Bergrun and Tasso Marn trailing.

The Lady Mori stood and rested her hands upon the tabletop. "There is much that is unclear to me still," she said without preamble. "But it is agreed, Merca Landré goes with you Tomas who goes with Lord Meyar and Lady Bergrun who travel to Hawke Hold. When we reach there, I will ask you both again what you wish."

She lifted her head to the Order Knights. "These two will be your responsibility but I must insist that whilst you and your Hands are under my auspices and wearing my house colours that you follow my orders. I will of course listen to your counsel."

Kal Meyar moved his bulk across the room to the fireplace, turned and let the heat warm his back.

"Of course, Lady Mori. I should tell you I have sent two of my Hand back toward the main road to Portisil to watch the way. But my advice is this. To leave before first-light. Take twenty men and ride north to the King's Highway and follow it east to Ellingbrok. There, take a boat up the River Ranning, through the Fenlakes to Outward."

"And the rest of my company?" Lady Mori asked.

"Let them follow but take the north road through the Mor towns. They should be quite safe even if they are waylaid, perhaps leave one of your Ladies in charge, a caravan on a simple trade mission for the Duncan."

Lady Mori glanced at Rogan her armsman who gave a nod of agreement. "Very well. Get some rest. We leave before dawn."

Tomas blanched and almost lost the bread roll from the pouch in his tunic when a hand landed on his shoulder.

"Come on Tomas. Let's get you settled," Marn said.

"I can't ride a horse." Tomas's thighs throbbed at the mere thought of it.

"Two days. That's all," Marn cajoled. "I'll show you how to sit right and I'll get you an easy-rider. It won't be so bad, smart as you are, you'll get the hang of it. Come on."

A leering Merca leaned across. "Bitch is lying. Ya legs are gonna sting like lemon juice on a cut. With any luck, you'll fall and break your neck you little shit."

The thousand barbed thorns scraped against her mind and Merca winced, her still tender head feeling every lancet.

Gods be cursed and damned, a girl can't even have any fun.

Chapter 33: The Hungering

The Trivium, Kingsholme, The Holme

The shade rippled across the room, alternating colours from the verdigris pattern of the rug to the grey stone of the wall. It gathered by the window, a formless, seething mass, unmoved by the cool breeze that gusted through it.

It had no eyes in an organic sense yet perceived as clearly as any creature might. More so, for its autonomy was an illusion, it being one small part of the Morhudrim, every sense, each thought a piece of a greater whole.

The Shade's focus shifted back to the room and fixated on a large, ornate bed and the bulbous, corpulent human that lay naked upon its covers.

The man's skin was pallid and blue-veined. Pulled by gravity it sagged, giving a melted, slug-like appearance. The liver and both kidneys were shot, by rights the human should be dead, yet he was not. For he was Taken.

The Taken's head thrashed upon the pillow and muttered in agitation. A drool of spittle ran from mouth to ear and a tear leaked from his eye in a parallel trail. The Shade could sense the distress in the man's dreams, taste the fear in its blood. It called, but the calling was easy to resist. For the Shade had partaken many times before and now that its power had sufficiently grown, it much desired a new flavour, a new trauma to consume.

Knowing the human would not awaken until its return, the Shade flowed out the window and into the shroud of night. Far below, a winding path weaved its way through neatly groomed gardens. The only light was from the stars and moons above and the tall lanterns below, which were strung out evenly along the path and around the perimeter of the gardens. In the near distance was the indistinct outline of another building.

The shade descended and followed the path, the flame from each lantern extinguishing as it passed, plunging the gardens into a deeper darkness. Then it waited.

* * *

Father Emmanual Vartis was tired and, he confessed, a little shaky on his feet. Too much Cumbrenan white. He gave Father Rigelun a conspiratorial grin. He returned it before teetering off in the opposite direction, the pair not too far gone in their cups to know not to speak, it would not do to disturb any of the bishops.

Pushing the door wide, Father Emmanual was met with a blast of cold air that freshened his cheeks and sobered him a little. Pulling his brown robes tight against the chill, Emmanual leaned against the door, shutting it behind him. Levering himself off, he wobbled into the gardens thinking of his evening.

The Red Conclave and its aftermath were all anyone spoke of. For his part, it was idle speculation that made him visit his friend, Father Rigelun. He'd wanted to glean the latest news from the Red Church first-hand, especially now that High Cardinal Tortuga had resurfaced.

It delighted him no end that the deeply unpopular Tortuga was the new Voice of Kildare. He'd met him once, as an acolyte, when the then, Father Tortuga, had given a lecture on Kildare. He'd found the oversized Red Priest sharp of wit and insight and had rather liked him. Not so Father Rigelun, according to him, Tortuga was a beastly, abomination of a man, derided and tolerated by the bishops and other holy dignitaries. Rigelun's vociferous bleating left Father Emmanual in no doubt that their prejudice filtered down to permeate most who wore the red.

He hiccuped, then grinned like a loon. When Tortuga disappeared after the Conclave it had driven the Red Church into a frenzy, not least amongst the bishops. Church scriptures and legal scrolls had been scrutinised exhaustively and in minute detail over the legalize of it. That Kildare had chosen Tortuga over all others to be his voice had caused much hand wringing and consternation. Any chance of rebuttal that the bishops found however was refuted, if not by one or other of themselves then by his own Lord, Rand Luxurs the High Cardinal of Ankor and Maris Jenah the High Priestess of Nihmrodel.

Emmanual chuckled and shook his head in amusement then wished he hadn't as a sharp ache rolled through his skull. He groaned, then cursed as his clogged feet tripped on the paving.

"Damn lightchs," he slurred, glaring at an unlit lantern pole as if it were to blame for his drunkenness. He clicked his fingers at it.

"Signaititum arhtim," he mangled the words badly. It elicited a flicker of spark-light which faded just as quickly. He lumbered past, thoughts turning to his dry mouth and throat. How can a man drink so much and still be thirsty?

Father Emmanual stopped and swayed, unsure why, his mind slow to pick out what his body sensed. His eyes had adjusted to the night but what little he could see had suddenly turned black. Squinting myopically up at the sky, it was filled with stars and the red smile of Kildare's moon leered back at him. Not blind then. He lurched drunkenly, stumbled back, caught himself then staggered forward.

"Shiit. Come on, Fadder," he babbled, afraid if he fell he would be found asleep in the gardens, or if it got much colder, dead. The thought stirred him enough to take another shuffling step, hand grasping forward protectively.

A cloying coldness flowed around his arm that sliced in sudden sharpness through to the bone. Skin split, flesh tore and Father Emmanual opened his mouth to scream only to inhale an oily blackness. It poured past his teeth and over his tongue, filling his cheeks and the back of his throat. He gagged, the scream dying before ever it was formed.

Lifted off his feet, Father Emmanual's eyes went wide in terror. He threw his head back and breathed through his nose, relieving starved lungs, it was the only respite to be had as the darkness enwrapped his body. Above, the canopy of starlight flickered then disappeared, the red moon's grin the last celestial object to vanish.

Was this Kildare's punishment for his irreverent thoughts? For his amusement at the Red Church's turmoil and their fall from lofty self-appointment. The thought fled as quickly as it came, replaced by an exquisite symphony of pain that cascaded through his nerves and up his spine to burst upon his parietal lobe.

His flesh prickled, the skin blistering on his feet, though from hot or cold he could not say. It was followed by sharp slicing cuts into the joints of his toes. Emmanuel screamed in silent agony, and the evil holding him soaked it in. Through the pain, Emmanuel could feel the thing pulsating in ecstasy.

He swooned but was jerked back to consciousness. *'Too soon'* whispered in his mind.

The nails on his toes ripped free and he thrashed violently. There was no traction as if he flailed in a pool of nothingness. He kicked and bucked only for his body to be pulled taut, rigid. He was helpless to affect his lot.

Veins distended, and then his toes ruptured, popping one at a time like corn nuts on a griddle. Flesh sloughed off the bone and an exquisite agony burst in his mind, more painful than anything that had gone before, overloading his senses. Piss soaked his leg and shit trailed down the back of his thighs. He prayed to Ankor for release, for death to take him.

'I'm your god now, mortal, and I've only just begun.'

* * *

The remains of Father Emmanual Vartis were found at first light by a priest of the White, the nauseous stench from the gardens drawing him to investigate. The Church physikers were summoned to identify the gelatinous glop of skin, bone, blood and flesh. Several heaved their morning victuals before confirming that, yes indeed, this was a man. Trawling through the soup of remains, the brown robe of a priest of Ankor was recovered, impossibly complete.

The Voices of the Trinity attended the grisly scene.

"I'll have Bishop Enning-Baye call a roster. This is one of my own." High Cardinal Rand Luxurs looked troubled.

"Have you heard of such a thing before? What could do this to a man?" Maxim Tortuga asked.

Of the three of them, Tortuga seemed most composed, least distraught.

"I've never heard of nor seen such a thing," High Priestess Maris Jenah replied. "I will ask the chief archivist. If he has not read of it, then maybe it is contained in one of the fettered volumes in the black room."

"They are prohibited for a reason." Rand Luxurs raised a bushy eyebrow at his long-time friend.

"This reeks of something otherworldly," Maris Jenah replied. "In shadows and corners, I've heard whispers of the Morhudrim. With all that is happening here, and in the world, we would be remiss not to consider every possibility."

Tortuga frowned. "It is empty rumours you listen to, spread, no doubt, by the Order. First the High King, now this. It would suit their cause to sow fear and further discord."

"Do you profess to know their aim, your Eminence?" Jenah asked, keeping a straight face, for Lord Renix had indeed discussed the return of the Morhudrim with her before his demise. Something stank in Kingsholme. First Tortuga's ascension, then Matrice, now this. It was, disturbing.

"No. Of course not," Tortuga responded. "I'm saying they should not be ruled out for this." He waved a hand at the pile of flesh.

"I do not believe the Order capable of this." Jenah held her hand up to forestall Tortuga's comeback. "Nor any man or woman. I do not mean the cruelty of it, for I have learned we are capable of the worst atrocities. No, I mean the manner. I think we should ask John Taran to attend us. The Enclave has been dabbling with demonology for a while now. Perhaps the Prime Magus and his magisterium can shed some light on things."

"Agreed." Rand Luxurs moved quickly to defuse the sudden tension between his two equals. He glanced at Tortuga. The man had made a remarkable recovery, especially for one as heavy-framed as he. He still looked ashen though and this must be tiring for him, Luxurs thought. "I think it would be prudent to station your Red Cloaks about the Trivium. As a safeguard. Whatever did this may return."

Tortuga inclined his head. "Of course. One can never be too careful."

Chapter 34: Ruminations, Cogitations and Lies

Waterdale, Cumbrenan

Marron always said he was a quiet man, contemplative, and Darion figured it must be so for she was rarely wrong. It was probably why he loved the Old Forest so much, perfect for 'cognitive ruminations' as one of his old masters used to say.

Alone in the wilds at night with Bindu curled next to him and nothing but the cosmos stretching in magnificent indifference above, he liked to philosophise about life. The duality of the forest and the way things fit together. Just like the seasons, everything had its time and place. How a tree would provide the leaf and the seed and the shelter to feed and sustain other life as well as its own. How in autumn when the leaves and seeds fell, they would rot into mulch and be shrouded beneath the snows of winter only for new life to rise from the detritus come spring. Nature was so eternal, just like the seasons and the stars in the heavens, but more tangible, more personal. More unforgiving.

Darion missed the peace of those times, wished he were back in the Old Forest now, with Marron and Nihm and the dogs. His world back then had been simple and honest and whole. But, like a ship leaving the shoreline, that life was gone from him, consigned to a memory slowly fading to the horizon. He felt bereft, his heart sundered by Marron's death, yet he had not the time to mourn her passing nor come to terms with her loss. Instead, he buried his grief. Layered duty and honour over it like old hoarding so that he could not touch it nor see it. But even after that, he felt conflicted, as two great weights pulled him in different directions. Nihm, their bond unbreakable in one, the Order and his oath of service, inexorable, in the other.

Nihm should have come with him. Why hadn't he made her? In his mind's eye, the memory of their talk back in Lower Rippleton played out. It brought a wry smile to his face, and he heard Marron plain as day. *'Nihm's stubborn as you are ya great lump that's why.'*

As he often did, Darion wondered what Nihm was doing. He knew she was alive, felt it in his blood and bone even before Castigan told him that Keeper said she was with Hiro again and on route to Midshire.

That had been last night, their third crossing the Shearing Flats. Now, in the watery, first glow of morning, Darion drew his horse to a stop and gazed down into a misted vale. Waterdale sat below, a small town, nestling against the dun-coloured waters of the Calda River. And, on the river's far side, hunched on a rocky bluff, stood a fortified grand-house, with crenellated battlements and a single, peaked tower.

His horse gave an impatient snort, expelling a billow of warm air and Darion patted a gloved hand against her neck.

"Come then, lady."

At Darion's voice, the mare obliged, crunching through the shallow snow that settled on the road. He led the way, Castigan and her grey knight, Ansel, just now coming up behind with the sound of the wagons further back, drawing nearer. Should he turn, Darion knew he would find Ironside and Rutigard holding the rear, which suited him just fine. For things had been strained since the farm outside of Thorn Nook and what had transpired there, or at least for him. Ironside seemed indifferent.

The mare followed the steep decline of the road as it curled down into the valley towards Waterdale. If they could have avoided the town, they would have but the next crossing was a day's travel according to Castigan and presented them with the same problem, namely, people.

On the slow descent, Darion tried to sort through his dour emotion, for a bleak greyness had settled upon him these past days which had steadily grown weightier. At first, he had put it down to angst, at losing Marron and with Nihm leaving him, but he realised now that was a false truth. One he had sold himself. Ironside had shattered that illusion. Made Darion look inside until he confronted what it was. He tugged at his beard, rueful at his foolishness. Marron would have seen it at once, it had taken him a ten-day…

The Order was his family. Every man a brother, every woman a sister and leaving that union as a young man had been both exciting and frightening. For the world outside was one of chaos, fraught with the vagaries of the entitled and the doctrine of the righteous. Darion never regretted his decision to leave with Marron, but he'd always maintained a nostalgic reverence for his brethren, a superiority of purpose. He could see that now. Could turn it over in his mind and know it for boyhood indulgence.

And the Order Knights? They might be family too, but they were also so much more. So very few passed the Trials of Ascendance that those who did and became Bonded were revered for their sacrifice and their service but also, for a young boy like Darion, idolised. Long-lived, they seemed never to age, were stronger and faster than any mortal, their martial prowess unrivalled. Though, as much renowned for their fighting skills, they were also masters of the arts and music, diplomacy and the sciences. When time is no barrier, much can be learned. How could that not capture a boy's imaginings?

Only now, Ironside had shown his sentiment for what it was. Wistful. Immature. Idealistic. The Order Knight might be a master of arts but Darion could see now that Ironside was as imperfect as any man or woman. No moral imperative prevented him from dispatching that luckless guard at Thorn Nook. The Order Knight had felt no regret, shown no remorse at having taken a life, needlessly. Long-lived he might be, but his flaws had been honed and crystalised every bit as much as his virtues.

It was an uncomfortable revelation and one that extrapolated not just to Ironside but to his whole family. Every Bonded, every Grey Knight, each brother and each sister. Even Keeper. Darion thought suddenly of Hiro, black sheep of the Order if ever there was one. Rumour had it he was one of the original Bonded. That he knew the founder, Elora dul Eladrohim, an ilfanum and the first of them. Given his revelation, Darion felt, maybe, that he understood his old master a little better.

His horse cleared the valley's slope and the road looped towards the river, following the rumpled contours of the land. In the belly of the valley, it was colder and gloomier, the barely risen sun too low yet to peek over the shoulder of the opposite rise.

Darion clopped past the first of the houses, wooden framed, wattle and daub affairs with thatched roofs. Each stood apart and appeared well kept. A shutter creaked open in one and the ever-present Bindu, padding softly by his side, turned amber eyes to stare at the dark recess beyond and the hidden faces watching them.

A dog barked in the background and an old lady, bent and leaning on a stick, stopped and stared as the riders and wagons moved past her towards the town square. She offered no greeting.

Darion twisted in his saddle. Castigan gave a nod, her face wary, mirroring his own. It was too quiet. He turned frontways again, eyes scanning the way ahead and every side street they passed. A child cried and was shushed.

A blacksmith's shop appeared on Darion's right. Smoke puffed from a chimney but none from the forge fire, its stack was cold and the workshop silent.

It was early yet but Darion knew that life awoke with first light or more often, before it. A town like this should be thriving with the sounds of crafters and merchants, with gong farmers making their rounds and muck-rakers cleaning the streets. But Waterdale was as drab as the churned snow, listless as if the life had been sucked from it.

They entered the town square, stopping to let the horses take water at the troughs in the centre, Darion and Ansel cracking the ice crust that had formed on top.

"Been here before and it was a busy market town. Nice." Castigan broke the silence, "I can sense people in their homes but not as many as should be. It feels half abandoned."

"Ai, summat's off," Darion said. He glanced around the square and his eyes stopped at a large stone building that rose above its neighbours. Lancet windows, evenly arranged, stood three apiece each side of a porch entry, their stained-glass panes an alternating, red, brown and white, though the colours were subdued in the morning shade.

As if awaiting his attention and with a plaintive squeal, the church door yawed open. Three priests emerged, a woman in the brown robes of Ankor, and two men, one in the white of Nihmrodel the other the blood-red of Kildare.

"An unusual reception committee," Ansel muttered. "Shouldn't they be praying or something?"

The kraa of a raven called and Darion looked up to find Bezal circling lazily above and hoped the bird would stay aloft. It would look strange indeed if she flew down and alighted upon R'ell's shoulder, especially attired as he was in the robes of a white priest. The thought made him glance towards Gatzinger's wagon in time to see Father Melbroth alight from the back of it.

Father Melbroth lowered his cowl then stretched his back out before walking to meet the oncoming priests.

The brown-robe called out. "Hail, Father. I am Mother Sessane, Highmarch of this parish, this is Father Hekbur," the priestess indicated the white-robed man to her left, "and Father Remual," the Red-Robe to her right.

Melbroth bowed, "Hello and well met, sister, brothers. I am Father Melbroth. In the wagon is Brother Welland and Sister Marin. Forgive them but both are indisposed."

"Indisposed? Are they unwell?" Father Hekbur exclaimed. "The Lady has blessed me with the physikers art, Mother Sessane as well. Though mayhap you are tired?" The priest directed this last with an arched brow at the Highmarch beside him.

Father Melbroth looked more intently at Mother Sessane and saw that her black skin looked waxen and her eyes sunken. "Thank you, but that will not be necessary," Melbroth replied.

"Come, Father. I must insist," Hekbur exclaimed, "We see few enough travellers down the Westway road this time of year as it is and from your accent, you are a Rivers man. Surely the three of you could spare a day in rest and regale us with news of the war against the savages?"

"And I for one would be interested to know," Father Remual interjected, eyes narrowed, "what could take three White Fathers so far from their parishes? And with such odd companions."

Now it was Father Melbroth's turn to arch his brow. He stared pointedly at the Red Priest. "Please moderate your tone, Father Remual, I too am a Highmarch. And since when does a White Priest answer to the Red Church."

"All paths lead to the One," Father Remual replied. Then at Mother Sessane's distempered look. "No offence was meant, Father, I assure you."

There was movement behind the priests of the Trinity and Father Melbroth watched over their shoulders as a Hand of Red Cloaks filed through the church doors with a crease of leather harness and clatter of mail. They formed a single rank in front of the church.

"In that case, none is taken. If I seem blunt then forgive me. It has been a hard month and my nerves are frayed." Melbroth turned and scanned the two white-robed figures sitting in Gatzinger's wagon, before pivoting back, "Our parish, was Greentower. Lost to the urakakule as is most of the Rivers. Rivercross is our last great bastion against the devils and it will, White Lady willing, hold."

"All the more reason to take your rest. You will be safe here, Father," Mother Sessane said. "I for one would enjoy your company."

Melbroth bowed, "You are too kind. However, we have lost days to the snow, and will no doubt lose more as we travel east. As much as I would enjoy fresh conversation, regretfully I must decline. I must complete my task and return to Rivercross."

"And these men," Father Remual indicated towards the wagons. "They look like mercenaries. I've not heard of such a thing. White priests travelling so, with an armed guard. One can't help but wonder why. If it is an escort you need then I and my Red Cloaks leave for Oling later today."

Melbroth gave a dry, humourless smile. "Unusual indeed but these are perilous times, Father Remual. These northern lands are filled with the dispossessed. Families stripped of their able-bodied to fight against these urak, leaving mothers with their children and the elderly to fend for themselves. Displaced, no home, many with no shelter and no food. In such circumstances desperate people will do desperate things to survive and Brother Welland and Sister Marin must reach Pik Lake unhindered. So we cannot tarry, Father Remual. Mayhap you will catch us on the road and we may share it for a time?"

"Pik Lake!" Father Remual exclaimed. Furtive eyes stole a glance towards the wagons and the two white priests sat in silence and swaddled with blankets against the cold.

Father Hekbur was not quite so quick on the uptake. "The leper colony? What mission could take you to such a place? Treatment is futile, the condition always returns."

Mother Sessane placed a hand on Hekbur's arm and stilled him, her eyes not leaving Father Melbroth. "It is a noble thing you do, Father. Transmission is rare but the stigma associated with this cursed disease is acute and with good reason. People fear what they don't understand and when a victim is healed of it, it returns, a month or a year later, stronger, more insidious than before. I take it whatever sanctuary our brother and sister had has been lost."

"It has. There are few places left for them in the north and the sanctuary on Pik Isle is guarded by the lake. My Primate, Hennim, maintains urak are averse to wide bodies of water. There is nowhere else for them to go."

"Then I would offer them the Saint's blessing," Mother Sessane began but Melbroth held his hand up to forestall her.

"Please, there is no need, the One shines in them already. The people of Waterdale need your blessing more." Father Melbroth cast a dour look. "This war in the Rivers is moving south and has already spread east into Norderland. Do not assume your parish is safe, the war is not that far from your door and there is no promise that winter will hold them until spring. Speaking of your parish, tell me, what has happened here? Where are the crafters and traders, where are the people?"

"That explains Lord Brennan's actions and High Lady Arisa's proclamation," Father Hekbur started, cocking his head toward Mother Sessane who in turn addressed Father Melbroth.

"One of Lord Brennan's captains turned up two days ago and posted a decree for conscription. He gutted Waterdale of every man and woman who could bear arms. This same captain also delivered a scroll to Lady Greymore who left with them the day before yester, leaving behind her servants and a Hand of armsmen to guard her children and manor. That is what has happened. The town is still reeling from the impact. Father Hekbur and I are doing what we can to help. Father Remual is visiting and bound to return to the church at Oling-On-Rake as he has already said."

Father Melbroth nodded his head as if this was no surprise to him. "Tis a sorry state we are in. I can only offer you my prayers, our Lady's strength and some advice."

Melbroth stroked a hand through his long, white beard. "You would do well to organise safe passage south for your parish. As a precaution. The river would be your safest road if you have the boats available. Just in case."

He bid them each goodbye, taking Sessane and Hekbur by hand whilst they offered hope of seeing him on his return journey. Remual folded his hands inside the sleeves of his red robes and bid a perfunctory blessing of 'safe journey'.

"Perhaps we will meet on the road, Father Remual," Melbroth teased.

"Perhaps," Remual said in leery reply, and Melbroth was satisfied, knowing full well they would not.

Back aboard the wagon as they rattled through town and rumbled onto the bridge that spanned the Calda River, Gatzinger couldn't help but comment.

"You lie very well, Father." He grinned.

"For a priest you mean?" Melbroth said.

Gatzinger chuckled. "Oh no, Father, that ain't got nowt to do with it. Every priest is a liar, every man, woman and child of us for that matter. But you, you ne'er so much as blinked an eye. Almost had me believing it and I know the truth."

M'rika joined in from the back of the wagon. "Lying is an aversion to ilfanum. That you humans practise it so casually is abhorrent. There is nothing purer than the truth."

Melbroth swung back to face the ilf, all but the glint of her dark eyes hidden by her cowl. "If I had told the truth things would not have gone so well, especially after those Red Cloaks turned up. If I hadn't lied so convincingly, I fear there would be five dead Red Cloaks and Lord Ironside stood over them with a bloodied sword in hand. Perhaps Mother Sessane, Father Hekbur and Father Remual too. I could not allow that, there has already been too much death, too much bloodshed. You should be thankful I lied so well."

Father Melbroth, swung back, eyes forward and brows furrowed. He was right to lie, knew he was but still, it left him feeling stained and dirty. Ahead, Darion swivelled in his saddle as if he had heard the conversation and perhaps he had, Melbroth thought, for they had not spoken softly.

Their eyes locked for a moment. The big woodsman was gruff and disdained him most of the time, so it was a surprise to Father Melbroth when he received the barest of nods.

Such a small gesture shouldn't have meant anything, Melbroth knew. The man was a heathen, a Watcher for the Order. But somehow it did.

Darion watched the priest stroke his beard like it was a cat or some such. The Father gave the barest hint of a smile and the skin around his eyes wrinkled, as Melbroth inclined his head.

Darion sighed a deep breath then swung his attention back to the road ahead. *Ironside was quick to take a life, Melbroth quick to save, was the priest any worse for following a falsehood or the Order Knight any better for living a truth?* The simple answer was no and yet it set his mind spinning. He thought of M'rika and R'ell and the conversations they had shared. He could see why M'rika was fascinated and understood R'ell's derision at the ambiguity of his kind.

"Trouble is, old girl," Darion said to Bindu who glanced up at him, "an open road leaves too much time for cogitating."

Bindu gave a questioning whine before turning her attention back to the road, parsing for danger. She was tired, her belly empty and her left flank ached where her wound had newly healed. It had been a day since she had sunk her teeth into anything satisfying.

Darion led the company steadily eastwards. The road was more often used than the Westway across the Shearing Flats and the snow on its surface was rutted and more compacted as a result making it easier to travel. Through the course of the day, they passed several small hamlets and a village and found each as subdued and languid as Waterdale had been.

They saw no sign of the Red Cloaks or Father Remual and Darion suspected they wouldn't the next day either. It was not without thought, Father Melbroth had mentioned Pik Isle. Lepers were shunned and a priest of the Red would not remain one should they contract the disease.

That night they took shelter in a farmer's barn, the farmer and his wife grateful for the coin, their two oldest they explained, a son and daughter, had been taken for the war effort just the day before leaving them short-handed. They would lose more livestock than usual over the winter months because of it and the money would help replace them come spring.

Father Melbroth offered them a blessing then treated the farmer for footrot and one of his young sons for a cut on his arm that had turned red and inflamed, his physiker ability, though limited, enough to deal with both. In gratitude, the farmer and his wife provisioned them with cold cuts, smoked meats, cheese and flatbread. Bindu even got a mutton shank much to the disgruntled whining of the farmer's dogs.

The following day they left before first light. Waved farewell to the farmer's wife and two of her young children who were already up and working. They saw no sign of the farmer.

The road east had many smaller paths join it, but it wasn't until they crossed a low hill range and reached the village of Ruonway that they had a choice to make. For Rounway straddled a crossway that led north to Oling-On-Rake, south to Midbow and east. There was no destination specified on the signpost for east but it was the one they took.

"At the end of it is Roadend and Pik Lake," said Castigan.

"Hate the leper colony, gives me the chills," Regus grumbled to himself, only for Ironside to clap him on the back.

"Don't worry, me and Cas will be perfectly safe," he laughed.

"Yeah well, it ain't you or Lady Cas I was worried about," Regus huffed.

They passed farms on either side of the road, fallow fields hidden beneath a smooth unblemished layer of snow, and pastures stained with grey, woolly sheep or clumped herds of cattle. A league outside of Ruonway, daylight fading, they made camp in a wooded copse that bordered the road and with a frozen stream running through it. The night was clouded, and the tri-moons and stars were invisible, plunging them in darkness so dense that the light of their campfire was like a golden bubble, extending only as far as the closest trees. Unconcerned, Bindu roamed, circling the camp before picking up a scent and loping off to hunt.

The next morning, as blackness resolved to grey, they headed east once more. They passed more farms and a few sombre looking travellers headed for Ruonway who stared overmuch. However, the further east they went the more infrequent both holdsteads and road farers became, so that by midday, they saw no more.

The road became narrower and more difficult to navigate, the snow upon it untouched. In places, they only knew the path was there because of the overgrown hedgerows and bushes that encroached upon its edge.

As evening beckoned the company cleared a rise, the five riders ploughing a path for the wagons to follow. From its crest, past a tangled, winter-dusted vista of trees and bushes lay the dark, mirror still waters of Pik Lake. A flat hummock of land rose at its centre, an island, with a dark smudge of trees lining its foreshore.

The other riders barely paused before following the trail downslope, but Darion dismounted to rest his horse and stretch his legs. He stood and stared. Bindu nudged against his thigh, and he brushed a hand over the wolfdog's flank. Pik Isle, he had heard it mentioned only in vague reference in all his years in the Rivers, and then only as a curse or some threat. It looked pretty.

M'Rika and R'ell moved one to each side of him and Darion glanced at them. Bezal sat perched on R'ells shoulder preening her feathers so vigorously it was as if she sulked.

"Bezal does not like that she has to stay away from me when humans are near nor why I need to drape myself in this cloth. She thinks I hide from her," R'ell said, catching Darion's look.

"You share a bond. Did you not explain it to her?" Darion said.

"No more than you could explain to Bindu why you left your homestead. Bindu follows you because you are pack, but she is no Tézani. She is smart like Bezal but cannot talk or comprehend in the way that we do."

"Tézani?"

Removing his hood, R'ell lifted his face to the sky as if basking in its light, the dark-green mottling of his leaf scale subdued. "Tézani. A higher being, like the bears of the Silver Lake or the Hrultha of the Verdant and Stoney Peak." R'ell lowered his head and locked eyes with Darion. "Like you humans, even the urakakule."

"There is nothing 'higher being' about those savages." Father Melbroth called from behind. "They were sent by the One to test our faith, challenge our resolve. To make us stronger and more united in our belief."

M'rika faced the priest, her hands calmly lowering her cowl and letting it settle about her shoulders. Her all-brown eyes, chestnut-dark, considered the priest.

"Your arrogance is only outdone by your ignorance, Father Melbroth. Humanity holds no divine right. For Tézani, you sit no higher nor lower than urakakule no matter what you might tell yourselves."

Father Melbroth bristled but when he spoke his voice was calm. "The Lady Nihmrodel guides me to the One. Forgive me M'rika, but it is not the ilfanum the urak murder and pillage. So, as much as you intrigue me, I will not be questioned on my beliefs or in my god by the likes of you or your kind."

M'rika's arm snapped up, so fast it made both humans startle. At the edge of his vision, Darion saw R'ell settle back on his heels unaware until that moment that the ilf had been about to move. It was not hard to sense the outrage emitting from the umphathi.

"Such potential," M'rika said. "Yet, your minds are like a lake sponge, absorbing and retaining whatever is first to fill it. Humanity has been here but a blink of time, so young and yet so filled with absolute superiority. If you do not learn, do not open yourselves to the world around you, do not temper your self-indulgence then humans will become nothing but dust in the wind. Forgotten and worthless. I tell you this not in threat or cruelty, but in the hope that you will challenge yourselves to see more than you are shown and hear more than you are told."

Melbroth tugged on his beard. "Nihmrodel the Pure shows me what my god needs me to see and know. The White Lady has my heart and my faith and it will not be swayed by you or any other."

Already weary of the White Priest and his dogma, Darion pointed. "Smoke. There must be buildings on the lakeshore." Remounting, he nudged his horse after the others who had broken the path downslope, the road now nothing more than a snow-filled track. After a moment he heard the laboured motion of the wagons and the snorting exertions of the horses. They would need a good day's rest in a dry stall, perhaps they would find it below.

Chapter 35: One Last Hunt

Roadend, Pik Lake, Cumbrenan

There were half a dozen box-like buildings in Roadend, all rustic and basic, the wooden beams of their construction weathered and stained, and their patchwork roofs capped with snow.

A man, swaddled in furs and wearing otter skin boots, stood waiting in its centre. He lent upon a knotted and gnarled, whitewood staff with two big hounds sitting like gargoyles to either side of him. Flakes had started to fall from the sky and collected like dewdrops in his lank, grey hair and straggle of beard.

"Didn't 'spect no visitors this side of the Drift," he called, the words lisping and lopsided. "If ya here for trouble then ya can get. Turn round, take it with ya."

The riders pulled their horses to a stop and two of them lowered their hoods.

"Thought the scurve would have taken you by now, Greybeard. Been a while." The horseman's face was sharp-edged and framed by black ringlets of hair.

"Ya seem familiar. Up here." Greybeard lifted a hand and tapped an index finger against his temple. "But fer ma life I can't recall ya. Dogs ain't gone fer yer so I guess ya better come in. I ain't got no food fer ya mind. I ain't no charity so don't be 'spectin none."

Greybeard shuffled around and held his hand out towards the largest building which had wide, double doors set in its front. With a slow twist of his hand and pull of his arm, the doors levered open with a scrape and groan, sweeping the snow on the ground to the side as if it was nothing.

"Put ya horses inside and park ya wains. I'll be in there when ya done." Greybeard pointed out the building closest to the lake, a dull light bleeding from the edges of its shuttered windows and door. With a scowl, he thumbed his nose at the newcomers then shuffled towards the house only to stop after a few steps.

Greybeard tilted his head. Lying in the snow, beside an impressively large man on a horse, was a wolf whose dull amber eyes studied him closely. With a sigh, his eyes rolled until only their whites showed. His eyelids fluttered and after a moment he blinked.

"She's spent." Greybeard turned back to his house and resumed his shambling walk before calling over his shoulder. "Best bring 'er when ya come inside."

* * *

The strangers took a while, so long in fact that Greybeard was wondering if he had imagined them. Only the dogs' unwavering stare at the door convinced him he had not. The pair missed nothing. It was they who had alerted him to the outsiders impending trespass.

Rocking forward to the edge of his chair, he stirred the pot on the fire. He had added to it, habit more than desire, the old codes ingrained so deep that they just were, despite not remembering the reason for them.

The crunch of feet, many of them. Uncomfortable with sitting, Greybeard rose and reached for his staff which stood, propped against the wall. Its familiar smoothness fit his hand, its touch concentrating his clouded mind.

A perfunctory knock, then the latch moved, and the door swung wide. Greybeard's grip tightened on his staff, the alluring tingle of magics exciting fingers and hand and running up his forearm. He remembered them then, the outsiders. The man with the wolf and the two who were not what they seemed.

"May we enter."

The voice was known to Greybeard but not the name it belonged to. He tsked, "Get in. Get out. One or t'other just shut the door. Ya, letting the heat out."

They filed in one at a time, even the two, hiding beneath their priest robes, but he had seen them earlier. Most new memories left him but some stayed longer than others. Last in was the big man, head inclining to clear the door lintel. On his heels came the wolf.

She was magnificent, standing as tall as his hip. As Greybeard observed her though a sadness stole upon him. There was a languid arch to her back and a torpid pain in her eyes.

"I've only three chairs but there are logs fer the fire ya can upend and perch on, or sit on the floor, don't care either way." His words came out slurred, and a drip of saliva drooled from the corner of his mouth into his beard. Greybeard wiped his sleeve at it as he shuffled to the tall stand next to the kitchen table and retrieved a bowl. He hobbled back to the fire and stirred the cookpot before ladling the stew it contained into the bowl.

Knees creaking, he set the bowl down near the fire before grunting upright again. He glowered at the big man. "Fer ya wolf."

He didn't bother asking the man for the wolf's name or his own. Knew he would forget them. Nothing stuck anymore. Greybeard ambled to his chair and eased himself back down, his two hounds, one on each side, eying the bounty on the floor. Neither so much as whined in complaint at the teasing smell or the bowl's enticing nearness.

"Rest of ya help yourselves," Greybeard waggled a vague hand towards the fire, watching as the big man led the wolf to the bowl. His beard rumpled, pleased when the wolf lapped at the stew.

"Do you not recall me?" said the man with black ringlet hair and angular features. His eyes were green and overly intense for Greybeard's liking, but some vague intuition told him that he knew this man, that he was, if not a friend, then friendly.

"My memory is not what it once was," Greybeard muttered.

"I am Ironside and that is Castigan, Lyra." The man indicated the woman beside him. "You knew us both once, do you not remember at all?"

Greybeard's teeth gritted, *did the man not hear him?* "I told you, my memory's NOT what it was."

His raised voice drew a slow rumble from the dogs, and he dropped a hand to their ruffs to quiet them.

"Where is Marius, your son? Is he about?" Ironside persisted.

Greybeard closed his eyes and dipped his chin and murmured to himself over and over again wracking his brain. Like a bubble of trapped air rising from deep water, it came to him. "Marius, yes Marius. My son. He is not here. Gone."

"Gone? Gone where?" The man's tone was impatient, "Will he be back?"

"He left today. Or was it yesterday," Greybeard offered. "He'll return tomorrow or the next day I expect, or another day, maybe." He could see the man, whose name he had already forgotten, getting frustrated.

The woman, whose close-cropped hair shone red-gold like a setting sun, rested a hand on the man's shoulder as Greybeard had done his dogs. "Leave him be Iron. He doesn't remember. We will wait a day or two and hope that Marius returns."

Greybeard did not eat. It might be he had eaten already, he couldn't recall, but he was not hungry so he decided he must have. He watched the outsiders avail themselves, emptying the cookpot, spooning in the lumpy broth as if they'd not had a hot meal in a ten-day.

He growled when two of the men gathered the bowls and spoons and cookpot and made to leave. "You're stealing my things." At his accusation his dogs rose, hackles up, their low-throated rumble silencing the room.

"They'll bring them back," assured an older man in white robes.

A priest. Greybeard settled, mollified. *There were priests on the island, he must be one of those.* He glanced about the room at all the people staring at him and felt suddenly overwhelmed. *What are they all doing here? Who are they?*

"Out. Get out, all of you, out. This is my home. My house. Get."

This time the dogs snarled and snapped, baring their teeth. The old wolf basking by the fire responded in kind and the atmosphere thrummed with tension.

Then, much to Greybeard's bewilderment, his dogs stopped their agitation, whimpered then sat, their large frames shivering with nervous energy. Another of the white-robes knelt before them, talking in soft tones in words Greybeard did not understand.

Greybeard struck his head with his palm, again and again. *There was something to remember about this white-robe and the other one but what was it?* He felt a hand on his shoulder and with it, a calmness settled upon him. The other white-robe knelt before him lowering their cowl and his breath caught. A feeling of wonderment overcame him. *Could it be?*

"My name is M'rika Dul Da'Mari, Visok and Kraal of the Rohelinewaald. You offered me food and shelter and I returned only silence, forgive me, Greybeard, for my lack of manners. I see that you are ill, that your mind is losing its path. That cannot be helped but I can give you respite for a short while if you would accept it?"

Greybeard had no words; his mouth was wet with saliva as it often was and he chomped his lips to keep the spittle in. He gave a nod and the smooth, leaf-scaled, feminine and symmetrically pleasing creature before him lifted her hands to his temples. He gazed into eyes as deep as the heavens that seemed to enlarge and grow until he was lost in their depths.

Then he remembered no more.

* * *

Greybeard awoke the next day to a call. A name. Someone was shouting. He levered himself slowly upright.

"BINDU."

It was not Marius. His son spoke in a whisper if he spoke at all. No, a stranger was here. He had a vague recollection from the night before, but it could just as easily be a memory from an after-dream.

His mouth was unusually dry and he took a drink from the cup on the nightstand. He had no memory of going to bed or how he got there but then he often didn't these days. As the cold water refreshed his mouth and slid down his throat he felt better than usual, his mind clearer.

The hearth fire had burnt to embers and the room was cold encouraging Greybeard to dress quickly. Pleasingly, his fingers did not fumble at the buttons or ties as they usually did.

"BINDU."

The dogs, curled by the dwindling heat of the fire, roused themselves as Greybeard stood and hobbled towards them. He threw a faggot on the dying flames sending a storm of glowing ash up the chimney. By the door, he pulled on his otterskin boots and shrugged into his thick coat. Grabbing his staff, he pulled the door wide and stepped outside, the dogs crowding around his legs as he did.

Snow fell from the sky in thick flakes, dancing like starlings whenever the wind gusted.

"Have you seen Bindu, my wolfdog?"

Greybeard turned. A large man, tall and broad stood at the corner of the house. His black hair and beard were dusted with snow.

"You showed kindness to her last night. Maybe you let her in? To share your fire?"

Greybeard could hear the hope in the man's voice and read the concern in his steel-grey eyes.

"Do we know each other?" Greybeard asked.

"We met last night. I'm Darion." The man raised an arm and tapped his chest.

"Agh." Greybeard puffed a breath and scratched his head. He remembered something about a wolf and other, stranger things. Mythical creatures, from a dream.

No sooner had Greybeard thought it than those self-same dryads, the tree spirits of his dreams appeared from the barn. Ilfanum. They walked toward him, and their every movement was lithe and graceful. The green mottling of their skin appeared vibrant against the snowy surroundings, their canted eyes seemingly black.

"Good morn, Greybeard," said the female, who bowed to him before turning to the man. "Darion, Bindu is not in any of the buildings. We should look for her tracks. Even with this snow, we should find signs of her."

The man called Darion spun without a word, head turning as if judging the lay of the land. Decided, he took several steps to the north but stopped at the flutter of descending wing beats.

Greybeard gaped as a large raven swooped down and alighted upon the wide shoulder of the male ilf. It kraaw'ed loudly and bobbed its head and the ilf spoke.

"Bindu is to the north by a fallen oak and a place of stones. Crows gather."

"Fallen oak, fallen oak…" Greybeard muttered, scratching at his bearded chin. "I know this place of stones. Come."

Greybeard shuffled off but the man, Darion, would not wait and ran ahead. Then the raven, with long, heavy beats of its wings, rose into the sky as if to show the way.

Lifting his feet, Greybeard increased his pace, feeling more energised than he could remember. He expected the mystical creatures by his side to run after Darion, but they did not. Content it seemed to walk in silence beside him.

It took Greybeard thirty minutes through drifting snow to cover the quarter league to the standing stones. By then his skin was biting with cold. His lungs burnt and his legs ached in a way that he had all but forgotten. It was invigorating.

The wolf was laid so still, Greybeard knew instantly she was dead.

The man, Darion, sat with his back to the fallen oak and he'd gathered the wolf to cradle in his lap, stroking the snow from her face and ears, his frozen tears like crystals beneath his eyes.

Blood caked the old wolf's snout and matted her side where she had been gored. A trail of ichor in the snow led past the standing stones and Greybeard followed it, whistling for his dogs to come.

Greybeard didn't go far before he found the source. A stag lay with its throat ripped and torn. His dogs gathered close, sniffing and licking at the wound. "Leave it be." He growled. "We'll come back fer it later with the sled."

Breath steaming, Greybeard made his way back past the standing stones to Darion who hadn't moved, still sitting with the wolf in his lap, eyes distant. Bizarrely, the ilfanum stood some distance away facing the opposite direction as if they could not bring themselves to look.

Greybeard took stock of things, *a man can't sit here all day. He'll freeze or cause hisself an injury.* He looked at the wolf and the dark, matted colouration of her fur and a memory, a precious impossible memory, surfaced from before. He couldn't recall when, but he had sensed inside this wolf the blackness of a canker, small but growing. He rubbed a hand over his mouth and beard then sniffed.

"Old wolf was dyin'. Reckon she knowed it too. The way I figure it the girl came for one last hunt. Died on her terms doing what she wanted, steada curled on a blanket like a dog."

Darion blinked and looked up at him with red-rimmed eyes.

"Bagged herself a stag. A fourteen-pointer," Greybeard said.

"Greybeard."

At his name call, he turned and saw the female ilf beckoning him. He gave a final glance at the man and his wolf. "Don't sit too long or I'll have two ta burn."

* * *

Greybeard felt the faintest of magics play across his aura. It manifested as a prickling sensation that stood up the hairs on his arms as if a cold chill had brushed over him.

With unerring, irrevocability, his eyes dragged to the north where he had left Darion, his wolf and the ilfanum. A slither of white smoke curled above the trees, barely visible through the falling snow but clear enough against the slate sky if one knew where to look. The smoke thickened and twisted in the wind, fraying into white threads before breaking apart.

Greybeard scowled. He felt almost whole again, more himself, more human. But it was as if he'd awoken from a deep sleep only to find that years had passed. Years he had no recollection of. It made the man's sorrow for his wolf all the deeper and more poignant as if all those lost years had condensed into this single day.

Darion, that he remembered the man's name and everything else since he'd awoken that morning was… glorious. Greybeard thought about the words he'd spoken to Darion and felt the truth in them. That the old wolf had taken herself for one last hunt and it pleased Greybeard to think that she had died in such a way.

A glumness settled over him and Greybeard knew it wasn't for the wolf's death. Magnificent though she was, he didn't know her, and it had been her time. No, this melancholy was for himself, for the cognizance that had returned to him was not permanent. Even now an insipid haze pressed inward, picking at the edges of his awareness, inexorable, waiting to consume him. To douse his mind once again in that occluding fog and trap him, returning him to his previous, ghost-like existence.

Once I have seen Marius again, I think that I, like the wolf, will take my last hunt. He swore it to himself and knew in his soul it was right. The wolf had shown the way and a final walk to the standing stones seemed only proper. It was as good a place as any for a final rest.

The cold stung his eyes and Greybeard blinked them warm and stared around the yard. Lyra Castigan was talking with Ansel by the barn. He recalled her fondly from years before when he had been a little younger and a lot more foolish. Apart from her hair, she looked just the same. He snorted, *hah, barking up the wrong tree there you old fox.*

The outsiders had taken the building next to his for their shelter and Greybeard's attention was drawn to it when its door opened. Ironside exited with Regus and another man he did not know in tow. He watched the three stroll towards the barn and Lyra, only to stop abruptly when Gatzinger appeared.

Greybeard could tell from the briskness of the man's walk and the look on his face that Gatzinger had news. Given that he'd been sent to watch the lake it wasn't hard to extrapolate that a boat was coming. Greybeard's heart began to beat a little harder, *Marius.*

Stomping his feet to get the blood going, Greybeard headed for the jetty, the two dogs bounding at his heels. He had been about to hitch them both to a sled to recover the wolf's stag but that would have to wait.

The outsiders soon joined him, and Greybeard knew who they were now, remembered them clearly. The Order were no strangers to this place, but it had never been for altruistic reasons that they came here, more for the fear that the Sanctuary engendered and the isolation it insured. It wasn't any different now just because they had a pair of ilfanum with them.

Swirling snow shrouded the lake. The boat must have been close by the time Gatzinger spotted it for it was almost at the jetty when they arrived.

Greybeard spied Marius on the tiller, identifiable by his comportment but more particularly that stupid looking fur hat he insisted on wearing that covered his head down to his neck. His son dropped the sail with perfect precision and lent on the rudder with practised ease.

The boat's bow swung around bleeding speed until it luffed and bumped against the jetty. Jumping ashore, Marius hitched the stern rope to a wooden post and then moved to the bow to do the same. As Greybeard knew he would, his son ignored the people gathered on the foreshore, instead, jumping back aboard to secure the sail and tidy the boat. He grabbed two roped bales and lifted them one at a time onto the jetty side.

"Regus, Gatz, lend the man a hand," Ironside said.

The two men hesitated only a moment before clomping past Greybeard. It might have been the wooden jetty was slippy but Greybeard sensed a carefulness in their walk. He watched the two talk to Marius before crouching and looping a bale each to their backs before marching with somewhat more purpose back past Greybeard and towards the tiny settlement.

"Father," Marius stood before him, his voice a nasal whisper that battled the wind. As was his want, his son's face was wrapped in strips of cloth so that only his eyes could be discerned with a break in the weave for his nostrils and mouth. "You should not be about in this foul weather. Come. I recognise one of our guests already but let us save pleasantries for inside where it is warm."

His son stuck an arm through his and steered him around, *like that damn boat of his*, Greybeard thought petulantly.

"I'm not an invalid, Marius." Greybeard yanked his arm free "At least not today. Today, my mind is my own."

It pleased Greybeard to see his son's eyes go wide in surprise. A sudden emotion overcame him, and Greybeard clamped his arms around and embraced his boy, felt Marius go rigid before slowly, the hug was returned.

"Father?" Marius whispered.

His son's breath brushed against his face and Greybeard forced himself not to recoil at its sweetness. He sniffed and broke the clinch.

"You are right. It's foolish to be outside. It's cold enough to freeze the antlers off a moose."

Greybeard led them back to Roadend, where they gathered in his house once again. He stoked the fire until it was roaring and lifted the pot he had prepared earlier over the flames, shooing Ansel away when he offered to help. "Do this with nought but my own two hands, every day. Don't need no outsider gettin' in me way."

"Marius." Ironside's tone was enough to cause Greybeard to turn and look. His son was by the door, disrobing still. He'd already removed his coat and that tomfool hat of his and was peeling off undergarments until he appeared half the size he was before.

"Marius. We need your boat." Ironside was abrupt and to the point. "And you of course."

Greybeard watched his son turn, hair all mussed and sticking up, the linen wraps still in place around his face. When he spoke it was in that same nasal whisper.

"Of course. Why else do you ever come here? But not today because it is late and not tomorrow because I am tired. The cold weather." Marius touched a hand to his cheek and then body in several places but did not elaborate any further.

"That's not acceptable," Ironside replied. "Time is critical."

Marius moved through the room toward the fire, the outsiders parting for him like a school of fish would a garpike, then settled with a sigh into his chair. He gave no reply, scratching one of the dogs between the ears instead.

Greybeard, knowing the real reason for his son's unspoken reluctance, turned to him. "You will take them tomorrow, my son, wherever it is that they wish to go. I will be alright," Greybeard assured, "You see, Ironside and Lyra have brought ilf who have cleared the fog from my mind."

"I see no ilf, father," Marius croaked. "No one has seen any ilf, they are figments, imaginings."

It stung Greybeard, his son's tone was that of an intolerant father to a disruptive child. It was Ironside that spoke up for him.

"It is true. The ilfanum are out with a companion holding vigil or some such nonsense. For a dog, if you can believe that. They will be here soon. Then you will see for yourself."

"So you say." Marius sighed. "I am cold and hungry. It is better to ask a man a thing when he is warm and fed. Until I am both I will make no judgement, despite what father says."

Leaning forward, closer to the flames, Marius picked at the knot of linen tied at his throat, then slowly, like peeling the skin from an apple with a paring knife, he unwrapped the bandages from his neck and face, the last few circuits snagging and sticky with fluid.

To Greybeard this was not unusual but the outsiders, he saw, were watching with morbid fascination as his son's face was slowly uncovered. Greybeard huffed at them, then lost his breath. The memory of his son was vague, years old at best. What was revealed was not the face he last remembered.

A wooden mimicry of a nose was strapped in place of the original. Like bruised fruit, lesions and pustules cratered his son's neck and face and his beard was piebald for no hair would grow where there was a sore.

"I don't feel the pain," Marius told the room. "And I don't want your pity."

* * *

The next morning, Greybeard stood outside in deliberation. Yestereve had been an uncomfortable one all told, even for himself. His son's leprosy had progressed to a startling degree and it shocked him. Even the White Father, Melbroth, had been perturbed by it. Only the Order Knights seemed unconcerned with his disease and they spoke with Marius long into the evening.

Darion and the ilfanum had returned just before nightfall. The woodsman though had been quiet and lost in his thoughts and retired before they had eaten. That the ilfanum had left with him, fascinated Greybeard, for there was some tie, some bind they shared that he longed to understand.

Greybeard lifted his face to the sun. The clouds had broken overnight, and the soft heat was pleasant against his skin. If he was honest with himself, he'd half expected to wake in the shadow world, reactive and responsive but unable to retain any thought or memory past an hour or two. To become once again an automaton that existed. Feeding, watering, doing what instinct and repetition dictated he do. It kept him alive but gave no substance to life, no meaning. Blessedly, he had not and his memory seemed sound.

A deal had been struck and the boat was being packed. Marius had agreed to take the Order and the ilfanum around Pik Lake and down the River Esta which flowed into the Rake. The Rake, in turn, would take them to the coast where its mouth emptied into the Sea of Prospero. A journey of two to three days, it would be at least five before Marius would return.

Plenty of time, thought Greybeard. He ran a hand through lank hair that was thinner than he remembered and wished he had worn a cap for it was cold and he'd been stood too long watching the frenzy of preparations.

It had been agreed that the wagons and the horses would remain at Roadend. Marius had negotiated a stiff price for their care until the spring. The coin would go to the Sanctuary on Pik Isle, who would provide feed for the horses. After deducting the cost from the price, they would have ample left to place an order with the priests at the Halfway for all manner of goods the Sanctuary needed but could not make themselves.

Marius was striding towards him. *No doubt some last-minute instruction stating the bloody obvious,* Greybeard cursed but then smiled. His son had wrapped fresh bandages around his face and was dressed once more in his furs. *Looks like a giant muerrat in that ridiculous hat,* thought Greybeard.

"I'll be back soon as I can, father." Marius leant in close to be heard, his words like a hiss of steam. Greybeard got another waft of sweetness. "I'll be stopping briefly at the Sanctuary to speak with Father Molenberg and give him the coin. I'll ask him to send Maxi and Jashena with the feed for the horses. They'll stay until I return."

"I'm not a child, Marius. I can feed a few damn horses and take care of myself. It's not like you don't leave me all the time."

"Only fer a day, two at the most. This time I'll be gone five maybe six. Sometimes you forget to eat," Marius said.

Greybeard scowled. "Told you. I'm better now."

"Maybe so," Marius said somewhat dubiously, "But would a bit of company be so bad? I was thinking they might stay over the winter. Nine horses is a lot of shit to shovel and you aren't any younger and I could use the help. Now, dress warm and by that I mean wear a hat, you're shivering. You want mine?"

"By all that's holy I do not. Keep that monstrosity, I'll wear my own."

Marius stared at him unmoved and Greybeard cussed. "I will damn it."

Greybeard was not one for goodbyes and neither was Marius but this time, as his son went to turn away, he reached a hand out to stop him. "I've always been proud of you. A man couldn't ask for a better son, Marius. Take care and… goodbye."

Marius' eyes squinted in concern. "Not like you ta be so maudlin, Da. Don't worry about me, I'll be back before you know it. It'll be good to talk like we used to do. I've missed our chats."

Greybeard watched Marius stride away, his heart heavy with the burden of what he must do, his thoughts bleak.

"I wanted to thank you before I go. For your words."

Startled, Greybeard spun. Darion stood several paces from him, the two ilfanum silent bodyguards behind.

"Eh?" said Greybeard.

"Yesterday," Darion said. "By the standing stones. The words you said about Bindu, the truth of them touched me. Thank you for them."

The big man dipped his shoulder and head before walking past, the ilfanum followed but M'rika paused and leaned in close. Her eyes studied his face to the point that Greybeard was starting to feel uncomfortable. Her words when she spoke were quiet and he had to strain to hear them.

"This respite will not last, and I can do no more for you."

Greybeard nodded in understanding, "Thank you. That you have given me this time has been priceless."

"Your aura is calm. I sense in you a peace," M'rika said. "The kind that comes from a truth understood or a difficult choice made. Whatever your intent, plan well and use your time wisely for I cannot say how much of it you will have."

Greybeard felt an overpowering sense of gratitude, not a feeling he was all that familiar with, but even that could not stymie his reawoken curiosity.

"You have given me so much Lady Ilf that I feel ashamed to ask this thing, but my meddlesome mind needs to know it."

M'rika looked intrigued. "To ask costs nothing."

Greybeard twisted his gaze to the burly woodsman. "Darion. There is a bond that you share I do not understand. If you can excuse the vagaries of an old man, I desire to know what."

The ilf tilted her head in thought. "Your enquiry is one with no easy answer. A debt is owed, he to I, and I to he, but it goes deeper than that. Let me say simply that circumstance and a shared ordeal played their part. The rest I am still trying to understand myself."

M'rika winked and it was so incongruously human that it startled him. By the time Greybeard thought to pry some more the ilf was gone.

He wandered to the jetty and by the time he reached it everyone had boarded. Rutigard cast off the fore line and Marius the aft. The wind was favourable from the west and Marius raised the lone sail which snapped and filled.

Greybeard raised a hand as they called out farewell, then the boat was before the wind and speeding away, Marius giving a last look back.

The dogs whined, sensing his mood.

"Come on, let's get you fed."

The walk back to the house was a slow one, for Greybeard dawdled, mulling things over in his mind. Father Charl Molenberg was an old friend and the nominal leader of the Sanctuary on Pik Isle. He was certain that once Marius asked Charl for help the priest of Ankor would be quick to act. Even before his mind grew cloudy and his illness had taken hold, Charl had been ever after him to move to the Sanctuary.

It went without saying he had refused, Greybeard had nothing against lepers, how could he? But it was the last place he wanted to die. That thought brought him neatly back around to his immediate problem. Maxi and Jashena could be here by this afternoon. Greybeard sniffed and a drool of spittle leaked from his mouth, he wiped at it without thought, his mind occupied by his dilemma.

Greybeard had hoped for a few days grace. To reminisce, write a letter or two. Prepare himself. *Maybe it's for the best, fortuitous,* Greybeard thought, *that M'rika set his mind straight and Marius forced matters to an earlier conclusion. You were ever one for procrastinating.*

Back at the house, Greybeard raked the fire before placing another log on the stuttering flames. He fed the dogs and left them inside before leaving to check on the horses.

After that, like the wolf, it will be time.

* * *

The old man, swaddled in furs stood in his otter skin boots, waiting. The sun was in the west painting long shadows on the ground. He lent upon a knotted and gnarled, whitewood staff. From inside somewhere dogs barked, calling to be let out. He ignored them.

"Didn't 'spect no visitors this side of the Drift," he called, the words lisping and lopsided. "If ya here for trouble then ya can get. Turn round, take it with ya."

"Hello Greybeard, it's me Jashena, and you remember Maxi?" said the woman. She walked with a limp and when she removed her mittens to brush at a loose lock of hair, two of her fingers were shorn down to the last knuckle.

"Charl sent us and Marius, and we saw a wonder. Ilf, two of them. Don't you remember them?"

Greybeard shuddered, her words triggered something inside, a vague memory, *he had to do something, go somewhere, what was it?* He slapped at his forehead with his palm, again and again, and muttered to himself.

Jashena limped up and placed her hands on Greybeard's shoulders to calm him and tilted her head to listen.

"What is he saying?" Maxi asked.

"He's babbling, repeating the same thing over and over." Jashena turned to Maxi as he moved nearer.

"One last hunt."

Chapter 36: A Road Hard Travelled

It began in Rivercross as a journey of hope.

On the fields of Dunning, they answered her call and many more besides came to glimpse her. She sat upon a white steed atop the rise she had spoken from the day before, where her voice had reached out and touched every one of them.

Lady White Crow. The name was whispered. A young girl, resplendent in a cloak of purest white who spoke with the voice of an angel. Some believed her a messenger, sent by our Lady Nihmrodel to guide them to safety, but whilst most did not, still they were drawn to her.

I confess that the Church of Our Lady played no small part in creating this imagery. It was not so much a lie but more a clouded portrayal, one we sought to use for good. For, in these darkest of days words are not always enough to repair broken faith and lost hope. Sometimes a manifestation of both is needed, and what better than a noble girl, pure of heart as yet untarnished by the Game of Lords?

We were none of us to know it would lead us where it did.

Mother Erwain Marr, priest of Our Lady, Nihmrodel the White (1017c 4A)

Camfyr Downs, The Rivers

It was a difficult journey, a painfully slow ordeal that was not yet over. The Forgotten, as they had come to be known, were six days out from Rivercross, a straggled column of humanity that stretched over two leagues along the King's highway, and they had yet to reach Lakeside.

Those first two days, the road had taken them east past cultivated land, through farms and holdsteads and abandoned villages before swinging south again to rejoin and follow the shoreline of the Emerald Lake.

Beneath its shroud of snow, the countryside had looked pristine and pure, ice crystals glittering refracted light from a winter sun suspended in a sky whose azure opus was marred only by an occasional high cloud.

Those daylight vistas though were as nothing compared to the panoply of stars and clouded nebula that patinated the night skies. Where Ankor's reverent orb gazed down upon them and Nihmrodel peeked out from behind her brother's corona, before racing him to the horizon.

However, as beautiful as it was the heavens remained mostly unobserved, for its majesty was barbed. With clear skies, the temperature plummeted and few of the Forgotten looked up to marvel at it. Instead, they gathered in barns and farmsteads and spread through villages appropriating anything with a roof. Most, less fortunate, camped upon the roadside wherever they could find shelter, huddling together for warmth beneath makeshift awnings.

Winter, though, claimed its due and that first morning, scores did not rise to see its new dawn. It caused much delay, for the living had not the fuel to build pyres for the dead and so release their souls. The priests of Ankor and Nihmrodel, realising this, sent wagons back to gather the fallen and ordered a great fire built at Hetting-on-Lake, the southernmost village they had yet passed. It was there they transported the dead and sent them onwards to One's embrace.

Thereafter, the priests kept a hand of wagons at the rear of the procession and more at its centre so that each morning they could gather the dead along the way with least delay.

The cruel season though was not done with them and on the third day, the winds changed from the south bringing warmer air and thunderous clouds with it. The tormented skies roiled and the wind whipped, a slurry of rain and snow bursting overhead as the storm struck. It turned the world grey and the road into a river of sludge.

The exodus of the Forgotten was reduced to a stuttering crawl, the footing treacherous and each step a wearying plod into a headwind of driving sleet. Many of them despaired but it seemed that just as spirits reached their lowest point, through the brume would appear the Lady White Crow. Riding back along the roadside she offered encouragement and hope to all. Wherever she went, morale lifted and for those that struggled most or fell, she ordered them to the wagons until they could carry no more.

Blessedly, on the fourth day, the storm broke and the clouds scattered. The winds swung again from the north bringing the promise of a new weather front as slate-grey clouds gathered like a rolled-up blanket on the horizon.

On the fifth day a cavalry, two thousand strong, overtook the Forgotten, forcing them to the verge as they passed. At their head rode a young Lord, heroic in burnished armour who looked neither left nor right at the dispossessed.

An old warrior, long retired, called out. "Peacock! The urak lie north not south." But, other than a few sullen glares from the brown clad riders, he was ignored.

On the sixth day, the troubled sky gave up its bounty and snow fell once again, large flakes that gusted in the wind and drifted the road and hedgerows. Progress slowed once more and the Forgotten were forced to find shelter earlier than they would have liked.

* * *

Sitting inside the women's tent, unmindful of the odour of warm bodies and damp clothes and trying not to worry about their slow progress, sat Lord Amos Duncan, a mug of black cha warming his hands. What was ordinarily a three-day journey had turned into a marathon of six but at least they should see Lakeside this next day.

Annabelle came and sat next to him and yawned before leaning her head against his side. Amos slipped an arm around her thin shoulders and she snuggled against him.

"You're tired, little one. You should go to your covers and get some sleep."

"Just a little longer," Annabelle pleaded.

He saw in her hands that she played with a stone, rolling it from one to the other. It was heated, a neat trick by Mercy to keep the chill at bay, at least a little. His sister had many uses.

"Okay, but if you fall asleep and dribble on my sleeve again, I'll dangle you by your feet from the nearest tree and leave you for the wolves."

Annabelle giggled but Mercy, overhearing, frowned from her seat. "You do not threaten children so, Amos. Mother would be horrified if she heard."

"Mother's ire. A fate worse than wolves. You would tell?" Amos winked at Annabelle. "Tis a pity, for the beasts must eat. Still, your scrawny sacka bones would not be enough to feed a wolf pup, let alone a wolf."

"I would too," Annabelle squealed.

"You've excited the girl. She'll not go to her bed now and we have matters of import to discuss," Mercy admonished.

"Belle is my chief advisor. What can I say?" Amos grinned, enjoying the acerbic look on Mercy's face all too much.

"I'm tired Amos and my bones ache. I've no time for foolery," Mercy snapped. "This is not like you."

Smiling at the interplay, a wearied Constance Bouchemeax interjected. "We're all tired. But we at least have been riding. All those walking must be exhausted and for them, Lakeside cannot come soon enough. It troubles me."

"Lakeside?" Mercy asked.

"Yes." Constance frowned in concentration. "Before it was a place to get to, but now I wonder what we might find there. Lord Idris said people were being held in camps and if urak have already crossed the Plago then Lakeside is hardly safe."

"Let's see what we shall find. No point worrying about things we don't know or can't change," Amos said.

Constance shook her head. "How can I not? Father Larson says the supplies are almost gone. How can I take the people further south if I can't feed them? And what of Lord Aric? Why did he lead two thousand of his Burning Cross south? Will they be at Lakeside? And will he help us if we ask him to?"

Amos gave a discerning look, his shadowed eyes appearing almost black in the dim light of the tent. "For one so young that is very astute, Conn, or should I call you Lady White Crow?"

"I'll put rocks in your boots if you do," Constance replied. She pulled a face at him, but Amos only raised his chin and looked down his nose. "What? I have turned twelve now. I have ears and I listen. To Lord Idris and at the High Lord's Council. Besides, I talked with Mal… Captain Kronke about it."

Mercy chuckled. "Kronke? Can that bear even read?"

"The Captain might appear gruff but I assure you he is quite perceptive," Constance declared somewhat haughtily. "I find no fault in his advice and what matters if he can read or not? If he can't then it is through no fault other than the circumstance of birth and lack of opportunity. I assure you his brain is fully functional, Lady Mercy."

The scar on Mercy's face creased. "It says well that you stand up for him, Conn. Each and every one of them in fact, even that shady looking fellow with one eye. For they are yours and if they are to stand by you and give you everything, including their lives then they need to feel that loyalty returned."

"The one-eyed man is Pieterzon... 'Zon' they call him. Names are easy to remember when you have only five to recall." Constance sighed. "I admit though, he does scare me a little. There is devilment in him. A taint in his eye that I do not trust."

Her shoulders sagged. "I'm still getting to know them. Sergeant Crawley is a little rough around the edges, but Mal assures me she is 'solid' whatever that means."

"It has only been days," Amos said. "Duty will hold them to you but loyalty takes time to come by. It will come though, of that I have no doubt."

At Amos's side, Belle yawned and rubbed at her eyes and Constance smiled at her friend before stifling a yawn of her own. It did not go unnoticed.

"To bed, my Lady." Junip Jorgstein said. "We will find what we will find in Lakeside. Ruminating about it will not help and you need your rest. Each day you cover four times as much ground as anyone else, riding up and down as you do. What would the Forgotten think tomorrow if you were to fall off your horse fast asleep?"

"Do not call them that, Junip, please." Constance pleaded. "I dislike the name as much as I do Lady White Crow."

A grunt of sucked-in breath sounded, loud enough that all in the tent heard it. An amused Amos twisted and gently gathered a sleeping Belle up in his arms and carried her to her bedroll. He laid her in it then unlaced her boots and removed them before tucking her in and laying her cloak over the top. He stroked her unruly mop of brown hair back and kissed her forehead before getting to his feet. When he turned around everyone was looking at him.

"What?" They looked amused and Amos felt his colour rising.

"Nothing, brother," Mercy said.

"You're staring. All of you," Amos accused.

Mercy grinned. "We're just wondering if you would tuck us all in before you go. Mayhap bestow a kiss upon our brows to speed our sweet dreams?"

"Droll, and beneath you sister. I wished to talk about Lord Aric and his Burning Cross, but I think it can wait for the morrow." Amos stomped from the tent their laughing eyes burning his back.

* * *

Dawn of the seventh day was clear. The clouds had fled south in the night leaving a refreshed carpet of white over the landscape. Amos dressed the black stallion, adjusting the stirrup leather whilst watching over the saddle-back the nearby Red Cloaks as they mounted and formed up.

There were two-score and ten of them and they were led by two priests of Kildare. They'd kept to themselves mostly. On the few occasions any did engage, it was only with their brothers and sisters of Ankor and Nihmrodel.

Their purpose was singular it seemed to Amos. The Red Cloaks escorted a convoy of wagons bearing hundreds of boys all bound for Killenhess and the Academy of Divine Right. Mother Erwain told him that some would be tested and go on to become acolytes for the priesthood, but most would swear a holy oath of servitude and train to become Red Cloaks.

It was abhorrent. What did a boy know of such things, none of them looked older than Belle and many were much younger. They had not lived enough life to understand what it was they gave up or were committing to. Not that they had been given any choice in the matter, Erwain told him most had been purchased. Desperate mothers had been offered food and money in exchange for their sons and many had accepted, for they had lost their homes and had nothing. The food, at least, would ensure the rest of the family would not starve. There was no doubt in Amos's mind that the Red Priests had oiled any remaining fears with promises of care and duty of service to Kildare.

That first day out, Amos had wondered why the Red Cloaks bothered to stay with them. For whilst it was their train of wagons that led the way, the Red Cloaks held themselves separate from the Forgotten. Mother Erwain, a fountain of knowledge, explained that promises had been made by the Red Church to the Primates of Ankor and Nihmrodel and they stayed to keep their word. But it was meaningless. They gave no alms to the Forgotten and offered them no prayer and certainly no protection.

It must frustrate them to crawl along so, at least I hope it does. Screwing his face up, Amos sniffed the crisp air to clear his nose then sighed it out in a wispy breath before focusing on his horse once more. He tightened the saddle's cinch strap causing his stallion to stamp a hoof.

"Sorry, Nera." Amos rubbed a hand against the horse's neck until the stallion settled.

A distant command was shouted and concertinaed calls rang out as the wagons and carriages of the Red Church moved off. Amos watched them leave, the fresh-faced boys squeezed into each wagon gazing back, looking lost and scared. It left a bitter stone in his gut.

A tug on his cloak drew his attention and Amos turned around and looked down at a wide-eyed Annabelle who stood back, casting a wary glance at the stallion.

"You said I could ride with you today," she mumbled.

Amos crouched. "Nera here would not hurt you, little one. He is big but gentle, as long as you let him see you and do not startle him. Here," reaching into his pack he took out a biscuit, "put that flat on your hand and hold it out to him. When Nera takes it, you will be friends and that will be that."

Annabelle shook her head at first, flinching when the horse twisted its neck and snorted at her.

"Nera can smell the treat. Lay your hand on mine and try not to laugh when he tickles you." Amos held his hand out.

Emboldened by the thought and reassured somewhat by Amos's calm tone, Annabelle reluctantly did as instructed. It felt as if she were offering her hand up to be eaten. Only, Amos was smiling, and Nera's eyes looked so big and brown, and the lashes, which she had not noticed before, were so thick and long.

Before Annabelle had the chance to make any further observation, Nera lowered his head and nuzzled her hand, scooping the biscuit up with lips and tongue. It did tickle. She giggled.

Amos grinned. "Now reach up and pat his neck. Tell him your name and that he's a good boy. That way he will hear your voice and know it."

Afterwards, Amos stood and looked down at Belle whose innocent face was filled with joy. "I think you've made a new friend. Nera will not mind carrying you, but you might find it uncomfortable. Are you sure you wouldn't rather stay and ride on a wagon instead?"

"No, I want to see Jerkze and Jobe and they ride at the back with Mother Erwain. I just know Jerkze will be picking at his bandages and itching his wounds. I need to keep my eye on him," Annabelle said in a serious voice. Then, in apparent afterthought, "Besides, I miss his stories."

Amos strapped his saddlebags on. "You do? I thought them long-winded and unfunny." Picking his pack up, he secured it between the saddle's cantle and rear housing.

"Some are I guess but he's good at explaining things," Annabelle replied.

Placing his foot into a stirrup, Amos hoisted himself onto Nera's back and stared down at the scrawny girl. "I want no complaining that you're sore or tired or that your boney little arse hurts. Deal?"

"Deal." Chirped Annabelle.

Leaning down, Amos grasped Belle's forearm and swung her up into the saddle and wedged her in front of him.

"Ow." Annabelle adjusted her seat. "I wasn't complaining," she added hastily.

Nera snorted and stamped a hoof. Amos clucked his tongue and laid the reins across the stallion's neck, steering them towards the road. He called out in farewell to Mercy, who was leading the trail this day, and lifted a hand to Lucky and Stama. They'd spoken already over breakfast, a stale roll and hard apple, he would be back after midday for the run into Lakeside.

The hand of Black Crows were ready and waiting by the roadside, the Lady Constance at their forefront slotting in beside him. She looked resplendent in her white cloak and sat with ease upon her white stallion.

"Good morn, Lord Amos," Constance said, her cheeks were rosy in the fresh dawn. Her face creased into a smile. "Hi Belle."

"Good morn, Lady." Twisting in his saddle as the two girls chattered, Amos acknowledged the others, his eye taking account of each of them. *It's good to know who you ride with.*

Junip Jorgstein rode a barrel-bellied piebald immediately behind her mistress, alongside the bearish Kronke who sat astride a tall, chestnut-coloured dray. Next behind leered the rat-faced, scruffy-bearded, one-eyed man and the farm boy in rustic holdsteader clothing whose face flushed under scrutiny. At the back rode a youth in full Black Crow livery whose cheeks looked like they'd never felt the kiss of a razor and finally, the trim figured Crawley, with dirt smudging her brow and whose dark eyes stared boldly in return.

They had been through much, according to Mercy. Fought urak in the grasslands northwest of Thorsten and were all that remained of a hundred-strong company.

Doubt nestled in his mind for they did not look like much to him. *Let's hope they are more than they seem.* The thought did not dispel his disquiet. Only Kronke looked formidable, but Amos sensed a deep malaise about the man. As for Junip, whilst they had fought together and she possessed a steely resolve, she was young and inexperienced. A mage apprentice only months ago. *They will need careful watching. All of them,* Amos resolved.

It was a short ride north to the fishing village of Whottin, a pillar of funeral smoke curling above signalling the way. Along the road, they passed shuffling lines of people, who had already assembled to continue the journey south to Lakeside, and so it began. The murmur for Lady White Crow and the calling for her blessing.

As much as she disdained the name bestowed upon her, Constance Bouchemeax never let it show. Offering encouragement to all, she urged the people to stay strong, to keep the One in their hearts and to have faith in the Trinity. It was a righteous and repetitious message that assumed a cadence of its own that must have grated with time. Certainly, it did with Amos.

It was only because he'd grown to know Conn so well these past weeks that he knew she struggled. Amos could see the subtle tightness around her eyes, the strained smile that over-reached upon her face, and hear the forced joviality in her voice. It was to her lasting credit that the young girl managed to maintain it.

In Whottin's small market square, they saw Father Larson directing the funeral pyre, his long pipe wedged firmly in the corner of his mouth, though no smoke puffed from betwixt lips or bowl.

The tangy smell of woodsmoke, straw and fish oil from the bonfire carried in the air and with it, the remnant aroma of burnt meat and copper, laced with a sulphurous afterscent that stuck in the nostrils. It was the by-product of the few bodies already committed to its flames. There would be more as the day grew and the Forgotten passed through.

The throngs of people parted as they pushed through the fishing village and continued northwards. The sight of Lady White Crow riding the trail had become a familiar one and the forgotten looked for her and called out continuously.

An unsettled Annabelle shifted in the saddle numerous times, but true to her word offered no complaint. Indeed, Amos thought her unusually subdued and he often caught her casting furtive looks towards Constance.

"What's wrong, Belle?" Amos murmured, after one fidget too many.

Annabelle shrugged slender shoulders but didn't say anything. Amos waited. The girl would tell him without his pressing if she wanted to.

The road north of Whottin was full. The air was cold, but the sun was bright and warm where it touched the skin. It was a day to make the most of. Alongside Amos, Constance kept up her youthful monologue of encouragement, touching people with her voice or a look.

"She's different," Annabelle said.

"Who?" Though Amos knew of whom she spoke.

Annabelle glanced towards her friend. The barrage of noise from the Forgotten and Conn's ceaseless response seemed to reassure her.

"It's like she's someone else. We don't laugh or talk like we did. Now she has her Black Crows to play with I don't think she has time for me."

"She is the same and is still your friend," Amos said with certainty. "But she has had to become Lady Bouchemeaux and take up her birthright and all the burdens and responsibilities that come with it."

"Why? She is a girl yet, like me. Why does she?" Annabelle moaned.

"She is not like you. Conn is a noble and whilst her father and brother are not here to lead these Black Crows it falls upon her shoulders whether she wills it or not." Amos could feel her tremble against his chest and sensed Belle was close to tears. It unnerved him.

"She will need you. You are the one thing outside of her station and duty that she needs the most. A friend. You must help her, Belle," Amos said.

"How? I'm a nobody with nothing. My Ma is gone and all my friends. I thought Conn had lost everything too, but she hasn't. She doesn't need me, not anymore. I miss her." A sob gasped out and Amos was flummoxed by her upset.

Constance turned suddenly and leaned over. "That is not true, Belle. Never say that." Moisture glistened in her eye corners which further disturbed Amos.

"You are my only friend. I'm sorry that I've been distant, but I have been so tired on a night. I've wanted nothing but sleep, only when I do it is disturbed by worry for these people and how to help them. But, as much as they need me, I need you. Believe me, Belle."

Constance reached out a hand and Belle clasped it, almost tilting herself off Nera's back in the effort. Only Amos clamping a hand to her waist kept her from falling.

To Amos the girls looked upset, both wearing cracked smiles and bright eyes. Once Belle had recovered her balance, he swiped a hand over his beard and tugged at its growing length.

"Well then. I'm glad that's settled," Amos said, in hope more than certainty. Conn's words though seemed to have done the trick, for he could feel Belle sitting taller in the saddle. She even waved at some of the children as they rode past.

The Forgotten seemed an endless line that carved across the landscape like a giant snake, stark against the white of the snow. They passed a handful of wagons, dotted along the road, the last of which was stopped with bodies being lifted into its back. The brown and white-robed priests called out blessings to them before news was passed along from the front and messages exchanged.

Amos would have liked to have stopped and rested the horses for a bit but knew that the Forgotten would gather. For as each desperate day passed in their journey south, the object of their hope grew ever stronger in their hearts and minds. The White Lady, Nihmrodel, was called the Traveller by those in the north and the belief that Constance was her agent had taken a deep hold amongst them. That the priests of Ankor and Nihmrodel did not gainsay this belief only seemed to underline the matter and promote her position.

It left a bad taste in his mouth. Constance was no messiah, yet Mother Erwain couldn't have made the White Church's intentions any plainer when presenting the girl with that damned ermine cloak, pure as virgin snow. It made of Constance a beacon and was a gross misuse of her person, one that could have serious repercussions if the Church of Our Lady could not control her as they might wish.

Around mid-morning, they reached the processional tail of the Forgotten and, spying Jobe upon his horse and Jerkze riding the back wagon, Amos broke into a wild canter.

Annabelle tensed and gripped her hands into Nera's mane as the stallion opened his stride. Jolting forward, she would have been unseated had Amos not clamped an arm around her middle. Unhelpfully, he whooped in her ear as she bounced up and down, too scared and too winded to open her mouth and join in.

Nera's snorting bulk scattered the Forgotten to the opposite side of the road and many less-than-savoury calls followed them. They passed the wagons at the rear of the column, waving to Mother Erwain as they flashed by. Reaching the last, Amos reined the black stallion in.

"Jobe, Jerkze. 'Tis good to see you," Amos cried, a large smile garnishing his face.

"Lord," Jobe said, giving a rakish bow from his saddle to Annabelle. "My Lady."

A beaming Annabelle chirruped. "I missed you. Both of you." Unable to contain herself, she drew her leg up and over Nera's back to dismount.

Grabbing a fist of her cloak an amused Amos steadied her slide to the ground. "Don't know what Belle sees in you two scoundrels but she was most insistent on coming."

"I came to check on Jerkze," Annabelle said. "Make sure he is not itching his wound. Mercy says it will need dressing or it will go rotten."

"It heals well, imp," Jerkze retorted. "Mother Erwain has attended it and her ministrations have aided my recovery. I'll ride a horse and draw a bow soon enough."

Jobe laughed, "Ai but for now it's me as cuts your food and laces your boots." His laughter died suddenly, and his gaze snapped to his left as a flight of blackbirds broke the skyline above a treelined ridge.

"Well I'm here now," Annabelle stated. "I will look…"

Jerkze thrust a hand out, and Annabelle's words trailed off. She felt chastised and wondering what for, looked to Amos then back to Jerkze.

"There is something in the woods. Belle, climb up beside me and take the reins." The urgency in Jerkze's voice had her scrambling up the side of the wagon.

Shades between the trees matched their direction of travel, distinct only because they moved.

Snapping the reins, Jerkze got the wagon moving again. They had become detached from the back of the line and were exposed.

"Here." He handed the reins to Annabelle, then, with a grunt of pain, reached for his scabbard and sword which lay wrapped in sackcloth and was tied to his pack.

"They are men," Amos announced. As he spoke the words, riders broke through the tree line and started down the slope. They wore the heavy furs of Nordermen and rode coursers rather than the smaller, durable steppe ponies the Northmen were renowned for. It was soon apparent from their angle of approach that they would intercept the lead wagon where Constance and her Black Crows rode beside Mother Erwain.

"I don't like it," Jobe said. "What are a band of Norders doing this far south?" Reaching behind, he took his bow from its saddle sheath and notched an arrow loosely on the string.

Amos frowned, his relief they were not urak turning to doubt. "Let's go find out. Belle, stay with Jerkze."

Touching his heels to Nera's flanks, Amos leapt forward, cantering the short distance to the wagons ahead, Jobe following. Passing the backmarkers, they moved up the line until they reached the lead wagon.

"Nordáas," Mother Erwain stated. "One wonders why they are so far from home with urak invading their lands." Her face though displayed curiosity rather than concern.

"Maybe they come with news or for help?" Constance suggested, intrigued as the riders drew nearer.

"That would require only a messenger and a fast horse, My Lady," Kronke replied. "They look more a raiding party on war horses. We should take care. They're a score and we only seven with Lord Amos and his man."

"Eight," Junip spoke out.

"Ai, Eight," Kronke conceded.

Amos noted that the newly appointed Captain had strapped a shield to his left arm, as had the young baby-faced Crow next to Crawley, who herself held a notched bow in her lap. They were ready for trouble; Amos approved. Ahead, some of the Forgotten had gathered, old men mostly and some of the older children, curious perhaps at the newcomers.

"What is it, Darri?" Mother Erwain asked of the youth who sat beside her. He wore the plain robes of an acolyte with a thick woollen cloak wrapped around his thin body. His round, hairless face was strained in concentration. He shook his head.

"I sense a wrongness in them, Mother," Darri piped up, his voice shrill.

"I have the sight and sense nothing untoward," Junip challenged.

"You're a magus but you do not see as I see," Darri mumbled, looking down.

Amos moved Nera past the Black Crows and into the snow meadow at the side of the road. "I'll ride and meet them. See what it is they want."

Seeing Constance lift her reins to follow, Amos growled. "Your place is here, My Lady."

A flash of annoyance crossed the girl's face but something in his demeanour must have registered for she gave a heavy sigh and reined in.

"Very well. Be careful."

Amos urged Nera through knee-deep snow, Jobe following just behind in the stallion's broken wake.

The Norders approached in a ragged single file, hard-faced and dead-eyed beneath their cowls. From the languid gait of their horses, Amos could tell that the mounts were spent. Their heads were held low and tossed side to side, the winded plume of their breath panting like forge bellows.

When Amos deemed them close enough, he sat back in his saddle, Nera coming to a stop. The Norders too came to a stuttering halt.

"Well met, friends," Amos called out. They looked travel-worn, their lead rider unkempt, the knotted blonde of his beard tufted, half-hiding the iron charms beading it. With growing wariness, Amos watched the man reach up and lower the hood of his cloak, his shadowed eyes turning blue in the full light.

Ignoring the greeting, the Norderman cocked his head to the side and peered past Amos, eyes sweeping over the road in a single glance, taking in the bedraggled wretches, the wagons and riders before settling upon the white-cloaked girl sitting upon a white steed. His eyes narrowed then returned to the man blocking his way.

"The girl in white. Who is she?" His voice cracked like parched leather as if it had not been used in a while.

For Amos, there was no mistaking the predatory tone it held. "She is my ward and no business of yours."

The Northman's mouth parted as if the answer amused him. "She's noteworthy, yet travels wid only a handful a warriors. A great risk in dangerous times. A man wonders why?"

"You did not ride from Norderland to talk about the Lady Constance. What is your purpose here? Why leave your homeland when it is at war?" Amos countered.

"Ma purpose is ma own, Black-hair. Our horses are spent. We need fresh ones and will have them."

With a nonchalance he did not feel, Amos shrugged his shoulders. "We've none to spare. Most of what we have are cart horses as tired as your own." He signalled to the south.

"Lakeside is just down the road. Even walking you will reach it before day's end. If the Traveller smiles upon you, you may barter for fresh horses there."

The Norderman's lip curled into a sneer and a wave of menace rolled off him that had Amos place a hand on his sword. Jobe must have felt it too for the corded strain of a bow sounded from behind. But then the man's eyes turned glassy and his head gave a tiny shake, then several times more as if he argued in silence with himself. His eyes blinked then cleared and with it, the unspoken threat seemed to pass.

Jobe's bow creaked as its draw was relaxed, whilst Amos dropped his hand from sword hilt to saddle pommel, in easy reach should he need it still. Amos flicked his eyes at the file of Northmen. There was something intangible and dangerous about them that rang warning. They had watched attentively but in hollowed quiet whilst their leader spoke, like attack dogs waiting for their master's command. His gaze settled once more on the leader, a man who had told him nothing Amos could not see for himself. As if reading his mind, the Norder spoke again.

"We murdered a hand of urak a day back. They'll nae be alone. Ya don't have the means ta post outriders nor pickets ta screen yar flanks. Ya need us, Black-hair. Even if'n just sittin' between them and you'n."

"You have a name, Northman?" Amos asked.

The warrior's jaw clenched, and a shadow passed across his eyes, gone almost as quickly as it appeared.

"Riekason." He said the name slowly as if dredging it from memory then more forcefully, "My name is Riekason."

"Well then Riekason, I am Lord Amos. If you ride rear guard I'm sure the people would be grateful. If not... well, it's a free road and I wish you a safe journey." Giving a brusque nod, Amos dragged his reins to the left. Nera turned neatly about and followed Jobe's mare back towards the road.

"I am none the wiser," Amos said as they reached Mother Erwain's wagon and the querying looks of those waiting. "Other than their leader's name, Riekason, and the fact they require fresh horses they were not forthcoming."

"Summat wrong with 'em," Jobe added. "Like they were spoiling for trouble."

"Sounds like most Norders ta me," Kronke rumbled.

"Ai," Jobe replied, grim-faced. "But most I know are full of wind and bravado. These weren't like any I ever met. Quiet like, but the dangerous kinda quiet if ya take my meaning."

Kronke and the Black Crows glanced as one at the Northmen as they meandered the trail created by Amos. They would join the road just as the last wain passed.

"Riekason mentioned an urak scouting party," said Amos, intruding on their surveillance. "Says they killed 'em but that there will be more."

"Murdered," Jobe said. "Riekason said murdered which is a strange way of putting it if you ask me."

Amos glared at Jobe who lapsed into silence. "We'll remain and keep an eye on our new friends." Amos addressed Constance. "But for now, I think it best, Lady, that you return to Mercy. I'll find you later this afternoon in Lakeside."

"I would like to accompany Lady White Crow," Mother Erwain said. "If I could borrow a horse, Lord Amos, I would be grateful."

"Ai, alright, I can see where this is going," grumped Jobe. Sliding from his saddle, he took his weapons and pack off and placed them in the wagon before helping Mother Erwain down then boosting her onto his horse. The skirt of her robe rode up, showing a boot and flash of stockinged calf and Jobe tugged the hem down.

"Thank you, my child. Rest assured I can ride well enough."

Jobe glanced up into eyes younger than his own and gave a rakish grin. "She's a good rider, Mother." He slapped the mare's rump and the horse skittered sideways only for Erwain to gather the reins and collect the horse.

"Take care of her and she'll take care of you," he laughed. Climbing aboard the wagon, Jobe settled next to the prudish-looking acolyte whose name he couldn't recall.

"Onwards my good fellow."

* * *

"You may not pass."

Captain Manis of Lakeside stood with a brace of guards to each side, hand resting casually upon his sword. He stood upon a wide bridge that forded a shallow waterway that was too small to be a river and too big to be a stream. The watercourse wove out of the hills in the east and would have been lost in the ridged landscape were it not for the ancient flood barrier that mounded its southern bank.

"And yet my Red Brothers crossed not an hour ago." Father Larson Bose chewed on the pipe wedged in the corner of his mouth and raised bushy eyebrows to each of the armoured men that barred passage. "Unless you wish to be named faithless and your souls condemned to the eternal damnation of the first hell you will step aside, my sons."

Captain Manis blessed himself self-consciously, "I meant no disrespect, Father. Of course, your Holiness may pass. I meant the people you bring. Lord Vandis has ordered that anyone fleeing the Rivers must remain outside Lakeside. There is a camp established on the eastern road to Thorn Nook with fresh water from the Synt and where My Lord provides what food he can."

Snatching the pipe from his mouth, Father Larson waggled it at the Guard-Captain.

"Utter madness. Where is your fool of a Lord? I would have words with him." Puffing his cheeks out his bulbous nose seemed to swell with indignation.

Manis bristled, "Lord Vandis is travelling to Killenhess with Lord Commander Whent and his army of Red Cloaks. I'm sorry, Father, but I have my orders. If you wish to entreat with my Lord, I am sure he'll hear you upon his return."

His eyes averted to a tall woman who strolled up and stood beside the scowling priest, a young girl cloaked in white by her side. A haughty bearing named the woman a noble as much as the quality of her clothing, travel-stained as it was. She would have been pretty too but for a scar that disfigured her left cheek. The captain opened his mouth to speak but the woman beat him to it.

"I am Lady Mercy Duncan of Hawke Hold and this is the Lady Constance Bouchemeax of Thorsten. These people need food and shelter. They are old and young, mothers with children. A few days rest and we will move on I assure you and no longer be your problem."

"My orders are clear, my Lady, I have stated them plainly. I can grant you admittance to Lakeside on account of your station and your retainers, but we cannot accommodate these," Captain Manis waved a hand at the Forgotten, "people. They are too many and it will take a few days to process them all and move them to the settlement, which, given your number, will need to be expanded."

"Process? An interesting turn of phrase by which you mean to take anything of value they might carry. Call it theft and be done with it, Captain but I will not abide it." Mercy snarled this last.

"We're at war," Manis argued. "Those savages are coming and everyone must contribute what they can if we are to see them off. Whether that is in weapons, coin or bodies it matters not for all three are sorely needed."

"Urak have crossed the Plago. Lord Aric and his riders must have told you as much?" Mercy's face turned a dangerous hue. "And yet you would take from these people who have already lost so much and stake them out like a shield wall for the enemy to crash against. Women and children will be slaughtered and for nothing. Where is your honour, sir?"

Affronted, Manis barked. "I have not seen this Lord Aric, nor his riders. As for my honour. It is to Lord Vandis and Lakeside, to Cumbrenan and High Lady Arisa Montreau. To the Trinity and through them the One. Do not question my honour, My Lady or noble or not I will have you detained."

Father Larson Bose placed a calming hand on Mercy's elbow before addressing the captain once more.

"We all must answer to the One, my son. It is not enough to blindly follow without question or hide behind oath and honour when it is clear what is the good and right thing to do." The priest steered Mercy away but proclaimed this last over his shoulder.

"All of us will pass this bridge, captain, or none of us."

Chapter 37: Lost Innocence

Lakeside, Cumbrenan

Covers rustled and grunts and snores filled the tent with arhythmic sounds that told Zon what he needed to know.

Someone broke wind, a brief toot of escaping air that added its stink to that of damp cloth, stale bodies and bad breath. It was Kronke, experience told him so as much as the area of emanation. The man was as flatulent as that big dray he rode and as constant as a town bell.

Despite his certainty, Zon listened to the sleepers for a further hundred heartbeats before sliding from beneath his covers. Like everyone else he was fully clothed, it was too cold not to be. He pulled on his boots and fastened his cloak around his shoulders before reaching beneath his bedroll for his sheathed daggers. He strapped them with blind efficiency to waist and thigh and tucked his finger-cutter into the hidden slot on his belt at the small of his back. All the while his ears strained for any irregularities.

Leaving his sword and scabbard in his bed, Zon rolled silently to his feet and eased through the darkness of the tent. Parting the flap, he slipped outside, stood tall and took a deep breath of chill air.

He was in a town of sorts. Not his town certainly, and not like any he'd ever been in but a town nonetheless. One of tents and lean-tos, canvas and cloth rather than wood and brick. The night air might lack the layered sophistication of a regular town but this one had a distinct odour and sound all its own.

Glancing upward, Zon scowled at the cosmos. It spread like a rash in half-clouded skies, adding a waxen light to Ankor's moon which hung high and bright. The smudged glow of Nihmrodel graced the western horizon and the red moon of Kildare was just rising in the east. Altogether it provided a bleached light to see by, too much light for his liking.

He moved off and the snow, compact underfoot, gave little sound of his passing. He made his way around the women's tent his mind leering with thoughts of young Jorgstein. Plain she might be and unworldly but she'd meat enough on her bones to keep him warm. *Teach her a thing or two about a man,* his crotch stirred at the thought and he paused to tug at his britches and adjust his cock.

'Ceptin' she's a mage ya fool and more like to burn your sorry ass to a cinder. As his rational side reasserted itself, Zon gave a melancholic sigh, recentred himself and walked on.

Their camp consisted of three large campaign tents abutting the canvassed and multi-hued encampment of the priests and their acolytes. Wagons formed a windbreak on the north side acting as both a perimeter and a corral for the horses whose coarse musk percolated the air.

A fire crackled nearby, casting a cheery glow over the four acolytes whose job it was to mind the beasts. They huddled, drowsing around its edge, lulled by the late hour and the fire's warmth. They did not stir as Zon stole past but if they had the firelight would have robbed them of any night sight and they would not have seen him.

Zon wasn't entirely sure what he was doing or why he was abroad in the cold and dead of night when any sane man rightly would be resting in his covers. Old habits he supposed. He'd lived for the night in his former life and the darkness was a familiar comfort to him.

A sniff of the air and the caress of wind on his cheeks had Zon angling south through the priests' tented village, the lure of a real town dragging on him like iron to a magnet.

He wandered past awnings and windbreaks where the desperate huddled beneath for warmth, and not all were asleep. He felt eyes on him but must have appeared a ghost to the woken, an indistinct shade that slipped by and was gone before they knew to say anything.

It was a short walk to the bridge and soon enough he crouched between a tent and an accacha bush gazing out towards it. Two guards, dark silhouettes in the moonlight, stood propped against the stanchions on either side. Across the span of the bridge led the road to Lakeside. A real town, with alehouses and whores and people with things of worth. Not like the paupers he travelled with.

He blew his cheeks out, *may as well be ten leagues away as slip past that bridge.* He couldn't swim the narrow channel and even if he could wade across the waterway, it would be ice cold and leave him soaked to the bone. No, what was needed was a distraction, both sides of the bridge and then again to make it back.

Unlikely and, much as he might wish it, Zon wasn't into taking risks of that magnitude. He'd taken a look-see and if, as he suspected, they were stuck here for a few days, he had time to dwell on it. He was about to turn away when his single eye returned to the guards. He squinted. They were too still. Neither had moved. Not a twitch nor a cough, he was sure of it.

Nervous energy coursed through his blood, instinct pushing at him to leave only he didn't. Desperate to piss, Zon eased his strides down and relieved himself in the bush, all the while his mind working. Shaking his cock, he tucked it back into the warmth of his britches, then gave a snort as a sudden chutzpah filled him.

Working his way towards the waterside he edged down the banked slope and waited, listening for any disturbance, any sign he'd been spotted from either side of the river. Satisfied, he stalked toward the bridge ready to bolt at the merest hint of movement. Nothing, not a hand scratching an arse nor a shift of motion from one foot to another. Neither guard so much as shivered and both his trepidation and confidence grew.

Yards away, Zon knew they were dead before his eye ever told him. The tainted smell of blood and urine accompanied a silence so loud it had to be so.

He sidled up to the nearest and brushed fingers over the guard's arm. Up close the black stain of blood was visible in the dark light, it painted the man's throat and soaked his tabard. Like a coat hook, the handle of a long knife protruded from his chest, punched with wild force through boiled armour and pinning the man to the bridge beam at his back.

Trepidation outbid his confidence and Zon's knees threatened to buckle in a spike of adrenaline-fuelled fear. They had been murdered neat as gutted fish and propped here to mask the deed. That both men had died without a sound meant there was more than one killer.

Instinctively, Zon's mind turned to the Nordermen that had trailed them all day. They weren't right that much was obvious. Nary a one spoke for a start and he'd never met a Norderman who didn't like the sound of their own voice. That their silence was accompanied by a brooding menace had set them all on edge, especially Kronke, Crawley and Lord Lardi-da.

Zon knew he should cry warning, but of their own volition his hands had slipped the dead guard's purse into his pocket and he knew where fingers would point if he were discovered at the scene and searched.

Let someone else find them, much as he was gripped by fear, Zon moved to the other guard, expertly patted him down and relieved him of his coin. It was foolish to tarry so but as he had already observed, old habits and all that. He jumped when the dead man gave a gurgle and would've pissed himself had he not already emptied his bladder.

The guard's head lolled forwards like a marionette whose string had suddenly been cut. Blood steamed in the moonlight, warm against the frigid air. Sucking in a relieved breath, Zon hesitated. He would like to have taken more time. Rings, necklaces, keepsakes, everyone had them but as his ass unclenched blaring reason broke the hold of his greed. These men had died recent, minutes maybe, and the thought the killers might still be near worried him.

He glanced across the bridge. There would be guards on the other side. That they had not heard anything meant it likely they too were dead. His mind taunted him. *I could cross unhindered.*

Backing away, Zon turned and fled into the night.

Retracing his route back through the makeshift shantytown, the eyes on him this time felt more sinister and it hurried his steps.

Zon passed through the priests' enclave, the acolytes still dozing benignly, and with a sense of relief entered the safety of camp. His addled mind was still trying to figure out his next move.

He was still wired, his senses surging, else he might have missed it. Edging around the women's tent a muffled sound, barely discernable, jarred him to a halt. He'd heard the sound before, the thrashing of a struggle. That it was so quiet made it more urgent. His single eye stared at the canvas, his mind registering what looked like a shadowed crease. A slit in the cloth.

Leave it be. Leave it... one hand reached for the split canvas, the other his short knife and Zon slipped inside.

It was dark and his eye, tainted by moonlight, struggled to adjust. There was an oppressive weight in the air that made his eyelid heavy. The tent slept, the night breath of its occupants mixing with the noise of the scuffle which, through some trick of acoustics, seemed less distinct now than when he was outside. But it was still there and it drew his attention to the right.

Zon blinked in the darkness as a deeper black registered. The faintest shimmer outlined it. He stood rooted, uncertainty weighing on him as to what he should do when a sudden, strange lucidity rose within him, clearing his mind like a cloud passing from a moon.

The ermine cloak.

Lady Constance.

He did not know where the thought came from or indeed why he cared but his knife reached out and touched the neck of the assailant.

"Fucking move and I'll spit you like a hog on Tenday."

Zon wasn't sure what happened next, it was dark after all, but he found himself propelled through the air to land with a screech on someone's legs. He wasn't sure if the scream was his or Crawley's but the woman was not sleep-touched. Her blade was out and at his throat before he'd taken a breath.

"What the fuck, Zon?"

"Lumousim echiguus." Words of power lit the inside of the tent and anything else Crawley was about to say died on her lips.

The fur-clad bulk of a Norderman knelt hunched. One hand pressed firmly into a distinctive white cloak that was draped over a bedroll. A child's feet thrashed feebly beneath.

The man's head turned, and dead, coal-black eyes regarded the tent. It chilled Zon to his core. He knew a devil when he saw one. Strange, because he'd never believed in the One nor the seven hells preached by the Trinity. Not until that moment.

The tent flap swished and Mercy stepped through. Whatever hold the devil had broke and everything happened at once.

A knife appeared in the devil man's fist. A hand shoved Zon in the back as Crawley levered him off and an ominous static filled the tent.

Bizarrely, without any thought to fleeing, Zon snapped his wrist and launched his knife at the furred man. It wasn't his best throw and with a thud, it embedded in the meat of the arm that smothered the Lady Constance.

The Norderman didn't so much as flinch or cry out nor release the hold on his victim. Soundlessly, the knife in its hand blurred and Zon saw death in the blade as it spun towards him, his reflexes were too slow to do anything other than tense for the impact that would end him.

With a kick, Crawley's tangled leg struck him in the back and a searing agony speared his shoulder.

Zon opened his mouth to scream, perfectly timed as a ball of fire sheared the air and struck the Norderman in his chest. It melted through leather and cloth and set his furs on fire but it did not carve a path through his flesh as it should have.

Baring its teeth, the creature smiled. Wreathed in flames, skin melting, it pulled Zon's knife from its arm then cocked it ready to throw.

Its head jerked back and with a spray of blood, a metal tip ruptured from its throat. Unmindful of the flames Mercy had stepped up behind and with a hand in the devil's hair thrust her blade through its neck. Its spinal cord severed, the thing that was not a man flopped to the ground.

"Oh gods, it hurts." Zon rolled over, clutching his shoulder. He'd borne worse when his eye was taken but sweet lord that was in the past and this the now.

***

Mercy stood with a bloodied blade in hand, her flesh crawling with called upon aether. She had been slow to react, shocked by what she had seen and hoped never to see again.

A high-pitched wail shattered the night, each rise and fall a different agony. Of despair then grief, torment and pain, abject pain until finally, like a deflating water bladder it twisted, subsiding into a frenzied snarl. It touched fear into the souls of all who heard it.

Calls echoed from outside the tent, but Mercy's focus was solely on the child.

"Belle? Bell…" A voice, young, laced with fright and uncertainty cried out.

"Don't come any closer, Conn." Mercy shook off her still smoking gloves and glanced at Constance who stood in fearful worry by the entrance to the tent. Her eyes returned to the thrashing, white-furred cloak.

"Stay away," the mage murmured, the memory of the man's black, soulless eyes bored into her skull. She had seen them before by the river outside Fallston. Taken. A Taken had come and killed Marron and now one was here. What did it mean?

The storm beneath the cloak suddenly subsided and the white fabric settled in a rumpled heap. Unmindful of Mercy's command, Constance tried to push past.

"I said stay back." Mercy's arm stretched out and stopped the girl. Her voice rang with authority, but Constance struggled against her.

"She is my friend. That man hurt her."

"Listen to me." Mercy kicked the dead man. "This thing was no man and it was here for you. Not Belle. She was cold, remember. You laid your cloak over her so she would be warm. Let me tend her."

Constance stood away, and Mercy gave a nod of encouragement before turning and kneeling by the becalmed bed covers. Taking a deep breath, she gripped the white cloak and threw it back.

A creature erupted from beneath. Dressed in the body of Annabelle its dead-black gaze was filled with hate. Snarling it clawed at Mercy who yanked her head away.

Nails raked the mage's cheek dragging skin with it and leaving four bloody contrails behind. With a grunt, Mercy shoved the girl down and pressed her into the bedding.

"You will die. You will all die," the thing hissed and spat. That it was in Annabelle's voice tore at Mercy's heart.

"What's wrong with her?" Constance cried, but the mage ignored her, ignored too her brother's voice that called to her in urgency, and dismissed Junip's cries of admonition. The young mage no doubt could sense her building power but there was no time to explain, no time to reason. They had not seen what she had seen. They would not understand as she did, that this was no longer a child.

The ink-black eyes cleared to hazel. A tiny red fleck in one that Mercy had never noticed before, glinted in the magelight.

"Don't hurt me. I'm just a child."

A tear ran down Mercy's cheek, the salt stinging her wounds. "Go in peace, Belle. May the One take you."

Annabelle cackled and her voice, when she spoke this time, was deeper, more ancient, more malign than a child could possibly utter. "There is no One. Only silence and eternal darkness."

With inhuman strength, the girl lurched, black clouds filling her eyes like a storm once more.

"Aaorus arctum."

There was a searing heat and a scream of denial.

Standing upright, Mercy wobbled drunkenly and then was shoved to the ground. There was a lot of yelling and cries but it was all just background noise, a homogeneous sound that wouldn't register. She lay in a daze feeling broken inside.

* * *

Amos had no recollection of entering the tent. He was sat cross-legged with Belle's head in his lap and a sobbing Constance by his side. The girl clutched her friend's hand, squeezing it as if she might find some pulse of life through sheer will.

She'll find none, Amos thought, his eyes travelling to the fist-sized hole in Belle's chest. There was little blood, Mercy's death strike cauterizing as it went leaving a charred ruin where the girl's heart should be.

Amos had known loss before but nothing, it seemed, had prepared him for Belle's death. It numbed him as no other had. He stirred, breaking his paralysis and brushed the tattered mop of mousy hair back from Belle's brow. It was unruly and would not be contained, always had been. The briefest of smiles twisted into something empty as her sightless eyes stared up at him. They were clear, frozen in perpetual accusation.

Wiping his eyes dry, Amos laid her head gently down and slowly climbed to his feet. She looked tiny and lost. An innocent who had suffered so much in her short life, lost so much, but who had always been filled with joy. As if life could not dent her zest nor contain her spirit.

His grief flipped to a rage that built from his boots, rising like a quick tide up his legs and through his body until it consumed him. Amos spun, eyes sweeping the tent. The white-robed Mother Erwain was tending to Mercy who sat in a fugue.

Four bloody grooves scarred his sister's right cheek, finger torn skin, damning as she was damned. Seething, he towered above her unaware he had taken the steps or that he bore a knife.

"You murdered her."

The accusation silenced the tent and awakened Mercy from whatever hole she'd retreated to for her head shook and tilted to regard him.

"No brother. Though it broke me, I gave her the only thing I could. Peace."

Mother Erwain was there. A hand gripping Amos's forearm with surprising strength. "Do not be rash, lord. Listen as I have listened before passing judgement."

Shifting her body, Erwain held a hand out. "Give me your knife, Lord. Or at least put it away. There has been tragedy enough for one night."

His nostrils flared, his jaws clenched so tight his teeth ached. The lines around his eyes tightened. "She was a child."

"I know you loved her, Amos. She touched all of us, but she was lost before I ever took her life," Mercy said, her voice cracking.

"A CHILD!" Spit flecked his lips and his body shook with fury. Amos could feel himself losing control and couldn't stop himself. Didn't want to.

Hands gripped his arms, restraining him.

"It's alright, boss," Jobe's voice was gentled like he was calming a horse. "We feel her loss too. Loved her as you loved her." His voice cracked. "But we need to understand what happened and why. It would dishonour Belle not to know the truth. You would tell us so yourself if you were not consumed by grief."

On his opposite side, Jerkze pried the knife from his hand. His friend, normally so stoic and unflappable looked crushed, his grief-stricken eyes a reflection of his own.

Mother Erwain stood back and helped Mercy to her feet.

"It happened so fast," Mercy started. "Constance could not sleep and I thought a walk might clear her mind. She stands out so much in that white cloak of hers that she took Belle's."

The mage spoke in a monotone, her voice lacking any nuance or offering any embellishment, eyes fixed and staring at no one and nothing.

"Returning, we heard a man cry out and Crawley cussing. I entered and found the Norderman crouched over Belle and bearing a knife. He was holding her down, I thought to smother her to death but knowing now he was not a man, I think it was to keep her silent."

Jerkze clasped a warning hand to Amos's shoulder to forestall him from interrupting, but it went unheeded.

"What was he, sister, if not a man?" Amos hissed.

"He was Taken. Same as that thing that killed Marron on the banks of the Oust." Mercy's faraway look grazed her brother's face before staring away. She could not hold his eyes.

"I told you of that time. His eyes were the same black, the same evil. Full of nothing but hatred and despair."

The one-eyed man in Amos's periphery blurted in excitement. "He was a devil, Milord. I see'd them. Black as a jailor's soul they was. Stuck a knife in its arm and it nay flinched. Ask Crawley here, she see'd 'em too."

The man bobbed his head and laughed. "She saved me." He pointed at Crawley. "You saved my life."

"It was an accident, cock-knuckle. I was untangling meself so don't go reading nought into it," Crawley growled. She caught the poisonous glare of Lord Amos and lapsed into silence. When someone was looking to knock something off it never paid to stick your head above the parapet.

"You think this funny, little man?" growled Amos, needing to vent his rage.

Father Larson intervened. "I've given Master Pieterzon a blend of knorcha oil, milk of the poppy and crushed dewslip to ease his pain and cleanse his wound. I'm afraid it is the medication talking. Another minute or so and he will be out cold."

"I will?" Zon waved his hand in front of his face. "Why do I see two when I have one eye?" With that, he promptly collapsed, deftly caught by Father Larson and a dour-faced Crawley.

"So you killed him." Amos turned back to his sister. "That does not explain why you murdered Belle."

"She was gone." Mercy's face reddened as her voice rose. "That thing came for Constance and instead claimed Belle. Turned her. Breathed its poison in and held her down whilst it took hold of her body and possessed her mind. She was gone and there was no coming back, so I did what I had to. And though it crushed me, I would do it again, Amos. Because I would not let that thing have her. Belle's soul is free and in the One's embrace. I can believe no differently else I've cast my own into hell."

Amos lunged but Jobe caught him, struggling to hold his lord back.

"You don't know that! You don't get to decide. She was a child. My ward. My responsibility. I swore to protect her, but never did I think it should be from you," Amos spat his rage.

"You are wrong, brother. I do know that. It is written."

"Do not call me brother. I cannot stand the sight of you, nor bear to utter your name. I want you gone. Gather your things, take your horse and leave."

"Amos…"

"Begone!" Tears warred with fury.

"My Lord," Jerkze began. "Perhaps we should…"

"What? Perhaps we should what?" Amos thundered.

Pulling her arm free from Mother Erwain, Mercy staggered towards the tent flap. She stopped momentarily by Annabelle and gazed at the ruin she had wrought, saw the indictment in Conn's eyes.

Bereft, Mercy walked on until she reached the tent's threshold where she paused once more.

"I'll have Stama come and gather my things." Mercy tilted her head as if about to say more, thought better of it then vanished into the cold of night.

Chapter 38: I Wish I Had Known Her Name

Skaag and the Forest of Helg, Norderland

A hand of men. Three rode tall horses and another a two-wheeled cart pulled by a pair of wiry and tireless mountain ponies. The last of them lay in the back of the cart, his leg wrapped in heavy bandages with a fur rug thrown over him, a shield against the frigid air and the sporadic dustings of snow.

They had been seven before autumn's end when they rode north from Jarlsheim. Now they were five and lucky to be so, Tannon Crick judged soberly, his mind turning to Jon Hodden and Dave Sanction. Jon had been with him nine years, Dave, an even dozen. More than friends, they had shared a warrior's bond of brotherhood and now they were no more, their life energy rejoined with the Allthing.

The soothing gait of his stallion lulled the pain of his loss but not that of his leg. Crick rubbed at the throbbing ache beneath his strapping. His bones had knit together quickly and well; he'd taken the splint off that morning but it hurt greatly still and he didn't need Marus Banff to nag him into using a stave as a crutch when dismounted. His orderly had complained vociferously at the removal of the brace and whilst Marus had not called him a stubborn fool out loud, Crick had read it all the same in his friend's face.

Besides, Crick told himself, pain was good. It reminded a man he was alive and helped concentrate the mind and he had much to ruminate on.

They had left Skaag in the pre-dawn of the day before and were on the road to Lonn, still another day or two distant. In Crick's opinion naming it a road was unduly generous; little more than a wide furrow gouged through the soaring trees of the Helg, it was comprised of hard-packed earth and crushed stone rather than the even paving stones of the southern roadways.

Against Crick's advice and in typical Nordáa fashion, Frode, Barle of Lonn, had remained behind. "Urak come. I'll no abandon Skaag, n'er run from a fight when ma five hundred could be the tellin' agin losin'." Crick shook his head at the memory of Frode's words.

To the left, an ice-encrusted river stood silent, waiting for the remote thaw of spring. Ahead, inching above the treetops, a slate-grey bluff appeared. The road swung eastward, matching the sweep of the river and the men followed it for another half-league before reaching a crossroads. An engraved boulder, a waymarker, declared Helvenin to the east, Lonn in the north and Skaag back the way they had come. Karl Hubert took them north and they crossed a stone bridge that straddled the ice river.

The road led them up a rising slope where the trees gradually fell away on their left, leaving a short, bracken-filled verge and exposing a steepening drop. It took their breath as the flour-dusted vista of woodlands and the distant, snow-capped peaks of the Torn Spurs unfurled before them.

The path began to level off and they found themselves atop an escarpment looking down at the road they had travelled only two hours before, tracing the vein of its path until the Helg swallowed it.

"Smoke." Merin Somar pointed.

The men stopped and stared. Their aspect from atop the bluff was south and west and all knew what it meant.

"We will rest the horses." Crick eased his good leg over the saddle and lowered himself to the ground. His body ached in familiar languor apart from the sore bones of his still-healing leg, which throbbed as he put weight through it. He slipped the stave off his back, leaned on it and then hobbled to the edge of the bluff.

The road so far travelled had steadily climbed towards the mountains and, looking back on the way, the forest of Helg stretched unendingly before him. He could not see Skaag Lak nor Skaag itself, they were too distant and hidden by the folds in the land. The far-off, leaden smog though gave a clear enough indication.

"It'll be night soon enough," Crick said to everyone and no one. Distracted by his thoughts.

"I'll find us somewhere to camp." Karl Hubert swung out of his saddle, hitched his horse to the cart then walked north following a trail that led off the road and through the trees.

Merin Somar approached his lord. "The smoke of war hangs over these lands and death lies beneath it. Though your heart denies it, leaving Skaag was the right thing, Tannon."

"Ai." Crick gave a heavy-hearted sigh. Turning, he patted the grey knight's shoulder. "Doesn't make me feel any less shit for running though."

**

Skaag's carn sat atop a rocky butte and dominated the town it was built to defend. Constructed of hardstone, quarried not more than a league away, it had taken a generation to build at great expense in both lives and material. The Helvenin called it Skaag's folly. For they considered a traditional palisade wall and Barle's Hall more than sufficient for defence.

Frode of Lonn looked up towards the carn's battlements, it was imposing and reminded him of his home in the mountains. He wondered briefly whether the Helvenin would think the carn so frivolous, now that urak swarmed the lands to the west.

That the urak were coming there was no doubt. It did not take the scouts that Magner of Skaag, sent out to know this. Not when the surrounding báers and holdsteads had emptied, bringing a tide of people to the settlement. Being forced from their homes was enough to rankle any Nordáa and Skaag overflowed with the displaced, each bringing a tale of woe and misery, anger and impotence.

The Lonn bannermen shifted around him, full of nervous energy and idle banter. Frode and his five hundred held a wide strip of the northern earthworks, which rose from Skaag Lak then east where it ended against a scarp, atop of which sat the carn.

Frode climbed the embankment, slipping on the bark strips and wood chippings that had been laid down for traction against the ice and snow.

Huorl Landa, Jarl and his closest friend, laughed at him. "Fallin' on yar' oon axe already, Laird."

Frode grumbled loudly. "Ai, that brose ya made is sittin' like a roak in ma belly. The only way ta get it ot is ta open ma guts." He held an arm out and Huorl clasped it with a firm hand and pulled him up the final yard.

"Brose, he says," The blonde-bearded, bull of a man feigned offence. "Ma porridge was cooked ya feck, it'll sustain ya and ya'll be thankful for it if ya have nae ta eat tonight man."

"A truth, but if'n its ma last meal, a sad one," Frode laughed before turning more serious. "Anything?" He asked, staring over the makeshift log and stone barricade, past the dismantled remains of the longhouses and the high fields, all the way to the treeline.

"Silent as a sinner on ten-day," Huorl said. "But I can smell 'em." The Jarl hefted his long-handled axe, his words seemed to hang like a promise in the air.

It was still. Too still.

Frode surveilled the woodland but the sun cast it in dappled shadow making it impossible to penetrate. His eyes swung westward, alighting upon the lake. Its waters had frozen in the past days, but the ice shifted restlessly, grinding and popping. It was thin, too thin to trust beneath a man's feet. It was one direction they need not guard against. Yet.

A horn blared a long note, a low-pitched dirge that vibrated the air and sank into bones. All eyes swivelled to the carn. A second lament blared after the first and their eyes returned to the front, searching.

A voice to Frode's right called out. "Smoke. In't woods."

As if answering the call of the warhorn, a deep drumbeat rumbled in the north and was answered moments later by another away to the south.

Frode called out. "Shield wall and spears ta the front. Archers, ready yar bows." His heart was pumping as he looked along the barricade, the command being repeated up and down its length. His Karls on the frontline unlimbered their shields and reached for their javelins and longarms whilst those at their backs nocked arrows to bowstrings.

Twisting, Frode checked behind. He had another two hundred archers spaced behind the earthen rampart with arrow buckets strategically placed among them. He had a team of healers, including a half dozen precious physikers. *They'll earn they'n keep this day.*

There were many more Nordáa besides his Bannermen. Báermen and Holdsteaders gathered with shields and swords, and many of them held bows for all Nordáas could hunt. It was the way of the land. Frode was drawn to a striking woman, as tall as he, her straw-coloured hair braided into a warrior's plait, her leather armour dark with re-grease. Her shrill voice commanded a squad of archers, chivvying them into place. She caught him staring and Frode of Lonn dipped his chin. The war maiden scowled but otherwise ignored him and a grinning Frode turned his eyes further back.

Older children darted between the longhouses, ferrying last-minute supplies to their elders, those too infirm to hold a sword or spear, and mothers who were busy organising what went where. It warmed his heart. These were his people. A fierce pride filled him as Frode swung back toward the forest.

Inky smoke fumed, thick and fast above the trees. *Fires burning but for what purpose?* In answer, a ball of flame as bright as the sun spun into view, rising through the smoke as if launched from a sling.

As the fire orb reached its zenith it hovered in the air before arching over the treetops gaining speed and momentum as it streaked across the sky, leaving an unnatural trail of yellow-green fire behind it.

Frode watched with thousands of others as the miniature sun, the size of a large boulder, rifled toward the carn. Fear and awe filled all who saw it, its intensity promised destruction.

Then, the comet started to veer. At first just a little but then more aggressively. Spinning and churning it deflected away from the carn, crackled over the heads of Frode and those defenders gathered on the earth wall, and punched with explosive force through the ice-skin of Skaag Lak, combusting in a violent eruption of fire and steam. The fire winked out.

Frode took a breath, his gaze traversing from the punctured ice and roiling water of the lake to the carn. An indistinct figure stood upon its battlement, the glowing light of a mage's staff raised to the sky slowly lowering. Jonah Terik, the Skaag's lone magus had batted the fire-orb aside as a warrior might a child's sword strike.

Mages were rare, especially in the north, as most children that showed signs of talent were sent to the Enclave in Kingsholme to become practitioners. A long, arduous and dangerous process that took many years. It was a harsh truth that few ever returned to their homeland.

A concussive blast struck in the south and the defenders were drawn to look and found a pillar of smoke and smouldering debris plummeting the air near the lake shore.

Another fireball, this one not so successfully defended. Sorina Tarlack a magus from Gannon-báer and her apprentice covered the south. Two mages against who knew how many urak spellcasters. Dread clutched at his chest, but Frode had no time to let it take hold.

"'ware the north!"

Frode spun to the front and lurched. Urak, a wave of meat and muscle a head taller than most men, were almost across the high fields. They sent up a bass roar that rumbled against the defenders like rolling thunder. They were so many.

Frode screamed, "Archer's three hundred paces. Fire."

An elongated thrum sent a staggered swarm of arrows into the air. Smaller volleys followed soon after from the Nordáa militia and by the time the last of them had launched, his bannermen were loosing their second.

Frode watched the first volley land. Urak shields raised to meet them but some few found gaps and thudded into neck and shoulder, chest or leg. Urak dropped, but it was like watching stampeding bison as the rest charged on. They cleared the high fields and some urak took position behind the remains of the plundered longhouses. Unlimbering bows they started to return fire.

The Nordáa volleys were coming in sporadic bursts but were more accurate as the range closed. The reply from the urak, the weight of shot, hammered into shields, splintering wood and staggering those that held them.

The onrushing urak were so close, Frode could make out their features, the wide-set eyes, large mouths and square jaws. Each urak face though was smeared with bloodred warpaint that gave their fearsome countenance a sameness. They charged through the torn-down buildings and streets, guttural war cries bellowing a promise of savage death.

The din made the giving of commands incoherent to all but the nearest of his Bannermen. Pulling his sword free, Frode bared his teeth and banged it against his shield, the time for talk was done.

The far slope of the embankment had been sluiced with water for many days preceding and the cold temperature had turned it to ice. The urak slipped and skidded, stalling at its base.

Nordáa behind the barricade launched javelins and spears. The wet thud of barbed points puncturing leather and flesh went unheard, drowned in the mangled howling of the wounded and dying urak, merging with the booming war cries of their brethren.

The second wave of javelins proved far less effective. The urak were prepared so as shields parted to deliver the strike a wave of thick, black-shafted arrows swept the barricade. They punched through boiled leather and chain-link as if they were made of cloth and the force knocked those struck from their feet, skittling them into the warriors stood behind. Gaps formed all along the barricade but were quickly filled as the living dragged the dead and the wounded out and slid them down the inside slope of the embankment for the healers to attend.

Axes cracked and hammers crunched, the urak hacking at the ice and edging up the embankment. When they reached the top, Nordaa spears thrust between shields seeking flesh. Behind the barricade, the flat top of the earthworks gave the defenders a steady footing and leverage, providing them with their best advantage. Frode jabbed over the shoulder of Cydric, a bannerman, aiming for the throat of a red-faced urak only for his blade to split the meat of its cheek as the beast lurched to avoid the blow. The urak would have slipped, dislodged, only it gripped a hairy-handed mitt on the long beam atop the barricade.

Cydric slammed his sword down, slicing through fingers and bone and with a squealing mewl, the urak tumbled down the ice. Frode took the momentary respite to step back and look along the line of defence. The urak were many but his bannermen would hold, he was certain of it. More worrying though were the defences to his right. The Báermen and Holdsteaders there fought ferociously but in isolated units and ragged holes were starting to appear.

Own sticks with own, Frode frowned, these Nordáa were fighters and could wield a sword or swing an axe, but they were mostly farmers and hunters and had not the discipline of trained warriors nor did their commanders possess the experience to move blades where needed. It was a known weakness which was why Frode had them placed near the scarp, hoping the added cover offered by the Skaagen bows in the carn would bolster them and compensate for their lack.

Frode shuffled along the embankment to where Huorl Landa commanded his Karls and gripped his friend's arm, pulling him close.

"The right is weak. Take half the reserve en bolster 'em. Dinnae let it fall, brother."

Huorl leered, his axe was covered in ichor and a streak of it smeared his face from brow to chin giving him a manic look. "Ai, Laird. Connaer," he bellowed.

"I'm right here, ya feck," said the man on Huorl's right. "Laird." He acknowledged Frode.

"I'm takin' the reserve. Yar in charge here, mon." Huorl thumped Connaer on the back, gave Frode a nod and leapt down the slope of the earthwork, shouting orders as soon as his feet hit the flat.

A streak of fire creased the sky leaving a sooty contrail in its wake before crashing into Skaag Lak like the one before it. It was followed almost immediately by another, accompanied by a sharp pain in Frode's ears which popped violently. This fireball passed overhead so low Frode thought he could feel the heat from it. It exploded much closer to shore, vaporizing ice and water in an explosion of steam and lapping flame.

The destructive force was worrisome and Frode winced, sparing a moment to stare at the stick-like figure of the magus atop the keep with his glowing staff. *How long can he maintain his mastery?*

A loose helm struck Frode in the shoulder and the Karl it belonged to lurched backwards with a gurgle. The man's face was sliced from eye to shattered jaw bone, blood spurting from his mouth and neck. Frode sidestepped the man, grabbed a fistful of chain-link and sent him tumbling back, down the embankment.

Stepping into the hole, Frode buttressed the shield man with an arm in the back who staggered beneath a blow, an urak blade lodging into the edge of his round shield. The man thrust beneath his shield with a short spear as Frode leaned to the opposite side and stabbed his sword through the gap, feeling his blade bite meat.

Leaning back, Frode brought his shield up to cover but there was no retaliatory blow. A man gripped the collar of his leather harness.

"We've got this, Laird," Connaer cried in his ear.

Fighting the bloodlust singing through his veins, Frode let himself get dragged away. He stood back and looked again along the defensive line of the earth wall. It had seemed but a moment, yet Huorl was already back at the front moving the twenty hands of reserves to where they were needed.

Frode wished he could see the battlefield more clearly rather than the fitful glimpses he got through the shield wall and barricade. It was impossible to read the ebb and flow of battle. To judge numbers and read the mood of the attacker. Did they flag or wilt under their losses or were they determined? Where were the urak strong or weak and when and where to shift warriors to counter any surge? He was all but blind.

A hum filled the air, quickly whining to a peak. The battle lulled as urak and humans alike clutched hands to heads, excruciating pain pulsing indiscriminately through ear and skull. The waterfall crash of sound exploded in crescendo and a wave of heat struck, instantly followed by a concussive blast.

It battered Frode, forcing him to crouch and lean to keep his balance. The sky rained soil and blood and larger debris which pattered on and around him. A dull buzzing rang his head and Frode could feel the liquid trickle of blood ooze from ears to beard. He shouted but his voice was muffled even to himself.

Frode straightened, fear seizing him, and he surged forward, even as others recovered from whatever magics had struck them. He peered between two shields and called a warning to the Bannermen that held them, but they gave no sign they heard his words.

A black, thick-fingered shaft thudded into the shield on his left, driving the rim into Frode's brow. He felt his skin split and wetness sting his eye and sheet his face. Staggering backwards, Frode shook his head, trying to clear the wool from it. A hand gripped his shoulder and a distended voice shouted in his ear.

"Urak bows are still singing, Laird." The belated warning cut through the ringing in his head but came to him as if he stood at the bottom of a well.

The fog lifted from his mind and with sudden clarity, Frode knew. Shrugging off the hand on his shoulder, he turned towards the lake. Frode stumbled and then ran. He could glimpse the destruction, the ground around the earthen bank was scorched black and a large hole gouged through it, gaping like an open wound. Scattered all around were broken bodies, those near the centre charred so badly he could not tell if they were man or woman.

For those unfortunates caught on the edge of the blast that yet lived; their furs smouldering, skin blistered and melted, Frode could do nothing and an unbridled scream, half despair and half horror ripped from his throat, joining the baleful moaning of the ruined. The piquant smell of burnt meat and the pungent stench of brimstone and sulphur filled his nostrils.

Frode cried out. Yelled until his lungs hurt. A hundred Bannermen, all that Huorl Landa had left of the reserve, seemed to have fared better than those Karls at the barricade. Whether they heard him or not they followed.

Urak surged through the hole in the earth wall. Arrows flew, the bottleneck making easy pickings for the Nordáa archers. More urak appeared above the earthen dyke, pulling themselves over the disrupted defences of the barricade, and the withering arrow fire shifted to sweep them.

The urak however did not drop so easily. In their berserker rage, it took two or three arrows to fell each one and inexorably the break-head began to widen.

Running atop the embankment, Frode lifted his shield and side-slammed an urak. His sword swept wide, slicing into the sinew and bone of another urak who straddled a shattered beam. The urak he pummelled with his shield, dropped its shoulder and hefted, sending Frode lurching and tumbling down the slope.

Rolling back to his feet, Frode looked up in time to see the urak gutted on a long pole, Connaer wielding it. His muffled hearing cleared, and the clamour of battle surged with an awakened howl against his ears and he swayed at its sudden onslaught.

Head swivelling, Frode tried to take stock. Battle raged along the embankment as far as the eye could see. Nordáa rushed by him, Baermen and Holdsteaders, charging the sloped earth around the breach. A wagon, stationed to carry the wounded, was being filled not by the injured but by sheaves of hay even whilst being pushed and pulled towards the gaping hole in the earth wall. The wagon steered into the rift and was set afire even before it came to a lurching stop. It would buy them time to shore up the defences.

Like a magnet, Frode was drawn to the tall war maiden he'd spied before the battle, her flaxen warrior braids hidden now beneath a steel helm. She stood a beacon of calm, her voice commanding and warriors running to obey. Frode felt admiration war against his shame, for she commanded more ably than he.

Behind the valkyrie, smoke belched like volcanic colonnades and unseen flames bathed the sky over Skaag's rooftops in a false sunset of golden pink. The town was burning. Through the press of warriors, Frode caught a glimpse of motion from deeper within Skaag's longhouses. Eyes flaring, he started walking, pushing through Nordáa to get a clearer look. Magnus of Skaag commanded the longer southern defences. More movement, this time in the roads and byways. Blocky forms that were too big to be men.

Opening his mouth, Frode cried out in warning, breaking into a run. Those warriors closest heard his call and followed his direction. Dreadful anger consumed him, even as a howling cry rose against the wind, bellowed war chants that announced better than he that the enemy was at their rear.

There was no time or need to wonder at Magnus or his thousands that guarded the southern flank. That the horde was here meant they were lost. Frode whispered a prayer, not to the Trinity or the One, but Trykís, of the old gods. *There is truth in death and I will face mine with a sword in my hand.*

With a battle cry, Frode charged. He did not know the warriors on each side of him, they were not his Bannermen, but they were his people, and they raised their voices with his.

They ran past the elders, the women and the older children and met the urak as they surged from between the buildings, a wave of death and fury that broke against the Nordáa wall in a deafening crash of flesh and steel.

Angling, Frode deflected a sword strike swinging for his head, the blow thumping against the shield on his arm and shaving off a thick, splinter of wood. Frode's sword slid between the exposed gap and inside the urak's guard, the red-painted warrior's momentum driving the steel through stiff leather and tough skin to lodge deep in its chest.

The urak's shield slammed upwards and struck Frode in the face. It smacked his chin and mouth and he felt cartilage break. The pain was immediate and excruciating even as Frode found himself tossed backwards. He landed hard on his back, the air driven from his lungs, mouth gaping as he struggled to scream and inhale.

His blade was still lodged in the urak, which leered, its lips and square teeth coated with blood. It choked, spitting a glob of claret onto its chin then stumbled and fell. Another brute stepped over the first, towering over Frode.

Scrabbling madly, Frode snatched the long knife from his belt and struggled to bring his battered shield to bear. A hand from behind gripped the back of his leather armour and hauled him to his feet. Blood sheeted Frode's face and he could taste it in his mouth and running down the back of his throat. He panted, his nose a riot of pain he could not breathe through.

With a growl, Frode spat out a tooth then hefted his dagger only for the man at his back to pull him away and step into his place. It was Connaer. His Bannerman yelled something at him, but Frode didn't register the words.

The urak struck, more circumspect than the last it did not overextend. Its heavy axe bit into Connaers shield, and the Nordáaman cried out as his arm took the full brunt of the blow. A spear lanced from the side, seeking the urak's flank only to be batted aside. A furred boot sent Connaer careening back into Frode, and the two men tumbled to the ground. Frode looked up into a spray of bone and brain, an axe blade splitting Connaers head like a dry log.

Scrambling backwards on his arse, Frode's hand struck a body lying in the reddened snow. He rolled over it, snapping a black shaft that protruded from the chest. Frode's eyes registered the blonde plaits and lake-blue eyes that stared vacantly at the sky. The war maiden's helm was gone, and her long limbs were bent in flaccid repose. *That she should die so, I didn't even know her name.*

A searing agony split his side and Frode slumped, his body spasming in shock. His shield was gone where he had dragged it with him and so was the arm that held it, blood pumping from its stump, pouring life onto the ground, adding its tincture to the canvas of slaughter he lay upon.

Frode waited for the final blow, welcomed death now that it was inevitable. At least it would take the pain. The sounds of battle faded away and a booted foot rolled him over.

"Your armour says you are a Lord." The urak was a mountain above him. A red-smeared face, a mockery of his own, gazed down upon him, long black braids full of bone charms swinging against the monster's chest.

The pain ebbed, diminishing to a dull ache. Frode felt himself fading as if sleep was slipping upon him. He was aware of other urak in his periphery, guards from the way they stood, their alertness. Somehow, Frode knew this urak was a leader, a chieftain among them.

"You fought well, human. In your next turn on the wheel, may Amhor-tun bless you to be born urakakule and Manawarih. Do you wish to speak words before I end you?"

Frode of Lonn looked up one last time to the sky. It was a deep blue with the lowering sun but stained with a veil of smoke. "Yes." The words came haltingly. "I wish I had known her name."

The blade arced.

Karth-Dur lifted the man's head. He hefted it in his palm. They had won a great victory, but it was tinged with anger. Anger that Krol had relegated the Manawarih and other tribes that opposed him, to fighting meaningless battles in the north whilst the Blood Skull War Chieftain, found glory in the south.

"Take his body and the female. Tonight we will feast. Drink of their blood, eat of their spirit." Karth-Dur looked up at the stone castle. "Tomorrow we will see about this house of stone."

* * *

It was night. Their camp was set not far from the road but deep enough back in the trees that the light from the fire could not be seen from atop the bluff.

Katal Zakpikt was settled near the fire's warmth. The Grey Knight was surly and spoke little but ate voraciously every morsel of food given. His wound throbbed as if every nerve ending was on fire, his leg itched and the skin pulled where it had been stitched and dressed.

It was quiet and the mood sombre. Merin Somar wandered over to the horses whilst Banff scrubbed the cookpot and the wooden bowls with snow.

Karl Hubert sat upon a log opposite Katal, eyeing the Mornayan from across the flames. "Fer a man what hates yams you ate enough of them."

"A hungry man will eat anything," Katal offered, white teeth glinting.

"Really?" Karl raised a sceptical eyebrow. "Northern pig fodder I seem to remember you callin' it yet here you are wolfing it down like it's the food of kings. You've eaten more than any of us."

"My injury makes me weak so a man eats what a man must to get strong," Katal said.

"Is that right?" Karl grunted.

"Stop baiting the man." Tannon Crick hobbled into the firelight. "If you're bored, Karl, I'm sure Marus would welcome your help."

The barrel-chested knight stood up and grunted. "Neither of ya are any fun. Think I'll take a shite instead." He strolled off into the woods, disappearing as soon as he stepped out of the light.

Katal glowered. "It is my leg that is injured, not my wit."

With a studied look, Crick nodded. "Get some rest." He raised his head towards Banff. "Marus. Lend me your shoulder."

Turning about, leaning on his stave, the Order man limped through the snow into the trees heading toward the escarpment. A jogging Banff caught him before he had gone ten paces and propped a shoulder under his arm.

"You should heed your own words, milord, and rest." Banff's blunt tone was full of reproach.

"You fuss like a mother does her children. I'm four hundred and thirty-six years young, Marus," Crick chuckled.

"Ai, you'd think being so old you would have learned some wisdom, ser, but I have yet to see any." Banff chided but with more humour than bite. "Now, what is it? You did not call on me to be a crutch. That much is plain."

"You're too clever by far to be my orderly, Marus," Crick said. "You know already why I called on you."

"Master Zakpikt," Banff confirmed. "Kat's injury was nasty, even crippling but all the signs are that he is healing well. There is no pus in the wound nor putrefaction of the surrounding skin hence no infection. I do not doubt that like you, he will be limping around soon enough. As to whether he makes a full recovery, it is too soon to say."

"Your bony shoulder is more a hindrance than a help." Crick shrugged free of Banff and resumed his walk with the stave. "Though Karl banters, he is right. Kat is not the same man. Something happened out in the wylds that he is unwilling to speak of. You know yourself. You've questioned the stitching of his wound."

Marus frowned. "What are your thoughts, Lord?"

They trudged on, skirting around the wide tree boles until the campfire was nothing but an obscure hint behind them. Crick stopped and turned to his friend.

"Tae'al, or aether as mages name it, is a living energy that resides inside of all things. A river flows as it flows and looks much the same from one moment to the next, but it is not. In constant motion, every instance it changes but the river is still the river."

"I'm not sure I follow, lord," Banff said.

"A person's aura is like a river, the tae'al beneath its surface is constantly shifting and changing but like the river, its flow and shape remain, more or less, constant. The person is still the person, the aura is still the aura. Having studied Kat, his seems to be as it should, only it is too static. It is subtle but the flow of tae'al does not reflect as it should upon his aura. I think it is a simulacrum. A mask."

"Are you saying Master Katal is manipulating his aura? I thought only mages, physikers or hedge wizards could manipulate aether like that. Could the trauma he suffered have awakened this talent?" Banff asked.

"It is possible, Marus, but unlikely. To awaken the talent and possess a mastery of it to the extent of creating a shielding aura is improbable at best. Certainly not with a hole in your leg and half-frozen. I will consult with Keeper. Say nothing to the others just yet but keep a careful watch on Kat. Now, wait for me back in camp."

Marus Banff said not a thing but neither did he move.

"My thoughts are clouded, and I need solitude to think them through. I'll be fine and I won't be long," Crick assured.

Banff turned away.

"Oh, and Marus," Crick called. "Do not leave anyone alone with Kat."

Banff returned a troubled look, gave a terse nod then left. Crick continued through the darkling wood, the path he had trodden earlier easy to pick out, his eyes already compensated for the low light. The trees gave way to scrub brush which in turn broke upon a snow-ladened edge with a precipitous drop. Crick rested his shoulder against the last of the trees and took the weight off his leg.

The sky above was clear with only a few high clouds, visible as a dead zone in the brilliant panoply of stars. Kildare's red moon hung over the Torn Spurs and Ankor's larger globe was high overhead, both casting a despondent light upon the land.

Wind rippled his hair; it was picking up and the scent of change was in the air. Eyes seeking the horizon, Tannon found the distant glow he looked for. A light beacon about where Skaag should be. It was no beacon though and the light offered no hope only despair for Skaag was aflame.

He felt a presence in his mind as the soft connection of the mind-link clicked into place. Tannon Crick focused on what had transpired since his last talk with Keeper, his mind shuffling through events with the speed of thought. No words were required.

<You believe Skaag is lost?> Keeper asked.

<If not today then certainly in the days to come. I should have fought harder to make them leave,> Crick answered.

Sympathy rolled across the link. <The Nordáa are a stubborn people. I doubt High Lord Janus, were he alive, could have persuaded Magnus of Skaag or his people to leave their home.>

Keeper continued, more brusquely. <Tannon, whether we are ready or not this new war of the Taken is upon us and, like the first, it will be one of attrition, of harsh defeats and small victories. At this most crucial of times, our beloved Order has lost its influence and its way. High King Edward lies dead, and a new monarch sits upon his throne. A High Queen no less, the first such.>

<Matrice!> Crick's thought hissed across the link.

<I did not perceive her ambition nor suspect her desire. A fatal mistake paid for by Renix,> Keeper replied.

<She is Taken maybe?> Crick mooted.

Keeper denied it. <I watched through Renix's eyes as she murdered him, and the malevolence and fervour were her own. I sense however the Morhudrim's hand in many things, not least the Red Church. The election of the High Cardinal during the Red Conclave was tainted by poison and murder. At its conclusion, only Tortuga remained, so we must assume he is compromised. This means we cannot approach the Churches nor the Crown and with the Order accused of Edward's murder our stock is low with the High Houses.>

Crick cursed. <What can we do?>

<I will consult with Da'Mari once her envoy arrives, but I fear until the Kingdoms realise whose hand guides this war our options are few. Until then we must speak the message and hope it takes hold in time.>

Crick's thoughts expanded in sudden clarity. <You knew. Before, when last we spoke you knew all of this. That is why your response in sending Rhool Dhunn to Jarlsheim was so limited. You're withdrawing our people from the Kingdoms.>

This time Keeper could not deny it. Not completely. <Not all. Many, like you, will not come if called and we still need eyes to see and ears to hear. These are desperate times, Tannon. You know we cannot fight a war where both sides see us as the enemy. Until the Kingdoms are ready to accept us, or we gather the ilfanum as allies we must protect our own and make Tankrit a fortress. The Morhudrim will come for us.>

<Isolating ourselves is not the answer, Keeper. It cannot be.> Crick faltered.

<We must face the truth however unpleasant it may be or wherever it may lead us. But do not despair my friend, hope is far from lost. We need to adapt and change our path as well as the narrative. To move to our plan rather than react to that of the enemy. Now, I sense you are conflicted about more than what has been discussed.>

Tannon Crick hedged, not sure why but disinclined of a sudden to discuss Katal with Keeper. Perhaps it was that Keeper had enough concerns. *<It is a personal matter. One I feel a need to resolve myself.>*

There was a slight pause before Keeper responded. *<Katal Zakpikt. His injury. Is there more to it you would tell me? You are not alone, Tannon.>*

The Order Knight shook his head at the night. *<Kat suffered great trauma, it can change a man. I will deal with this my way. Help him if I can.>*

Tannon Crick could sense Keeper was not entirely satisfied but whatever wisdom he had to give he kept to himself.

<You should reach Lonn in two days. We will speak again soon but until then say nothing to your Hand about what we have discussed. Especially Katal.>

The link terminated and Crick wondered why he'd not confided in Keeper his worry about Kat. *He knows already.* Keeper's last words proclaimed as much. The thought was a disquieting one.

Crick's eyes refocused on the distant smudge of light. He'd come seeking clarity but had found no joy in the answers he'd received. He watched Skaag until his limbs stiffened and the cold seeped into his flesh.

Knowing Marus would not leave him be, Crick turned and trudged back toward camp.

Chapter 39: Master of Birds

Anglemere Castle, Kingsholme, The Holme

"How hard can he be to find?" Matrice stamped her foot in frustration and then immediately regretted it. It played to that of a petulant fifteen-year-old girl rather than a queen. Stalking to her chair, black mourning dress rustling, Matrice forced herself to sit and gripped the padded armrests.

They were in the drawing room of the royal apartments. Present were Sir Gart Vannen, the Queen's First Sword, Master Piert Wendell, the Queen's adviser and Ricard Loris, Captain of Matrices' Personal Guard.

"Father has been dead a ten-day, yet that pampered buffoon eludes my justice. Explain how that is possible." Matrice asked, the new calm in her voice fooling no one in the room.

Loris glanced at the other two then cleared his throat.

"Not you, Captain." Matrice's dagger-like stare settled on Vannen who grimaced before answering.

"The city watch and Queensguard have trawled every street and alley and found no trace, my Queen. Every lead has turned out blind. I have reached out to other, less law-abiding contacts and the early promise that showed has proven misplaced."

"Does this Lord of Thieves slight me? Play me for a fool?" Matrice tapped a finger against the chair's armrest, a metronomic tic to her idling temper.

"The Targus has everything to gain and nothing to lose in finding your broth…," Vannen paused and corrected himself. "In finding Herald."

"You have been my strength, Gart. Never before have you failed me. That you do so now, and so," Matrice shook her head in disappointment, "so… completely, pains my heart."

Gart Vannen dropped to his knees before the elfin queen and bowed his head. "I strive with every sinew in my body to please you, my Queen, but I am no bloodhound. No skulker in the shadows. Let me back to your side. I can't protect you if I am not with you."

"Desist. Your whining and excuses are beneath you. I will not listen to them." Lifting her hand, she placed it on Gart's head and curled her fingers through his pepper-brown hair. She could feel his scalp shiver beneath her touch though he had the good grace and sense to keep his head lowered. She gripped a handful of hair and yanked harshly, eliciting a grunt from Vannen as she dragged his head up. Her green eyes fastened on his brown and she rewarded him with a knowing smile.

"The task did not suit you, my Sword," Matrice said agreeably. "But there are few I know to trust and none as much as I do you. I have many enemies and many more besides who see me as a child queen and they pray to see me fail. I will not give them that satisfaction. With my reign just begun and tenuous, I must do disagreeable things as must you all in my name. Now, off your knees, for surely you cannot protect me whilst you are upon them." Her mouth pinched into an impish grin as she released his hair and dropped her hand back to the armrest.

Her lost touch was like the warmth had left him and Gart quivered as he rocked back on his heels and stood. She was so tiny but there was steel in her and a fire of purpose so hot he basked in it. Gart stepped back and to the side, unsure whether she had granted his wish or not and too afraid to enquire.

Addressing the room, Matrice clapped her hands together, "You are all to attend my council in the war room at the next bell. Now, leave me." She clapped her hands twice more, then took pleasure in watching as the three men bowed to her and called her Majesty before filing out. She waited until the door banged shut then took a sip of wine and waited some more.

The air stirred, disturbing the drapes that fell on each side of the drawing-room's seaward window. All the windows had been closed and the diminutive Queen got up to investigate. She stopped halfway across the floor realising she was no longer alone.

"You're late." Matrice spun and addressed the slim, non-descript woman who stood next to the chair she had just vacated. How the woman got there and from where was both a mystery and a worry.

The woman was dressed in a servant's grey garb, of loose trousers beneath a three-quarter length robe, cinched around the middle with a wide, brown sash. How she could move so quietly in such attire baffled Matrice.

"No, I am not." The surety in the woman's voice was unequivocal, her clipped words, what few they were, held the accent of Holme, though Matrice did not trust it. They had met only a handful of times and the only certitude about the Master of Birds was that nothing was as it seemed, the woman's honorific only one such example.

Moving to the door, Matrice slid the bolt home, using the time and the silence to collect her thoughts. Rhin Malraven, Master of Birds made her uncomfortable. Matrice had neither heard of the woman nor her title until the night of her coronation when Malraven appeared in the small hours of the morning in her royal bedchamber. A hunched shadow in the black of night, Rhin had sat by the open window of the bedroom, though how she had opened it from the outside, Matrice had no idea.

Rhin's first words to her were, "To scream would be a mistake."

The fear of murder being a real one, Matrice had very nearly done just that, but some instinct held her silent.

Rhin's second words answered her first thought. "An assassin does not announce themself. A few drops of ariqksen in your night wine and you'd be none the wiser until your lungs seized."

"Who are you?" Matrice had asked.

"I was your father's Master of Birds, his spymaster. Now I am yours." Rhin's answer to her had been a statement as much as an oath and it had changed everything.

Matrice left the door and returned to her cushioned seat.

Rhin Malraven glided to the centre of the room and spoke in a monotone that only just carried to Matrice. "Herald fled the city six nights ago and travels north in the company of Lady Mori Duncan. The logical assumption is that they head for Hawke Hold."

The queen's face darkened. "I'll have the Duncan hung by his balls, that cogitating, interfering old fuck. Are you certain?" The coarseness sounded unnatural coming from Matrice.

Malraven gave a terse stare. "Few things are certain, the sun rising and the moons in the sky, but I am sure enough that I mention it. The night of the fire in the Stack's was a distraction. Whilst it was burning the Lady Mori left the Shorune Plain, your uncle's Blackcoats had no cause to hold her and none had the authority to stop her. Lord Henry, you see, was busy in the city taking the knee and assuming office as your Lord Marshall. It was a well-orchestrated escape."

The Master of Birds wandered to the sideboard near the window as she spoke. Lifting the carafe of wine she filled her nostrils with its scent before returning it. The queen's eyes flickered towards her goblet and Malraven's gave the faintest of smiles. "Sorry, a habit of mine. Few poisons are completely tasteless and odourless. Assassins tend to veer toward wine rather than water for that reason. The heady bouquet of a good wine can hide much, you see. It's the tannins."

"Do you toy with me, Rhin?" Matrice's voice was flat, her jade eyes turning flinty. "Many have mistaken my youth and inexperience as ineptitude and have already paid the price for it."

"I am not many," Malraven returned. "I serve you, Matrice, but I am not subservient. I tell you my truth without fear nor favour. I mentioned the wine for two reasons. The first is that you drink too much of it. You are young, too young yet to claim wine as a vice. It is a false crutch.

"The second is because you cannot trust anyone, even those closest to you. Having chosen this path, you will need a clear head and no small amount of good fortune if you are to reach its end. A final coda, a suggestion if I may. Order your wine as before, but do not partake of it. Instead, pour it away, discretely, and drink only water. I will give you a tab of powder that is a counter to the most common of the tasteless poisons. Keep it on your person and use it if you suspect your water has been tampered with. It will make you shit and vomit but delivered timely enough you may survive."

"Any other pearls of wisdom?" Matrice asked, unimpressed with the woman's attempt to unsettle her.

"Yes. The Duncan's word can be trusted which makes him the best of allies and the worst of enemies. I urge you to the former and caution against the latter for you have enemies enough already and not just the existential threat of the urakakule. It is the Order's belief the Morhudrim is returned and the second war of the Taken is upon us." Malraven raised a hand to forestall the Queen who looked ready to explode, to no avail.

"How very convenient," Matrice sniped. "A distraction to cover the Order's scheming and lies. I warn you, Rhin, do not challenge me on this. I will have my father's murderer. I will take my brother's head and if the Order seeks to use Herald, and the Duncan to protect him, I will crush them all."

Malraven gave a pointed look and waited for Matrice's tirade to subside. "I told you at our first introduction that I am a truth dealer. I provide information and advice and it is yours to do with as you will, but in return do not peddle me your false narrative, it insults us both. Keep it for those who need to hear it."

An agitated Matrice glanced toward the door. That this woman mentioned poison in one breath then all but accused her of patricide in the next and all in the tone of an equal, were compelling enough reasons to have Rhin Malraven killed. Matrice just wasn't sure how to go about it.

"You are wise to be concerned, Matrice, you never know who might be listening," Malraven smiled and her face looked almost pleasant. "But have no fear, I have warded the room. None will hear us speak. Now, hear my truth.

"The Holy Quarter is afflicted by a spat of murders. Priests fall victim almost nightly, brutalised and turned to boneless lumps. What remains is beyond recognition as human. The Voices of the Trinity cannot explain it. They consult with the Prime Magus who has assigned a pair of Enclave Arbiters to investigate. But the Prime knows already. The Prime has read the forbidden tomes and the ancient scripts."

"Knows what?" Matrice could not help but ask, nor wonder how the Master of Birds could know all this and more.

"Knows that murders like these have been seen before. Just not in a thousand years." Malraven paused to let her words sink home.

"If the Morhudrim is here, working in the shadows, sowing discord and terror, then you and the peoples of these Nine Kingdoms will have need. Read the forbidden histories, Matrice, and you will see the wisdom in my truth. So, I warn you, do not close off all avenues to the Order, at least until we know. Now, for today, let us put the matter of the Order aside.

"The Duncan." Malraven moved on. "He is a reasoned man. Send him a reasoned message but no threats. Threats need to be delivered upon, and the Duncan will understand them without the need of statement."

Decidedly more circumspect, Matrice blew out a sigh. These conversations with Malraven were always unsettling but Rhin's advice had always proven invaluable. It gave her insights she lacked and an edge when dealing with, well, everything. "Very well. I will have Harris contact the Duncan with a polite enquiry."

"You have a garrison at Crickwillow, as does High Lady Hardcastle," Malraven said. "Order them to Outward. The Lady Mori's caravan will have to pass it to reach Hawke Hold. With luck, it may net you Herald but otherwise, it will remind the Duncan of the stakes at play."

Matrice nodded approval at the suggestion. "You have more to say."

The Master of Birds gave the barest trace of a smile. "High Lord Zacorik docked in Sudda two days ago. My birds tell me thirty thousand of the Defosi were assembled and waiting for him. They rode this morning, destination unknown, though I posit several potentials."

Clasping her hands together, Matrice stood. "Your news, whilst welcome, merely confirms my own intelligence from Sudda. I am not incompetent, Rhin. My father was a great strategist and I have his gift. Do not think I sit idle or worry only about what I see before me."

Malraven inclined her head. "My apologies. I would be interested in hearing your thoughts on the matter."

Ignoring the sense she was being indulged, Matrice moved to a landscape map of the Nine Kingdoms that hung upon the chamber wall and jabbed at Sudda then dragged her finger westward. "If the Defosi move to Lamá it is to counter the brewing rebellion in the far west. If the Defosi continue along the East Way to Ventara then it is to fortify the Ventris Gap. Zacorik will look to barter his support for the war against the urakakule. He will seek concessions from the Crown or worse, look to secede from the Kingdoms by closing the border, knowing our troubles in the north strengthens him and weakens the Kingdoms."

"It is as you say, Highness," Malraven agreed. "However, the situation may well be more fluid for Zacorik. If he holds at Malvaris it tells us his hand is uncertain. That he covers both the south road to Lamá and the northern route to the Kingdoms. However, having studied the man and knowing his character, I would suggest another possibility.

"In his youth, Yanik Zacorik was besotted by a young woman, a cousin thrice removed, Suran of the Sumar Isles. A love that was reciprocated but was lost when Suran was betrothed to the then Crown Prince of the Nine Kingdoms." Malraven gave a discerning look. "You look much as your mother did if I may say, Matrice, and possess many of her qualities."

The waif-like queen returned a thin-lipped stare.

Giving an insouciant shrug, Malraven continued. "Yanik Zacorik is cunning and precocious. A worthy adversary. He is honourable in the way all great men like to think of themselves. However, like most born of privilege, he is a man of appetite and ambition. The mother is beyond his reach but not so the daughter."

Matrice's eyes flashed dangerously.

"To lend his Defosi, the price Zacorik will demand will be your hand in marriage, to become the Queen's consort. He will seek to put his seed in your belly and his child upon the Kingdom Throne."

"I would rather slit his throat," Matrice growled.

"A child's response. Do not dismiss it out of hand," Malraven said. "You have Southland blood in your veins but a union with Zacorik would further bind the Southlands of Olme to you and offset the threat of your uncle, Henry Blackstar. For if you think he has given up hope of the Kingdom Throne you are sorely mistaken. You might consider making an overture to Zacorik, after all, he is not displeasing to look upon and he treats his current wife and concubines favourably. If you tire of him, then once the High Lord of Sudda has played his part and given you a child, preferably two, he can be disposed of. All problems have a solution."

"I will think on it," Matrice mumbled, unhappy at the prospect. "Anything else?"

"Nothing that won't keep." Malraven moved to the door of the bedchamber and opened it but looked back over her shoulder at the queen in her mourning gown. "Wear red, the time for black is done. To become the Red Queen you must dress for it. And remember what I told you at our previous meet, of the High Lords and Ladies. You will need it for your war council."

The Master of Birds stepped out of the room and the door closed behind her. Matrice didn't bother to go and look, knowing Rhin would be gone by the time she opened the door to see. Instead, she unbolted the drawing-room door and called for her maids.

* * *

"We just don't know enough. We're dealing with broad strokes rather than detail."

Lord Marshall Henry Blackstar stood at the northern head of the large map table. His gaze lifted from the blocks and markers which sat upon the map, to the war council attendees who were seated around its edge. His piercing eyes swept anti-clockwise around the table, from the High Lords' Ostenbow of Branikshire, Trevenon of Eosland, Dumac of Westlands and the High Lady Hardcastle of Midshire, past the three Voices of the Trinity who sat opposite the Southlands of Olme, barely paused at the queen's close council which comprised Rudy Valenta Master of Coin, Magnus Harkul Lord Commander of the Queensguard, Piert Wendell of no title or office and Harris Benvora the queen's mage. They rested briefly on the Prime Magus John Tarran before alighting finally upon Matrice, first of her name, High Queen of these Nine Kingdoms. Apart from himself, she alone stood, her eye-catching crimson dress form-fitting from chest to waist before flowing in voluminous bulk to the floor.

"What do we know, uncle?" Matrice asked. Her voice was calm and assured.

With a vexed grunt, Black Henry returned his attention to the map. "Urak have taken everything north of the Plago and the Fossa with some reports claiming they are as far south as the Sindhow Plains."

Leaning in, he swept his hand over the Rivers, then east to the Torn Spur and Norderland. "The fortress at Highwatch is lost and urak flood the forests of Helg. The Barle of Skaag reports they are preparing their defences."

The Prime Magus, John Taran interrupted. "No longer, Lord Marshall. The Enclave received word as I was leaving. Magner of Skaag fell in battle. The town is lost but the castle still holds, though for how long is uncertain. Jonah Terik, Skaag's magus, claims the town and castle were assailed by hellfire and that thousands of the enemy occupy Skaag and many more hide under cover of the Helg."

"Hellfire?" The Lord Marshall raised a quizzical eyebrow. "This supports the accounts from Thorsten. It seems the urakakule do have spellcasters to counter our own."

Rising to get a clearer view of the Norderlands, the Prime Magus flicked his robe back. "Historical scrolls name them Shaman but there is little written about them. Their prior involvement in conflict seems non-existent, which means either our histories are inaccurate or something fundamental has changed in urak societal culture."

John Taran glanced at the table and the tiny mark upon it notated with the word 'Skaag'. That such a tiny spot symbolized a whole town, represented thousands of men, women and children, was a wonder of humbling insignificance. He could reach out and cover it with his fingertip and convey more immediately than any words that it was no more. He looked up. "I beg your pardon?"

Henry Blackstar gave a pinched look, a muscle along his jawbone spasming. "I said 'I don't give two fucks about urak societal culture from a thousand years ago.' You should have spoken of this to me before our council, Prime."

"It's my council, uncle and the Prime Magus mentioned it to me," Queen Matrice said. Stepping back, she sat and reclined in her father's chair, now hers. *It needs a few cushions.*

The Lord Marshall spun to face her, his eyes like schist-rock.

"Don't look at me like that, uncle. There was no time to inform you," Matrice said. "Besides, that was not the only news, was it Prime?"

"No indeed, your Majesty. Mage Terik reports that High Lord Justin Janis was murdered on the Skárpe Steppes whilst on his way to relieve Highwatch. Purportedly by Marlik Riekason, one of his sworn men." John Taran glanced at the queen. "May I?"

Matrice bowed her head in the affirmative.

"Tannon Crick, an Order Knight, rode with Janis. Crick told Magner of Skaag that Riekason was not himself. That the Jarl was a Taken, possessed by the Morhudrim from legend," Taran stated.

"Preposterous," Maxim Tortuga rumbled from where he was seated. His flaccid bulk filled the chair. "More artifice, Highness. It can be no coincidence that the Order was present at both your father's assassination and the High Lord's."

The Prime Magus lowered his bushy eyebrows at the interruption. "Except, Your Holiness, that Barle Frode of Lonn confirmed Crick's account. The Order man arrived after Janis was murdered and many of the High Lord's Karls witnessed Riekason's guilt. I know that the Church of Kildare holds cause against the Order but do not let it interfere with truth. The matter should be considered rather than dismissed out of hand."

The truth. Matrice had heard the word said far too much this day. High Cardinal Tortuga had been instrumental in her succession, but she was not blind. Everyone wanted something. It was more than likely that rather than the vision he proclaimed having, Tortuga saw her patronage as an opportunity. That she was easier to obtain, more pliable, simpler to manipulate and influence than her uncle, Black Henry. It made sense. Rhin Malraven had said as much that first night they had met. Matrice parted her lips showing a flash of teeth. She had grown up watching the Game of Lords and was no stranger to it. Other than the players, the petty rivalries of the churches were no different.

Matrice lifted her voice to the room. "Lying upon his deathbed, High Cardinal Tortuga was graced with a vision. Kildare showed the Nine Kingdoms in blood and flame and, though still in the grips of his malady, he told us in this very room, uncle, what you have today. More, for he named the urak clans involved. That the White Hand invade the Rivers and the Red Skull the Norderland. So, his words should not lightly be dismissed."

"Thank you, Your Highness." Tortuga's fleshy chin wobbled as he spoke and he patted with a scented cloth, at the sheen of moisture that coated his face.

Matrice could sense the smile hidden behind it and gave one of her own. "Kildare's vision as you have conveyed it, however, does not preclude the possibility of the Morhudrim or some other power at play. Something prompted the urak to traverse the Torns and invade my lands."

Matrice raised her voice, letting a little anger seep into her tone. "There are other happenings that are of concern to me. Ones not accountable to the Order. Happenings in this very city, of murders most vile. They should have been reported to me by those I should trust the most. That they were not, begs me to ask the question, why not?"

Her eyes sparkled as they moved from Tortuga to Rand Luxurs in his gold-embroidered brown robe and Maris Jenah in her pure white. Tilting her head, Matrice included John Taran in her sphere of displeasure. "Murder in my city. Yet you deigned not to tell me."

Giving a glance to the two men beside her, Maris Jenah took it upon herself to reply. "Your Majesty, the murders happened solely upon the consecrated grounds of the Trivium and targeted only at our Holy Fathers and Revered Mothers. We are still trying to understand the nature of the murders as well as apprehend the perpetrator. If we had something to offer concerning either, we would have informed you. Until then, Ma'am you have the business of this war and the Nine Kingdoms to manage. There is no ulterior motive other than we did not wish to distract you from your greater task."

"Your Holinesses, Prime. We will speak after this council," Matrice said.

"Indeed," Henry Blackstar barked, wresting back hold of the conversation. "This is a discussion for another time. If we could get back on topic."

"Agreed, uncle, please continue."

"This council is for war planning and is based on what we know, not idle conjecture." The Lord Marshall exhaled heavily.

"Losing Janis is a grievous blow. He was a strong leader, a fierce warrior and his death leaves a hole in our northern defences, for his son, if memory serves me, is a child." Blackstar's head pivoted from the map to an unmoving, Matrice. "He is too young and unfit to take his father's mantle. In war, a land needs its strongest, most experienced sons to lead it."

Gart Vannen, standing in silent guard behind the queen's chair, placed a hand on his sword hilt but did not draw it, though his gesture was seen by all.

"You would make a poor drape, uncle. Should I fetch you the Kingdom Crown or perhaps a box for your head?" Matrice tapped a slender finger to her lips.

"I meant only that you should appoint a seasoned Barle as High Lord of Norderland rather than rely upon the tactical nouse of a boy," Henry growled, unperturbed by the threat.

Matrice gave a winsome smile. "Master Wendell informs me Kaygó Janis is seven and the Norders will declare him High Lord as his father was. I will no more interfere in that matter than I would any of my Kingdoms. Not directly at least. I understand until Kaygó attains his majority of fifteen a Warmaster will be appointed. A man, or woman, most suited to the task I am sure, as are you uncle. Please continue with your briefing."

Henry gave his niece a begrudging nod and returned his attention to the map table and the room at large. He pointed to the Rivers.

"Rivercross is the spearpoint of our defence in the nor'west. It has high walls and is protected by rivers to the north and guarded by the Emerald Lake to the south which can be used to resupply the city. It will not succumb easily."

"Urak have been sighted but distantly and High Lord Twyford reports they seem reluctant to attack or siege the city. The scouts sent out fail to return which means we have no clear idea of their numbers nor disposition, only that they control from Fallenfaire in the east to Confluence in the west. It is a front too wide to cover and with snows inflicting the north we are limited in our response. What we do know, courtesy of the Lord of Thorsten, is the urakakule have brought not just warriors but whole tribes."

"All of this confirms two things. First, they are here to stay and second, where they can avoid it, urak will not waste themselves against our fortifications."

With barely a pause and used to being heard, Henry Blackstar's voice rang with conviction and authority.

"Every indication is they push south, taking our smaller towns and those settlements less well defended. But there are vast tracts of wilderness in the north, the Sindhow Plains, the Dherin Dales, the Camfyr Downs, where they can roam and we wouldn't know it. Even if we knew where the bulk of their forces gathered, given we do not have the numbers at present to bring them to battle, we must instead try to contain them."

Leaning over the table, Black Henry moved several blocks from Revis to Rosenmouth and Whaling. Then, several more from Hardcastle to Peatbrook and Sull, and finally a block from Morport to Arden.

"All these towns are walled and, except for Sull, lie on the High Road from Morport to Rosenmouth. We reinforce them as we can. Then, if one is attacked support lies no more than two days away. We can do no more in winter than this."

"What do you mean by 'as we can'? Matrice queried.

"He means," said High Lord Dumac, "that moving armies is challenging at the best of times. But these are not the best of times. A winter conflict is a madness none of us has prepared for. We have neither the food nor the supplies needed for such a wide and enforced campaign and, now the snow has arrived in the north, we do not have the means to acquire it. We are hamstrung until spring."

"I asked for plans, not excuses," Matrice stated. "If you are suggesting we sit and do nothing until the snows melt you are mistaken. Every town and city boasts armsmen. Call them up."

"Oh, the order has been issued, Highness," Henry Blackstar replied. "From Morass and the Blue Mountains to the Bite. But High Lord Dumac is right, and I estimate at best only a third of any standing garrison will ride or march, for no lord nor lady is prepared for a winter campaign and none will leave their towns undefended. Reinforcing these towns as I intend will present additional logistical problems. Feedstock, grain, meat and the accoutrements of war, will all need to be found and moved from our stocks in the south. That will not be easy or come cheaply."

"I will sign a writ and give a war bond for the standard value of any goods or materials requisitioned," Matrice declared, exasperation creeping into her voice. "Anyone who refuses or barters for a higher price will be drafted and sent to the north to stand upon the walls with their brothers and sisters. I will not be defied in this. Once the war is done, we will look at how best to honour the bonds issued."

Matrice leaned forward from her chair and glanced to her left. "Lord Valenta, as Master of Coin you will coordinate with the Lord Marshall after we are done here. Draw up a list of goods and materials, then price them based on the cheapest seasonal cost for each."

"Your will, Your Highness." Rising from his seat, Valenta bowed to the queen and then gave a nod to Henry Blackstar before reseating himself.

"You have covered the Rivers' western borders but what of its eastern?" Matrice said.

Henry Blackstar spared the High Lords and High Lady a look. Other than Hardcastle, none seemed too pleased with Matrice's proclamation, and he smiled inwardly to himself. *Discord sows the seeds of discontent*, his father Kenning Blackstar used to say. *Nurtured correctly its harvest is opportunity.*

With a cat-like grin, the Lord Marshall returned to the map. "We will hold at the River Thun. Killenhess will anchor the Emerald Lake and there are watchtowers of old along the Thun we can use to watch for any crossing." He started moving blocks from Eosland and Cumbrenan to places along the course of the river, from the Emerald Lake to Mox Thun in the northeast. "Many towns and villages along the Thun have fortifications we can use but I intend to concentrate most of Cumbrenan's forces here, here and here." Black Henry indicated Thorn Nook, Tunning and Rapid Lakes.

Afterwards, Henry Blackstar spoke briefly once more of the Norderland. In many ways, they were the hardiest, most resilient of the Nine Kingdoms. Renowned for their warrior code and fighting spirit they would rally as a nation to the banners at Jarlsheim. Until they knew more, however, such as who the Warmaster would be and what was needed, the Norders, he declared, would have to fend for themselves. The only concession to this was High Lord Trevennon of Eosland being tasked to ready his fleets. If chance permitted and the opportunity arose they could land men and horses by ship up the coast to provide support or flank the enemy.

"And what of the Holme and the Southlands?" asked an irritated Trevenon after giving his grudging agreement. Whilst he addressed the Lord Marshall it was plain from the intensity of his stare who his ire was directed at. "You seem content to order my fleets and our lords around like pieces on a Shojek board whilst treating us like those blocks on the map. Why don't you explain where the Holme's forces are to be deployed and why?"

"You know already, High Lord. Do you not? As does everyone here," Black Henry answered his eyes roving the table. They hesitated on the queen's close council. "Well, most of you at least."

"It's alright uncle, I believe High Lord Trevenon meant the question for me." With a rustle of red silk, Matrice rose once more from her chair and moved to the head of the table.

"As you are aware, High Lord Zacorik left Kingsholme before my ascension to the throne. He faces trouble in Great Olme, rebellion in the west at Kampok and the Sunset Isles and increasing pressure from at least three of the Five Hosha of Sudda, to break from the Kingdoms.

"I need stability in the south. The Kingdoms demand it. And of all our great lands, Olme is least afflicted by the privations of winter. They provide grains, fruits, sugarcane and cotton, silk and other commodities we have all come to rely upon. That trade cannot be lost nor used to hold us to ransom. Not at this time and not ever," Matrice declared.

"We also need the Defosi. When winter passes and the snow has melted, we will need the horsemen of Olme. To combat the urakakule in open battle, cavalry will be our most destructive weapon, mages aside."

Derek Trevenon rose, face flushed and slapped his palm down with a clap on the Endless Sea. "You talk and talk and tell us what we already know. Tell us what we do not."

Like kindling on a bonfire, a fury sparked in Matrice's eyes. "Have a care for your tone, High Lord. Whilst in council I wish all to speak freely, but I will brook no slight or refusal to my command. I possess neither the tolerance of my father to overlook it nor the luxury of doing so. I pray, do not test me on this, for you will like the outcome far less than I. Now sit. You as well uncle, if you would."

Matrice watched as Trevenon sucked in his cheeks, his eyes blinking in agitation. She could almost hear Rhin Malraven in her head, laughing at her clumsy attempts at control. *Show a threat, imply it by all means but if you declare it, you must be prepared to act upon it. If you have to act upon it then by definition you have lost control, you are simply on a path you cannot leave.*

Matrice exhaled slowly whilst she waited for the two men to be seated. *Bitch was right.* She took a breath. *Again.*

"Since some of you seem disinclined to listen to my context, I will tell you what is and you may draw your own conclusions." Her gaze shifted to the High Lords and High Lady.

"Zacorik is my problem, and I will attend to it and bring him to heel. How I do so is none of your concern. Your business is north as is the Lord Marshal's. Uncle, you will leave and take direct command of our forces. You may take your Blackcoats with you but no Lords of Holme. They are mine. I would suggest Morport as a base, it is only partially walled but the Rivers Marr and Lothern guard its flanks.

"Prime, consult with the Lord Marshall. I expect the Enclave to do their part. I have heard tell in ancient times that cadres of battle mages were formed. If you have not already looked into it, do so. I need as many of these cadres as can be made to combat these shamans you speak of. We need to know how they compare with us."

Matrice looked down the length of the table, across the breadth of her kingdoms in miniature, to the Voices of the Trinity. "Likewise, I expect the churches to offer assistance. Priests for service, physikers from Ankor and Nihmrodel and Red Cloaks and Battle Priests from Kildare.

"High Cardinal Tortuga, it is my understanding Bishop Whent, Lord Commander of the Red Cloaks has been called to Kingsholme and that he brings an urak captive with him. That is good. I would like to meet both. I will take the urak to Southlands and show them what they face. What we all face if we divide ourselves."

Tortuga's sunken eyes, too small in his large head, looked almost black for a moment but Matrice had already moved on to encompass the room with her gaze and rhetoric.

"Listen to the Lord Marshal. Do as he says. Provide what is asked for so we can hold this flood of urak to the north. Otherwise, they will be on your border, invading your lands. Make no mistake, they will end us unless we are one. So cease these rivalries you play, at least until the urakakule have been defeated."

"Now, some final news." Matrice took a more conciliatory tone. "Though heavy checks will be implemented the gates to Kingsholme have been reopened. My High Lords, my High Lady, you may return home and carry out our will. However, I do require family representation from you all at Kingsholme. I have left written instructions in your quarters in this regard. If you have any issues, please raise them with Master Wendell. He is the new Lord Chamberlain and will bring any concerns you have to my attention.

"Prime Taran, High Priestess, High Cardinals. If you would remain. The rest of you may leave."

Her uncle, Henry Blackstar was closest to her and when he stood and bowed, the look he gave when he straightened was telling. *You should have discussed this with me it said.* The conceited smirk implied she had erred and he was pleased by it.

Had Rhin Malraven coached her wrong these last nights? The look ate at Matrice as Black Henry left the room, ushering quiet words to the High Lords though excluding, Matrice noticed, the High Lady Hardcastle. Her worry vanished of a sudden and she smiled. *Rhin was right.*

You may be a wolf, uncle, and these others. But you are no pack and you will all find out soon enough you play with a Hrultha.

Chapter 40: Winter-Meet

Forest of Arden, Midshire

Hiro sat opposite his old comrade. The firelight played across Maohong's face, animating it with a vibrancy that was a lie. His thoughts drifted back to when they had first met.

Originally from Maritq'ha in the Chezuan Imperia, Mao was more than he seemed. More than anyone knew. He was the son of a Kan and a summoner. A powerful one at that, but youthful and prideful with it.

Barely a man, Tasao Maohong, son of Tasao Honsuho third Kan of Maritq'ha reached too far into the void. Summoned a being so powerful he could not contain it nor control it. By the time the elders had subdued the demon, it had killed half a village, women, children and warriors. It had torn them to pieces, bellowing its outrage.

Of course, Hiro had not seen any of that. Nor did he witness the elders tame it with their magics. But he came, intrigued when the wind carried rumour of the tragedy. Sentenced to death, the Kan had interceded at Hiro's suggestion and banished his son instead. Releasing Mao to him under oath that neither man return to Maritq'ha.

Hiro blinked his idle musings away then stared. He knew Mao was in there staring back at him but so too was Q'tox and it was the demon that held sway now.

The mark of contract itched his hand and Hiro rubbed it absently and berated himself for being a sentimental fool. He should have ended this at the caverns. Buried a knife in Mao's heart and robbed the demon of the sanctuary of his friend's body. It was his duty, only Hiro couldn't bring himself to do it. Companions for almost sixty years, that time was not so casually dismissed, and Mao deserved better than a quick death by his hand. Now though, he had to live with the consequence of his inaction and the infernal agreement he had reached with Q'tox.

The air hummed and a shiver of energy brushed over Hiro.

"Is that wise?" Hiro asked.

Q'tox-Mao, still as a rock, answered. "The ilf dressed in the skin of a human knows of my presence, as does the mystic, the rest don't matter aside from the boy and girl. Those pair are an intriguing conundrum."

"I see."

"I am not sure you do, but I digress. I wish to amend our agreement," Q'tox-Mao said.

Hiro sat straighter on his log, "I'm listening."

"The agreed destination is no longer relevant to me. I wish to make it flexible."

"Thought what you wanted was in Kingsholme?" Hiro's voice held a note of enquiry. "Perhaps if you explain what you need, I could better help."

"Help me, human?" Q'tox-Mao chuckled. "Fifty-nine of your sidereal years I was bound, an insignificant period for me but an eternity for your kind. In all that time never once did you seek to speak to me let alone offer aid. Am I to believe you would do so now."

Hiro's eyes narrowed. "You murdered people. Half a village perished by your hand, and you didn't just kill them. Skin blistered and sloughed from the bone at your touch, their internal organs ruptured and reduced to slush. You deserve death and worse."

"You were not there. You understand nothing. Those deaths were on Tasao Maohong, not I," Q'tox-Mao intoned, his voice even but his eyes bright with anger. "That stripling had the temerity to summon me. Me! Q'tox, Tetriarché, second rank Sházáik of Sházarch. Pulled against my will through the void as if I were nothing more than a Bezalgets."

Hiro shifted on his log. "Mao's crime was pride and arrogance. He was young, barely a man and has paid his due every day since. What he did was wrong, but he did not do murder. What you did was evil."

Mao's head shook. "Is a Hrultha evil? No, it is a fearsome creature, vicious, volatile but one of nature. If you instantaneously took a Hrultha and dropped it into a village leaving it disorientated, what do you think it would do? No more than I and yet you deem me evil?

"I have witnessed you, Hiro of the Order, as long as I have Tasao Maohong. In that time, you have grown no older and yet Mao has aged and turned frail. I fear his death. That the trinket I was bound to would become lost or broken. If you truly wish to help, then send me back."

Hiro was silent for a time, lost in thought as he considered what Q'tox had said. "Maybe the summoners of the Chezuan Imperia could help but we would need to cross the Great Expanse to reach them. It isn't a quick nor easy journey to make and in case you hadn't noticed we are at war. The Morhudrim has returned and spreads its darkness across the land."

"I care not for your woes," Q'tox-Mao replied. "And you forget yourself, I possess a summoner already to open the rift. What I need is the Vox Léchtar Fai-ber to read the signs and etch the symbols then, either a place where the veil between worlds is thin or a source of power strong enough to fracture the way."

"Vox Léchtar Fai-ber? A Wordsmith. There is Razholte, Master of the Library on Tankrit but I presume you speak of another. One that has perhaps left Kingsholme recently?"

Q'tox-Mao's grin widened, showing a mouth full of yellow, crooked teeth.

Hiro nodded as he collected his thoughts. "It might work. My binding with you leaves me no choice so the sooner you are gone the better. I will help but you must return Mao to me unharmed when we are done."

A dry, humourless chuckle greeted Hiro's demand. "I fixed bone and mended flesh, but Maohong's spirit is weak. I cannot promise it will cling to life without me. That he lives long enough to maintain the rift is my only concern."

"Then allow him more freedom," Hiro beseeched. "Let him come to the fore and experience life as before. Let his tae'al recentre and bring balance. It will strengthen his will and aid with the sending. In return, I will tell you what we must do."

"Q'tox listens," the sháadretarch said.

"Ekan Maul, the broken city. No life grows within a league of its fallen walls. Ancient texts say it is not of this age nor built by man but little else. I went many years ago and saw it for myself and it was not a pleasant experience for it was tainted and I felt great despair. The power I sensed, the life energy surrounding Ekan Maul, was corrupt and alien as if it did not belong. Perhaps it does not?"

Mao's face remained placid, but his eyes shone bright with interest. "Ekan Maul. I have not heard of this place. Where is it located?"

* * *

Nihm was frustrated. Something was going on between Master Hiro and old Mao and she hoped to learn what. But, as fine-tuned as her hearing had become, she could not for the life of her understand what it was they said. It was like listening to someone speak underwater.

<Perhaps you should just ask Master Hiro rather than spy upon him?> Sai suggested.

<You're pretty smart but you've got a lot to learn about people. Grownups only tell you what they think you should know. He treats Renco like a child and would me too given half the chance,> Nihm said.

A memory of her eight-year-old self sneaking into the homestead when she was meant to be doing chores flittered through her mind. The grunting and groaning from her parents' room caused a flush of concern that turned to embarrassment when she entered their room. <It didn't end well last time if you recall,> Sai commented.

<Stop that. I don't need that memory repeating thank you very much. Besides, that was different. I was a child then and didn't know any better.> Nihm shuffled her feet and Ash, sensing her agitation, whined and brushed his nose against her hand.

Mao and Hiro glanced into the wood towards the tree she hid behind and Nihm placed a quieting hand on Ash then froze. After an exaggerated moment, the two men returned to their conversation and Nihm took a breath.

Whatever they talked about was coming to an end. Hiro stood and walked around the campfire and Mao warbled something before the two clasped hands, Mao taking Hiro's in both of his. More words were spoken then their hands released and Hiro walked off towards the Wylder wagons.

Mao for his part sat staring into the flames, head cocked to the side as if reading something in the glowing embers. He held a hand to the heat and the fire hissed and spluttered. Flames leapt from the burning kindling and coalesced above Mao's fingertips which snatched at the air as if they played some unseen instrument. Faster and faster his fingers moved and with it, the ball of flame grew tighter and brighter. Its colour changed from a red-yellow to a blue as pure as a summer sky.

A flick of motion sent the blue-ball soaring above the treetops. Then, with a snap of Mao's fingers, the flame orb exploded in a shower of golden sparks that floated tantalisingly before winking out of existence.

Nihm's mouth opened in wonder. When her eyes returned to the glade, adjusting to the new darkness, Mao was gone.

"It was a neat trick, don't you think?"

Nihm spun, placing the trunk between her and the voice, her heart pounding even as she recognised it as Nesta's. Mortified that the ilf had snuck up on her, she jabbed an accusing look at Ash by her side and then Snow who sat next to the ilf as if it was of no matter. "Lot of good you two were."

The wolfdogs gave a whine.

<*And you weren't any better,*> Nihm directed at Sai.

<*De'Nestarin has considerable skill at moving undetected and he is downwind,*> Sai stated.

"I didn't know Mao could use aether like that." Nihm peered at Nesta, her enhanced sight easily picking out his features in the dark light.

"There is much you do not know, Nihmrodel Castell. This way you have chosen is open to misinterpretation. Perhaps the answers you seek are best asked."

<*That is what I said,*> Sai observed.

"You know, don't you?" Nihm accused. "I see you and Hiro and Mao all in Mama Besom's wagon. You're up to something. I want to know what. Don't think I'll just tag along like a lost puppy as Renco does."

Nesta scratched Snow between her ears. "Humans. Always so impatient. Almost everything you do centres on yourselves, hence the reason, I suppose, that you view the world through such narrowed eyes. Is that you, Nihm, or can you open your mind to the truth? When you are ready to listen I will answer your questions."

The ilf left as soundlessly as he arrived, feet barely breaking the snow upon the ground. In contrast, Nihm stomped towards the Wylder camp.

<*Your anger is not for the act of spying but at being discovered,*> Sai prompted.

<You need to work on your pep talks cause they stink.>

Computing that a response would yield no meaningful benefit, Sai withdrew from the conversation. The wolfdogs reached a similar conclusion because they loped behind with their tails low.

The Wylder camp was never silent even at night, and several dogs growled as Nihm passed, and the Wylder on guard duty commanded them to silence. Nihm raised an arm to the man who gave an acknowledging nod before turning back to the brazier and holding his hands out to its warmth.

Reaching Mama Besom's wagon, the dogs settled beneath its bed whilst Nihm climbed the steps to find her own. Mama Besom snored gently as Nihm disrobed before slipping beneath the covers of her narrow bunk. Sleep, though, did not come, her mind instead turning over Nesta's words. He knew things. Maybe everything and he had challenged her. The more she thought about it though the less sure of what it was she should ask. What was it she wanted, what was she looking for?

A feather touch of enquiry blossomed in her mind, similar but different from her link with Sai. <What's eating you? You're riled up. I can feel it from here.>

Nihm could almost sense Renco's yawn. <Nothing,> she returned.

<Well, unless you want to talk about this 'nothing' that's bothering you, get some sleep. Then maybe I can too.> Renco left the link without waiting for a response and Nihm huffed, he could be so infuriating. Always so calm but smug with it, like he thought he was better than her.

Just like that, Nihm's mind shifted from one problem to another, Renco. This bond they shared, the link, she didn't ask for it and didn't want it and he could be such an ass. Or was it her?

Sleep slipped over her as she tussled with the issue of Renco and that night she dreamed again of the burning woman and cried in her repose.

* * *

It was their third day in the Arden Forest and the fifth since the training fight incident that led to Renco's half-naked run through bitter snow, all to fill a cup with water from the Emerald Lake.

That whole episode had been madness of course and all at the instruction of Master Hiro. Nihm had been mortified and more than a little distressed for it was her mistake, not Renco's.

Sai made the rather astute observation that had Master Hiro given her the endeavour to fill the cup she would have refused point-blank to go but had run along unreservedly when Renco had been given the task. As vexing as that was to know, Nihm knew she would do no different.

Recalling their nighttime run, Nihm glanced across at Renco. The only ones who had enjoyed that freezing escapade were Snow and Ash. However, as cruel as it was at the time, it also hadn't bothered Renco. The cold barely touched his naked torso, and he did not seem put out at his task. The strangest thing was the trace lines appearing on his body and face. The intricate patterns of interwoven lines and geometric circles on his front were all but invisible to the naked eye but appeared in bright relief to Nihm's night eyes. They provided a stark contrast to the lumps of scar tissue that crisscrossed his back.

Feeling her gaze, Renco caught Nihm's eye and signed at her. 'What?'

Renco could have spoken over their mind link but, much to Lett's chagrin, he was teaching both Nihm and Morten how to sign. Morten possessed a knack for it and, thanks to Sai, Nihm picked it up effortlessly which further rankled the young bard who had been learning a lot longer but found it a struggle.

'Nothing,' Nihm signed. 'Just thinking about our run.'

'You think a lot.'

'And you don't think enough. What Hiro did was cruel. You should have refused.' Nihm glanced ahead at the old monk but his back was safely turned.

'You did not have to follow, it was my mistake, my penance. Master asked for what he knew I could give, and I succeeded,' Renco replied.

'I could have killed you.'

With a snort of amusement, Renco signed. 'But you did not. I blocked your strike and prevailed. My error was retaliating, and my punishment was a fitting one.'

'Boys are so stupid,' Nihm's fingers snapped.

'Hey!' Morten signed.

Nihm rounded on him. "Were you eavesdropping, Morten Stenhause?"

Morten grinned. "Hard not to. You were shouting, though I only understood a few of the signs ta be fair, 'tis rather inconsiderate ta sign so fast. Makes it hard for a fella ta follow."

"What did I miss?" Lett scowled. She was riding behind and hadn't seen the silent exchange.

"Nought much," Morten chuckled. "Think they were arguing. In public. Bad form that."

"We were not arguing," Nihm protested, but one look at Renco, tight-lipped and trying not to laugh, made her repeat her admonition. "We weren't."

"Was it about dat fight agin?" queried Kaid Dax in the affable timbre all Wylders seemed to possess. The young man rode beside Lett, his sable hair every bit as lustrous as the bard's golden mane. "It was magnificent. Controlled and t'en so explosive. It was close. Ya almost had him, Nihm but t'en, on his first attack, Renco had you. It took me breath."

"He did not have me," Nihm growled. "I stopped. He carried on. At best it was a draw." Her glare swept from Renco to Kaid, who shrugged, then Morten.

"I don't know." Morten offered, "It was close."

"Stupid boys," Nihm said, repeating aloud her earlier assertion. Yanking on the reins of her white dappled mare, Nihm turned and trotted down the line to Mama Besom's wagon.

'She did stop.' Renco signed but no one saw, busy instead talking with each other.

"She's got fire in her blood d'at one," Kaid's voice was full of approval.

"Sore loser more like," Lett huffed.

"Hey now, she ain't sore." Morten scowled. "Stubborn as a rock is all."

***

For the rest of that day, Nihm rode with Mama Besom as the caravan rumbled ever southward through the Arden. They should have cleared the forest already, but Kafelie Dax had left the main road days back, weaving an improbable path between the mighty beams and underneath the evergreen arches, taking secret ways, known only to the Wylders.

Their purpose, explained Kafelie Dax, was to reach the winter meeting grounds of the nor'west Wylder families. Here, tradition dictated, they would remain until the winter solstice though most families, Kafelie said, stayed until the first kiss of spring. It was a time to renew old ties and forge new ones, for the young to meet and matches to be made. A chance for the mystics to convene and the family heads to hold council. This year, with urak infesting the lands from the north, that would need to change.

The trees grew denser, and they soon came upon a wide but shallow river free of winter ice. Fording it, the Dax-Wylders turned eastward and followed the river's winding path through a changing forest, the evergreens intermingling with ancient oaks and eldas.

Night came early beneath the boughs and a grey light was settling when they reached a standing stone covered in vines and moss. Turning away from the river they traced a path under the glooming trees.

Ash and Snow pricked up their ears. Beneath the song of the forest, of birds and creaking beams, a discordant sound reached Nihm. The eddying breeze was from the north, but a tenuous smell percolated the air and grew perceptibly stronger. A short while later, Mama Besom had Nihm call the wolfdogs onto the wagon.

"There are Wylders in these woods and we do not want them to be mistaken for wild beasties," she declared.

The mighty beams began to thin, and the undergrowth grew thick, sprouting between the trees like weeds. The path though remained unbroken and led them through the foliage into a large clearing, one that was far from empty. Wylder caravans occupied the space in clustered groups, each bordering the surrounding woodland.

Dominating the centre of the clearing was an open-sided, multicoloured pavilion, stretched around an immense tree whose lower branches had been shorn away. The pavilion however was incomplete, triangular gaps appeared at several junctures around its circumference.

Forewarned of their approach, a crowd had gathered to welcome them and calls of 'isha Dax', welcome Dax and 'hacana', peace to you, rang out. Many of the Dax-Wylders riding in the wagons dismounted, shouting greetings of their own, before merging with the crowd in a riotous mishmash of colour as the green and yellow coats of the Dax mixed with the rainbow blends of the other Wylder families.

"I did not know there were so many of you," Nihm said to Mama Besom.

"Ten of the twelve families are here," Mama replied. "Only the Horgan and Ishmun are still to arrive. We are all of the Wylder from the Vorsa Delta in the west to the River Lothern in the east. Little more than two thousand souls give or take. It is not so many."

"You're worried?" Nihm said, reading the old woman's furrowed brow and the set of her shoulders.

"If you look for it, life is nothing but worry," Mama deflected. "Unless you can do something about it, worry is wasted energy."

The tall wagon began moving through the crowd of people and Nihm's eyes flittered like a sparrow over their heads, absorbing the sights and sounds without focusing on any one thing until they settled on the multihued tent in the middle. It was like a much larger version of the one erected by the Dax most nights.

<There are twelve segments of which three are missing.> Sai mentioned. <It is in the high percentile of probability that each segment represents a Wylder family. If that is so, then the Dax will fill one of those missing segments. The Wylders are nomadic but I would contend each familial group follows the same circuitous route each year. Ask Mama Besom about the Horgan and Ishmun. If my perception and analysis routines are correct and they range to the north like the Dax, it may give some indication as to their delay.>

<You mean urak, right?> Nihm said.

<Correct.>

"The Horgan and Ishmun are late to the gathering," Nihm began. "Do they range in the north like you Dax?"

A piercing gaze settled over Nihm and held her eyes but Mama said nothing.

"They are happy to see you?" Nihm nodded at the milling Wylder, "But I sense relief in their greeting as well."

The mystic's thin lips tugged into the faintest of smiles. "Most your age, seeing a Wylders meet for the first time, would ask a different question if they asked any at all." She glanced at the unfinished pavilion and gave a wistful sigh.

"Wylder men all have a touch of panache. Or like to think they do. These Winter-meets, the young ones strut like peacocks to catch the eye and woo the heart and the habit follows them ever after. The boy never entirely leaves the man in my experience."

Nihm gave a puzzled look which drew a proper smile from Mama Besom who continued.

"Kafelie Dax is a good man and a great leader but not immune from this condition. A showman young Lett might call him. Kafelie prides himself on arriving last to the Winter-meet. 'A late entrance leaves the largest impression' or some such nonsense. That we Dax are here and the Horgan and Ishmun are not is a concern. Both, as you surmise range to the north but these are the earliest winter snows for twenty years and it is just as likely the cause of their delay as the urak that plague your mind."

"Mama!" The shout drew their attention past the horses pulling the wagon and ended their discussion. A black-haired bear of a man stood head and shoulders above his nearest neighbours with his arms held out wide and a grin plastered to his bearded face.

"Torgot." Mama Besom glowered.

"Elsa said you'd arrive today and here you are. What's that on your face?" Torgot rumbled affably. He waited for the wagon to draw level and walked alongside it.

Mama touched a hand to her cheeks. "What do you mean?"

"Agh, it's gone. I think it was a smile but I'm not sure." Torgot laughed. "Now stop the wagon and give me a hug witch."

"I will not. You smell like a moose, even from here," Mama hissed. "Tell Elsa I'll come see her tonight."

"I will, Mama." Torgot turned at hearing his name being called. "Jul Hass, you old goat!" He bellowed and swaggered out of sight.

Mama Besom looked to Nihm.

"Boys!" Nihm offered.

"Boys!" Mama cackled. Still chortling, she shook the reins and the wagon lurched on.

Ahead, Kafelie Dax veered through the crowd, calling out names as he did so but not stopping as he led the Dax-Wylders towards their traditional campsite. Nesta rode beside him and behind came Master Hiro and Mao, followed by the others. Morten was wide-eyed, head swivelling to take it all in whilst Kaid Dax was pointing something out to Lett and laughing. Renco barely turned his head and sat relaxed but immobile on his horse a dichotomy to the restlessness and agitation Nihm sensed from him across their bond.

<You're uncomfortable?> Nihm asked.

<I don't like crowds. It's hard to see danger with so many people this close,> Renco replied.

<There is no danger. They're just Wylders.>

Renco didn't respond but his disquiet remained and Nihm found herself surveilling the crowd.

Mama Besom made her own observation. "You are wise to be watchful. You're the first Holders in memory to see this place and some of the Wylder families will not like that you are here."

She clicked her tongue at the horses. "Holders for the most part deride us or tolerate us at best, and it leaves strong feelings with many of my people. Kafelie has offered you sanctuary and you are under his protection so there is nothing to be concerned about. However, it would be well to caution the others, in particular Morten and Renco, to tread carefully. Young Wylder men as we have established are hot-headed boys, full of bravado. This is especially so at the Winter-meet. They will not take it kindly if they perceive outsiders are intruding on their rights and traditions, especially where the young Wylder women are concerned."

Nihm looked at the mystic and gave a lopsided grin. "I don't think we'll be here long enough to worry about that. Master Hiro is taking us south. To the Duncan."

Mama Besom nodded sagely. "Maybe so, maybe so. But it will not be tomorrow, nor the next day. A storm will be here by mid-morn. A big one. You'll be with us at least until it passes."

Nihm looked overhead at the stars that had started to appear. Stuck beneath the forest these past days the sky had been mostly obscured and she missed its grandeur and story. She glimpsed her moon, Nihmrodel, a faint crescent in the west and the red, slanted eye of Kildare. To the north of the clearing, fringing the treetops, a thin tumble of clouds gathered, touched violet and yellow by the setting sun. She breathed deeply of the air and searched for the ionised scent of a coming storm but got only the whiff of the encampment and the damp wood-moss smell of the forest.

"Not all things can be seen or felt. It will come," Mama assured her.

"Mama, what's wrong with Mao?" Nihm said. Abrupt. Asking before the courage left her.

The wagon rumbled on, an oasis of silence in the exuberance all around.

"I can read aether you know but Mao's aura is like a mask, hiding what lies beneath," Nihm said.

"An aether sensate." Mama raised her overly hairy eyebrows in surprise. "You have not asked Hiro or Nesta this question?"

Nihm shook her head, no.

"I too read auras amongst other things. Do you want me to tell you what I see?" Mama stated.

"Yes," Nihm said.

"I see two souls, intrinsically bound each to the other both seeking purpose. One unaware, the other adrift looking for the nearest piece of flotsam to cling to. To be clear, I do not speak of Mao, Mao is not your purpose. He is not your story, and it is not my place to tell you his." As Mama spoke, Nihm deflated, her shoulders slumped and her gaze sinking to her lap.

In a rare show of empathy, Mama reached across and patted Nihm's knee. "Your purpose will find you, child. You do not have to snatch and grasp for it. It will come. For Renco too. And, when it does, it will not be the concern of two old men nor this old woman for that matter."

The wagon rumbled to a stop, pulling up in the newly forming camp, taking its usual central position. "Now run along. Take joy where you can for tomorrow is always uncertain."

Nihm hopped down from the wagon, Snow and Ash following from beneath the padded riding board where they'd lain and brushed around her legs. She paused a moment, then looked back at Mama. "Thank you."

The mystic gave a curt nod and watched Nihm wander towards the horses and her friends. Mama knew her gifts were a blessing from the gods but tonight they weighed heavy.

"Whatever your destiny," she whispered beneath her breath, "the God of Fate has dealt you a dark hand, child."

Chapter 41: The Mouth Of The Viper

River Borq, Cumbrenan

Bartuk's body ached from being cooped up. The cage, two paces wide by three long, was all he had known since being taken. The blood-cloaked humans, his captors, provided a straw bale as if he was some tamed carvathe but he could neither eat it nor use it for a soft seat. He'd tried the latter early on but was too tall, his bowed head pressed hard against the iron bars above. The straw was no use for bedding either, most of it got blown through the palings of his cell. In the end, he used the bale as a bulwark against the wind, as much as that was possible.

Those first days of his capture, the humans tried to interrogate him but Bartuk feigned ignorance of their mangled common and after a time they seemed content to leave him stewing in this rolling jail. Why humans would waste metal on such a contraption rather than just bind him in chains and make him walk, he could not fathom. The idea seemed senseless but then so too did taking a prisoner for no purpose. Where was the honour in that? When urak fought it was to the death. In battle, whoever carried the fight killed any wounded left behind, and those survivors that retreated would seek to fight another day and regain their lost honour. It was the way of the warrior. To do otherwise was to invite the wrath of Varis'tuk or Nos'varg.

Humans are strange creatures, Bartuk decided, they were as artful as they were cunning yet weak as their false gods were weak. That they bred like riguts, along with the pale mimicry of their spellcasters and their stone walls, meant they posed a challenge. However, in the end, shunned by the true gods, humans were no better than game, to be hunted and slaughtered like any other.

These thoughts did not console nor appease Bartuk. He could feel the ire of the gods every waking moment these bars contained him, their will urging him to seek death rather than endure capture. It scalded his blood but shamefully it wasn't enough to overcome his desire to survive. He wanted to live. Unwilling to risk Nos'varg's Gate, he needed to live. For surely he would not pass through it to the halls beyond. No… undoubtedly, his lot would be to return to the wheel, where his next station in life would be pinned lower than it already was.

I will suffer to live. Show Nos'varg and Varis'tuk I am more than they deem me to be. That I am worthy. Bartuk swore it.

The wagon rattled and bumped, and his arse throbbed as the wheels slushed onto a bridge that stretched over a slow, wide river. It emptied into the lapping waters of the lake that had been his companion these last ten turns.

Shuffling to the bars, Bartuk gripped them and lowered his head against the backs of his hands and stared out across the white-capped waters of the lake. *Much colder and it'll freeze.* His eyes stretched to the basalt-coloured banks of turgid clouds which swept the western horizon. A storm and a big one. It had moved down from the north throughout the day like a tide that refused to turn. The wind gusted against his face and cold fingers reached through the gaps in his hide coverings to nip at his flesh. He smiled. It was nothing but a gentle tickle compared to what his kind endured in the Norde-Targkish.

He flexed and rotated his ankle. It was stiff but much improved, the sprain healed but untested. If he could escape, he'd have a chance if he picked his moment. *If the storm moves east maybe I will find it.*

As was sometimes his wont, his thoughts strayed to the human youngling that braved his cage and got too close. Belle. Incongruously, the human chala had appeared out of nowhere in an armed camp full of blood-cloaks and given him a soft crust and a hard fruit that was sweet and crisp. Then, like a qu'ri, she had disappeared. Belle didn't return as she promised and Bartuk wondered again where she had come from and what had become of her.

The hollow grind of the wheels changed pitch as the wagon left the bridge and returned to the road, it broke his distraction. His eyes examined the sky. The light was fading, soon the humans would set up camp. An over-elaborate affair that took too much time in Bartuk's view.

Ahead, the column of blood-cloaked humans curved into sight as the road bent to follow the lakeshore. Their numbers were much diminished and resembled a warband rather than an army. Several turns previous they had passed a small settlement and stayed overnight at a complex of large fortifications containing more of the blood cloaks. In the morning when they left most of the humans remained behind.

They liked to build things and hide within them when the Gods knew it was safer to move with the herds and follow the food. How they fed so many all squeezed into such a small area confounded him.

So too did their tongue. Urakakule spoke several distinct languages of which there were many dialects, but all tribes shared a common tongue for trade and bartering. That the humans spoke a heavily inflected type of common was a mystery for the shamans, but it meant he understood them and Bartuk had gleaned from broken, overheard snippets of conversation that they were headed south to meet the blood-cloaks war chieftain in his great stone citadel.

Frustrated, Bartuk's hands tightened on the bars of the cage testing the strength of the iron and he growled. Every moment took him further away from his people.

His wide-spaced eyes returned to the storm. He watched its distant chaos and violence, finding solace in it. Bartuk willed the tempest closer, but the storm did not care for his wants and paid him no heed.

The sky began to darken as Marq-suk's light faded; the life-giver claimed by the far-off thunderheads. Calls rang out, now familiar to Bartuk. The humans would make camp.

Perhaps tonight will be my moment.

* * *

Brother Thomas Perrick's untimely death meant Holt got the luxury of a two-man tent to himself by dint of no one else wanting to share with him. It was no surprise to anyone, not least Holt. A brute of a man at just under seven feet tall, with a face like a kettle pan and missing an eye, he was imposing to look at but even more intimidating to be around. He was no conversationalist.

Holt found the sealed missive in his pack when he rummaged for his whetstone. He didn't waste time wondering how it got there. He simply turned it over and held the seal close to his one eye for inspection. The subtle stamping around its edge held the correct markings so he knew it was genuine. Not that he'd had any doubt.

Rough fingers broke the seal and a heavy key dropped out. Holt read the message it contained with slow deliberation, silently mouthing the written words. He grunted then rolled it up, opened his lantern and touched the parchment to the flame, watching it ignite and letting the cinders fall and hiss into his slop-pail.

He pocketed the key. Reclaiming his cloak from his pallet, Holt fastened it around his shoulders then reached for his sheathed sword, wrapped around by its belt, and ducked outside.

* * *

Henrik Zoller's face was a mask of neutral passivity. Lord Commander Jon Whent's officers' meeting was beginning to wind down and the only topic that held Zoller's interest, albeit briefly, was the report on the health of Maxim Tortuga, the new High Cardinal of the Red. He lived.

In a twist of perverse irony, given Zoller's unaccounted and spectacular fall from Tortuga's good graces, the Lord Commander had asked him to lead a prayer for their Holy Father's continued recovery and his future good health. As much as it rankled to deliver it, Zoller had known it for what it was. A not-so-subtle reminder of his still precarious position and need for the Lord Commander's protection.

Captain Warwick rose to take his leave now the mundanity of their order of march and state of supplies had been discussed; Zoller wished he could likewise depart. Instead, he had to endure whilst Brother Henreece, The Lord Commander's personal physiker, reported on their captive.

"Your Grace, you have made plain your intent to bring the urak to Kingsholme, whole and in reasonable shape. That being the case the creature could do with some exercise to aid its conditioning." A young man, the physiker was at least ten years Zoller's junior but spoke with clipped preciseness and with confidence in both tone and demeanour that belied his years.

Zoller did not care for him. The man lacked deference to the Lord Commander and his betters, namely he, and Zoller was yet to decide if it was impudence or arrogance. In either case, Henreece needed to know his place.

"And its injury?" Whent asked.

"I have not braved its cage to make a proper assessment, Your Grace, but I judge it healed," Henreece replied.

Whent nodded softly, "Your recommendation?"

"With a suitable guard, I would chain the beast and let it out of its cage for twenty minutes each night. Then I can more readily assess its recovery and, if all is well, perhaps consider tethering it to the wagon and letting it walk for an hour or so each day."

"I would be sorely displeased if the urak were to attempt an escape and be injured or killed in the subduing," the Lord Commander said.

Zoller could not help himself. "If it did, it would not be the first prisoner to have escaped your Brothers, Brother."

Whent smiled in wry amusement. "You mean Our Brothers, Father Zoller. Red Cloaks and Red Priests, we all serve our Lord, Kildare do we not?"

"Of course, Your Grace. I am corrected," Zoller bowed his head in agreement.

Henreece continued in an even voice. "I would make clear to the urak the repercussions should it try, and there are measures we can take in addition to restraints. A powder that can be administered to its food to make the creature more docile."

"You still believe it understands what we say?" Whent questioned.

"I am almost certain of it, Your Grace."

"Almost and certain," Zoller spoke. "Two words which do not belong together."

Whent watched the byplay. Both men were ambitious, and, like anyone in a position of authority they had their own agendas. Henreece, who he knew well, rarely let anything break his veneer of calm but the slight tightness around his eyes told Whent enough. Zoller was harder to read, an air of disdain a more difficult shield to pierce but one thing was clear to him. The one did not like the other.

"Certainty. An absolute only the Trinity and the One may claim, Father." Whent cupped a hand in thought to his chin. "Still, you may have a point. You're a man of intellect and, I understand, an expert at getting answers from the less enlightened, of which this urak certainly qualifies. Go see the beast. Make your judgement, then report to me in the morning. Let me know if you concur with Brother Henreece."

Taken as a dismissal, Zoller rose and bowed, "Your Grace."

Leaving the tent, Zoller's head never turned, and his eyes did not waiver, but he could see both men in his periphery. Jon Whent was stern-faced and difficult to fathom whilst Henreece wore a placid mask that did not fool him. *Both are dangerous, tread carefully Henrik*, he told himself as he pushed through the inner folds of the tent.

Outside, one of his Red Cloaks awaited him and lead the way, turning for the good Father's pavilion.

"To the urak first, Brother Sebastien." There was no point delaying the matter and besides, he'd already decided to support the physiker's position. There was no benefit to be gained by putting himself so openly against the pompous upstart. Not when there was time yet to sway the man's loyalty. He just needed to find the right lever.

Having been with Father Zoller a while, Brother Sebastien knew enough not to speak. The Red Cloak turned down an aisle between the tents leading towards the horse corral and wagon park. It was dark but torches stood positioned at each junction and they were enough to light the way.

As was usual, the prison cart was set apart in an open space ringed by the supply wagons. The nicker and snort of horses could be heard and their heavy musk ladened the air. A single, large brazier smouldered in the centre, casting light shadows against the bars of the cage revealing the hunched outline of the urak inside it. The beast-man could have been mistaken for a boulder were it not for the gleaming, pinprick reflection of its eyes.

"Where are the guards?" Zoller demanded.

"I do not know, Father," Brother Sebastien replied.

A displaced mass moved in the darkness behind the wagon and Brother Sebastien stepped in front of the priest and drew his sword. "State your name and purpose."

The mass disappeared as it rounded the wagon before stepping into the light revealing a mountain of a man busy lacing his britches.

"I sent the guards for their victuals." Holt's voice was like shifting gravel. He looked up and blinked his cyclopean eye as if only now seeing who they were. Falling to his knees, Holt bowed his head. "Forgive me, Father."

Zoller shoved past Brother Sebastien. "Get up, Holt. In the name of Our Lord, what are you doing?"

Holt lumbered upright. "I was taking a piss, Father."

Zoller glowered and the giant winced before glancing at the urak and then back to the priest. "A word, Father."

"I was hoping for several, Holt, preferably strung together in some sort of order that made sense and answered my damned question," Zoller rasped.

The big man gave a brief but pointed look at Brother Sebastien who was busy sheathing his sword.

It was not missed by Zoller, who paused his tirade finding himself intrigued, which was not something normally attributable to his brutish bodyguard. "Brother Sebastien leave us," Zoller stated.

"Want me to wait for you beyond the wagons, Father?" asked Brother Sebastien.

Zoller turned and placed a hand on the Red Cloaks forearm. "Thank you but no, our Brother will escort me back once the guards are returned."

Sebastien shrugged, disappointed to miss the tattle but pleased at least with the early end to his duty. "Your will, Father." Turning about, he marched past the wagons and back the way they had come.

Zoller watched the shape of the man vanish into the night before turning once again to Holt. "Well, Brother, I'm waiting."

Holt strode to the brazier and picked a torch out of a bucket then held it over the flames until it took. He towered over the priest but both men knew who held the power between them. "It's something best seen, Father." The giant grated before walking back around the wagon end.

Zoller hesitated, a sudden unease lodging in his chest. Something troubled him but a quick survey of the inky murk around the cordon of wagons revealed nothing. It did not alleviate his sense of foreboding and he wished perhaps he had not sent Brother Sebastien away.

"Father?" Holt called out.

Lighting another torch, Zoller made his way around the wagon, the cats-eye glint of the urak tracking him all the way. He gave the beast a wide berth.

On the far side, Zoller found Holt crouched low to the ground. It was dark but for the flare of Holt's torch which extinguished as he thrust it into the snow but not before Zoller caught a glimpse of something. A bundled lump.

"See here, Father."

See here, indeed. The great lummox had just put his torch out, how could he see a thing. The light cast from Zoller's torch marched across the ground, illuminating the giant's broad back which threw a shadow upon the ground. "What is it? Is that a body?"

"You can trust nobody, Father. Not even your own." Rising, Holt stood back revealing two men, red cloaks pooling like blood beneath their lifeless bodies.

Zoller gaped. "Are they dead?" His words were redundant but not his next question. "How?"

A deep rumble sounded from behind and Zoller's robes swished as he twisted wildly to look. It was the urak. Its hands clenched the bars of the cage, its feral grin pressed up hard to the iron. Torchlight cast shadows across its face. Then it spoke.

"Run fool. Death comes for us both."

Zoller had to concentrate to understand the words and an icy chill shot down his spine as their meaning registered.

The snow on the ground crunched and Zoller spun back around, lurching as a colossal frame loomed above him. He opened his mouth to scream but it never came. A vice-like hand clamped his throat and he was lifted onto his toes. Zoller gurgled, his throat constricted, the breath in his lungs trapped. His eyes popped wide with fright.

Choked to death by an imbecile. The ignominy. Defiance mingled with fear lent Zoller a desperate strength. Somehow, he still held his flaming torch, and he swiped it at Holt's broken face and one eye only for the giant to bat his blow aside with a chuckle as if he were a child.

A choked cough, then a tremor shook Zoller's body. Holt gripped a paw around his wrist and squeezed. Zoller's bones cracked, and he dropped the torch which sputtered and smoked in the snow at his feet.

Leaning close, Holt leered, his sour breath washing over the priest. "Think ya so clever, Father, scheming and manipulating. Those smug eyes, reading everyone and everything yet all this time blind to what was in front of them. I was never your man, but Tortuga's. A pity, I always admired your cruelty, Father."

The fingers around Zoller's throat began to tighten and spots swam before his eyes even as his vision dimmed. Zoller didn't have the strength to kick, the fear became everything and nothing. A gagged whimper escaped his snarling lips. He stared hopelessly into Holt's bloodshot, glee-filled eye, knowing that when his own eyes closed, they would not open again.

Holt gave a sudden, pained grunt, slipped and then staggered. The weight settled back over Zoller's feet as the grip around his throat loosened and blood rushed back to his head. Zoller sucked in an agonised breath. Relief, however, was short-lived, as he was propelled with abrupt ferocity through the air like a discarded rag. He crunched against the wagon's front wheel and collapsed to the ground, stunned.

"Tuko, you tiny puke. Guess it was too good to be true, you dying."

Zoller's eyelids felt heavy, and his head lolled but he forced both up. He couldn't see past Holt's broad back and wondered if he had misheard.

"Big and still stupid. Some things never change," a familiar voice drawled. Zoller would have smiled but his body ached, and his throat was raw so that each ragged breath was a tragic gasp. Insolent, irreverent, dangerous, Zoller had never been more pleased to hear the wiry assassin's voice in his life. He shook his head to clear it.

Holt stepped to the side and scuffed a boot at his sword, which lay in the snow along with his belt and sheath.

Tuko laughed, "I should be grateful your trews stayed up when I cut your belt loose. That's a sight no man wants ta see."

Holt leapt backwards as a sword cut the air and Zoller got an umbrous glimpse of Tuko beyond. The torch on the ground spluttered and Zoller crawled to it and picked it up.

The faltering flame wobbled and then strengthened, casting its light around the wagon, washing over the dead bodies in the snow and illuminating the dusky-skinned Tuko.

Holt gave a drunken wobble toward him and Zoller stumbled out of reach. The giant red cloak sank to his knees. He swatted at his neck and his hand came away bloody.

"What you fukin' do?" Holt slurred, teetering like a tree before the felling, then crumpled onto his side.

Tuko sauntered into the light, a callous smirk on his face. "Lucky for you, Brother, I'm out of deeproot. You got the good stuff instead. Black Janus. Fuckin' shame to waste it on ya, it's a pain to get."

"Sssit do?" Holt stuttered like a drunk.

Tuko knelt beside Holt and started to pat him down, slapping an arm away when the drugged man lifted it to grab him. Tuko sniffed and hoicked a wedge of phlegm, pooling it in his mouth before spitting it into Holt's face, then laughed.

"It does a lot of things. Numbs your mind and body, slips a man into a nice sleep. The amount you took it'll wear off by morn. Course, by then ya'll be dead, an hour maybe two layin' here and the cold will take you. When ya get ta one them hells you like sending folk to, you'll be pleased it was so painless. Fuck knows I wish I had the time to make it otherwise."

Holt didn't answer. His lone eye gave a lazy blink then closed and didn't open.

"Aha, got you." Tuko held a rough iron key up to the torchlight. He glanced across at Zoller. "What do you want to do, Father?"

"He betrayed me," Zoller croaked. His throat burned and he rubbed at his neck as he hobbled over. "All these years and he fucking betrayed me." He walked to Holt and laid a kick to the man's head then winced at the blow.

"You're done here, Father. Holt came to kill the urak but didn't hesitate ta do you too when ya poked your nose in. Tells me someone here wants ya dead. Tortuga certainly does. Ya heard the big cunt say his name."

Zoller inhaled through his nose, calming himself "Kingsholme…"

"I've saved your life. More than once," Tuko blurted. "And I'll save it again when I tell you Kingsholme is death. It's the mouth of the viper and you're a mouse, Father. Now release me. My debt is more than paid."

Zoller shook his head in denial. "The debt is not paid. I saved your life once again in the Defile else you'd be hung and quartered."

"Ai and you beside me, Father." Tuko twirled his blade.

"I presume that key is for the cage. What is your plan?" Zoller asked.

Tuko's face creased into a smirk. "Give it to the beast. Then go. The guard will change at around midnight. When the dead are found the Red Cloaks will pin it on the urak and give chase. They won't be after me and, until morning, they won't think to come looking for you. I suggest you make the most of that time. Do not go back to your tent."

"Our time," Zoller snapped. "We leave together."

"What makes ya think I won't gut your body and leave it in a ditch, Father," Tuko asked.

Zoller smiled, "A lone man, armed and on the road, will be conscripted. A priest of Kildare, travelling with his guard, will be unmolested. Come, if we are to leave let us go. We can argue our differences when we are safely away." He held his hand out and with a shrug, Tuko handed the key across.

Zoller moved until he was just out of arm's reach of the cage. "You understand our words, beast. You know what has been said. This key is your freedom. Tell me your name and you may have it."

The urak scratched its whiskered cheek but barely hesitated. "Bartuk." Its arm extended through the bars and its hand uncurled.

"You will be hunted, but at least you will have a chance. Morport lies a day to the south, maybe two. The city marks the southernmost point of the Emerald Lake. Once you are around it the west and north are open to forest, hills and plains. Good luck." Zoller dropped the key onto the urak's palm. Turning, he extinguished his torch and followed the dark smear that was Tuco as he led them toward the horse corral.

Chapter 42: An Endless Path

Fallston, The Rivers

'Life has a way of complicating things. A simple need or singular desire, when acted upon, opens new paths, morphs into wider, more complex possibilities that in turn lead to ever increasing choices. And, my young Lord, before you ask, yes, there is always a choice. Even when sometimes it may seem like there is none.

'Life, you see, is an endless path. The choices we make upon it are what define us and make us unique. For no man nor woman ever walks the same steps. Consider this moment. Every decision you have ever made has led you to this very place and time, as mine has me.

'Now, what is the most important lesson?'

'Knowing the choices before us, Master,' the boy replied, confident in his answer.

The master's cane swished and the boy yelped as it cracked against the back of his hand.

'Wrong, boy. It is understanding that each choice has a consequence and a cost, many of which only become apparent after the choice has been made, as I have just ably demonstrated. I trust you'll remember this lesson.'

The memory of Master Lutico and his lesson never faded and never grew old. *You've still to master it. Perhaps that's why.* Jacob Bouchemaux smiled as the words formed in his mind. Even they sounded like his former master. He remembered hating Lutico at the time. Grumpy, brusque, intolerant, the old bastard was difficult to like. Now, with distance and time, Jacob recalled it all with a certain fondness.

"Pity the miserable sod isn't here now," he muttered scratching at his ruff of beard.

"Pardon, milord?"

Jacob glanced at the man by his side. Mahan looked haggard. His face was gaunt and dark bruising shadowed his eyes. Fear or shame, Jacob wasn't sure which, seemed to nestle just beneath the guardsman's skin giving him a nervous, haunted disposition.

We are none of us what we once were. Jacob gave a pasted smile. "I said I'm glad you're here with me now."

"Aye, well nay offence, Lord Jacob, but I'd rather I was in Thorsten with a mug of ale in one hand and John sat across, complaining about that good woman of his." Mahan fell silent. Unable to maintain eye contact, his gaze drifted off.

Jacob didn't respond. Talking to Mahan was like picking at a scab on a wound that refused to heal. Their easy banter from before the Grim another casualty.

The bushes rustled and Jacob drew his sword and Mahan a knife, but both relaxed when the shrubs parted and Nils Baka appeared. He glanced at both men and their drawn weapons. "Heard ya both from twenty yards away."

Even though the Grimmer was right, the rebuke nettled Jacob who glowered in response.

Baka shrugged, "Ned says ta come. Quiet like." With that, the Grimmer turned and disappeared back the way he'd come.

The winter-dressed bush, grasping and stiff, snagged Jacob's cloak as he made to follow and he felt a tug as Mahan pulled it free. Neither man spoke.

Baka led them through dense undergrowth along an animal trail that was barely discernable in the hanging light. They climbed a rise, passing through a copse of bone-fingered trees with laurus shrub and spiky shojo bushes, ripe with red berries, nestling between them.

In a bush-lined hollow just beneath the crest of the rise, they found Ned Wynter gripping a bow with an arrow ready on the string. Relaxing his draw, Ned gave a nod of acknowledgement before handing Baka the bow.

Signalling for quiet, the bow master and former Grimmer signed for Jacob to follow. Like a stalking cat, Ned disappeared through the brushwood and Jacob tucked in behind with as much stealth as he could manage.

On the far side of the ridged hummock of land, disguised amongst the damp of winter bark, earthy loam and fresh snow, the merest hint of wood smoke tickled the air. Voices reached up to them, hushed and indistinct, carried by the breeze.

A stone outcrop extended several meters and Ned crawled to its edge. With a grimace, Jacob stretched out flat in the snow and inched himself forward until he was side by side with the ranger. The smell of wood smoke was stronger now, though no smoke trail was visible it seemed to cling to the rock.

Stretching his neck out, Jacob peered into the gulch below. Boulders scattered the ground and in the dim light between them, there was movement. People, their voices clearer now, soft but unmuffled.

"…tomorrow, or next. Ain't no point moaning, can't move 'til we get more boats." A woman, hard to distinguish in the bad light but she wore the variegated, patchworked cloak of a Grimmer, Jacob was certain of it.

"Or more men," challenged the man she spoke with. "Should have gone to Fallston. This was a mistake."

Jacob's eyes narrowed. The man was no Grimmer. The voice, foreign yet familiar, tugged at him. His heart surged, it wasn't possible.

"I told ya." The woman snorted. "Urak lie thicker 'un maggots on a corpse east of the Oust and there's some near about's. If'n ya don't believe me then go. Lord Grim might want ya but ain't no one holding ya here."

A hand nudged Jacob's side but it took an effort for him to tear his eyes off the man below. With a gesture, Ned backed away and with reluctance, Jacob followed.

Back in the hollow, they huddled together with Baka and Mahan.

"That was a Grimmer with a Black Crow," Jacob effused. "I couldn't see clearly but I'm certain of it."

"Ai. Well, that's Braunecks Gorge they're in. There's a breach in the rock face that opens into a cavern. I know it well enough and scouted around before you came," Ned replied, "seen two Black Crows but there are others back in the cave, I'm sure of it. Seems Black Jack is offerin' sanctuary to 'em."

"Crows!" Mahan clutched Jacob's forearm. "We have to warn them. Can't leave 'em with those scum. Not after what they did to you, milord and ta John."

A light burned in the guardsman's eyes and Jacob's mouth twitched. He seemed almost like the Mahan of old.

"Agreed." Jacob turned to Nils Baka and Ned Wynter. "How many Grimmers are we dealing with?"

Ned wiped a finger under his nose and gave a disgruntled sniff. "A brace."

"Two?" Jacob frowned. "I wondered where you got the bow from. How many were there before?"

"Does it matter? Two's left is all that counts. But they'll know summat's up soon enough if they don't already."

"You should have told me before taking action, Ned." Jacob gave a hard stare but the bow master just shrugged his shoulders.

"Ai, well, I had no choice." Ned glanced at the heavens as if the fickle gods were to blame. "Stumbled on the first. A lookout. He saw a Grimmer and looked relieved I wasn't no urak before he recognised me. Bought me a split second else I might not be here. The die was cast then."

Choice, the word chimed with Jacob, evoking the memory of Lutico and his lesson. *Him or me, life or death.* It was the most primal of decisions, one made with the unconscious bias of self-preservation. Now, he had one to make.

"It sounds like more Grimmers are on their way. Baka, head back to the caves. Bring Nip Rokan and Sis. Varla as well if she'll leave Aousa."

"You ain't my lord and this ain't my fight," Baka rumbled unhappily. "The ones Ned took; I say we carve 'em into bits. Leave a bloody mess no man would rightly make then string 'em up and slide away. Let 'em think urak done it. Might keep 'em off the west bank."

"We aren't leaving them behind." Jacob glared.

"Ya think I want more Black Crows about? Ya can think again, Lord Assling."

"Enough, Nils." Ned's words silenced the man. He turned stone-grey eyes to Jacob who bit back the retort on his lips.

"If ya want ta do this, lord, it's now. There is no waiting," Ned said.

Jacob scratched at his cheek and went through the motion of consideration but knew in his bones that Ned was right, the decision was made. It had been the moment he saw the Black Crow and heard that voice. In the bleached light, he gave a brusque nod.

Without further instruction, Ned turned and left the hollow and after a moment's hesitation, Jacob followed with Mahan at his back. Baka swore profusely, then, with a shake of his head, he tagged along behind.

Wynter led them south along the ridgeline a hundred paces or more before crossing over the rocky crest and down the far slope. The rocky peak gave way to scrag bush and snagging undergrowth that lay hidden beneath the snow. It forced them to a crawling pace, each step thought and placed with care, each man treading in the tracks of the one before.

Reaching the bed of the gulch, they turned and traced a path back towards the rocky promenade. They followed a glazed stream that meandered between giant knucklebones of stone and a wall of granite which rose on their left casting a dusk-like gloom. The crunch of their feet in the snow and rock shingle seemed overt and echoed off the rock face.

Raising a hand, Ned brought them to a stop behind a large slab. He circled two fingers then waggled them. Baka broke off and disappeared into the scrub brush and undergrowth to their right.

Ned arched an eyebrow at Mahan. "You up for this?"

"Just tell me what ya want," Mahan rumbled.

"The cavern is forty paces ahead. Cross the stream, hug the rock face. Don't be heard. You'll know it when you're needed."

Mahan looked to his lord, who gave a permissive nod, then moved out.

The two waited while Mahan crossed the frozen brook, then pulling their cloaks around them they moved warily between the boulders and further up the draw until a dark gash in the rock face revealed itself.

Glancing from cover, Ned made a furtive observation of the cavern. Fallen rubble from a rockfall half hid the entrance.

"They know summat's coming but not who or what," Ned breathed, leaning his back to the stone. Then, at Jacob's quizzical look, he cast a thumb back over his shoulder.

"No lookout where there should be one and the fire under the overhang is out, but I can still smell it. Reckon a narrow entrance like that they'll be waiting in the dark with a couple of bows trained for anyone foolish enough to stick their head in the hole. You ready?"

Jacob shook his head. "For what?"

In answer, Ned stood, leant over the granite and raised his voice.

"Skunk Munro. Talk or die it's up to you."

Jacob peered around the side of the boulder, eyes travelling up the scarface to the rocky outcrop he'd lain upon not long since. It was lighter up there, argent clouds blanketing the sky. His gaze slipped to the lop-sided maw of the cave mouth. One end was curtained behind broken stone. Black upon black eddied, stirring like cha in a mug, hinting at movement.

A flutter of grey, gone in an eye blink had him draw a sharp intake of air. Jacob exhaled it in a cloud then glanced at Wynter.

"May as well smoke a pipe. Slow, shallow breaths, Lord, else they'll know two is here and not one." Nostrils flaring, Ned's low whisper barely carried but still managed to convey his ire. "Now, stay outta sight and let me do the talkin'."

Jacob's blood boiled at both the man's tone and his assumed command. *Not all of us are trained in skulking.* Taking a calming breath Jacob held his tongue. Then, mindful he had drawn a lungful of air, released it in a slow stream and was rewarded for his effort by a shake of the ranger's head.

Ned stood tall, chest and head appearing above the boulder. "Got no time for games, Skunk. I see you and now you see me."

A fleck of movement by the rockfall.

"Don't like the name Skunk. Least of all from the likes a you, Ned Tullock. Best ya fuck off 'cause once Black Jack gets a sniff a you, ya'll be wishing you died back on Morqhill."

Ned spat, then wiped his mouth. "Well, if we're getting' names straight, Munro, mine's Wynter. Ned Tullock died when he left the Grim the first time. As fer Morqhill. I survived it. Don't matter how. Makes me free and clear so Jackson can go hang hisself."

A throaty laugh belched across the divide. "Tell him yaself, Ned. He'll be here soon, and he'll want you and what you took; those lordlings. You got 'em still?"

"Nah, they're long gone. They'll be in Rivercross by now or more probably urak food. Damn fools had no bushcraft and wouldn't listen ta no reason," Ned called back.

"Ya know Hett's gone. You got her, Ned? And the boy, Tom. Black Jack might be amenable ta… "

"Look, Munro," Ned interrupted. "I ain't here ta trade insults, negotiate, nor answer any damn questions."

The ranger raised his hand then drew it down in a single, sharp motion. A moment later, a strained grunt sounded, and a ball arched overhead. It landed then rolled with a skewed bump before coming to rest near the cavern's entrance. A head, eyes glazed but open, stared vacantly at nothing.

"Charlie Flute ain't feeling your confidence, Munro. Nor the others. No one knows ya here but me." Ned let the smile on his face seep into his voice. "How'd ya think I found ya?"

"Fuckin' goat shagger. You want us, Ned, come in and get us. I got me and four murks. We'll be waiting. I'll be waiting."

Ned laughed, "You got yourself and Bonny Boyd, a piss poor excuse for a murkhawk if ever I saw one, and some Black Crows whose fight this ain't." He paused as if considering matters. "Look, Munro, I'll give 'e three choices. Ya' can take an item of whatever ya filched and go. Unharmed, on my oath."

"Your oath don't mean shit, Ned."

"Or, stay put and I'll smoke you out. Then I'll murder you and Bonny Boyd, rob your corpses and take everything you got stashed."

Ned sensed more than saw the subtle motion in the greyness and ducked as the thrum sounded. The air parted and the loosed arrow was eaten with a rustle by the foliage in the woodland behind.

"That ya answer then, Munro?"

"You said three," came the sullen reply.

"Ai, I did. The third was that you could join me, but you did just try ta stick me with an arrow," Ned replied.

"You was threatening murder and rape," Munro said.

"Ya've spent too long with Torgrid. I said nought about rape."

"This is going nowhere," Jacob hissed. Raising his head above the boulder, he glanced toward the cavern. He felt a hand grasp his cloak but too late.

"Endo Rayne. To arms." Jacob's commanding voice boomed off the rockface. He was pulled unceremoniously down, unaware until the spark of metal on stone and the snap of branch behind that an arrow had glanced the rock where his head had been.

"Are you trying to get yourself killed, boy?" Ned growled. "Your timing is ill-judged, lord."

The honorific was spoken like a chastisement and Jacob felt the heat rising on his face once more, but the ranger was not done.

"You've played ya hand. Trumped ma own. Now we must see how things play out." Ned drew his sword, a crude, simple blade and risked a glance toward the cavern.

Shouts could be heard coming from within but not the expected clash of steel on steel. Moments passed, the commotion growing louder and more fraught.

There was a scuffle of motion in the cave mouth and a figure appeared, a merged man-beast with four arms and four legs. As it moved out from the shadow of the maw it resolved into two, one man holding another from behind, a momentary glint edging the steel held to the other's throat.

They shuffled away from the entrance, the taller hostage almost slitting his windpipe trying to keep his feet. He was an older man with a paunched belly and what in normal times would have been a jolly face. His receding hair was swept back leaving a splash of red-gold fringing his ears.

Skunk Munro hissed at the Grimmer who snarled something back before stopping and hugging his hostage closer.

"We're walkin'. You twitch funny and I'll cut this fuck from ear to ear," Bonny Boyd yelled.

Ned shook his head, amused. "Think I wouldn't stick an arrow through a fat man, Bonny? I'd do that and more if I wanted ya dead but ya've my word. Leave him be and you can walk free."

"You're a lyin' sack a'shit, Ned. But that lord there, the one as you said was in Rivercross. That's different. See this is one of his people. So, thinks I'll keep him close." Without moving his eyes away, Boyd hissed. "Clara, go."

A darker shade of black appeared at the cavern's entrance. Munro, edging away from the cover of the rockfall, gave the shadow a wide berth, an arrow taught on her bow. She spun and stepped behind Boyd and whispered to him.

Boyd shook his head, vehemently.

"Munro's gonna leave. Then me and the fat man here will follow. First, I want his Loftiness ta give his word there'll be no funny business. When I'm safe I'll let him go, unharmed. That's my word on it."

Jacob stood and stepped out from behind the boulder, hands splayed open and wide. "You may both leave and on my oath as lord and heir to the estate of Thorsten neither I nor my men, Ned included, will hinder you. But you will release that man before you go."

Bonny Boyd gave a sardonic chuckle. "Release. Take your word just like that? Too fuckin' funny. Clara, go."

Munro moved out from behind Boyd, eyes flicking nervously between Ned Wynter and the dense undergrowth where the head thrower must be. She moved hurriedly down the gully, so intent on what was in front of her that she didn't see Mahan step out from a cleft in the wall face and club her to the ground.

With a scream, Bonny Boyd yanked back the chin of the man he held, pressing the knife blade so tight against his neck it drew blood. The man whimpered, damp staining his crotch.

"Hold, hold, damn it!" Jacob raised his hands. "Mahan, stand down."

"They're filth, lord. That man's dead whatever that cock says." Reversing the pummel of his knife, Mahan stood over the prone Grimmer.

"I said, stand down damn you!" Jacob's voice bristled with authority.

The shadow in the cavern moved, stepping out into what remained of the light. It revealed a man in a black cloak and padded armour, his dark surcoat emblazoned with a crow on a red field over the entwined emblem of the rivers. His sword made no sound as it was raised and pressed into the back of Bonny Boyd's neck.

"My Lord. What is your order?" The Black Crow spoke with the melodic twang of the Morass and the Blue Mountains and he wore the amber-skinned complexion of its people.

Jacob blinked. There were few foreigners amongst the ranks of his father's household guards but Endo Rayne was one of them. He acknowledged the guardsman with a slight tilt of his head. He'd a hundred questions on his tongue but this was no time to ask them.

"Provided Boyd here releases this man they may go. I gave my oath, Rayne, I'll not be the one to break it. You too Mahan. Stand down." Jacob repeated.

Taking a step back, Endo Rayne lowered his sword. After a moment, face curdling, Mahan did likewise, his knife arm dropping to his side. The woman at his feet gave a disconnected groan but lay unmoving.

Jacob returned his attention to Bonny Boyd. "Let that man go and you may walk away."

Boyd licked dry lips. Though the sword had been removed from his neck he could still feel the sharp kiss its point had left, burning against his skin. He'd almost slit the old bugger's throat at its touch and doomed himself then and there. He snuck a look at Ned Tullock and saw the same dead stare Black Jack wore. Obdurate, unforgiving, it held no mercy. His eyes returned to Jacob. The young lord held sway here though and was almost the polar opposite to Ned. *Noble foolery, fucking eejit.* He gave a jittering laugh.

"Swear it on ya soul, lordling. Swear it on't One and on't lives of ya wife and children. Ya father and mother. If I believe ya, we have an accord."

Though Jacob could feel the antipathy rolling off Ned beside him, he didn't hesitate.

"I have no wife nor child but, as the One is my witness, I do so swear on the lives of my mother and father and upon my immortal soul that you may walk free from this place, unharmed by me or my men on the provision you release your hostage now, uninjured. Otherwise, I'll have you run through and damn the consequence to my honour."

Boyd sneered. "Well then, an accord it is, my lord." The plump cunt he held stank of fear and piss and as Boyd removed his blade, he pushed a hand into the small of the man's back and sent him stumbling away. Bonny Boyd took a clean breath of air.

A blow hammered the wind out of him. Unseen, it struck Boyd in the chest sending him sprawling into the rock wall. He didn't feel the sharp stone edges dig into his skin, nor remember dropping to his knees. He couldn't breathe, it was like a hand gripped his lungs, squeezing them.

The numb ache in Boyd's body spread like a stain to his limbs. Abstract shouts rang out, but they sounded distant, muffled. The fist in his chest tightened and panic filled him. Tasting iron, Boyd choked. His head, suddenly heavy, lolled forward and he stared at the shaft and fletching that jutted from his flesh. *I've been shot.* Bonny Boyd keeled forward, driving the arrow deeper before it snapped beneath his weight.

"God damn it. I gave my oath." Jacob was raging.

The Grimmer was dead, Endo Rayne knew it without looking but knelt anyway and pressed two fingers to the man's neck. Nothing. As Lord Jacob stomped over, he shook his head.

"Trinity save me. Baka!" Seething, Jacob spun and faced the gentled slope opposite and glared as if his eyes might penetrate the dusk blighted bracken and undergrowth that covered it.

"Keep your voice down. Control your temper, Lord." Ned Wynter placed a calming hand on Jacob's shoulder, but his eyes looked elsewhere, roving their surroundings with a worried frown on his face.

A screech had both men spinning back towards the cavern in time to see a tall lady with greying hair scoop the portly gentleman into her arms. "Vic, I was so worried. I thought you dead."

"I've wet meself," Vic mumbled.

"I can see that dear. Let's get you back inside and cleaned up."

"Speak softly, Viv," warned Endo, "your words carry and there has been too much noise already."

The woman gave a brusque nod, then, steered her husband back toward the cavern, dabbing at the blood on his neck with a scrap of cloth. She passed a second Black Crow as she did, a squat, burly man, built like a barrel but who was taller than he seemed.

Jacob didn't know the name of the new Crow but recognised him from the Keep. Brown-bearded, the man's features held a squashed nose that had been broken more than once, a fleshy mouth and water-blue eyes.

"Lord Jacob." The man sketched a bow that was rustic at best.

A rustle of leaf and the snap of a branch had Jacob turning back around as Baka appeared, bow in hand with an arrow held loose on the string.

Anger that had never truly left him, boiled up inside Jacob at the sight. "I gave my word. You had no right…"

"I had every right," Baka spat. "Told ya afore. You ain't my Lord. This ain't some game of chivalry where y'er word is worth a lick-spit-a-shit. Look around. There ain't no high walls here. Nae courts to pander to. Ain't nuffin' but the wild and if you want ta survive it you'd best put away any miss-notion ya have of fair play and honour."

The Grimmer pointed at Skunk Munro, who was only now just starting to come around. "She's next. Shoulda let ya man there do his job, but since he cannae cause of ya fool word I'll 'ave ta do it."

Jacob moved and blocked his path.

Baka snarled. "If ya let her go, Black Jack will know we're about and it won't take his evil arse a minute to suss out the dozen or so hideaways we could be using. Ya honour ain't worth a shit if ya'r dead now, is it?"

"Everyone dies, Baka. It's how we choose to live that's important. A man's word matters else we're no better than the beasts," Jacob retorted.

"Nice. Read that in one of they'n fancy books of yours." Baka sneered. "Ya nae grafted a day in ya life. Nae worked till ya fingers bled or eaten things that were pure boggin' a dog wouldn't touch it."

"Enough, Baka." Ned Wynter interposed himself between grimmer and lord. He could sense Endo Rayne at his back and knew the man was not to be trifled with.

"Both of you are right. We can't let Munro go else she'll lead Black Jack to us. I know my half-brother and once he gets wind we're about, he'll not rest 'til we're dead." Ned turned to Jacob. "This concerns more than just you, lord. Baka is not your man so does not impugn your honour if he were to act outside your order."

He held his hand up at Jacob's glare of defiance. "By the same token, I know you'll not stand for Skunk's murder even if it is by another's hand. The choice then is plain. Stand aside and let Baka do his job or take her with us."

Baka opened his mouth to complain but Ned silenced him with a raised finger without taking his eyes from Lord Jacob.

"The Grim never truly leaves a man. I know Baka is right and back in the day, her blood would already be spilt. But see, your father gave me something I ain't never had afore. A chance and a choice. He taught me summat when he did that but it took me a while to realise it. That any man can have honour. That his word ought ta mean something."

Ned stepped away and stood beside a sullen faced Baka who shook his head.

"What the fuck 'ave they done ta ya?" the grimmer muttered.

Ned shrugged. "We need to move."

Baka thrust the bow at him. "Fine. She lives. But I'll bind her, guard her ass and if she gives any shit I'll do the necessaries. No question about it."

Baka stomped around Jacob, who, at a nod from Wynter, let him go.

"Lord?"

Jacob turned. "Endo Rayne. It is good to see you. My father, mother?"

"Well enough, lord, when last I saw them both."

"I've questions but most will have to wait. But tell me, how many do you bring? How many Crows?"

"Just John Tanner and I, with a dozen of our people." As Endo was speaking those self-same people started filing from the cavern.

Jacob turned and watched. Ragged, dirt-stained, they looked more like vagrants than citizens of Thorsten and most had seen more than forty winters. The hope many wore upon their faces at seeing him humbled Jacob, but it did not disguise the brittleness behind their eyes nor lift the weariness from their limbs. They were near their limits.

A knot of unease nestled at the back of Jacob's skull, a despondent malaise that slipped down his spine. He was still trying to figure out what to do and here now was a new burden to bear, another fear to manage. What could these folks offer other than more mouths to feed? He grimaced. The thought was unbefitting of a lord. He gave what he hoped was a reassuring smile.

"We have a place of safety. I will lead you there, but you must keep quiet, and you must keep up. It's an hour's walk to the Reach over some inhospitable terrain. Once there, we'll make camp and send for boats to ferry you."

An older man, who looked to Jacob like a plump beetle with his small head and thin legs sticking out from a carapace of multi-layered clothing and a thick cloak, gave a derisive snort.

"That's what this one said." The beetle tapped a boot against the dead man. "We've already wasted a day on his say so and we've not eaten. Have you got any food?"

Jacob locked eyes with him. "We'll share what we have when we make camp not before. We must make the most of what's left of the light so gather whatever you have."

The man gave a bitter laugh. "What I have? I've nought, lord. No home, my wife taken in the night by urak, one son dead fightin' the beasties and t'other waiting to die back at Thorsten with your father."

The brawny bulk of John Tanner stepped forward. His voice was oddly gentle for such a thickset man. "We've all suffered, Ernst. All of us lost what we had. But this is what we got now, and we need you, old-timer. Come, I'll walk with you but no talkin'."

"Ai, I know it. You and that bronze heathen told us enough times already. I'm sick a hearin' it."

Relieved at Tanner's intervention, Jacob turned to Ned Wynter who, at his nod, started chivvying the newcomers into some semblance of order.

Watching the ranger organise them, Jacob suppressed a surge of envy, knowing it was unworthy. But the clipped efficiency with which Ned Wynter handled his people and the way they responded to him told Jacob this man was a leader and probably a better one than he.

"Life and death decisions have lived with that man his whole life."

Jacob jerked, unaware until that moment that Endo Rayne stood beside him. Had the man read his mind as well?

"Command comes easy to him it seems," Jacob replied.

"Experience has made him what he is," Rayne replied. "An artisan knows every tool and every instrument they have to work with. They know which to employ and when. It is no different for a lord, only your instruments are people. Keep him close, lord. Make him your man as your father did."

Endo Rayne walked off and Jacob watched as he angled towards Mahan and Baka who were bent over Skunk Munro and arguing it seemed over how best to bind the murkhawk.

It was a short while later that Ned Wynter led the ragtag group out of Braunecks Gorge, Jacob just behind him and the others stretched out in single file with Baka and Rayne bringing up the rear. Climbing the hill they retraced their path east, the sullen waters of the Reach beckoning them on.

* * *

High on the far slope, hidden eyes observed the dead man at the foot of the rock face and tracked the progress of those who had left. A red deer, a juvenile doe taken earlier, lay forgotten on the ground as the watcher followed. A new hunt and bigger game beckoned.

Chapter 43: The Sanctuary of Caves

Fallston, The Rivers

Night was settling by the time Jacob and Wynter and their band of refugees descended the escarpment to the Reach. The beetle-like Ernst fell, slipping on the ice and snow as they navigated the steep decline. Only the trunk-like legs of John Tanner arrested the older man's fall but by then his back and side were bruised and he had to be aided the rest of the way down.

With the escarpment at their backs, they were shielded from the buffeting wind, though an occasional gust still reached them and carried with it a wasted knot of ripe air. A telling reminder of the proximity of the Grim Marsh.

Above, the skies were overcast and clouds roiled to the north. A storm was brewing and Wynter knew they would do well to get back to the sanctuary of the caves before it struck. Despite the encroaching darkness, Wynter led them unerringly around the edges of a beechwood grove that bordered the Reach and located the skiff he'd left hidden in the tall reeds.

There was no debate and no discussion when Jacob ordered Ernst into the boat along with Vic and Viv, the husband and wife from the gorge, and an older lady whose name Jacob had been told but which had slipped his mind. It was not just the refugees that were tired.

A gruff-faced Baka took the paddle and promised to be back by the witching hour with boats for the rest of them.

"Keep ya eye on, Skunk. She's a crafty bitch and won't think twice a' stickin' a knife in ya throat if she gets free," he groused at Mahan. The two of them had been nettling away at each other since Morqhill, the possession of Skunk Munro only the latest of contestations between them.

"Hold the stick with the wide end down or you'll no get anywhere," Mahan retorted.

"Fuck you, Crowbait." Dipping the paddle into the water, Baka pulled, and the boat vanished into the stygian night.

After some debate, they lit a fire in a bush-lined glade situated between the tall reeds and the beech wood. The hairless branches of the trees would somewhat shield the light of the flames from anyone inland unless they stood directly upon the bluff they had descended, and lakeside its faint beacon would give a signal to Baka of their location.

"Let's just hope no one else is out upon the lake this night," Wynter said to Jacob. "I'll watch the woods. I suggest ya post Endo Rayne to the south, John Tanner north."

Time was hard to judge in the bleak, starless skies and it proved a long night for those left waiting. All were hungry with little food to go around, and they were exhausted, limbs sore from days of travel and their energy depleted by the constant fear of urak.

Their meagre fire provided a much-welcomed warmth and spread a pocket of light that encased them in a lustreless cell. One they could not see out of as they sat, huddled together, their cloaks wrapped tight.

True to his word, Baka was back in the witching hours just after midnight, leading a quartet of boats paddled by Sis Lafferty, Nip Rokan and Nadine Varla.

Jacob left it to Ned Wynter to organise the even loading of each vessel which he did with calm efficiency. Few words were spoken, people moving with a quiet urgency to Ned's instruction, eager to be gone and happy to be told what to do, even when that meant plunging their boots into the frigid waters of the Reach.

Skunk Munro was placed in Baka's boat with Mahan still guarding her. The broad-shouldered, barrel-chested John Tanner helped a civilian in before climbing into the bow and taking a paddle. "I know the water some," he said to nobody in particular.

Ned Wynter and Jacob were the last to board, taking Nadine Varla's boat which was already occupied by Endo Rayne.

They slipped out onto the quiet of the lake, the ripple of the paddles in the water and their laboured breathing the only sounds. The wind picked up as they left the shelter of the escarpment, gusting hard against their left flank, its touch chilling where it found flesh.

The storm struck in the hours just before dawn, the howling wind driving the snow horizontally at them. Huddled beneath their cloaks and blankets they endured and as the eastern horizon turned to ash, Nip Rokan in the lead boat angled them towards the shore. The ambient rumble of the falls grew ever louder with each stroke of the paddles until its power crashed around their ears, adding its voice to the tempest.

The boats pulled for the shore and as they came into the shelter of the rising bluff they could feel a current working against them, swirling and eddying until suddenly its grip dissipated and the water calmed. A forest of wilted reeds rose around them and Nip Rokan steered them through a channel until the prow of his skiff ground against mud and beached. Not waiting, he leapt from the back of the boat into the lake, sinking up to his thighs, the cold catching his breath as water lapped around his balls. Wading ashore, he grabbed the bow rope and dragged the boat higher, its hull slipping and sliding across the slush of mud and snow.

"Come." Holding a hand out, Rokan helped the passengers, one by one, from the skiff.

"Wait over there. You," Rokan pointed to a middle-aged man with narrow shoulders and a paunched belly, "grab the front and lift when I lift." He waded back into the water, this time only up to his shins and grabbed the back of the boat. Empty of its cargo the vessel was surprisingly light and, with a grunt of effort, the two men lifted it free of the Reach and marched it onto dry land.

They gathered by the roar of the falls, the noise oppressive and the air heavy with moisture. They were nineteen souls and ten of them were wondering what they were doing there.

"Fallston is just the other side. Why stop here?" shouted one, a balding man with a flat nose and a line-creased face that bristled with stubble. His cowl was pulled up over a woollen cap too small for his large head.

"Fallston is a husk, nothing left but burnt timbers and despair," Jacob answered, voice raised against the sound of the falls. "Just follow Ned here and try not to break any branches when you do."

Squelching over the soft mud and slush, Wynter led them onto firmer ground, frozen and crisp with snow. Moving away from the falls, he guided them through bushes and tall ferns that looked brown and dead but still held their shape. He followed a barely revealed path that twisted west into a grove that abutted a towering cliff face.

The long, low cleft in the rock side, half concealed by vegetation, would have gone unnoticed in the predawn light but Wynter knew it was there. He gave a fluting bird call, then, ducking low, parted the vines and shrubs and disappeared beneath the lip of the cave.

A dim light flared as a lantern was unshuttered and Wynter blinked in the glare.

"It's true then?" Trilled a young voice as the boats were hauled inside and stored out of the way.

"Ai, Tom. Survivors, all the way from Thorsten." Ned answered. "They're cold, wet and tired so ya'd best be prepared for 'em."

"As much as can be. I caught plenty of fish, enough ta feed everyone at least." Turning, Tom Trickle led them into the caves, following a well-used path that had been worn smooth over countless years.

The sound of the falls had dropped to a faint vibration when they'd first entered the caves, but the deeper Tom led them the stronger its muted rumble grew. The way ahead lightened until, of a sudden, the passage opened onto a large cavern.

As they spewed into the underground chamber, they found it was decorated with the flotsam of humanity. Crates and boxes were piled haphazardly around its edges with a dozen or more camp beds staggered down one side and there was a table of all things with chairs and cut logs to sit on. In places, strange calcite deposits extended like teeth from the floor and hung from the ceiling but the wonder of them went largely unnoticed for it was the fire pit in the centre that drew their attention, casting a cheery glow and throwing distorted shadows against the nooks and crannies of the walls. The people crowded forward. Drawn by the irresistible lure of food cooking and an open flame.

A squat, toad-like woman with a perpetual frown on her face rose from her seat by the fire. She squinted one eye closed and glared at the interlopers with the other.

"Sofia," she rasped, prompting the woman stirring the cookpot, who was focused on her task and seemed oblivious to the sudden intrusion.

Turning at her name, Sofia watched impassively as people gathered around. They were old, or at least older than her twenty-eight years. The soft glow of the fire did little to mask their reddened, wind-chaffed skin or disguise their fatigue. Another time and another place she would have clucked and fussed over them but now their plight barely touched her at all.

Sofia blew subconsciously at a strand of auburn hair that had broken free from her ponytail and tickled her cheek before turning back to the cookpot. Picking up a bowl she ladled fish broth into it and held it out, not looking to see who would take it.

"I got it," Tom murmured grabbing the bowl and passing it out but she didn't acknowledge him. She never said much these days. She bent and took another bowl to fill.

Casting a half-glance at the dour-faced Hett, Tom took the offering and passed it along, before turning and taking the next.

"You'll find we've plenty of room," Jacob said as the food was passed around, "even if it's not the most comfortable of places to call home it's dry and we've plenty of clean water. Once you've finished eating, get some sleep. There are cots and blankets over there." Jacob pointed. "We'll sort out something more permanent once everyone has rested."

Endo Rayne proffered a bowl and Jacob took it with thanks. His stomach growled with impatience at the aroma, and he chugged a mouthful of hot broth, watching as a complaining Skunk Munro was led away by Baka and Mahan.

"Shut ya trap," Baka warned. "I'm hungry and wet and no in the mood for ya whining. Behave and Mahan'll get ya some stew."

Jacob didn't listen to the murkhawk's reply, his eyes had fastened on a figure, stood at the opening of a passageway. The shape and build, the stance and subtle tilt of the head said it was Sand, and yet his cousin was unrecognisable to the man he had grown up with. He was pale as a corpse which exacerbated the dark shadows ringing his eyes. They, too, were different. The same startling blue as his own but the whites were bloodshot and pink, and, whereas before they had always held a mischievous warmth, now they were only penetrating and cold. Sand's wavy blonde locks were gone as well, the stubble that had grown back was as black as jet.

Jacob could live with all that. After what his cousin had survived it was a miracle he was alive at all, and yet the biggest change in him was one that could not be seen. It was as if the fires that burned Sand had scoured and consumed all the joy from his soul. Sand never smiled nor laughed. There was no banter, just stilted dialogue. *You're in there somewhere cousin, I know it.*

"Have you finished, lord?"

Jacob looked down and found Sofia at his elbow. Her gaze though was locked upon the same space his had been.

"No, I've not had chance yet." Jacob took a sip from his bowl.

Sofia's stare remained fixed on the passageway. She remained silent for a moment longer then turned and walked away.

When Jacob looked up again, his cousin, too, was gone.

* * *

Vic Stenhause launched the contents of the waste bucket into the wall of water, feeling the rope around his girth tighten at the motion. The foul contents disappeared in an eyeblink and with it the smell. Well mostly. Dipping the bucket in the channel beside him, he scooped up water, swirled it around before sending the dregs the same way.

He stood a moment, enjoying the natural but fractured light that filtered through the falls. He'd not felt the sun on his face for four days or was it five? It was easy to lose track of time in their underground sanctuary.

The rope around his waist tugged. Grinning, he about-faced and held the bucket up to Viv in salute. She shook her head at him but couldn't hide the crease of a smile. It was her tolerant smile; one he knew well enough and one that could just as easily turn into something sterner if he didn't stop his dawdling. Vic navigated carefully around a shallow rockpool, then feeling emboldened leapt a trickling rut of water, slipped, caught himself then stumbled to an awkward and inelegant stop in front of her.

The water cave, as it had come to be known, was thunderous, the noise from the falls reverberated against the walls which gathered and reflected the noise. It was painfully loud, and Vic appreciated the fact that it would buy him a little respite before Viv's admonishment undoubtedly came.

Untying the rope from around his waist, his wife coiled it in a loop before she led the way down a passage toward the central chamber. The noise from the waterfall dropped dramatically as soon as they rounded a bend and Viv started unwinding the scarf tied around her head and which covered her ears. Vic decided to leave in the wadded cloth bunging his lugholes just a while longer.

"Don't think I don't know you can't hear me, Victor Oscar Stenhause."

Unable to help himself, Vic gave a trite grin. "Pardon dear?"

Viv pursed her lips, but her eyes twinkled in the half-light of the torches that filled the cavern.

"Very droll. You're not as spry as you think you are. If you slip and put your back out or turn an ankle you've only yourself to blame. And I'll tell you now, I won't be the one running around after you if you do. There is far too much else to get on with."

Leaning close, Vic pecked her cheek, "Right you are. I'll… a, return the bucket to the latrine."

"Meet me in the third chamber and don't dally. I need you to shift some of those crates for me."

Vic watched fondly as his wife marched away, her back upright and her stride determined. He knew some of it was a façade, but not all. Viv had always been a doer and it had taken her barely a day in their new refuge before starting to organise things. His heart lurched and he shucked his shoulders at the sudden melancholy that threatened to overcome him. All this tragedy, their inn burnt to ash, everything lost, and Morten gone the Trinity knew where. Yet despite it, they still had each other and all the stress and worry only served to make their bond stronger. It would be enough. *It has to be.*

Vic made his way through the main chamber. That first day underground he had marvelled at its enormity, so large it could fit the entirety of the Broken Axe Inn beneath its vaulted ceiling. But that wonder had soon faded and now all he saw were dark walls and looming rock.

Four or five days since their rescue. Four or five days of living underground. It wasn't natural and some had taken to it badly like old Mrs Madrigar who had gone in on herself and barely spoke. Or Stannis Ruddlan who railed and moaned, though never in earshot of Lord Jacob or the former grimmers. He didn't much like Ruddlan if he was honest. He was belligerent and a complainer, a vegetable seller off the market who liked the sound of his voice a little too much.

Pausing by the passageway, Vic glanced back at his wife and saw her talking with Hett, the squat, troll-like woman who, according to Viv, was a physiker and apothecarist. For some reason he had yet to fathom, Viv liked the troll.

His eyes moved a fraction and alighted on Sofia who stood nearby but was removed from whatever conversation was being had. The woman's body was listless and her face slack with disinterest. What with gossip and tales being part of a taverner's lot it hadn't taken his wife long to glean the reason why and according to Viv, Sofia's daughter had died and the enigmatic and rarely seen Lord Sandford had something to do with it. Which was the reason, he supposed, for her unkempt appearance and vacant demeanour.

As if feeling his scrutiny, Sofia tilted her head and returned his stare with eyes as dull and lacklustre as her auburn hair. With a half-smile, Vic gave a brusque nod of acknowledgement only for Sofia to blink then swivel her head away.

Vic coughed, awkward at the one-sided exchange and took a step toward the passageway, eager suddenly to resume his chore. A distant echo spun him in his tracks. It was a cry, a bellow and though he could discern no words there was no mistaking the urgency in it.

Heart pounding, Vic watched as Lord Jacob leapt from one of the cots and began strapping his swordbelt around his hips. Endo Rayne appeared, the Morassian Black Crow was never far from Lord Jacob, and the two of them marched across the floor towards the noise which was growing closer and louder with every passing moment.

The shackled fear inside of Vic that he thought had gone, broke free. Urak, they must have found them. Someone must have left a trail in the snow or been seen out on the lake and followed. "One save us. Trinity aid us." His breath ghosted the old words.

He looked for Viv who, unlike him, was not frozen like a witless fool and was striding purposefully towards him, pulling Sofia by the hand.

The troll began barking out orders to the room like an innkeeper clearing a bar after final orders, and this more than anything, had people scampering towards the tunnel at Vic's back.

There was a passage, Vic had learned, that led into Fallston but its entrance was blocked town-side according to the ranger, Ned Wynter, and it was yet to be scouted out and cleared. It offered them no escape and with only one way in or out, the corridor of rock at his back was their only option, one that led, inexorably, deeper underground.

If the enemy ever came, non-combatants were to gather in the furthest of the storage caves where a seam of rock created a barricade of sorts making it highly defensible. At the back of this cave, a craggy corridor wormed deeper, joining a labyrinthine network of cutouts and caves. No one had said anything about them, and it was Vic's impression that no one knew much at all of what lay beyond.

Like a doorman, Vic stood to the side as people filed past. Someone battered his shoulder causing him to stumble against the wall. Ruddlan. His eyes were wide but they did not see Vic as he barged by.

The sharp pain digging into his back was enough to break fear's hold and Vic reached out as Viv rushed up to him. "Go through, I'll be right behind. I just… let me see what's happening and I'll be right there. I promise." He stammered.

Viv squeezed his hand, the worry lines around her eyes bunching. She opened her mouth to say something, shut it, then opened it again. "No further than here. Don't you leave me alone, Vic."

"Never." Eyes glistening, Vic bent and pressed his lips to hers. "By One's grace, I'll always be with you. Now go. I'll be along soon."

Bringing Vic's hand to her mouth she kissed it. Then, in a rush, she stepped through into the passage, Sofia dragging along behind.

Vic felt for the long knife on his hip. Reassured it was there, he turned his attention back towards the commotion in time to witness two men stumble from the passage that led to the Reach. One was John Tanner, the Black Crow that had been with them since Thorsten. He had a shoulder under the arm of the other man, one of the grimmers, who had an arrow protruding from his chest and was half dragged, half carried into the room.

Tanner coughed and spluttered, sinking to a knee as Endo Rayne and Lord Jacob took the wounded man's weight and lowered him to the ground.

Immediately, Hett was there, pushing the two men away as if they were annoying children and growled. "Guard the passage. And where's that bloody boy."

"I'm here, Hett." Tom Trickle hurried across the cavern from a passageway near Vic's own, the ranger Ned Wynter and Lord Sandford walking briskly behind him.

"Nip's been shot?"

"Fool of a boy." Hett rolled one beady eye up at Tom, even as she closed the dead man's eyes. "I'll need a ball of flame. Gather what ether you can and be ready when I call for it."

"Yeah, sure," Tom stammered, eyes fixating on the arrow in Nip Rokan's chest.

Vic about jumped out of his skin when someone brushed past him, then another. Two more of the grimmers, Sis Lafferty and Nils Baka.

Ignoring Vic completely, they loped across the cavern to the gathered defenders and stared at Nip Rokan's body. The stillness of it told them all they needed to know. Screwing her face into an angry frown, Sis Lafferty moved to the weapons rack and pulled a bow from it and a quiver of arrows.

"Fuck," John Tanner swore as he climbed to his feet, "I lugged a deadman here?" He glared back the way he'd come, hand resting on his sword hilt.

"Report, John," Lord Jacob commanded.

"Grimmers. They musta knowed we was 'ere. Never saw 'em till Nip got hit. I hauled him inside and took two of the buggers when they tried ta follow. Next thing a barrel rolls in spewing hell smoke everywhere. I couldn't breathe nor see so I dragged Nip back here."

Vic felt the knot in his gut unravel a fraction. Grimmers were bad news, but they weren't urak.

"How many?" Jacob asked.

John Tanner shook his head. "Didn't see but they was prepared, so enough I reckon."

Vic watched a smoky finger curl around the sconce on the cave wall, flickering and dimming its light and he thought he could detect a bitter, acrid tang in the air even from where he stood.

"They'll block the entrance and let the smoke draw in." Ned Wynter said. "When they're ready they'll be in behind it and we'd best be ready for 'em. This ain't gonna end well."

Chilled by the bleak assessment, Vic turned to go. He'd heard enough.

"What're you doing?" Nadine Varla blocked his way, one hand on her knife hilt, the other clutching, Aousa. The fierce look on the young girl's face was the opposite of her mother's, who for once looked concerned.

"Miss Varla," Vic nodded, ignoring her question. Instead, he dropped to his haunches and looked at the little girl. "Hello, Aousa. Why don't you come and wait with me? Viv is back there and will be pleased to see you."

"Can't. I'm going with mama. I got my knife." Aousa brandished it. "I can use it too."

"Aousa, go with Mr Stenhause. He will keep you safe until I come get you," Nadine ordered.

The little girl glared fiercely and braced her feet.

"You're strong and brave, I can see that," Vic cajoled her. "But some of the old folk back there aren't. They're scared and need someone to protect them. Someone like you."

The girl frowned and pursed her lips.

"Of course, it's a lot of responsibility protecting so many. I guess I'll have to do it if you can't." Vic pulled his knife from its sheath but fumbled and dropped it clattering to the floor.

Aousa glanced at her mother who shook her head. "Useless. Guard them, Usa, and show Mr Stenhause how to hold a knife properly. We wouldn't want him to cut his fingers off by mistake would we?"

With a giggle, Aousa's scowl vanished. "Okay, mama."

Recovering his knife, Vic stood and gave a nod to Nadine Varla whose eyes had fastened on his. He waited for her to say the words. To take care of her little girl. To keep her safe. It is what he and Viv would have said, only she didn't. She simply held Aousa's hand up for him to take and when he did, marched past.

Vic looked down at Aousa. "Hmmm, I can't quite remember where to go. Was it this way?" He pointed.

"You're stupid," Aousa announced, "It's down here silly."

The girl dragged on Vic's hand and led him down twisting and turning passages and through several caves littered with crates and chests. The sound of voices reached them. High and echoey they grew louder with every step until they left the passage they were in and came upon a cavern full of people.

A chest-high seam of rock crossed the room and a box had been dragged to it to act as a step. He helped Aousa over, where a relieved looking Viv was waiting.

"What in hells is going on?" Ruddlan demanded.

"Keep your voice calm and I'll tell everyone what I know," Vic said, waving his hands for quiet. He went on to explain the situation.

"Lord Jacob should'na had that grimmer killed." Ruddlan moaned. "They were taking us somewhere safe. Not this pit in the ground. I say we give 'em what they want."

"And what's that exactly?" Vic asked.

"Ain't no secret. Ned Wynter and his merry band of cutthroats is what. Hand 'em over ta this Black Jack fellow and maybe he'll take us in. Get us out of this hellhole." Ruddlan glanced around at everyone, but none would meet his eye.

"I'll stab you in your neck." Aousa brandished her knife and lurched toward the stout man. "Your piss stinks of fear. I can smell it on your leg."

"Aousa Varla, that language is appalling," Viv cried. "Where did you learn to speak like that?"

"My mama," she snarled then hissed at Ruddlan. "Black Jack would feed you to the sallies."

Vic stepped in, trying to keep the grin off his face at the child's fierceness and Ruddlan's fear but only half succeeding.

"No one is handing anyone over." They were Vic's words or near enough, but they had been uttered before he could speak them. Everyone turned toward the entrance where the voice rang from and saw a man peering over the rock wall.

It was Mahan, Lord Jacob's man and behind him was the female prisoner, Skunk Munro. Even in the gloomy light, Vic could see he was pale and sweat beaded his brow.

"The little girl's smarter than the lot of ya," Mahan said. "Black Jack's a monster. Any of you wanna cast your lot in with him, climb this wall and make your way to Lord Jacob. He'll let you through I'm sure, and then see how ya fare."

Silence filled the cavern.

"No one? Good. Any more talk like that and you'll have more than just Aousa here to answer to."

Aousa beamed, whilst Ruddlan sank back through the people behind him.

"Get your hand off my ass," snapped the grimmer woman as Mahan encouraged her over the wall of rock.

"With a name like Skunk, I want nought to do with ya ass Munro."

Once Mahan and Munro had joined them, they waited mostly in silence for what seemed an interminable amount of time, straining for any noise that might give a clue of what was happening. They had only one torch lit and it cast eerie shadows along the walls and ceiling.

Though most there did not know it, supplies had been stacked in the back of the cave, where a dark rent split the rock, a rent filled with stagnant air. But Vic knew it and so did Viv. They had inventoried and helped prepare what they thought might be useful. Food, flint, oil and torches. Along with ropes and grapples and all manner of things needed to survive in the lower caves. Vic prayed silently to Nihmrodel that they'd not need it. He felt a tug on his sleeve.

"I'll show you how to hold your knife," Aousa said.

* * *

Dense smoke billowed into the cave, its toxic fumes biting the back of the throat and leaving an acrid taste in the mouth.

"We cannot stay here, lord," Endo Rayne said. A bow thrummed as Sis Lafferty sent an arrow into the smoke only to hear a sharp report as it clattered against rock.

"I'll not scurry away like a mouse to die in a hole in the ground," Jacob snorted.

"We're already in a hole underground, lord. What matters if we go a little deeper?" Rayne said.

Ned Wynter was stooped low against the cavern's wall, flanking the passage belching smoke.

"Summat ain't right, here." Wynter peeled away and crouch-walked to the upturned table Jacob was using as a barricade.

"What do you mean?" Jacob asked.

"This smoke. Hinders them more 'n us," Wynter reasoned. "That passage will be filled with it and they gotta come through it ta get ta us. Even if they wait for it ta clear, it's gonna take time. Allows us to set our defences and still limits them to a narrow entry point. Smart thing woulda bin ta rush us at the start."

"Your brother, this Black Jack, is a cunning man?" Endo Rayne asked.

"As a snake, and he's my half-brother," Wynter replied.

"Then it is a distraction. It draws attention here and the question is why? What for?" Rayne observed.

Ned closed his eyes and raised his head to the ceiling. "Awww shit. Fallston. The entrance from Fallston. They fuckin' cleared it. Has to be."

Bounding to his feet, Wynter lurched towards the opposite side of the cavern, calling over his shoulder. "Baka, Sis, Varla on me."

Jacob rose from his position only for Endo Rayne to place a hand on his arm.

"We cannot abandon this entrance, lord."

Jacob cursed roundly. "I feel useless just waiting."

"It's a soldier's lot." Rayne gave a crooked smile. "Along with boredom, long marches, bad food and rough sleep. Oh, and fightin' and dyin'. Send John Tanner. The two of us and Lord Sandford should be enough to hold this post long enough if needs be but really, we should consider moving back to the next cavern and restricting them to one point of attack."

Jacob sighed heavily, knowing the advice was sound. "John, go with Wynter. They'll need a strong blade and your shield."

A sturdy finger prodded Jacob's right shoulder blade and, twisting about, he found himself face to face with Hett. She held a leather bladder up in offering.

"I'm not thirsty," Jacob said, although now that he had said it, he found he was. Bile from the smoke sat like a slug at the back of his throat. Tom Trickle stood behind the witch with big eyes, *the most useless mage in the history of mages,* Jacob thought, harshly.

"It ain't fer drinkin'. Throw it at the hole when the time comes, and Tom here will light it up. Then take cover. It'll buy ya time." Not waiting for an answer, she waddled off towards Wynter.

Loud cries rose from across the far side of the cavern followed by a clash of steel that had Jacob spinning to look. Grimmers had burst in through the Fallston passageway and Wynter and the others engaged them.

"Throw it now," Hett yelled over her shoulder, before angling her path toward the deeper passage they were to fall back to.

A whoosh of sound and orange heat washed over Jacob as a ball of oscillating flames sprang into being, rotating slowly over Tom Trickle's hand.

"The pouch, Lord Jacob," the lad squawked.

With a grunt of effort, Jacob tossed the skin of liquid into the smoke-filled passageway and with a surge that stood up the hairs on his arms, the fireball followed its trajectory.

Rayne pulled Jacob down and Tom ducked below the tipped up table as a concussive whump detonated. The table shivered as it was splattered by debris and ribbons of woodsmoke began streaming off its top.

Jumping to his feet, Jacob shielded his face as bilious smoke and yellow flame curled and danced in the passageway adding to the smog cloud already there. He had no idea how long it would last but Hett said it would buy them time.

"Come on." Drawing his sword, Jacob sprinted towards the fighting and Endo Rayne was quickly on his heels.

Nadine Varla was down and writhing on the floor. Ned Wynter stood over her, parried a blow and slipped his knife into the gut of the man he faced. Nils Baka fought at his side, blood sheeting one side of his face, his off-hand balled into a bloody fist and held tight against his chest.

Sis Lafferty stood further back launching arrows into the mouth of the passage as fast as she could loose them and John Tanner was guarding her flank.

Shit, thought Jacob doing a quick assessment. The grimmers had cleared the passageway and forced enough of a gap that they could reinforce their numbers. They couldn't hold for long. Once flanked they would quickly fall.

With a berserker cry, Jacob crashed past John Tanner, his sword leaning over the blade of a man and into his face with a crunch. Whipping his blade out he drove his shoulder into the dying grimmer and levered him into the ones behind.

Rayne slid by on the left, deflecting a sword that would have taken Jacob's arm off, catching it on his blade before running it to his crossguard and driving it up. He punched the knife in his left hand through boiled leather and into a kidney. Pulling back to Jacob's side he lectured, "This is no training ground. Try not to over-extend, lord."

Jacob grunted, hacking at a new assailant who had pushed aside his dead comrade. Their blades screeched as they connected and Jacob forced it wide before slashing his blade back, its keen edge biting into the man's neck with a gout of blood.

Another dropped at the entrance to the passageway, an arrow in his chest and the tide of Grimmers stuttered. Endo Rayne's blade flicked out slicing a hand, drawing a pained cry from the murkhawk he fought. He drove forward, forcing the man to scramble back, heel catching on one of the fallen. As he stumbled, Rayne's sword skewered his thigh and he screamed and dragged himself towards the passage.

A ball of fire lanced between John Tanner and Sis Lafferty making both flinch away from its heat trail. It burst against the bodies in the entrance emitting a sizzling roar as leather and clothing, skin and hair ignited. It sent the Grimmers waiting beyond into a panicked retreat.

"Sprung their trap early, they'll be back," Nils Baka panted, through teeth gritted in pain.

Sis Lafferty sent an arrow through the fire and into the dark light beyond. "That were Torgrid in the back. Spineless fuck."

Ned Wynter bent over a groaning Varla and pulled her hands from her stomach to inspect the wound, his face turned grim.

"Lord, we are two down and cannot hold both sides," Rayne prompted, wiping his blade clean on the cloak of a dead man.

"Okay. We fall back." Jacob ordered glancing at the grey-faced ranger. "Ned. We can carry her."

Ned didn't respond but gathered Nadine Varla up in his arms.

They retreated in haste, Tom Trickle leading the way, John Tanner bringing up the rear with his shield and Sis Lafferty covering them with her bow.

They passed through the adjoining cavern and headed deeper underground, extinguishing torches and removing them from their brackets as they went. In the next cave, they rested and those able set about hauling crates back down the passage they had just left, blocking the way. It would not hold the grimmers long when they came but it would give them some warning. They then set about fortifying the cave's entrance.

Ned Wynter laid Varla down, bunching her cloak up as a pillow for her head. Blood the colour of her red bandana stained her lips and dribbled down her chin. She coughed and then screwed her face tight.

A squat figure loomed over them both and Ned tilted his head enough to take in the scuffed boots, worn hose and frayed skirt-ends.

"Hett, can ya…"

"It's a killin' wound and nought I can do about it," Hett muttered looking past his shoulder. "I'm sorry, Nadine. I… you're a good sort and I always liked you. May you walk in Jarekicar's light." The grizzled physiker held a hand out to Ned, in it was a small thin blade.

With a sigh, Ned hung his head. "Got ma own," he mumbled, watching the feet as they turned and shuffled away. He glanced at Varla and saw that she was watching him, her eyes wide like a startled deer, though whether it was in pain or fear he could not tell.

"I'll mind the girl. With my life, I swear it, Nade."

"Screw…hu…you…hu," Varla gasped.

Ned smoothed the bush of hair off her forehead. "I ain't never knowed love. Spect I wouldn't recognise it even if I did. But I reckon you're as close as I ever got. I treated ya wrong leavin' like I did and I wish it were different but I can't change that, Nade. All I can do is move forward and try ta be better than I was. Lord Crow taught me that."

Varla's eyes closed, and tears gathered like dewdrops between her lashes. "I…hu…hu…hu," her breaths came shorter and closer together, "scared…hu…hu…Ao…Aou…Usa…hu." With a grimace of blood-stained teeth, her head went back, and she gave a low, mewling groan.

Leaning low, Ned brushed his whiskered cheek against Varla's impossibly smooth one and whispered in her ear. "I'll not leave her, my black soul on it, Nade. I'll give my life ta see her safe." *Is she mine?*

Ned couldn't bring himself to ask. In the end, his courage failed him. Leaning back, Ned cupped a hand to her cheek, and they stared at each other. Their eyes conveyed what words would not and with a thrust, his dagger stopped her heart. Varla spasmed once, twice then was still.

Ned felt a hand on his shoulder and looked up to find Nils Baka's blood-smeared face staring down at him. Nothing was said, for there was nothing to say that each did not already know.

"Sand…? Where's Sand?" Jacob cried, shattering the moment of quiet. "Did anyone see him?"

"He did not come through," Hett supplied from the far side of the cave where she was gathering some things and packing them into Tom's backpack.

"We have to go back. While we can." Jacob moved toward the barricade of crates.

"It's too late," Ned growled rising to his feet. "If he is not here it's cause he chooses not to be. No, we go on."

Jacob cursed, then glared. "Go where? I'll not leave him Ned, and these passages and caves mean they must come at us in ones and twos. We can bloody them and make them pay."

"To what end?" Ned shouted.

"You are sworn to me," Jacob snarled. "Sworn to my family."

"I know it, boy." Ned stalked forward.

Endo Rayne stepped between them and laid a hand on the ranger's shoulder. "Careful."

Jaw clenched, Ned restrained from driving a fist into the Black Crow's gut and refocused on the lordling. "Sworn maybe but I'll tell a truth when I see it and speak when I need ta be heard. I asked to what end, lord? Cause we cannot fight and win. We've lost two already and we'll fall one by one if we do this." He jerked a thumb over his shoulder. "An' what about your people, eh? What happens ta them when ya bravado gets ya killed."

"Lord? Everything alright?" A voice called from the far side of the cave, and they all turned to see Mahan framed in the low-slung passage leading out.

"Just discussing tactics, Mahan," Jacob said after a moment before addressing Wynter again.

"We go deeper in the caves, what then?"

"We survive. Whatever it takes. No one knows how deep or far they go but there are rumours, tales that they extend for leagues. Maybe we can find another way out? Besides, we have summat they don't," Ned said.

"And what's that."

"Light." He nodded towards Tom Trickle who had wandered over to look down upon Nadine Varla, oblivious to their conversation.

"Yeh, the lad surprised me with the fire back there." Jacob conceded. "I didn't think he could cast."

"Been spending time with Lord Sandford. Now ya know why," Ned said, watching as Tom knelt and muttered something to Varla's lifeless body. Ned knew the boy thought a lot of her and the lad looked crestfallen.

Reaching out, Tom pulled the red bandana from Varla's head and tucked it into his belt. Then, reverently, he lifted Varla's hands and crossed them over her heart. Standing, he pinched and then rubbed angrily at his nose, but his eyes remained dry.

Ned had told the lad once when he couldn't have been more than six, *Tears are wasted in the grim. They show nothing but weakness.* And it was true, thought Ned, but still, seeing the honesty and emotion in the boy made his own feelings of loss seem inadequate. *Since when did you care about anyone but yaself,* his mind whispered.

"Ned!"

Wynter turned back to Lord Jacob. "Sorry, what?"

"I said okay. We'll try it your way." Jacob turned to the others. "Let's go."

Mahan walked forward. "I'll… wait here a bit, Lord Jacob. If ya leave a bow, I can slow them up. Buy some time."

Seeing the denial on his lord's face Mahan spluttered. "I'm a wreck. Even in the big cavern the weight and the pressure, the walls and ceiling they bear down on me. The blackness waiting behind every torch, every lantern light. I can barely stand it. These smaller ones, I can't abide. I've seen the hole you'll be going in and I can't do it, I know it and I'll not be unmanned again. I'll not lose myself like before. I'd rather ya thank me for ma service, then take ma sword and a bow and have ya send me on my way. I'll take a few of the bastards with me."

"Mahan, Alban. You've been with me since I first swung a sword in the practice yards. I cannot," Jacob began.

"You must. This ain't no time for sentiment. Just take my hand, one last time." Mahan held his arm out.

Jacob stared at it, wiped at a tear that tracked unbidden down his cheek then clasped it, wrist to wrist.

"Warrior to warrior, brother to brother," Mahan invoked the pledge all Black Crows gave one another and gripped his lord's arm tightly. "Bin an honour and a privilege. Now, piss off, lad."

Jacob gave a fierce yet brittle grin. "Kildare steady your arm, brother."

The others had already gathered ready to leave and waited by the farside passageway. With heavy feet and an aching in his chest, Jacob joined them, following as Nils Baka led them out.

Mahan watched Jacob leave, backlit by the torches he followed, then turned back to the barricade. He thought he could hear noises coming from the otherside.

"It'll nay be long now, John," he murmured to the ghost of his friend. Setting his sword down in easy reach, Mahan picked up the bow and fitted an arrow to the string.

"Fuckin' hates the bow."

Chapter 44: Fire and Ash

Paulsen, The Holme

In the small hours just before dawn, Lady Mori left the village of Paulsen with a company of thirty-nine riders. The trail they took led them over the foothills west of Portisil where it joined a path that later fed like a tributary onto the road to Larn-Mor.

For Tomas 'The Mouse', a boy from the Stacks who had only ever known Kingsholme, the journey was a feast of other-world delights; of hills and trees and countryside that, despite winter's touch, seemed vibrant and wholesome compared to the big city. Yet, for an adventure, it was also disarmingly boring.

An adventure it may be, but Tomas did not enjoy those first few days on the road. On the one hand, he was still alive and removed from the death warren that was Kingsholme, something he should be grateful for, and was. On the other, his ass throbbed with a dull ache, the pain only diminished because that of his chaffed thighs had been so much worse. It was as though someone had taken a sanding stone to them and rubbed the skin raw. So his relief at the former was tempered greatly by the persistence of the latter.

Of course, it hadn't helped matters that Tomas didn't know how to ride. It always looked so easy watching people doing it on the streets of Kingsholme. He tried to emulate the neat, concise form of Tasso Marn but his elbows stuck out and his feet pointed the wrong way and his horse, a supposedly placid, grey-toned mare, didn't take kindly to his skill. Thrice the she-devil had dumped him off on that first day alone and, for someone unphased by the high roofs of the capital, the ground suddenly seemed a long way down.

The worst of it though had been whenever they broke into a trot or canter. It set his head rocking in time to the grey's gait, up and down like a bobbing apple at the Green Fair. No, those early days on the road to Ellingbrok had been torturous.

It had taken them two days to reach Larn-Mor. Tasso Marn said it was a large city, though to Tomas its battlements were half the height of Kingsholme's. Disappointingly, he never got to experience its interior for rather than entering Larn-Mor and seeking lodgings, as Tomas hoped, the Lady Mori led them around its walls and their company continued eastward, toward Ridlowe, making camp that night in a farmer's field.

Another day saw them passed Ridlowe and into Ellingbrok and for the first time 'The Mouse' got a real sense that the world was so much more than Kingsholme. So much bigger. Always inquisitive, it awoke in Tomas a longing he couldn't articulate. His world compass had skewed and expanded to such an extent that he felt smaller, more insignificant than he ever had. He had no idea where he was or where they were going, other than a name, Hawke Hold. It was a name that held no meaning for him and yet despite that, it was a place Tomas was excited to discover. He'd even gotten used to riding Greybitch and though his muscles and skin were still tender, the accompanying aches and pains lacked the intensity of the previous days.

Ellingbrok signalled a new phase in their journey. The city retained no wall and its sprawling expanse was built just beyond the southernmost edges of the Fenlakes and straddled the River Ranning, whose waters it was said could be traced to the High Moors of Jorin far to the north. The river itself flowed from Hawke Lake, winding its way southward past Hawkewood and through the Fenlakes before emptying into the salty waters of the Deeping Rift.

Taking them through the streets of Ellingbrok, Lady Mori led them to the river docks where she arranged for the charter of three longboats to ferry their company upriver to Fenwater, a town on the northern fringes of the Fenlakes. For Tomas, it was a welcome relief. Instead of riding Greybitch, he got to ride a boat, another new experience and one far more pleasant.

The journey upriver to Fenlake took two days. A bank of oarsmen on each side pulled them with ease through the wide, calm waters of the Ranning or rested when the wind was favourable and the square sail could be unfurled.

It was not exactly quiet onboard but it was peaceful in its way. The timber seemed to groan both in rhythm to the oars and the song chanted by the oarsmen. When they were quiet, the snap of the sail in the breeze and sigh of wood over water replaced them. The horses, corralled on the boat's main deck, accompanied it all like a badly tuned orchestra, snorting, nickering and farting with gusto, hooves clomping discordantly against the straw strewn boards.

Tomas's only chore was Greybitch, something that was made clear to him by Tasso Marn that first day she handed Tomas the mare's reins.

"A horse is the rider's responsibility. I'll teach you as we go but you will do everything from now on. Feed, muck out, groom, check and pick out her hooves. In return, she will bear you wherever you ask. Look after her, Tomas and she will look after you."

Tomas had heard stories that a horse could kill with a kick and up close their size was intimidating. But after three days spent around the brutes, he'd gotten over his initial fear and grown used to their bulk and power. Each horse, Tomas had been intrigued to discover, possessed a different character and temperament and Greybitch, he conceded, was pretty agreeable when he was not sat on top of her. Now though, with the horses penned so close aboard, some of that earlier anxiety returned. Walking between their flanks, checking on their water and feed, he took to cursing at them in soothing tones. It made him feel better. The horses for their part ignored him. Only Greybitch cast a doleful eye at him as if to say she understood every cussword and was not fooled by his soft voice.

The horses however only occupied a small part of his day. The rest Tomas spent at the prow keeping out of the crew's way and everybody else's for that matter. Old Town and The Trades had always been crowded with people but most never saw him and Tomas wasn't accustomed to nor liked the attention that had come his way since leaving his old life.

As for O'si, the sháadretarch remained in his ring. The 'little demon' hadn't made an appearance since Tomas's set-to with Murder in the back of the wagon that day. And P'uk, well, P'uk never came out, *apart from that one time, even then I never saw him…her…it…whatever the fuck they are.*

It was cold sitting upfront, his oversized tabard fluttered like a flag whenever the breeze gusted, but Tomas liked it well enough. Watching the flat, whitewashed landscape slide by was soothing at first but his contemplations inevitably turned maudlin. He mused over that night at the Enclave and everything that had happened since. Meeting Renix had been the best of things, losing him and Sparrow the worst. Would that he had never taken the Targus's bloody commission.

Tomas spun the ring on his finger, then adjusted the bracer on his left wrist, a habit he'd developed whenever he thought of what they contained. His two, unwanted travel companions were bothersome. If he concentrated on his hands, he could feel the seal in his flesh binding them together. *I need to do something about that.* Just what however was beyond him.

What small solitude Tomas found did not last. Others had a similar notion it seemed, as the wide bulk of Mordan 'Mord' Mordignus made his way forward, fingers twizzling that ridiculous moustache. Tomas groaned inwardly. The man was likeable enough and always ready with a tale, but Tomas was not fooled by his easy manner. Mord had a way of getting Tomas to talk and that made him leery, not least because Tomas couldn't seem to help himself. He supposed it could be worse, Herald could be here onboard. Instead, the fallen prince was in the second boat with Lady Mori and the Order Knight, Grema Bergrun.

"Saw ya waddling like a duck before, my lad, how are ya holdin' up?" Mord clapped a hand on Tomas's shoulder as he heaved his bulk down and continued as if Tomas had answered.

"It's a lot to take in I know. Ya life is something else now. Better. With a little luck, you'll get ta see the world." He swept a theatrical arm wide at the river ahead and the snow-covered landscape. "And there is so much of it out there."

Mord cast a conspiratorial look at Tomas. "I wasn't much younger than you when I took my first boat ride. Nothing small like this wee thing." He clomped his boot against the boards. "Mine was a two-masted brig called Seawitch. Fer two days I heaved my guts out as Seawitch plied the Prospero. Thought I was gonna die until I got my sea legs. I saw things ya wouldn't believe. Beasts twice the size of the Seawitch. Some with spines that could've skewered us in an instant and others that spat water plumes higher than our masthead."

Despite himself, Tomas's eyes went wide, and he leaned in to hear better. "Weren't you scared?"

Mord gave a toothy grin. Fish landed, he rubbed his hands and proceeded to regale Tomas with his exploits upon the high seas. So engrossed was the one with the telling and the other with the listening that they never heard nor saw Merca Landré arrive behind them.

"Leave us."

Mord paused his tale and cocked an eye at the black-skinned woman. Her face would be pretty were it not for the hard set to it.

"We're in mid-discussion, woman. Come back later."

"No. I will not."

With a leery smile, Mord twisted to face her. "Well, darlin' park yaself down and wait, there's a good girl. Might be ya hear something ta put a smile on that pretty face, eh?"

Merca bent low until her hair brushed Mord's cheek. "You will move, now. I will not ask again."

Worried, Tomas looked between the two. "It's okay, Mord. Ya can tell me later how ya won a Kraken's tooth." It was as if he spoke to the wind.

"Or what? You'll move me? You're just a wee slip of a girl and Mord here ain't fer movin'." Mord stood and tapped a finger to his knife butt then mused out loud. "I hear ya dangerous, darlin' but unarmed and after washin' your puke off my wagon boards fer a day ya don't look much ta me. Ya should eat more. Put some meat on ya bones. No one likes a skinny wench."

Tomas's eyes flared wide as Murder tensed like a bowstring being drawn until she stood straight-backed. A flash of white teeth transformed her face and Tomas thought she looked almost joyous. He sensed the subtle shift of her body, her left foot sliding back a fraction as if she was about to turn away. She did not.

Her right boot caught Mordan Mordignus square in the chest from less than a meter away. Her leg straightened in the instance of contact and the portly teller of stories was propelled with comical ease backwards over the gunwale.

His tumble over the railing though was arrested when Merca Landré grabbed his legs as they cartwheeled up and she held on, jamming her feet against the post rail.

"Applied correctly a small mass can control a big mass. You just need to find the correct fulcrum. Have I found yours, fat man?

"Ermm, yeah, yeah I think so. Now pull me up. My back!" Mord cried, arms flailing.

Grinning fiercely, Merca nodded at Tomas to grab a leg and together they levered Mordan upright enough until he could clutch the railing. He stood, panting as if he had run half a league and rubbed his chest.

"I am not your darling, your girl or your woman and most definitely not a wench," Merca sneered. "Say these words to me again and I will repeat this lesson only next time there will be no fulcrum to lever you back from. Do you hear my words?"

Mord's stomach bulged as he arched his back, a line of fire lit it where he had lain across the gunwale. "Yeah, sure. Next time ask nicely, eh. Save an old man his blushes."

"That was my nice," Merca replied.

Puffing his cheeks, Mord cast a glance at the boy and then brushed cautiously by the woman. She was dangerous, he decided. To his chagrin, the altercation had not gone unnoticed and amongst the onlookers were Tasso Marn and his master Kal Meyer. Both seemed amused. "Fuckin' spit in her food," he mumbled under his breath though apparently, not quietly enough.

"Do so and I will take your knife and stick it in your eye," Merca replied.

Moustache quivering and still panting from the ordeal, Mordan Mordignus walked on with as much dignity as he could muster.

Conscious they were the centre of attention, Tomas turned from Mord to Murder. Her mouth was wrinkled but he wouldn't go so far as to call it a smile. Whatever it was, it vanished when she caught him looking, turning altogether more serious. *Fuck.*

"You've been avoiding me."

Erm, no I haven't. I've been trying not to fall off a godsdamn hell horse. He did not voice the thought though. The sight of Mord flailing half overboard was still too vivid. "Sorry," he mustered.

"I would talk. Sit." Merca indicated the rope coil he'd been using as a seat.

Tomas cast an eye back towards the stern and saw Tasso Marn and Kal Meyer talking together nearby. He knew they watched however much they might pretend otherwise. Abruptly, he folded onto the rope.

With the languid fluidity of a cat, Merca crouched on the deck beside him, ignoring the wooden block Mord had used to sit upon. She did not say anything at first, to the point that Tomas was starting to feel even more uncomfortable than he already was.

"I... apologize."

Tomas risked a glance at Murder. She looked as if she had tasted something bad. For some reason, he found it funny and pressed his lips tight together.

"Am I amusing, little Mouse?" Merca purred.

"Nah, you just suck at sorry," Tomas' grin broke free only to fade when Murder remained stone-faced. He sniffed. "You have a right ta be mad, I guess. But I can't give ya what you want."

"What I want." Merca mused aloud. "What do you know of what I want."

"You want ta be free right? I know that much. As fer after," Tomas sighed, "don't even know what I want, let alone anyone else."

"I like you, boy," Merca said.

Tomas couldn't help himself. "Course ya do. Worth a lot of gold to Bortillo. Bet you like Rald even more right? Gilders more."

"You chitter like a mouse, perhaps that is how you got your name, eh," Merca replied.

Yeah, nice apology, Tomas thought but remained silent. Murder never seemed far from violence and though the binding upon her kept him safe, Tomas couldn't shake the feeling he walked upon a razor's edge.

"I come from Berins-Low. Have you heard of it?" Merca asked in a sudden change of topic.

Tomas shook his head.

"Course not. Street rat like you."

Merca's voice was low and Tomas remained silent, sensing in her an urge to talk like Sparrow used to when something bad had happened and she needed for someone, him, to hear, because she had no one else. With the unencumbered insight of youth, it struck him that the assassin was alone like he was alone. Like Sparrow had been alone. He waited and after a time, Merca began.

"My first woman's blood was born of fire and ash for it came the day the outsiders did. That day I was no longer a child but also no longer a woman. No longer human." There was a distant quality to her voice and Merca stared ahead at the silent waters.

"I remember that day better than I do my mother's face. We knew the outsiders were coming but did not run for our warriors were proud and strong and had never tasted defeat. My father, Merca Jasou was the best of us and killed many, but it was not enough. Afterwards, we watched as they hacked his body into pieces and fed the bits to their hounds. Then they turned on the rest of us. Herding us like cattle they culled those they did not want, the old and the children too young to walk or feed themselves. They raped who they wanted and pillaged what was not burnt. Then they took us and sold us to the Reavin." Merca tilted her head and cast a hard, sideways glance at the Mouse.

"I do not tell you this to garner sympathy but so that you may understand how I was reborn and reforged into what I am. A killer whose blade always thirsts. Relentless, I bear no remorse and am faster than anyone I've faced, but that is not what makes me the best. I have a hunger, a desire that drives me every moment of every day." She tapped two fingers to her temple. "It is this that makes me the best."

Merca's nostrils flared in exhale before she turned and stared straight ahead, letting the flat waters of the river calm the fire in her eyes. When next she spoke it was with a distant air.

"When I sleep, I relive the massacre and subjugation of my people to the point that I now can barely recall life before it. Horrendous as that may seem it is nothing compared to the impotence of being bound into slavery and subjected to the whim of another. To be used for their purpose rather than my own. That was my life."

She turned both eyes onto his again and Tomas felt the weight of her need in them.

"I saw him. For the first time in all these years, I saw the man who killed my father. Who raped my mother and slid his blade across her throat as he did so. And I have his name. A name protected by the Targus. One he forbade me to kill despite me... begging, begging him!"

"Now I find the Targus' shackle removed only to be replaced by another and every day, I am further away from my purpose. Set me free."

Tomas wriggled on his rope seat. "Why tell me any of this?" He cast his eyes down at the angled prow where the boards tapered and met the railing.

"You could compel me as Bortillo Targus did before you," Merca said. "To know my every thought, my truth. This way I've chosen the time and the place. Small freedom I grant but any is better than none. I take what I can."

Tomas lifted his chin and met her green-flecked eyes. "If I could free you I would have outside Kingsholme as I promised. But I cannot."

He flinched as her hand shot out and gripped his forearm. She gave a gentle squeeze. "I know that Tomas. I've had plenty of time to think. That is why I am not talking to you."

Tomas blanched when Murder canted her head like a bird of prey, her eyes piercing his and forestalling the denial ready on his lips.

"When you own a thing, Tomas, possess a person so completely that their loyalty is never in question, it can make you lax. Complacent. So it was with Bortillo. It was the nature of my work to listen without being seen. To know things that are hidden. That knowledge did not vanish with my change in ownership."

Tomas grimaced at that last word and the assassin's lip curled into a sneer at his discomfort.

"For instance, I know that the Targus sent you into the Enclave to steal something and that the commission originated from Korban Mercer, a magus. One reputedly researching the dark arts of plane portals and summoning."

Tomas blinked, he had just heard something he did not know before. Merca Landré held her chin and tapped a finger to her lips, the flecks in her dark eyes seeming to dance.

"Such a secretive place the Enclave. It seems odd does it not for a magus to commission a job to steal from himself. Very puzzling. As for that great tome you lug about in your pack that you take out and read when you think no one is watching. That too tells a tale, for I have looked at it when it has been unguarded. I can read but its script is strange, incomprehensible to my eye. The pictures and diagrams however tell me what it is, a book on demons and summoning.

"So, Merca, I say to myself. This is what the mouse was tasked to steal. A magic book on the forbidden arts. It is what Bortillo seeks and the mage wants. Stolen, so that Korban Mercer can keep it secret from the Council of Mages, for why else commission its theft?

"Logical it seems and yet wrong." Merca abruptly stood and leaned on the railing. She signalled him and reluctantly, Tomas joined her.

"I believe the book to be incidental, a theft of opportunity," Merca confided. "It was not what you were sent for. I was bested that night on the rooftops by magic, but I have observed you closely since and I do not believe you possess the talent. No, I think it was someone or something else and don't try selling me that fool prince, he was out cold."

Tomas's face was frozen. He could not refute her claim. Not without lying and she would know it.

"You know, when my slave contract was first bought by Bortillo, it took his pet mage hours to replace the Reavin's binding with the Targus's own and yet that night it was unravelled in an instant. You, an untrained boy, undid in a moment what a trained magus took hours to make. Foolishly I did what we all do, I fit the narrative to the truth I believed. After all, what else could it be but a boy out ensorcelling a mage and defeating, if I may say so myself, the Targus's deadliest assassin?

"Thinking on it now, it doesn't make sense. Doesn't sit right. Whoever cast this binding has a deftness and elegance of touch that comes with experience. That is not you, Tomas the Mouse. I've seen you talkin' to yourself sometimes, only you're not, are you? You're talking to someone I can't see but maybe a magus can or these Order Knights cause you ain't done that since they showed up.

"So, Tomas, I am not talking to you. I am talking to whoever it is you stole. An imp may be or shaitan, a demon? I have heard of such things and seen enough of this world to know it is not as plain as people think it."

"I..." Tomas licked dry lips, unsure what to say. Renix had worked it out and now Murder. Did Marn know? Did Renix tell her? What should he say and to whom? Who could he trust?

No-one.

Merca intruded on his flailing thoughts as if he wore them plain upon his face. Maybe he did. "Your instinct is to lie. I get that. Trust no-one. Words to live by in our world, Tomas.

"Look. This shaitan. Can it hear me?" Merca asked.

For Tomas, it was as if someone else controlled his body. His head gently rocked in the affirmative.

Merca waved a hand over her body and hissed. "Well then. Release me. My oath, my bond is to protect the boy not you ya piece of shit. There are a thousand ways I can make your existence miserable and dangerous without threatening the boy. I am more trouble than you need or could possibly imagine."

Leaning over she gripped Tomas' wrist. The electro-static snap of power was felt rather than heard and it jolted Merca to silence. The boy's eyes rolled up in his head until only the whites showed and when Tomas spoke it was with his voice, but it was not the Mouse, of that there was no doubt.

"Your incessant mewling is unseemly mortal. Your cloak of self-pity abhorrent. The Vox Léchtar Fai-ber must be protected until his vow is complete. Until then, what you want is irrelevant. What you need is nothing. You are but a pinhead of light in an incandescent sky filled with a thousand suns. You are worthless but for this single task. Like Tomas, your only release will be in the fulfilment of his vow or death."

A seeping agony crept up Merca's fingers where they gripped the boy. It went from painful to exquisite in a heartbeat, every nerve strand and fibre in her hand, scratching in excruciating concert. Merca would have snatched her hand back but found she could not move, her body locked in rigor-like paralysis. Her eyelids fluttered in distress before her eyes turned blood red and then ruptured into a bloody pulp. Her snarling mouth contorted into a rictus of pain, and she screamed before her jaws clenched tight with such ferocity that her teeth snapped to bloody stumps and shredded her lips.

The pain vanished as instantly as it had appeared. Merca gasped, her eyes could see again, and she worked her jaw, tongue probing the inside of her mouth and tasted no blood, found no broken shards of enamel, just whole teeth.

"That is but a slither of what I can visit upon you, Merca Landré of Berins-Low. I liked your story by the way, but it is extraneous to our discussion. All that matters is Tomas. Protect his vow or death. Decide now."

Merca released the boy whose white eyes blinked clear before staring back at her.

Tomas sniffed and swiped the back of his hand under his nose at the snot that coated his top lip and looked at it before giving Merca a puzzled look.

"Sorry 'bout that. Must be gettin' a cold. I never get colds. You okay? Look like ya seen a ghost or summat." He wiped his hand against his trouser leg and cocked an eyebrow at Murder.

Merca straightened, legs shaking and clutched the railing. The pain had been so great its absence hurt, the memory of it reverberating like twisted phantasms inside her skull. Leaning forward again, she retched, heaving the contents of her stomach out until only bile came up. Gods, she was sick of being sick.

Tomas watched Murder heave over the side and pondered what to do. It had all happened so quick, one minute they were talking only he seemed to have zoned out because he could not remember the last of their conversation, the next this. He placed a wary hand on her back in comfort expecting her to snap him in two. When she did not, Tomas produced a cloth from beneath his tunic with his other hand and held it out, he could feel her trembling beneath his touch. Maybe she too was sickening for something?

Merca snatched the cloth and dried her mouth with it before rotating her head, looking up at the sky and then round to the soft-sounding water as it washed past the prow.

"I'm guessing you met one?" Tomas surmised.

Merca spat to clear her mouth then cocked an eyebrow at him. "There's more than one?"

"O'si and P'uk." Tomas fidgeted, the look in Merca's eyes he'd not seen before. He couldn't place it.

"Here I thought I was fucked. You're possessed by two shaitans?" Merca coughed, snorted and spat again over the side.

"Oh, I'm not possessed. I just carry them about. We've got an agreement of sorts. A contract I can't break I guess you could say." Tomas was babbling but found he could not stop himself now that Murder knew.

"O'si is not so bad. Bit of a prankster but has saved my butt more than once. We talk sometimes. P'uk, not so much. Quiet. I get the feelin' P'uk don't like us. People that is. Did you speak to O'si? O'si can make you see things that aren't there." Tomas blushed scarlet and lapsed into silence.

"No, Mouse. I think it was the other one. I a... I need some space." Merca turned back to the railing and stared vacantly past the prow of the boat.

Dismissed, Tomas turned and took a step before stopping himself. Murder's distress was obvious. Right then, the assassin seemed more vulnerable than when she'd been disarmed and hogtied in Old Town. Back then she had still seemed dangerous. Here she did not, she seemed deflated and small.

"I'm sorry. Never meant to drag ya into any of this." Tomas moved off towards Greybitch, thinking to check her water bucket and feed. He never heard Murder's reply nor saw the fire rekindle in her eyes.

* * *

A strong headwind built up on the second day of their river journey, turning the placid waters of the River Ranning choppy. It caused delay and the longboats pulled into Fenwater the morning after they were due to arrive. With the wind came overcast skies and snow showers. Awnings provided some shelter from the inclement weather, but the wind always found the gaps so that by the time the boats docked Tomas felt half frozen.

Hoping for a reprieve and a day in a tavern to thaw out, Tomas was once again thwarted. Not one for waiting, Lady Mori drove them northward with singular determination. At least climbing onto Greybitch's back his saddle seemed more comfortable than he recalled, and his body found the mare's balance and rhythm all on its own. Small mercy.

Another change, and the only thing that had thawed, was Murder's attitude towards him. She manoeuvred her mount so that she was behind Tomas and Marn and when they broke at midday she spoke with a civil tongue, telling Tomas they would begin training that evening. Tasso Marn seemed less than pleased when she heard and the two women squared off like two stags ready to butt heads.

"I am responsible for Tomas and will see to his training." Marn stood in front of Merca ready to respond to any violence.

"You cannot teach what I know." Merca flicked a dismissive hand at the Order woman as if she were a bothersome fly.

"A murderer with no moral compass? I don't think so." Marn shook her head.

"Who better? Knife work is a dirty business. Mouse ain't built for anything else. Not yet. Besides, you've had days and taught him nothing but how to sit on a horse. Too busy mourning your lost love."

Tasso Marn's hands balled into fists, the only visible sign of the brooding tension. "Think I would trust you with a knife near Tomas or around any of us for that matter. Why are you still here?"

"I'm as wanted now in Kingsholme as the Mouse and my path forward lies with him. I don't like it any more than you do but that doesn't matter any more 'n a poke in a brothel. I am bound to him until I am not, whatever the fuck you and your precious Order think, eh."

"I can use a knife already," Tomas exclaimed pulling out the blue-tinged blade Renix had given him. The look of disdain from both women was like a punch in the gut. That each wore the same expression would have been comical if Tomas hadn't felt so inadequate.

"Never draw it unless it is to use," Merca chided roughly. She turned to Tasso Marn. "I need nothing to train the boy, but he'll need to practise with a blade to get used to its weight and balance. I begin tonight."

Tasso Marn and Tomas watched her strut away then glanced at each other.

"She really can't hurt me," Tomas stated only for Marn to huff.

"I wouldn't be so sure about that, young one." She tussled his hair as Renix had occasionally done, drawing a scowl. "She is right though. I have been neglectful. I will remedy that."

Tomas grimaced, Marn's words sounded bodeful.

That evening, they stopped at a large holdstead and by arrangement with the holders, took over a large barn and two outbuildings. After Tomas had attended to Greybitch and eaten, Murder came for him and led him behind the barn where three torches burned in sombre illumination over a small course studded with logs that had been symmetrically arranged.

Much to Merca's annoyance and Tomas's discomfort, a small host gathered to watch.

"What am I entertainment?" Merca grumbled spotting Marn, Lady Mori, the fat man with the outrageous moustache and Grema Bergrun in the crowd. Tuning them out, she pulled the Mouse around to face her.

"You are puny. I cannot make you taller, bigger or stronger. What do you have?"

Tomas shrugged.

"Speed, agility and quick-wit. You're a master thief, I have seen you display all three myself. You must use these gifts you have, not wish for ones you do not. Now, in a standup fight what do you do?"

"Nothing, I usually get slapped and beat. If I fight back, it goes worse," Tomas said, glancing out at the dark fringes of the makeshift training circle.

Merca tsked loudly, "You shame your name, Mouse."

It drew a few laughs from the darkness. Murder spun and threw her arm, sending a sliver of silver spinning into the night. The solid thunk as it hit wood seemed loud and stilled the laughter.

Tomas reached around his back and felt the empty sheath where his knife had lain.

"Interrupt my lesson again, and next time my target will not be a post," Merca promised. "If you cannot remain silent then go. Now."

No one left. Merca's malignant glare circled those gathered before settling on Tomas once more.

"A mouse does not face the cat but runs. As you must do. However, sometimes that is not possible. Where you can, you must draw your opponent away from their strength and towards your own. In Kingsholme that would be the roof where your size works for you and their's against. Always you must look to your advantage.

"From your lackless expression, I see my words are like rain on a lake, unheeded. Maybe I state the obvious and you know these things? No matter. You will learn. For now, we will work on your speed of body and mind. Pay attention." Merca touched three random logs.

"This is Marn, this is Mord and this is Merca, me." She qualified the latter as if it needed clarifying. "These are good. When you hear each name, you will touch the correct log with your left hand."

She touched another three logs situated at different points around them. "Mika, Mengis and Moose. These are bad. These you will touch with your right hand. Do you understand?

"You threw my knife. Renix gave it me," Tomas complained. "Thought you were going ta teach me how ta use it, not throw it away."

Merca's fingers flexed. "No one will touch your knife. If I am satisfied, I will return it. Now. Do you understand the game?"

"Yeah, touch the logs. I got it."

"Mord, Merca, Moose."

Tomas flailed, touched the log for Mord with his left hand then Moose right next to it. Then swivelled to Merca's log and touched that.

"Speed Tomas. You understand speed is needed?" Merca stated.

"Well, yeah. I got them," Tomas replied. "You caught me off-guard that is all."

"That is not all." Merca touched the logs. "Only Mord was correct, in order and hand. One of three is all you achieved. I think I overestimated you. Again."

Prowling around the logs like a she-wolf, Merca called three names. This time Tomas was ready and touched them in order and with the correct hand. *There that was not so difficult.*

Merca however was far from impressed. "That took five resting heartbeats. Far too long, Mouse. Go again. Faster."

Tomas was faster, he flew around the circle of logs and touched each one only messing up the hand order on the second and third repetition.

"Again."

The process was repeated. Again, then again. The crowd, at first amused soon grew bored and started to filter away until only Tasso Marn, Lady Mori and Grema Bergrun remained.

Tomas had improved but he was tired. The circle of logs was no more than three meters in circumference, but the short sharp movements burned his thighs in a wholly different way from riding a horse. The problem wasn't that he couldn't do it, it was that he barely finished a set of three when Merca called the next and the next and so on. Always he would slip up, get the names mixed in his head or the wrong hands snatching at a log.

"Marn will keep your knife until I say otherwise. Tomorrow we will train again," Merca Landré left the circle of light, leaving Tomas on the ground, wearied and panting for breath.

"Did I do okay?" he called after her but only the sounds of the night replied. "I can go again."

"It has been over an hour, Tomas," a soft voice intruded. He glanced from his crouch and found Lady Mori standing by his shoulder, her elfin face framed by blonde hair. He took the hand she proffered and as she pulled him to his feet felt his heart swell.

"I'll get bigger," he blurted.

"Of course." Lady Mori's blue eyes twinkled in the torchlight. "But only if you eat well and rest." Releasing his hand, she walked toward the barn until she too vanished in the night.

Tomas jumped. Darkness moved beyond the light, but he relaxed as it resolved into Marn.

She waggled his blue blade at him and chuckled. "I'll get bigger." She shook her head. "Come on, ladykiller, let's get some rest." Tucking the knife into her belt, Marn draped a hand over his shoulder and steered Tomas away.

The following few days settled into a routine of riding, tending Greybitch and taking Murder's lessons each evening. He still hadn't touched a knife and the exercise expanded from six logs to eight and then ten.

His reactions improved, speed and stamina as well though he never received a word of praise. Each night he was left exhausted and Murder as stony-faced as ever.

Their path northward tracked the River Ranning and the countryside changed from the lowlands of the fens to thin forests of asper and hardwoods. Hills climbed away to their right, but they were soon past them and the landscape morphed into rolling moorlands of heathers and gorse. The holdsteads also dwindled until there was nothing but the beaten track to give any sign of civilisation. Marn pointed out a herd of deer. They were the first Tomas had ever seen that hadn't been skinned and hanging from a butcher's hook. These looked big and watched them with wary disregard.

On the third day out from Fenwater, the moorlands turned to grasslands in a blanket of white that stretched to a matt-brown horizon. Holdings started to appear again, lesions on the pristine landscape.

Over the next hours, the dark fringe on the horizon thickened and changed hue, extending toward the distant sweep of the river.

"That is Hawkewood. When we pass beneath its boughs we will be in The Duncan's demesne," Tasso Marn explained, pointing out the forest. "We'll reach Outward tonight and sleep in a proper bed. In four days we'll be in Hawke Hold."

"Then what?" Tomas blurted.

"Then we shall see." Marn looked ready to tussle his hair again, so Tomas lent away in the saddle, catching a hand on the pommel as he started to slide off. Marn looked amused and he heard a snort from behind that could only be Murder. The two women had settled into an unlikely truce and Tomas wasn't sure he liked it.

Up ahead the column came to a halt. Craning his neck forward, Tomas could see Lady Mori and Kal Meyar talking to a man on horseback dressed in rustic, homespun clothes. A homesteader or farmhand, Tomas had seen the like on the journey north. After a brief discussion, Lady Mori proffered the man something, but he refused, bowing instead from his saddle. His horse sauntered down the column and past Tomas and Marn.

They didn't move off as expected and Tomas' glance at Marn was enough to tell him something was up. Looking ahead to see what the delay was, Tomas could see Lady Mori, Kal Meyar and Grema Bergrun in discussion. It broke up as he watched and the two Order knights turned about and ambled back down the column calling out names as they went. Both stopped when they reached Tomas though it was Marn they addressed.

"We go our own way here," Kal Meyar began. "The Red Queen has been busy since we left Kingsholme it seems. Two hundred soldiers from Crickwillow, flying the gold and black of Holme, blockade the way north and Hardcastle's browns hold the western road outside Outward. We'll cut east cross-country a few leagues then turn north and make our way through Hawkewood. Lady Mori will wait for us by the Gurding bridge."

Grema gave a piercing whistle and fourteen riders peeled out of the column. Amongst them, eyes ringed yellow with bruising and face looking like thunder, Herald and his ever-present giant, Horyk Andersun. Tomas groaned inwardly; he had managed to avoid 'Rald' most of the journey but with their company halving that would be a lot harder now. He didn't relish taking Greybitch off-road either.

Marn nudged the flank of her horse against his and a reluctant Tomas steered Greybitch in behind Grema as she led them south, the holdsteader that had brought them the news was a distant figure down the road.

Herald urged his horse, forcing his way past and Marn clucked and reined back forcing Tomas to do the same. A hiss from Murder and muttered expletive expressed her disdain for the prince better than Tomas could manage and it made him smile. The lady could swear.

They waited, letting the hard-bitten men and women that comprised the Order Knights' Hands ride past. Mord waggled his eyebrows at Tomas but wasn't inclined, it seemed, to stay with them and regale them with his stories. Stories, Tomas found, he missed for Marn wasn't made for telling them and Murder, well Murder's stories all sounded like a threat.

They appeared to be following the holder for the man turned off down a path towards a distant holdstead and Kal Meyar and Grema Bergrun took the self-same route. Tomas looked to the north for Lady Mori, but her column of riders was nothing more than an indistinct smudge. *At least you'll be sleeping in a proper bed.*

Murder snorted from behind. "Missing her already, boy? Little cock all stiff for her?"

Marn gave a pinched frown. "Merca, please, hold that vile tongue of yours. The lad is twelve, thirteen at most."

"Little pukes think a nothing else. Think he's innocent? No one's innocent, least of all men with more blood in their…"

"Enough, we get the picture," Marn snapped.

"You were innocent," Tomas said. "That day of fire and ash you said you were born in. When they took you."

"If you think that, you weren't listening." Merca's dark eyes grew darker. "If I could murder you boy, you'd not breathe another word. Since I can't, just shut the fuck up."

"You started it," Tomas stated.

With a hiss and snap of reins, Murder cantered her horse past and pulled in several riders up, beside Mord who looked less than thrilled at seeing her.

"Born in fire and ash?" Marn raised her eyebrows.

"Ai, so she was. Want me ta tell you?" Tomas asked.

"Story like that is not yours to tell, Tomas," Marn replied. "It'll keep, for now. Instead, tell me what you know of the Order."

Tomas groaned. Another lesson. He glared ahead at Murder wishing he could swap places with her. Mord had still to tell him how he came by that Kraken's tooth.

He glanced again to the north, but the riders and Lady Mori were gone.

Chapter 45: Better Not Get Yourself Killed

Forest of Arden, Midshire

It was the morning of the third day of the storm. The wind whistled outside, and the pelt walls of the tent grew taut with every gust. It was different than before, Renco could tell. Less intense, the subtle pressure inside their conical shelter diminished from the storm's peak during the night.

The preceding days had been discomfiting. Renco had spent much of his short life with two old men for company and there was an agreeable familiarity and rhythm to it. But Master Hiro was not here, nor Mao. In their stead was Morten, a red-headed taverner's son who Renco found affable and easy to like. And Lett who had affected his life completely, her beauty arresting but their history, brief as it was, tarnished.

Renco's eyes sought out his last companion, picking out her shape in the dim interior. Nihm.

Just thinking her name made him uncomfortable but in the quiet moments his mind plagued him with nothing else. They barely knew each other and yet she had come for him. In his most desperate hour, she had saved him, but in the doing had created a bond between them that neither of them fully understood. No. That was not entirely true. The bond was made when they first saw each other on the road outside Fallston, they just hadn't realised it at the time. Two lost souls, inextricably linked by a moment.

An opalescent glint reflected in the shade of her form. She watched him back. Renco slid his eyes away at the realisation. How long had he been staring?

Nihm leaned forward, her features coming into relief by the dying firelight. "We need more wood."

It was meant as a peace offering. A quiet statement of fact yet it set Renco's hackles rising. They had argued over the past days, mostly in the silent conveyance of their mind link but not always and not just the two of them. A discussion between Lett and Nihm over Master Hiro and Mao broke down into a disagreement in which Renco was presented as an evidential point of proof. It was as if he wasn't sitting there at all. It galled him at the time, as did Lett's shrill admonition, which rose in pitch and volume as she made her argument. Ever the peacemaker, Morten had intervened on that occasion and the women had retreated to their pallets.

Renco pulled on his boots and got to his feet. In his mind, the feather touch of Nihm's uncertainty was a reflection of his own, for he knew his ire was unwarranted. Had he not insisted on fetching the firewood? The chore was nothing compared to the daily ones he'd grown up doing and even with the storm, it was no burden. For, since the Defile, his body was different. It had undergone a fundamental change and the winter cold was a sensation to be felt rather than endured. Besides, in the bleakness of the storm, collecting wood for the fire gave him something to do.

Not just Nihm watched as he slipped outside, but Morten and Lett too, and he was grateful when the flap closed behind him. Even then he was not alone, Renco could sense the amber-eyed gaze of Snow and Ash. The wolfdogs had made a den of sorts beneath Mama Besoms' wagon and often accompanied him to the woodpile, their altercation forgotten. On this occasion, they did not follow.

The wind tugged at Renco's hair and snow raked against his face and neck. He supposed he should have worn a cloak, but it did not bother him as he trudged away from the tent and toward the stacked woodpile or what was left of it. The canvassed mound from two days ago had been reduced to a snow-covered lump.

It was dark, the sun yet to appear, and a short distance to his right a bonfire burned. It illuminated several Wylders and cast the nearby wagons and mountain-shaped tents in flickering shadow.

He heard a babe crying, a shrill harmonica to the wind and an accompaniment to the cadent crunch of snow. Dysmorphic darkness appeared ahead and to his left, moving toward the woodpile. As they converged it resolved into the tall figure of De'Nestarin del Eladrohim, still wearing his man-guise.

Renco had not seen Nesta since before the storm.

"I've been waiting for you." The ilf-man signed the words as he spoke them and Renco had no trouble seeing, his night sight uncommonly good.

Renco hooked his index finger. 'Why?'

"To talk."

A puzzled frown crossed Renco's face.

'I was meditating whilst immersed in ki'tae. You should try it, I recommend it.' Nesta divagated, his fingers playing out the words. 'It is hard among so many to find a private moment but the tail end of a storm before daybreak provides such an opportunity.'

'Talk about what?' Renco signed back.

'Auras,' Nesta replied. 'Each is unique but yours is unlike any I have seen. You have been taught how to shield yourself but now that you are changed it is rudimentary at best. With minimal effort, I can see past the walls you project and what I sense troubles me.' Nesta switched from sign to sound.

"You are tae'alénn-vos, runemarked and unprepared for such a thing. I would instruct you, here among the Wylders, Nihm also, and offer what insight I can." Nesta raised the staff he rested on. Lines of iridescent gold blazed along its length, tracing out signs and symbols until the entire shaft was covered. He held it toward Renco.

Rippling power emanated from the staff. Though it was not hot, Renco could feel it as if fire warmed his face. Intrigued, Renco lifted his arm and tentatively extended his hand until his palm hovered inches above it.

"Take it if you can."

He couldn't. Renco's eyebrows knit together in concentration as he tried. The more he reached for the staff the harder it became to close his hand. His palm and fingers tingled. The sensation grew steadily stronger until Renco lost all feeling.

Without thinking, Renco dropped into ki'tae and like a shutter dropping the mundane world vanished, changing to one of kaleidoscopic colour. If he had tried, he could have sensed the life around him, nestling among the wisp-like clouds of aether. But he didn't, his attention was wholly on the crimson slash before him. It arced; a rip in the fabric of space, magnetic swirls rolling out of and around it like steam from a kettle pan.

There were no straight lines in this hidden sense, just soft edges and curlicues of energy, however, perpendicular to the crimson arc, a rival band of aether roiled. Renco knew it was his, could feel it in every cell of his body, only his tae'al had changed so much it was unrecognisable. A solid, electric-blue instead of the green and brown threaded white he was familiar with.

The two energies crackled and snapped but did not merge. Could not. Their polarities, alien to one another, held them inexorably apart.

The deep red winked out of existence leaving an echoing bloodmist behind. Immediately, Renco's tae'al lost intensity fading to a veined, blue-tinged white.

<Renco. What's wrong. Why won't you answer me?>

His arm was gripped. Renco blinked and transitioned back to the ordinary to find Nesta peering at him. Releasing him, the ilf's eyes swivelled past his shoulder toward the hurried sounds of someone approaching.

'It's Nihm,' Renco signed feeling dazed, unsure what it was he had just experienced.

Nesta leaned against his staff, the markings had faded to nothing and the white wood was plain and unadorned once more.

Nihm appeared through the snow, flanked by her wolfdogs. Her boots were unlaced and she carried a sheathed sword in one hand and like Renco was uncloaked. Nihm slowed to a walk her eyes taking them both in.

There were more footsteps and Hiro came out of the darkness with Mao at his shoulder. Unlike Nihm, both men were fully clothed.

"What happened?" Nihm asked.

Renco glanced at Nesta who gave an incongruous smile.

"A lesson. For the both of us," the ilf answered, eyes spanning the group.

Hiro frowned. "We have spoken of this, neh. I thought you would respect my wishes?"

Barging past the ilf, Mao clamped a hand on Renco's shoulder and panted. "Master Hiro run very fast. Very worried. Drag Mao from bed." His bleary eyes peered close and his fingers pinched Renco's cheek.

"Bah, boy fine. Mao no like cold, go back bed." The old man gave Renco a fatherly pat before retreating behind Hiro, though he did not leave.

"I listened to your words, Hiro. I respect the truth and I will speak mine," Nesta said. "Your path lies with Maohong but taking these children to Ekan Maul with you is dangerous. Renco is tae'alénn-vos, a runemarked. The energy in the Blight will poison him as surely as this world is anathema to the creature within Maohong." Nesta's eyes narrowed.

"As for Nihm, I believe she is the Lightlost. Even were she not, she is newly awakened and the two are bonded, their fates intertwined. Both have much to learn. If they are willing, I would teach them what I can." The ilf-man cocked an eye toward Nihm, then Renco. Neither said a word.

"Renco, Nihm, go back to your tent," Master Hiro instructed, his jaw set.

<I came for wood, Master,> Renco projected back. He hurriedly knelt to lift the canvas only to feel a surge of annoyance wash over him. Standing, he gave a contrite bow before turning away.

"No."

The word seemed to still the wind and hang in the air and it stopped Renco cold.

"I will not be dismissed like a child," Nihm said. "I want the truth. All of it. Not just what you think I should know. Renco deserves the same. More so than me probably."

Mao gave a lopsided grin.

"Stop smirking, Mao." Hiro barked without turning about. It only made the old man grin all the wider.

Hiro tilted his head to the sky and into the snow slanting out of the darkness and gave a resigned sigh. "Mama Besom's then. The dogs stay outside."

* * *

The Wylders emerged from beneath their awnings and wagons and the protective arms of the forest and set about repairing the Winter-meet. Part of the main pavilion had collapsed on its north side under the weight of the snowdrift. A team of people set about clearing the snow and raising the canopy anew.

It was quite impressive, Renco thought, taking in all the activity as he went to check on their horses. The Wylders seemed unfazed by the storm or its aftermath and the huge encampment proved surprisingly robust. The wagons were being dug out and the cleared snow was piled and compacted into walls that ringed each of the ten family enclosures.

Before the storm, the Dax-Wylders had moved the high-sided wagons to act as windbreaks. Inside this screen, a dozen conical tents were erected which took several hours to construct using wooden poles and a combination of fabric and furs to line them. Two were given over to the outsiders. Master Hiro and Mao shared one, the rest of them the other.

During the storm, Renco only saw Master Hiro or Mao when dropping off their firewood. As for their own, Nihm would often practise the technique Nesta had taught her, touching him and drawing on the reservoir of aether he had built up to heat the wood until it hissed and steamed before bursting into flame. After two days, she could manage the feat without the furrowed concentration it had taken before. For Renco, it was a contradictory experience. The drawing of aether felt natural, pleasant even, yet Nihm's warm touch made him highly conscious and uncomfortable of her nearness as did the disagreeable look on Lett's face every time it was practised.

At night, by the light of the fire, Renco had taught Morten the slow forms of combat. Morten had received some training but his control, concentration and shaping left a lot to be desired. However, away from prying eyes he had been less timorous and eager to learn. With a combination of signing and demonstration, Renco had shown Morten the five basic stances and how to move between them. Never having trained anyone before, he had found the whole experience strangely rewarding.

There was a crunch of snow behind and from the sound, Renco knew it was two people. He puffed a resentful breath. It wasn't enough they'd spent the last few days cooped up together. They had to follow him.

"It's damn clever really," Morten enthused. "The whole place'll be up and running by day's end. Mark my words."

"Well, I'm frozen, I've slept horribly and I've not washed in days." Lett wrinkled her nose. "Neither have you."

"So sorry mi'ladyship, I'll just go run a bath. Unpack some clean clothes and lay'em out for ya." Morten feigned a bow.

Renco had observed that the red-headed, innkeeper's son seemed to rile Lett. The two constantly sniped at each other. First Lett with some less than gracious observation and then Morten retaliating, it had made his meditations challenging. Renco stopped so abruptly that Lett ran into his back with an exclamation of surprise. He spun and signed at them.

'Shutup. For two minutes, just shut up. Else go back to the tent. I don't need you to check on the horses.'

Lett stood back, her brows knitting together. She cocked her head back at Morten. "Renco's grumpy. He always signs too fast when he's grumpy, but I think he said he wants you to stop talking."

"Fer a bard, your voice is very shrill. I think he means you," Morten retorted.

"My voice is not shrill," Lett shrieked

Renco glared. Pointed a finger at one then the other and made a slashing gesture across his mouth.

"Both of us?" Morten sounded affronted.

With a shake of his head, Renco resumed his march, the two behind bickering briefly before realising he was getting away and running to catch up. He felt a twinge of amusement from his link with Nihm.

<Morten or Lett?> Nihm asked.

<Both and I'm glad you find it funny. Next time you can stay behind, and I'll take your place on the hunt.>

<Ha, no chance. Lob thinks I'm blessed by their god of the woods,> Nihm said.

The levity across their link dropped away, replaced by a more serious, concentrated sense as Nihm's focus switched to something else. <I've got to go.>

His brief interlude with Nihm had lasted a mere half dozen paces and Renco blew an exasperated breath as the other two fell into step behind.

Their horses had been roped in with the Daxs', beneath a copse of evergreens fringed by bushes, and next to a corral of the larger shires. Renco could see they had been well cared for, with horse blankets and plenty of feed.

He spotted Kaid Dax sitting around a smoky campfire with several other Wylders, a long pipe being passed around.

Ducking beneath the rope, Renco stroked a hand over the dappled neck of the nearest mare who snorted and nudged her head against his shoulder.

"Ya survived the storm then," Kaid called out leaving his fellows and striding over to meet them. "Yer horses are fine as you can see." Pulling his mittens off, he swiped the hat from his head and brushed fingers through his tangled hair whilst bestowing Lett with his best smile. Morten stood excluded on the outside looking less than impressed by the young Wylder.

Renco ignored them all, bending over he ran a hand down the mare's foreleg before lifting and checking the hoof. He pulled a tool from his belt and picked at some debris that had accumulated before moving onto the hind leg.

"I hear the old men are leavin' and you're stayin' till they get back," Kaid said.

"What are you on about?" Lett frowned.

"Mama came round with Hiro and spoke to me Da. Ask yer boy, he knows." Kaid nodded toward Renco who moved around to the far side of the horse to continue his inspection.

A grinning Kaid waved Lett closer. "The family heads are meeting later ter talk about the Horgan and Ishmun. Me Da will ask you be allowed ter stay then."

Lett shook her head, "No. We're going on to Hawke Hold to see the Duncan. I'll not stay here in the middle of nowhere with a..." she caught herself.

"With a what? A bunch of Wylders yer mean. Didn't hear you complaining none when we took yer in," Kaid flared.

"That's not what I was going ta say," Lett said.

"Ai, tell yer face that."

Morten insinuated himself between the two. "There's a war on and Lett's a bard. As fascinating and thankful as she is to the Dax, as we all are, she ain't made none for sitting still and watching the world go by. Songs and tales are being made and she'll not find them here."

Lett elbowed Morten aside. "I don't need some tall strip talking for me. I can speak for myself."

Kaid folded his arms, the anger on his face gone as quickly as it came.

"What?" Lett growled.

"I'm waitin'. Let's hear it then," Kaid challenged.

Lett's nose wrinkled. "Well. What he said, obviously."

Her cheeks flushed at Kaid's laughter, and she knew, should she look, Morten would have some stupid grin on his mug as well. She turned her back on the both of them. "Renco, what's going on?"

There was no answer, not that she expected one from Renco of course. The mare he'd been working on gave a frosted snort.

"Renco?" Lett ducked and looked beneath the horse's girth but he was gone.

* * *

Renco headed north away from the encampment by happenstance rather than intent. Loose snow pattered from the tree limbs above dusting his head and shoulders and he pulled the hood of his cloak up, a habit more than anything since the cold flakes did not bother him like they once might have.

As he walked, the events of the morning turned over in his mind and he let them, waiting for some equilibrium to settle where he could sort through them. Then he would be ready to disseminate them as Master Hiro and Mao had taught him.

A rushing burble of water intruded, pulling on him like a lodestone, a soothing song to his troubled mind. The gentle rise he was climbing levelled out and the treeline cut to a tumbledown edge that overlooked a river. It was the same river they had crossed the day before the storm landed, though here it was narrow and fast as it was drawn through a ravine.

Renco's eyes traversed left then right, tracing the path of the river before settling upon a distant, grey smear that crossed the divide. A fallen tree, a victim to the storm maybe, he mused. Curious for no other reason than it was there he set off towards it.

Mao is possessed.

The thought floated to the forefront of Renco's mind as he picked his way around a tree bole. That morning was the first time since their reunion that Mao had seemed like his old self. He recalled vividly the assault by the giant Red Cloak, Holt. Tough as old boots Mao might be, but it should have killed him or left him broken only it had not. Mao's strange abstraction, the withdrawal into himself, Renco had put down to the after-effects of that beating. Ancient to his young eyes, Renco worried Mao might never be the same.

I was right but for the wrong reason, Renco reflected dour-faced, for things were not as they seemed. In Mama Besom's wagon he had learned that Mao harboured a Sházáik, which sounded suspiciously like a demon to Renco. It was a Tetriarché, which was some kind of Lord according to Master Hiro, called Q'tox.

"Words hold power, names grant dominion. Q'tox is not mine but it is what you may call me." Mao's eyes had turned black, and his voice grated like two rocks scraping together.

Renco blinked at the remembrance and shook his head. He would never forget that look or tone till the day he died. It was when the surreal became real.

Renco moved lower down the slope, around a thornberry bush that crowded up to the lip of the ravine, hungry for the light offered. He stomped back up the far side as Q'tox-Mao's dissertation percolated through his mind.

"This sack of blood and bone I inhabit, dragged me unbidden to this corrosive perdition of a world which eats away at my being. I will not rest nor offer respite or mercy till I am returned to my own. Hiro bears my mark and is bound to me and Mao my vessel until such time as this charge is fulfilled."

In his distraction, Renco trod a little close to the edge and a slurry of earth and stone dislodged, clattering down the rockface to plunk into the water. Duly cautioned, he moved back a pace and passed on the downslope of the trees in his way.

Master was leaving. Again. This time with Mao and it worried him. The last time had not worked out so well.

"Five, six days there my boy. Maybe a few more for this wordsmith to show then back again with Mao, grumpy as ever he was, neh." Hiro had patted him on the shoulder in reassurance, but the words rang hollow. The clenched fist in Renco's gut told him so, leaving him with a fearful certainty that he would not see them both again.

"De'Nestarin will see to your training whilst I am away. He is a Ke'pa of the Antén-Wahr and you will attend him. You too, Nihmrodel Castell. I will send word to Keeper of where your father may find you. Though our destination remains Hawke Hold."

Renco's foot snagged on a hidden bramble buried beneath the snow and he stumbled, sending a watch of ghost shrikes whirring out of the nearest tree. Embarrassed at his clumsiness, Renco righted himself and dusted the snow from his leggings. His eyes scanned the woodland surrounds before sweeping out across the ravine. They fastened on an obscuration.

Smoke. It settled like a low fog over the treetops to the north, visible only because of the gap in the forest that the river and ravine provided. He sniffed and thought he could detect the faint, musk of woodsmoke.

The uprooted tree was close. Tall and thin, it lacked the girth of its former neighbours, leafy boughs stretched forlorn across the divide its tip barely reaching the far cut. Fresh earth and revealed roots ringed the base of the tree some still suckling at the ground, it was a wonder the river and ravine had not claimed it.

Not the safest of bridges. The thought affirmed what he would do. A nag in the back of his mind told him it was needless and foolish to attempt any crossing, but he ignored it. *Master is leaving.* The endeavour would be both a freedom and a rebellion against the tumult of emotion he felt. This decision was his, not Master's, Nesta's, nor even Nihm's. Foolish or not, to turn back from the challenge would rob him of something tangible, of self. *'So much has changed.'*

Removing his cloak, Renco folded it and tucked it in the crook of the tree then rose and climbed easily up upon the trunk. It felt solid beneath him, the rough bark offering good traction. The haze of smoke made him wary, and he scanned the far tree line. He could see nothing untoward, but then the woodland hid most of everything. He dropped into ki'tae and extended his sense outward. Nebulous wisps of energy surrounded him, weak and transparent. Weblike veins threaded the mist like spiders' silk and telltale globes of white appeared, some buzzing like fireflies, as his focus shifted through the cloud. Life, most of it tiny, all of it natural. He returned to himself and blinked his eyes, waiting a moment for his normal senses to reassert themselves.

Taking a breath, Renco walked out along the tree. The headwind picked at his tunic, but it did not trouble him as he made his way across, testing through his boot soles the solidity of each step. Just before the mid-point of his passage, the first of the larger boughs sprouted from the trunk and Renco navigated it with care, resting briefly in its support before moving on. The trunk began to narrow as he progressed, and the branches became smaller but more thickly populated. Rather than getting easier as he had thought it would, Renco found it more precarious. The bark of the trunk became less rutted and lost much of its abrasiveness as the beam grew tighter. His weight started to be felt by the tree, shivering first under his tread, then seeming to flex. The edge was close but there was no clear space to leap the last few yards and Renco was forced to the very tip, wobbling and creaking the branches before alighting on solid ground.

Renco puffed his cheeks out in relief then extended his senses. His sight was foreshortened by the trees and the rush of the river was loud in his ears masking other sounds. Lifting his head, he sniffed. The hint of woodsmoke was more obvious. He tapped the knife, sheathed at his hip and wished his sword was not back in the tent. With a shrug, he set off, following the smell of the woodsmoke.

Despite the recent storm, the snow underneath the boughs was only shin-deep, though it clumped in piles like bleached termite mounds where the canopy above grew thin or refused to overlap. Renco moved with care but, looking behind, winced at the trail he left. It made him nervous. He had assumed the smoke was from one of the missing Wylder families, or perhaps refugees from the north seeking shelter from the storm but what if it were not? His tracks would lead unerringly back to the Winter-meet.

A morbid dread settled upon him. The fortified townships of Wooliston and Dalby Mead stood as gatekeepers to the north but there were plenty of ways around them and he'd seen for himself how quickly urak could move.

I'm a fool. A dangerous fool, Renco chided, knowing now he should have returned and reported the smoke to the Wylders. Only now that he was here, Renco could not bring himself to turn away. His tracks were there to be stumbled upon whether he stayed or not. He had to know.

Crouching low by a wide trunk, Renco transitioned into ki'tae, once again extending his sense outward. His awareness passed through nebulous swirls of indigo and smaller clouds of turquoise, above a bed of coruscating greys and sparks of white. To his surprise, the ache in his head as he pushed up to his limit never materialised and the opaqueness of the aether clouds remained constant rather than thickening into obscurity. He pushed past it.

A flare of golden energy appeared stuttering and flickering, vapour plumes of mustard pillaring above. Renco had studied enough under the influence of ki'tae to know it for a campfire. It drew his consciousness like a beacon would a ship in the night, but it was not what stopped his breath.

Orbiting the fire's energy were white clouds laced with thick beads of purple and red. One, in particular, was brighter than the rest; the non-human threads of tae'al glowed deeper, richer than the others. It alone was stationary and hovered like a bird against the wind.

Urak. It startled Renco so much that his concentration wavered, and he fell out of ki'tae with a gasp of breath.

The distant snapping of branches brought him around. The sound grew louder and more urgent. *They know? Somehow they know I'm here.*

Turning, Renco retraced in haste the puncture marks he'd left in the snow. His mind reached for Nihm, and he sensed her away to the southwest. He sent a burst of fear-laced thoughts down their link and a warbling echo of concern reached back to him. Renco couldn't make out Nihm's response. It was as if they stood at opposite ends of a long, winding tunnel, her thoughts reverberating and incoherent.

Crunching snow and the rustle of vegetation sounded closer behind him but also wider, cutting away to his right and left. The urak were flanking him.

Renco picked up his pace, running harder, unmindful of the noise he made. He burst from the wood at the edge of the ravine and leapt, letting the branches of the fallen tree catch him. The crown buckled and swayed, several smaller limbs cracking beneath his weight, threatening to dump him into the turgid river below. Renco barked his shins as his feet scrambled for purchase before he managed to pull himself up. He pushed violently through the canopy until he reached the slender tip of the trunk which trembled and shuddered as he moved along its length.

The river roared beneath him, but the sonant hiss of contracting snow must have reached through it for Renco glanced back in time to see an urak explode from the woods. It was male and hairy. Seven feet of sinew and muscle, his broad face and squashed nose curled into a feral snarl.

Without breaking stride, the urak threw himself up and out at the tree, crashing into its leafy arms. The tree tip bent ominously beneath the urak, whose large hands clawed at the branches to arrest his fall.

Fear coursing through his blood, Renco heaved himself on. A whip-crack cut the air and the trunk shuddered then tilted toward the river. With a despairing lurch, Renco grabbed for safety that wasn't there and, in a moment, both human and urak were gone, dumped into the water below and swept away.

* * *

Nihm let her breath even out before raising her bow.

Though it felt like cheating, a rush of anticipation coursed through her veins as a contact arc appeared in her line of sight. It was one of Sai's many miracles and as the bowstring grew taut the arc straightened into a line that she placed over the elk.

The breeze was into her face which Sai had compensated for in the arrows projected line to target. If she thought to inquire, Sai would provide the exact wind speed and direction.

With the elk quartering towards her, Nihm moved the arrow's projected impact point to just below the base of the elk's neck and the point of the facing shoulder. A guaranteed quick kill and a good-sized target to aim for. There was no point sticking an arrow in a beast to have it run away and die of a festering wound days later and in agony. Her Da had taught her better than that.

Nihm took a slow breath with her draw but as the feather tickled her cheek, a sudden alarm crashed against her mind. Her aim wavered as she released. Unsure of the shot, Nihm flexed her wrist at the last possible instant and sent the arrow skidding high and wide to clatter into the depths of the forest. The elk bolted and Snow and Ash burst after it from opposite sides, where they lay in wait.

Nihm was oblivious to it, the elk forgotten. A surge of confused thoughts washed across her link with Renco, jumbled and too indistinct to make out anything other than he was in grave peril. She centred herself as Lob appeared at her shoulder with a quizzical frown on her face.

"You pulled your shot?"

Renco was to the northeast and some distance Nihm judged as she oriented herself toward his location.

"There's trouble." Nihm pointed straight ahead before shouldering her bow.

Reaching out, Lob gripped Nihm's shoulder. "What are you talking about? What trouble?"

"Not sure exactly but I need to go. Send someone to warn Kafelie and the other families then, if you will, follow me as best you can."

Nihm's head rocked as Renco's garbled thoughts abruptly terminated and the whole of her body vibrated like a plucked harp chord. Looking up into worried eyes, her body still shivering, Nihm placed fingers to her lips and issued a piercing whistle. The dogs would follow if no one else.

Shrugging free of Lob, Nihm bolted through the trees, leaving the bewildered Wylder woman behind.

A green line appeared in her vision.

<I have placed a transit line for you to follow, plotting the fastest route through the trees.>

Nihm barely acknowledged Sai, as she settled into a languid, ground-eating pace she could maintain indefinitely. She sent her thoughts back toward Renco but worryingly there was no response. That she could sense him still gave her some small comfort.

Nihm gave a belligerent huff. "You better not get yourself killed."

Chapter 46: From Sea to Sky

Rakemouth, Cumbrenan

The sea foamed and heavy rollers battered the land, the remnant rebuke of a storm in the Sea of Prospero. The small breakwater at Rakemouth was scoured by the waves, each collision crashing over the boom of rocks, threatening to sweep it away. As each assault retreated however the defences stood resolute and defiant.

Beyond the breakwater lay a small, natural harbour split by a wide inlet swollen from the surge of a tri-tide. Its north shore and riverbank were littered with islands of broken stone that had fractured and crumbled from a towering cliff face. In contrast, the opposing bank was smooth, where a seawall had been built to guard against the waters of both the sea and river. The wall swept from the river mouth to the southside harbour foreshore until the rising ground made it unnecessary. Perched upon this bastion of stone lay the fishing town of Rakemouth.

Darion wandered its cobbled streets. Alone, for the most part, M'Rika and R'ell remained in the Red Lobster and Ironside and Castigan didn't question his need to clear his head. He did spy Bezal from time to time, usually when the skuas and gulls shrieked at the raven's trespass, and it was his impression the bird was keeping a beady eye on him. He grinned ruefully, Bezal would like the upcoming sea voyage no more than him, of that he was certain.

The boat ride from Pik Lake to Rakemouth had been the calm before the storm; quite literally, thought Darion as the wind pressed his cloak tight against his body only to turn a corner and have it whip out behind him.

Greybeard's son, Marius had seldom spoken during their journey here. The leper found it difficult to raise his voice and so had not bothered talking unless required. After dropping them off, he did not tarry. Merely gave a nod to each, eyes lingering longer on the ilfanum, then reminded Ironside of their agreement on the horses. Darion liked that about him. To the point, no time or words wasted.

As for Rakemouth, it seemed sad. If the town had ever had a heyday it was long past. The buildings were tired, scoured by the elements and more than a few were boarded up. Whatever economy Rakemouth had once enjoyed was gone and what was left looked barely enough to sustain its seawall. It was like a long slow spiral into death that for some reason made him think of Greybeard.

He walked up the sloped street towards the Red Lobster. Reaching the inn, Darion pulled open the door and stepped inside. A fire crackled in the hearth and the cold light from the windows blended with the warm yellow of the room. The smells of woodsmoke, straw and cooked food teased him further into the room. He spied Castigan with her red-sunset hair, standing by a farside table gesticulating to Ironside who was seated at its head. Around the table were Rutigard and Ansel, all that remained of their two Hands, along with the orderlies Regus and Gatzinger. The table erupted in laughter though Darion was too far removed to hear at what.

Ironside spied him and waved Darion over.

"Our ship, *Royal Blue*, is out to sea. We'll be leaving when the tide turns. If you could inform our travel companions. Maybe get something to eat before we go?"

Food was the last thing Darion wanted with the upcoming sea voyage. "I'm not hungry." He turned for the stairs.

"Better to have something in your gut to throw up than nothing. Otherwise, it's like choking up a kidney."

The mirth in Ironside's voice rankled, "Ai," Darion returned, "I remember."

Navigating the tables and chairs, he climbed the narrow, stone staircase to the upper floor. His room was sea-facing and when he knocked and entered, he found M'rika and R'ell staring out of the window. Bezal had found her way inside and the dishevelled raven was preening herself on a nightstand.

"There is a ship out to sea," M'rika said.

"Ai, she's the *Royal Blue*. A boat will take us out to her when the tide turns." Darion unfastened his cloak and hung it on a hook by the door.

"Her," M'rika pondered over the word. "I wonder why humans genderize inanimate, lifeless things. Do you know, ilf-friend?"

"You should not call me that here. We have a saying, 'behind every wall and door is an ear'." Darion said. "As for the ship, she bears and protects them, so to her crew she is life, and it's easier maybe to bless or curse a her or him than an it."

"Strange," M'rika returned to gazing out of the window and after a moment spoke again.

"By your standards, I have lived long. I have passed and renewed many times, as Da'Mari needs, yet I have never been upon the sea. I have never seen these waters. What is it like to sail them?"

"Beautiful and cruel, so they say. For me, awful." Darion shrugged. "I've only sailed once before, from Tankrit to Deepwater in the north and I spent all of it sick in my bunk."

M'rika faced him and tilted her head, the dark orbs of her eyes as unfathomable as ever. "The water makes you sick?"

"It's the motion. Never found my sea legs. I'm sure you'll be fine."

There was a knock at the door. "It's me," Father Melbroth called from the other side.

Darion unlatched it and pulled it wide. "Come in, Father." The room was starting to get crowded.

Needing no further invitation, Father Melbroth entered, white robes swishing about his ankles. He pursed his lips at the sight of the giant raven then wrinkled his nose at the mess she had shit on the floor.

"She is not used to being inside," R'ell stated.

"I can see that," Melbroth grumbled. "I'a, heard you talking, and wondered if our 'friends' had any news on our departure."

"The tide is set to turn on the hour, we leave then," Darion explained.

"Well, we should eat. I've heard ship food leaves a lot to be desired and a man should not travel on an empty stomach."

"Ai, so I've heard. You go ahead, Father. The others are downstairs with that self-same thought." Darion watched Father Melbroth shuffle for the door.

"I'll bring some fruit," the priest called over his shoulder to M'rika and R'ell.

Darion closed the door and latched it, resting his head briefly against the wood. *I'm really not looking forward to this.*

* * *

The waves had calmed somewhat in the last hour but the pinnace ride from Rakemouth was still horrendous, especially once they cleared the breakwater and hit the open sea. The *Royal Blue* sat at station two hundred yards adrift of the harbour mouth, luffed with only a topsail unfurled for steerage. She seemed so close, but it was the longest two hundred yards of Darion's life. His guts had already started to rebel, grumbling with each sweep of the oars.

By the time they reached *Royal Blue*, his limbs felt leaden and weak. They tied a rope around him for the treacherous climb up the netting which hung over the side of the ship. He'd half clambered, half been hoisted and when his feet found the tilting deck, Darion stumbled for the side gasping for air, the sickness rushing upon him now the fear of the boat ride had gone.

It was a miracle then when M'rika gripped his head between her hands. Where her fingers touched, a warm heat suffused, radiating from his temples to his eyes and ears then deeper, beneath skin and bone. Darion's mind cleared, his nausea shredding and the tatters blowing away like ash in the wind. So amazed was he at the sudden release, Darion reciprocated, clasping his hands to M'rika's smooth leaf-scaled cheeks and kissing her forehead.

"You're amazing. What did you do?" he cried, releasing her as strength flooded his body. "I can breathe. I can stand tall."

The ring on his finger burned cold and M'rika frowned in confusion. It brought him down from his euphoria. "Sorry. I did not mean to cause you upset."

M'rika tilted her head, "I am not upset, ilf-friend." But she had gone. Turned away with the ever-present R'ell at her shoulder, who carried Bezal in his arms. The ilf gave Darion a stern look before following M'rika and Father Melbroth below deck.

A bell tolled. Calls cried out and moments later the wind shrieked through the rigging as the ship came about, her sails cracking and snapping as they unfurled. With a dip of her bow, the *Royal Blue* sliced through a wave, sending sheets of spray across her fo'c'sle deck.

Darion felt his lungs fill with ice-cold air, tasted the salt on his lips and felt… exhilarated. The ship swung into a trough and rode its farside, cresting another wave with a hiss that shivered the boards beneath his feet.

Lurching from the ship's side, Darion climbed the steps to the quarter deck and swayed towards the stern rail. He passed two wheelmen on the rudder and another two who looked back over the main deck, their eyes alternating between the sails and rigging to the grey, corrugated seas.

These last two wore tricorne hats and their demeanour was one of command. Captain and First Officer, thought Darion, though which was which he could not tell. Both looked grizzled and wore neatly trimmed beards, but one was older, his face more lined and the creases deeper, his speckled hair mostly grey. Both men rode the ship as easily as Darion did a horse. Words were exchanged and the older bellowed an order which cut through the wind making Darion pause momentarily, but the order was not for him, and he stumbled to the stern rail and clasped it with a sense of achievement.

A pennant, black with a white circle in its centre, fluttered stiffly back across the quarter-deck, pointing to the wheelmen. Darion stared at it a while, it had been a long time since he had seen the Order Flag. Dragging his eyes away, he followed the spume of the ship's wake, trailing back towards Rakemouth. The fishing town looked small, a nugget on a horizon of rolling hills and lofty cliff faces.

With nothing but the roiling sea and receding landscape before him, Darion felt an angst surface from deep in his bones. It was as if he stood upon the waves and who he was, where he should be, diminished with the land. Insignificant, alone. Everything was gone, lost but for the memories. He twisted the binding ring on his finger.

Marron. His heart panged, crushed beneath the weight of her name. Her loss thrummed in woeful lament through every nerve and fibre of his body. Tears came unbidden and unseen.

Bindu. The homestead. The life they had worked so hard to build. Would that he had savoured the time more.

"What do I do now, love? My duty is almost done, and I swear, I am done with it." He swiped a hand under his nose and brushed at his cheeks, his fingers like icicles against his skin.

Nihm. Her name whispered to him as if carried on the wind. She was out there somewhere, headed toward Hawke Hold and the Duncan. Not everything was lost.

"I should never have left her," he told the wind.

Her path is hers alone. Darion shook his head in denial.

"I will find her. I will come for her."

The promise settled like a tattered shroud around his shoulders, feeling hollow and already broken, and he watched in silent turmoil as the land reduced to a blur on the horizon.

Behind a wall of clouds, the sun began to set, and the sky was darkening but a break allowed a singular, russet beam of light to penetrate the canopy and he felt moved by it. It promised freedom or hope, maybe both. It lifted his spirit.

Darion felt a hand on his arm and twisted. M'rika's tall, sinewy form stood by his side. Her eyes furrowed as they fastened on his, penetrating. Knowing.

"I feel your sadness. The pain in your eyes reflects my own." She took his hands in hers and her mouth wrinkled. "They are like shards of ice. Come. You have been out here too long ilf-friend."

M'rika tugged his hands, gently but firmly. Her simple touch seemed to earth him, and her words lifted his despondence. Enough at least to return a melancholic smile and allow her to lead him away.

They made their way below decks and with each step, Darion locked away the hurt and stiffened his resolve. He would deliver M'rika to the Order Halls in Bastion. To Keeper. Then he would be free.

* * *

Blessed with a following wind, the *Royal Blue* crossed the Sea of Prospero to Tankrit Island in three nights and two days. She navigated the tempestuous northern waters around Tankrit and berthed at the deepwater port of Baylok early on the third morning.

Baylock. It was many years since Darion had last been here and yet to his eyes, beneath its winter coat, it looked unchanged.

The port's sea defences and stone jetties were as impressive as ever and, though they lacked the size of those at Deepwater and Cambryn and its harbour mouth was unadorned by the giant statues that bracketed those harbour cities, it had a stalwart grandness to it. One that said it had faced the seas for a thousand years and remained undefeated.

Apart from a cluster of buildings around dockside the rest of Baylok sprawled in lazy sweeps across the surrounding hills seemingly without plan or purpose. The houses were nestled in small pockets, each separated by trees or sloping meadows. In the spring, after the snows had melted, it would be even more picturesque, Darion knew, with the bloom of meadow flowers and the vibrant greenery of the trees colouring everything.

There was little time however to reminisce or for Darion and the ilfanum to admire the view. Carriages, each with a team of horses, awaited their party as they disembarked the *Royal Blue* and they set off without delay.

The road taken led south through a valley, the carriages weaving around contours and struggling up icy inclines until they passed some unseen town limit. Here, the carriage drivers stopped and Darion and the others stretched their legs whilst steelwood runners were fit to the coaches, locking through some mechanism to the wheels. The reason for the change became evident once they set off again, as the snow on the road deepened and the newly fit runners slid smoothly over the surface.

Their journey from Baylock took them through woodlands and plains. Darion saw more wildlife than he did people. The settlements they passed through were few and far between and most had only a smattering of buildings. There were other signs, holdsteads sprinkled here and there, but mostly the land seemed devoid of humanity.

That all changed on the second day as a range of low mountains loomed ahead. Holdsteads became more frequent, and they passed travellers on the road who waved in cheery greeting as the carriages slid passed. On their left, the ice river, the Tomé appeared, winding its way ever eastward where it would eventually empty into the Great Expanse.

The plains changed into wrinkled hummocks of land that gradually transformed into hard-edged hills and rocky spires until the carriages were surrounded by stone. Ahead, rising imperiously, loomed the mountains of The Zon.

As the road weaved, Darion could make out the familiar walls and towers of Bastion, carved high into the side of Apog, the northernmost mountain of The Zon. Darion felt his heart skip. As a boy, he'd grown up on the shores of Lake Kilda but on his eighth nameday, he'd been offered a place at the Order Halls, for study and training. It was a great honour and his parents had been immensely proud. He'd spent his formative years there and at first, he had hated his new home. Compared to the lake and forest and grasslands of his childhood, the rock and stone of Bastion and the Order Halls had seemed harsh and unforgiving.

Now Darion found those self-same feelings of excitement and trepidation that he'd had as a boy assail him once again. He would see Keeper, deliver M'rika, and then his duty would be done. He would be done.

The carriages scrunched through the snow as the road steered them around the side of Mount Apog, the going turning more treacherous as they rose ever higher. Passing through a canyon of rock they found themselves in a crowded hub of buildings that seemed to grow from the stone surrounds.

Basetown. As bleak as it looked it held some fondness for Darion and he smiled in remembrance of the alehouses he once frequented as a young man. This is where he had first summoned the courage to ask Marron for a dance.

People in thick furs and woollen hats lined the side of the road as the carriages slid by, their faces knowing and their eyes keen with interest. That they were expected shouldn't have surprised him, for not much happened in Bastion and the Order Halls that did not make its way down to Basetown.

The carriages turned down a narrow lane and passed beneath a stone arch into a courtyard that was surprisingly large and extended under the side of the mountain.

As soon as they stopped, a groaning Father Melbroth alighted from their carriage, twisting and stretching his limbs. Darion disembarked feeling stiff himself though M'rika and R'ell seemed unbothered by the long journey and were surveying the undercliff with interest, the dark orbs of their eyes taking in the stables and storage barn that were hewn into the rockface.

Though the wind did not reach them in the courtyard, it was bitter. The cold permeated through the ground with a deathly chill and Darion was keen to move inside.

"M'rika, R'ell."

Both ilf had foregone their priest robes back aboard the *Royal Blue* and wore instead their forest cloaks over garments of dark, almost black, material that hugged their bodies. The ilf had pulled these latter from a pouch on their weave belts; tiny, folded pads of fabric that unwound like a bandage. Darion had watched in fascination at the time, as the ilf wrapped the strange material around their torsos, arms and legs. Observed as tiny moss-like shoots grew before his eyes, thickening and weaving until they merged, knitting together to become seamless. As entranced as he'd been, Darion never felt the subtle, brush of magics against his skin so whatever sorcery the ilf employed remained a mystery to him.

At Darion's call, M'rika moved to his side with R'ell at her back and Bezal crawing unhappily on his shoulder. The raven had been grumpy ever since Rakemouth.

Darion led them towards a large, iron-bound door where Lyra Castigan, Gatzinger and the Grey Knight, Ansel waited for them. Ironside and the others it appeared, had already passed through to the promised warmth of the interior.

"Bastion and the Order Halls are above us," Lyra Castigan addressed the ilf as she pulled on the door, swinging it wide. "The road ahead is deep with snow and impassable for horse or carriage, so we walk from here. There is suitable food for you inside and something warm to drink. Take both. We leave within the hour."

M'rika did not acknowledge the Order Knight but followed Darion inside. If Lyra Castigan was perturbed at the snub, she did not show it, instead trailing behind the ilf and leaving Gatzinger to attend the door.

Chapter 47: The Envoy Tree

Basetown, Tankrit Island

The road from Basetown to Bastion was not for the faint of heart. The sloped side of Mount Apog towered above and below, anchoring one side of the way but offering nothing but air and a drop to oblivion on the other. The road was wide enough for a carriage but not much else and in winter, choked with snow and ice, it felt much narrower.

Darion had made this trip more times than he could recount but the last was a lifetime ago and not in the heart of winter. Each step seemed more unstable and treacherous than the last. His breath streamed and his legs, idle these past days, burned at the effort.

Directly ahead was Father Melbroth, wheezing in the thinning air, panting clouds that whipped away in the gusting wind. He should not have come, Darion thought. He was old and whilst the priest's body was lean, he was not built for this sort of rigour.

"If I await better weather and a clear road I'll be here til spring," the priest had insisted back in Basetown. Darion wondered if he regretted his decision.

A swirl of fog, streaming like river water, enveloped them and the priest vanished into the white. Darion could barely see his own hand and heard Melbroth gasp for Nihmrodel, the White Lady. As if in answer to his plea, the fog turned wispy and translucent before vanishing as quickly as it had come.

Melbroth stumbled on. Rutigard was ahead and walked in the tracks of Regus and Ironside, who led the way. The Order Knight did not seem of a mind to wait and had already disappeared around an elbow of rock.

"Come on, Father. Just a little further," Darion encouraged as Melbroth stopped and sank to his knees, breath rasping in and out.

The priest raised his head to the sky, eyes closed as if the effort to open them was too much and shook his head.

Slinging the pack from his shoulders, Darion unlaced it and sorted through it for the flask Ruith had given him back in the Old Forest. Then, it had chased the cold from his limbs and re-energised his body, perhaps it would help Father Melbroth. As he pulled it free though, M'rika crouched by his side and stayed his hand.

"Eld'rein water is not for your kind."

Darion frowned. "Ruith gave it me. I did not take it."

"I know," M'rika said. "I meant only that it is more like to harm than heal. Ruith is a dúr-phr-ta, a healer. That he gave it to you means he read your tae'al and saw that you have some compatibility for eld'rein water and its properties. A rarity amoung humans."

Nodding his understanding, Darion returned the flask to his pack and re-laced it, aware all the while of Lyra Castigan, trudging her way forward. No doubt to see what the delay was.

Crunching past R'ell, the Order Knight's steel-grey eyes took in the scene.

"Bloody fool," she said, grumpily.

"I'll take him," Darion said.

"Nonsense." Striding past, Lyra grasped the priest's cloak and hauled him unceremoniously to his feet.

"Just give me a minute," Melbroth wheezed.

"Ai, then two or three." Levering a shoulder under his armpit, Castigan clamped a hand around the priest's waist before hauling him like a sack of bones up the path.

Darion and the others followed the Order Knight who seemed untroubled by her luggage.

They passed the elbow of rock. A long, rising sweep stretched before them, carving into Apog's side. After they cleared the next bend, the way opened onto a small plateau surrounded on three sides by the mountain. Cut in the wall of rock opposite, there yawned a cavernous mouth as tall as three men and wide enough for a drawn carriage. The jagged teeth of a portcullis jutted from its roof just inside the entrance and they were in time to see Rutigard as he disappeared beneath their lethal points.

Lyra Castigan didn't hesitate as she half dragged, half-carried the priest across the open ground and into the breach. For Darion, who followed, a weight settled upon him that grew heavier with each step. Bastion lay on the other side, a homecoming of a sort, only this was no longer his home, and he found the weight was not the welcoming one he'd grown up with. *I do not belong here anymore.*

The realisation should have pained him, but it did not. By his side, Darion sensed M'rika absorbing it all, both her surroundings and his mood, but he did not look at her, his head never wavered from the hole in the rock. Not until he passed into its maw.

The sparsely lit tunnel opened after a hundred paces onto a wide, quadrangular courtyard that narrowed towards the rockface. The other sides were open to the world and enclosed by elegant buildings, crowned with towers and spires all made of the same imperious, black rock as the mountain. As wondrous and imposing as the architecture was it was not what drew the eye. Lined ranks of people filled the courtyard and at their forefront stood a solitary figure.

Keeper.

Darion felt the ilf bristle beside him, rubbing rough to the smooth of his own emotions.

Keeper was a leader and a teacher. Wise beyond the wisdom of mortal men and as ancient as the Order itself. He had helped Darion, helped them all to find meaning and purpose.

Darion found himself stumbling forward and sinking to his knees, oblivious of the gathered assembly. With a loud tsk, Keeper reached out and pulled him to his feet, holding him at arm's length and gazing up into his face.

"Though it was seventeen years, two hundred and sixty-three days ago, I remember your leaving as if it had been this morning." Keeper's voice held a hint of amusement, its lyrical tone as comforting as hot bread. "You and Marron, fresh-faced, excited with the prospect of a new purpose and the adventure of making a life together." Keeper beamed, the all-dark rounds of his eyes warm and deep. "Then too you sank to your knees. Do you remember my words that day?"

Darion nodded, a grin weaving across his face. "Yes. You said, 'No man nor woman should kneel to another.'"

"You are much hairier than I recall." Reaching out, Keeper tugged Darion's beard then grasped his chin and turned it side to side. "And a little greyer. They say your first grey hair arrives the day your first child is born. A nonsense of course, but a pleasant one that I rather like."

"Ai, well I can attest that Nihm is responsible for most of mine," Darion replied, his smiling eyes searched Keeper's face. It was as unchanged as Baylok and Bastion, the same as it ever was. Smooth brown skin, unwrinkled by time, hairless but for a thin, dark slash of eyebrows. His features were soft, perfectly symmetrical and unblemished by age but for the eyes. The eyes were ancient. All black pools as deep as time. They marked Keeper as different, as other than human, yet despite this, they held a warmth, a knowledge that drew a man in.

Keeper released Darion's chin and clasped his arm instead. "I mourn Marron's death with you. She was a good person. We will talk later. About Nihm too. But now, I think you must introduce me." He inclined his head toward the ilfanum.

Darion took a step back and to the side, twisting unconsciously at the ring on his finger. He locked eyes with M'rika. They were a brown so dark they were almost a match for Keeper's and just as unreadable. The subtle tightening of her jaw and the wrinkled pinch to her nose, however, conveyed what her eyes did not. She was troubled.

"Keeper, this is M'rika dul Da'Mari, Visok and Kraal of the Rohelinewaald, and R'ell, Visok and Umphathi." The raven on R'ell's shoulder gave a loud caw.

"And, um, Bezal." Darion trailed off as M'rika stepped forward. She flashed him a tight-lipped grin.

"We know each other, ilf-friend. Do we not, Elora, Ke'pa of the Eladrohim?" M'rika's words turned from soft to hard as her regard shifted from one to the other.

"I have not heard that name spoken for longer than I care to mention," Keeper replied, unperturbed by the ilf's tone. "It was taken from me along with who I was. I am no longer the being that you knew."

"You're an abomination," R'ell stormed, his angular frame pushing forward, obsidian daggers smoked from each hand.

Darion stood in the ilf's path. Behind him, beyond Keeper, there was a hiss of drawn steel from the front ranks of those gathered.

Raising his arm, Keeper's voice rang out, crisp and clear. "Stop. Sheath your weapons and return to your places." Then more softly. "You too, Darion."

Keeper's eyes, calm as a cave pool, fastened on R'ell's rage-filled ones and waited.

"This is not Da'Mari's wish," M'rika uttered, the words enough to gentle R'ell.

"Forgive me, Kraal. I forgot myself."

"We are both here at Da'Mari's will. Do not forget again," M'rika admonished.

Chastened, R'ell stepped back, retreating to his former position. The daggers in his hands twisted into black vapour before dissipating, pulled apart by the breeze.

"I would complete my purpose," M'rika said as if the interruption had never occurred. "Show me the ground you have prepared."

A snort of breath from Keeper. "You think me the great betrayer. All these years, after everything I have given, everything I have sacrificed, still, you see me as a pariah."

M'rika's nose creased. "You speak like a human, of I, I, I. Well, we did not come to hear you speak 'Kee-per'. Save your words for Uma."

"Anger taints your tae'al. Do not let it cloud your mind, M'rika dul Da'Mari. I am not the enemy." Keeper folded his hands into the sleeves of his grey robe and his gaze shifted to the white-cowled figure leaning heavily against Castigan.

"I will take you, ruua-uma, to the seeding ground, but first perhaps I should attend to your travel companion who appears in some distress."

Keeper glided past M'rika and R'ell and stood before the white priest.

"Father Melbroth, I presume? Brave and foolish are twins and sometimes it is hard to tell them apart. It would have been more prudent to have waited at Basetown. At least until you had acclimatised to the altitude. Still, you are here now. May I?" Keeper's hands uncoupled from the sleeves of his robe.

With a boneless nod, Melbroth gasped his response. "Indeed. It would seem I have over-taxed myself."

With a wry smile, Keeper fastened long fingers to Melbroth's temples and cheeks. It was much like M'rika had done when dispelling his seasickness, Darion thought, watching from the side.

The sudden caress against Darion's skin could have been mistaken for the kiss of a summer breeze, only it was not summer and the freezing wind that swirled in the courtyard could not reach beneath his clothing as this did.

Father Melbroth groaned. Colour returned to his face and the exhaustion in his eyes lifted. He took his weight and shrugged free of Castigan's supporting arm with a muttered. "Thank you, my dear."

Standing taller, the white priest looked up a fraction into the endless depths of Keeper's eyes. The leader of the Order was not quite what Melbroth had expected. He seemed almost youthful in an ageless kind of way, as if time held no power over him. Keeper's golden-brown hair was knotted into queues with charms and spangles threading each strand which were gathered in a bunch and fell down his back.

"Welcome to Bastion, Father Melbroth. A little rest and some warm food will go further than the giving you just received. Now," through some art, Keeper's voice raised and carried to all assembled, "as fine a winter's day as this is, it is too cold to be stood around passing pleasantries." With a clap of his hands, the packed courtyard started to disperse.

"Father Melbroth, we will talk later. Until then, Lyra here will take you to Master Attimus. He looks more his age than do I and has a fascination for the Trinity and your One God. Attimus will talk your ears off but will also answer any curiosity you may have."

"Thank you," Melbroth said.

"This way, Father." Lyra Castigan led the way and the priest fell in behind with Ansel and Gatzinger bringing up the rear.

Darion watched them pass but was aware when Keeper's attention shifted back to him.

"You know where everything is. Your old room is unoccupied," Keeper began.

"Darion stays," M'rika interrupted. "The ilf-friend and I share a debt. Each to the other. He will bear witness."

One of Keeper's dark eyebrows rose as he considered the two anew. "As you wish."

Folding his hands once more into the sleeves of his robe, Keeper walked them across the courtyard, which seemed much larger now it was mostly empty of people. He led them to a tall pointed arch set into the side of the mountain, its stone border etched with black runes and golden symbols. Immense, ironwood doors stood closed, but a small gate set in one of them was open. Keeper led them through it and into a cavernous hallway.

The air inside was warm and held an earthy, chalky scent instantly familiar to Darion. He'd almost forgotten that smell. Like the strange bioluminescent light, it came from vines that wrapped around several trunk-like pillars. Small moats encircled each column and were interconnected by a central water channel that bisected the room.

Darion's eyes climbed the nearest pillar to the high ceiling above. The light was weaker up there, more diffuse as if gravity pulled on it, though in reality, the vines had ceased their clambering sprawl twenty feet below. It was enough though to make out the spider work lines of text and murals that covered it.

Like the runes and symbols around the Ascendants Gate, Darion knew the writings were not human. They had remained indecipherable for centuries until Master Razholte, a visiting wordsmith, had unpicked them. A historian as well as a wordsmith, Master Razholte had never left.

Waátori góyn Hqrik they were called. Dead and gone millennia ago though no one knew exactly when or why; for the writings uncovered gave no indication. The Waátori had carved these halls and passages and called them home and the ceiling above told some of their history and the murals gave imagery to it.

"Interesting. I was never told." M'rika stood at Darion's shoulder and followed his gaze. "Would that I had time. I'd like to have read their story." Before he could ask what she meant, M'rika walked after Keeper towards the nearest of the stairwells bordering the room.

They went up. The steps were wide and deep but shallow as if built for a child. They climbed above the entrance hall and passed a gallery that was rough-hewn and glittered with quartz light and gemstones. They left that below as well as they continued their spiralling ascent.

They passed more landings, each as strange and different from the last. Some they would exit onto and walk along but always it was to another stair and always they moved up. Darion's thighs ached, first the path up Apoq and now the interminable climb through the various Order Halls taking its toll. *Come on old man.*

The next floor was a landing of marbled stone and panelled walls and was lit by glowing orbs that hung suspended from the ceiling. It lacked the mysticism of the 'Waátori' levels and felt altogether more human. Keeper led them down a wide corridor, nodding politely to several people as they passed. Darion had suspected their destination several floors ago and was vindicated when Keeper took a left at a junction and the glow globes faded out, replaced by natural light that streamed through a wall made of clearcut crystal.

Keeper placed a hand against the glass and a pink pulse of light surrounded the contact point. A crack appeared in the centre of the wall, tracing from top to bottom before the crystal sides swung open on silent hinges revealing a wide portal. A cool lick of wind eddied through it.

The Stone Arboretum. In his twelve-some years of training and studying at the Order Halls, Darion had experienced it only a handful of times and each had been as fresh and vitalizing as the first.

Below the doorway lay a bowl-shaped mesa, its eastern side sheared away to a cliff edge and revealing a soaring, purple vista of the land beyond. Standing stones girdled the base of the bowl, each menhir formed of a different rock, providing a contrast in colour and shape.

The ground beneath these stone giants was sprinkled with snow, which was unusual, Darion thought. Given the altitude, the rocky monuments should be buried in the stuff, yet the Arboretum was different, the elements more muted as if they disregarded the rocky plinth perched on the edge of the mountainside.

They took a curving path down the sloped incline to the flat, before it cut between two monoliths. It led them to a pool, which sat, like an unblinking eye, at the centre point of the stone circle. A narrow waterfall, untouched by winter, pattered down the nearside wall and fed a small brook which meandered its way to the pool before it continued its journey to the cliff's edge.

Keeper waited on the path whilst M'rika walked alone to the pool. She paused by a square of turned earth, nestled between the still water and the stream, the naked soil a stain against the white coat of the mesa. Kneeling, M'rika kneaded fingers into the rich loam and pressed, knuckles deep before scooping aside handfuls of dirt, creating a small but surprisingly deep hole. Sitting back on her heels, Mrika's eyes closed and she stilled, as calm as the pool beside her.

Darion glanced at R'ell who stalked the outside of the stone circle, his hands touching each monolith before moving to the next. Unmindful it seemed of what was happening elsewhere.

M'rika rose and Darion's eyes snapped back at the motion and watched as she walked the crooked path of the stream to the precipice. Darion held his breath, from where he stood it looked like another step would take M'rika over its edge.

Somehow, he knew this was a seminal and deeply personal moment for M'rika. Though not as grave, a solemnity was in the air every bit as poignant as that back in the Old Forest when M'rika had found the remains of Groldtigkah, her soulbound. Darion found himself moving toward her. It felt right, and he would not bear idle witness to whatever was about to happen.

R'ell stopped his circuit inspection of the stones and glared at Darion as he trudged across the centre space to M'rika. Unwavering, Darion ignored the ilf and was thankful when the umphathi made no move to intervene.

M'rika's back was straight, head held high, toes tight against the lip of the drop. A strong gust of wind could carry her over. Darion was cautious as he approached, uncertain what to say.

"What is this about? You seem… different," he tried.

"It is better than I had hoped for," M'rika replied. "It is beautiful, is it not? I can see the land stretching below and the ocean beyond. From here I can watch the new dawn and the world pass. Truly it is a fitting place to rest."

Darion did not fear heights but from where he stood, M'rika seemed to be surrounded by air, the lip of the precipice surely too fragile to support her weight. The stream next to where she stood plunged into space, noiseless against the howl of the wind which had picked up out here on the edge, plucking at his ilf-cloak so that it danced around his shoulders.

"Ai, I can see that. From back here where it is safer."

M'rika laughed and took a step back. "I did not mean to scare you, friend Darion. Did you think I would fling myself off like one of those lost souls your storytellers sing of?"

"Well, not on purpose maybe," Darion grunted.

Turning, M'rika looped her arm through his, a bizarre and human thing to do that caught Darion by surprise.

"You seem different," Darion repeated.

"I would tell you some things and seek two favours before I go. One you will find hard to give but I will ask it nonetheless."

"Go? Go where? We just got here." Darion frowned. "As for any favour. Ask it, if it is within my power, it is yours."

M'rika looked at him, "Like every human, you speak without thought. What if my favour was for you to leap from this cliff. That would be entirely within your power to do, yet if you did, it would be catastrophically stupid. Yes?"

"It's an expression, kind of," Darion said somewhat defensively. "And you would not ask me to do such a thing."

"Words have power, Darion. Use them wisely."

Darion nodded agreement and waited, knowing M'rika had more to say. *Not least these favours.*

"Seeing this home of the Waátori góyn Hqrik awakened many memories inside me. None of which are consequential to you, but it has given me pause for thought. If you grant these favours, we will have time to talk, and you will learn much about what has been lost."

Darion stopped and untangled his arm from M'rika's and turned her to face him. "One moment I feel you are saying goodbye, the next something else entirely. I thought you ilf were plain speaking?" Though dread gripped his heart, his eyes wrinkled in good humour and M'rika smiled in response.

"I deserve that I suppose." They slowly ambled towards the pool. "I feel a need to talk with you, and yes, in a way this is goodbye. Let me explain."

"Ilf in your tongue most closely translates to 'child' and ilfanum 'children of'. Da'Mari has many children. R'ell and I are Visok, children made by Da'Mari in the image of humans." Her canted eyes pinched in afterthought and she offered further explanation. "Da'Mari considered the similarity would make it easier to interact with your race."

Except that you do not, Darion thought but held his tongue.

"Whilst at our core all ilfanum serve Da'Mari, Visok possess a certain autonomy and self-reliance many of her other children do not. We have an awareness and knowledge of the greater world for example."

"Most male Visok, like R'ell are umphathi, wardens or guardians made for a singular purpose, to protect. Female Visok perform the same roles as their male counterparts, but we are also more, for we carry raka-caeed, a special type of tree seed if you will. A female Visok bears a single raka-caeed, be it kaorak, taotoa, ronu, manaka, asper or even baobab. It all depends on what part of the forest they inhabit and how they, themselves, are grown. I, however, am also Kraal. I carry a single raka-caeed the same as any Visok, only mine is not preordained. As a Kraal, my raka-caeed can become any type of raka, tree, that I choose, and as may be required. Which brings me to my purpose here." The two of them had reached the pool at the centre of the stone arboretum and stood by the freshly turned earth.

R'ell, having completed his inspection of the stones, stood with Keeper at a distance. The pair watched on in silence as M'rika stepped into the hole in the soil she had dug earlier. Her feet wriggled, worming deeper. She touched a hand to her throat and her cloak slipped from her shoulders and heaped around her legs.

"I am Da'Mari's chosen. My raka-caeed will be that of the huron, the envoy tree. Through me, Da'Mari and Keeper will commune."

M'rika fumbled at the flax-weave belt, encircling her waist. Pulling free a pouch she held it out to Darion. "Our debt, Darion, each to the other will be fulfilled by dawn tomorrow. These favours I ask, however, are as your friend."

Darion took the pouch which settled comfortably in his hand. It felt surprisingly heavy as if it were filled with sand.

"These are some of the ash remains of Groldtigkah. My wish is for you to keep vigil with me tonight. Then at dawn's first light, bury Grold's ashes at my feet. In some small way, we may sustain each other."

Darion's eyes pinched and his brow wrinkled as he contemplated her words.

"Understanding will come," M'rika preempted, her mouth curving into a tight smile. "When it does, do not be sad, my friend. And please, do not be angry with me."

"I don't want this," Darion murmured, unsettled.

M'rika held her hand out and he gripped it, felt strength in her clasp and it eased his worry. She released him and touched a hand to the dark, seamless clothing she wore. At first, nothing happened. Then the black of the cloth seemed to swirl like mud in a puddle, the dark fabric changing hue to dark browns and dappled purples. It spread, discolouring the garment until it started to fall apart, at first in flakes then larger clumps that settled like rust chips on her discarded cloak. The flax belt and skirt soon followed until M'rika stood in nothing but the green and gold mottled leaf-scale of her skin.

"Already my blood is thickening. The change is coming upon me. Soon I will speak no more." M'rika's arms moved to her sides and Darion watched in mute despair as it fully dawned upon him what was about to happen.

"I do not want you to do this," Darion said, his voice cracking.

"I will face east and see the sunrise usher in the new day. It is a nice view." M'rika twisted toward the cliff she had stood upon. Darkness was falling, night came early on Apoq's eastern slope.

Darion moved so he could face her and stare into her eyes. He opened his mouth to speak but words failed him. It seemed to amuse M'rika.

"Finally, you show wisdom." Her face was bright in counterpoint to Darion's concern. Her words though became deeper and more sluggish.

"My second request; I cannot ask. It will become plain… I hope… during our vigil… together."

M'rika yawned and settled. Where her arms lay against her sides, the leaf-scale seemed to shimmer and flutter, as if ruffled by the breeze. They merged seamlessly, the arms becoming part of her trunk even as he watched.

Darion reached out a hand but snatched it back. Her skin felt rougher than it should, her flesh firmer than before. She did not speak again.

Time passed unnoticed.

Night fell and Nihmrodel and Ankor rose, the moons casting their gaze down upon the stone circle which seemed to hold and reflect the moonlight.

Keeper left at some point, but Darion could not say when. R'ell remained though, standing as still and immobile as his charge.

In M'rika's slow-changing state, her mouth yawned open, slow as treacle down a frozen windowpane, as if to take a final, long breath. The dark orbs of her eyes turned glassy, lost their lustre and the light behind them faded to nothing.

Darion felt tears on his skin and realised he cried, though strangely he felt no sadness. Once, his hands touched her, brushing against M'rika's skin only to find it rough and bark-like.

The cold of a winter's night, halfway up a mountainside should have frozen him, but it did not. Instead, it was temperate and of no consequence. The pool glowed in the moonlight and, together with the stone sentinels surrounding them, bore witness as M'rika dul Da'Mari completed her transformation. She was no longer an ilf. No longer his friend for she was gone.

When the first ray of sunlight grazed his shoulder, Darion recalled her request. Taking out the pouch filled with Grold's ashes, he emptied it onto the churned earth then, with his hands, dug it in around the trunk of the envoy tree, *a sorry poor excuse of a tree if ever he saw one*, thinking to bed the ashes and keep them safe from the wind.

Darion's fingers brushed against something smooth that yielded to his touch. It was spherical, about the size and shape of a grapefruit. Darion dug and scraped around it and lifted it free. A single root clung to it like an umbilical cord but broke away, sinking back into the soil. *What in seven hells?*

"It is M'rika's caeed. It carries her essence, all her memories and thoughts since her first caeeding." R'ell's voice was abrupt, its usual hint of disdain replaced by ire.

Darion glanced over his shoulder. He had not heard R'ell's approach, but the tone was not unfamiliar to him. He turned back to the tree and shook his head to clear the cobwebs from his mind. He felt so tired.

"What does it mean?" Darion asked. But already he knew the answer. Had done the moment he lifted her free of the soil. It was M'rika's unasked favour. The coherence of what it was and what that meant though eluded him. It was as if he was at the bottom of a lake and M'rika's caeed floated above him on the surface. Darion knew he had to reach for it, swim to it, but instead was sat in the mulch looking up, slowly drowning as she floated away. *No*, surging for the surface he stretched out and grasped.

His mind became hazy, a fog sinking into his brain. *What is wrong with me?* A great lethargy stole over Darion, and he shivered. He was so cold of a sudden all apart from his hand. The hand holding M'rika's essence. That was warmth. That was life. It kept the stupor at bay but could not banish it entirely and Darion found himself slipping into a dream-like fugue. Aware but unable to act.

He sensed movement behind. Heard a rustle and a muttering in a strange tongue that sounded oddly like cursing. Then, a shadow fell across him and something pressed tight against his lips and teeth. His mouth parted and moisture rushed in. A mouthful, no more.

A streak of warmth oozed down his throat, spreading like an inkblot through his body as it went. Feeling returned and his mind cleared. He took a breath and felt the sun on his cheek.

"Get up. Move. And hide that. Keep it secret. Keep it safe."

Darion felt hands pulling him up, so he stood and took an unsteady step before righting himself. He turned in time to see R'ell pack the flask of eld'rein water back in his pack.

"Thank you," Darion said.

R'ell grunted.

Darion lifted the caeed in his hand up to his face for a closer inspection. It was ruddy brown, the colour of a horse chestnut, only this shell was warm and pliant. Indeed, it seemed to mould to his open hand as if it were made to fit.

"Put that away," R'ell snapped. "I do not like this place. I feel eyes upon us."

"That door is the only way in or out. We are not overlooked." Kneeling, Darion opened his pack.

"Not there, fool. Your ilf-cloak, give it the caeed and wish it safe and the cloak will hide it for you."

It's light enough, Darion thought, weighing the seed in his hand, but he had examined the cloak many times and there were no pockets. Certainly, nothing to hold an orb this size.

R'ell's obsidian eyes glared at him.

With a shrug of his shoulders, Darion opened the cloak and held the caeed within its folds.

"Think it," R'ell growled.

Take this caeed and keep it safe, Darion wasn't sure what to expect, was accommodating an increasingly riled ilf more than anything. The cloak swirled in the wind and the gentle weight in his hand was lifted.

"What?" Darion grasped the cloak and swished it around.

R'ell glowered, a look of impatience upon his face. "It is within the cloak. Think it and M'rika's caeed will be returned to you. Now, let's go."

"Go?" Darion asked. "Ai, I want ta leave. Have ta find Nihm but we've not been here a day. We'll need supplies and passage across the Prospero. For that, we need Keeper."

"No," R'ell shook his head violently. "If you had relinquished the caeed you could do as you will. But you did not. You are the bearer, and you must return M'rika's essence to the Rohelinewaald and Da'Mari."

"Oh, no. I said I would go for Nihm, and I intend to. M'rika knew that, so did you." Heat pulsed through Darion's veins.

R'ell bared his teeth. "M'rika told me you were not like other humans. I told her she was wrong. Was she, hu-man? Her caeed will last no more than a month. Unless she is returned, then everything she learned, everything she was since her last caeeding will be lost."

Darion's anger faded to despair. "I would. If not for Nihm I would, I swear it, but I can't. You take it, this is what you came for. I know it."

"You held M'rika's essence in your hand," R'ell accused. "Her caeed bonded with you; your tae'al sustains her, not mine. You chose."

"I didn't…"

R'ell grasped Darion's tunic and with a grunt of effort lifted the human off the ground. "It should have been me, umphathi, not a worthless human. But M'rika would not listen and chose you, as you did her. Now you must accept it, ilf-friend." He spat this last and thrust Darion away from him, sending him stumbling into the envoy tree.

The ilf walked off but stopped when he reached the path. "I will wait for you by the entrance to this citadel, but I will not wait long. M'rika's fate is yours to decide."

Darion watched the ilf climb the path to the crystal doors, pull them wide then vanish beyond. With a heavy sigh, Darion faced the envoy tree. It wasn't much to look at. A green-barked trunk and not much else. He laid a hand against its surface, the tactile roughness a comfort.

"I'm angry with you," he told the tree. His foot tamped the ground around her base where he had buried Grold's ashes. Her words from earlier returned to him.

'These are some of the ash remains of Groldtigkah. My wish is for you to keep vigil with me tonight. Then at dawn's first light, bury Grold's ashes at my feet. In some small way, we may sustain each other.'

"I thought you spoke of Grold sustainin' you, but now I think ya meant me."

With a final pat on the trunk, Darion turned away from the envoy tree and headed up the path.

Epilogue

Thorsten, Rivers

The Black Crow stood upon the curtain wall looking down between the crenellations at the makeshift shanties and tents that covered Thorsten's central square. He breathed in deeply the smoke-scented air. Tarnished with the foul undertone of human squalor, it was a smell he would never grow accustomed to.

Behind him was the Black Keep, uncaring of the ripening tragedy beneath. For its ramparts stood above the mire, the malodour washed away by the winter wind before ever it breached the summit, and its height rendered faceless those that suffered the deprivations and degradations below.

No. The keep would not do. It was too clean. Too easy to retreat to its anonymity when this burden was his. The failure to protect them on him. So each morning, Lord Richard Bouchemeax, Lord of Thorsten walked upon these walls. Looked out upon his people and asked himself. What can I do for them this day?

Invariably the answer was, not much. Everything that could be done had been, long since. Barricades were erected, thoroughfares made and foraging parties sent out. Water was drawn from the numerous wells both inside and outside the castle, which was one mercy at least, but every morsel of food was stringently rationed.

That had oft been the cause of trouble in the early days. Accusations that those inside the castle ate well while those outside starved, but ten-day upon ten-day of privation had taken a toll and morose hopelessness filled the bellies of most of the survivors these days.

It wasn't all bad news. Whilst numbers had diminished through urak raids and some few that decided to take their chances and flee, many others had been evacuated down the Black Keep's escape tunnel to the Oust and sent down river on anything that could float and hold out water.

This however had limitations and Lord Richard knew it was not sustainable. The number of boats dwindled quicker than they could be foraged and making them took time, materials and skill, of which they lacked all three. As well, groups could only be sent on the blackest of cloud-filled nights and it was into the unknown. Whether anyone made it past Fallston and to the Grim was unknowable. It was just as likely as not urak were aware of this exodus and he was merely sending people to their doom.

The Black Crow sighed, he churned these self-same thoughts over day after day, yet knew the bigger enemy was not the urakakule but winter and the season had only just started to bite. Richard rubbed the heels of his palms into his eyes, then scrubbed at his face, clearing the frost off his beard and warming his cold cheeks.

"My Lord."

Richard turned bleary eyes at the familiar voice and raised an eyebrow. Bartsven, his First Sword stood a yard to his left and at his side was a guardsman he recognised as the one from the boat that day. The day this all became real. He wracked his brain but could not recall the guard's name. Bartsven nodded his head at the man who stepped forward.

"Lord Richard." The guard bobbed his head. "Mage Lutico is atop the Black Keep. He um, he's asking for you. Captain Greigon too."

"Very well," Richard said. The guard stood there.

"Means you can go, Lebraun," prompted Bartsven's gravel voice. The guard ducked his head, turned and made his way back along the wall, searching for Captain Greigon.

The Black Crow spared a tired glance at his people below and exhaled a steamy breath. "Let us see what that crotchety old goat wants then."

"Ai, milord."

The two men made their way into the Black Keep and up the half-dozen floors to the ramparts. Three guards, stationed as lookouts, snapped to attention as their Lord appeared. Two stood together with a lone guard at his post on the south-facing wall.

The Black Crow had eyes only for the dark-robed old man by the western battlement who stood, oblivious, with arms outstretched and peering between his hands. Bartsven's glower, however, told the two guards their idling had been noted and sent them scurrying back to their respective compass points.

"What is it Lutico? More tribes from the north?"

Lutico never moved, his hands twitching as if twisting some imaginary object between them.

"Thankfully, no." The last arrival to the plains around Thorsten had been six nights ago. "One might even say the opposite."

Intrigued, Lord Richard strode to the breastwork and peered out past the rooftops and the town wall to the fields beyond. He had become used to the ever-present grey-brown smudge of tents that surrounded them and the curling smoke of endless campfires that fed the clouds above. There did seem fewer of the steaming pillars. His heartbeat quickened and his tongue moistened dry lips.

Lutico moved his arms to the side and the Black Crow shuffled closer to peer between the mage's hands.

The air distorted. The sight between them blurred before coming into focus. It revealed a dozen of the tall, conical urak tents and at least half of them were being stripped down by teams of urak. Smaller urak, adolescent by the looks of them, rolled skins and tied poles. Further back, past the tented villages stood beasts of burden, shaggy-haired and long-tusked they stood docile, the urak fussing around their flanks and loading them up were only half their height.

"It is not just the western tribes either," Lutico stated. "Here." The mage panned his arms slowly northward and a similar scene played out. The fluttering pennants and standards that announced each tribe were coming down, fires smouldering as they were left to die.

"They're leaving?" Lord Richard could see it but asked the question.

"Yes. Look." Lutico dropped his arms and clasped his staff from where it leant, wedged between crenel and merlon, then tapped his way to the southern castellation.

The guard on watch glanced at the puckered countenance of the mage and took several steps to the left. The Black Crow followed the old man, his piercing blue eyes fastened on him.

"Report," Lord Richard asked.

"Gert Vanknell, lord," The guard stuttered. "It's as the magus said, my lord. They are striking camp. One lot has already left." Vanknell pointed a hand toward the lumped outline of the Weswolds on the horizon.

Lutico raised his arms again and the air distorted once more. The sight revealed to Richard, replicated what had already been seen.

Lebraun and Captain Griegon appeared shortly after. Lebraun moved automatically to the western battlement, his original post, whilst the captain strode to his Lord's side. Greigon, having questioned Lebraun on their way up, had some inkling of what was afoot. Seeing his lord standing tall with shoulders back made it real and a seed of hope took root in his heart.

They observed over the next several hours the urakakule pack up en masse and leech away, looking like ant trails as each tribe took a different path in a different direction but never northward.

The Black Crow watched the lifting of the siege with growing certitude and unanswered questions. "Where are they going? Why now? The dead of winter is still to come, yet they move the heart of their tribes, the elders, the women and children into the wilderness. It makes no sense to me."

Lutico snorted a stream of air. "The Norde-Targkish is said to be a harsh land. If so, I imagine they find ours far more pleasant to roam, even in winter."

Captain Greigon shook his head. "I sense more to it than that. Magus, you said the Council of Mages expected Rivercross to come under siege or assault any day. That they expected it sooner. Maybe these tribes move south to join them?"

Lord Richard scratched a hand over his chin in thought. "That seems credible."

"Not to me," countered Lutico. "If that were so, why rush? Why not follow the roads south rather than spreading like leaves before the northwind. No, I fear your thoughts are clouded by what you know rather than what you do not. You answer the question you want to answer rather than ask the question you should."

Greigon looked from the mage to his lord with a wrinkled frown.

"Be grateful you didn't have him as your teacher, Captain," Richard murmured with a rueful smile. It didn't hide the worry creasing his eyes, "even now he cannot help himself."

"How so, lord?"

"Come," the Black Crow turned and crossed the roof of the keep to the northside and the two men followed. They stared out across the emptying Northfields.

"Lutico, in his inimitable way, is saying we should not be asking who the White Hand run to, but rather what they run from?" Lifting his hand, Richard pointed north.

"The question unasked and unknown. What is coming that the urak fear?"

Principal Characters

Nihm	Pronounced Nim. Daughter of Darion and Marron Castell
Renco	Pronounced Ren-co. Apprentice to Hiro
Tasao Maohong	Pronounced – Taz-a-o Mow-hong. Hiro's companion.

The Order

Darion Castell	Homesteader and Orderman.
Marron Castell	Homesteader and Orderwoman.
Keeper	Titular head of the Order.
Hiro	Order Knight (Sometimes)
Renix	Order Knight, Kingsholme ambassador
Chivalry	Order Knight
Ironside	Order Knight
Lyra Castigan	Order Knight
Attimus	Order Knight, Master at the academy
Tannon Crick	Order Knight at Norderland
Grema Bergrun	Order Knight
Kal Meyar	Order Knight
Meredith Chancer	Clothier and Orderwoman in Confluence
David Chancer	Adopted son of Meredith
Regus	Orderman and steward to Ironside
Gatzinger	Orderman and steward to Castigan
Rutigard	Grey Knight, Hand to Ironside
Ansel	Grey Knight, Hand to Castigan
Tasso Marn	Orderwoman and fabric merchant in Kingsholme
Tasso Chiguar	Orderman and husband to Marn
Steinling Razholte	Wordsmith and Orderman, Tankrit isles
Marus Banff	Orderman and steward to Tannon Crick
Katal Zakpikt	Grey Knight, Hand to Tannon Crick
Jon Hodden	Grey Knight, Hand to Tannon Crick
David Sanction	Grey Knight, Hand to Tannon Crick
Karl Hubert	Grey Knight, Hand to Tannon Crick
Merin Somar	Grey Knight, Hand to Tannon Crick
Salu Kimer	Grey Knight, Hand to Grema Bergrun
Rasicus	Grey Knight, Hand to Kal Meyar
Mordan 'Mord' Mordignus	Orderman and steward to Kal Meyar

Lords of the Rivers Province

Trenton Twyford	Pronounced Ty-Ford. Ducal Lord of the Rivers province.
Richard Bouchemeaux	Pronounced Bow-She-mow. Known as the Black Crow. Lord of Thorsten.
Jacob Bouchemeaux	Son of Richard.
Constance Bouchemeaux	Daughter of Richard.
William Bouchemeaux	Lord of Redford – brother of Richard.

Robert Bouchemeax	William's 1st son.
Bruce Bouchemeax	William's 2nd son.
Sandford Bouchemeax	William's 3rd son.
Jason Chadford	Lord of Greenholme.
Ivern Menzies	Lord of Fallston.
John Trant	Lord of Marston.
Winston Brant	Lord Duke of Greentower.
Victor Nesto	Lord of Charncross.
Aric Nesto	Eldest son of Victor, Captain of Charncross.
Idris Inigo	Lord of Confluence.
Mical Hanboek	Lord of Fastain.
Jenis Rakoman	Lord of Wooliston.

Men and Women of the Rivers

Kilé Bartsven	First Sword to Lord Bouchemeax.
Sir Anders Forstandt	Knight-captain in the Black Crows.
Mal Kronke	Sergeant in the Black Crows.
Jannick Pieterzon 'Deadeye' 'Zon'	Black Crow guard.
Jess Crawley	Black Crow guard.
Morpete	Black Crow guard.
James Encoma	Black Crow guard.
Sir John Stenson	Captain of Jacob Bouchemeax's personal guard.
Greigon	Captain in the Black Crows.
Mortimer	Sergeant in the Black Crows.
Mathew Lebraun	Black Crow guard.
Geert Vanknell	Black Crow guard.
Endo Rayne	Black Crow guard.
John Tanner	Black Crow guard.
Lutico Ben Naris	Mage of the third order, master of the arts magical, emissary for the council of mages and councillor to Lord Richard Bouchemeax.
Junip	Mage apprentice to Lutico.
Johanus Elling	Weapons Master, Thorsten.
Cyril Dechampne	Master of Arms, Thorsten.
Annabelle 'Belle'	Young girl, Thorsten, charge of Lord Amos Duncan.
Ned Wynter	Bowmaster at Thorsten.
Witter	Sergeant at Greentower.
John Nesbitt	Duke Brant's chamberlain.
Sir Vincent Dulac	Commander for Lord Inigo, Confluence.
Harton	Guard Captain, Confluence.
Osiris Smee	Mage of the third order, master of the arts. magical, Councillor to Lord Inigo, Confluence.
Si Manko	Swordmaster and First Sword to Lord Inigo, Confluence.
Sir George Flik	Knight-captain, Master of the Guard, Rivercross.
Sir Ardin Lucspar	Knight-captain of the Burning Cross, Charncross.
Frederick Manus	Lord Chamberlain of Rivercross.

Victor 'Vic' Stenhause	Landlord of the Broken Axe, Thorsten.
Vivienne 'Viv' Stenhause	Landlord of the Broken Axe, Thorsten.
Morten Stenhause	Vic and Viv's son and only child.
Leticia 'Lett' Goodwill	Bard apprentice.
Ernst Stigar	Clothier, Thorsten.
Stanis Ruddlan	Fruit seller, Thorsten.
Ruth Madrigar	Shop owner, Thorsten.
Master Ertu Gúl	Owner of Eastlight Traders, Wooliston.
Mistress Molpa Gúl	Owner of Eastlight Traders, Wooliston.
Captain Maveison	Captain of the Eastern Promise, Eastlight Traders.

Grimmers

Jackson Tullock 'Black Jack'	Lord of the Grimhold.
Hissings	Reaver.
Tom Trickle	Hedge mage.
Hettingly	Physiker and herbalist.
Torgrid	Murkhawk reaver captain.
Jessop	Murkhawk reaver captain.
Odd-John	Murkhawk reaver, Producer of Whiskey Mash.
Nadine Varla	Murkhawk reaver.
Aousa Varla	Nadine's daughter.
Egg	Murkhawk reaver.
Busk	Murkhawk reaver.
Nils Baka	Murkhawk reaver.
Sofia Grainne	Captured scribe, from Thorsten.
Millie Grainne	Sofia's daughter.
Sayzan Trickle	Mother of Tom.
Rogar Sanning	Murkhawk reaver.
Mattie Nieker	Murkhawk reaver.
Sunny Mordrunski	Murkhawk reaver.
Sis Lafferty	Murkhawk reaver.
Nip Rokan	Murkhawk reaver.
Clara 'Skunk' Munro	Murkhawk reaver.
Bonny Boyd	Murkhawk reaver captain.
Menin	Murkhawk reaver.
Seth Crombie	Murkhawk reaver.
Mallory Lorcini	Murkhawk reaver.

The Duncans

Atticus	Lord and patriarch.
Morgenni	Lady and matriarch.
Samual	First son.
Lemuel	Second son.
Amos	Third son.
Angus	Fourth son.
Loris	Fifth son (twin with Lucan).
Lucan	Sixth son (twin with Loris).

Morgan	Seventh son, Magus (in training at the Enclave).
Pris	First daughter.
Hope	Second daughter.
Mercy	Third daughter, Fire Magus.
Prudence	Fourth daughter.
Mori	Fifth daughter.
Rayne	Daughter of Samual Duncan.

Duncan Bannermen

Jobe	Amos's friend and companion.
Jerkze	Amos's friend and companion.
Stama	Amos and Mercy's friend and companion.
Lukas 'Lucky' Lucson	Amos and Mercy's friend and companion.
Milak	Guardsman for Mori Duncan.
Rogan	Guardsman for Mori Duncan.
Remus Fitch	Steward to the Duncan.

Red Priest's – Church of Kildare

Henrik Zoller	Priest, Tortuga's former protégé.
Maxim Tortuga	High Cardinal.
Eruk Mortim	Abbot of Thorsten.
Jon Whent	Archbishop of Killenhess, Lord Commander of the Faith Militant.
Pieter Manning	Priest, Secretary to Tortuga.
Per Torsten	Cardinal of Norderland.
Renton Barroso	Principal Bishop, Order of Service.
William Wentworth	Bishop of Charncross.
Fren Milgorin	Battle priest assigned to the Defile.
Tigh Remual	Priest from Oling-on-Rake.

Red Cloaks (Brothers all)

Tuko	Zollers guard.
Holt	Zollers guard.
Patrice	Zollers guard, Physiker.
Diadago	Zollers guard.
Hector Henreece	Physkier in Whents army.
Comter	Sergeant, in Whents army.
Warwick	1st Captain, in Whents army.
Maesons	Captain in Whents army.
Richard Morgan	Guard in Whents.
Hamish Johns	Guard in Whents.
Mackey	Guard in Whents.
Stokes	Guard in Whents.
Mercer	Tortuga's guard.
Rashud	Guard in Whents.
Canting	Guard in Whents.
Welling	Guard in Whents.

Darding	Guard in Whents.
Jesmon	Guard in Whents.
Smit	Guard in Whents.
Ricar	Guard in Whents.
Junna	Tortuga's Guard captain.

Brown Robes – Church of Ankor

Rand Luxurs	High Cardinal.
Enning-Baye	Bishop at Kingsholme.
Marie Sessane	Highmarch of Waterdale.
Charl Molenberg	Priest on Pik Isle.
John Korring	Primate of Rivercross.
Larson Bose	Priest at Rivercross.

White Robes – Church of Nihmrodel

Maris Jenah	High Cardinal.
Jen Sophia	Abbess of Cross Wick.
Father Kilan Melbroth	Highmarch of Greentower.
Bernardo Farley	Abbot of Confluence.
Loren Hekbur	Priest at Waterdale.
Joshep Hennim	Primate of Rivercross.
Erwain Marr	Priestess at Rivercross.
Darri	Acolyte with Mother Marr.

Men and Women of Kingsholme

Edward Blackstar	High King.
Margot Blackstar	High Queen.
Herald Blackstar	Crown Prince.
Matrice Blackstar	Princess.
Rudy Valenta	Lord, Chancellor and Master of Coin.
Malcolm Reibeck	Lord Chamberlain.
Harris Benvora	Mage to The High King.
Magnus Harkul	Lord commander of the Kingsguard.
Rigard Lowenstow	Local Lord.
Elwin Wolsten	Sir, Master of Horse.
Gart Vannen	Sir, First Sword to Princess Matrice.
Piert Wendell	Master, Tutor to the Royal Family.
Marta	Companion and Lady-in-waiting to Matrice.
Horyk Andersun	First Sword to Herald.
Grayson	Chamberlain to Herald.
Ricard Loris	Captain of Matrice's Kingsguard.
Adler	Sergeant in the Kingsguard.
Sayers	Corporal in the Kingsguard.
Loren Cripps	Royal physiker.
Rhin Malraven	Master of Birds (spymaster).

Kingsholme Underworld

Bortillo Targus	Leader of the Syndicate, Thief Guild.
Willie 'the Hand'	Fence in the All-Ways.
Tomas 'The Mouse'	Child Thief and Wordsmith.
Sparrow	Child Thief.
Benny Four Fingers	Old thief and philosopher.
Merca 'Murder' Landre	Hunter for the Targus.
Rooq	Acozi, a syndicate hardman.
Greik	a member of the syndicate.
Rimul	a member of the syndicate.
Mengis	a member of the syndicate.
Mika	a member of the syndicate.
Moose	a member of the syndicate.

Cumbrenan

Arisa Montreau	High Lady of Cumbrenan.
Lord Ferec	of Thorn Nook.
Lord Vandis	of Lakeside.
Rollo	Holdsteader outside Thorn Nook.
Marley	Holdsteader outside Thorn Nook.
Lady Greymore	of Waterdale.
Greybeard	Old magus, Roadend.
Marius	Greybeards son.
Manis	Guard captain in Lakeside.

Norderland (Nordáalund)
Note: Barle is a Lord, a Jarl is a captain and a Karl is a bannerman.

Justin Janis	High Lord/High Barle of Norderland.
Kaygó Janis	High Lord's sonm and heir.
Johanus Ulrikson	Lord of Highwatch.
Marlik Riekason	Jarl to Justin Janis.
Utarr Gant	Barle.
Ebba Darjhalen	Jarl from Ead.
Borik Shan	Magus to Justin Janus.
Frode of Lonn	Barle of Lonn.
Orik of Lonn	Frode's kinsman and Jarl from Lonn.
Huorl Landa	Jarl from Lonn.
Connaer Hagenson	Jarl from Lonn.
Cydric of Rúk	Frode's Karl.
Magner of Skaag	Barle.
Jonah Terik	Magus of Skaag.
Runé of Helvennin	Barle.
Sorina Tarlack	Magus from Gannon-báer.

Notable Others

Costa Ostenbow	High Lord, Branikshire
Derek Travenon	High Lord, Eosland
Yanik Zacorik	High Lord, Southlands of Olme
Henry Dumac	High Lord, Westlands
Elizabeth Hardcastle	High Lady of Midshire.

Sházáik (called Demons or Shaitan by humans)

O'si-binsaléq-xu 'O'si'	Sháadretarch (Third Level Sházáik)
P'uk-samnew-zix 'P'uk'	Sháadretarch (Third Level Sházáik)
Q'tox-killanan-vor 'Q'tox'	Tetriarché (Second Level Sházáik)

Urak

Bartuk	Pronounced Bar-Tuck. Toreen, White Hand Clan – Scout
Mar-Dur	Pronounced Mar-duur. Clan Chief of the White Hand
Krol	Clan Chief of the Blood Skull
Tar-Tukh	Pronounced Tar- Tuck. Hurak-Hin (bodyguard) to Krol clan chieftain.
Nartak	Pronounced Nar-Tack. Hurak-Hin (bodyguard) to Krol Clan chief.
Grimpok	War Chief in the White Hand.
Muw-Tukh	Pronounced Mow-Tuck. Hurak-Hin (bodyguard) to Mar-Dur Clan Chief.
Baq-Dur	Pronounced Bak Dur) Bortaug tribe chief. White Hand Clan.
Nasqchuk	Pronounced Nas chuck. Raid Leader, White Hand
Karth-Dur	Tribal chieftain of the Manawarih, Blood Skull clan
Narpik-Dur	Tribal chieftain of the Toreen, White Hand clan
Grot-tuk	Pronounced Grow Tuk. Toreen, Warband leader, White Hand Clan
Murhtuk	Pronounced Meer tuck. Toreen, White Hand Clan
Rutgarpok	Pronounced Rut gar pok. White Hand Clan, Huntmaster
Makjatukh	Pronounced Mak jat uk. White Hand Clan, Scout
Maliktuk	pronounced Mal ik tuck. Toreen, White Hand Clan, Huntmaster
Orqis-tarn	Toreen Shaman, White Hand Clan

Ilfanum

Da'Mari	Pronounced Da- Ma-re. A Nu'Rakauma – a world tree bordering the Rivers to the west.[1]
Eladrohim	Pronounced El-Ad-Ro-Him. A Nu'Rakauma – a world tree to the west of the kingdoms.
Elora	Pronounced El-Ora. Visok and K'raal[1]
M'rika	Pronounced Ma-Rik-ah. Visok and K'raal.
D'ukastille	Pronounced Du-kas-steel. Visok and K'raal of the Rohelinewaald.
De'Nestarin 'Nesta'	A Ke'pa and Wahr[1]
Ruith	Pronounced Roo-ith. Dúr-phr-ta[1]
R'ell	Pronounced Ray-ell, Visok and Umphathi.
Bezal	Pronounced Bez-al. R'ells bonded Raven.

---

[1] See Ilf Dictionary that follows for pronunciation guide and meaning.

Ilf dictionary

Ilf	Means child/children
Ilfanum	Means child of
Nu'Rakauma	Pronounced Nu-racka-uma means in literal terms world tree mother
Nu	World
Raka	Tree
Uma	Mother
K'raal	A type of Lord/Lady
Visok	the term for a High Ilf
Anum	Means several things of/from
Umphathi	Warden/guardian.
Ka'harthi	Gatherer/gardener.
Fassarunewadaick	The name for the Fossa River near the Torn Mountains (The Torns).
Fassa	fast/quick
Rune	Running/flowing/moving
Wada	Water
Ick	Ice/cold/frozen
Rokulinewaald	Ward of the north forest
Rovalinewaald	Ward of the south forest
Rohelinewaald	Ward of the east forest
Ronilinewaald	Ward of the west forest
Rokuline	North/northern
Rovaline	South/southern
Roheline	East/eastern
Roniline	West/western
Waald	Forest
Tézani	A higher being
Dúr-phr-ta	Healer
Tae'al	Pronounced Taa – al (tail), essence or binding force
Ke'pa	Wanderer
Ruua	Little/small
Caeed	seed
Antén	Tower
Wahr	Mage

Look out for - Chaos Reign
Book Four of the Morhudrim Cycle
Due for release – 2025

If you are reading this, I'm impressed. You've made it through the Principal Characters **and** the Ilf dictionary, that is what I call commitment, so well done. I would also like to say thanks for devoting so much of your time to my little tale.

Darkness Resides has been a real labour of love. It took longer to write than I anticipated and took me to places I hadn't planned or foreseen. Alas, some of my beloved characters did not make it with me. Life can be cruel like that.

Book sales can also be cruel and apart from my editor, Michelle and my band of faithful beta readers I am doing this all on my own. So, how can you help, you never asked. Well, it is as easy as leaving a rating on Amazon and Goodreads (if you use it). It's as simple as clicking on a star, or, if you feel so moved, you could leave an actual review, you know with words and everything, just a few or a dissertation or anywhere in between, it is up to you. Whatever you can do, your support matters massively. It gives me a lift to see them (and trust me, some days I need one) and every rating or review helps my books flex their might with Amazon's unknowable algorithm, giving them visibility so that others might find and enjoy my work.

What? You're still here. Well, if you want updates on book four and beyond, or just want to get in touch to say hi or provide me with any feedback, or, **gulp**, you find a faux pas of some description. You can get in touch with me via my website at https://adgreenauthor.com/ it is packed with useful information on my books, maps, and lore, and you can sign up for my newsletter as well as contact me privately.

You can also follow me on:
Amazon https://www.amazon.co.uk/A-D-Green/e/B0825861Q6 and never miss one of my book releases.
Facebook @adgreentheauthor – for news and book reviews
X (nee Twitter) @adgreenauthor – for shameless flogging of my own book and the odd philosophical mumblings.

Thanks for reading.

A D Green

Printed in Great Britain
by Amazon

e1f2505e-bcb1-4ee8-97c6-605a210fe752R01